T0166416

SHERBROOKES

OTHER WORKS BY NICHOLAS DELBANCO

FICTION

The Count of Concord
Spring and Fall
The Vagabonds
What Remains
Old Scores
In the Name of Mercy
The Writers' Trade & Other Stories
About My Table and Other Stories
Small Rain
Fathering
In the Middle Distance
News
Consider Sappho Burning
Grasse, 3/23/66
The Martlet's Tale

NONFICTION

Lastingness: The Art of Old Age
Anywhere Out of the World: Travel, Writing, Death
*The Countess of Stanlein Restored: A History of the Countess
of Stanlein ex-Paganini Stradivarius Violoncello of 1707*
The Lost Suitcase: Reflections on the Literary Life
Running in Place: Scenes from the South of France
The Beaux Arts Trio: A Portrait
Group Portrait: Conrad, Crane, Ford, James, & Wells

BOOKS EDITED

Literature: Craft and Voice (with A. Cheuse)
The Hopwood Lectures: Sixth Series
The Hopwood Awards: 75 Years of Prized Writing
The Sincerest Form: Writing Fiction by Imitation
The Writing Life: the Hopwood Lectures, Fifth Series
Talking Horse: Bernard Malamud on Life and Work (with A. Cheuse)
Speaking of Writing: Selected Hopwood Lectures
Writers and their Craft: Short Stories and Essays on the Narrative (with L. Goldstein)
Stillness and Shadows (two novels by John Gardner)

SHERBROOKES
NICHOLAS DELBANCO

DALKEY ARCHIVE PRESS
CHAMPAIGN / DUBLIN / LONDON

Originally published by William Morrow and Co. as *Possession*, 1977; *Sherbrookes*, 1978; and *Stillness*, 1980
Copyright © 1977, 1978, 1980
Afterword was originally published, in slightly different form, as "My Old Young Books"
in *The Writer's Chronicle*, February 2011
Dalkey Archive Press edition and afterword copyright © 2011 by Nicholas Delbanco
First edition, 2011
All rights reserved

Library of Congress Cataloging-in-Publication Data

Delbanco, Nicholas.
Sherbrookes / Nicholas Delbanco. -- 1st ed.
p. cm.
ISBN 978-1-56478-587-9 (pbk. : alk. paper)
1. Vermont--Fiction. 2. Domestic fiction. I. Title.
PS3554.E442S54 2011
813'.54--dc22
                                    2011016861

Partially funded by a grant from the Illinois Arts Council, a state agency, and by the University of
Illinois at Urbana-Champaign

www.dalkeyarchive.com

Cover: design and composition by Danielle Dutton, painting by Wolf Kahn
Gray Barn, 2010 (detail), oil on canvas, 52 x 60 inches
Courtesy: Ameringer|McEnery|Yohe

Printed on permanent/durable acid-free paper and bound in the United States of America

As ever, for Elena

POSSESSION

PART I

I

It is cold where he sits. The Big House too is cold, but there at least they can set fires.

He has laid in forty cords, just having the fence-lines trimmed and thinning out the hardwood lot by Bailey's. What with fourteen fireplaces, he figures on a cord each week. It has taken more than that—but not a bad season for snow, not as high as the window where he sits. Still, the winter has been dark and wet, with a March that set Harriet muttering: why not California, she said to him, why not North Carolina; why not anyplace but *this* place; what keeps us here this winter?—answer me that.

He made no answer, of course. She never in her life had left and would never leave. You can lie here, Hattie said, all right, I'll grant you that; you can be buried here, we'll all of us be buried here, but what's the matter with a trip to Carolina in the winter?

Or maybe New Orleans; you said you loved New Orleans; remember how you said that once?

The cords line the front of the cow barn. He had had them stacked there in October, starting on the north wall, to keep at least that much wind back. It took ten cords to front the wall, and then they'd gone eighty feet east and eighty feet south and west. "Biggest log cabin around," Judah joked. "Now all's we need's the roof."

Yet it is a charmed enclosure, four foot high and four foot wide and trim. They took the deadwood first, from the south. He had walked in November through the space the ash logs left and stood in the center of his heat fort. "Lord, give me one more winter," he prayed. "Lord, grant me one more spring." Early on, he had had the habit of prayer and then, as he grew older, the habit of blasphemy. Now he mixed the two and wasn't sure of the proportion. "God, let the sap in me run."

"You've got no earthly reason," his sister complained, "not to waste this time. Not to visit New Orleans instead of just lying up here."

But lie here he would, or sit, or stand in his diminishing fort. From the window where he sits now, in April, the wood is a single squat line. There is sugar maple left to burn, and locust, and hickory wood. He'd not permitted sugaring this year. He'd lost his sweet tooth anyhow, and the profit wasn't worth the trouble, and he wanted sap in the trees. There'd been bloodletting and leeching enough in his time.

So he cut a hole in the pond ice and took the thousand sugaring taps and funneled them down through the hole. Then he took an awl and pierced the thousand buckets three times through each bucket base. It had been slow work. The buckets stood in the sugarhouse, piled ten high and in one hundred piles. Judah spent the best part of an afternoon each afternoon for a week. He'd take a bucket and upend it and drive the awl through in irregular patterns, working it around so just a drop of solder wouldn't fix the leak. Then, when he'd finished with a pile, he'd set it back in place; his right arm tired easily, even in methodical destruction, and he took his time.

The sugarhouse was empty but for the buckets and vats. The rafters had been charred. There were raccoon leavings at his feet. There was wood by the north wall, though not from this year's cutting, and Judah remembered, fifteen years back, working with the men. The vats would bubble, boiling, and they cut the syrup down with fat. They'd string lard across the pans, maybe four inches over, and he never tired watching how the froth would bubble and accumulate and mount to the fatback, then fall. He tired of nothing, those years. He never tired from the heat or the twenty-four-hour work shifts or the taste of Scotch with syrup. "It sweetens the whiskey," he said, "and sours the sugar water. Best of both possible worlds."

Weak sun shines through the twelve-pane window to his left. He turns his face. He shuts one eye, then the other. With one eye shut, his nose appears, and he concentrates on his nose and shifts the closed eye and watches his nose-line shift. Harriet would want him in for lunch and, before that, for a drink.

"You mix," she'd say. "I'll have what you're having."

"I'll have a whiskey."

"Not that again," she'd complain. "How about a whiskey sour? Or a sloe gin, maybe. Or a Manhattan; why don't you offer me that?"

"I'm having whiskey," he'd say. "You have whatever you want."

"Make me a Manhattan, please," she'd say. "I can't abide whiskey straight. And one single maraschino cherry, for the taste."

He would have started already, since he knew the game. He would select the bottles and glasses from the sideboard, measuring her cocktail with deliberation.

"Your health," he'd offer.

"*Your* health."

There would be ice in the ice bucket, and maraschino cherries on the silver tray. Judah watches his nose, in the sun's light, go incorporeal; he rearranges his scarf. He fills this space. It isn't over-windy, but he's brought his sheep rug and has some deciding to do. His sister can wait on her noontime maraschino cherries, and he can wait on his scotch. He thinks himself a hunter; his first quarry is his wife.

There are ways and ways, Judah says to himself. *All kinds of ways. There's fifteen ways to skin a cat, and the whole town's studying. I got to bait them with the prettiest. There's lawcourts, come to that. I got to know what I'm about before I get untracked on it; I got to bait my traps.*

This satisfies him, seemingly; he puts his hand on his belly, then thigh. The chair he rises from is a child's settee. The Toy House had been designed for his grandfather's children, and his children's children and their friends. It is a replica of the Big House, scaled one to ten, but without the fireplaces, since there should be no risk of fire where young people play. His grandfather had caused equivalent gables and the clock tower to be erected; the Toy House, in faithful imitation, is built of white clapboard and slate. Four stories high, the Toy House is just tall enough for Judah to stand at his ease. He measures six foot two in socks; now he has boots on, and stretches. His right hand touches the upstairs landing, outside of what was Maggie's room; he puts his middle finger on the place where she would sleep.

Past seventy, Judah Porteous Sherbrooke started counting. Numbers were a code he'd cracked when young: six is consistently six, and six times six is thirty-six even if you have to multiply it, in 1976, by six again before you get what six could buy when Judah had been born. He'd lived through the nation's lean times. But there'd been food enough to eat, more than enough to go around, and they'd shipped apples and eggs and beef down in the club car to his cousins in New York. He wondered if his Wall Street cousins sold apples in Manhattan. And though he's joked for years that what this country needs is a good five-cent cigar, it isn't funny anymore; it makes him sad to think that nothing worth the buying costs a nickel now. They've wiped the silver, he would say, off of that buffalo's ass.

Still, eighteen times eighteen is six times three times six times three; he can verify that. And a square has equal sides, though the sides can be eighty feet or eighteen inches, and the sides will enclose equivalent angles, each of them ninety degrees. He recollects license-plate numbers long past his memory for cars, or who was driving them, or why. He recollects telephone numbers long past the time when his wife and son relinquished those numbers and left. He has Social Security numbers and license plates and bank account numbers, and he knows them all by heart; they are the ciphers of integrity, so he ranks and musters digits with the certainty things fit.

Elvirah Hayes had been the daytime operator, and Lucy Gregory had been the nighttime operator. For their small town's small switchboard, they needed no one else. He knew that they kept apple trees, so Judah sent them pears. Sometimes he'd ask Lucy to call up Elvirah for him and inquire how she was feeling that night.

"Who wants to know?" she would ask.

"Your devoted admirer," Judah would say, courteous. "J. P. Sherbrooke calling."

"Why, Mr. Sherbrooke," she would say. "How very kind of you to ask. I might have known it was you. You and your consideration that would call."

"Considerateness, Ellie."

Her voice would flute and twitter, scaling octaves when not on the job. He imagined that the earphones kept her orderly; she raised Dalmatian dogs.

"Yes. I'm fine. It's a lovely summer breeze this evening. It's kind of you to ask."

But telephone operators now are long-distance, or information operators out of Burlington, and their voices are not voices he can trust. Sometimes he calls to verify his memory of numbers, and they are bored or rude.

"If you knew the number, why'd you ask it?" one of them complained. "We don't have all that much time."

Numbers segment the visible world; he knows each fraction of his thousand acres, and the way the fields and woodlots edge up against each other. He remembers Maggie's legs by the lilt of her last four telephone numbers in Manhattan; six-eight-two-three was the rhythm she beat out when walking: *rings on her fingers and bells on her toes*. Once, at the Rutland State Fair, he had guessed the quantity of pickles collected in a pickle barrel to the nearest dozen; once, at a Bulova Watch Display, he guessed the grains of sand in an hourglass to the nearest hundred and won the Bulova Watch. "Them that's got shall get," he said. "And them that's not shall lose"—and handed the trinket to Maggie and told her to hoard time.

Harriet sounds the gong. The gong is electric but she can set the frequency of beats; a bronze fist beats on the shield. The gong hangs on the porch in summer, and Judah remembers hearing it from the far pastures, summoning him. "The sun is past the yardarm," his father used to say. "Time to wet the decks." His father had booked passage on the *Titanic's* maiden voyage, but had had to cancel three days previous. He liked to talk thereafter about his brush with death; he had, his wife complained, a sailor's tongue.

They say a baby whale's six foot by fourteen foot. And when it feeds it swallows waves entirely, then spits the salt part back. The pasture where he lay would swarm with bees, there would be timothy grass and butterflies above him, and the gong's call would sound, in the windy distance, like the call of mourning doves. Sometimes he packed a picnic lunch (his first horse was an Appaloosa and stood fourteen hands; he remembers that, and the Morgan's height, but not the horses' names) and rode to Shaftsbury Hollow or followed the Walloomsack six miles down to Eagle's Bridge. *The whole damn town's a salt lick,* he pronounces to himself. *An edifying sight, my Lord, all those tongues in that one groove. The central declivity, yes my Lord, and envy up the shaft. They've salted down the crops and laid the region waste and are proud of it into the bargain; they plant mothballs now and concrete. They print brochures.*

He shuffles to the Toy House door. It opens out; he opens it and finds the April noontime warm; he locks and padlocks the door. There are lilac bushes to his right, and a tamarack tree; the tamarack is starting to go green. Judah crosses the gravel driveway and makes for the Big House porch, stepping on the flagstones, sidestepping mud. He brings both feet together on a single stone, gathering himself. He uses his left foot first. His boots are Dunham boots, with enough tread on them still to pick up all the mud he'd need to bank a ditch, or enough mud anyway to set Harriet screaming. They are eyelet boots and trouble to unlace, and he hopes to keep them on and therefore takes care with the path. His familiar chorus starts on the seventh step; he rests and waits it out.

All things begin again, young woman. Maggie. Except this one thing, since it never stops. She's coming back to you. There's venality abounding on your chosen plot. He holds his hand up, imperious. There is wind in the lilac branches, and the gong has worked itself to equanimity. He mounts the Big House porch.

"Finney"—he had used the phone in the garage—"I need advice."

"Shoot. What can I do you for, Jude?"

"Advice," he said. "The sort that takes some thinking out. Not just off the top of your head."

"I'm with you," Lawyer Finney said. "I'm listening."

He leaned against the pony cart. There were swallow's nests above him; the floor was cement.

"Let's say about snowing," he said. "Let's say it doesn't snow by night and there's no snow on the ground. Then you wake up in the morning and it still ain't snowing but there's snow two inches deep. Well," he rested his left hand on the black telephone. He coiled the cord. "It's circumstantial, ain't it, that it snowed? I mean that's circumstantial evidence, correct?"

"Correct," Finney said. "That's a valid inference."

"How valid?" Judah asked.

"About as good," said Finney, "as the one that says the sun will rise. No law to prove it, I suppose, but nothing likely to disprove it, and the inference is sound enough to argue on."

"In front of any judge?"

Finney ruminated. "In front of any I know."

"So no one's got to see the snow to prove that it's been snowing?"

"They got to see the *ground* snow. They don't have to witness the act."

"And what if they was in another county when it snowed?"

There was noise on the line between them. "You're losing me, Jude. I don't exactly follow."

The cord was split. He saw the wires through the rubber casing. He put his finger on the rubber's oval separation. "What if they arrive too late, I mean, to witness it? What if the ground's gone muddy again, and there's no snow left excepting only that I tell them it's been snowing?"

"Hearsay evidence," said Finney. "Inadmissible in court."

"I thank you," Judah finished. "For your trouble."

"No trouble. That'll be a triple Scotch and one ham sandwich, thank you."

"Sold," he said. "Don't be a stranger"—and hung up as he always did, without saying good-bye. He needed no further permission now; he knew Finney's license plate number, but not the make and model of that blue sedan. They call cars after Indians who never got to drive.

He had kept Maggie's car washed. It would gleam, awaiting her, and Judah made certain the chrome had been polished and the insides scrubbed and swept. The Packard sat like some gray chariot with dark blue trim in the first of the four garages that were stables once. There was the pony cart she called a carriage and, in the farther bay, his truck. She left him messages. She would write CLEAN ME on his fender, in the dust and grime that settled there daily, or "Darling, don't forget. At eight o'clock the Clarks are coming," and leave it on the seat. When she left him, the first time—taking Ian to New York, saying their son required proper companions—Maggie drew a heart around the handle of his door. He found it two days later: her farewell.

Judah had been drinking. He clattered off the porch, into sun that made him squint. His mouth felt like the bottom of a birdcage, and by the time he reached the truck he was sweating; by the time he backed it out he had the shakes. It was July. The maples had a sleeve of dirt; the bottom of their leaves went brown with his raised dust. So he got out and pumped up water and drank. He soaked his red bandana, rolled it tight and tied it to his neck. He turned back to the truck and raised his hand to the door handle and saw it shaped an arrow in the center of a heart she'd drawn. He could not rub it out. When he sold the truck the next day on a trade-in for a Ford it was there still: fading, smudged, a Valentine with the rust-pitted chrome latch to prove where his heart cracked.

Names stick. You name a thing and that's the shape it takes. His grandfather's father, writing from California (where he had gone to practice law and ended up railway-rich, crony to Frémont and Stanford, sporting fur and silver in the oil portrait Judah possesses), had named it the "Big House." "I have always maintained and will maintain," he wrote, in his elaborate left-handed scrawl, "that Vermont is where you find it. It being the true repose of the soul, whereas this Western paradise delights the flesh exceedingly."

Judah has the letters. He has every laundry slip or bill his ancestors received. They were pack rats, all of them, and assiduous in accumulation and transaction-proud, and he sometimes thinks he and Hattie keep the mansion just for storage space. "Yet we return from Babylon, though these be not waters to weep near but praise, and in our private coach, I wish the latest architect arrived from London to be retained, on an appropriate retainer, and set to building us a Big House against our soon retirement. I dream in these long nights of family and friends from school-time clustered to the several hearths, of faces flushed with God's exertion, not the demon rum. I wish the house to be of a pleasing façade, yet particular in shape. The fashion of the time is ornament, a glass to grandeur. We shall be fashionable only in restraint."

Nothing Judah knows of Daniel Sherbrooke accorded with restraint; his Vermont kin called him "Peacock" and were by turns awed and outraged. The construction process took six years. Sherbrooke was meticulous, in his transcontinental planning, with an attention to detail that others might call interference but he called the key to success. He made all the final designer's decisions and gave the final go-ahead— from problems of siting to patterns on the parquet floors—but never traveled east.

An architect was hired and brought from New York. "I wish him godly yet mondial," the magnate wrote, "and with some comprehension of our local stuffs." The architect built scale models of country houses in the Cotswolds and shipped them, according to Sherbrooke's instructions, to Vermont. "Peacock's" answering letters were hortatory, full of praise, but each would mention some new wing that "might be an addition of some slight extent. The House needs be a meeting house; I must have space wherein to meditate upon the narrow final confine we each of us inhabit. How but by contrast might the shelter prove exemplary, or offer to the wearied Spirit its adequate reach?"

Therefore porticos were added, and porches and trellised walkways and even, at Sherbrooke's insistence, a widow's walk.

"Though two-hundred miles from the ocean," he wrote, "and sheltered from its ceaseless surge nor yet an intimate of watr'y Storm, I wish continual reminder of the souls gone screaming down in ships-wrack, and their attendants on shore. These are Pleasing Protuberances, with grillwork that testifies to the vigilance of watchers in God's sight. I wish the widow's walk to circumnavigate the cupola and gables and be of ornamental iron painted black."

His pious architectural injunctions, over time, produced the largest and most lavish house in the region. It looks, Maggie said, like that prose style of his; it's crazy and ornate and out-of-date. Neighbors dubbed it "Peacock's Palace" or "Sherbrooke's Showplace" or "Pride's Peak." But the first became the final name and it was always now, only, the Big House. There are stained glass windows in the tower, and a ballroom on the second floor, and a central staircase that is foot for foot the equal of the central staircase in Mark Hopkins's home. It is a Victorian extravaganza, with four flights of servants' quarters that Judah's father leveled, raising a greenhouse instead. Maggie tended the greenhouse in winter, loving the luxuriant heat and the profusion of blossoms where she stood—except for that one width of glass—waist-deep in the wet snow.

The magnate, Peacock Sherbrooke—for that name also stuck—journeyed east in 1869 to die in his ancestral town and newly finished house. His voyage had been arduous, even with a private railway car, and a retinue that filled it of servants and daughters and his son-in-law.

"He suffered from a wasting fever," the daughter, Anne-Maria, later wrote, "but was upright and upstanding to the last. What wrack it was I dare not think nor scarcely venture to recall that caused the sweat to form upon his noble brow. That brow that frowned at each Malignity but lightened at the footfall of some loving tread. So pity us who watched him and could prove no comfort save the Book we read from and provided him to touch and kiss continually, which is of course Sufficing comfort & abundant recompense. We brought him from the station on a kind of litter, bundled as an infant 'gainst the Weathers importuning, and the rude shocks I myself was sensible of administered by these towpaths and oxtrails they call roads. My father as you amply know was a man of Sunny Countenance & also Determination & Will, but I who witnessed saw the Sun bedimmed by Rain clouds that started from his staring Eyes, as Will & Can may sometimes war, the latter in ascendance. We attained the gate at four forty-seven o'clock; I remember he queried the Time.

"There were Workmen standing, caps in hand, on either side of the Approach drive, nor did he stint to thank them with the hand that shook with palsy but was firm in Christ's close Grip. We made a grim Processional, that had thought to be a glad. For when the Big House rose before us, starting from the Maple trees that garlanded it greenly, and in the gathring dusk that was the Dark he voyaged through before—I do profess it—entering Eternal & Absolute Light, then did he raise himself upon an elbow and commend His works. I thought for an instant my father intended the architect's accomplishment, not Christ's, and turned to make some slight rejoinder, adding praise to praise, but saw his dear Orbs sightless and his Head cast back. His last words were—as sev'rally attested—'I pronounce myself content.'"

II

At nine o'clock that morning, he'd left the Toy House for a haircut—and it proved a gauntlet to run.

"Long time no see, Mr. Sherbrooke." The barber welcomed him, "A pleasure to see you again."

"Yes. Well. I've been busy," Judah said. He took the middle chair.

"At what, if you don't mind me asking?"

"I don't mind," Judah said—but did: minded the habit of gossip, minded the ease of the flourish and that oversize napkin he had in his collar, minded the man's name even, Vito. There was a *Playboy* calendar tucked in the mirror's edge and not even registering April but only a girl on a picnic blanket, serving up herself instead of food.

"Nice weather we've been having," Vito said.

He held to his silence.

"They say it'll snow later on."

"Ayup."

"We've had too much snow already," Vito said.

The room was empty. There were three chairs.

"Well, what'll it be?" Vito snapped his scissors like a soldier coming to attention, and his left hand brandished the comb.

"Just trim." Leaning back, he shut his eyes, remembering the manicure jobs of his youth. When they took you in the back room there it meant you bought whatever they were selling; there was whiskey in the lotion bottles and gin labeled "Shampoo."

"A head of hair like this," said Vito. "Makes you look like nobody's been caring for you. Not enough, Mr. Sherbrooke."

He opened his right eye. The white shocks about his ears were on his shoulders now. The thatch had been reduced. Vito bustled behind him, snipping. He hoped the family was well; he had seen Miss Harriet inside the Stitches Shoppe. He hoped the town would vote against the trailer ordinance and vote for one with teeth; there were so many regulations it was a wonder you could spit in your own driveway nowadays, not to mention what he had to do with towels to keep his license to cut hair, so why not rules for trailers, Vito asked. Would you believe the washing-down and mopping-up he had to go through; would you care for some hairspray this morning?

"I would not," Judah said.

Next he walked to Morrisey's and ordered ten pounds of sirloin.

"How's that, Jude?" the grocer asked.

"Ten pounds. And wrap it in one chunk."

"You've got a party?"

"I got a black eye, Alex, from walking in that door. I'm told that sirloin steak is just the thing."

"All right." Morrisey busied himself with his apron. "Ten pounds. Ain't sure I got that much in sirloin."

"You used to," Judah said.

"Not in one slice. Never."

"Well, cut it up then. And get me some Camembert cheese."

"Yes, *sir.*" Morrisey was mock-deferential to cover his true deference. "Coming right up."

"And have them send it to the house. But not before lunchtime, hear? Not till three o'clock."

So he who geared himself for battle never got to fight. He'd donned his manhood's armor at fifteen. He had been, Judah decided, witless to begin with—a giant of a rich boy who would rather be a farmer because lock, stock, and barrel it had been his father's farm. Then he filled out. It had been perceptible: a lengthening, a thickening, an equality with field hands who came to hay or pick. And once the line was crossed you couldn't backtrack or beg for delay; you didn't notice, passing it, that there'd been a rite of passage. But the world about you noticed and the upstairs maids would giggle and the field hands tell a different sort of joke.

And because it had been owned outright he was able to keep what he owned. "I'm a gentleman farmer," he'd say. "But not much of a gentleman and nothing of a farmer." Still, he fought a rearguard action and held on. There has been some work to that—what with supermarkets and tax laws changing and roads going up on the land's perimeter, and his neighbors selling out to make motels. He's held on sixty years. He had been old enough for the Great War just when the war was over, and the Second World War came too late. He could have joined up somehow, he supposed, but they'd have given him some desk job in Montpelier or D.C., and if he couldn't fly or man a tank he'd rather, he decided, shuffle lumber mills and farms around than some stack of papers. The farms and lumber mills were useful, and Judah expanded their output fivefold.

So the wars went on without him, and stock-market fortunes won or lost were not his fortunes, really, and the cities prospered or went bankrupt somewhere else. It had been sentry play. He stood and watched while men went out with bayonets or wire clippers and came back triumphant or dead. They came back on their comrade's shoulders or in their comrade's arms or sometimes slung in a fireman's carry, already a carcass and stiff. And he, who was weaker than no man and stronger than most, stayed home to mind the store. He minded the storekeeper's wives. He fought mostly holding actions, while the world was in that flux about him they called progress and advance. Then (sudden as the one before, he crossed a second line that said: this far, no farther, boy, take off your chain-mail suit) it was retreat. Then his manhood fled from him, and sentry play was too much work for one winded codger with a heart condition. Then he laid his armor by and shriveled into winter clothes and shivered cutting wood and stacking it and shivered feeling it burn.

He hears a plane. He hunts it, squinting, and sees it off by Woodford Valley, catching the bright light. Will Carr owned a Cessna, and once they flew to Brattleboro and circled back above his land and Judah recognized it all, knowing which way the drainage ran and where the sumac needed clearing, knew all of it in March because the leaves were down and nothing green or growing yet, but Will declared come August he'd be baffled. Can't tell the Green Mountains from the Alps or Burma, he said, and Judah wondered why he didn't say the Allegheny Mountains or the Adirondacks. "You've been there, I suppose," he asked, "flown over them?" and Will said no, but I can imagine; I see them clear as that set of foothills there. Imagination, Judah thinks, is like a hand shaking in the plane's loud clatter, with what looks like an old Boy Scout ring on Will's fourth finger where the wedding band would be, and some vague comparison tricked up as truth that lies.

Forgetfulness: he covets it, has lived the life most men would live, has kept some standards up with what—depending on the mood of it—he'd call stubbornness or mulishness or fierce determination; which standards has he kept, he asks himself, and comes up with a wash of words all meaning *loyal,* all meaning *live with what they call fidelity or die*; he's sidestepped less than most. The record players now boast high fidelity; there's a marching band that marches right across the living room. And when the violin comes at you it comes from a speaker where you don't hear flutes; he'd swear he tells the left hand from the right hand when the radio plays piano music, when he goes to shut it off. He uses his right hand. In Arab countries, Judah's heard, you use one hand for eating and one for wiping yourself, and it's a mortal insult to offer the wrong hand to a stranger; he thinks *fidelity is eating-hand; high-fidelity is shit.*

His sister stands in the hall. She wears a thick-ribbed red sweater and the shawl he gave her; she has been preparing, she announces, to wind the gong again.

"Shut that door," says Harriet. "It's cold."

"It ain't that bad."

"The radio says snow."

"Yes. Well."

"It's too cold for almost May."

"April seventh," he reminds her.

"You had a haircut, finally. Is that the reason why you didn't hear the gong?"

"I heard it."

"Where were you then? There's some sort of bird in the chimney, and I don't dare light the fire; there's feathers all over the logs."

"Just put down a piece of bread to catch the drippings," he jokes. "What are you having to drink?"

They are in the study, and Judah pours. Measuring her Manhattan, he reflects he's made it past the front parlor with boots on. He has left his blanket by the door.

"You don't believe me? About the birds?"

"I believe you. But there's wire on that chimney, sister. Your health."

"*Your* health. Where were you at this morning you didn't hear the gong?"

"I heard it," Judah says. "I didn't mean to worry you. I'll have them look at the chimneys. You'll want a second cherry?"

"To sweeten my disposition"—Harriet makes their old joke.

"Sweets to the sweet," he says. The cherry stem stains his fingernail pink.

"I thank you, brother." Harriet is eighty-one, five years his senior, and accepts such gallantry as due her age, not sex.

"What did *you* do this morning?" He is anxious to appease her because of his plan; he has intended to announce their afternoon surprise at lunch.

She lists telephone calls. She embarks upon the history of Ida Simmons's health, and who was right with regard to sciatica, and which shots helped and for how long; she, Harriet, knows there is no remedy for sciatica, but doesn't want to tell poor Ida or be the bearer of discouraging news, since Lord knows Ida's discouraged enough, considering her boy's arrest and the way they're building the highway right past her pantry door.

Trailblaze. That was it, Judah thinks. That was the name of his horse. Fourteen hands high and dappled musculature, fat with proper feeding and curried till he shone. The two of them would take the day and spend it on the land's far reaches, hunting or mending fence or just on the say-so, asleep. The herd was Ayrshire then. Now the herd, or what is left of it, is Holstein and nowhere near as difficult to keep. He caught trout in abundance in the river's shallows, and the smell of trout in his tote bag—mingled with the sweet pine air, and Trailblaze, and his saddle's wet leather—is a smell he still can smell.

"Maggie called," Harriet says.

"*What?*"

"She called."

"Who? When?"

"Margaret Coburn," Harriet says, redeeming her error by blushing. "At eleven o'clock. She wants to ask you not to just join the Library committee, but to be its honorary chairman."

"Tell her no," Judah says.

"She wanted to ask you herself."

"Tell her no. Tell her not ever to call."

It's a kind of blasphemy, he tells himself. *One time it sings on your tongue. One time it's the loveliest name that ever was invented, and for the loveliest woman, and now it's for some blue-haired bitch who's drumming up attendance for her rummage sale. Take that name in your mouths again,* he threatened the men at the bar, *and I'll take all your teeth out and the tongues that do the licking: I'll split you back to front and leave you for the crows to clean. They're used to filth in their beaks*—he finished, his excitement spent. The men looked down at their drinks.

"She meant no harm," Harriet says.

"And she'll accomplish none."

"I meant no harm by it either."

"No, likely not. But her name is Mrs. Coburn. You remember that."

He shod his horse himself. He said I put his shoes on, and Trailblaze does a sight better walking that way. The pines were antler-stripped; he marked them where he fished.

Coincidence, he tells himself. *There's nothing accidental now. She reads my mail. She washes out the toilet bowl and found the letter-scraps and because the ink ran wants to provoke me to telling. Hattie's a cat and the cat's got her tongue and we're none of us telling catty Hattie what's-a-mattie,"* he jingles, vengeful, remembering. *Wife, you should be here.*

Ten days before, he had had Finney come see him in the Toy House, while Hattie was off volunteering at the Library. The two men jostled, fitting in the children's space.

"Well, what did she say?" Judah asked.

"It's cold in here. You ought to have a heater, Jude."

"You think so?"

"Yes. I'm freezing."

"What did you tell Margaret?"

Finney rubbed his hands together. His breath steamed. "She said she'll come."

Judah sat. His legs gave out.

"She said she'll write you that it's her idea to come."

He sat on his hands. There was a rising motion in his chest. He heaved and breathed and his stomach plummeted.

"I told her what you told me to," the lawyer said. "That you're dying anytime now and she'd better come up soon."

"When?"

"Soon. That's all I can tell you."

"How soon?"

Finney rolled his shoulders, anxious. He adjusted his coat. There was mucus hanging from one nostril; he inhaled it back.

"How did she sound?" Judah asked.

"The same. She sounded like she always does. I'm freezing, Jude."

"You've said that."

Finney sniffed. The drop descended.

"Well this is what I want," said Judah. "Tear up everything you've got. I want three wills." His chest had cleared. He felt Finney's heat too palpable beside him and spoke quickly: "Hattie's got her portion and she'll keep it like before. The same with the charity leavings. But everything else: one will says it's Margaret's; one will says it's Ian's, and one says fifty-fifty—got that? Otherwise I'll die without and they can fight over it."

"Judah?" Finney said.

"What?"

"I've got to ask this. You might call me legally bound."

"It's nothing illegal. Now is it?"

"No. Not till you've got witnesses and signed. But morally I'm bound . . ."

Judah interrupted him. " 'Being of sound mind and body.' It's my decision. Mine."

"When I said you were dying, was it true?"

"Yes, but"—Judah considered this, shifting where he'd settled.

"But what?"

"But not"—and he lowered his lid ponderously—"right away."

"So it's a lie," Finney said.

"You knew that."

"Not for certain."

"We none of us can know for mortal certain . . ."

"You made me make a fool of . . ."

Judah brushed this aside. He raised his hand to his ear, palm out. "I want three testaments. That's what I want from your office. And make each of them binding," he warned. "Come to supper when my wife comes back and bring them with you, OK? I'll sign one."

"And Ian?"

"Write him. Say the same."

"I don't have an address."

"Use the last one you've got," Judah said. "Just write him. Just don't call."

He loomed above his friend, extracting a red linen handkerchief. "Here," Judah said. "Don't say I never gave you proper compensation. Wipe your nose."

There is a pianola by the wall, with music rolls that feature John Philip Sousa and music from New Orleans. Maggie played the piano, and there had been a Steinway grand where the pianola stands. She schooled him to love music then. He would sit at her stool's edge, behind her and a little to the left, watching how she tucked her lip in at the louder parts, astonished at her fingers' lightsome agility. He marveled how she knew the notes, or when to turn the page. She played with a rapt stillness and the hands of earthly angels but, to hear her tell it, out of tune. He complimented her. "Rachmaninoff," he said, "himself couldn't play that piece better. Artur Schnabel's no more musical than you."

"Oh, Jude," she said. "You're sweet. You're a dear to say so. But you've got a tin ear, darling, and don't think I don't know. Or you're lying to make me feel proud. Or taking the intention for the deed."

"Not so," he had protested. "I love to watch you play."

"But not to *listen,* darling, and that's the point of it."

"All right. To listen, then."

"That was Chopin," Maggie said. She touched his sleeve. "This is a mazurka."

Smiling, she'd choose another sheet and play some other melody that set his heart delighting. When she left him, later, he had had the piano hauled out to the woods. He'd learned Rachmaninoff's name, and Artur Schnabel's name to please her, and had taken her to concerts in Boston and New York (with Maggie on his right-hand side, in silk, her gloved hands emulating the prodigious maestro's hands; they'd have box seats always, and she'd press her elbows in with pleasure, clapping, while he watched her breasts expand) and maybe she was right and maybe he did have wax in his ear and maybe couldn't change. She'd said so, at the end. He'd change, he told her—not begging, but announcing change. "You simply can't do it," she said.

So he doused the sounding board with kerosene and filled the works with paper and wrapped the legs in soaked rags. It had made a pleasing conflagration, and the strings snapped, jangling; then he bought a pianola and played that instead.

There is the portrait of Daniel Sherbrooke and a portrait, done from memory, of Peacock's wife. Most of the Big House paintings, Judah knows, had been ordered in bulk lot from a supplier in London; the supplier charged less for the paintings than frames. "Send us suitable representations," Peacock wrote, "of scenes both lively and Inspiring. Also I require Floral arrangements and Pictures of apples and two or three scenes from the Hunt. Like unto the fox is man when pursued by conscience-demons in the guise of that goodly baying Pack. We must sniff out Iniquity, e'en to Reynard's lair."

What friends they have are gone from them, dead or estranged or fled south. There was a time the Big House seemed continually lit, and he'd find strangers sleeping in the corridor, or come back from the river to find dinner laid out for twenty and the cook in a desperate bustle; they'd kept cooks then, and maids, and he wondered whether Ian thought the world was mostly peopled with maids and visitors and drunks.

There are cameos above the mantel, and scrimshaw cornucopias; there is a wooden sailor with a carved ivory leg. "Who says we can't change?" Judah complains now to Harriet. "Who said so; answer me that?"

He had been avid of instruction, wanting to learn the mazurka and how it differs from the waltz or *valse polonaise*. He had turned the pages for her, not reading the notes really, but reading the toss of her head. Her teeth would bite her lower lip and he would chew his, hard.

He had been to see the doctor three weeks before. There he got his plan. Dr. Wiggins's face was grave; he listened routinely to Judah but was listening to some heart-speech the stethoscope would translate, attentive only to that.

"Fred, let me ask you something," Judah said.

"Yes."

"We've been friends for thirty years."

"Mm-m."

"Thirty-five years, nearly."

"I came here," Dr. Wiggins said, "in '45. After the Pacific."

But Judah was not tempted into reminiscence; he watched the man across from him unblinkingly.

"Fred, what are my chances?"

"What are you asking me—*chances*?"

"Let's put it directly. Am I sick?"

The doctor looked down at his charts. He tapped a ruler on his desk; he snapped a tongue depressor. "Directly, no."

"But could I be?"

"Of course. You've got that heart of yours."

"Could I say I was dying?"

"You could, in that respect. But not because your doctor says so."

"I wouldn't quote you."

"In that respect," said Wiggins, "none of us can win this gamble. Specially with angina. We're every human being bound to lose this bet."

"I wasn't asking *if* I'll die. I'm asking when."

Dr. Wiggins looked at his hands. They were pink from scrubbing and his nails had perfect crescent moons.

"Jude, I just can't tell you. It's a guessing game. What are you, seventy-six? You might go on for five years, ten; you might go on till they haul you out kicking maybe fifteen years from now; on the other hand, and with that heart of yours . . ."

He spread his hands. They were expressive. They told Judah everything he needed to tell Hattie, and what to tell his lawyer to notify his wife. Leaving the office, later, he practiced the gesture—spreading his hands and fingers and letting the fingers contract.

His sister had been handsome once. Or so he can remember thinking, and so Macallister had thought, and Jamie Pearson and the widower Powers from Manchester. Judah hopes she's taken pleasure when it was available to take; now she sits behind the lamp, a raw-boned woman, fretting. She'd never married—though Jamie Pearson had proposed, and maybe the widower Powers; she'd called that first proposal more a proposition than offer.

"What's the difference?" Judah asked.

"It's a business proposal. He wants to be married to the family, not me."

And she was right, he'd thought; Pearson drank too much and couldn't hold his drink and therefore couldn't hold his bank job without some protective influence. But half a catch is better than none, he had declared, even if the catch is half-baked—or, like Jamie, boiled.

"Brother, you insult me," Hattie said.

"That's not my intention."

"And the family. You insult them too."

So she married history and took an uncle or great-uncle or second cousin once removed or grandfather to bed each night. She'd wedded herself to their letters and daybooks and bills. She kept file boxes in her room with all the clippings she could find, right down to Daniel Sherbrooke's second cousin, Augustus Cobb. There was a great-great-uncle lost at sea. He'd gone down with a clipper ship off Hatteras, "cut off untimly," a survivor wrote, "in his manhood's beauteous prime." Judah knew she mourned him, and he joked she got more heat from Tommy Sherbrooke drowned at sea than from her hot-water bottle. He wished her joy of their ancestors; he wished her joy and consolation in the watches of the night.

34

"You misunderstand me."

"Not at all."

"You're doing it a'purpose. You're being a tease, like you always were."

She said the same about Samuel Powers, who had lineage to equal theirs and therefore wasn't in it for that kind of gain. His mother was a Colonial Dame; his father's forefathers fought with Ethan Allen in Bennington and then at Saratoga Springs. But he scarcely knew his people's names and didn't care when she told him, and didn't read the articles she left for him to read.

"They were probably bastards," Samuel said. "Thirteen percent of all the children born back then were out of wedlock. That's something to think about, when you get to thinking."

Judah agreed. "The man's got sense," he said to Harriet. "And knows how to laugh besides."

"It's no laughing matter." She disdained, she said, all such easy-earned disdain. There were things worth taking seriously, and why should she trust Powers to take her into his family—with his sham family sense? What kind of proof could he give her that he honored what she stood for if he didn't also honor where she stood?

"You're talking in circles. You just don't want to leave our house."

"Why should I?" She had smiled at him, coquettish. "It's a losing trade."

So Harriet aged and solidified, her flesh gone gray. She was the one who first used the word "spinster." "I'm your spinster sister," she would say—deflecting the pain of it, lifting her hands—"the one who's left behind to mind the store."

Jamie Pearson drank until his liver quit. Samuel Powers married a redhead from Connecticut, who was divorced and already had two children. They flew to Nassau for their honeymoon, and the plane went down. Doc Macallister was long since dead, and Harriet, surviving, put their obituary notices in her Miscellany file.

Now he finishes his drink. He opens the dining room door; his sister precedes him, bustling. He pulls out her chair for her, then pushes it forward to the table with her slight added burden. Harriet had been thin then plump then fleshy then corpulent and now is thin again. In the old days she had candied apples and Indian corn and peanut brittle ready when the children of the village dropped by for Hallowe'en. "Oh my," she would exclaim—as each child shuffled in, sack at the ready, big-eyed behind masks—"don't we look marvelous tonight. Tell me what you want to do for trick or treat."

The cowboys would yodel or brandish their capguns, and Pocahontas war-whooped while she filled her sack.

"My goodness, we're near out of chocolate." Harriet came from the kitchen with a basket full of chocolate kisses, and packs of Hershey bars.

"You'll like this," she told Davy Crockett. "Only don't murder raccoons."

"I didn't do it, ma'am," he said.

"But would you? Would you do it if you had the chance?"

"I got three woodchucks," he announced. "With just my .22."

"You'd do it," she lamented. "All those dear creatures slaughtered for the sake of coonskin caps."

"I got it for my birthday," Davy Crockett said. "It was give me. Trick or treat."

The Big House porch would be lamplit—Judah had rigged jack-o'-lanterns—and they played movie tiptoe-music on the pianola. In the rare lulls, when no one was there or could be heard arriving, Harriet would clasp her hands and bow her head and say, "My, my, brother, but they do exhaust me so. The girl with all the crinolines—Scarlett O'Hara, I think she said she was—is Maisie Petersen. Isn't it *astonishing?*"

"This is her last year in that kind of outfit."

"How much she's grown," Harriet marveled. "How quickly she'll be beautiful."

"It happens," Judah said.

None, no single one of them would ever equal Margaret. She was and is and always will be his definition of grace. She had hair the color of wheat and cornflower eyes and legs that made him think of jumping deer. He knows these words are cheap but prizes them nevertheless, and would not call her simply blonde and blue-eyed and long-legged. Nor does she wither and stale in his recollection; she is always twenty-three, running flat-out from the house to meet him, arms pumping, feet raising dust. He would have trouble focusing, from all those hours in the sun, and she would be a doubled, jerky vision, wearing a white dress. He cracked two ribs from squeezing her, but there was no fragility in her athlete's stride. Or thirty-three, her long hair longer but not one whit altered in its coloration (though later he'd suspected and accused her of hair dye and she'd said so what, so what if I just touch it up?) nor five pounds fatter to mark the decade, standing at the staircase, dressed, lifting her dress to come down. His sons had kicked her belly out, and he saw her nine months pregnant, a moon. An arm or leg would shove at her, and he'd watch her bunch and ripple; she'd smooth her skin and rearrange herself on the three extra pillows in bed.

Judah found the Toy House windows soaped on mischief night. Once someone stuck a toothpick in the doorbell, and he had to pull the wiring apart. Maggie, their last Hallowe'en, had dressed herself up as a witch and climbed the maple by the porch and lowered buckets of cooked but cold spaghetti on a rope. She cackled it was worms and raised and lowered the bucket, intoning: "Take, take, take." He himself had worn a beard. He had strapped on the sword that belonged, once, to Ulysses Grant. He had watched her in the tree's fork, luminescent, ghostly, and known she'd go for good the next time gone.

III

"If you please," says Harriet, "I could use a touch more Sanka."

"What?" She has startled him. "What?"

"If you please," she repeats, and slides her cup toward him.

"I'm sleepy," Judah says. "I must have been about asleep."

"You've not been all too talkative," she says. "I guarantee that."

"How much?" he asks. He lifts the pot and poises it.

"Half a cup," Harriet says. "Not even."

"Say when."

"When."

There is liquid on her saucer. He sloshes her saucer's leavings into his own empty cup.

"Sugar?" he asks.

"Yes."

He measures out one teaspoon of sugar. She does the serving if they meet for breakfast, and he does the serving for midday meals, and she serves at night.

"I thank you."

"I must have been sleeping," he says.

His wife had called them goblets in the early years, and chalices. Judah called it just a drinking glass, but Margaret insisted they were chalices replete with her love draught for him, and her desire's potion. That had been early on. They had clicked their glasses, no matter from what distance and every time they drank.

His sister's voice is shrill. "You missed the gong," she said. "You took ever so long with the whiskey. You dawdled with the servings and shouldn't wonder it's late."

He clears his head. He shakes it.

"Sanka doesn't trouble me," she says. "You know that, I expect. I could have a third cup if I wanted and still not have it worry me. I could drink the pot."

"You know what I've been thinking?" Judah asked.

"No. What?"

"Been thinking I should take her back."

He had not known how to say it, had not known how it sounded but knows it for the truth.

"Her. Who?"

"My wife. Margaret Sherbrooke." He looks at Harriet. She colors.

"That's a name," she says, "I thought we'd agreed not to use."

"Yes."

"Well?"

"It's over." Judah stands. "The agreement. I'll take her back when she comes."

"What makes you think she's coming? What makes you so certain?"

"She'll come," he pronounces, "by suppertime. She's making the four-forty bus."

Hattie slides her spoon along the cup rim. "I mention Maggie Coburn and you bite my head off."

"That's different. It isn't the same." He edges his chair to the table again. "I got to get some rest."

Jude, he tells himself. *Keep on. You've done it up properly now. Seven lean years and sixty-nine fat.* He shuts the dining-room door behind him and makes for the hall, performing his familiar calculus. *There's a Rhesus monkey twenty-seven inches long that hangs from a branch by both hands. It drops and you have to shoot it, and it's ten feet from the ground. Where do you aim to be sure of hitting; ask the doctor that.*

The wind slaps at the Big House shutters and he hears it in the chimney, humming. He would wet his finger, sometimes, and circle a glass rim till it sang; the wet wind rimes the chimney now with that low single note. There had been omens enough. He'd known when Lawyer Finney said, "It's five years since you seen her, Jude. And seven since she left. You want to change the will?"

So when the letter came two mornings back, he had not been surprised. He'd recognized her script at once, and the mocking deference with which she'd written, "J. P. Sherbrooke, Esq." There'd not been a return address, though the postmark was Grand Central Station, New York. She'd used a three-cent and a ten-cent stamp that said: "It all depends on ZIP code," and showed planes and mail trucks and trains. The stamp was multicolored and, Judah decided, expensive to print. The plane and parcels were yellow, and the train two shades of red. She'd used no zip code for him, not even his post office box, but only "The Big House."

He sliced the letter open, using his right hand. It was folded over, twice. He smoothed and held the letter, waiting for his breath to quiet. She had used blue ink. Her hand had been the last hand on this paper, he reflected, and she'd tongued the envelope flap. He has watched her at it often: she'd tear the stamp from the stamp roll, not abiding by the perforation and tearing half a head off presidents, then licking the stamp and placing it at the envelope's edge. *"Jude"*—he peered at the inscription. *"I've been away. I'll keep this letter short because I'm not certain you'll read it."*

He switched on the light. He'd burned her early letters, or flushed them down the toilet, torn into eighths, unread. He'd refused the ones with postage due or written on them: Return to Sender. Addressee Unknown. *"But there are things I have to tell you and things I have to ask. You'd do me a*

kindness to let me visit soon. As you know, I'm not one to beg. I'll be at the
Bus Station Wednesday, arriving at 4:40 from New York. If you meet the
Greyhound Bus, I'll be happy to get off; if not, I'll understand. Or try to. But
please do meet the bus, for auld sake's sake if nothing else; it's more than auld
acquaintance surely, and we owe each other that. I'll not ask another time.
I'll travel on to Rutland and not bother you ever again. But I come in hopes
the love I bear you and you said you bore me once will alter your opinion of
the proper way to act. I hope this finds you well. Meg."

He takes her signature for a good omen, and the tense of "bear." He
takes her memory of his catchphrase, "For auld acquaintance sake," and
the fact she's used blue ink. It had been Monday. Monday was the day they
married, and Wednesday the day they first met. *"I'm not, as you know, one
to beg."*

Ian was a breech birth, and difficult. Maggie had her first contractions Friday night, and she had gone into the garden and pinched and staked and
bound up tomatoes all next morning.

"Don't overdo it," he warned.

"I'm not overdoing it. I'm doing it, that's all."

"You're in pain."

"I *want* to do it." She was flushed with bending and had a sweat moustache.

"Well, do what you want," Judah said.

"Yes."

"I worry about it, is all."

"You mustn't worry, darling. I need some distraction. I'll stop when it's
time to stop. Promise."

He wondered what would prove to her that it was time to stop. He put
his hand on her stomach and felt the muscle band.

"It feels like the world's biggest girdle."

"The tightest, leastways," he acknowledged.

"Oh, Judah P," she sucked down her breath. "It hurts me so much when
it hurts."

He took the green twine from her, and the scissors. She exhaled. Later, eating or staking tomatoes, assaulted by their pungency, he would remember her nest-building bravado and the way she'd distributed weight. She smiled at him, hands on her hips.

"It's better now. He's got the hiccups, maybe. But he's got an elephant kick."

When Ian came he did come kicking. There were forceps creases on his head. Judah heard her (down the hall, he could swear it, and one flight up, bellowing for him, her husband, telling the doctors there'd been some mistake, and she could go home now, go quickly, he, Judah, was waiting and she wasn't ready for delivery at this particular moment, he'd endow a hospital, and where was the promise they'd made her, where the nurses' estimate that it'd be over by noon, then three, then seven, then eleven, and where was the gas they'd promised to give, where the injections, the relief since she'd rather be shot) screaming: "Please! Please stop it. Please."

They stopped it at dawn. Ian Daniel Sherbrooke weighed eight pounds. He was a solemn baby and lay and mused for hours, wide awake. He cried without rage, dutifully, flailing his arms and legs as if he knew that's how an infant cried—but out of choice, not instinct, and not out of need. His mouth distended later in what was more a rictus than a grin. Judah, watching, cooing, understood that things were serious and life no laughing matter—no matter how much Maggie laughed. She had had levity scooped out of her with that first wailing son—as if all body blitheness was ejected with the afterbirth. Sheep eat the afterbirth. Sows eat their farrow, given the chance. There are nutrients a mother needs and loses when she loses the fetal food sack. He'd have taken that placenta gladly, had they thought to offer it. He'd have separated out the waste lines from the veins for humor and for body blitheness, and made Maggie swallow them back.

Now he ascends. His father had had the elevator shaft constructed when his mother was bedridden with phlebitis. The machinery is in the attic, underneath the cupola. When she was sick with more than phlebitis and too weak to close the doors—too weak, even, for the buttons, though he put her hand on the buttons and helped push—she nonetheless insisted on a ride each morning. She had had nurses, of course. But she depended on him—"Only Judah's strong enough," she'd say.

So he would wheel her on the tour. The upstairs halls were long and narrow, and he grew adept at maneuvering through rooms. She'd point to bedspreads or curtains that needed cleaning and say: "You must note that. Inform Maria. It's outrageous what has happened to the house. She'll sweep that carpet by tomorrow or she'll be dismissed."

"Yes, mother."

"Don't *yes* me like that, Judah, or take me for a fool. I know what's happening here. There's laxness and corruption and I know what made that bedspread dirty. Just don't take me for an idiot. Maria cleans that carpet or hey-presto out she goes."

Maria swept the carpet. She had been engaged to Harry Jackson who left his job in the lumber mill and died in the ditches of France. She used that expression "died in the ditches of France" to amplify her grief, and Judah would watch wide-eyed while she bent to unlace herself, sobbing. He had been seventeen. His mother, the next morning, accepted the guest room carpet and curtains but pointed to the hanging lamp; the lamp needed polish, she said.

So he manipulated her through storage closets and in bathrooms and along the upstairs landing. "Oh, Judah," she would say. "Don't suffer this indignity. I wouldn't wish indignity like this on my worst enemy. They take me for an idiot, forgetting I have eyes. Forgetting I know what I know."

He held his breath in the oak box. The front and back were doors. The doors alternated on each floor, so he could wheel his mother in and stand behind her, hands on the chair rim, and then continue pushing in the same direction. She hated to be pulled. When she had made the full inspection and he consigned her again to her room ("Don't leave me, Judah," she would say. "Don't forget your mother. And don't take me for an idiot or think I don't have eyes."), he'd jump the steps three at a time and run to the stables and saddle up and drop his head to the horse's flank and breathe deeply, cinching the girth. He would inhale the smell of oats and animal expectancy, then swing himself up and be at a canter by the time he'd cleared the barn.

So when his mother died he closed the elevator up. They inspect the hoist rig every six months and keep the wires oiled. Margaret made him love her in the elevator once. "I want to do it," she whispered, "in every single nook and cranny of this whole house. In each individual bed. In every place you've ever been, my darling, or anyone has ever been. There. Here." She'd rubbed against the dust-dulled walls and brought them to a sheen.

His son is his principal rival, he knows: the reason Maggie left. "I'll not abandon him," she'd said.

"Sooner or later you've got to."

"No. It's hard enough . . ." Her voice trailed off.

"What?"

"Nothing."

"Finish what you started," Judah said.

"Ian is my only son," she said. "I think about Seth always. That's as it should be and I'm not complaining but I won't lose Ian also; he's worth the world to me and you'd better know it, Jude."

"I do."

"Not really. Not deep down."

"He's my son too."

"Then how could you imagine that I'd let him live here, hating it? There's a world outside. There's high school to finish and college to go to and maybe law school and medical school and all sorts of people to meet. Musicians. Women. Politicians."

"Whoever," he said.

"And the point is Ian's young and needs to get outside these walls. He's like a prisoner here, Jude. You can't invite the world."

"If he's lonely . . ."

"I know: 'Let's invite some friends up for the weekend.' That's not it. He's got to learn that city life means more than Rockefeller Center and a boat trip on the Hudson and the Empire State Building. He wants to go and I'm taking him with me since it's what you'd call abandonment to stay."

Judah'd tried to warn her she should leave Ian alone. He'd tried to make it clear: the Sherbrooke place was world enough for two and it could hold their son. Go and you take yourself with you, he'd said; that's the thing about departure; leave but don't ever come back.

"It is important," Peacock wrote, "that the stair-crest be sufficing Broad. I wish it an Adequate Perch for the announcement of Arrivals, and jollity to be surveyed by the Provider thereof. But let there be currents of air. Else the pestilential vapors will foregather and Accumulate as unwelcome guests at such festivity, and rioting in secret in that lecherous Enclosure soon make their noxious Presence known, infecting the Host unawares. There shall be Crimson Carpeting in the center of each stair-tread, which Carpet is to be secured by a Brass Rail."

"Good afternoon," he calls to Harriet.

"Good afternoon." She is at the stairwell, watching.

"Sleep well."

"Yes. Thank you."

She too takes an afternoon nap. "Give Tommy Sherbrooke my best," he says.

"I'll rest," she says. "I've had two cups of Sanka but it doesn't trouble me."

"That's good. You've got a clear conscience. That's good."

"I hope I'm not the only one." She squints up at him, meaningful. "I hope *your* conscience is clear."

"As mud," he says. "As always. Happy dreams."

"I'm not reproachful, brother. I wouldn't want you to think that."

"Then don't reproach me, Hattie."

"I can see," she calls to him, "that the subject is closed."

"What subject?"

"You know very well. The one you raised."

"No. Which?"

"The subject of your wife," she ventures. "Margaret."

"I raised so many subjects," Judah turns again. "You're right. Yes, the subject's closed, and she'll be here on the four-forty bus. And yes, my conscience is clear."

"Happy dreams."

"And when the subject opens up again it's her and me who'll open it. All right?"

"I'm not being reproachful. Don't think that."

"I don't," he concludes. "I don't think about it at all."

But that's not true, he tells himself, ascending. *Reproachfulness is all we think of. And recrimination. There's nothing openhanded in the house.*

His plan is ready, his trap set. He will call them together about him and announce it: he'd little time left, the doctor had warned, and could wake up any morning dead and before that he desires to settle up accounts. Let no one say he left them owing, or he's been ungenerous. His room is the fourth on the right. Their room had been fourth on the left, at the hall's opposite extension, facing south. There is one leather chair in his room, an oil lamp, a water pitcher and a drinking glass. There are gilt-framed standing photographs of Ian on the bedside table, but nothing on the walls. The walls are green. The floor is parquet squares. There are no rugs or curtains nor any ornamentation beyond the ornamental moldings and the single-sleigh bed. The bed is gray, its tracery is green. He removes his boots laboriously and sits on the bed, facing out. Winded, he sets the alarm for three thirty, in case. Snow eddies past, so lightly that he thinks (what with the lamp's reflected glare, and the day's chill reckoning, and whiskey) it is his eyes.

He shuts his eyes. The snow continues. He puts his right hand out and touches the window and, opening his eyes again, tracks the pane's frost filigree. His fingertips stick to the glass. He runs his index finger across his gums and teeth. When she forsook their plush sunlit room, he thinks now, leaning back, she perhaps relinquished comfort also. She was in Grand Central Station, maybe, with only the price of a stamp.

There is the afternoon to get through. There had been the night before and Tuesday night and this day's dawn and morning and noon since her letter arrived. There have been the ten days since Finney told him she'd come. Judah has till the four-forty bus and still can change his mind. He thinks of not meeting it but driving to Rutland instead. She would look out the window and scan the station and wait two minutes and maybe get out and ask at the desk if there were any messages for her, Margaret Sherbrooke, and the attendant would say no, and she would ask if he were certain, and he'd riffle through his notepad and check the board again. "No, ma'am, nothing," he'd say and she'd turn and exit and climb back on the bus (it would be snowing, maybe, or the snow would turn to rain, and just a single taxi and pickup truck that she'd know at a glance wasn't his. Still she'd check, irresolute, because he might have bought another pickup, because he might well have hired a taxi—but knowing all the time, knowing from the instant of arrival, and while the driver cut the motor and opened the doors, he, Judah, wouldn't dream of showing and what had she been dreaming of, and why?)

The tarmac would be wet. There would be slush on her window. The air would have that bone chill that passes for spring in Vermont. ("You know what they say," he used to joke. "About the weather here. Nine months of winter and three of poor sledding." She, Margaret, had laughed but later on insisted he take her to New Orleans . . .) The bus would shudder, starting. "Next express stop, Rutland," the attendant would announce. "Arriving at five fifty-two. All aboard for Rutland, please. Next stop."

So there she'd be, abandoned, who had abandoned him once. She'd watch the roadside markers and the motels and restaurants in town. There would be half-glimpses of a car or face she thought she knew, but soon the bus would gain momentum in the gathering half-dark. It would run through the gearbox and clatter out onto Rte. 7 and she'd settle back. She was marked "Return to Sender" and had not been claimed.

Judah smiles. He feels himself smile. There would be tinted windows and the bus would have its lights on as it bowled north through Manchester. His wife, Mrs. Margaret Sherbrooke, would put dark glasses on—and maybe her neighbor would notice and think it strange since outside it was more than halfway dark, though the weather would be clearing, though the storm clouds emptied somewhere short of Equinox, and there, to the west, was the moon, scudding through the sky beside them—and bend to the window, throat working, shoulders hunched. "Are you all right?" her neighbor would ask—would think of asking, rather, since the woman brooked no interference, even in discomfiture, and was forbidding now as she had been forbidding the whole trip from New York. "Yes, quite all right, I thank you," would be the answer surely, glacial and inviolate and false.

So Margaret, his second wife, would be delivered to the Rutland bus depot. She would deposit herself on the tarmac again, this time with her canvas bag. She'd tighten her cloth coat. She'd breathe and blink and find him, Judah, there before her, grinning at the game he'd played and won. There would be explanations but no need of explanation, and she'd be in his arms again, unstrung.

"How could you do it, Jude?"

"Do what?"

She sobbed but would not let him see her sob and inclined her face away.

"Do unto others," he said.

"That's not the golden rule," she said. "It's cruelty, pure cruelty."

"I wanted to surprise you."

"Nothing you do now surprises me."

The conversation is wrong. He had had the advantage and she takes advantage from him, pressing where he yielded and compliant when he pressed.

"I meant no harm," he said.

"You did. You do," and she was racked with tears and on his shoulder, trembling.

"There." He stroked her. "There. I'm sorry. Come into the house."

"Yes."

"Megan. Maggie. Whatever you call yourself nowadays."

"Meg. Mrs. Judah P. Sherbrooke," she smiled.

"Welcome what the cat dragged in. Margaret, welcome home."

Pleased with his imaginings, he climbs into the bed. The ceiling pattern is familiar; there are plaster cracks the shape of a spring-tooth harrow. He courts sleep. Tonight, he tells himself, he will have most need of it. He puts his arms behind his head and presses his elbows back as far as they will go and lies there breathing, stretching, remembering the license-plate numbers of every car he's owned. He chops the second willow down—the one by the pond that's dying anyhow, and killing tamaracks to boot—and sees, in his mind's eye, how he will notch it and in which direction it should fall. Then he chops the limbs off and segments the trunk and then chops the trunk into log lengths and splits and stacks the wood. Willow wood is stove wood, no good for burning by itself but useful in a mix. He turns to his right side.

Meantime he occupies himself, singing "Begin the Beguine." The word "beguiled" sticks to him like a burr. He would beguile the time until she arrived, as she had been beguiling and he had been beguiled. There were guileful people and there was the town of Guilford and there were wiles and guiles. Giles Cavendish had lost his arm in Normandy on D-Day, and that reminds him of Maria and "dead in the ditches of France." He had taken catnaps standing, though Maggie called them "horsenaps." She had complained he wasn't horizontal ten minutes, ever, before she heard him snore. She would lie reading, or brushing her hair with the silver-handled brushes that had belonged to his mother, and he would look at her and shut his eyes; he had coveted wakefulness, once, as now he covets sleep.

"Jude," she whispers at him. "Judah P."

He makes no answer.

"Judah. Jude, I say."

He turns.

"Come a little closer. Just this close."

There are rocks. She positions herself on the high forward rock. She is combing out her yellow hair. It cascades.

"I'll tell you a secret, J.P. I'll tell you something I've never told to anyone."

"Not anyone?" He finds his voice.

"Not anyone. And I'll never tell it ever again. Not to anyone but you."

She employs an amber comb. He has presented it to her. Her hair is amber also, and has teeth.

"Come closer, Jude. Come here till I tell you."

He advances. There is water. He swims.

"It's not the sort of thing," she says, "one ought to beg to say."

He flails his arms and flutters his legs and is advancing.

"Not to a gentleman . . ."

He rises.

"Judah, darling." She exhorts him. "Judah P."

She bends and holds her hand out and her hand is at sixty degrees. He reaches for it but she is receding.

"Try," she sings. "Try harder. Husband."

There is water in his mouth. There is water as well in his nose and eyes and, catastrophically, water in his ears.

"Lover," she calls out to him. "Love." But he is unable to hear.

"I wish a cupola to Crown the house," Peacock wrote, "and be its Glittry Diadem werewith to catch the Morning Sun and honor Him who made it, as He created light and every living Creature. There must be variegated glass, and of as many colors as was Joseph's Coat. I see a Signal Beacon to the footsore traveler or pilgrim Pelerinating with his eyes cast up at dusk to catch the fading warmth and certify Direction. He shall see our constant Rainbow and take his bearings thus and know, I do devoutly think, heart's ease. It is no small consolation to see a Steeple rising at the forest's rim. Often have I lingered at the Path's fell turning, with such the final sight. It affords no little Comfort to hear the mellifluous church-chime breast the Tempest's howling like some Sturdy Swimmer with consistent stroke. And surely every Mariner must say a Thankful prayer when he spy the lighthouse winking in the Blackamoor and minstrel face of Night. What tho the dawn will scrub the nigger Visage clean, and each Ship prove its goodly Harbour and traveler attain his Resting-place, yet would I have our Cupola be th'unchanging Watchman, a *twelve-sided* sentry of the Soul . . ."

PART II

I

He is at the depot, in the increasing dark. He stands by the green metal bench, in front of the soft-drink machine. Descending, she sees Judah and misses the last step; her ankle twists in. So Maggie limps toward him, transferring the bag to her left hand for balance; she had expected Finney, or a taxi sent to bring her to his bed.

"Well, hello," she says. "Should you be here?"

"Who else?" He takes a step toward her. "Let me help you with that."

And reaches and takes the bag and hefts it with a strength that does not seem a dying man's, and she who has prepared for shock is shocked that there is nothing changed, is suddenly back from a weekend's excursion and not seven years.

"So," Judah says. "You made it."

"Yes."

"It's been raining this last hour," he gestures. "First, snow. Like it can't make up its mind what weather we're having tonight."

"You're up and about," she says.

"As you see me."

"I can't quite believe my eyes. I thought . . . "

"Believe them," he tells her—slipping into his protective condescension, opening the car door for her, shepherding her in. "I'm here."

Sitting, she asks, "When you got my letter, were you surprised?"

He starts the car. "Power steering helps."

"Were you expecting it? Or was it a shock to you?"

He drives with both hands on the wheel, and the attentive caution of the aged.

". . . But once you get a problem in the power steering unit, it's harder than all hell to fix. Might as well walk."

She settles back; she knows he won't answer till ready to talk. Her father thrives. Judah, give or take a year, is her father's age. "How's Finney?"

"Fine," Judah tells her. "He's coming over for dinner."

"And Hattie?"

"The same."

"Ian? Have you heard from him?"

"Not likely."

Things are familiar, not strange. So this is it, she tells herself, this squalid litany; how's the grocer's nephew with the harelip; how's Elvirah—she marvels at her memory for all of this inconsequence—Elvirah Hayes?

"And you?" Judah asks.

"I'm as you see me."

He signals for a left turn at the Library. "Pretty."

"We're none of us immortal," Maggie says.

"Pretty always."

"Flatterer."

Remembrance is a trick time plays; the world is déjà vu and everything repeats itself, with nothing new under the sun. Elvirah Hayes and Lucy Gregory live in that brick cottage to her right, behind the picket fence.

"Why did you come?"

"Why not? What else is one supposed to do?"

"Don't laugh at me," he says.

Embarrassed, she looks out the window—seeing sleet and the huddled houses. They relax, she thinks, with summer—they sprout awnings and porch furniture and the accoutrements of easy weather. "I'm not. I wasn't laughing."

"Maggie," her husband pronounces. "Is that what they call you these days?"

"Whatever you want. Mrs. Sherbrooke."

"You're being nice," he says. "You'd never been this well-behaved before you took that bus."

"I'm a little surprised to see you."

"Don't be," Judah says.

He has the possessor's vanity; her vanity had been to do without the claims of ownership. His love had been exclusive, but hers had been inclusive: all of God's chillun got wings. So Maggie had opposed him term for term—insisting jealousy was shopworn, and marriage a convenience; her dream had been of liberty, his of unfettered constraint.

"We'll take the long way round, through town. That way we'll miss the hill."

"Is it very slippery?"

"I wouldn't want to lose you now you're here."

He says this with such force she takes it for the first true note of all his praise and banter; she raises her left hand and rubs it on his cheek. "Feel Daddy's scratchy face," she says. "That's from *Pat the Bunny*. I remember Ian used to raise that fist of his before we even turned the page, before we'd get to Peekaboo."

"Hide-and-seek. Seems like every game there is is one we tried to play."

"Succeeded in playing," she says. He tries to kiss her hand—still staring forward, still driving, and misses and smacks his lips.

There had been purple martins by the pond. Judah wanted purple martins to keep mosquitoes back. They rarely settled this far north, and had to be enticed. Before she married him he coaxed the birds with houses set up on poles, the proper distance from the pond and built to Amos Sandy's satisfaction; Amos said they liked their houses just so. He had waited for three seasons, with no luck. Then Maggie settled in and with her came the purple martin families; they settled that fourth season and returned. They skimmed and flitted across the pond, and she took them—the first evenings, so swift was their flight—for bats. Maggie joined him in the evenings on the Big House porch, and they watched the swooping birds and heard them in the trees.

"An owl," she'd said. "A wise old owl."

"A mourning dove."

"This time of night?" she asked him. "Wouldn't it likely be owls?"

"It's not that kind of morning. It's what you do with sorrow, not the time till noon."

Maggie could feel herself color. "I never knew that," she said. "I thought it was morning A.M."

"They're nothing like you think them"—Judah was expansive. "They're fierce birds, matter of fact, and even in a cage. Put two turtle doves together, they make fighting cocks look tame."

> *Oh don't you see yon turtle dove*
> *Who flies from pine to pine;*
> *He's mourning for his own true love*
> *As I will mourn for mine—*

She sang to him. He complimented her with the condescending kindliness she had heard in Hattie when the choice of a fabric or color reflected well upon her own astuteness in the choosing. "Keep at that song, it's fine." He believed her, said her husband; he had taken the stanza for truth. He figured purple martins were as good a sign as any that his luck would change, and then not change again.

In any case she sang:

As I will mourn for mine
Believe me what I say.
You are the darling of my heart,
Until my dying day.

Now it all seems foreordained. It makes sense, looking back. Of course she would work as a model and hate it; of course come to the Big House hunting some father surrogate (as she'd told her analyst long since, but been bored with the pat equation even in the telling) some memory of a male presence to dandle and comfort and change her. Of course he, Judah, would fit that bill in every particular: titanic and comfortable both.

"A thing done that's worth doing," he said, "is worth admitting you've done it."

"What if nobody asks?"

"Then nobody's any the wiser. And that's all right."

"But what about being sworn to silence?"

"There's some things we don't talk about," he grinned at her. "And some we talk about doing and some we only just do."

Maggie loves her father, wanly, still. He lives alone in his retirement home in Cape Cod, and she would spend stray weekends there, dutiful, admiring his seashell collection. He is full of sea lore but has never been to sea. He'd pace the Wellfleet wharf or the trails to Great Island for all the world like a retired admiral, jaunty, sheltering his pipe. He limps and somehow manages to suggest it is a sailor's roll, and that his parquet flooring is a pitching deck. He sports yachtsman's caps. She hears him out but hears within the babble only, "Help. Meg, not the man I was. Have some sort of patience, it's holiday season; it's the way we used to be, remember, in a southwest gale off Hatteras, the tuna sinking everything in sight . . ."

She walked with him where fishing boats weathered the winter—swept up to the wharf as though by an outlandish tide and stranded there on cinder blocks and jacks. She lagged behind. The prows were huge, rotting, barnacle-streaked. Boats with names like *Mudlark* and *Norman Scott* and *Li-Burt-E* towered above her, their cabins painted jaunty colors and their decks piled high with nets. Her father spoke of basking sharks the size of whales and how the whales would dance around the boats. There would be ice on the dock. He picked his way with care: an old man in the wind. Maggie listened to him with a familiar yearning—that he not be consigned to muttering his tales alone. She leaned her head on his shoulder, but was too tall to make the gesture more than mawkish, embarrassing them both. She straightened. "I've been to New Orleans, Dad. And San Francisco since I saw you last."

He smiled at her vaguely, obsessed. "But when a whale is sickly," he continued, "and the herd knows it's a goner—this is true for dolphins too, mind you, and seals, and anything with the slightest spark of compassion or instinct for decency, mind you—then they shove it in to shore. That way it can go in peace; that way the sharks won't get at it; it's the fish equivalent for burial at sea."

And suddenly she knew she'd answer Judah if he called. Suddenly she made a covenant: The Golden Rule. Do unto others. If somebody watches over my father, anyone, she told herself, I'll watch out for my husband forever and ever, amen. An ancient Dodge appeared. She heard it the length of the dock away, noticed its shape in the far distance. It made for them; she made out a man at the wheel. He was sitting erect, using both hands to steer down this wide and empty avenue; his car had been repainted, black, and he brought it to a halt. Gulls wheeled above them, dropping and shattering clams. He rolled down the window, rolling it all the way, using his entire arm to crank. Polite, he doffed his cap. "Hey, Harry," he said. "You fortunate man. Who's this young lovely with you?" There was rheum at his eyes' pouches and a red waxed moustache. "Must be your daughter? Afternoon, miss."

"Not so young," said Maggie. "But thanks just the same."

The chromium was pitted; she put her hand on the headlight's bright abrasions. They "geezerized" for minutes—it was her father's word for conversation—in the wet wind. She would go to Judah when he called.

Maggie had spied on him once. She had been in Providence but came back unexpectedly, telling Junior Allison who drove the cab to let her off at the gate. The night was dark, and clouds obliterated what she guessed was a half-crescent moon. The mountain ash trees had bloomed in her brief absence; she was thirty-two years old. She believed in psychic age, though she thought her own had shifted and might shift again. Men were born a certain age and stayed that way; Judah, for example, in her mind's eye was always forty-five.

Dogs barked at her, then quieted. She walked on the driveway's grass rim. It was not spying exactly, she told herself, stepping out of her shoes. It was looking at the life her husband lived without her, in her absence; it was hunting some new access point to his walled enclosure.

"How long will you be off?" he'd asked.

"A week," she said. "Maybe less."

"And maybe more?"

"Maybe, I doubt it. Ten days at the most."

"Your uncle needs your help?" It was a question really, but she took it as his answer.

"Yes, there's so much furniture. There's so much we've got to decide."

"Don't bring it here," Hattie warned her. "We don't need anything else."

"His ladder-back chair," said Maggie. "Maybe the rolltop desk."

"Ship what you like," Judah said.

She stepped, therefore, secretly onto the porch. The watchdogs wagged their tails. Later she would tell him how the cousins divided up family spoils. She needed nothing and had taken nothing but her uncle's ladder-back chair. Later she would tell him how she missed him there in Providence, walking in the chill bay wind and seeing the house lamps light up. The living room lamps, here, were lit. Judah sprawled in the green leather chair. His sleeves were rolled to his elbows, and she saw the white hairs riffle on his arm. He bent above the yellow stoneware plate to eat a sandwich, leaning forward, mouth making swallowing motions, and something about that gesture—a weary domesticity, the time he'd taken to make and arrange his sandwich, adding lettuce, a sweet pickle—touched her, moved her as none of his elaborate courtesy could, nor any of the regal meals she had pictured him consuming.

He was six feet from her, maybe, with glass and gauze intervening, but she saw his head in profile as though he slept beside her on the pillow. He sucked on his cheek. He wore his brown corduroy pants. She had mended them more times than she would care to count, and offered to buy him a new pair, but he said not until I wear it through, but thanks, but what about this button, can you manage that?

Later she would tell him that she hated Providence. They were crows over carrion, she'd say. They'd argued over furniture and even stamp collections, like a flock of crows. It's good, she'd say, to be back home where nothing was in question or out of its accustomed place or on some sort of auction block, with legatees bidding. Judah moved. He looked at her. He craned his head to the left and was staring at her, she could swear, staring *through* her at the willow. She flattened herself. "I'm crazy about you, mister," she whispered. "Crazy mad."

Hattie comes to the door. They greet each other, constrained. Her voice is high-pitched, querulous. "What brings you to these parts?"

"I wanted to see you. Both. You know that."

"Well, look your fill," says Hattie. "*We're* not leaving, him and I."

Maggie takes her bearings. Judah used to say that any liar dreams he'll be caught and pardoned; any faithless person reasons faithlessness is faith. There's something in a clown, he said, that needs to get egg on his face and to take a pratfall walking in or out the door. But women have a harder time of it these years, she believes, than men. Not only do they have the housework and child-work and beauty-work to keep up with, but they also feel dishonored if they honor it as work. When a man has a profession the world calls him a professional; when a woman pursues a career, they call her a "careerist."

"Yes, well," says Judah, entering, carrying her suitcase. "We'll let her alone a little bit, sister. Just long enough to wash."

"I don't mind," Hattie says.

"I didn't guess you would," he says. "Well see you in a while."

"How long?"

"Twenty minutes?" Maggie says. "I do want to freshen up."

In her own way, her sister-in-law has kept to what she stood for, standing fast. Hattie tried. She loved the boys. But sometimes it had seemed more standing pat than fast, and then there was change all around them so that standing still was change.

"I'll be in my room," Hattie says.

Hair in the flanges of his nose, hair in his ears; a nose like an Indian's, where rain could practice skiing. Eyes that were blue in daylight, gray at night, and green in the pine woods or when he looked at grass—the only changeable thing in him, Maggie thinks, an absence of color really, not a hue to name. Big ears to hear her where she walked, a mouth like Cupid's crossbow, with the skin so often cracked and healed it seemed scarified. That was how his whole skin moved, independent of the bone struts beneath, so that when he squinted his checks would fall, not rise; that was how he used his hands, wrapping them like swaddling around the fork he held. There was stubble on his chin and cheeks; she has been robbed, she tells herself, of his resplendent youth. She has the photographs. He stands there pole-trim, erect. His white hair had been yellow then, as everything was yellow in the print. He is, she hears herself telling Mary, just the most beautiful man. He's everything I dreamed of, he's the strongest man in the whole wide world, just dreamy. He's rich, her city friend says. Yes, he's very rich. He's old, she says, not all that old, just graying at the temples. But— and Mary drops her voice, sybilline, insistent—do you love him? Love him, Maggie answers, oh my, yes. I'm mad about the boy. He has this team of horses that he broke himself. He has a carriage—you know, the old-fashioned kind, with plush seats, all the trimmings and a place to put your parasol—and he takes me in it sometimes and we ride for hours and don't ever leave his land. It's a one-horse carriage actually, it's for the Belgian workhorse that he got in Canada. But Mary says it's boring; it isn't boring now but will be twenty years from now, she'd rather shop at Bendel's. And twenty years from now is eight years ago, and everything they'd argued on or prophesied had come to pass, is past. Judah stands there, her sizeable beast, her leonine husband twice the size of that dead emperor they called the Lion of Judah. And his eyes are yellow now, and the pouches of his flesh reek of the dying animal that he, the container, contains.

II

Across the hall, she hates them. She hates Judah's offhand dismissal. She had said, "I'm not reproachful," but he had reproached her nonetheless. He hasn't, Hattie knows, the right. She'd done some things that merited reproach—as which of us hasn't, she asks herself now—and other things to anger him that merited his righteous anger. She'd not deny that. She never denied it, in thought or in deed, and no matter what it cost her in his teasing disrespect. He doles her maraschino cherries out like alms. She can afford to buy all the maraschino cherries in the state of Vermont, and all of New England if pushed to it. She could have hoarded or have swallowed them in clumps. She could drink cherry pop or cherry brandy or Cherry Heering, come to that. But she prefers to be modest and ration her pleasures and not to be discourteous and to await his toast. "Your health," he'd say, and she'd answer, "*Your* health," noting how the sweetness bobbled and spread out and sank. There was little enough, otherwise, to sweeten up the bitter draught Judah made her drink.

She imagines, sometimes, a maraschino cherry tree. She has heard that somewhere they tie bottles over the fruit bud and let fruit grow in the bottle and then pour liquor in. That way you get a pear or peach too big for the bottleneck but in the bottle anyhow and saturated, growing. The maraschino cherry trees would line the streets of Washington and the banks of the Potomac, and springtime there would be, completely, bliss. George Washington chopped down a chokecherry tree. She is certain of that. She is certain that our nation's father spared the proper cherry tree and cleared the nuisance—the chokecherry—out. He tossed a silver dollar straight across the wide Potomac and never lied and could have felled the chokecherry with three mighty strokes.

There are other misconceptions. There is the misconception that he had silver teeth. In fact his teeth were wooden, and he spent the night of Valley Forge inspiriting the troops. He proved his gay insouciance and his scorn of prideful Redcoats by whittling at his lower teeth with his honed bayonet blade. She, Harriet, has no problem with her teeth. She is blessed with every single one of them, and they do not corrode. Her brother said that cherry acid was as good a paint remover as any, and better than most, and that he'd filled a bathtub with it once and worn out the enamel.

He was always teasing her. He's teased her since she can remember and is at it still. She supposed his teasing was a surrogate for courtesy, his way of saying: "Harriet. I'm glad you're with me, sister. It makes it easy you're here."

"Thanksgiving's not a harvest feast," he'd say instead.

"Of course it is."

"You're wrong. I'll prove it."

"Prove it then," she challenged him.

"It happens in November, right? The final Thursday of the month."

"That's Roosevelt's doing," Hattie said. "That's when he regulated holidays, remember?"

"But it was somewhere around then anyhow. Well, give or take a week."

"All right."

"And it started in New England."

66

"Yes."

"And they're bringing in pumpkins and corn from the fields."

"Of course."

"It's not 'of course'"—he triumphed. "There's nothing growing then. There's not a pumpkin left to harvest, or even Indian corn."

It was a misconception, and she'd set him straight. Samoset had brought in corn from the storehouse, not lifted off the stalk. But Judah pointed to her picture books that showed the pilgrim-settlers coming laden from the fields. Samoset walked down to meet them, grinning, arms filled full.

"Well, then, the artist got it wrong. That's not how it happened at all."

"You don't know, Hattie. You weren't there either. It must have been slim pickings is my point."

"All right," she said. "All right."

"Admit I proved it," Judah said.

"You didn't."

"Admit it. I did."

So they would fall to bickering and squabbling as they'd squabbled seventy years before. He'd bested her at checkers, though she had taught him the game. He'd bested her at riding and in their mother's heart of hearts. He'd bested her by the involuntary arrogance of size. But there was voluntary arrogance also, and she had curbed that in him. She'd made alliance with her sister-in-law, and they bridled him for years.

Then the alliance was broken, and everything in the Big House broken, shattered by Maggie's departure and the way Judah went wild. He teased her about the family tree, calling it scrub oak only, or like the poison sumac that mostly was display. He told her how the doctor said a bottle of maraschino cherries can cause what's called insulin shock. He teased her that she never married and wasn't the marrying kind. "Love 'em and leave 'em," he'd say. "That's my sister Hattie—got a string of broken hearts there knotted around her finger. Only none of us knows just exactly what she needs to be reminded of. Or who. She keeps her own counsel on that."

She kept her own counsel continually. She could have told him things. She could have told him, for instance, how the women of the house first fashioned their alliance. Maggie had been making quiche lorraine. She called it "quiche lorraine," but it was really only pastry crust and eggs and onions and bacon. She, Harriet, was in the kitchen (watching the wreckage, thinking this young person cooks as if she'd all her life had someone who would clean up after, scrubbing up the pots and mixing bowls as if it were a privilege to rinse what Maggie dirtied . . .)

"I hope you like the way it tastes. And that this recipe pleases you."

"Of course."

"I mean it," Maggie said. There was a pastry smear beneath her eye.

"Why do they call it quiche?"

"It's a peasant dish," she'd said—and Harriet wondered, was that the answer? "It comes from Lorraine."

"Lorraine who?"

"It's a place, not person." Her sister-in-law straightened, smiling. "It's an area in France." Maggie wiped the pastry smear but managed only to enlarge it. There was flour on her hand.

"You're making it for Judah"—she let resentment surface. "You're making it for him and for his guests."

"For you too, Harriet. For all of us."

"You don't care a, a—what's the word?—a twopenny damn. You're being polite."

Then Maggie made their alliance. She laid the mixing spoon and the eggbeater on the table (not on the bowl, Harriet saw, not in the tray set aside so the drippings wouldn't puddle or trail to the floor) and put out her hand. "Don't despise me."

"Despise you? Why should I despise you?"

"You've got your reasons, I don't doubt. But don't despise me. Please."

Nobody on God's bounden earth could have resisted the woman; she, Harriet, couldn't resist.

"I don't hold you responsible"—she staked one final claim. "I don't think you intended harm."

There was evening sunlight on Maggie's white cheek. The cheek was smudged. "I married your brother for love."

And money, she might have responded. *And position. And the house. And for his salt lusts.* She would have said that earlier—five minutes previous she'd been watchful and suspicious, been the sentry of the Sherbrooke clan. *And for the name, to lord it over people with. To eat up his substance with whorishness. Who knows your reasons, lady?*

"I did,"—Maggie joggled her hand, palm out. "I do love Judah Porteous. And his sister therefore is someone I shall come to love—if she'll permit it. Will you?"

So they became domestic partners, banding together and bonded. They clucked and bustled in the kitchen like a pair of broody hens. Even then the woman was, Harriet suspicioned, no broody hen but an eagle at rest—and her arms were mighty wingspans and her hands sheathed claws. Yet she had followed Maggie, chattering—from kitchen sink to countertop to stove to chopping block to sink—picking up her droppings, setting things straight. Judah said they'd got a pecking order, and that made him (teasing, kneading Maggie underneath her apron) the roost's cock. His wife had slapped at his hands. She told him to behave himself, and laughed.

But this was her wan, private knowledge, and she forgot it for years. She had taken Maggie for an ally—but had been taken in, mistaken. They had bridled Judah with conspiratorial efficiency—making him take off his shoes when on the ballroom carpets, making sure he came on time to meals. He had been docile, gentled, as her sister-in-law had been docile—so Harriet believed for years she was witnessing family love. She had partaken of it also, partaking of their bed and board and knowing there was room enough to spare. It had been a mistake.

Except Maggie, in those first few years, never made mistakes. She wronged them all repeatedly but seemed to do no wrong. Nothing she ate or drank made any difference to her figure, ever; she could guzzle all night long and gorge herself on cakes and bread but not accumulate a single pound. Her skirts would billow about her like sails in a stiff breeze. Harriet baked cakes, despairing, and then baked rhubarb and pecan pies and fudge brownies and presented them topped off with homemade ice cream and shared it all and felt herself bloat and go greasy while Maggie ate, delighted, licking her fingers in the kitchen and licking the spatula clean. She had the complexion of a Camay model, and it would not mar.

"How do you do it?" Harriet asked.

"Do what?"

They were allies now—but Harriet still baked cakes and cobblers and brownies, letting Judah have a tuck-in on plain New England food.

"I've burned the crust," she said.

"Don't be silly, Hattie. It's perfection."

"You think so?" she'd ask, shy.

"Yes. *Perfect*."—and Maggie'd pare the drippings off the pie pan and swallow and make a perfection sign, curling her index finger to her thumb. She'd raise her other fingers and squint past her hand's circle, appreciative, nodding.

"Sugar and spice and everything nice"—Judah smacked his lips. "This ain't half bad, Hattie. I'll have another slice."

"Tell her 'if you please,'" said Maggie.

"I do please," Judah said.

"You don't—you unmannerly man." They were allies in this also in making him say "Please" and keep his elbows off the table and wipe off his mouth when he drank.

"OK, ladies. Hattie. I'll have more, please."

"Why, certainly," she said.

"Why, thank you," Judah said.

"You're welcome, I'm sure."

"Pretty please," he pronounced, "with sugar on top"—and she knew he had bested her and heard Jamie Powers crackling through the underbrush, whistling, laughing, and felt her face flame and threw the cake knife down.

"Now look"—Maggie scolded him—"look what you've done."

"I'll take a second piece."

"Not while I'm sitting here," her ally declared—who would not, would never be bested.

"Thank you," Judah said. "It's been a lovely meal."

"*You've* spoiled it. You're the one who spoiled it, Jude."

"I said pretty please," he said.

"You didn't mean it. You meant something else."

"I've been studying good manners."

"But you're not learning them," his wife pronounced.

"And you,"—he said, his face suffusing with dark blood. "You two are such excellent teachers."

"It's your fault," Harriet echoed. "It isn't us who spoils it"—and he overturned his plate and coffee cup and stalked out of the room.

They had had a second son, Seth, born two years after Ian. Unlike his elder brother, he was a sickly baby, but patient and pleased with the world. He died at six months old, of what Wiggins called crib death.

"What's that?" Judah demanded. "What sort of sickness is that?"

The doctor said it was a name for no name, for something they hadn't figured out but maybe was a sudden fever in the night. "He had no fever when he went to sleep," said Judah. Seth lay there, extinguished, in blankets that doubled his weight. "I'm truly sorry," the doctor repeated. "We don't know enough about it." Hattie feared it might have been God's judgment, that He who giveth taketh, and for reasons that we know not of.

"What reasons?" Maggie said. "What are you implying?"

"Nothing. Only that He passeth understanding." They talked about Seth often, then rarely, then avoided talking till avoidance was a habit and he became mere memory, a bit of breath and trustfulness and bone.

"Hattie, I need you."

"Yes."

"To be my friend," said her sister-in-law.

"Yes."

"What do you mean by that 'Yes'?"

"Just yes. You need me for your friend."

But it was a "yes" of concurrence and not agreement; it was a "yes" that recognized the rightness of the statement, but not the statement's case. She made no acquiescence with that "yes," nor any sort of pledge.

"You offered me your help once, Hattie. He's insane."

"Excitable," she said. "Judah was always excitable."

"He's *insane*. Your brother is stark raving mad."

"That's not true and you know it." She was being loyal but the loyalty was fair. "He just gets fighting riled."

("Brother," she had ventured. "Won't you tell me what's the matter. Please." There were foam flecks and spittle on his lips.

"You've been provoked. All right. Something was done to provoke you."

She watched his sinews working. He moved his fingers, and his forearms indented and swelled. For Judah was rampaging. The veins in his temples were blue. He stood, feet spread for balance, on the hearth. He had on a work shirt, and the muscles in his arms were knotted cords. His skin seemed flayed. He had coal lumps in either hand, and he clenched and broke and pulverized the coal. That was, she knew, a feat of strength. No ordinary man could do it, nor could Judah in his ordinary mood. But he stood there grinding the black rock together, with coal dust streaming from his hands as though he'd picked up coal dust to begin with. His hands were black; his forearms blackened and caked. He sprayed small bits and shattered fragments of the coal—in a black semicircle, his back to the mantelpiece, silent. It was the silence, Hattie knew, that meant his true rampaging. Nothing of him moved except his hands and arms. His arms were working only from the elbows in; he kept his elbows splayed. She did not fear his trumpet bellow by comparison, nor his wall-tumbling word frenzy; *this* was the leveling rage. He held them all, she told herself—and all their perquisites and ancestry and expectation of a decent life, and why was that too much to ask for her who'd never done much asking, always satisfied or saying so at least, and her allotted portion an adequate allot- ment—in those closed clamped hands.

"Please. You're frightening me. Us."

His smile had no teeth.

"Judah," she had pleaded. "Please."

But nothing would avail until the seizure itself had availed, and he would stand there empty-handed, shivering. He would have crushed a scuttleload of coal.)

"I told you," Maggie hissed in the kitchen. "I told you he's impossible. I told you you'd not get a word."

"It isn't me he's mad at," Harriet said. "It isn't me he's destroying out there."

Judah drove a wedge between them, therefore, and split their alliance apart. He'd split her off from Maggie—she recognized it now—like some skillful herdsman herding sheep.

"Well, what's he mad at?" Maggie asked. "What did he tell you I'd done?"

"He didn't tell," she said.

"I never gave him cause. There wasn't any reason, Hattie. Believe it."

"He's mightily provoked," she said.

"And you're mightily frightened, I see." Maggie raised her long white arms and took her hairpins out. She shook her head and freed her hair and that meant no more kitchen work. "I see that much."

"You see it, yes."

"Oh, Hattie," Judah's wife said. "You shouldn't let him cow you. It's insane."

"I'm not"—she stacked the dishes. "Not letting him cow me, I mean."

"Of course you are."

"I'm not."

Judah stomped out through the parlor, and his boot prints were black.

"Those schoolboy antics," Maggie scoffed. "That show-off strong stuff." She gathered conviction. "Me heap big he-man. You Jane."

Harriet laughed. She hoped Maggie took her mouth-stretching rictus for laughter.

"The Johnny Weismuller," said her sister-in-law, "of the northern counties. Another county heard from. But it's ballot-stuffing, Hattie, don't you see? It's a rigged election and one he has to win."

Harriet poured Ivory soap in the sink. She let the hot tap run.

"You don't even know," Maggie said, "what it was we argued about. You don't even want to know, seems like. You didn't ask him, and you won't ask me."

"It's not my business," she said.

"It is. It is, it has to be. But it isn't, oh, your business to quake in front of that huge bully. He's your younger brother, Hattie, think of that."

"I do," she said. "That's what I think about. That's all I've been thinking while you let him stand there. You and your fancy charities that don't begin at home . . ."

"It's my home too," Maggie said.

"It wasn't always and it won't be always, maybe."

So what was enmity then friendship turned to enmity again. Push come to shove, she told herself, she was allied with her brother and the born Sherbrookes, not wed. She was a born Sherbrooke, and not above announcing it or taking some pride-pleasure in hearing it announced.

"What do you mean by that?" Maggie had straightened.

It meant she stood for something, where she stood. It meant the time-tried values of decency and loyalty and truthfulness were in the room. "Just what I said."

"You mean it?"

Straightening, she came to Maggie's chin, and breathed, and watched her breathing.

"I do," she said. "I mean just what I said."

III

"So I've come back," she thinks. "So nothing much matters but that. A nice enough place to return to." Andrew's apartment was nice enough too, on East Sixty-Third Street and with a balcony with green outdoor carpeting that simulated grass. He liked to practice putting, and the automatic putting green spat shots back at him. From the next floor, Maggie was certain, or from across the courtyard anyone looking would believe the carpet was actual lawn. They had to vacuum, not cut it; that gave it away, she supposed. But she found the whole thing comical and pleasing and kept Andrew's telescope inside the balcony door. She did her yoga there. Whenever she caught the binocular's telltale flash from 14D (that white-haired man in undershirts who was, inexplicably, her father looking down at her from the hill's height in Wellfleet, and not some sex-tormented dotard in a service apartment) she stepped inside and fetched the telescope and trained it ostentatiously along the sightline of the watcher watched.

The apartment walls were gloss white. Andrew said there was little enough light in New York, and he needed what light he could get. So, leaving, she had emptied the shoe-polish box and used his shirts for rags and smeared black and brown polish on the bedroom and living room ceilings and walls. She stood on the sofa to get at the ceiling and tied a black rag to the broomstick— but this was more trouble, somehow, than it was worth, so she concentrated on the walls. She rubbed Kilroys and toxin signs and crosses on the bedroom wall, then rubbed them over and wrote ViVA, and NIXoN LIvES!!!

She knows Judah is dying, of course. She has expected it for years, and that he would require her to give and get his final blessing. She acknowledges she owes her husband that much anyhow; they live on a battlefield site. Their farm had been a theater of the Revolutionary War. Maggie laughed at the phrase. She asked Harriet to tell her what about war was good theater, and how many actors took how many curtain calls.

"Who buys ringside tickets?" she had asked. "What's so theatrical?"

"That's not what the expression means."

"What does it mean then?"

"Theater of war. It's an expression, that's all—it's a way of saying Seth Warner billeted troops."

"Who's Seth Warner?" Maggie asked.

"You have to be joking. Seth Warner and the Green Mountain Boys— they made all the difference hereabouts."

"Not to me," said Maggie. "All right. George Washington slept in this bed. No wonder the man was universally loved. I mean, the father of his country—he must have fathered thousands, sleeping in all those beds."

"You're not being funny," Harriet said.

"Well, neither is it funny to prink about theaters of war. I wouldn't be boastful," she finished. "Not about that."

"Seth Warner was a decent man. And committed no atrocity and defended in an upright fashion what was his beholden township and his duty to defend."

So they took picnics to the battlefield and drove where the Green Mountain Boys had shinnied up hills and down gullies. Judah said, "It's always a shock. I mean, to see this half an acre and to think how many men were dead in it once."

"I thought Vermonters never died," she said.

"They died that evening."

"With their boots on," Maggie declaimed. "In rightful conflict and with noble mien."

"Something like that," Judah said.

"With thistle in their face. And burdock. And probably cow patties."

"What is it?"

"What is *what*?"

"The problem." Judah turned to face her. "Tell me."

A hawk spiraled past them, rising. She wanted to warn every sparrow.

"Nothing," she said.

"That's not true."

"Well, something," she admitted. "You know I'm pregnant."

"I guess so," he smiled down at her. "I was in on it."

"And it'll be a boy maybe. And he'll be a Sherbrooke and proud of his rifle and end up on a field somewhere with his face in cow crap and someone will be saying, 'Wonderful. You died for your country. Good boy.'"

"He isn't born yet," Judah said. "You don't have to worry he'll die."

"Christ, I hate these proud memorials. I hate each marble slab. I hate what they did to them and everyone who comes to glory in the memory of war."

"We came for a picnic," he said.

"I didn't mean to spoil it."

"We can go," he said.

"Yes. Please."

So he became solicitous and watchful, and would have kept her on the sofa bed the last ten weeks. She hadn't meant it that way, she explained.

She'd been upset, and war was still a topic she'd prefer to avoid, but that didn't mean she couldn't climb stairs or fetch her food or go to the bathroom alone. Judah thought all women were helpless, of course. He'd wheeled his mother around too long and too considerately to consider any woman other than an invalid who needed help with washing and needed her pillows plumped up. It hadn't been that way at first. At first he admired her seat on a horse, and the ease with which she ran or swam, but it was like some armor-suit he had to find the chink in. He had to find the way she cracked, the place where she was joined together and would tear along the seam. Maggie knew her fear for Ian's life would be a seam that showed. She had been fearless for herself, and hadn't thought to lock the door, but now each open door was risky and each crowd carried polio, even with the Salk vaccine, and every drinking fountain was a place she drank from, first.

"You'll make a sissy of him," Judah said.

"I'll make a survivor."

"A lot of people drink from fountains without contracting polio."

"What does that prove?" she asked.

"He'll drink from streams. He'll swallow a lot worse than water."

"In his own good time," she said. "And not until he wants."

Therefore Judah fastened on her fear of guns. He taught Ian to hunt, although he knew she hated guns and feared the two of them shooting each other while they hunted deer. There would be a clearing; it would be rimmed with spruce. Her son would face her husband and both would be wearing russet, having taken off their red hunting jackets because it got too hot.

"Be careful," she would warn them.

"Yes, Ma," Ian would say—with that impatient knowingness she herself had mustered once.

"I mean it. Judah. Ian."

"Yes."

"Yes, you'll be careful?" she asked.

"Yes, we know you mean it."

Largely, however, she feared for his weakness, not strength. She felt herself protective of the boy-man who needed protection. "Feeding time at the zoo," she had called lunch, laughing. "Come and get it. Nice raw meat. Nice bloody cutlets, boys." Yet it wasn't always funny and she saw the great swatch of muscle and sinew, hacked back from the bone with a needle-bright blade, the animal bellowing not with sensate grief or pain but only amazement, only how could they do this to me, only what fair-weather friends have turned foul? That's what Ian said they thought; that's what cows were good for if they weren't good for milk. "Hey Mom, what's for lunch?" he'd ask.

"What's always for lunch?" Maggie asked.

"Food."

"Drink," Judah concurred. They washed their hands. She made them wash their hands for thirty seconds under the tap, no matter what was said about the Salk vaccine.

"It's Wednesday," Maggie said. "It's always spaghetti for Wednesday."

"Psketti," Ian lisped. He mispronounced on purpose what had eluded him before.

"And dessert?" they chorused. "What's for dessert?"

"Your just deserts," she joked. That too was a Wednesday tradition—angel food cake. Her stripling coarsened while she and Harriet fed him and observed it, and she watched even-handed, balancing scorn and relief.

"Margaret," Finney said ten days ago. "Or do I call you Mrs. Sherbrooke?"

"Whatever," she said. "How are you, Samson?"

"Tolerable," he said. There was static on the line. His voice approached. "I'm better than Judah is, Margaret."

"You always were"—she teased him. "You were, what's the word, exemplary."

"It's not a joking matter. I'm calling to tell you he's sick."

Voices intervened. She heard the operator ask if this was Akron, then asking for the routing code to Akron, Ohio.

"How sick?" she asked. She lit a cigarette. "Did he tell you to call?"

"Can you hear me?"

"Yes. I hear you."

"Good," he said. His voice was higher-pitched than she remembered. She thought, perhaps so big a man impressed her with flesh resonance, so that at a distance one forgot his speech's squeak. "Good," he said again, and paused.

"Go on."

"What was the question?" Finney temporized.

"How sick?" she repeated. "And did he tell you to call?"

He paused, considering. "I'm calling on my own say-so; he wouldn't want you to know."

"Then why did you tell me?"

"I'd better correct that," he said. "He'd want you to know, but not want to know that I told you."

"Samson," she said. "Don't play the lawyer, please."

"I'm sorry," he said quickly. "I didn't mean to joke with you. It's no joking matter"—he coughed.

She let his cough subside. She listened to it echo and wondered if it echoed all the way to Akron. Stubbing out her cigarette, she watched the ash disperse. Death, she told herself, he's dying; why won't he dare use the word? "What word do lawyers use?" she asked. "What's the danger of decease?"

"Demise," he corrected her.

"Death. Death," she nearly shouted. "All right, how sick is he?"

"I'm not a doctor," Finney said. "You needn't shout."

She lit a second cigarette. "I'm sorry. Thank you for calling."

"I thought you should know. You're still his wife."

"Of course. Thank you."

"I'm only his lawyer," he said. "I don't know the medical facts."

"The coroner's report," Maggie said. She was sleepy, suddenly. She wanted to lie back and sleep.

"What? How's that?"

"Can you hear me, Akron? Over and out," Maggie said.

"There's trouble with the lines. Bell Telephone," Finney said. "It's the second-most mismanaged company. It's impossible . . ."

"Which is the first?"

"Consolidated Edison Electric. I'm not even a customer, but Con Ed's famous for mismanagement. It'll bring the country down. It'll bring us to nuclear war."

Then she remembered his theories. He and Judah traded theories over coffee as to who brought the country lowest, and in the service of which foreign power or infidel belief. General Motors, Judah claimed, was the country's curse. "What's good for GM is good for the nation," he said. "I believe that. I grant it for argument's sake. But also in reverse—and since those rattletraps they make are all tin and tinsel and glitter, why in hell should Americans be pleased?"

"Why not?" Finney asked. "We still make more cars."

"With—what do they call it—planned obsolescence? With a motor that won't take you fifty thousand miles and body work I'd kick in except it just might dent my shoe. Better do it barefoot," Judah said.

So they argued while she listened—first carefully then carelessly, then as to actors rehearsing. She had had water in her ear. She heard the sea continually. It was as if she held a conch shell there, suspended, hearing the sea's tide—but in her right ear, there where Finney theorized, she heard only babble, a small stream hauled over rock.

"So I wanted you to know," he said. "I think you have the right."

"Yes."

"It's up to you of course. I wouldn't want to interfere."

"I'm coming," Margaret said. "I'll write him that it's my idea to come."

There was a Cole Porter song. It came from *Kiss Me Kate,* which came in turn from *The Taming of the Shrew.* Bianca—whose name rhymed with Sanka when her suitor chided her—sang a song explaining her flirtatiousness. "I'm always true to you," she sang, though her fashion of truth ran to lying. She sang about millionaire playboys and what they tried to offer her in exchange for what she offered. She whirled through stanzas, getting fortunes, driving her true love wild. He had fits of jealous haggling while she swore her faithless devotion. The audience applauded. It pounded its approval night after night. The song was a showstopper, and even her stage lover had to smile and approve and applaud.

She made Judah take her, twice, to *Kiss Me Kate.* He was not happy in New York. Other men might be impressed by the Empire State Building, for instance, or overawed or bored or busy calculating costs, but Judah, she knew, calculated only his chances should the wind blow him off of the tower. He would gauge jumping distance and check the ledges for toeholds and be an animal at bay.

So his pleasure in the theater would be mixed. He could not forget himself. He gauged the strength of men beside him and in front; he thought the woman who handed them programs was lighting the wrong row on purpose or making him shuffle thick-footed down the wrong aisle. "Darling, in my fashion," Bianca sang—and Judah would be grim. There was nothing humorous, for him, in all those Texas millionaires and Oklahoma tycoons she sang about, nor did he find it funny when she flounced away. They argued betrayal; they argued pancake makeup as a substitute for flesh tint, and buttressed body garments as a substitute for flesh.

"Sit back and enjoy it," she said.

"I am." Judah was stiff-lipped. "I am."

"Oh, Jude," she said. "It's a *play.*"

"I am enjoying it, I just don't like our seats."

"When was the last time," she asked him, "you laughed out loud in public?"

"In aught-seven. At the hanging."

"You mustn't be threatened," she said. "There's nothing here to threaten you, except only people who laugh."

"I'm not feeling threatened. I just don't find it funny."

But *threat* was never far from him, nor the guises of challenge or menace. She threatened his possessiveness, she knew. She was the last best challenge to his habit of control. They locked in mortal combat that was nothing like the comic "battle of the sexes" she saw in musicals and that ended, always, in bed. It was a kind of struggle that continued on past pleasure, a question of dominion and boundaries cut back.

Now Maggie inspects the house. She walks through each of its floors. The kitchen calendar shows deer in snow, standing alert while Santa flies above them; the white-tail deer wear comical expressions. They stare from the lower left corner at the reindeer apparition that is harnessed and stepping in unison across the clouds like turf.

There is no light left outside, and Maggie moves from room to room without adjusting lamps. If there is a switch nearby she turns it on and leaves it on; if she cannot find the light, she does without. Sometimes she cannot remember; reaching for switches that do not exist. Her hand's assurance alters. She brushes at plaster and wood, certain that the room will come illumined instantly. It does not. She has no purpose, surveying, other than to walk the house entirely, from room to hall to stairwell to the cupola. She can remember waiting for him, earlier, in the gathering half-dark, whispering *Jude*, darting from some thicket or the barn door when he walked home after work. And there would be fireflies and thick odor in the air, and she would feel herself electric to her very fingertips. Then there was no question of juggling, or light; then she'd needed none to know her way around their world; then she'd been, he joked with her, his Eveready battery and charge.

They'd walk home that way, or she'd lead him back into the barn. In those years she could name the constellations and the times of night they'd appear, and in which sector of the sky. Now Orion merged with Cassiopeia, the North Star with a planet, and all she'd recognize for certain were the drinking gourds; now she'd identify satellites, or radio stations, or planes.

Maggie consults her watch. It is nearly seven o'clock; she has dawdled in the halls. Dinner is to be at seven; she must wash. Descending, she feels light-headed nearly, as if a maiden once again and holding the hymnal, singing till she hyperventilates and thinks herself transcendent: *walks in beauty like the night*, bedecked with flowers and later with straw where her lover lay with her, *and all that's best of dark and bright*, the aspect and the eyes of it; when he asked her if she's tired she said she's short of breath.

The two women meet in the second-floor hallway. Visibly, Hattie masters herself. The one thing Sherbrookes sometimes fail in is politeness; she will do the proper thing.

"You're welcome here," she says.

"I thank you," Maggie says.

"You're welcome."

Then there is silence between them. Hattie peers upward. "You've not changed," she offers.

"Oh, but I have," Maggie says. "It's been seven years."

"Not so you'd notice."

"Is that a compliment?"

"I meant it that way."

"Thank you, then. *You're* looking well."

"Now that's a compliment," says Hattie. "But I look like something that could crack a mirror."

The women laugh.

"My goodness," Hattie finishes. "It's been a while since there's been laughter in this house."

"How is he?"

"Him?" She drops her voice.

"Yes."

"He doesn't change much, either. You travel light," she says. "You just brought that one bag?"

The hall ends in a west-facing bay; there is a sudden single lance of light. The sun is red, is going. Dust dances in the beam.

"So Jude's all right?" Maggie asks.

"Or maybe you've got luggage coming?"

"No."

"Well, anyhow your things are here. They need a bit of airing."

Maggie wears high two-inch heels. For Hattie, she imagines, this must be adding insult to injury and make her seem six feet tall. She bends down to her sister-in-law. "What do the doctors say about it?"

"I don't follow."

"Doctors"—Maggie says again. "How bad do they think it is?"

"What? Judah's health?"

"Yes." She is impatient. Hattie no doubt wants to tell her the stuff of decency is patience; the young must wait their turn and take their proper place in line. "Has it changed?"

"Not so you'd notice."

"Would he tell you if it's gotten worse? His heart? I don't mean would the doctors tell . . ."

This time Hattie interrupts. Now it's her turn, it appears, to lose patience. "He wouldn't need to. Not to me."

"Yes, but . . ."

"Some people, maybe. Some would have to get a phone call, I don't doubt. Or read about it in the papers. Some people come on up with just one little suitcase, thinking that's how long he'll last, that's all the time it's going to take. I'm eighty-one years old," she finishes, "and Judah's a sight stronger than *I* ever was. I never . . ."

Maggie reaches out and takes her wrist. Her fingers make a bracelet over bone. "Don't be offended," she says. "I didn't mean it that way."

"What way then?"

"Of course you'd know," she says. "You'd be the first. And they wouldn't have to tell you anything," says Maggie. "You could tell the doctors all about it if they thought to ask."

Therefore she seems mollified. "What ails my brother," Hattie says, "isn't for doctors to fix."

They reach the stair's crest. Hattie returns to her room; "I'll just get ready for dinner," she says and withdraws. Maggie gathers herself. Her skirts fill as if they were sails. "Why, Jude," she cries, descending, "it's so very pleasant to be back."

Lately her dreams have been troubling: she knows herself in woods but lost. Men chitter at her from the trees like monkeys, and all the elms are blighted, falling, and she stands beneath their rain of leaves as once she stood beneath a waterfall. She'd pressed against the rock and breathed in the air the air pocket made within the water's arch, wet enough just from the spray, but knowing she'd have to pass through the loud solidity and liquid pounding anyhow. ("Why?" she asked. "Why do I have to do it?" and the answer was "Because." She'd said that wasn't any sort of answer, that wasn't reason enough, and all they repeated was "Because . . .") Because, she knew, they'd laugh at her; because the water on the pool side was limpid and quiet and like, they said, a puddle; because the waterfall might shift its crescent arc, descending, or with a strong enough wind. Then she would get cold at night, ensorcelled by the white wet arc; because her parents would miss her; because there never was a dare she hadn't dared to take; because Sammy Underhill was waiting, watching, and she'd jump through hoops for him if hoops were what he wanted—dreams now the elm is slippery elm and excellent for chewing, what time she had to sweeten breath before he sucked it out of her, dreamed illustrations in the trees and her husband dying, disconsolate, his trunk the elm's girth easily but yielding to disease.

IV

Judah met her first in 1938. He remembered the influenza scare of twenty years before. "You opened the window, and in flew Enza"—that had been a chant of the time. Maggie flew into his window at thirteen. She knocked on the Big House side door. She was up for the summer, she said, and out riding her bicycle for the afternoon and would be late for supper and was lost. Judah had been balancing accounts. He liked the work: it had a neatness of notation and there had been that summer a deal more black than red, so he looked up not unkindly to set this girl stranger straight. She stood in his door like a stork. Long-legged already, she was rubbing her left leg with her right instep where it itched above the ankle. She was fighting back crying, he saw, and had grass stains and dirt and burdock down the side of her dress.

"You take a spill?" he asked.

"Yes." She pulled at her left side.

"Hurt much?"

"Yes," she admitted. "But not now."

"Well, where are you going to?"

She told him, and he knew the place and was impressed by her cycling diligence; give or take a couple, she'd traveled twenty miles. Later, when he'd married her and they had children and the birth announcement was a picture of a stork, he remembered how she could have been his own child then, was more than young enough, her angularities just bone and raw-lunged stridency. She rounded off, in time. The stridency diminished and became contempt. The bone fleshed out, and the twenty-five-year difference between them was a quarter of a century, not years. He'd lived through "years," and first they were to his advantage and then his disadvantage, and "years" was a word they worried at like dogs disputing ownership of some cow's cooked rib. But "quarter of a century" had no age implication; it did not implicate him; you couldn't strip or splinter it or lie in the chair's shade, digesting. It was a time-lump, single, simple, and Maggie swallowed it whole.

Only then she was swallowing dust; he'd offered her something to drink. "I'd like a glass of water, please," she'd said.

"We can do better than that. Have root beer. Have some cider."

"I'd like water, please."

He went to the kitchen and let the cold tap run and drew a glass of water for her, seeing the glass bead. "You come on in," Judah said. "You can use the telephone if they've got a number to call."

He offered her the water, and she sniffed and swirled it, then drank. He watched her watching him. He saw her yellow bike propped against the fence. He was feeling generous (and knew the generosity not typical, knew even then it was compounded of the afternoon's accounts, and the honeysuckle smell in that soft air, the chill of his right hand's wet palm and the suspicion she had evidenced about the glass he gave—her city manners nicely according with this new country necessity—knew that he liked the bravura about her, not tears she had been fighting back, but not not-tears either, and the distance she'd traveled since breakfast; knew also he could circle back by Harry Nickerson's and settle up about the silo and visit with Harry and find out what was happening to Tim, knew suddenly the house had held him for too long and why not break a habit and accommodate this once, since she too was mistrustful and polite . . .) and offered her a ride.

"I couldn't do that."

"Why not?"

"It's too much trouble," she said.

"Going that way anyway . . ."

"I've got my bike."

"I got a truck. We'll haul it."

"I couldn't," Maggie said. "Thanks anyway. And for the water."

"Put that glass down."

He stepped around her and down off the porch and picked her bike up and slung it in the truck bed and tied it to the crossbar, then laid it on burlap so it wouldn't scratch. "Get in," he said. "We're going," and climbed into the cab.

She had obeyed him, of course. She edged the door shut, and he told her to slam it. She did. Yet there was something peremptory in her submission, a kind of acquiescence that made the favor conferred seem not his favor but hers. She accepted compliments as he'd seen some men take insults— as though it was the rightful portion, properly bestowed. Praise was her rightful portion, even then. Later she would enter rooms as though she knew he'd rise, expectant, and would walk to the room's door knowing some man would sweep it open. Beauty was conferred on her, he understood, and was its own authority (though at thirteen the conferral had been tentative, mawkish, a first rehearsing only of the spectacle to come— and she sat there stork-legged, voluble, pitching her voice high against the engine din.) He asked her name; she announced it. "Margaret Cutler."

"Where you from?"

"From New York City. Manhattan Island."

"Where in New York City?"

"Eighty-Third Street," Maggie said. "In the just about exact middle of town. Between Park Avenue and Madison. Do you know where that is?"

"Close enough," he said.

"Well, I think it's the very nicest part of New York City. Because there's a museum there and I've a real bike, not like that one"—she tossed her head—"and I ride it to school if I'm late, or Mary doesn't feel like walking, or for any reason mostly, as long as I wait for the lights."

"And don't get lost?"

"You can't, really. Not in Manhattan. You'd know that if you knew it well. There's Central Park. There's the East River to the east and the Hudson to the west, and the even-numbered streets run east . . ."

He cut across Route 7 and took the old East Road. She chattered while he watched her, idly, and he'd forgotten now (if indeed he had ever remembered, had then seen fit to remember or had listened even to her singsong litany of how to get to where you're going, and her game of naming trees) what else she had told him or asked. She asked though, he remembered, to be let off two miles from her house.

"My mother would be angry," she explained. "At me making you come all the way. I can make it back from here, really. Really and truly. I take the first left turning, and then it's just down that hill. Please."

He stopped the truck. The clutch was giving out; they settled, lurching. She smiled at him (the images coincident again, girl become woman, though practicing, and with her bite plate still) and pedaled off. He was not sorry. He started up and turned at the fork and made for Nickerson's. She'd known enough, he knew, not to bring some stranger back and maybe knew enough to work the sweat and dust up on her on her trip's last leg—arriving breathy, cheerful, just in time for supper and not admitting how she'd lost her way or found it, giving a fair imitation of hunger and hungry enough anyhow to do justice to the soup.

(He taxed her with that later. "Why me?" he'd ask. "Why me?"

"You're fishing for compliments, darling."

"Maybe," he acknowledged. "What made you pick me then?"

"When?"

"The first time. Later. Whenever."

She smiled at him, showing her teeth. She had had a toothache in her right incisor, he knew, and touched it with her tongue.

"Why not? No reason not to. It was such a lovely house.")

Now Judah knows, with bitterness, her talent for deceit. He wonders if he'd been a part of her sin-schooling then, and source to some white half-lie or omitted truth. He's watched her late arrivals often enough. He wonders how many doors she's knocked at, or been asked to enter, and how many times he himself has waited two miles from her drop-off point, consulting his watch. Her appetite was checked. She's reined it in too many years to give it its head now. So she'd arrive—not cheerful, not breathless to get at her plate—and ring for wine and have a cigarette. He hated cigarettes. They slaked her hunger, she said, as a glass of chill white wine would slake her thirst. She could puff out smoke rings and did so, coolly, while he watched. She was the only woman ever to dare to smoke rings in his house. She crossed her legs and sat there smoking, drinking, in pure opposition. He knew she used the smoke stink to cover up her body's stench from love. He broke or hid the ashtrays, and she dropped her matches and ash on the floor. It hadn't been an accident, he came to decide, that she knocked on the Big House door—and not at some farmhouse or barn.

Yet what he calls deception she had called tact. She was a reed bending before him, pliant, at first even obsequious in public, but Maggie never broke. She took the Big House over as if it was a toy house, something manageable. She charmed them all—just sitting there, crossing and un-crossing her legs, engaging in discussions as to Adlai Stevenson ("Christ," he had asked her. "Who's this Adlai Stevenson to get so worked up over? An egghead with egg on his face. A politician like the others, but a bit less expensive to buy . . .") or practicing her scales. She read aloud. In the evenings she would read him Tennyson or John Greenleaf Whittier or Henry Wadsworth Longfellow, and he found himself suspecting there were messages in what she read, some code he failed to crack. She read them with a deference that was kissing cousin to mockery. She read of babbling brooks in a voice that made him think of babbling brooks. She read of leafy copses and the azure empyrean in a way that made him see both woods and sky.

Yet she did so—he hunted the term—holding back. She was always holding back. Even in her hurtling run, or the way she came at him headlong, or the ferocity she showed him when he had her cornered—there was something inside her inviolate. It was like those Chinese boxes on the windowsill. There was Meg inside of Megan, and Megan inside Margaret. But inside Maggie—his final pet name—in the epicenter of her, impenetrable, there was a stranger he could not touch or name. He had gone clumsy-fingered at the end. He could not pick that lock. Even penetrating his wife, with her beneath him pinioned and Judah at his full extent, there was some final love veil that he could not lift. She stared at him, eyes hooded, and he never knew for certain what she, tilting, glazed, had seen.

Nor did he want to know. He was nearly, for the one time of his manhood, fearful. He had loved her, nearly, for the limitation of her love for him—he who had been limitless in love. It was that hooded glare he feared, her head thrown back, neck arched, and the veins in her neck working while he worked above her. He had power in reserve. He had his wealth and history of women in reserve. He had had, for the first years, the advantage of years. So he pitted his battering strengths against her receptive inertia; he pitted his heat and her chill. It was a standoff mostly, though he sometimes thought he won, exulting in the warmth of her—then found it reflected, or fox fire, maybe heat she got in Providence those weeks she spent there with what she said was her cousin, maybe heat from a mazurka, or *valse polonaise*.

So Judah traded off his leverage and gave her cars, or permission to smoke cigarettes, or not to visit with him when he visited their son at elementary school. He knew he looked the clown. He knew what they said of him in the village, and what his sister must think. He guessed what

"Cousin" Alexander said of him, in that pitch-pine-wainscoted third-floor walk-up in Providence, on Benefit Street. He knew what the dairy hands said, even, and Margaret's own mother—although none of them would venture, in his impeding presence, a syllable aloud. It didn't matter anyhow; he shrugged off gossip like flies. He always had done so, and would, though envy and malice abounded. What mattered was her laughter at Alexander's jokes; what mattered was the way she kept no protective distance when talking to the dairy hands, or watching Artur Schnabel; what mattered was decorum gone, the love veil peeled away.

He saw her again that summer, at the summer's end. There was a carnival in town, and Judah went the final day. Samson Finney said the carnival strongman held the world's weight-lifting record for the two-handed curl and press. And maybe it was so and maybe wasn't so, but any man who'd lift that fat bearded lady was strong—and any man who'd do it more than once was, Finney joked, a world-class jerk.

Judah shot at sitting cardboard ducks. He studied the construction of the carousel. There were eleven horses on the outside ring, and seven on the inside ring—painted, in alternating patterns, brown and pink and white. The horses rose and dipped—he calculated by the pole's rubbed sheen—four feet. The carousel began. The music was the music of the Sheik of Araby. She clattered past him, wearing red. Her hair was in a cap, and plaited, and he knew her but not how he knew her. She swooped and circled, not sidesaddle, but riding as a man would ride, flourishing her cap. She was there with friends, he decided, and playing Calamity Jane. He drifted to the ball toss where they tossed for kewpie dolls. His aim was inexact. He found—he said to Finney—this particular carnival dull. There was a time this sort of thing seemed cause for celebration, and he'd down a bottle of applejack brandy on anybody's say-so to celebrate the world.

"Let's do it," Finney said. "Let's celebrate the world."

"It's going to hell in a handcart."

"All the more reason. All the greater opportunity for this little drink."

"There's not any reason not to," Judah said.

He took a pull from Finney's flask. He was standing there, tasting it, feeling the heat course through him when she waved—he'd got her name now, Maggie, and the circumstance (though he hadn't been sure at the carousel's gate-edge and wasn't over-certain now—was thinking of that mad house-painter in Munich and his chances for wrecking the planet, was thinking of the sluiceway his intestines made, how the applejack dispersed out even to his elbows, was calculating the profit at a nickel a ride, and eighteen people to the ride, assuming the carousel full, assuming the barker could fill it fifty times a night . . .)

"Good evening," the girl said.

"Good evening. Maggie."

"Mr. Judah Porteous Sherbrooke." She smiled. She shook back her plaits.

"You've got a memory."

"I never thanked you properly. I inquired your name. You never told me 'Porteous'—I asked after that."

"You thanked me," Judah said.

"I'm going to New York tomorrow. I've had a lovely summer. I've got to go now, but thanks."

She bobbed and moved off, quickening. He knows the child is father to the man. The wish is father to the thought, and necessity the mother of invention. Her propriety and laughter was a seed then, germinant. White clover, Judah knows, stays in the ground upwards of seventy years. She planted something in him (though he would not know it, would forget her name once more, and this their second encounter until she reminded him, later, in their proper courtship, of how he'd rocked back on his heels and neglected to acknowledge how she'd grown, was growing, had won a picture of George Washington at bingo—would plow his bedfields under, repeatedly, and labor enough in his time to tire of it, nearly; would reconcile himself to widowerhood, and bachelorhood, the two indeterminate, fusing, since his first wife had died early on) that took a decade to sprout.

The ordination of the chromosomes, he thinks, *that's my true ministry. That's what I ought to preach.* From that first spawning instant, the sex and size and wit of his sons was ordained.

Maggie had been twenty-three. She called herself, then, Megan. He met her at Morrisey's Grocery, selecting cheese. She was studying the label and the price on Camembert. He had taken Camembert from the same counter two days before, and the cheese had been inedible. He had returned it, of course. He complained to Morrisey that the stuff was so damn overripe the cow that produced it was ten years buried, and the cowhide wallet worn away with all those doctor bills. "Matter of fact," Judah said, "I shouldn't wonder if this was the milking that killed it."

Morrisey had laughed and credited him and produced a new Camembert cheese. Judah told this story to the girl at the cheese counter, and she turned to face him and was familiar.

"I know you," Judah said.

"No."

"I've seen you before."

"It's possible," she said.

"Yes. Not lately."

"No. I haven't been here"—she calculated, lifting her index finger— "since 1938."

"I knew you then," he said, recollecting. "You lost your way on that bike."

There was nothing timorous about her now, no trace of that thin supplicant. She was model-slim still (was indeed, she told him later, working as a model in New York—but hated it, hated the hair dryers she sat beneath for hair dryer ads, the vacuum-cleaner parts she assembled and disassembled for vacuum-cleaner catalogue ads, the people that she worked with, and their whole notion of chic—).

"Have dinner with me," Judah said. "We'll have to fatten you up."

"I can't," she responded—but speculative, smiling. "Thanks anyway."

"Of course you can."

"You're kind to ask . . ."

"For auld acquaintance sake," he said, and wondered why he pestered her and why he felt persistent.

"I'm with friends."

"Well, bring them."

She replaced the Camembert cheese. "My name"—she held her right hand out—"is Megan."

"And mine is Judah Sherbrooke, Megan. Maggie. Welcome back."

"I'm passing through," she said. "I'll tell the others."

"Yes."

"They're waiting outside. I'll be back. Mr. Judah *Porteous* Sherbrooke."

She turned, with her hair swirling, and he watched her out the door.

"Look at that," Morrisey said.

"I'll take ten pounds of sirloin," Judah said. "Now get behind that meat shelf and behave. You ought to be ashamed."

Morrisey wolf-whistled. "I am, lawsie mercy. I am." He listened to *Amos 'n' Andy* and was working on the accent. "Lawsie mercy. I'se gosh-all get-out ashamed."

Judah stood by the cereals shelf. He remembers wishing, for a moment, that she'd get back on her bike—or car, or motorcycle, whatever conveyance she used now, or some second stranger's pickup truck—and leave him to his evening's plan (a walk, a meal, a smoke, the solitude he broke from only in his aimless grazing). She said to him later that week: "Three coincidences. That's one too many to take for granted."

"How else do people meet?"

"Through introductions," she said. "Because of school friends or through family or work."

Her friends had come and stayed for drinks, then left (were never present really, were moustachioed absences between the bookcase and the standing lamp, were twittering there like magpies, wearing cameras, asking for gin). He asked her to remain. He barbecued ten pounds of sirloin and dropped the whole thing on her plate. It dwarfed the plate's circumference, bleeding out onto the cloth.

"You're joking," Megan said.

"No."

"You'll spoil me with that kind of joke."

"Spoiled rotten"—he sat down. "If you haven't spoiled already. Like that cheese."

He leaned back, pleased with himself. He studied her gestures, engorging. She sliced and chewed with delicacy, theatrical. She would eat his life.

Even across the continent's span, Peacock felt himself a native of Vermont. He sent ten thousand dollars home, as his subscription to the cost of levying troops. "We pay John Chinaman," he wrote, "so why should not the Slave receive like Wages and proud Liberty? All bondage—lest it be to Christ—is heinous in His sight."

They stand there poised on the shore's brink, reflected, wavering, in an immobility that is motion arrested for the instant only. She is in the ocean, of it, turned three-quarters to Ireland, the sun in front of her so that Judah, squinting, sees the foam-nimbus smudge her body's edge—the outline of her indistinct in that spume halo, and all of it shifting, her feet hunting purchase, the sand floor accreting (so that he no sooner puts his foot down than he finds it swallowed up, is up to his ankle in silt), the tide continual and treacherous (though this too seems a code to crack; waves come in sequence, he has learned; there're maybe seven big waves, maybe nine, then nothing much—as if the trough and crest were components of a level whole, the subtraction of one water mass massed up against the next). Then there are riptides, she tells him, and crosscurrents and circle currents that they call a sea puss, lazily coiling, and though he's not afraid of it, can subdue what fear he has and enter the water behind her grinning, thumping, dominating the waves, he never thinks of it as better than an armed standoff or some sort of watchful truce: not his element, nor one in which he takes his ease, though the marble quarry up at Danby made a fine place for swimming, and he'd stand in some streambed for hours, snagging trout. But she has wished it and her wish, he jokes, is his command, and therefore they have driven to this coastal outcrop and she is in her element, disporting like some glad sea otter, though he's never seen an otter and doubts they wear pink two-piece suits; still, Megan loves lobster and oysters and clams, and he promises to have a seaplane bring them lobster. Still she laughs that he's like some forlorn stranded Neptune who's forgotten how to swim, standing there on that rock jetty, needing only a pitchfork for trident—huge, she teases him, and cranky and bedraggled as a soft-shelled crab.

"What kind of crab is that?" he asked.

"The kind that's good for eating." She licked her lips. "The kind that steams up pink and ain't as tough as it looks."

"A hermit crab. That's what."

"A god of the sea"—she touched him—"who loves his water sprite."

"Yes," he acknowledged. "Very much."

"And likes to watch her swim."

"Considering the tasty morsel she herself might make."

"Yum yum." She put her fingers in his mouth. "Old Neptune's hungry again."

He's forty-eight years old, he tells her, and not the sort of person to joke with or make jokes about; she pulls her fingers from his mouth, salutes, and dives from the rock jetty cleanly, into the crest of the waves.

"Since we cannot take Material Substance with us," Peacock wrote, "I am persuaded that a Christian man must make display whilst still in the Possession of Appreciative Faculties, and health. The fireplaces shall be marble, not Parian marble nor the stuffs of Italy, Carrara and suchlike, but from our neighbor quarries in Vermont."

He had traveled home via the Isthmus. The train across the Isthmus was a train he scorned. There were blockades in the Mexican Gulf, but they were under escort and out of danger's reach. They took a steamer up the Hudson and a train from Troy.

Peacock fulminated against imprecision in trains. His mine trains had a gauged wheel that could hold the track in snow or rain or ice. If he could keep, he argued, twenty tons of ore from falling off of mountain passes, why couldn't this rattletrap conveyance arrive on time? "The camel finds the Needle's Eye," he wrote, "more readily than I find easement for what they call Pneumonia. Strait is the gate . . ."

Through his law practice, Sherbrooke had acquired real estate and mining properties; he accepted notes in lieu of salary and was a paper millionaire by 1852. He bought Montgomery Street. He was, a letter-writing wit observed in the *Alta California,* "*Golden* tongued. There be a stream of language issuing forth from Lawyer Sherbrooke's mouth with its proportionate amount of fool's gold, but by all accounts worth panning at sixteen dollars the ounce. His opponents would wish him *dried up.* His admirers say the *vein* is inexhaustible and will *run on* to the Supreme Court and dwarf the *Mother Lode.* Myself I do account him a *natural asset* to our fair state, babbling as the stream does babble or rumbling as the *mine-shaft* when it buries some unfortunate within. I propose a monument to Lawyer Sherbrooke's *weighty words* and will be thereof the first subscriber. I herewith pledge two *pounds* of *pebbles* for our Demosthenes' mouth . . ."

"If the mote is in thy neighbor's eye," Peacock wrote, "pluck out the mote in thine own. Thus do we learn the gentleman's comportment—since I never yet knew scoundrel but could bandy reputations with the best. Truly to learn humility is, I think, the Christian's highest art—for many's the mock-humble man who thrives on Pomp and Praise. I pride myself on nothing half so much as this: that never have I claimed as due more than the bond's redeemable Value, nor ever left notes unredeemed."

There is Italian marble everywhere, and columns that his father ordered shipped from Greece. The house is what he labeled sizeable and others call huge. Judah moves through it with habit's ease, not noticing the glitter or the gimcrack elegance his mother had insisted on as *comme il faut.* He'd asked her what that meant, and she said, "What it means is place. It's knowing your position in this town, and how to keep it up."

So the Big House is ornate in ways he only sees when seeing it as others do: Maggie, for instance, batting her eyes at him, staring at the mirror that had silver Cupids at the top. They had married three months later, in the upstairs ballroom. They had a civil service, with a justice of the peace presiding, and only a handful of relatives and friends. Her parents motored north from New York. Her father was his, Judah's, age and none too pleased about it—but not, when he arrived and saw the farm, any too displeased. They got along. They got through a bottle of sour-mash whiskey that first afternoon. He remembers Maggie's father with affection— a dapper man wearing pinstripe suits and a moustache like Thomas E. Dewey's moustache.

"We could go the whole hog," he had offered his bride. "If you'd prefer."

"No. This is between us, not them."

So they'd stripped the guest list back and made no fuss about it, keeping private covenant and swearing private marriage vows and saving the parties for later. There would be parties enough.

V

"Hattie," James Pearson called. "Hey, Hattie."

"Yes," she'd said.

"Come on over here."

"Why?" she inquired.

"Why not?"

"Not till you ask more politely, Mr. James Pearson, sir," she'd reprimanded him, smiling. "Not till you ask the way a gentleman would ask it."

"Please."

"That's better."

"Come on over here, hey, Hattie, please."

His face was red. His hair was red. He flamed at her from the room's dark corner.

"Well," she acquiesced. "Since you insist. *Parce que vous insistez.*"

"I do," he said. "I do."

She'd taken that as augury and walked toward him, blushing. He reached out his right hand.

"Say please," she'd chided him.

"Please."

His hand was freckled, and the knuckles sprouted hairs.

"Say pretty please"—she took his hand—"with a cherry on top."

"Pretty please with a cherry on top."

"Say pretty please with a cherry on top, and marshmallow dressing, and sugar."

He placed his left hand on her waist.

"Pretty please," he'd whispered. "With a cherry on top, and marshmallow dressing, and sugar."

"No," Harriet pouted, withdrawing. "I don't like marshmallow dressing."

This completed their routine. She had learned it when learning the way to jump rope. This was her posed, phrased resistance, and now she let him fondle her and gave herself up to his arms. He smelled of licorice. He pressed and mauled at her for minutes, for what seemed like hours though she kept close track of time. He disarrayed her clothing, and she let him paw the disarray. Then Harriet pulled back and kissed his freckled chin and said, "No, please. We mustn't."

"Yes."

"No. Pretty please."

The licorice transmuted and became the smell of gin.

"Why not?" He had turned sullen.

"Mr. James Pearson"—she chaffed him—"you know the answer to that."

"Christ, Hattie . . ."

"Don't blaspheme."

Later, when she met him by accident—Jamie, just come from propping up the Drop-Inn bar, whose nose had gone bulbous and stomach distended and red hair lost its fullness and sheen—she had reconsidered. She thanked her lucky stars. She watched him shuffling down Main Street, doffing his engineer's cap to women in comic obscene deference, doing a jig on streetcorners as he waited for the light to change—and thanked her luck he did not see her or doff his cap when she passed. Obscurely, she had been offended that Jamie stayed in town. He should have vanished from the streets and bars when he vanished from her embrace. He had sworn to. "Hattie, I'm leaving," he said. "I can't stay around here like this."

"Don't go."

"I know when I'm not wanted."

"Please stay," she said, not meaning it and he knew she didn't mean it and, to spite her, stayed. He weaved and hiccuped past her as an emblem of decorum lost; he lost his job at the bank. She noticed, when he did the hornpipe, he clicked his heels twice in the air. Therefore she wished on him, in retribution for her broken heart, a broken leg. He should, she thought, twist an ankle at least and not prove so monkey-agile, capering.

"You'll break my heart," she told him.

"There's nothing to break," Jamie said.

"You're cruel. You're being unfair."

"All right," he had leered at her, stinking of gin-sweetness. "Show me your heart. Let's have a look."

So, breathless, not daring to breathe, not knowing why she did it but knowing that she had to, once, not knowing how she dared but knowing his juniper-berry fueled bravado was a dare she had to take, she took off her blouse and unlaced her chemise. She had been cold. There were goose pimples on her arms. She dropped her chin because he might still put his rough hands on her neck, and there was a chill wind blowing that made her naked neck contract. There were willow trees. They stood in a bower the green branches made, and he reached out and twined his fingers in the willow strands.

"Keep going," Jamie said. "All I can see is ribs."

Her brassiere was white. It had lace eyelets and four hooks. She reached around and fumbled with the clasps and closed her eyes to concentrate so she would not be fumble-clumsy, and because the cold wind hurt her eyes.

"Jamie?"

"A-yup."

"James Pearson-person," she said.

"Keep going."

"I've got a heart," she finished and dropped its final protective layer and stood there shivering. She screwed her lids tight shut. Her heart was in her throat. "Well, haven't I?"

"That's all you got," he said and laughed and turned on his two heels and left her in the willow's shadow and crashed across the stream still laughing, whistling. She hated him implacably. She wanted to put out his eyes.

Harriet closes the bathroom door. It squeaks, requiring oil. The door drinks oil, it seems, the way Judah drinks whiskey; no matter how well lubricated, it soon enough dries up. That had been Maggie's joke. Most of the wit and levity within the household had been hers; she, Harriet, grants that. But there is such a thing as too much levity, as jokes in bad taste following the jokes in good. Their mother had a saying: "There are six senses," she said.

"Which?"

"How many do you know about?" her mother asked. "How high can you count?"

"To five. One two three four five."

"And what are the five senses?"

"Sight and sound and smell and touch and taste," Harriet said.

"That's right. And then there's *good* taste, darling: the sixth sense."

So Harriet would chant while bouncing, "Sight and sound and smell and touch and taste and *good* taste," or skip rope to the rhythm of it, counting six. There was a sixth sense she learned of later that meant you saw for distances you couldn't possibly see. It meant you heard things too far away for sound to carry, and smelled smoke when there was something burning, though you couldn't smell the smoke. It happened to her, Harriet, sometimes; she walked into a room and looked at the clock on the mantelpiece and the clock started to chime. She shivered when she heard Fred Rowley's name and learned, next day, that Fred Rowley had died in a car crash twenty-four hours before. She saw a painting on the Millers' wall (of the Connecticut River, with an Indian poised on the bank, wearing war paint and feathers and a loincloth) and decided she didn't much care for it and the instant she made her decision the oil painting fell.

That was coincidence, maybe; she's willing to grant that. But she had run out screaming from the Wittens' parlor at the very minute of the day her mother died. She'd known (though in the Library, attending to the Periodical Shelves) when her nephew Seth was born. It was her day to volunteer, and Judah said, "Go on, we'll manage without you. We've managed before," and Maggie said, "If this one's half as long in coming as the last, why, there'll be plenty of time." So she had been arranging *National Geographic* and marking down the issues missed or out of order. They had a complete second set. There was no smoking in the Library, of course. She herself had never smoked. But suddenly her lungs filled up, and there was the smell of Judah's cigar smoke, and she had known beyond coincidence there was a baby born.

Harriet arranges herself in the sheets. She uses an electric blanket, but also a hot-water bottle, since she does not trust the blanket while she sleeps. There could be short circuits or a defect in the wiring or faulty connections she would not notice till the morning, till too late. Hilda Thornhill had suffered first-degree burns on her back. If the hot-water bottle broke, Harriet thought, all she would wake up was wet.

"Lord," she murmurs. "Save my brother Judah from the ravages you visit on us all. Preserve my nephew Ian according to the love we bear him, and his just deserts . . . "

She cannot continue. The prayer does not soothe her, nor is she composed. The junket had been excellent, she knows. It was just the right consistency, and neither too tart nor too wet. The Sanka did not trouble her—not even that second cup. She, Harriet, breathes with a sweet and inoffensive breath. Judah can tease or ignore her or flaunt her need for maraschino cherries, but her teeth are much better than his. She wonders what sort of wood George Washington used for his incisors. She imagines Martha Washington held in the crook of her husband's right arm, face tilted back and breathing deeply, but breathing in the smell of cedarwood, not Crest.

"Hey, Missie Sherbrooke. You there! Hey, my maiden lady."

Her next suitor, Samuel Powers, was bluff about her chastity and found it a fine joke.

"Don't shout," she'd said to him. "I hear you."

"So you ain't deaf?"

"No."

"Not deaf to entreaty, neither?" He chuckled. "What about that?"

"You hush up, Mr. Sam," she said.

"Not deaf to my proposals? Not deaf to argument?"—he winked at Judah hugely.

"No," she said. "Not all that deaf. You'd wake the sleeping dead with that bellow."

"OK,"—he slapped his sides, delighted. "All right then. OK."

"But hush your mouth and mind your manners, Mr. Sam." She was reading Southern novels then. She dropped a curtsy to him from her imagined carriage height but also dropped her handkerchief.

"Accidental a-purpose." He pounced. He gathered up her handkerchief and wiped his cheeks and kissed the handkerchief. "Hey, Judah," he bellowed. "Looky here. Look at this moo-chwower."

"*Mouchoir*," she had corrected him.

Her brother laughed, sardonic.

"It's mine, you unmannerly man. Give it back."

She stomped her foot in what she hoped was a heroine's coquettish fashion. He crumpled up her handkerchief and put it in his waistcoat pocket, covering the watch fob and the silver chain.

"Not likely," Vice President Powers declared. "I found it and I'll keep it. To console me, Missie Sherbrooke." He winked at her this time, and she checked to see if Judah was watching—then saw her brother at the fireplace, back turned.

"This memento," Powers continued. "This fragrant memory, if I may so describe it"—his chest and belly shook with pleasure. "This, this, this moo-chwower."

She stuck her tongue out at him and bit the end of it. She turned away to hide her tongue's sudden pain (like burning it on gravy or licking at the sharp edge of a piece of paper) and he resumed his chat with Judah as to railroad stocks. They were engrossed in a prospectus by the time she turned again, and he flung her compliments like bones.

"Hey, Missie Sherbrooke," Powers said. "Sashay this way, why don't you? Do a poor fellow a favor."

He and her brother swapped stories. They slapped each other's backs. Grimacing in the corner, they huddled over balance sheets and toted up credits and debits. They bickered together the way old friends bicker, and she was only an accessory, she knew. Widower Powers consoled himself with whiskey and gin rummy and poker and cigars. There were other forms of consolation, no doubt, to judge by his burbling smug whisper when he came back from Bridgeport, Connecticut.

"There's things"—he grew expansive—"things to *see* there. Yes."

"What sort of things?" she asked.

"I can't hardly begin to describe them. Don't know as it's proper in— saving your pardon—mixed company."

"Why, Sam,"—she fluttered, letting her voice break—"you've learned something after all. After all these weeks."

"A-yup," he chortled, nudging Judah. "You can say that again."

"Bridgeport, Connecticut," she continued. "It's on the water, correct?"

"Right. Leastways I think so."

"You didn't notice?"

"Nope. Not me."

"I thought you said you saw things there."

"Hattie," Judah intervened, "he never got out of his room."

And she was tired suddenly, tired of their self-delighting schoolboy antics. She was weary of their glib obscene fraternity in lust. Powers would be boastful. "I've joined in the amorous lists," he would say. "I've entered the fray. I've thrown my gauntlet down and plan to be a-jousting soon"—he winked—"in amorous lists."

So when he married that redhead from Bridgeport, Connecticut, Harriet was not surprised. Instead she felt, perceptibly, relief. She was relieved of Samuel's importunities (smoothing his hair past the bald spot, crinkling up his eyes in heavy-handed laughter at some heavy-handed joke, clinking the silver together in his side pants pocket, fist working at the coinage, cloth-swaddled, huge) and at peace.

Nor did she feel embittered by Judah's teasing title, "Spinster." She selected it herself. It was an honorable name—the spinning sister—and her chosen fate. Time passed, and the passage was simple. She gave up on vanity. She had been young, then youthful, then a woman in her prime, then middle-aged, then past her prime, then old. She had eaten sweets and then forsaken sweets in order to preserve her figure and now ate sweets again. She had tried, persistently, to battle her increasing age, but it had been a losing battle and better not to fight. Time was, she joked, the perfect diet; time has brought her weight back down to what she'd weighed when seventeen. She'd thought her girth irrevocable—but it was time-revoked.

Nor did she feel requital when Powers and his wife died on their way to the Bahamas in a charter plane. She had not wished him—as she wished Jamie Pearson—dead. She bore no grievance that would demand requital in some coral reef off Nassau in the Bahamas. Harriet has never been to Nassau in the Bahamas, nor, for the matter of that, to water warm enough for coral reefs. But she owns coral necklaces and bracelets, and she had seen photographs in *National Geographic* of the Great Barrier

Reef. Magic fish and eels can snout their way through coral, whereas men would flay themselves on contact with the pointed nubbins of the rock. Their skin would shred and bleed and sharks would follow the blood trail and make a noonday snack of Samuel Powers and his bride. She wonders, idly, if sharks eat human hair. She wonders if they'd lop off his wife's head entirely, or leave the strands of orange hair to coil through the coral like weed.

Now she feels sleep slipping up. She has twenty minutes to rest. She switches off the electric blanket; "Lord forgive them their trespasses," she prays, "as I would ask forgiveness of my own." She thinks of Thomas Sherbrooke, whose knowledge of ships had been meager; he had piloted a rowboat once, on Parrin Lake. He had learned to swim and had bought boats in bottles, she imagines, and watched the firelight gleam off their rigging and sails. He would have watched for hours, his elbows on the desk.

Whales would spout to starboard. Dolphins would follow the ship. He lay on the forward deck, thinking of home, noting how the water underneath him was moving so much faster than water in the near distance, or at the horizon. There were bands of water. He knew the waves were demarcation points. ("Dear mother and father,"—he had sent one letter home—"Forgive me if you can. I'm off on what we sailors call the 'Bounding Main.' I have no regrets or uncertainty in making my fortune this way, and sure I am to do it because the ship runs four boats and is fitted out with 3500 barrels and for a voyage of 3 years. We are going 'round Cape Horn and to the South Pacific Ocean in a voyage after sperm whales with a crew of 27 men, and very pious Officers. I am satisfied with my situation and Prospects except only in the grief I caused by the manner of my leaving but you *must not worry* for me, not you particularly mother. There were contrary winds and averse currents but we weathered them and recruited off Payta as also recruited off Tecamur and stand now at a full compliment of men. Tell Daniel to be a good boy and not to do as I have done unless he wishes also to be a burden to his parents. Tell him remember me.")

She pictures her ancestor, gold-haired, blue-suited, laying down his quill pen to breathe and sigh and stare and brush away hot tears. The ship would heave in the windless swell; the smell of rum was rank. She pictures him rereading—as she herself has countless times reread—his single letter: "It is impossible to describe the misery of the slaves both here and at Rio in particular you would hardly conceive that with all its fine palaces and grand houses with the King of Portugal riding in his splendid Gilt Coach and officers attending him there could be so much misery but while your eyes would be dazeled with all the splendor you will turn them away and see twenty or thirty poor slaves chained together bearing heavy burdens. Your soul sickens at the sight. But I am forgetting my story I went while there to see the place where the slaves were whiped there was one about to be Punished as he was tied to the post his back stripped and 150 lashes given him he uttered not a groan and when the horrible scene was finished the blood lay in pools at his feet and his body was so mangled and torn that he could not rise but lay senseless until he was carried away. Give my love to all the children tell them to forgive my faults and if possible to forget them. Give my love to all my relations and friends if I have any. I hope to be a steward shortly in the Captain's mess, and share his rations and musick what time he has musick to share . . . "

He stands in the whaleboat, balancing. There are harpooners behind him. The harpoon is intricately carved, and the blade has a green sheen. It is polished. There is blubber and blood and, astonishingly, reefs that rise like candelabras from the troughs of waves. ("I have hopes you will forgive the rash step your son taken, signing on at Falmouth for which I am undutiful but repentant, and if ever I return again which God grant I shall endeavour to make good in esteem but no more for the present it is too much . . . I get in common with the rest of us the 1.75 lay or one barrel out of 1.75 . . . ")

The harpoon shaft rests on his shoulder, and the shoulder acts as a fulcrum; it is tattooed. She peers at the tattoos but is unable to decipher them—they do not signify. They are black and red and bulbous. They are changing, self-wreathed shapes. His shoulder aches. He weeps. He fingers the tattoos. She knows there is a message there, but not for her to read.

VI

They eat. He eats in silence, mostly, while Harriet makes conversation. "I want you to remind me," she says, "to have them plant shallots this spring. Shallots would be wonderful with meat like this, and I can't buy them anywhere—not Morrisey's, not anywhere. We could have them every day all winter long. They keep."

Finney has brought the three wills. He has followed Judah's instructions; they are alike and brief. Hattie has her constant portion, and there are bequests. The charities amount to one hundred thousand dollars—ten of them each getting ten. The principal beneficiaries, however, change; one testament allots the bulk of the estate to Ian, one to Maggie, and one to an agreed-upon division, half and half of an assessment of the whole. There are copies in the briefcase Finney carries. He will be one witness and will take them to his office for a second witness and to have them notarized and filed.

The lawyer has learned not to offer advice. Some clients want his opinion, but it's wasted time with Judah and not worth the fuss. He knows that Ian has no chance, that this entire dispensation ceremony is no more than a charade. He had been tempted, almost, to try to track Ian down. He had wanted to see Judah's face if both of them arrived—but then Finney thought that this too might have pleased his client. And then he thought that Maggie might inform her son, or maybe the letter would anyhow reach him; then he thought the simplest thing is do what Judah asked. He bills for his time, whichever way, and each of them will be a legal binding document once signed. If pressed to it, he'd say that Judah's crazy like a fox. "Ours not to reason why," he reminds himself, "ours but to do and do it properly." He'd set the briefcase by the sideboard and received a Scotch from Judah and ventured a joke: "It's your funeral," he'd said.

Finney drinks. He requires the hair of the dog. He needs an entire kennel, based on what transpires here, based on what these people think is sensible; he swirls the whiskey in his glass, watching the water separate out from Scotch. The Big House isn't big enough to contain Margaret Sherbrooke; the state of Vermont isn't big enough, and he's heard she'd flown the coop as far as San Francisco, figuring the whole East Coast wasn't sufficient, thinking maybe she'd try for Hawaii. Finney knows the type. He knows the ones who go to court with a black eye from a door or maybe some Italian who obliged them, and wail and say it was their husband and can they please have everything he owns. He knows the ones who sign on late then want to leave early, taking fifty percent of the whole. But though he heaps them all together—with the ambulance chasers and the malpractice people and the ones who run to Canada, then ask for amnesty—Maggie is one of a kind. Finney figures her at fifty, and maybe a year or so past it, but you'd never know by looking and you'd have to do the arithmetic twice. She's playing Florence Nightingale tonight. She is all smiles and chatter and hot compresses and sympathy; Judah'd got what he wanted by getting her back. But Florence Nightingale contracted syphilis, Finney knows, and died in the Crimea of a dose. That was the hell of a thing—he finishes his drink and jangles the ice cubes and figures maybe he'd best pour the second go-round himself. You pick a model of charity and decency and selflessness, and make her a model for nurses, and she gets the clap.

He pours. He is here to safeguard the Sherbrooke interests. Heavily, he toasts her; she smiles up at him sideways, batting her eyes. But she is a Sherbrooke also, and an interested party, and Judah's never even entertained the notion of divorce. He himself suggested it, and Hattie no doubt suggested it often. But Finney got a flat-out no, and Hattie probably got worse, a mind-your-own-business-not-mine.

"Are you happy to be back?" he asks.

"Yes."

"Does it still feel like home to you?"

"Of course it does."

"Why did you leave then?" Judah asks, interrupting them.

"You know."

"No, really . . .

"Let's not start that, Jude," Hattie says. "Not now."

"Why not? No time like the present . . ."

"I never heard you say that," Maggie says.

"All right. What brings you here?"

"The love I bear you." She says this with the precision of a prerehearsed recital, looking at Finney instead.

"Bore," Judah says.

"*Bear.*" She cites her letter to him. "And you said you bore me once."

"How was the trip?"

"When did you get my letter?"

"Monday."

"What did you do with it?"

"Tore it up," he lies. "Flushed it down the toilet. Gave it to Hattie instead." She turns to her sister-in-law, but Harriet asks for the salt.

It had happened to him with his son. Feeding Ian, watching how his baby learned to swallow or stick out his tongue, inserting the small spoon with its quotient of apricot or carrot or banana mush, Judah remembered feeding his mother—with her on her final bed, drooling. Lavinia Sherbrooke lingered for months, force-fed by him or one of the nurses—eating from china, and with the best silver and crystal. But she ate only mush or a boiled egg maybe on a strong morning, with maybe a sip of champagne. She ate with the witless deliberation that signaled bodily function and not her spirit's purpose; her intention, she declared, had been to call it quits.

Judah fed his mother patiently, announcing how the egg was fresh; he'd plucked it from the chicken coop five minutes before boiling. "It should set up," she said. "There's such a thing as over-fresh." She said the glass she drank from stank, and that it smelled of onions, or possibly garlic or scallions, she wasn't certain which. He brought her day-old eggs, and she said they were too old.

Still, the room is peopled. There had been birthday celebrations and dinners for the Governor, when the Governor came south. There had been eighteen servants quartered in the servants' wing. Directly above his bedroom, in a third-floor storage hall, dresses hang. His grandmother had had the habit of preserving the year's most beautiful dress and selecting it on Christmas Eve. She would give the rest away to charity or servants or nieces—or, if she were fond of the fabric but not style, would have the dress remade. The storage hall was cedar-lined, and the commodes and chests were cedar, and therefore the clothes stayed moth-free; Harriet strewed camphor on the floor. His grandmother, commemorating, would pin a note to the left shoulder of the dress—so Judah, holding a yellow lace-embroidered flaring full-length gown would read: *1882. June 25th The Adams Ball. I danced till 2 A.M.* In 1883 she wrote: *January 23. Reception for Anne Watts*—and chose a dress that was predominantly violet, an oriental-influenced arrangement of silks. There were ball gowns and picnic outfits and gowns she wore to christenings, but after 1907, with her husband dead, she wore only black. It pleased him, sleepless, to think of his grandmother's portly promenading form, and the grave gaiety of Christmas Eve, when she made her selection. There were hats and riding habits and gloves and shawls in profusion. There were mantillas on pegs.

"I, Judah Porteous Sherbrooke, being of sound mind and body, hereby declare . . ."

"Don't," Hattie says.

"I do declare," Maggie mocks him. The women lean together.

"And dispose as follows . . ."

"Jude," she says. "Remember the day we got married? You flustered the J.P. so—what was his name again, Thompson? We were married in this very room—Paul Thompson, that was it."

"Yes," Hattie says. "He lived in Eagle's Bridge. He ran for Sheriff, later, but he lost, remember, and every time he did a marriage he warned about breaking the law."

"What I remember"—Maggie reached around the glasses and put her hand on his—"was when he came to the part about goods. I still don't know if it's 'earthly' or 'worldly' because you had him flustered . . ."

"*You* did," Judah says.

"What I remember, anyway, is how he mixed the two together and came up with 'worthly goods.'"

She will not leave off teasing, Judah knows. She takes his declaration on her terms.

"And then we were all out on the porch. And he said he'd take the wedding picture and you focused it for him and came to stand beside me and he must have sneezed or something because when we developed it he'd missed the two of us entirely."

"Legs," Finney says, "He got those."

"So what we have is 'worthly goods' and a bunch of steps that needed painting. That's what I remember," Maggie says.

"Are you finished?"

"No. You don't have to announce," she says, "every little thing you're planning. It works out different, anyhow, it's never the way we expect."

"Amen to that," Finney says.

"He's got the papers," Judah says. "There in that briefcase. It's yours."

It is water, always, that he works his way through—water where she sports and luxuriates, the liquid that surrounds her so she is *of*, not *in* it.

"Ninety-eight percent of our body, Jude," she'd said to him, "is water."

"Fact?"

"True fact. And every single body cell is mostly water too. We come from it and swim in it our first nine months"—she pointed to her stomach—"like little Ian-Betsy is swimming in there now."

He managed swimming well enough and had been a strong swimmer. He flailed at the Battenkill, going upriver, and didn't give ground to the current. But it had been assertion always, and not relinquishing, not lazing on his back. He gauged his progress by the river snags and branches and rocks on the bank; she made no effort he could see but wriggled and flipped her way past him with slithering ease.

"You're fighting it, Judah," she'd say.

"Talking of onions," Harriet says, "we're mostly out of them. There's water in the cellar now three inches deep. It doesn't seem that way *above* ground, not the worst mud season ever, but it's bad enough below, I tell you, and very lucky I looked."

"The wet went deep," he offers.

Maggie fiddles with the cutlery. "What else can you tell me?" she asks.

He says, of course, no question; it has been in his mind all along. It had been the first thing he intended to discuss. But somehow he got sidetracked, someway it was hard to raise the subject: Do what you want with the house. Judah has no wishes, none that count. Mouse droppings on the carpet she had prized so highly, and squirrels using insulation for their nests—what happens happens anyhow; a stitch in time saves nothing; anyhow the fabric rends. No question, Judah said, he'd been meaning from the first to make some fitting dispensation and quittance for all claims.

That's why he summoned her; that's why he'd wished each heir and legatee to come. Ian, of course, failed to show. Ian has been busy with whatever busies him. Finney had no address they were sure of; nor did they try much more than middling hard to notify that missing person of the chance he'd missed. You couldn't put a wanted poster up, you couldn't have the post office print an announcement: Ian Sherbrooke, come on home; collect your proper inheritance, your parcel of the acreage and floor of the

117

house and three hundred thousand dollars at the ticket window, please. That's what drove him off to start with, and it wouldn't haul him back and if it did he wasn't worth the finding anyway.

So everything gets sidetracked, he tells her; every talk they had would trail off into bickering. You get to telling someone how jade plants require water. You tell him how the axle on Harry Turley's Packard split like a toothpick that time. It was like the differential was all teeth, like murder with malice aforethought when the front end dropped. You get to tracking little live things every which way, busy in the scurry of it, keeping up your prattle and dispensing Kaopectate to the very young or elderly, and there is somehow nothing left, no time and not much inclination for the rolltop desk and settling up accounts. You've worked your way through balance sheets before. You do it to your satisfaction, toting up a deal more black than red, then looking up and squinting to see an angel of some sort of mercy or death hover stork-legged in the hallway, waiting for your verdict as to which is suitable, water or the undiluted wine.

He himself was open-handed. He'd said why not, what the hell, there's plenty more and he'd elected wine, saying come along, step on it, Maggie, hop in, we're going for a hop-step-drive along the Old East Road. There are potholes. There is Harry Turley's Packard to remember. There is, Judah tells himself, every blunder that you ever made or might still be about to make, rankling so your ears would hum; there is this creature telling you Manhattan Island is a better place for bikes. It isn't memory. Your memory is good, is maybe better than most. They told you that in school or at the auction barn, and you never lost a number series once you learned it. And anyhow he needs no reminding, knows the present forms the future and is a kind of prophecy that will be history when the future is also the past. I meant to tell you, baby, it's been in my mind all along. There is *yon valley* and her pursed lips on him and her hand and her thin cheeks puckered, and the strands of her hair on her cheeks, the way the sweat adheres to skin; there is the jingle of *adieu* and *whatever I do*.

"Please pass the salt," Finney says.

"Yes."

"These are excellent potatoes."

"Pepper? Butter? What else can I get you?"

"Are you still taking seconds?" Hattie asks her sister-in-law. "I remember you shoveled in heaps of food and never put on weight."

Judah hears them hunting comfort in the topic of the food. He has his chin to his chest. He stares at his wife, seeing where she has coarsened, sees the lines around her neck that had been seamless once. They talk about him now as if he cannot hear.

"I've been tending to him," Hattie says.

"Yes."

"Night and day."

"I'll bet he takes some tending to." He takes this as a compliment.

"Seven days of the week," Hattie says.

"I'm glad I'm here. I hope to be some help."

"I've not needed help," Hattie says, "I've done it night and day these seven days a week. He just needs attention is all."

"I do know that."

"You simply can't imagine," Hattie continues. "I look at him sometimes in church. And it's just the saddest face; you let him settle down and think there's no one watching and it's the saddest face you'd ever want to see."

"I wouldn't want to see that," Maggie says.

"No. Of course not. Not if you can help it."

"We . . ."

"He may have been your husband once, but"—and there is sniffing virulence in his sister's face again—"let me tell you, he's changed."

Judah shaves with a strop razor; that is consistency in change. What he touches has grown pliable and takes on his palm's sweat. The blue spruce tree he planted to signal Ian's birth was higher than Ian to start with, then smaller since it grew less quickly, then taller since it continued to grow. He wonders why he has no memory of pain. He would will himself into remembrance or anticipation, but the pain is not corporeal, any more than pleasure is corporeal when done. Judah is glad about that. If he could balance pain and pleasure off, he figures pain would weight the scale considerably; he'd have to have been sporting fifty or five hundred times to cancel out one broken leg.

He'd heard the heart stopped beating in three different ways. It stopped, Doc Wiggins said, when you sneezed or climaxed or died. You only die once, Judah said, and you come maybe five thousand times, or if you're lucky ten. In the oblivious intervals he tended to his business—not pleasure and not pain.

"Well, what about sneezing?" asked Wiggins. You could sneeze six times in succession if you breathed back hay chaff, say, and it would take a lot less energy than sporting; it would wring him dry a whole lot more efficiently. So one was pain and one was pleasure and one was by and large indifferent, and he would choose, if forced to choose, that heart-stopping sneeze as the best way to go.

Wiggins recited his ditty, "I sneezed a sneeze into the air. It fell to earth I know not where. But hard and cold were the looks of those, in whose vicinity I snooze."

Judah laughed. "Still and all," the doctor winked at Judah. "Still, judging by available receptacles, I'd a deal sooner hope to empty myself by that other device for emission. If you take my meaning."

"Yes," Judah said. "I do. You piss-ant simple son of a whore. I take it well enough."

"What did you call me?"

"If recollection serves," said Judah, "a piss-ant simple son of a whore. But I meant it kindly," and he grinned at Wiggins who backed off, bristling, abject.

"Jude."

"Yes?"

"Jude, I say."

"I hear you," Judah says.

120

"Judah, are you listening?"

"I heard you the first time," he says.

"What was I saying?"

"Well, what was I saying," he mimics, word-perfect.

"Before that?"

"Jude-boy, are you listening?" His voice rises, parroting hers.

"You never listen to me," Maggie says. "You don't hear a thing I tell you."

"I'm listening," he says.

Why does she counter him, she asks herself; what drives her to it, drove her north and to his side like a night nurse who prefers hot mustard poultices to balm, who uses rubbing alcohol to staunch each wound; why not submit if all he needs for peace is her enforced submission? The guises multiply and then persist and then it isn't clear which one is truthful, which a disguise; *age cannot wither,* she remembers, *nor custom stale.* But age does wither and custom does stale and there's no infinite variety to what she's learned or where (has said this to her analyst also—that she'd left Sarah Lawrence after two years, not seeing the point of it, not wanting to call Bronxville the Athens of the Bronx, wanting real grape arbors and not the hundred yards of trellised walkway they thought of as a conduit to universal learning, not needing little needy men to tell her there were large ones once, nor willing to believe her breathless labored whirling would be the future of dance); her grasp and reach an octave only, not enough.

So she argues with him just to keep her hand in: forgive but don't forget. That's her motto, she tells Judah, you say tomato and I say tom-ah-toe; you say potato and I say pot-ah-toe, *salad days,* the wilted scrap of what had seemed to be love's feast. We're old-time adversaries, husband, and I'd rather disagree with you than agree with most.

Now each of them wonder, is this all? Is habit's hold unbreakable and will they sit to supper forever and ever, as if betrayal and revenge were topics like the quality of meat? Good manners, Hattie said, mean never discuss what you're eating. You can compliment the cook, but that's as far as it goes; you should never talk about the food being tasted at table. There had been stews, she'd heard, in which men were served up their sons. The proper thing to do would anyhow be compliment the cook and then, when you learn what you've eaten, to provoke a duel.

So politeness is the order of the day. Politeness means that Maggie serves Finney, and no one hurries Judah's carving when he drops the knife. No one says, "Here, let me help," or "Would you like to let me try?" or any of the phrases that might make things bearable (his shaking pronounced now, the blood leaking out of the undercooked steaks—not rare, not raw even, just bloody and expensive pulp, the blade making scant progress against that ten-pound fibrous lump, and none of them hungry anyhow, none of them able to do justice to Morrisey's best). No one refuses potatoes when the white slop sticks to the spoon; nobody mentions that the carrots should have been washed and peeled. It has to be deliberate, Maggie tells herself; it has to be a parody of meals they shared before. Yet Judah eats with concentration, chewing on his mouthfuls like something in a stable, shifting it from side to side in the forefront of his mouth. She herself—she answers Hattie—has no appetite.

"Why's that?" the old woman asks. "You always used to eat."

"I ate on the bus," Maggie says.

"They've got nothing there."

"In Albany," she says. "At the terminal. There's a cafeteria and I wasn't sure what time we'd be eating."

"Correction," Judah says. "You weren't sure you'd get to eat."

"What does that mean?" Finney asks.

"It means she didn't know for certain I'd be there. It means she worried where her next square meal was coming from, that's what."

Candles flare. In the soft light and flicker, his skin smoothes. Hattie toys with her food. She arranges it in segments on her plate, then shifts the right-hand portion to the left, the left right. She mashes her potato, the fork tines giving slightly when she forces. She makes a pyramid of meat.

"You're not eating," Judah says.

"Yes I am," says Hattie. "It tastes good."

"You're lying," Judah says.

"We call it table manners," Maggie says.

So they attempt to please him, bending to their plates again, and suddenly this seems to Maggie the story of her history: a supervised consumption when all appetite is gone. She straightens, rejecting her food. "Jude, I'll be sick if you force me to finish this."

He grins at her and says, "That's the little lady. That's the one I married."

"Why serve us this?"

"Because I need to see just how much shit the others will swallow," he says, and touches her arm, conspiratorial. "Because there's no limit to what certain people can eat."

"Judah," Hattie says. "You'll make yourself sick."

"These slops"—he gestures. "These pig leavings. This crap I had prepared for you to watch you at the trough." He sweeps his plate backhanded and it crashes against the fireplace wall and falls and spills but does not break. They watch it teeter. "I been waiting," Judah says, "for one of you to say just one thing all this meal. Just once to tell me what you thought of what we put before you. Every step of it's been planned."

"Fine," Maggie says. "So you serve us a second-rate dinner . . ."

"Who in heaven's name cares?" Hattie asks.

He had been making it, was faking weariness and sickness when it came to him that she needed someone young and hale as he, Judah, was once; he presses his legs together and feels his pants' fabric compress. He does not move. He hears his heart's pulse amplify and echo from his chest to ears, then wrist. He is his own best audience, the kid who gapes forever at the card trick that he never learned, the one who always says "Again, again," and sits there openmouthed, letting flies feed off his tongue. He says four queens, hell, that's terrific, hell, I could have sworn—when every second card's a queen, except he doesn't know it; riffle the deck in the other direction and it's only queens; his legs go weak. His lungs are weak. His arms that had been tempered steel ("Like a sword," she'd say. "You draw your arms out from that undershirt like some proud swordsman") are rust-riddled, breakable. He can remember toting water to the house; the wells went bad one summer, and he had to fetch and carry everything they drank. With clarity now for the first time he feels that what he'd faked is real, that all the fraud was worthless since it also stood for truth, and Judah is in mortal straits, is mortal, is cut out to die.

They draw back from the table. He says he'll sit a little while; it isn't all that often you give the world away. Maggie leads Finney into the room's far alcove, then turns to him, speaking softly. "What is it you're after, Samson?"

"How do you mean?"

"You understand what I'm asking. Just tell me what's the point of this and I'll know how to play."

"It's not a game."

"It's not all that serious either."

"For Judah," Finney acknowledges, "the point is that you're here."

"One bus trip. One afternoon. I didn't even have to change at Albany; they've improved the service."

"Yes."

"One one-way ticket, it's nothing to fuss about, Samson. What's the fuss?"

"The will," he says. "You heard him."

"Yes, it's mine. I've said my thank-yous; I'll say them again. So what?"

He stares at this quicksilver creature and thanks God he never married. There were times, he wants to tell her, when he'd been tempted to get on his knees and there'd been candidates enough for Mrs. Finney, in case she thought the opposite, in case she didn't know. He eats a Ritz cracker, no cheese, and the crunching sound seems loud.

"You haven't answered me," she says.

"It's a legal document—or will be once I get it witnessed."

"And then?"

"It's watertight, like seeing snow on the ground and deducing it snowed. Which would stand up in court . . ."

"I don't . . ."

"Been thinking how best to explain it," Finney says. "You get the place lock, stock, and barrel once it's notarized."

"Aren't you forgetting something?"

"What?" He pops his tongue. He selects a second cracker from the bowl.

"Someone."

"Not that I know of. It's provided for. I'm sorry about Ian, but it's the way he wanted it."

"I'm not talking about Ian."

"Seems your boy wanted it this way. He's the one who didn't show. If he'd only come . . ."

"That's not what I mean," Maggie says.

Now it's his turn to stand there quizzical, awaiting explanations. Finney runs his tongue across his teeth.

"It's Judah you're forgetting."

"I don't follow."

"He's got to die first, Samson. That's what makes it legal and a—what did you call it?—binding document."

He focuses. He had taken off his glasses when they sat to table.

"Until that time"—she nears him—"it's a piece of paper, right? Just a statement of intention, am I right?"

"Well."

"I could give it all away, correct? I could give it all to Ian, for example."

"In your turn," he starts to say—but she is hissing at him, so near now he smells the perfume.

"Correct?" she says.

"That's true. There's no proviso . . ."

"But *after*. Not till after. While Judah lives it's his and I am his and he can rearrange it anytime. Just call you in one afternoon and say, for instance, today my wife forgot to squeeze the orange juice, I want her out of the will. She talked back to me this noon and I don't like her yellow dress so I'm writing her out, understand? He's done it before; he did it this evening to Ian, so who's to say he won't again?"

"People don't just . . ."

"Judah does," she finishes. "There's nothing changed here, Samson. So I ask you one more time, what's all the fuss?"

He swallows his answer since Judah approaches. She puts her index finger to her lip and kisses it, then blows him the kiss. "Why, darling," Maggie says, and crosses to her husband. "How lovely you were well enough to eat with us. How nice you could come down."

Finney makes excuses. He has his work to do; the bowling league started at eight. He likes the weekly routine of the league—the feel of his personalized ball and the friendly competition and the beer. Sometimes, with his second glass swallowed, he stares at his shoes on the sheen of the alley, watching the pattern his teammates make when running. The red-and-blue striped shoes tumble forward, and he thinks the laminated wood beneath him is a triumph of carpentry. This is all there is, he sometimes thinks; this is ballet, war, law, friendship, everything that counts: the rush and release and the clatter of pins. He has a one-hundred-and-sixty-three-point average for the last ten games; that's just this side of bad, says Finney, but preening, plucking at his coat sleeve, meaning just this side of good.

Judah says don't go just yet, let's smoke one good cigar.

It has been simple for Maggie, a kind of acquiescence, not revolt—and that the path of least resistance happened also to be primrose is a lucky break admittedly, but not her intention or fault. It has been natural, this sitting down to supper with her husband and lawyer and sister-in-law; fortune comes full circle like a wheel.

And there were surprises. She had watched him chew, bone-weary, head to one side and mouth making preparatory motions, as a blind man might.

The attentive way he paused to swallow, the effort that it clearly was for Judah to down anything who when she met him gorged on flesh—the weakness in him fortified some fierce protective tenderness she might as well call love.

"Should we talk about it?" Maggie asks.

He makes no answer.

"About how long I'm staying?"

"Yes."

"What's your opinion?"

"As long as you need to."

"Which is why I want to talk about it."

"The doctors . . ." Hattie begins, but Judah is impatient, spitting smoke.

"Doctors know shit from shinola. As long as they collect the fee it's operation successful, patient dead. If you're lucky you come out no worse than you went in."

"I wanted to tell you . . ." Maggie says.

"What? What? Don't tell me lies about doctors."

"That I'm here," she offers. "As long as you want me to stay."

So the seven lean years succeeded seven fat; so she sojourned in what Hattie would call wilderness. Yet the Big House and its owner have not changed. "You are," he said, "my only prized possession. My prizewinning entry at the fair."

"That's sweet," she said. "You're sweet."

"I'm being truthful," he said.

"You flatter me."

"No."

"Yes. What a generous comparison. The best homegrown turnip. A cow."

"My prizewinning entry," he repeated.

"Impossible"—she spread her hands. But he was impervious, possessing her, as he had been impervious to cows. He said they'll treat you how you treat them, and you get as good as you give. Now Sam, for instance, had no use for Ayrshires. And they know it and can use their horns; they're mean cows, Ayrshires are, and he's got to watch them all the time, not like with Jerseys, they're sweet. I mean there's more than half a ton of cow, and you don't want it disliking you . . .

"That isn't my point," Maggie said.

"What is, then?" He contrived surprise. "What am I saying that's wrong?"

"Oh, Jude," she said.

"Tell me and I'll fix it"—he spread his hands, palms out. His lifeline was black.

"I was trying to be serious. There's ways and ways."

"I'll mend my ways," Judah said.

So he joked and parried with her, inattentive. She never could touch him with words. He paid no heed to speech but heeded her motion and shape. She had been angry at that; it was what they called sexist now—the body's degradation via compliment. Maggie fell back on body claims and was angry with herself and angrier with him for forcing that language upon her—language she'd learned since puberty, or since her first pink sheets. She had grown facile, using it, and fluent in her limbs' articulation when she walked. She knew that, where she walked, men watched. They followed her with their eyes or in imagined deed and some men followed her actually. She swiveled her hips, she sometimes thought, in comic counterpoint to the way their heads would swivel—or advanced across the room in order to elicit an advance. But she'd been at it long enough and—she remembered Judah's expression about the game of baseball—had retired undefeated, hanging up her spikes.

She could delight him, at first. She pleasured him in simple ways, but they were a complex delight. She wore no underwear, for instance, beneath her evening gown. She perfumed herself and smacked her lips when watching him approach in the hot candlelit dark. She kept her stockings and garter belt on and lay down like one of those magazine pinups, Judah told her; when he entered her, she gasped and was

appreciative and wanted, she would whisper, to be his garden of earthly delights.

"You've got the house now," Hattie says.

"Yes."

"Congratulations."

"Thank you."

"May you have much joy in it. I wish you that."

"Don't be so serious, Hattie. Nothing's changed."

"That's not how I see it," she says.

"Why not?"

"You're thirty years younger than I am. You can laugh."

"I wasn't laughing," Maggie says.

The phone rings. Hattie goes to it. "Hello," she answers. "Sherbrookes."

There is silence.

"Sherbrookes," Hattie says again. "Who is it?"

Their mother had said, "Sherbrooke residence" is for the maids to say,
but you never just answer the phone with "hello." "Hi" is a way of measuring height, and "yes" is short for "Yes, who may I say is calling, please?" So
Hattie had settled on "Sherbrookes" as a way to answer, and she says it a
third time.

"Hello"—her voice goes querulous. "Is anybody there?"

In the instant it takes for her to cradle the receiver, Judah divines that
the caller is Ian, calling his mother in code.

"Nobody there," Hattie says. "Just breathing."

"Maggie's back," he says.

"How's Ian?" Hattie faces Maggie. She drops her voice.

"Who?"

"Ian. Have you heard from him?"

"Yes," Maggie says. "Last week in fact. He's fine."

"I'm glad to hear that."

"You don't have to whisper."

She points to where the two men are puffing cigars. "I wouldn't want Judah . . ."

"What?" Maggie says. "I'm sorry but I just can't hear you."

"Do you hear from him often?"

"Yes. Well," she pauses, judicious. "Not all that often."

"How often?"

"It's not that he's been too busy to call," Maggie says. "You understand that."

"I don't," Hattie tells her. "I do not."

"Well, your brother does."

"Don't shout at me."

"I wasn't shouting."

"You were," Hattie tells her. "You are."

"This is silly," Maggie says. "We can do better than this. He doesn't ever call me, if that's what you're wanting to hear."

"I thought so," Hattie triumphs. "He's run out on every last one of us, I do so hope he's well."

Maggie believes, and tried to tell her husband this for years, that joy's a thing to share. You spread it around. You do that with butter, he says, not land. Good fences make good neighbors. She knows what he's saying, she says, but he doesn't hear her when she declares the opposite, bad fences make bad neighbors; and why should he mistrust this idea of neighborliness anyhow, why isn't everybody in the same house always, sharing everything? A goddamn hippie commune, he says, in the days they used to argue; nobody gets in my bed but the lady I put there, you hear? I hear you, Judah, Maggie says; I get the message. Loud and clear, he asks her, and she cups a hand to her head like an earphone, tilts it, saying, "Eh?"

But it isn't always comical, Finney knows that; it's been a bone of contention between them as long as he remembers. If pushed to it he'd say, indeed, that's been the rock they foundered on, the bedrock of the squabble where belief enters in, saying enough's enough. They're peas in a pod, as he sees it, two of a kind.

"You'll excuse us," Judah says, not making it a question. "I want to talk with my wife."

"Yes," says Finney.

"Good night."

"Night." Released, he gathers his things.

"You can go now," Judah says. "Hattie."

"I'm not the one who's tired," she says. "You mustn't mind me."

"I don't. I want to talk to this one who's come all the way from New York City."

"Good night then," Harriet says.

"Good night.

"He'll try to fool you," she insists to the room. "He's tireder than he lets on. I promise you that."

"Hattie, you can leave us now."

"I'm leaving. It isn't so easy"—she turns to Maggie. "I sit all day in that chair. And you can't imagine how it bothers the sciatica, how it irritates the nerve. It's probably a pinched nerve, Ida Simmons says. But the courtesy to let me take my time going, is that too much, plain gratitude, a simple thank you . . ."

"Hattie," Judah says, and this time is commanding. Finney takes her arm; they make their way. And as Maggie turns to follow Judah, smiling at him, Finney, with a captive's sheepish smile who nonetheless would wash the feet of captors and dry them with her hair, the lawyer feels that Maggie wanted company not for the celebration but its mournful aftermath, not the night but day. She would cross that bridge when the bridge came; she would make the mountains come to meet her, shifting on their axis as the world continually shifts.

VII

Lately, Hattie has been seeing things. She walks into a room and the walls whir. Cats flash across the edges of her sight. Sometimes she sees birds there also, flitting, with that quick lift and shift of direction that mean they sense an obstacle, and sometimes no beast she can name. She would rather call them "cat" and "bird" than nameless changeling presences because her eyes are weak.

Tonight, however, she can name the ghost she saw. It is—she was sure of it—Seth. The Big House is not haunted, but her dead infant nephew is a presence at the windows and outside every wall. She would not voice her fear to Judah or ask if he sensed something too, but she is certain—in a way that beggars doubt—the crib death was no accident. It would not have happened to another family or in another house. It had not been vengeance so much as retribution for what they'd failed to learn. The lesson was humility; they'd scanted that. They'd thought themselves above ill luck, but all the time it had been brewing, always there in some dark corner, fermenting, heating up.

The Sherbrookes had been fingered by a finger dipped in blood. That moving finger moved across the village, Hattie knows, hovering above the roofs and chimneys, sparing firstborn sons and families that lived with due humility. But above the Big House it wavered and then pointed down, like applewood for water, or any dowser's stick. She sees forked lightning that way, sometimes, as if it were God's dowsing stick, eradicating what it touched in order to point to the depths.

Seth had been a candle snuffed out before its time, is what they said at the service: a brightly burning light. And she had been bereaved. She'd mourned and wailed in silence for as many months as Seth had lived—neither daring to commiserate with her sister-in-law nor comfort her brother out loud. Judah had studied gain and pride, not the difficult lessons of loss. His wife proved his equal in that.

"I'm sorry, Maggie," Hattie would venture. "If you must make me say it."

"For what?"

"For what happened to Seth. For the way it happened."

"But no one knows what happened. You're not responsible."

"We're all of us responsible."

Maggie said nothing, of course. It would have been simpler to dowse for water in the desert than to find the source of tears in her, or to strike a rock and make it gush. She cast no aspersions and said nothing bitter and named nobody by name. But she was tormented by guilt. Hattie herself was unable to sleep and sat awake as now she sat, hearing lamentation fill the corridor. Wherever Maggie stood or rocked there was the sound of weeping; when she, Hattie, went down to breakfast her sister-in-law would be in the kitchen already, wide-eyed, staring, fixing coffee.

"Did you sleep?" Hattie asked.

"Yes, thank you," she'd answer. "I only just now came down."

So they kept up appearances. They pretended—as Judah too pretended— that nothing was so badly wrong it couldn't be set right. What the doctor called crib death, he said, cannot be predicted and therefore by care or precaution avoided: it's water gone under the bridge. And therefore Baby Seth was scrabbling at the walls and windows—still waiting for a proper burial ceremony and the proper mourning period—at her sight's outer edge.

Lately she has dreamed day-waking dreams. Thomas Sherbrooke tumbles, in her vision, through the ocean's depths and whirlpools the way washing does in a fluff-dry cycle. He spins past her, sleeve over leg. His sleeve is empty and unbuttoned but does not flap; it waves. This gravestone lies if it says that it marks the place of my burial, Thomas Sherbrooke says. She, Hattie, hears him out. He is mourning the sweet sun and how his eyes were eaten by the barracuda, and how he'd been undutiful.

"You see me, Hattie," Thomas Sherbrooke says, "in Davy Jones's lock-up. You see me 'twixt the devil and the deep blue sea."

"Don't blame yourself," she pleads. "It's not your fault."

"Whose, then? Who was it went to make his fortune on the bounding main?"

"Put it out of your mind, Thomas, if only for my sake. Don't blame yourself."

"The devil spar," he burbles at her, inconsolable. "That's what I'm tied to, me hearties. That's where I spend my time. Forever and ever and ever and . . ."

"Don't. I can't bear to hear it."

He silences. He raises his leftover arm at her with all the sweet grace of Ian, and he doffs his cap. Striped fish swim at his ears. "I'll have this dance," he says. "If you'll permit me, Miss Harriet. It's written on the dance card."

"Yes," she says.

"It's what we call a hornpipe jig," he says.

She waits, collecting her breath. It is difficult to breathe. "I can't swim," Hattie tells him, but he guides her through shoals. The water, once she holds his waist, does nothing to her garments, and they spin together, laughing. He murmurs compliments. He says she is a natural-born dancer, and she says he lies. He protests his whole life now is spent in the service of truth.

"That's right and proper," she commends him. "That's as it should be."

Pilot fish maneuver past. He points to them: "It means there's a big one nearby. A killer whale, most likely. Some kind of shark."

She struggles, in over her head. He whispers courteous things to her, and his manner does not change—but what had seemed a dance transforms itself to writhing. She falters, loses step. She opens her mouth and the water roars in and she swallows, choking, while Thomas weaves himself around her like a willow branch, or weeds.

"Your manners, Mr. Sherbrooke," Hattie pleads.

He continues dancing, swimming, smiling his death smile.

"Please."

His hair, she sees with horror now, is water moccasins.

"A gentleman needs no reminding when to take a lady home."

But he is oblivious, as she knew he would be; his arm is an electric eel. His legs are octopus legs.

The death of Seth that night in his crib had been, she understands, the beginning of the end. There had been trouble beforehand, of course; every marriage has some trouble, and this May–September marriage was slated for its share. Still, she'd thought it for the best and thought they'd handle difficulty when difficulty came; they'd talk it out and fix it the way they discussed what's for supper. In the first years of their marriage, they gabbled over weather and the news and music and what Maggie was planning to do for the day and what Judah'd planned for the morning and, later, what Ian did or was about to do. They chattered and whispered and told the same stories until it seemed they'd wear the language out. They wore their tongues out, surely, what with kissing each other and licking their lips. Those early years were hard, of course, but if she'd been a betting woman and been asked to bet she'd have plunked her money down

135

on luck and love enduring; she too forgot humility and dreamed no ill-omen dreams.

Then Seth died a crib death and was gathered up by God. Then the banter ended, and there was silence at meals. Judah could talk with his mouth full, she told herself, relenting; he could mumble nonsense all he wanted to at suppertime, just so he shared some of his bereavement and lightened it by sharing with those who were also bereaved. Ian took no notice or, if he noticed, didn't much mind. That was understandable; he was only three years old and too young to care. But there was selfishness abounding in the silence of the Big House, and it made a breach too wide to fill.

"He's the strong but silent type," Maggie complained. "Know why? Your brother has nothing to say."

"Still waters run deep," she had said.

"Come off it, Hattie, still waters don't run. They sit there and stagnate, that's what they do. They get covered over with weeds."

Soon Maggie started traveling, who'd been a stay-at-home. She'd say where she was going and take a trip and visit friends to fill up the silence-breach. First she'd stay the day away, and then the day and night, and then stay days at a time. To begin with, Maggie took her son along and he'd come back from Concord, Massachusetts, or Mystic, Connecticut, or New York City with stories to tell of every ship they boarded and each museum and what the grizzly bear looked like, standing on its hind legs in the hall. Then, with him, at summer camp, she went off alone. Judah would be in the fields or at his accounts or off at auction somewhere, and she'd back the Packard up and race away and should never, Hattie thought, have been permitted to drive.

But she had always known her sister-in-law would return. She knew it as she'd known that time on School Street when the collie ran after the bus. Hattie saw it coming though she'd seen the dog go after cars and trucks and buses every morning for what seemed like years, and veer and fade off barking. She'd known it a part of the morning's arrangement, part of the proportion of things that the bus would angle left because the Oldsmobile in front of the Carters was parked a foot farther away from the curb, and the collie would maybe lose footing or maybe scent something for once on the wind or off the tire's rim that wasn't danger but delight, would hurtle ahead as the bus shifted gears (the driver so used to this noisy assault he'd not even bothered to check, certain the dog was in sham earnest only, more worried about Oldsmobiles than someone's pet in any case and not overly worried about either, worried most about his watch, which if it wasn't running fast was telling him he'd better). The pattern held; she'd seen it; the dog was entirely crushed.

The chills were mortal here in April, what with the weather changing and snowing the one day and raining the next and then being sixty degrees. So there is also, Hattie knows, the question of her brother's health. He shouldn't get over-excited; he shouldn't tire himself. "You'll catch your death of cold," she warned.

"Don't baby me," Judah responded.

"I wasn't," Harriet said. "I wouldn't dream of it. I only said you ought to be more careful."

"There you go again."

"All right. I didn't mean it badly."

"Again," Judah said. "Again."

So she'd wished him vanquished who had lately been invincible, and is glad now (she decides, scrubbing her teeth and then using dental floss and then mouthwash) that Maggie has returned. Teeth are the mark of class distinction, Harriet maintains. They are the surest yardstick in these times of changing measure. No poor people have adequate teeth, and if poor or ignorant people have adequate teeth they are the exceptions that still prove the rule. She likes her sweets; she will not gainsay that. She keeps mints and toffee candy by her bed. But she attends to her dental hygiene and scrubs and rinses with a scrupulous regularity after every meal. She will die without a false tooth in her, and only a few teeth removed.

It is raining loudly now; snow funnels from the eaves. She can remember building snowmen with Maggie and Ian and maybe one of his friends. They gathered and rough-shaped the snowman while she fetched the props: a scarf and porkpie hat and carrots and old coat and coal. Ian rolled his snowball down the hill, enlarging it, and by the time he reached them the snowball was up to his shoulders. The friend did the same and brought them what would serve as the snowman's round white head. They hoisted it up and smoothed the balls together and Maggie said, "We need a belt. Hattie, is there a belt for this big-bellied man?"

"We need arms," Ian said. "We have to give him arms."

"And shoes," said Ian's friend. What was his name, she asks herself; was it the Harrison boy?

"That isn't possible. He'd melt."

Nonetheless they set to it, smoothing and adjusting him and inserting the coals for his buttons and the carrot for his nose. She went back in the house to carve potato ears, then fetched a pair of Judah's boots and an old dressing gown sash.

"His feet are fat," the friend declared.

"And flat," rhymed Ian. "His feet are fat and flat."

They skipped with the pure pleasure of it, fashioning the snowman until their gloves were soaked. Their noses, Maggie said, were just as red as any carrot, and dribbled a good deal more. "His feet are fat and flat," they chortled and placed Jude's boots, Charlie-Chaplin style, pointing out wide-angled at the snowman's base. Maggie tilted the hat down at a rakish angle, so that it shaded one eye.

"Now let's do Mrs. Snowman," Ian said.

"Mrs. Snowlady, you mean," Maggie said.

"Let's do *you*, Mommy."

"Snowladies," the friend—Joey Harrison?—said. "What do they get to wear?"

"Well," Maggie said. "Coal and carrots and potatoes, like the others. Then maybe an apron and bonnet. You know, something housewifely, so no one gets confused."

"I'll get them," Hattie offered. "I know where."

"And don't forget the lipstick," Maggie said. There had been an edge in her voice.

"We'll build *you*, Mommy," Ian said. "From the bottom up. We'll give you straw for hair."

So they set to work again and fashioned the snowman's companion. Hattie fetched an apron and a broom. The house was hot, or maybe it was the temperature change, or the afternoon which before had been cloudless was suddenly cloud-shadowed and her energy was spent; maybe it had been the vengeance with which Maggie shaped and jammed on breasts and buttressed her ice hips—but what had been a game was earnest now, and not much fun, and she told Ian that she'd lost the stomach for it.

"But where's the bonnet?" Ian asked. "You promised."

"I couldn't find one," she said.

It had been evil, obscene. Her breasts were melon-large and pendulous already, dripping with the heat of hands, and Maggie forced the broomstick in between and said, "Well, what do you think? Do you think that should satisfy Mr. Snowman? The lord and master here."

Another argument was when the Toy House was repaired, and Maggie asked, why bother with those pygmy slates; why mullion the windows just so? She called the structure an extravaganza, saying it wasted both money and time. But Judah told her it isn't so much a bother as duty, and if he had had the patience he would build a dollhouse inside the Toy House, and a midget dollhouse inside the dollhouse and so on. There are ivory elephants, Judah said, that split down the center to disclose further ivory elephants; he'd seen one set of eleven white elephants—the first ten hollow and segmented. They ranged from the size of his two hands to the size of his thumbnail—and all of them hand-carved. Now why bother doing that, he asked; why worry over imitation and repeating shapes?

"There's a difference," Harriet had said—still siding with Maggie back then—"between what maybe takes one Indian man a week to carve in his spare time, when he's got nothing better to do. And setting Albert Wills at a Toy House this whole summer, when you've got no toys. When there's no little girl to love it as a place to play."

Lord knows where Ian has gone off to, and she, Hattie, certainly doesn't and doubts that Judah knows. It is the gypsy in him, Hattie said. There were gypsies enough in the Sherbrooke generations, without adding Maggie's portion—his legs just built for running, his hand to wave good-bye. "You take yourself with you," she'd warned him, "wherever you travel. Ian. There's nothing you don't carry when you go."

"A backpack, Aunt. A single suitcase, maybe."

"Lock, stock, and barrel," she said. "It's foolishness to think you travel light."

He has always been her darling. Now they mention him in anger, if they mention him at all, and she maintains to Judah that it's pure plain calumny. "If you've got nothing good to say, don't say it," she had said. "If there's no kindness in you for that poor forsaken boy."

"The kindest thing is say nothing," Judah said. "That's right. He about doesn't exist."

"Of course he does."

"Well, there's trouble where he's living, that's for sure," her brother said. "There's floods and earthquakes and general uprising."

"Judah," she protested. "He's your son."

"That's no excuse."

He had been teasing, she knew. Ian was a chip off Judah's block. He looked the spitting image of his mother, and therefore those who didn't know him thought he came mostly from her, and even whispered sometimes, leaning to their cups or in their cups and insinuating, that maybe he was straight out of Maggie with no intervention, or maybe intervened with by some other blue-eyed blond whose last name wasn't Sherbrooke by marriage or birth. They had candidates. They listed them, though Hattie wasn't listening. Such talk was simple foolishness, for Ian was as like her brother as son had been to father since the start of time. He was look-alike with his mother, she said, all surface angles and skinny and fair, but inside he was pure plain Sherbrooke to the core.

And so his enmity with Judah was the enmity of near and dear, not strangers. They knew each other's thoughts so well there was no need of talking, and those who heard only silence thought there's nothing between them to say. It was a man in a mirror, not needing to articulate what he tells the shaving mug, or how he feels that morning, but plain as the nose on his face. It was the prodigal's story all over again; there were those who left and those who stayed at home, and the stay-at-homes were wayfaring strangers when the stranger-son returned.

"Well, anyway he's growing up," she said.

Her brother drew air in his nose.

"Twenty-five years old he'd be."

"Thereabouts," Judah said, "I forget."

"You can't have forgotten."

"Why not? It's not like there's been birthday cake."

"Whose fault is that?" she flared.

"Nobody's," Judah said. "Twenty-five. I remember now, because that was the year the Jerseys ran milk fever, and we lost every single lamb at lambing time."

They were peas in a pod, she maintained; they were spitting images which is why they spat. She remembered when Ian had the whooping cough, and Maggie nursed him until she too fell sick with the flu, and the boy's cough got worse. The doctor said keep him quiet, keep him easy since we mustn't strain his heart, that's the danger with babies, and fever—so Judah sat by his bedside three nights running, not shutting his eyes and not letting anyone else use the washcloth or thermometer but only in-sisting on beef-marrow broth and grated apple and toast. She'd wondered where he learned that gentleness, and how he has forgotten it since—but knows he's not forgotten, really, only learned to lock it in when he locked Maggie out . . .

So she had known at lunchtime—what with his long delays and haircut and the way he'd fumbled with her maraschino cherries—that Judah had an announcement. He made preparations with each shift and set and mo-tion of his mouth. She'd heard him out often enough. He'd talk and talk and what would matter was the single thing unsaid.

She'd tried it out by naming Margaret Coburn—and knew, by his reac-tion, that she'd gauged the tide drift right. Margaret had called, indeed, but not to ask Judah to be the honorary chairman of the Library Com-mittee Funding Drive; she'd white-lied though not really lied about that. Margaret had called to say his thousand-dollar pledge was welcome, as it had been welcome every year since she, Harriet, joined the volunteer staff. And surely Margaret Coburn would have been daunted had Judah (who rarely set foot in the building, who didn't read worth mentioning and then only agricultural circulars or histories he took six weeks to fin-ish, then forgot) been willing to serve. It would have meant a pledge hike and Margaret called about that. The Library expenses had increased. There was inflation everywhere, and books were hard-hit by inflation and maga-zine subscription prices, and the cost of heat. She explained these things to Hattie—who had known them anyhow—and also knew that Judah would maybe increase his pledge but not serve as an honorary chairman of the Funding Drive.

So she'd sounded Margaret's name—calling her "Maggie" a-purpose, not risking much. He exploded as she'd thought he might explode. She remembers their father's dead face. It had a smile upon it past the art of any undertaker; it must have been the hand of God that turned the corners up. So natural, she'd said to Judah, so like him to the life. She'd prayed that he would leave this world with all his limbs and wits about him, able to walk without assistance the path to Heaven's gate. Their mother had had to be wheeled. She wished their father Joseph in the full possession of his strength. And that wish has surely been granted, Hattie knows; she'd laid red roses on his chest, and he'd seemed to settle in the coffin, dapper, smiling lightly, in the middle of a dream it was too good to leave. The cuckoo sounds ten times, then pauses, then sounds once on a higher note; it is ten-fifteen.

VIII

She has been his lawful wife, now, for twenty-eight years. He had married for the second time when he himself was forty-eight, and Margaret twenty-three. He had amused her with percentages. In two years she'd be half his age; three years before she had been, Judah calculated, forty-four percent, and eight years earlier—with her fifteen and him forty—she'd been thirty-eight-percent. Therefore she was catching up but would never truly catch him; last year, for example, she was sixty-seven percent.

He had thought their marriage would continue. He had been a gambling man and thought it worth the bet. He had known the odds against them and been lectured on the odds—though not aloud; they'd not dared that; he'd been instructed instead, in the bars, by his friends' backslapping hilarity, then lectured by his sister's noisy silence, and Samson Finney's attention to detail when it came to rewriting the will. It was a good deal more expensive than betting an inside straight or drawing to two pair. He knew it was a deal more risky than bluffing on a four flush; he needed no lecture from Finney, or reminding of the odds. Instead the lawyer grinned and said, "Judah, you were always unlucky at cards," and rewrote the will.

With Ian and Seth born, he thought his gamble won. Ian had been born the third year of their marriage, and Seth two years thereafter. Meg would spend glad hours with them, suckling, crooning, contained in the enclosure of her sons' small reach. She bent above them, hair cascading like some hay bale with the twine untied. He reclaimed Daniel Sherbrooke's cradle from the storeroom; it was birdseye maple, and had spools for slats. She sang: "Mama's little baby loves shortnin', shortnin'; Mama's little baby loves shortnin' bread." She made the song an incantation, using only that verse. He watched her, never breaking the motion of rocking or the rhythmic chant. Ian kicked and squawled and raked his nails across his face, they had to cut his nails repeatedly and glove his hands at night.

"He's got your spirit," Judah said.

"Your stubbornness." She smiled.

"I hope he gets your looks, leastways."

"And brains, don't forget about brains."

"He'll get them also, Maggie, if he's got a brain in his head."

It hadn't all been prideful then, or easy rearing, or companionable banter while she gave the baby suck. But he remembers it mostly that way. She would sing "Mama's little baby," and his sons' eyes would glaze over with that same distant stare their mother had when beneath him, in bed. Judah is relieved by now they had no daughter. She would have been, continually, a torment; she would have been echo and shadow and an adversary always who called his four-flush bet.

"What about Ian?" he'd asked her, the first time.

"What about him?"

"You can't run away like this."

"I'm not," she said, "I'm taking him, I wouldn't leave him here a minute longer than I had to. Not one day."

145

Yet when she left the Big House Maggie took a single suitcase only; she could, when it came down to it, travel light. He forced himself to keep from her closets, or from ransacking her bureau drawers to find out what she took. And Judah could guess anyway, could rub between his empty fingers the silks and lace she would have been wearing so as to have them torn off . . .

"Bring fine clothing," Peacock wrote, "when you come to settle here since Coarse Cloth is available, and Linens. When you travel through the Isthmus, I should advise wool Underwear, because it proves more healthful even in the heat. And make certain to embark before the Rainy season, if Providence and Planning permit, since April is the time when Vapors do not cling to the commercial Pilgrim as more than a Miasm of the coming Storm. But June is Tempest Weather for that which you consign to Cargo Ships, & you must hazard Cargos and be sanguine of their quick Arrival, else the brine encrust our Bounty, as with so many ventures before. The Land Grant Commission, Judge Hall presiding, has made good my claim on the two thousand acres at San Rafael. It is a healthful Place."

Maggie left town driving, taking the Packard. He subdues the memory but cannot quite erase it—her soft-brimmed hat angled toward him, the Packard spraying gravel as she pitched it down the drive and himself at the French doors, holding to the handle so as not to put his hand through glass, thinking he could be in two strides at the railing and ten more at the car. Maggie would lift her foot, surprised, and the Packard would sputter, throttled, and he'd reach in through the window or break it if need be, reaching, and take the keys and throw them over the roof. But even then he'd known enough to let her go, knowing it was best though worst to let her be, and locking the door handles therefore, holding himself at attention, biting on his pipestem till it shattered, then spitting the black fragments out, praying: *God deliver me. Deliver me from this witch-*

woman and her beauty spell. Let her drive the car to Nevada or to Mexico and buy whatever it is they sell there that passes for a severance, a sundering in Your sight.

The chandelier behind him had been lit. He stood, not seeing anything, not moving till the dust of her departure settled and aroused again, the wind rigadooning so that even her tire tracks were erased. All else will be, he had promised, erased. He brought his nose to the pane's nose, and pressed.

They call it, Judah knows, the green-eyed monster. It had a wintry aspect, but the man who courted jealousy was skating on thin ice. There was a joke about Canucks. One Canuck went ice fishing, but he was so stupid he never cut his ice hole and stood there freezing for hours, catching nothing. A friend passed by on a snowmobile and called "Hey, Pierre, any luck?" Pierre said, "No. Not a bite." So the second Canuck pointed to his snowmobile and said, "Hop on. We'll go trolling."

He told that joke repeatedly. He liked to think of the two men zigzagging over the ice floes, slapping their arms as they fought with the reel, cursing at the weather and the fish that would not bite through ice. He told the joke to Finney, and Finney got hiccups from laughing.

There were jokes about jealousy also, but Judah never laughed. There were jokes about husbands with horns on their head, and faithless wives, and the inefficacy of chastity belts. He knew it silly not to laugh, knew the joke about chastity belts and the queen with quadruplicate keys was as funny as the joke about ice fishing. But he had no stomach for that kind of humor—has never had, not even with the tables turned and himself the lover of some faithless married woman who had married and deceived somebody else. He stomached it no better than Hattie brooked jokes about family pride. There were certain things you held on trust, and certain things you trusted in, and he trusted in the notion of fidelity, once wed. There were jokes about men in closets, and stories about the milkman or television repair man, but anyone who knew him, Judah, knew not to tell those jokes.

He remembers Maggie in the rope hammock strung between two apple trees. He sat beside her on the grass, and she used her horsehair riding crop to ward off flies.

"You've got nothing to complain of," she had told him. "Not any single thing."

"The thought's the deed"—he pressed her. "You've sinned in thought and that's as bad as deed."

"Come off it, darling," she said.

"I'm not accusing you. I'm just observing that the thought's the deed."

"You're positively biblical." She pushed the ground with her left leg and started the rope hammock swinging.

"No."

"Yes. It has to be Sunday today."

He watched her body's pumping motion—the whole of her rhythmic, suspended.

"Yes."

"Yes, it's Sunday, and yes, you're vengeful and jealous and biblical, and no, you have nothing to complain of."

("Jude-ass," they'd called him once. He'd broken the right arm of the boy who started that. It had been Billy Harrison, and they were both thirteen, with Judah half a head taller but fifteen pounds less fat. He'd taken Billy's arm and twisted it behind his back and elevated it till Billy shouted "Uncle!"

"Uncle what?" Judah asked.

"Uncle Jude-ass," Billy said, and Judah took his arm and raised it to the shoulder blades until he heard the crack.)

She was wearing riding boots. He helped her pull them off.

"You've got to trust me." Maggie splayed her toes. "Just like your bank"—she grinned at him. "Bankers' Trust."

So he had worked at and endeavored trust. It had seemed plausible then. She rubbed his cheek with the black horsehair crop.

"All right?"

"All right."

"All right as rain?" she cajoled him. "Or just all right all right?"

"As rain," Judah said. She'd blandished the pants off of him often enough, and no doubt she'd done it with others and no doubt could do it again. He acknowledged that. She'd have taken him at poker for every cent he was worth, or sold the Brooklyn Bridge twenty times over with such cajolery. She'd smile and stare at him and he'd forget his witness proof, would twist to her finger like string.

"A penny for your thoughts," she said.

"I'll give them to you free."

"A penny anyway. They're worth that much."

She twisted, set the hammock jumping and reached for the pocket of her riding breeches. They were tan, and tight.

"I can't quite make it," Maggie said. "Not from this position. You reach in and take what you find."

"I'm thinking," Judah acknowledged, "this isn't the worst way to be."

He cupped his hand on her and pushed. She swung away from him, then back to his hand's shield.

"What's better?" his wife asked.

"What's better is believing what you tell me to believe."

"Believe it, Judah P. You've got no right," she'd say, "to worry me like this."

"It's me who's worrying." He was an old, fond, foolish man, with nothing to mourn for and nothing amiss.

"You've got no right to that either. You'll give yourself ulcers, darling."

"It's not a joke."

"No more are ulcers," she teased him. "My darling Judah P."

So he took the bait she was, and every love hook and the crookedness. She said he was a bigmouth bass, just waiting in the shallows for her to flit by near enough. He would lie there, Maggie teased, disguised as some mild mud stick till he lunged. He had thought himself the catcher but was caught.

Judah had been married once before. But looking back he can scarcely remember the two years spent with Lisbeth McPherson when they were both beginning; he has put her out of his mind. Yet he consults her portrait sometimes, seeing, yes, she'd had brown eyes and a firm-fleshed face which would, he thinks, have ripened and rotted in time. She wears amethysts. It is a strand his mother gave her, set in gold and imitating a basket of fruit— so one amethyst is pear-shaped, one shaped like an apple or banana and one with gold tooled around it in order to resemble grapes.

Lisbeth would have made him, Judah supposes, a proper wife. Their courtship had been proper, and the engagement no surprise, and the marriage ceremony had been a sort of contract for the families to sign. It had been *their* wedding, not his. It was, somehow, the two families' idea. He had married the McPherson place, and the McPherson's second daughter and together they established a company called McPherson-Sherbrooke. But when she died it was no flesh loss or any sort of amputation; they had not known each other long enough for him to know how to mourn. She'd been soft-spoken, dutiful, and no doubt kept her eyes shut when he came to her in darkness and no doubt had them lowered when she crossed the street. Therefore Lisbeth noticed nothing when the truck jumped lanes and swerved to miss her, missing her by maybe five feet but instead hitting a tree that hit the power line that fell—snaking, making a murderous skip rope she caught her ankle on and tripped.

Yet the loneliness when Maggie left was absolute. It was as if his fingers were divided down the center, nail from knuckle—as if his arm were wrenched from its socket and he walked one-legged. There was nothing of his body that had not been their body, so he falls back on arithmetic. *One is not a fraction; it's indivisible. Integrity means,* he tells himself, *oneness, wholeness, a prime number, the number as it is . . .*

Lisbeth sewed. She constructed lavish dresses that she dared not wear. She knew her place, as Hattie said, and kept it at the bottom end of the table, and when she left there was no absence, nothing to replace. So for twenty-five years Judah said he had been married but would not marry again. He missed nothing notable. He'd learned about the nuptial state and wedded bliss and what they called uxoriousness; he'd learned about other men's wives. Nothing of it mattered much and he felt no need or wish to double his integrity. She had had dark brown hair that, when he came to her in darkness, framed her face.

Still, there are memories. There is the time he found her in the summer kitchen, with an armful of flowers for drying. He said those flowers weren't good enough for drying, and Lisbeth bent her head, submissive, and he took her in his arms to take the edge off insult. She'd seemed entirely compounded of lilac fragrance then.

There is a memory of mourning clothes, her stiff-faced family about him and the oak box she lay in. He had gripped the coffin rail in order to feel something, *anything,* he told himself, *whatever it is that bereaved husbands feel,* and made his knuckles white with gripping and popped the seam on his shirt. There was music; there were the comforts of faith. There were professions of sorrow, and Judah waited in the parlor, in the stillborn center of his infant marriage, professing sorrow with his upright silence and hearing them tell him: "Too much. It's just too much to take." Even then they'd called it freakish, calling the accident a freak, saying somehow something intervened to blight his purpose and thereafter bring him to his knees who stood a head taller than anyone else, who cohabited on the top floor of the highest house on that high hill. They whispered, Judah knew, that the Sherbrookes had had their comeuppance, and it was a long time coming. Add it up, they whispered later; he marries a twenty-three-year-old because he lost one earlier; it all of it adds up.

And, in a sense, this was so. Yet his comeuppance came with Maggie; he'd learned about loss and bereavement with a living wife. He sometimes thinks there is a Woman's League, a kind of bluestocking alliance to get even every single way now they've got the vote. So Maggie was the last, best version of Lisbeth—though Judah had thought them opposed. He'd elected blond for brown and tall for short and hard for soft, forthright instead of retiring and fire over smoke. And he had been watchful,

151

watching Maggie at the door or on the carousel or, ten years later, at the cheese counter where she shopped in Morrisey's. But what he watched, he knows now, was his passionate embrace of error, their last best chance to bring him down.

So Maggie is Lisbeth incarnate and their shared revenge. When his first wife jerked like a puppet on that electrified string, convulsive to her very hair-ends and he felt no sympathy, or when he was convulsed atop her, emitting what he thought was life into that doomed receptacle—when he stood unbending by her open grave to wonder what was closing now (*What stops,* he'd asked himself, *what ends with this beginning?*), Judah had broached rules. The rule is do unto others; the rule is where there's smoke there'll be a fiery second wife to flame at you from every recess of the Big House and the Toy House and the barns. The rule is press dry lilacs and they turn into perfume, and men will lap that scent up from behind your wife's earrings like dogs; scorn not lest ye be scorned.

Later, Maggie flaunted faithlessness in front of him, bringing what he knew were suitors to the house. Still, he had restrained himself. The meat knives trembled in his hand, sharp-honed enough, and he dreamed of carving up her dinner guests. Ian had admired and then emulated his precision with the carving tools. "You keep your brush hook sharp," Judah had said. "And sickles. And your ax blade and your hatchet, right? So do the same with knives."

He, Judah, would simply lean across the table and take the piano teacher or Cousin Alexander or Andrew Kincannon by the throat and, holding them with his left hand, slice off their earlobes with his right. He'd use downward strokes on the right-hand side and, inverting his wrist, upward strokes on the left. Then he'd release his choke hold and they'd cover their faces, moaning, and try to stanch the blood while he'd reach down and geld them, removing the creased, cloaked parcel that had sought its pleasure between his wife's spread legs. They had rooted at her, and he would stick them like pigs. He'd put their mangled, fabric-swaddled manhoods on the salad plate.

"It used to be a delicacy"—Judah had worked out his speech. "Leastways some of us present believed so." He'd impale the shriveled testicles on the fork-tines or his knife. "Take a bite. We're ever so proud of the blood sauce, though you might prefer the stuffing. My wife preferred it, once."

They made conversation. The subject was a long career, and who was up to it or bound to stop; Margaret was asking if Horowitz would play again.

"I don't think so," her piano teacher said. Judah cannot remember his name. "That's my opinion."

"Why?"

"It's only my opinion, mind you, but a considered one. I think there's a limit to the pressure. We go so far and snap, if you see what I'm driving at, like a string, say—yes, just like a string. We replace it, do you see, we don't knot it up and start again."

"We tune a piano," Margaret said. "It's a question of degree."

"Yes. A good point there. I see what you're driving at. But it's a false analogy, if you'll permit me, Mrs. Sherbrooke. The point is really one of snapping like a string."

"Well, what about Rubinstein?" she asked.

"Now, him. Now, Artur. He'll bend and stretch forever but he'll never snap. That's my considered opinion; he'll be playing piano till he's ninety-five years old. And enchanting the audience too."

"There's so much hair oil there." She laughed. "There's ever so much lubrication for the moving parts."

Judah snapped his wineglass. He had tightened his hand on the stem. The crystal shattered and his red wine spilled.

"Darling"—his wife had half-risen—"are you all right?"

"Yes."

He watched the wine stain spread.

"You're certain you didn't get cut?"

"Yes. The goddamn stuff's so thin you break it just by breathing."

"You're absolutely certain?"

"Don't mind me, folks. Just pay me no mind."

So she would ring for another glass and bottle and the maid would bring them to him and pour salt on the stain. He would note with satisfaction how the gossip lagged. The piano teacher's windy exuberance would slacken, and Margaret would focus on her plate, and Andrew Kincannon would go thoughtful, toying with his cutlery and glass.

"You were saying?" Judah prompted.

"We were talking," his wife said, "about concert careers. We had been discussing that. But we don't have to, really, there are other subjects. We could discuss, for instance, the quality of shit you spread this morning on the fields."

She was feisty; he granted her that. She had had more balls than all of her suitors combined. That was why he spared them, not bothering with the knife; they were just accessories, like hats she tried on and discarded or lace mantillas stored against some dress-up occasion. She sat at the table's far head, lit by candle glitter, and was his equal adversary—crystal he could neither warm nor crush.

"My cup runneth over," he said—and proposed it as a toast to both his wife and guests.

Now he reaches the lumber trail's end, or not its end so much as evanescence, the track of it faded, those wheel bruises finally healed where first they leveled trees then leveled the undergrowth, hauling trees down. All Judah sees is second growth, or even third growth maybe, the biggest standing tree his body's girth only, trunk congruent to trunk. He thinks of the gigantic labor it once was to raze these hills and how his great-great-grandfather's logging teams had spent the summer cutting and the winter using ice sleds, clearing, season by year till the mountain shed growth like a man going bald and was its rock face only, with streams for the blood lines and high white patches and the skull showing through fuzz. Daniel Webster spoke once, Maggie discovered, at Glastonbury, the confluence of valleys that was the Woodford Mountain Pass, and forty thousand men came to hear him, she said, and even if she multiplied by twentyfold his true attentive audience, even if there'd be no man without a megaphone who could make himself heard, no matter how high the soapbox or how high-pitched his bellow, over the stertorous breath of the wind; even if she multiplied by forty how spellbound he held them and how long without coughing or pausing to swallow he spoke, the speech presumed vitality where all was death-thralled now, and absence, no living thing beyond Judah's voice range but sparrow or sparrow hawk, squirrel and deer (there were mountain men he'd heard of who ranged these hills still, toothless, unlettered, begetting new idiot-get). So he bears left from the lumber trail and finds the beaver bog he recollected, dams intact, the three beaver houses seeming empty but trim, and knows them therefore not empty but that his crashing passage through the undergrowth signaled the beavers to take shelter and wait this his alien presence out in their wet safety, remembers having ridden there with Maggie (she was the better rider, really, though he could stick to any horse he's known or force it to yield to his own unyieldingness, who had been thrown often enough but not beaten, who clambered back grinning and clamped his legs to that shallow-breathing belly like glue—though that was not the point for Maggie, never at issue somehow; the horse would be completed by her, suddenly intact, so that when once again riderless it would look halved, bereft, deprived of that airy and sweet-smelling weight it had been released by, not burdened) taking picnics, with maybe a chicken and wine in the hamper, and hard-boiled eggs and cheese and fruit, and they'd clear themselves an area and tether the horses and spread out the blankets, then use the blankets both as a table and bed—"A jug of wine," she'd said to him, "a loaf of bread, and thou." "What's that?" he had asked her, incurious. "And thou beside me in the wilderness," she'd said. "That's poetry, you dodo, that's the *Rubaiyat of Omar Khayyám*." "Makes a pitiful picnic," he'd said, and she flailed at him, laughing, pummeling, till he folded both her fists in his one hand and held. So Judah torments himself, returning, looking for the flattened grass where last they'd lain, a score of years before, where a century previous maybe Daniel Webster also took his pleasure, the beaver bog a streambed then, with limpid and inviting pools to slake the body's thirst, and falls to his knees in the thicket and is assaulted by mosquitoes and the branches lash his arms as he scrabbles beneath them for some sort of signal, *her trace.*

What is it he hunts there, he asks himself, circling, and answers with what he can't find. First, and predictably, the ground has shifted, grown over so that he won't even know (except this is the southern bank, their chosen exposure) if the patch of earth he picks is near the one they sunned and spawned on, if that tree had been the sapling at the center of her Morgan's forage circle, if the brackish water before him has receded or advanced, making the lakebed their bed. Second, he remembers losing nothing and strewing nothing that lasts (stowing the wine bottle back in the hamper, though empty, forgetting neither shoes nor watch nor anything corporeal, but *everything*, he whispers now, *every single thing that matters*) for chicken bones won't make a chicken, nor cheese rinds the cow nor eggshells the egg, the fruit pit turned to humus maybe but surely not an orchard. Third, his memory's gone fitful and he can no longer distinguish the dream from remembrance, so she torments him only incarnate as mosquitoes, the flesh he presses flaccid, long since slack. Yet Judah makes obeisance and rims his poor perimeter with stone and kneels facing in the four directions, arms at a northwest axis and feet splayed, pointing south-southeast, and shuts his eyes and bends his head and rends her garments gently, kissing the breast-dust.

IX

She came for her old love of him, she says. She came for her continued love, and because he'd let her.

"Come running when I call?" he says. "That isn't like you."

"No. But it's been some time."

"Yes."

She smiles at him, attempting to kindle an answering smile. "Since last you called, I mean."

"I didn't have no telephone number. Finney did."

"You could have whistled." She bats her eyes, slipping back into their mockery like camphored clothes.

"Ayup."

"You still got all your teeth."

He purses his lips.

"You're a handsome old goat, Mr. J. P. Sherbrooke, even if you *are* my husband . . ."

"I thank you, Mrs. Sherbrooke."

He inclines his head, and she watches him carefully. He does so out of weariness, Maggie decides, and plays their courtship game indifferent to the rules.

"Don't take it as a compliment," she finishes. "Take it as the truth."

She sits beside him, takes his hand in hers and traces the lines on his knuckles. There are crosshatchings and little white hairs. There is dirt in the pores. Always, no matter how hard she had scrubbed at him—or he for her—with soap and pumice stone and nail brushes, there had been dirt in the pores. It was, he said, cleanly dirt.

"That's a contradiction," Maggie had argued. "It doesn't make sense."

"There's dirty dirt," he said. "Not all of it's sweet-smelling."

"Well, it's distinctive filth, I grant you that."

They argued then for conversation's sake and not because it mattered, not because she meant it or would hold to her argument's side. Had he apologized, saying Maggie, I'm sorry, I just can't get rid of it, she would have told him, why should you, it's honest and justified dirt. The house is built with bricks and wood, and both of them come out of the earth; why try to hide where you come from or what you did today?

She feels Ian is correct. He has severed himself from their lives with a finality so absolute he can even afford to be kind. His postcards are cheery, always, as is his voice on the phone. She wonders how he knew so much so early—knew to get out when the going was possible, since the Sherbrooke knots around him would tighten, not loosen, with time. She knows no context for him and therefore has various dreams. Always his eyes are the same glacial gray; always he calculates odds. Seth remains her suckling infant, doomed by crib death to consistency, but Ian is the principle of change. She dreams of him sometimes, resplendent, in rodeos or bank board meetings or in the Himalayas, coiling rope. He sends her cards from Mallorca and Dakar and calls from Albuquerque or, once, collect from a hotel lobby in Bombay. She too has many addresses, and sometimes she wonders if Ian is trying to reach her, needy when she is unreachable—sometimes worries that he'll fetch up penni-less or sick.

By contrast her own separation felt sham. She had maintained it ur-gently, knowing anyhow for certain she'd see her husband again. His hand is heavy. She hefts it. They are in his chosen room, though she had expected he would lie in their shared bed and not on this single gray relic with its cotton sheets. His weight impedes her; she finds the phrase "dead weight."

"Husband?"

He makes a sound in his throat.

"You warm enough?"

He coughs again.

"Or maybe too warm?"

"Just right."

"Tell me whenever it changes, OK? If you get too cold or hot."

His fingers move. They have their own volition. They cramp and curl.

"I'll tell you that," he says.

"Hattie would blame me, don't you think? I'd catch it good and proper if you get a chill."

"She's a taskmaster, yes."

Maggie asks herself, this night, what is she trading for what? Put safety in the scales against the sweet wine of risk; put roots against pure rootless-ness, the determined creature against the self-determined. She looks back for turning points that she'd not seen when turning—for what their poet called two paths within a single wood. There had been options, of course. But Maggie understands (in this first year of her sixth decade; who was it, she tries to recall, which friend that said the first years of any decade are the difficult ones, so she's spent time preparing, through the last five years or so, for being fifty, can handle it, is managing nicely, I thank you) the way nostalgia trumps truth.

Therefore she tests herself in mirrors and men's eyes. The mechanics of flirtation are easy for her still, as the gearshift is simple for garage attendants and the heating system for the fuel oil man. She knows which strings to pluck and how to strike the tonic note and, bending over her husband, which card to play.

The water is warm. Maggie is swimming at night, in phosphor; it is their honeymoon. Her feet and arms are wands. He snorts and wallows while she noses through the incandescent water, igniting galaxies of diatoms. She has brought a mussel steamer and they are hunting mussels on the water-covered rocks. There are weeds and kelp and crabs attached, and she separates them carefully; she distrusts free-floating mussels, she says, because one mussel filled with mud and not meat can spoil the entire concoction. Nor should there be grit in the brine. He says, "You know about salt water," and means it, not scornful of her shoreline certainties. She takes it, however, not as a compliment and says: "I've lived here, you know. Always by the sea in summers—with one exception, that time in Vermont."

Their honeymoon house is on stilts. He likes to lie face down on the porch, watching the landscape through slats. The gray sand eddies beneath him, and the spear grass traces perfect circles; he cuts his feet on the sharp spear-grass points.

("Are you glad about it?" he asks.

"About what?"

"That single exception? That time they hauled you to the mountains."

"Kicking and screaming." She smiles.

"And giving you a bicycle."

"I'm glad," she says. "I wasn't at the time, you know. I wanted a canoe."

"We'll get you one."

"Oh, Jude, you promise?"

"Yes."

"Cross your heart and hope to die?"

"Not hope to die," he says. "But cross my heart."

For which she rewards him by kissing his hands, then putting his hands on her breasts. "Cross mine instead," she says.)

"You've been hearing from him."

"Who?"

"Ian. Our son."

"Yes."

"Well?"

"I never denied it," she says.

"How often?"

"He sends his best. He wants you to know he's thinking about us together."

"It's big of him."

"He's busy now. He's got a life to live."

"So where is he living it at?" Judah asks. He picks out a thread from the coverlet. The thread is brown; he winds it around his index finger, tight.

"In New York mostly."

"Where?"

"He'd tell you, Jude, I'm certain."

"I'm his father," Judah says. "In case you've forgotten I'm fifty percent of his family. I've got a right to know."

"No one's denying that."

"You are. You both of you have got it figured so he'll be a stranger when I die."

She lifts her eyes. He reverses the spool on his finger and jerks it so it snaps.

"Tell me what he says," says Judah.

"I've already told you. He sends his best wishes."

"For a speedy recovery, right?"

"For everything."

"Well, where's my card? Where does it say 'Get Well Soon'? Why doesn't he call us just once?"

"That's his business," she says.

"It's what you put him up to. Why can't he just come visit?"

"He's not a child now anymore. It's *his* choice, his decision."

Judah, she knows, has set traps. His enticement is his legacy, the house and land and wealth. Whoever wants, he seems to be saying, to get into this house of mine must eat the fish head at its center; whoever backs in can't back out.

"What do you want?"

"Nothing I'm aware of," Maggie says.

"They all of them want something. They're sniffing around this place."

"For what?" she says.

"For real-estate development. For the state highway extension."

"Don't let them do it," she says.

"High-rise dwellings, I believe they call it. Condominiums. Museums. Doesn't matter what they call it, they all of them want something."

"Not me," she says. "I don't even want to be questioned."

"Why not? If you've got nothing to hide."

"It isn't a crime yet to visit your husband."

"Why did you leave?" he asks her, insistent. "And why did you come back?"

She tells him that she loves the place, making her mouth work. She had had, that afternoon, to change the bulb in her bathroom; the light burned out. She went to the pantry and selected the right size—and standing there, among the insignia of some strange family order, in her chill shuttered seclusion (the tomato soup next to the peanut butter where she, Maggie, never would have placed it; the lightbulbs stacked by salad oil and aluminum foil) she felt at home.

"You look well."

"Thank you, Judah."

"Every compliment I paid you was the truth," he says. "You do look well."

"My goodness." Maggie smiles at him. "You've gone and gotten courtly."

"Just paying dues," he says. "Giving out praise where it's due."

"You didn't used to do that."

"I would have," he tells her, triumphant. "You just didn't used to deserve it."

There was a hole he dug and covered over carefully, with brush laid crosswise and long grass and leaves. It looked to be substantial ground, but was a pit with thorns. There was a net he slung and covered with branches and leaves and when his prey ran through, Judah chopped the net's draw-lines and hoisted his catch. There were decoys to set and red herrings to drag on the trail. There were chipmunks who would tackle musk-melon rind, if the winter up ahead looked difficult enough.

"The time is past," she ventures, "when we should beg for favors from each other. When everything you have the right to ask for is denied."

"It isn't my intention," Judah says, "to beg."

"No."

"There's things I own and things it's mine to give away. And there's been a pack of them after it, believe you me."

"I believe it."

"You see them off in corners whispering, or dickering about the best approach. Which way to sidle up to Uncle Jude . . ."

"It can't be pretty to watch."

"No," he tells her, triumphing. "Not half so pretty as you."

All through the autumn squirrels hoard, and chipmunks, and the black bears accumulate fat; so everything about him, that had slept a dull slow season, stirs and is grasping and trapped. Judah hears them plotting; they rooted for his leavings and shat tomato plants. They were mistaken, he told the town planners, to think they could reap what he sowed; a man's entitled to the distance he can travel in a day, on one horse and in one direction; then take that line as radius and cast it in a circle, not forgetting mountains, not forgetting riverbanks and the valley that they fashioned, not forgetting trees.

Now he raises himself and sits upright. He does this with a smooth swivel motion, shifting his hips. It is the gesture of a farmer—rolling out under the tractor or carrying a feed sack or vaulting over the gate.

"Hey," Maggie says. "I thought you would be sleeping."

"Maybe."

"What woke you?"

"I don't ever sleep these nights. I give myself twenty minutes. It's a way to let Hattie get rested, see, to tell her I sleep straightway through. And"—he moves his mouth—"to give me some left-alone time."

"I can take a hint."

"I didn't mean that. Not from you."

"You want a dance band?" Maggie stands. "You just moved like you've been practicing."

"What do they call it? The Twist?"

"It's the Black Bottom," she jokes. "That's what's in fashion today."

"I knew you'd know the name of it. You'd know every one of those dances. Be in on the latest."

"The Black Bottom isn't the latest," she says. "It's been replaced."

"The Yellow Belly, then. You'll know them all."

"If you only want to argue, Judah, why did you let me come back?"

"You're my wife. You're not some money-grubbing climber come to lick my hand and bite it when they think I'm sleeping; you're not that."

This is said in accusation and with a spitting venom that makes Maggie stare.

"You wouldn't show up smiling just to wish me dead now, would you; you'd not quit the house then come back smiling when there's money in the wind. When I've got a will written out for notaries to stamp. There's others who might do that, but not you."

Seth had suckled at her; his perfect hands had ten perfect fingers with perfect crescent nails. They fitted themselves to the curve of her breast and were a perfect fit. His eyes were blue as blue could be and he shut them in appreciation while he drank. They stayed that way. Then the suction lessened; then his lips stopped working; then the action of his throat, in its turn, ceased. He slept.

"You let me come. You *asked* me to."

"No. Finney did."

"You haven't got to wreck it, Mr. Sherbrooke. We could maybe like each other."

"Don't take me for a fool," Judah says. "It isn't too much to ask, now is it, just don't take me for a fool."

"I won't," she says. "I never have."

"Miss Black Bottom. Miss Yellow Belly," he derides her. "Maggie the Queen of the hop."

Then Judah shuts his eyes. There is a regularity in his breathing that makes it seem to be sleep. She imagines husbands a century or so before who'd leave for seven years and go to cross a continent or ocean. Gone to make a fortune or shore up failing fortunes, they would come back wearing earrings maybe, and carrying parrots or malacca canes, smoking strangely fashioned pipes. Or centuries before that, even, bounding home to tell of wondrous voyages, and three-legged natives wearing palm fronds for shoes, and nothing else but musk oil to disguise their animality. There would be news to give and get, and the oil lamps would have flickered and the windows misted over just the same way for that pair of strangers, those fraudulent avatars also . . .

Old sons would visit mothers who had lost their sense and sight. Sons would come home to fling themselves after the last handful of earth strewn on a new-dug grave. They would return, Maggie imagines, with a week's hard ride, with no chance to favor their horses or thank the ferryman sufficiently (who was not used to night trips, who didn't like the weather and was half-deaf anyhow, who heard no apologies therefore and waved the tip away in a gesture of derision, muttering about horse pucky on his loading ramp). Sons returned without left legs or six inches taller or bearded or bald, returning through malarial swamps and taking the shortcut past the tamaracks where two thousand died that first August—skirting the bogs and rapids, but losing their packhorses anyhow to gopher holes, a kind of indignity always attendant, mosquitoes rampant and the storm-felled oaks impassable, the message ("Come Home if you Can; Mother Faring poorly and would like to see you Once") deciphered, worried over endlessly, the paper of it worn and rubbed dull with folding, edges furled . . .

"I'm dying," Judah says.

She makes no answer.

"You know that."

"No."

"Finney must have told you. You got to know that much tonight."

She takes his hand.

"I'll die if I sleep here alone," he says.

"We'll watch over you."

"How can I be sure of it?"

"I promise." She spreads his fingers with hers. She strokes his palm.

"How do I know you won't leave me?"

"You don't."

"You always have."

"I always came back," Maggie says.

They are adept at this gambit also, and she marvels at how quickly she resumes their ancient play. Men return from wars or bounty expeditions or mental hospitals; their parents say, hey, boy, fix me this gatepost, hey, boy, go brush your teeth.

"Don't leave me. Don't run out."

"I won't."

"How can I trust you?"—he stares at her, unblinking. She waits for him to blink.

"You can," says Maggie.

"Come sleep with me."

"All right," she says. "I'll get an extra blanket. I'll be back with pillows."

"No," Judah says. "In this bed."

He releases her hand and pats the space beside him.

"I need someone to hold me. When I die."

He would, she knows, spare her nothing; he has worked out his punishment in every fierce particular. "If you ask me, Mr. Sherbrooke, you're a mighty lively corpse."

"I'm not asking your opinion, I'm asking for your help. For charity's sake."

Her hands are shaking. Her voice shakes. "The condemned man ate a hearty meal."

"Or send up someone who'll do what I ask. Find me some other lady."

"No," Maggie tells him. "I'll stay."

He looks at her. She could swear he smiles. It is a grin he turns—she could swear intentionally—into a cough.

"Go," he says. "I'll manage. Just find me somebody else."

"Who else would have you, Judah? I'm your wife."

So now she tries to comfort him, who has little comfort to spare. She says the world is full of things that frighten her, because you're never certain where they hide at night. Best keep the closet doors open, she whispers; best keep chest-drawers pulled out. Best close your eyes; best pluck your brows; best wish upon and blow the lash that falls.

"You win." He lifts his hands in submission.

"And you."

"I'm tired," Judah says. "Let's both of us get into bed."

She sits beside him. She has felt the same way, sometimes, after drinking too much or not good enough wine. Her very bones have stiffened; nothing works. No single limb or digit makes its customary motion.

"Get in," he says. "Under the covers."

"It's hot here," Maggie says.

"Not for me," he tells her. "It's as cold as that night was we slept out in the winter. Remember?"

"Yes."

"Get yourself here next to me."

She commences.

"Not that way," Judah says. "If you're so hot and I'm your husband anyhow, take off your clothes."

She is sweating.

"I'm not hot," Maggie says.

"Of course you are. You're sweating. You're a furnace."

"I'll get used to it."

"No," Judah says. "Take off your clothes."

She tells herself it doesn't matter—that this is her husband in health, not sickness; in his prime, not mad old age. She unbuttons her blouse.

"I'm dying," Judah says. "Tonight. You'll see."

"Please," Maggie says, "Don't say that. Please." She drops her blouse to the chair by the bed.

"I'm not trying to scare you," he says.

"But you're succeeding, Judah."

"The skirt. What about taking off that?"

And so he wheedles and coaxes her out of her clothes. She lies rigid beside him, watching the gooseflesh on her arms prickle and subside. It is, she tells herself, a caricature scene: *Death and the Maiden* or perhaps *Virginity Defended and Preserved*. But there is only his breathing, and she had yielded up her maidenhood thirty-four years earlier, in the changing room of the cabana in Alan Seligman's family's Easthampton beach house.

"Hold me," Judah says.

She holds him. She busies herself with memories: the way that Alan Seligman's swim trunks' elastic intaglioed his stomach, and the burnished gold his body was above the line contrasting with the flaccid fish pallor below. He had pretended competence but was a virgin also, and they fumbled and poked at each other. Maggie shuts her eyes. Alan Seligman had been eighteen and won the freestyle relay and was flexing his pectoral muscles and biceps and triceps for her; they went steady afterward and improved their shared technique.

Judah keeps his ear cocked although she thinks him heedless, and keeps his right eye open behind the lashes' web. He is peeking out at Maggie like a schoolboy, inching the curtain aside. She would be his audience and join in the applause, be stomping her feet in the aisle. There are others. It is dark. The footlights flare at them, not him. He will leap to her side with agility—and not be caught in the bedclothes or crippled, or spavined by arthritis like some out-to-pasture Clydesdale collapsed with its own weight. You have to be quick-footed to steal a march on Jude.

He feels a man's life signifies; it matters how he walks upon this earth. He has been schooled from childhood to believe that actions ramify, a Sherbrooke's more than most. He says the Lord giveth and taketh away, but so does the federal government, and so can any man who's self-willed, self-reliant, self-defined. Therefore he will give his house and barns and land for love; therefore he withdraws from anxious husbandry. His world is the visible world. He owns everything he sees of it, and that has been enough. Lying beside him—two feet to the side, and half a head shorter, she looks at a different world. It's only natural, he tells himself, it's one of the laws of perspective. But he owns all *she* sees to boot—even lying, feigning sleep, in the bedroom of the house he fingered in its replica that morning. He can confer it, and does so. She takes it as her due.

X

Hattie finds herself with slogans now when what she wants are words. She despises supermarkets and the jingles she finds herself singing in supermarket aisles. They pipe in music from every corner, and she is pursued while hunting rope or camphor or tomato juice or corn. In those newly built and lavish emporiums, Hattie feels her age. She stumbles down the corridors of canned goods and household supplies, pushing her pushcart as once she pushed her mother's wheelchair, but with a deal less agility. She—who'd admit to many faults but never indecisiveness—is assaulted by competing claims and labels and products and stands there indecisive, trying to sort matters out. Like as not she'd reach for camphor and there'd be mothflakes and mothballs and mothcakes to choose from, and when she'd choose at last and reach she'd knock the whole stack down, or scatter cans. She did the bulk of their shopping at Morrisey's, or had it done by Judah— but once a month, maybe, or once every three weeks she negotiates the shopping plaza, tormented by such opulent look-alike choice. Soda water, for instance, would be marked at thirty-five cents the bottle. There were five-or-ten-cent additional deposits to pay. So she'd accumulate bottles at forty or forty-five cents the bottle, arranging them in her cart and checking the stamped price each time. Once she found a bottle marked at eighty-five cents and pointed out the error to the girl at the checkout machine.

"Look here," she said. "Someone marked eighty-five cents."

"Where?"

"Right here," said Hattie, pointing. "Right at the spot where my finger-nail is. On the cap."

"I'm sorry, ma'am, I'll only charge you for thirty-five cents."

"I expect so," Hattie said.

But her point would be lost, and her precision wasted—except for the fifty cents saved, and that was hardly saving. The girl would sweep her goods along, and someone else would pack them, and Hattie would be out of there before she even knew it, sorting the change. She'd be out on the tarmac, hunting the taxi she'd ordered, still hearing the loudspeaker bray organ music behind her and taking her first deep breath and breathing in gas fumes and heat and the smell of hamburger fat from the restaurant section.

Judah cursed modernity and every tinsel accomplishment; they were salvaging nothing important, he said, although they saved some time. "A stitch in time saves nine" had been her motto, but he asked her if she truly thought they required this frugality, and what did it save anyhow—nine stitches or nine times?

"Nine stitches," she had said, "and please don't forget who does the stitch-ing." He granted her her point but said she should throw the old clothes and sheets and tablecloths away.

"If I did that," she said. "We'd see how long you'd let me do it."

"Long enough."

So she hoarded their history's leavings; she is like a magpie, he complains, lining her room with silk scraps. "A penny saved earns pounds," she said. "Waste not, want not," she urged. Then Judah told her they earned more each year than they knew how to spend. She said that wasn't possible, and he explained to her that money made money without half trying; funds accumulated on the trust funds and investments, and even after taxes there was all they'd ever need. "Necessity's a difficult teacher," she reminded him, and mended the living room curtains where he didn't see they needed mending, and wouldn't have cared if they did.

But Maggie had spent money like she spent herself on everything—flat-out. It was as hard to hold to, Judah said, as a greased squealing pig. Not that he minded it, either; there was as much fun spending as there was in getting, and he lavished gifts on her. He gave her earrings and bracelets and cars and would have given a fur coat if she tolerated furs. "I can't abide it," Maggie said.

"What?"

"Shooting and trapping and poisoning those animals. A seal for a seal-skin coat, a lamb for lambswool. Leopards."

"They ain't defenseless. And some of them is pests."

"Don't play the trapper, please. Did you ever notice that you put your bumpkin accent on whenever you're not certain?"

"Sartin," Judah pronounced. "Shorely."

"Well, I don't want a coat that comes from killing. Thanks anyway. No thanks."

Hattie listened, envious. Words were a kind of coinage they melted down from slogans; Ivory Snow is a dish soap, and Gleam and Crest are toothpastes, and Joy is a detergent, not a state of mind.

Now, moving with caution, soundlessly, she readies her own bed. It is a tester bed, not canopy, because there is nothing inside it to cover, no shameful goings-on; the fringe around the bedposts is pink eyelet lace. She allows herself that much. It is an extravagance, of course, and frilly the way little girls dream about frills. Sometimes, staring past the bed's frame at the rectangle of ceiling, Hattie thinks maybe that's how you get to heaven, that's what ascension means. Maybe you go through a space that's called a tester shape because it doesn't close you in and is a trial. There's tribulation inside, and pleasure for the best part of a quarter of your life. Lately she's been sleeping poorly, but still she calculates six hours on the average for, say, sixty years. She's done better than that to begin with, and nowadays does worse, but it all evens out. Along the way there's been temptation that came in many guises—call it luxury, then restlessness, then sloth. The eyelet lace would be a comfort-temptation and test, but her soul would hurtle past it into the cold space beyond and butt against the ceiling and knock for admittance. It would be smoke without a chimney, lifting to the topmost part of rooms to hover, coil, and dissipate—or birds caught in a barn or, like the bluejay in the entrance hall that time, battering at windows, seeing only the blue sky beyond. It was like the way heat rises to cool upper air, or the way she went lightheaded after bending and straightening up and thought she'd grown six inches. Everything would rise about her, and what seemed like plaster with a crack in it would be, entirely, smoke. Where there's smoke there's fire, but this would be a screen to shield her from impurities and smoke the hellish remnants out and leave her in the perfect welcoming empyrean, breathing without luxury or sloth.

Hattie smiles. She permits herself day-waking dreams if the visions are not harmful, and no one could claim daydreams of heaven ever did anyone harm. Her heaven is snow-white but warm. It is a storm of miracles, with everything unblemished and intact. Vermont is her heaven on earth. It is a kind of paradise, free from the disasters that beset the countries she reads of and almost every other state. It has no tidal waves or hurricanes because it has no ocean; it has no poisonous snakes. There are no earthquakes and no one dies of jungle fever, and no one ever dies because of rabid bats. There are rabid bats, all right, behind the Big House shutters, and she hears them squeak and rave but knows they will not bite her if she offers nothing to bite. There are no floods worth mentioning, or not enough to kill you, and few drought years in Vermont. It is Eden on earth except for a blizzard that maybe could cause you to freeze. But even then you had to be improvident and not amass the firewood, and there are no avalanches like she's seen on TV in Canada. Men fire off their guns and mountains fall. There are wood ticks in abundance that Judah picks off the dogs, but they do not carry Rocky Mountain spotted fever. He'd sit there squeezing and applying rubbing alcohol or matches to the ticks, and she'd be appalled at their blood-sucking tenacity—but it is not fatal in Vermont.

And so this earthly paradise stretches around her, comforting. There are high winds, admittedly, but not so high you perished out of breathlessness, and if you stay away from falling trees. No place in the Bible does it say what happened to the tree once they ate the apples from it, but Hattie thinks the tree went rotten and was hollowed out by woodpeckers hunting for insects and fell in the first high wind. Eve knew enough to get out of the way, but Adam cast a backward, rueful look. Get thee behind me, he seemed to be saying, at least until I'm full of sinful knowledge and have honed my ax.

Still, paradise is warm. It is a stepped-up version of September. There are skies so deep the deep she knows means shallow, with no bitter cold or natural catastrophes or enemy to man. If only for that single fault, the landscape would be Eden, so she warms it up in daydreams just the way that New Orleans is warm—and then the snow is duck down in angelic sheets.

She'd populate it differently too. She'd pay no attention to color or creed, since paradise is democratic and without regard to that. But He regarded manners at the entry portal, and if your hands are presentable, scrubbed, and cleanly after labor. He regarded works, of course, and kept them in a ledger, keeping neat accounts. But mostly He decided if you'd done willful harm, or not, and if you've done no willful harm in thought and deed you were just about guaranteed access to eternal life. It would be bliss; it would be cherry trees in blossom and no neighbors running neighbors down and nothing spoiled or soiled. It would be a profusion of delights. The people would be openhanded and glad-hearted and their wings have eyelet lace through which you can see arms.

She waits at the window seat. She has never been a lazy woman; no one gainsaid that. No one denied that she woke at first cockcrow and worked at the day's tasks unflaggingly—glad for the chance to be useful and not meddlesome or lazy but only helping out. Busy hands keep out of cookie jars, she said, and empty hands are never full and weak ones aren't worth shaking if they daren't shake you back.

But this night she does feel lazy and will stay that way. This night there are others asleep in the house, and Judah'd made it plain enough her presence was crowd-company, and that he'd do without her now who hadn't done without her day or night for seven years. There is nothing to do in the room. She'll stay in here till Maggie leaves, or noon, though she doubts that Maggie will make it till noon. She'll stay until they come to get her and find the door's been locked.

For exile even self-imposed is exile, with nothing to read she wants to be reading and no television set or silver to polish, and her afghan in the billiard room. She ought to have remembered that. She could have swept in, leaving, and swept it up and taken it but couldn't creep back down there now and get her work. It is purple and yellow, which are Millie Ferguson's favorite colors, and Hattie plans to finish it by May Day for Millie Ferguson's niece. It had been unkind of Judah, but she was used to his unkindness and inured long since; his wife should intervene, however, and take Hattie's part. Yet she wishes Margaret no willful harm either, for having failed to intervene or say with loving-kindness, "She's your sister. She could stay."

She sniffs. She wouldn't have wanted to stay. There had been goings-on enough in that room, and will be likely again; she, Hattie, has no need to know. Curiosity, she used to tell Ian, doesn't always kill the cat, but if he sticks his nose in garbage cans he'll come up smelling bad. It makes no difference if there's a pile of roses; sniff around it long enough and you'll find the stench of compost at the bottom of the barrel; there are certain things it's better not to know. They huddle in the rooms beyond her, bickering or reconciled or lustful, and everything would be arranged and rearranged in any case. So she is glad of her privacy and has left the room of her own free will and not been ordered out. She wishes she had the silverware or afghan anyhow; it would have passed the time. "There's no natural catastrophes," she'd said to Judah. "Not in Vermont."

"But what about unnatural?" he'd asked, only half joking. "What about my wife?"

"That isn't fair," Hattie said. "You don't mean that."

"I do," he assured her.

"Not really."

"A manmade disaster. Just like her son."

Ian, their glory, their hope—who'd make all well in this world and was an image of perfection in the next. A long while after Eden, she had been bursting to say to her brother, there were lights in the house the first family built. There was someone inside sweeping up. There was silver to polish and canning to do and the sampler for the downstairs hall is frayed along the edge. There are bills to pay. There is always someone leaving and someone left behind, and ingratitude rides on the train of departure like thistles on a skirt. You pick your steps and have picked them before and know the way the path heels over and where it would be, likely, mud, and anyhow the thistles find you out and follow you and find themselves a brand-new site at breeding time.

Hattie listens for the furnace and can distinguish its noise. Water clanks beneath her in the hallway pipes. It sounds like iron croquet balls on carom shots; she loves croquet. She'd beat Judah handily when he consented to play. She knows the pitch and obstacles and takes on every comer and never ever had lost. "You're a tough customer, ain't you," she'd tease him—and then go through five wickets without losing a turn and knock his ball into the uncut grass for good measure on her last. "Some tough customer," she'd say, and wipe her hands on her handkerchief, since they'd grown damp on the stick.

Hilda Payson had beaten her, once. But Harriet had been overconfident and lazy and let Hilda get the jump on her and then was knocked into the wet uncut grass herself, and was just getting over a cold. So her shoes were soaking and she sneezed and missed the recovery shot, and then Hilda, who was gleeful and cantankerous and not to be trusted with the liquor cabinet key, knocked her back again. She'd nearly lost her temper. She said dreadful things, nearly aloud. Hilda Payson had pretended not to care. But Hilda cared—she, Harriet, could see that—cared tremendously, was cawing to herself in triumph and her knees were set so far apart you'd think she sat on a horse.

"Croquet's a game," she said. "You win some when you're lucky." Harriet was ill and shivering and her next shot hit a rock and bounced right back. That was the trouble with Vermont; no matter how you fine-toothcombed it there were always, anyhow, rocks. It was inhospitable country for a proper round of croquet. "It doesn't matter," Hilda chortled. "You'll have better luck next time, I'm sure."

"It isn't luck, it's skill. I'm off my game."

"You couldn't know about that rock, of course."

So Hilda inched her out. She, Harriet, is near to sleep now and upholding truthfulness and therefore bound to qualify that judgment. It hadn't, in plain truth, been close. It was closer to a country mile than inches, and Hilda brayed with pleasure as she hit the stick. Her upper plate was loose. Harriet pointed that out. "Don't be a spoilsport, dearie," Hilda said. Harriet had not been any sort of spoilsport, then or ever; it was just she'd had no practice losing at croquet. So she'd had the borders trimmed, and Judah levered up the rocks for her and she took every comer on again and beat them handily—but she had lost her taste for it and was glad, that year, for snow.

Ian was meticulous. He spent hours preening—or what seemed to Hattie like hours—turning in front of the mirror, studying himself with what at first seemed vanity and then something harder to name and accuse. It was the kind of study he'd accorded puzzles, or spelling, or the internal combustion engine when he took his first motor apart. There were parts and wholes, and somehow the sum of the parts, Hattie knew, had to add up to the whole. Somehow those eyes and ears and eyebrows made up the whole of a face, and Ian studied it to puzzle out the mystery of things. She hesitates now, though she had not at the time, to call it being vain. There was nothing personal in that slow study, as if he might have studied any available skull—providing that the skull would smile and wink and scowl on order and not lose patience or leave.

He had learned degree and size. Hattie made this clear without saying; her lessons were none of them spoken but written on the blackboard of the air, and just as quickly erased. The neighbor's homes are none of them big as the Big House, and theirs is the biggest around. The Sherbrookes that spilled over went to Canada and started up a place called Sherbrooke there. Our family was sitting here when neighbors came in wagons, and they took their shoes off when they came into the parlor, and the shoe still fits.

So that way they were similar; that way vanity was utilized by each. When the sun sinks over Woodford Ridge it is the sun, not Hattie's world sinking, and no one speaks her name if she isn't there to hear. Ian had occasion to be vain; he was his mother's picture in a man. Everything that passed for beauty or handsome was his, and handsome is as handsome does, Hattie said. You couldn't help but notice how the phone rang nightly, and how they always picked him in the partner's choice.

She hears the sough of Judah's toilet, and the trickling refill in its tank. There are voices raised in what she thinks is argument, then thinks is maybe song. If her Redeemer liveth, He knows without half trying all the goings-on in the Big House, and he too clucked his tongue. Pins dropped in a haystack are silent, she knows. Yet across the hall, inside his room, she hears the sound she has tried to avoid: Maggie saying "Judah," and what sounds like springs, like slamming doors, the sound she hears unceasingly, the slap of flesh on flesh, *Judah, Husband,* while Hattie curses her hearing, her ears that have to endure this, *Judah, Jude.* The bustle of the two-backed beast is loud, continual, and even in this seven-year silence it's all she's ever listened to from that cage three doors away where Maggie prowls, her heels going clickety-clack on parquet—and places her hands on her ears and hears in her cupped palm the sound again, blood thumping *Husband, Judah, Judah, Jude,* and presses her elbows together like knees and forces her ears shut.

XI

"I'm dying," Judah says.

"Don't say that," Maggie says.

"I'm dying."

"Fifty years from now." She snaps her fingers. "Just like that, remember? It used to be your joke."

She presses herself to him and is again the cocksure twenty-three-year-old who's met her husband-match. Then Judah had been superb. He was the strongest man she'd ever known or would have wanted to know; he set her teeth on edge. He set them chattering, then ground them down, it seemed, until her teeth were nerve ends too. When he hugged her he had done so with such suffocating pressure that even her teeth felt compressed. He'd cracked two ribs those years—and when she remonstrated or drew back he was, absurdly, hurt.

"It's me who's hurting," Maggie'd say. "I'm the one who can't breathe deeply."

"I'm sorry."

"You don't know your own strength."

"All right," he'd promise. "I'll quit."

But he wouldn't quit, would never leave off pawing at and pressing and compressing her until, for sanity's sake, she made him keep hands off. He called her "Hellcat" since there was a play about a football hero, and his wife who was Maggie the Cat. Elizabeth Taylor played the movie part, and they went to see the movie and he told her, meaning it, she looked better than that Maggie or the movie actress anyhow, and by a country mile. She rewarded him for that. It came to be a system of reward. When he grew submissive she'd submit in turn to his manhandling and lie there underneath him while he worked his ardor off. It wasn't all one-way, of course. She took pleasure enough for herself. But there was always panic at the edge of it—that he would take more than she had to give and leave her sucked dry, dessicate, bone pounded into bonemeal and her pelvis crushed. She'd seen a dog that way once—run over on its hind legs but not yet dead, but howling, running with no way to run. Hattie came and fetched her, seeking help. It lifted itself impossibly from the roadbed, swiping at its body that had no dimension left—and she, Maggie, ran to the house and found Judah in her turn and told him to bring his rifle. He did, but the collie was dead by the time they got back to it, with the blood not running. He shot it anyway, point-blank, twice in the head.

"Hold me," he repeats.

"How?"

"Here," the old man mutters.

"Are you all right?"

Her husband makes no answer, turning to the wall. So once again she is his helpless totem, sprawled beside him on her back. The dog had shifted twice.

"Harder," he says now. "I'm dying."

Maggie sighs. It does not help. She tries to see him in his towering possessiveness and marbled perfection, stripped to the waist while he sponged himself clean after work. The division of the sun line on his arms was absolute.

"I don't know you," Judah says.

"Yes you do."

"This isn't my wife."

"Oh, Judah, yes but it is."

"No. Outen here," he warns her. "This isn't the way my wife works."

She knows when things went bad. She knows when the whiff of mortality became a mortal stink. When Seth died the world went bitter, difficult, and everything that seemed to fit was formless after that. That was the path's true turning; that was when the woods grew dark and trails criss-crossed and doubled back and things she took for granted were no longer hers to take.

Seth had been a sunshine child. He lay contemplative, grinning for hours in his crib or the rocking chair Jude rigged for him or on her lap. She was sure he understood things as he suckled, blue eyes wide and huge. They had been drinking when Seth died, disputing in their practiced way about the way to be and behave. She remembers that much. She has spent the intervening years forgetting, and there are many things about the night she never could remember. But she remembers an argument with Judah as to squatter's rights. She'd said the nation had been built by squatters, and like as not his ancestors got what they'd gotten by squatting, and the early bird catches the worm's a phrase for birds and worms. Therefore those who took land today had no less justice in the taking; more, seemed like, since the government made it a good deal harder to keep. He'd scoffed at her. He'd said how about the three hundred acres of bottom land; how about everything that abuts the river; we're not using it this season are we, so why not just give it away? Why not, she'd answered, and been serious, and he'd looked at her and seen as much but said you can't be serious. Why not, she'd repeated; what are we holding it for? For our sons, that's who for,

Judah said. Men who'll make the proper use of it in its proper time. I'm glad of that, she'd said, of course (but thinking back on it thinks maybe that's when she thought she heard Seth; maybe that was pride's signal and the time that outrage settled in, suffocating and betraying and sucking every bit of air up from her infant's room; maybe that was the self-congratulatory shepherd penning the wolf inside his fold, then ticking off his blessings as he heads back for the hut). I'm glad for them, repeated Maggie, and grateful, but it doesn't change the argument; it doesn't mean that those who need the land should get no pasture rights. I've built this place, Judah said, with these two hands I've tilled it. Your great-grandfather built it, she said. You've tilled it for lack of anything better to do. There's been no necessity here—and thinks she hears it once again, thinks as he looms above her, furious, passionate, the advance he makes upon her prelude to some sort of grappling, but whether to beat or embrace her she's never certain till joined; thinks later the susurrus she heard was the whistling, whimpering final breath Seth drew, and had she not taunted her husband so, had they not finished the bottle, had the night been less loud with cicadas or had she not insisted on Chopin in their lovemaking's aftermath, bedded by him on the library couch and therefore not even stumbling past Seth's bedroom to their own—had she only been less idle her son would somehow live.

There's no blame to attach. There was no way to prevent it, and nothing to have done. But Maggie takes the blame up anyhow and knows that otherwise nothing makes sense; if his death is wholly senseless then the world is wholly evil, and she'd rather think there's meaning she can't as yet quite grasp. Hattie said the same. Only Hattie said it, saying there was meaning in the soul's salvation and punishment for evil ways, and Maggie told her, never quite saying it, say that again and I'll pull out your tongue.

Now she is using the toilet and lifting her hand for the chain. She hauls at air with her right hand, then lifts her left hand instead and finds the chain and pulls. She washes both her hands. They measured land in rods here, Maggie remembers, and remembers thinking it's a better word than acreage. She knows that millions of children die yearly, and crib death is the sort of graceful gathering to God a theologian might describe. She knows that, by comparison, death by starvation or cholera or bombing is a fate far worse, and the best thing of all, say the ancients, is not to have been born. Next best, she knows, is to die young and in untrammeled innocence surrounded by your loved ones in a world they appear to control.

Yet that suspicion of a whisper was enough—that susurrus on the second floor while she strained against her husband underneath. It meant Seth suffered while she took her pleasure, and she hears it now more loudly than any scream of pain. From that time, she herself had aged; from that fell turning she hacked her own way. Light changed in the afternoon, and woods that seemed benign were suddenly hurtful, threatening; birds fed on putrid flesh. Owls that seemed wise were ferocious; mourning doves were fierce. From that time on her beauty was a weapon—and she wielded it both as a shield and spear. She would endure, she said to Judah, no third child. They'd lost one altogether, and the firstborn, Ian, would make his way, gain or loss, out in the world without them. Hostages to fortune, she says, that's what we are, wife and child. Whose talk is that, he asks her, feigning interest, and she says William Shakespeare's, or maybe Francis Bacon's, and he says big talk, big talk. Don't feign illiteracy, Jude, she says, it's bad enough as is. What's bad enough, he asks her. Being a hostage to fortune, she says. Being for an instant on the top of fortune's wheel. It means you have to drop.

She rose again, of course. Folks rise, he told her, sententious; can't keep a good man down. That's a dirty joke, she wants to tell him, it's only manly boasting. That's the sort of purblind optimism she's earlier embraced; all it is is turning; all it is is evil, evil chance.

Maggie tells herself to think of other things. She will not think of Seth or any of the accoutrements of beauty nor her vanished own. She will instead think about cats. She'll concentrate on cats and dogs and raining cats and dogs and dog days and dog pounds and penny wise, pound foolish. But the word that sidles up and lodges next to foolish is careless, and the word next to careless is love, *careless love*. And so she is word-trammeled, circling, caught in the web he's spun that is this bed. She studies the brown leather chair and the three photos of her son. Judah lies like a vast spider next to her, at home in his intricate tangle—and all she herself can manage is a set of nonsensical songs. Come into my parlor, said the spider to the fly, she sings; come fly with me, let's fly away; *away in yon valley, in a low lonesome place . . .*

That had been Judah's verse. That had been his courting tune, and he sang it with a plangent grace that never failed to move her. It overpraised his ear to call it tin. She didn't know if there were cheaper alloys even than tin; she could call his ear aluminum foil, she supposes, or plastic, or claim it was made out of mud. But he sang "Saro Jane" with an emotion that beggared complaint—believing it, believing he was some rejected rancher and she, Maggie, had elected comfort while he rode the range.

Range was home on; range was kitchen; kitchen was the place she came from when he called. The distraction succeeds. Maggie sighs. She is carried from this evil room to her apartment's kitchen, or memories of Judah with his caterwauling earnestness, or how she'd seen Gene Autry at the circus once, his belly all over his pants.

"That's better."

"Yes," she says.

"That's what I want from you," he says and turns to face her.

"Your servant, sir."

"For better or for worse," he says, only half mocking. "In illness as in health."

(He had wanted, he told her, to offer a no-nonsense speech. He had been straightforward in the taking, as in asking, "Will you be my wife?" That was honorable discourse, and she should know it for a New Englander's plain speaking, without embroidery. Generations of Sherbrookes had gone to their knees and cracked their joints before generations of soon-to-be-Sherbrookes, he joked. He'd not get off his knees, he said, till she said yes.

"Is that a threat or promise?"

"A promise to keep."

"You'll hurt yourself"—she bent above him—"down there on that hardwood floor."

But she had looked down at him swaying, not so composed as all that, not certain if he meant what he never would ask without meaning.

"It doesn't surprise you," he said.

"No."

"You've known it was coming, likely."

"I thought so, maybe." Maggie opened her eyes.

"Well, what did you think"—he rocked back on his heels—"when you thought it was coming?"

"I thought I'd tell you yes."

He put his hands on her knees. She stooped above him, then knelt where he was kneeling and smiled and said, "That's settled then." He kissed her, elated, pleased she had accepted him and only told her afterward she'd taken the words from his mouth.)

So it had happened offhand finally, after all his preparatory scheming, his traps and teasing preludes—happened as she knew it would, looking back, coterminus with her not caring that it happened anymore, with his decision that the legacy was trivial and separation trivial and who cared how he handled it or fouled or let fall the reins: Jude kept his seat, was graceful as he'd been when in his riding prime, was mastering that comic turn the world calls circumstance and giving his wife what she'd anyhow always possessed—his house, his lands, his body to dispose of in the way that she saw fit. "Thanks anyhow," she told him, "but no thanks. It's kind of you to offer but I'm otherwise engaged."

"You can't mean that."

"I do."

Later still he tells her, "Take it," and she says, "All right." She takes it with the negligence she'd always shown to favor, as if a debt redeemed.

"So tell me where you've been," he asks.

"New York mostly. San Francisco."

"New Orleans?"

She smiles at him. "A little."

"To visit your cousins?"

"To visit the queen."

"Do you have an apartment?" he asks. "A house?"

"It's still the same apartment. In New York City. On the river. In just about the exact middle of town."

"You've said that before," Judah says.

"I know. Which is why I repeated it."

"You've got a memory."

"No. It's you who used to quote it—that thing I said the day we met. I wouldn't have remembered."

But she controls herself. She is creature-comforts Maggie who knows her way around. She is mistress to the house and wife to the man in the bed. He holds her, vehement. She is fifty-one years old and, without much adjusting, a blond. She had, she tells herself, been asked for help by him who'd never asked before—though much of that begging seemed malice and some of it certainly fake. She thinks of the endless demands on devotion that devotion, once constituted, makes: it isn't a question of manners, or habit, isn't a question of needing to hurt what seems so vulnerable now; it is for Maggie simply that she doesn't know how to refuse him this night; what he asks of her she gives because for years she gave or gave in or gave over.

"I don't need charity."

"This isn't charity," she says.

Yet she is startled by his near-divination of her thought. He always had been generous—with that offhand largesse of the rich who need no money since it all was earned before. She used to tell him he threw checks at foundations like scraps at the bluetick hound, only with less careful aim. He'd not even read the brochures.

"You're wasting it," she'd say. "These people use ninety percent of their funding for office space. None of it goes to the needy."

"I give a tithe to the first takers; it's simpler first come and first serve."

"But unfair," she'd protested. "Immoral."

"Then slip your envelopes on top of the stack," Judah said. "It won't make any difference. But if it makes you glad . . ."

So she selected and directed his charity for years. He'd spent less on himself than anyone; she granted that. He wore the same old coats and boots till they were worn to patches, and then he had them patched. His car was always ten years old (though he'd flung that Packard at her, and tried for furs, and the Steinway concert grand). It wasn't self-denial or a planned austerity, just that he had no use for what she labeled useful. Somewhere Judah must have heard that men who loved their women gave their women gifts—that husbands who could manage it would manage a fur coat, or car, or diamond rings. So when he remembered he took her out shopping—rampaging through George Jensen's with pockets full of hundred-dollar bills, and emptying those pockets out, floor by floor, as she trailed behind him, protesting. It was luxurious, of course, but not her sort of luxury since he paid more attention to the cattle at an auction barn than to the silver service, or the goblets he bought her, or plate. His gift-giving was so dutiful it undermined desire—and he'd thank her, frowning, for her own few gifts to him, then fold and store them away. It was a frown of puzzlement more than reproof; he just didn't know what to do with a second overcoat, or a carryall with stamped initials on the flap.

"I got no need of charity," he mutters at her now.

"No," Maggie says. "You're self-sufficient, darling. I know that."

"Correct. One hundred percent."

"I'm not dispensing charity. I hate that word. I'm glad to be here and glad you let me come." She wonders, is that true? "Truly. And grateful for the house."

"You're not"—he twists his mouth—"the lying kind."

"Be quiet," she commands him. "You'll tire yourself with this talk."

And then he is obedient and she takes his flesh between her hands. She prods and rubs and massages his shoulders, feeling him quicken then ebb. He is a white-haired elder lying at her side, and she dispenses charity. She soothes and strokes her husband, making circling motions on his lower back. Maggie rises above him, not mindful now of the sheets, warm with this familiar exertion, watching her breasts sway and dangle as she works.

"That feels fine," he mumbles. His mouth is in the pillow.

"Hush. Don't talk."

She labors like this for some time. She finds herself caressing him and making for his buttocks like an alien, secret place.

"It's good to be here," she whispers.

He makes no answer.

"Judah."

He shifts his head.

"J.P." She hears herself whispering, hoarse. He draws his hands down to his sides.

"Jude, are you listening?"

Ponderously, he draws up his knees.

"It's good to be back, do you hear?" She touches herself, expectant. "It is."

He pushes himself up on his hands. He is on all fours in the bed and turns to face her, focusing. She watches him watching her. He licks his lips.

"That's not polite. You shouldn't stare so"—and places his hand on her left breast and lets it settle. "Touch me, Judah."

He balances. She feels his hand veer.

"Please."

He falls upon her and is a great weight; she flattens herself and supports him.

"Talk to me," she says.

He does not move.

"Say something, won't you? Anything."

Still he is silent. She listens for his breathing and does not hear but feels it, in concert with hers. She holds her breath. He does not breathe.

"Jude?"

She feels the panic's edge again and tries to force him off her, but he does not move. She scissors her legs shut. His cold leg moves in consonance, and he lies atop her two closed legs.

"Are you asleep?"

He does not answer.

"Sleepy, darling? That's all right. We've plenty of time in the world," Maggie says. "Rest."

His hair is lank. She reaches to brush it back from his forehead, then stays her hand. She holds it there suspended, shaking, and shuts her eyes again. Now panic enfolds her utterly and fills her mouth and pours itself into her ears. It stops her nose and fingers her and runs rough fingers down her body, squeezing. She drops her hand. It holds her hands. It plays upon her spine as though her spine were something like a xylophone, but with no sheathing for the hammers, with nothing to cushion her; there are no blankets; she shakes. Panic is efficient; it tongues her without haste. It licks its chops and tastes her and is not perfunctory; she vises her legs against it but it pries her easily apart. It has a throat and makes percussive noises in its throat. She weeps but keeps her eyes closed, screams but keeps her lips together and is dry-eyed, soundless. She cries out, "Judah, Jude." She has a sudden memory of Ian, eight months old, with a flu and croup and fever that reached one hundred and five degrees in the first two hours; Judah took their son and plunged him in the bath, with ice and cold water, and Ian screamed and shivered while they brought the fever down. She remembers Jude's huge hands, the size of Ian easily, and how they held and tormented their son, but helpful, but healing, and she tries to marry panic and embrace it now. It enters her. It is practiced. It penetrates her with a thick rigid member of ice. It scrapes her womb and fills her mouth and reams her asshole out. It ejaculates everywhere, grunting, spewing ice. Its sperm is like sea spume where even the tideline has frozen. Ian was blue in the face. He spat and had been mottled and outraged. Panic assaults her, stiffening, where there is no pleasure left. It continues. She lay beneath her ancient husband, and he knew her not.

PART III

I

Judah wakes, as he always does, quickly. He is asleep, then wakeful, with no intervening period. He focuses on the pillow beneath him, then the sheet above his head. There is light in the room. The dials of his alarm clock are luminous, radioactive, though Hattie said that if you wear a wristwatch with radioactive dials you get cancer of the wrist. He shakes his head. He disagrees with her, disproving it by proving how many men wore wrist-watches with dials like that for how many years. No cancer has ever been reported, to his certain knowledge, that anyone has ever traced to radioactive dials.

It is like strychnine, he said. Swallow a small dose and you build up resistance; swallow a big one without any practice, and it's your final dose. She had been adamant. What about sciatica, she asked; what about that? They thought they knew about it ever since the word was invented, and here they'd been using it wrong all along and now they'd swear on Bibles what they gainsaid just last week. She made him swear to wear only his uncle's gold vest watch, with its slipcase and chain. She'd made him send back Finney's Christmas gift, which illuminated the date. He'd promised, to humor her, and had been out of the habit of timepieces anyhow. He raises himself to joke to Maggie about her sister-in-law's grim insistence, and how time flies if you throw your watch out the window. There is a janitor at Smith College, he jokes, who's worked for thirty years. When the girls ask him what he wants for a retirement present, he says, I wanna watch. So they let him. He chortles and slaps at his side. He turns to see how Maggie takes the joke. She is not there. He swivels, scanning the room. There is a bloated form beside him, its breath laborious, and he shrinks from it because his wife was always whippet-lean and a light sleeper. He had not dreamed her, did not dream. He cannot remember his dreams. She has slipped away again, and that is once too often in this life.

Judah extends himself from the bed. It is no distance to the closet, nor any real accomplishment to stand. He acknowledges, departing, that the shape beside him is in fact his wife. She owns the house now and will not leave. It is his turn to go. He will gather up his errant son and they will leave together; Maggie lies there in the bed as bait, for his new quarry will be Ian, and the trap is this woman lying in the middle of the house. He turns his attention to his son, attending to that. There are rings on Ian's fingers and bells on his toes. He will track and seek his lost son out and force him to return. Ian has a banjo, possibly, or a beer bottle to whistle in or guitar or Jew's harp or piano; he makes music wherever he goes.

The oil lamp by his bedside gutters down. The shape on the bed rearranges itself. Judah chooses a duck-hunting jacket to clothe his nakedness and stands there hefting it in the closet's warm oblivion. He fits his arms into his sleeves. The sleeves are thick. He rests, standing as he used to stand in duck blinds in the darkness, a piece of the surrounding space. His coat has the stench of raw health. He needs no boots. He has his cane and body-cunning and will find whoever lies with Maggie where they lie.

Then he makes his way into the hall. He pads down the center of it, se-cretive. It is a thing he'd noticed early on that men go down the centers of streets, or skulk on the paving, or can't make up their mind and cross the road at puddles or for the sake of the sun. But early on he'd chosen to walk each walkway's center. He'd give way to cars, of course, or a team and cart, but not concede dominion to some engineer's idea of who should walk in which direction when. It is a habit now he won't break for the sake of stealth, although he walks on tiptoe, without shoes.

"They're giving out tickets in New York City, Mr. Sherbrooke," Sam Bur-gess said. Sam Burgess lost the use of his left arm in a driving accident, so they made him stand outside the elementary school, whistling and waving at cars.

"What for?"

"Jaywalking's what they call it. It costs you fifteen dollars to cross be-tween the green."

"I call it freedom of movement," Judah said. "I call it my own skin."

"I wanted to warn you," Sam said.

"You've done that. But there's no car coming, and we got no traffic light."

"Just don't say I didn't warn you if you get to New York City and they throw you in the clink . . ."

"Not likely," Judah said. "But thanks all the same." And anyhow it is his hall, and anyhow they'd see him if they chanced to look.

There was a riddle Ian asked one morning, after school. "Hey, who's the strongest man in the world?"

"I don't know," Judah said. "What's your opinion on that?"

"Superman. You're supposed to answer 'Superman.'"

"Superman."

"Wrong again," his son crowed. "A traffic cop. Know why?"

"I can't imagine."

"Because he holds up a hundred cars with just one hand."

"Except it's all he has," said Judah. Ian veered off to the kitchen to try the riddle out on Mrs. Sattherswaite.

(Judah Sherbrooke lies, they whisper, on his deathbed now that was his marriage bed. He believes he can hear the doctors consulting. We could schedule a quadruple bypass next week, they say, or give him mustard poultices. We could make him take his morning constitutional and see whether yogurt would help. It's the mitral valve, they say, it's an infarction; it's all of that beefsteak for all of those dinners for years. He lies, he hears them say, in splendor, in great pain, in peace. They lie. He is merely husbanding his strength. Bears hibernate, and ducks go torpid in the wintertime, and many beasts are sluggish until heat quickens them. The bedsprings creak and complain. The frame's securely jointed, he knows about that, but the rails of the sleigh bed need sanding. There where he flings his legs to the floor, or sits at the bed's edge winding his watch, the inside of his legs has rubbed the edges smooth. There's nothing like the action of the flesh; it gives a sheen to wood no varnish can accomplish. It's endocarditis, they say, it's angina certainly, all his sins upon him at long and final last. What can't he shoulder by bearing; which trick or two remaining is the trick to play? He asks himself who let the doctors in, the lawyers out, and where is Maggie, and why should they whisper if he hears them anyhow whispering. It's blockage on blockage, they say, the LAD, the widowmaker, enough to fell an ox. Nonsense, he winks, no such luck. Come here till I tell you: there's caterpillars coming out of moths. There's beasts in air and water that will walk upon this earth. It took him three shots through the head to kill one snapping turtle, and the jaws were moving even after that. He'd hunkered in the long grass by the pond, sighting, waiting for the thing to surface, and it surfaced not six feet from him and was an easy shot.)

In his mind's eye he sees the letter to his son. Its edges curl because the envelope is larger than the paper it contains. Finney has a new secretary, and she insists on folding things twice, the letter turned in on itself, when a single fold would do. She has, Finney tells him, advantages. She can take shorthand faster than he talks, and her typing is acceptable, and she has many talents in the field. In the hayfield, Judah jokes, and Finney—as if he could manage to make hay in hayfields nowadays—winks. The letter has been postmarked March 30th. It says *Please Forward If Necessary* on it, but

Ian leaves no forwarding address. It requests him to contact his father or his father's lawyer and be present at discussions of the terms of the estate. It suggests such presence would be vital to the nature of the settlement, and proposes a per diem allowance and, of course, that travel expenses would be furnished at the estate's expense.

The envelope is cream white. Finney's title and address are printed in green ink, on the upper left-hand corner. He employs an IBM Selectric typeface for Ian's address, but resists a postage meter as a mark of the impersonal. There's not so many letters, Finney says, that you can't lick and stamp them by hand. They've tried, Lord knows, says Judah, to haul him home before. It lies on a hall table, under magazines. In time the dust will form a diagonal consistent with the left upper edge of *Popular Mechanics* that lies athwart it, protective. The table, Judah imagines, is a plain pine table with walnut stain. Its two front legs are on the hall runner, its two back legs on the floor. There is therefore a slight downward tilt to the angle of the whole (though not above an eighth of an inch) since the table weighs sufficiently to mark the purple runner, and the runner's threadbare anyhow. Ian's off to sea, he thinks, and in this seaport town the mildew happens quickly. It's as if the envelope was sweated on, or steamed; it's as if the formal furtive language is a circular, and any lost son everywhere is welcome home.

The stairwell is another matter, since it gives on the library door. He would be discovered, and his sham would be exploded and his illness turn to health. He considers the parapets and windows, and of the back servant stairs. But they lead past Hattie's room, and he knows her far more wakeful, even sleeping behind a shut door, than his careless wife. So he turns toward the elevator shaft. He pads to the door and pulls it open carefully and peers within; the cage is there.

Judah shuts the door again; it is solid oak, and squeaks. The door to the library, too, is solid and windowless oak. They are in the library, discussing him, he is certain. The elevator reeks; it is memory's confinement and a box for invalids. Still, it fits his spying purpose and will make little noise.

Pleased with his contrivance, he rests for the count of ten. Then he pulls the door open and steps inside and unscrews the elevator's lamp. Next he feels in the new darkness for the button, pushes, and feels himself fall. There is a soft whirring and complaint from the elevator cables, but he knows they cannot hear him or distinguish this new sound from the surrounding noise of the house—the furnace, for example, or water in the pipes. He settles himself for his vigil, breathing carefully to ten.

("Count to a hundred," Ian had said, "before you start to look for me. And keep your eyes closed or it's cheating."

"I won't look," Judah said.

"But keep your eyes closed. OK?"

"OK."

"Now count to a hundred," he yelled, distancing.

"I'm counting. One one hundred, two one hundred, three"—and Judah leaned his head against the wall and listened for his son. Ian hid in closets or would bang doors then shut them without running through, and early on he'd fitted underneath the couch.

"Oley, oley infree; ready or not here I come."

What, he wonders now, does "oley oley infree" mean; how had he clambered over furniture, shouting "Fee-fi-fo-fum, I smell the blood of an Englishmum," in pursuit of that elated boy he could not locate now? Then they played "Thing in the Room," and Ian chose an object and Judah guessed which one it was by circling and pointing, while Ian cackled. "Getting cold. Ice cold. A little bit warmer. Getting warm now getting hot, getting hot as a person can get." So Judah, nosing up to the vase, would know it was the vase and turn on his heels and point to the painting of oranges. He would step past the still life and the mantelpiece and Ian would pretend to freeze and shiver, beating his elbows and saying, "Brr-r it's cold in here. So cold.")

"Though there be severall who think it improper," Peacock wrote, "we will not heed the world's scurrility but take our bounden pleasures in that almost-Eden whence my thoughts continually fly. Oh to be in Vermont where the first green things this week will testify to spring and to His ceaseless

Husbandry Who watcheth over all. I seem to see the Easter lambs at their frolics, and freshening cows, and the season's wheel which here on this Pacific Coast seems not to turn, or grudgingly, though th'Inhabitants call it healthful and breathe this salt-slime down. Had they one taste of Mountain air, once filled their lungs as I have with the sweet pine-scent of our beloved pasture-land, they would choke with every inhalation or keep Cambric pressed to the nose. There is profit to be made here in the better class of lace . . ."

There where he keeps his ladle the stream runs all summer long; the ladle is tin and large enough for two to drink from—not together, though they've tried that too, her head butting his, their noses opposed, but one after the other, his wife going first—and in April or June he only has to dip, not even bending, to fill the cup full; later it tastes of metal, and then of leaves with a flavor not so much the residue as presage of decay, the maple and oak leaves thickening the streambed banks, and clogging the rock sluice he'd chosen. Nearby he built a salt lick and an apple stand, building it at Maggie's urging and high enough to clear the snow so that the deer might have unimpeded winter access, and when they snowshoed in to see they saw that the apples were gone and the salt lick troughed hollow by tongues, so she laughed and held him and said, "There, we've helped that many at least," and he didn't answer, "For a week maybe. For the dogs to kill," but only pressed her where she held him and said, "You've eaten those apples. They're in your cheeks," and she answered, "Lordy. Lord, I married a romantic. The last of the red-hot romantics," and he scooped the snow's crust back and dug till he uncovered the stream and thrust through the crystalline surface to the sluggish trickle beneath—the ladle's cup was snow-stuffed and he knocked the powder back and filled the cup with icicles and chill white water and drank and made her drink: the tin adhered to her lips and, tearing the ladle free, she shredded her lips' flesh.

He has tried to reach Ian by phone. He called the last numbers he knew. There had been no answer or the phone was disconnected or the parties that he reached had never heard of Ian Sherbrooke and couldn't be bothered to look. He didn't really blame them. It wasn't a question of blame. But he had known that Maggie knew where Ian could be reached, and tried the phone in Wellfleet and hung up on her father when he heard the first "Hello."

He thought of telegrams and about taking out ads. He tried to send a letter but the words evaded him. Maggie had been fluent, and she would have found the language, but his own stock phrases stuck. He could not bring himself, he knew, to beg for what was his by right and what each man could anyhow expect: a son beside him in his house. He imagined protestations that would haul his son back, hat in hand, protesting that he also left for love. He imagined Ian reconciled and by his bed, saying, "Why didn't I understand sooner? What a fool I must have been!"

"Not foolish," Judah would say. "Just a bit stubborn, that's all."

"A willful piggish fool," Ian would accuse himself, and the tears would blind him. "How can you ever forgive me?"

"No need. Just stay here is the only thing I ask."

"Done," Ian said. "You didn't have to ask for that. My stuff is at the station, Dad. I'm here to stay."

When Judah comes to, there is silence. He does not recognize the space; it reeks of lemon oil. The air is bad. He breathes and stretches and opens his eyes but is in blackness nevertheless. Stretching, he touches two walls. He remembers, then, his place and purpose and gathers himself to his feet. He reaches for the light switch, and finds it and presses and remembers he unscrewed the bulb. He takes mincing, sideways steps around the floor's perimeter and toes the bulb in the last corner and leans to retrieve it, then rests again. There is silence in the library; he feels for matches in his hunting pockets. Patting at the pockets, he drops the bulb and hears it bounce and shatter. He curses himself for a loose-fingered fool, and continues. There are empty shotgun shells and a handkerchief and sand grit and a penknife in his pocket also, but nothing like light. He sighs. He hears his breathing echo. He decides to ascend and presses the button for the second floor but does not move. He thinks perhaps he's pressed the wrong button and fingers each button beside him, then presses his palms against the instrument panel entirely. There is silence. There is not even a boiler below him, or any sort of clanking in the elevator chains. Hattie had been claustrophobic. She had feared just such a breakdown, she told him, just such a short in the lines. What if I'm riding, she asked him, between one floor and another, and lightning comes and knocks the power out, what then? You pays your money and you takes your choice, Judah said, not wanting to coddle her fears. For every fire, he maintained, there's twenty false alarms.

So he collects himself and breathes again—the air denser this time, acrid—and counts to ten. He shrugs himself out of his coat. The insides of his arms are wet; his right foot itches. He wants to sneeze. He can always, he tells himself, open the door. He tries the door. It does not give. He tries again, leaning his weight on the slab. He knows enough of circuitry to know the circuit holds. It clicks and does not give. He had known, somehow, in the dream from which there's no escape, that the door too would be locked. There is air and space and time in abundance, he tells himself; there are people in the house to find him when he calls.

He blames himself, at times. It isn't a question of taking the blame or whether he deserves it so much as whether he is willing to admit the possibility. Judah admits the possibility. He could have bent a little who had been unbending, could have guessed the way the wind would blow and made his own adjustments. He should have checked on Seth that night and should have checked on Maggie on a hundred nights. But he'd thought that not reacting was a reaction also: a man of his stamp sits and takes it till there's nothing left to take. Lately he's suspected that his nothing done or doing was to blame; "You can't take it with you" was a fool's compliance. He would take it with him since there was nothing to take.

They stand there attentive, awaiting him, eyes left, though what they see he can only question, seeing in their stance the marines at Iwo Jima, scaling the rock face to plant a bronze flag—or perhaps the imitation of a statue he saw once in school, the Laocoön, an old man muscled as is he, Judah, surrounded by sons and a snake that surrounds them. His eyes are blood-engorged and blind with possibility—mottled with effort, the rock-veins bulging—and so they clasp each other and embrace with a concentrated fury that proves this combat mortal, proves the opposition absolute of arm to arm, knee-knee. His right knee fused with his opponent's left, the fulcrum there where one must surely topple, go flailing full-length out over that rockbed as base. Once spread-eagled, Judah asks himself, once felled and pinioned and made to cry mercy, what variety of mercy might be his to beg—since he had asked no quarter nor offered any ever—mercy not his strong suit, never his strong suit, and not the kind of quality to outrank justice—or not in his ranking, at least. Put them in a scale and he'd put on his thumb for punishment, weighing it with probity and willing to accept and pay whatever was assessed as his fault's due—and at the door's unyielding handle thinks collapse a kind of comfort, the promise not threat of thirst finally slaked. Perhaps "The Kiss" is the statue he sees, or one of those headless, handless statues that Maggie made him study while she enthused about proportion and he waggled his toes in museums, trying to see what she saw. Or some time-blunted frieze of centaurs raging, drunk with undiluted wine, through courtyards where the women cower yet—does he imagine it?—exult. He is exultant anyhow in the knowledge of completion, and finality inhering, *whatever it is this is it.* Nor will the lazy circling birds bother to investigate who surfeit on the easy scavenge and are heavy-bellied by noon, those legs that were so pliant now rigor-stiff, unbending—men in the streets with naked swords, the swords aloft and wavering, seeking that unguarded entrance to palpitant flesh, or ambushed, upended in wells, the well-throats stuffed with this wet clot of carrion. Judah shifts his stance just slightly, imperceptibly rocking on his toes and heels to make minute adjustments, the motion imperceptible to those who watch, if any might, except only perhaps as the witnessing eye's nictation, or the sun glinting off some new flesh facet, or a sudden breath drawn, and offers and acknowledges and yields up his arrogant shame . . .

Then there is light. Then he sees himself naked, holding his duck-hunting jacket, and there is blood on his foot. There is no light in the elevator, but there is light in the room, and he is in the room since the door-latch had released. He has fallen forward as the door gave way. It opened without warning, since his weight was on the door. He has not harmed himself. He stands. There is no one in the room. There are fire remnants. There is the smell, still, of cigarette smoke, and he wonders has she been blowing smoke rings and did Finney admire her pursed-lip dexterity. It is—he considers the grandfather clock— two twenty-three. The minute hand moves slightly backward, always, before it moves the minute forward; Judah thinks of springs uncoiling to advance.

The blood has dried. He broke the bulb; he recollects that. He turns again to the elevator, propping the door back, and retrieves his locust stick. The mess is negligible. The door should be oiled, he reminds himself, and the lock system changed. He hears house sounds above him, but they have not opened his door. He has not been found. Fleetingly he wishes he *had* been discovered—here, sprawled on the landing, bleeding, blinded by the sudden light burst, a hero spat back. She would have bent above him and been solicitous. She would cradle his head in her arms. She would ask if he were hurt, and he would answer not too badly, and then she'd say, in a low voice to Finney: "Run for the doctor. Quick."

Finney, less solicitous, would pause. "Do as I say," Maggie would order. The man would scuttle off and she would bend above him once again, protective. Now Judah stands half naked in the room he fears she's fled forever. He breathes. He walks, without disguise or limping and precaution, to the mud room. He takes three rights and one left. There he pulls on his brown wool pants and a red shirt, and his walking boots. He replaces his hunting jacket, stuffing himself through the sleeves, but leaves his cane.

"We none of us," Peacock had written his daughters, "should forego the Pleasure and Profit of Travel. There is instruction in the temples and the

205

Pagan mosques where no man has a pew to call his own, nor can he keep his shoes on in the sight of God. For whatsoever they name Him He is immanent, as if Allah or Buddah or Thor be the nick-name childishly put on by youthful Pleasantry, until we learn that Nick himself is but the Devil's label, and there prove one proper appellation only. Just so with methods of Food preparation and marriage and ornament and all the Customary appurtenances of this life. First custom seems peculiar then it seems but quaint then regular then normal then the rule, and by these slow succeeding ventures we who were Parochial become what now they call Cosmopolites. It is a stage, as any Other, to endure."

II

First he walked with Ian or took him pickaback. His son was long-legged even then, and Judah made him stretch his legs. He tried to teach him pace. But Ian would bustle and dart along and get tangled up in grapevines or make a game of puddles, jumping, stomping flat-footed into the deep center to see how much water it sprayed.

"Don't do that," Judah said.

"Why not?"

"Because it gets your pants all wet."

"They're not all wet," said Ian.

"OK. Because it gets me wet."

"You're not either. It doesn't."

"Because your mother would be angry."

"It'll dry. I promise." Ian jumped three feet across the flagstone path and landed like a geyser in the mud.

"Because I tell you to," said Judah.

"It's not a *reason*."

Judah leaned and lifted him and held him up, spread-eagled, eight feet above the ground. "This'll dry you off."

"Carry me, Daddy."

"Not wet like this."

"I'll dry, I promise. Please."

So Judah eased his son's soaked legs around his neck; he held to Ian's ankles and they continued.

"Giddyap. Let's canter. Let's jump that old fence."

"How much do you weigh now?"

"A lot," said Ian. "Forty-three pounds."

"Well, that's too much for this old horse to jump a fence with."

"We did it yesterday. Giddyap."

"But yesterday you weren't all wet. That makes it heavier. You've got to add the water," Judah said.

He pressed his son's knees to his ears. He heard only Ian's burbling instructions, felt only the self-willed warm extension of his flesh. "That one," yelled Ian. "Get the ram!"

"Horned Dorsets," Judah instructed his son. "Those bigger one are Suffolk. The most of them is culls."

"We'll get them at the pass."

"What pass?"

"The gate," said Ian. "Up ahead. That's where we'll head them off."

"Not this horse."

"Giddyap."

"You're not checkreining. You haven't given me signals."

Ian pummeled at him and he veered left. For all his gruff disclaiming, Judah felt the victor when he lost.

Now he sits in the kitchen's deep dark, having placed himself precisely in the center of the space between the sink and table. He knows the room's

coordinates. He is at the apex of a triangle with the cutting board and faucet at the base; Judah tucks in his arms. He follows his nose. He is someone
sitting, he assures himself, in the middle of the kitchen that is the middle
of the downstairs wing in the middle of the house.

His chair is painted white. It has three slats in the back. It has a solid seat,
and the legs have been squared off. There are three additional chairs drawn
up to the table's three sides; Judah bisects the chair that had been opposite his.
He draws the line from that apex (where Harriet had used to sit, and splits her
down the center, imagining her intestines and esophagus coiled around the
perpendicular bisector that makes of man a mirror) and connects those two
legs across the table's plane, and has an isosceles triangle similar to that which
his chair fashions with the far legs of the flanking chairs. Except he himself
has moved. The room will not stay vacant. No matter how hard Judah stares
at the wall as though it were Euclidean, he sees his parents backed against it,
wearing evening clothes. They are gesturing and fretful in the middle of some
argument he cannot hear, but feels himself involved in. It is summer since the
screens are in, and he hears the june bugs clattering against them. His father
had his arms upraised; his mother was not cowering but shrinks from him,
is wearing silk, and the rustle of her dress is like the rustle of the june bugs
on the screens. Then Judah sees himself with Maggie on the cutting counter,
watching her reflection in the kitchen window as she bounces above him and
jiggles. He balances on his toes. "We'd best not wake the boy," he says. She
makes appreciative noises although he covers her mouth.

Therefore he does his roots. The square root of four is two, and the
square root of two hundred and fifty-six is sixteen. The square root of one
is one, but the square root of minus one is an imaginary number, i.

Ian was a real result and Seth an imagined result; they multiplied an "i"
by "i" and got minus one. "Don't talk arithmetic to me," said Hattie when
he tried to explain. "There's no such thing as making a mistake with roots.
Square roots indeed. You water children and feed and love them and they
grow; our family tree, Judah, is as long as anybody's in America. Don't ever
be ashamed of that."

"I'm not."

"There's glory in it," she said. "It's no disadvantage to know your own roots."

The root of nine is three, and three has a fractional root; the root of eighty-one is nine, and nine squared is eighty-one; things fit. He can imagine apples doubling and contracting and being bushel after bushel and then stacked crates. The world is a warehouse of numbers, and if you keep close enough track you'd know where everything is stored and when it had been put there and labeled and how it stood with reference to everything about it. There are no memories, no panting wives or generations scrabbling at the edges of composure like june bugs at screens. Maggie played cat's cradle for him, and he watched the intricate interlocked twining; there were patterns she could twist and fatten or reverse and then she'd flick her fingers at him and there'd be only string.

As the years went on, however, Ian lost his interest in games played on the farm. The boy was studious. Judah read him Peacock's letters and he liked them well enough but said that history had passed the old man by.

"What's that mean?"

"You know the frontier thesis," Ian said.

Judah waited.

"Frederick Jackson Turner says you have to keep on going if there's wilderness in front of you."

"What of it?"

"That's what makes America. That's why we're so busy moving all the time."

They were in the study. Ian had his Hammond Atlas and a sheet of copy paper and was making maps.

"I follow," Judah said.

"Well, the way Mom sees it, Peacock got to the Pacific but he had to turn around. He should have stayed there, maybe."

"Is that how she sees it?"

"Yes. Then we could all be California people. It's an improvement, Mom says, it's the Gateway to the Orient, and warm."

"Your mother talks that way to you?"

Ian drew the Mississippi, using blue. He made the delta just above the gulf and put a big black spot at Hannibal, the birthplace of Mark Twain.

"She says that Peacock's partner, Colonel Frémont, was a brave man with men's lives as long as they weren't his own. She says that General is just another word for coward, and we won the west by genocide."

"By what?"

"By genocide. What's that mean?" Ian asked.

"It's when you kill off everyone. But there's people left in California."

"Well, anyway," said Ian. He crosshatched the Texas panhandle and Oklahoma in red.

When Ian learned to paint, Maggie bought him easels and sketch pads and a box full of oil tubes and brushes. Then Judah set a gallon can of Barn Red beside them and asked which was likely to last.

"That's not the question, is it? Look at this sunset, darling."

"Look at this barn," Judah said.

But more and more, as the years passed, he set out alone. He took the pickup or a tractor to the bottom land and saw his fields splay out, untenanted. He watched his son, come back from school, practicing lay-ups at the basket he had rigged behind the sugarhouse for twenty minutes only, then practicing the piano for two hours every afternoon. It grew dark while he played.

"Aren't you proud of him, Jude?" Maggie asked.

"Why?"

"Listen to that. Grieg. It took me years to learn just the first movement. He'll play it in the school recital Thursday."

"What time is that?"

"What time will that be, Ian?"

He looked up at her from where he sat on the piano bench. He used no music.

"Three o'clock," said Ian and commenced the phrase again. Maggie bent above him, nodding, tapping her foot and wiggling her fingers in time, and Judah—watching from his leather chair beside the fireplace—saw that his son's eyes were closed.

"It's beautiful," said Maggie.

Ian continued.

"Sixteenth notes," she explained to Judah. "Every one of them clear as a bell."

"They're muddy." Ian said.

At two o'clock that Thursday, Judah got stuck in the Shed field. He had been seeding alfalfa, and turning on the western slope he sunk his right rear wheel. He tried rocking free, then led his length of chain around a locust tree and pulled. The tractor stalled. It settled. He had one pass left to make and took his work coat off and tied the sleeves around his neck. He filled this sack with alfalfa and completed the seeding by hand.

"Let the buildings be laid out," Peacock had commanded, "in the Shape and Memory of our Savior's ransom, with the four points of the compass being the four of the Cross. Let the barns be due west of the house, pointing as His strong arm pointed to where I scribe these lines. Let the Carriages and suchlike be stored on the easterly Axis. South at a suitable distance, where his feet were nailed, you may build in whatsoever fashion but not above one story's heighth, the farmer's house. Thus even to the eagle's eye, and surely to him who stands on the Cupola, will we furnish instruction. Somehow I seem to see the Holy Spirit hovering, in the bird-guise he assumes wherewith in safety he may visit this nether pit, and to avoid a suchlike crucifixion—for what are the yearly migrations but testimonial also to the Flock's disgust? And do not greylag geese example this search, scanning the Compass-points for some clear sign that our

Redeemer prospers—espying the Reverent arrangement of our Severall buildings, and reporting to the august Captain that in this township anyhow there thrives one Honest man!"

The order in the house assures him. He knows what each closet contains. He knows the way the servants' stairwell curls around the dumbwaiter and laundry chute, and how the elevator shaft takes up the southeast corner of what had been the ballroom. He knows the hall's dimensions, and that it takes seventy-two steps descending from the room she used to sleep in. There are plaster ornaments Judah can trace, eyes shut, and he distinguishes the feel of the oak fireplace from those that are sided in walnut; he knows who bought the billiard table for the billiard room.

The difference between four and fourteen, he knows, can be ten or the first integer or he can multiply by three and then add two or subtract two from the square of four; they're all of them fourteen. And it had been the same with steamer trunks or women's protestations and the jobs he held then quit. Within the seeming random sets there was always this arcane rigidity—always his own sense of system and logic and the exact opposition of loss to gain. From one to two, Judah knows, you either add one or double the original number; you also multiply by seven and then subtract five.

Yet these rooms contain no series he can plumb. Nor did his age and illness seem sequential to his block-hard rock-thick middle age. Nor is Maggie's disappearance and return and disappearance a series; you go from one to four to one to six to one to eight to one, and someone on a contrapuntal series thinks you've never left. He was running home mud-crusted, with the taste of metal in his throat. He was hiding in the laundry room behind the wicker baskets, staring at the shapeless, starched gray uniforms of maids. He was chewing on a syrup stick, his hands full of beet sugar, and he added water to it until it was a paste. He shuts his eyes and focuses and creates color: red and yellow and the sun's orange arrangement. He wills it, this one dawn, to turn as he turns, motionless, and slip around the world the way a sleeve might on a scrawny pointing arm. He opens his eyes and is gratified: flame comes from the west.

Fire: he sees her also as flame, though this is more his element, and of the four he'd qualify for earth and fire, she for air and water (he knows this; they have worked it out in the game called "Essences": "What animal is Jo-jo," she would ask. "What time of day?" And he'd answer "Skunk," or "Three o'clock in the morning," and she'd swat at him and grin and say "Raccoon. Early evening." Then he'd ask, "What color is Hattie? What scent?" And she'd answer, "Mauve. The smell of pressed lilacs," and he'd say "Green, because you ate my second piece of apple pie . . ."), but still he sees her firelit, her face become a kind of screen with shadowplay, that hair of hers alight ("Enclosed air spaces," he would say, "it's the secret of flame. And build it back up tepee style, and far enough back there to catch the draft." "Why are you telling me this?" she would ask. "Because," he'd say, "although I hope not, there may come a time when you need to make a fire and I'm not here to build it. Check the flues." "You're always here to build it," Maggie said. She mock-shivered, then stretched. "You're my heat source, husband . . .")—so flame was domesticated for her, a source of comfort not terror, and he thinks of her always as "toasty," which also was her word, or bending to the match flare with which she'd light her cigarette, or standing by the chunk stove with her hands out, fingers spread. He gave her a rotisserie one Christmas, and she used it often, so he'd stand in the kitchen watching while she trussed the chickens up, or ducks, and pricked them with her long-handled fork and added seasoning, then skewered them with what he could only call relish, ramming through. While the bird was turning they would watch it sweat and pucker and his wife would say, "That's it. That's heaven. Name every pleasure and the chicken has or is it now"—the fat igniting underneath the broiler coils, and liquid sizzling that would later coalesce. If they had an argument it was how she hated winter (and it was true, he came to acknowledge, that their first three meetings had been in the summertime, that she maybe thought Vermont a place of green abundance, not mud and granite and ice): fire her servitor somehow, so that she'd have only to breathe on the last white ash heap of the last set of embers on some abandoned hearth to kindle the household again, to set the stewpot bubbling and the ice-stiff clothes to dry . . .

"We'll walk the lines."

"No."

"Yes. You ought to know them."

"Why?"

"Because it's important. A person should know what they live on."

"I'm hungry," Ian said.

"We'll take something. We'll bring yogurt with us."

"I hate yogurt."

"Pretzels then."

"Why can't we just eat it here?" asked Ian. "Why do they have to get all soggy?"

"Come on. We're wasting time."

"My ankle hurts."

"Come on, I said."

"It hurts me. Mom said I shouldn't stand on it."

"I'll take you part way pickaback."

"I know the lines already," Ian said.

"Not the part we're going to. Not north."

"I do so."

"OK," Judah bent. "No more discussions. Not another word from you, hear?"

"But I've got to go to the bathroom."

"Go ahead. I'll get us the pretzels and Coke."

"Can we check traps?"

"Yes."

"Can I take my .22?"

"We'll see."

"Can I? Promise?"

"Yes. I thought we said no more discussions."

"Promise double-promise?"

"Yes."

"It's muddy out there," Ian said. "I hate those boots."

"The hell with it, I'll go alone. You stay."

"Well you might ask," wrote Peacock, "why I promote this Residence and what purports its Excellence of size. As well ask the midge in the evening wherefore he Elects to bite. As well inquire of the leaping Salmon why it should scale Rock!"

When Ian sprained his ankle jumping from the Toy House roof, Judah had been jumping with him, and he took the blame. "Thirty-two feet per second," he said. "It's true all right. We timed it."

"Are you hurt bad?" Maggie asked.

"Of course not," Judah said. "The shingles just broke loose is all."

"Tell me where it hurts you."

"He's all right."

"Let the boy answer, OK? Let him say so for himself."

He had carried Ian to the house. He laid him on the daybed by the porch and put a blanket over him and then called Maggie. She came running. "What *happened*?"

"We were doing roofing. Look, his toes move. Ian, wiggle them at your mother so she'll know there's nothing broke."

Ian spread his toes. Then he raised and lowered them while the face he had built for his father came undone: his lips jutted out, the skin around his eyes bunched up and wrinkled and his nose went white.

"Don't cry."

"He isn't crying."

"He can if he wants to."

"Who's stopping him?"

"I want some chocolate," Ian said.

"I'll get that," Judah said.

But in the pantry, hunting chocolate, he could hear his son's high wailing two rooms over and across the porch. There was a row of soup cans and chickpeas and tuna fish in front of him; he put his hand at the edge of the shelf and swept it, right to left.

Wind: he thinks of her also in that; always there are breezes where she walks, and he thinks she could float if she stretched her arms out far enough and let hair billow on the updraft, a flaxen parachute to let her down securely wherever she might land. Judah thinks her the air's consort, easy with airplanes and landing and what they call jet lag. It was always windy when they played at badminton, and though he said it was stupid, a grown man batting at a bit of fluff with feathers on it, swatting at nothing with wood and catgut that weighed next to nothing, no heft to it or solidity, she made him play and skipped happy circles around his aggrieved opposition, contesting his service and forehand assault, not ever sweating though she jig-stepped all over the court while he stood planted, immobile, in the court's dead center, stamping the grass into mud. Using wrist flicks that he barely saw and a scampering grace that caused him to teeter from frustration to envy to desire, winning always, she defeated him with the wind at her back or in her face or coming at them sideways, gusting. There was the created wind they rode or drove in, with the windows open, and the winter's continual probing, ice fingers fisting down chimneys or where they hadn't caulked or through the storm-window sash, under doors. Air is what nobody does without; air is what you needn't notice till it goes bad or stale. Next he remembers fire drills with Maggie and Ian, so they'd know how to blanket flame and close off all air sources and where he stored the plywood to cover up the fireplace if there were chimney fires, and how to keep low under the heat and, more important, the smoke, how to crawl not for the nearest exit necessarily but the smartest, how to take short breaths and hold them, how to follow his two golden rules, Keep your head, and Keep your head down. So Judah follows those instructions, keeping his own head and keeping it down and exits where he entered through the kitchen door. Air is something that you watch at sunset maybe, or when it's coming on rain and there's a field to load yet, reminding him of when he'd burned the bottom land by accident, and how it smelled: they had a brush fire going, trusting to the windless March day's wetness, and there were only embers when he broke for lunch—returning to the Big House and taking his ease, sitting in the kitchen's warmth and washing with relish and putting so much sugar in his coffee that the spoon got sluggish, going back at noon to hear the whole field crackling and the ground already crepitant, but there were marshy spots and snow at the field's edge and what wind there was stayed southerly, herding the small flames to water. So he'd not been overworried and stood watching the bottom land gutter, smelling what he smells again now, and the field indeed sprouted greenly in April and gave a thick first cutting by June, and they took three cuttings off it that summer and by September he was claiming to have set the blaze on purpose. Air's inconsequential until you need it for fire or to let the liquid out of cans or just to put some sort of God above this earth.

III

"You'll want to make your peace, Jude."

"Yes."

"You'll want to set your house in order."

"And lands."

"How do you prefer it, then?"

"The way I always did," he says. "No nonsense. Straight up and down."

"How do you mean?" Finney asks.

"You know the one about the millworker. Who's so dumb his cronies convince him he's pregnant. He says that isn't possible, and they bring a doctor into the joke and the doctor examines him and says, yes, Sven, you're pregnant all right. So he goes home and wags his fingers at his wife and says, from now on none of that fancy who's-on-top stuff. From now on it's straight up and down."

Finney laughs.

"Next question," Judah says.

"That isn't what I meant," his lawyer says.

"There's no peace to make," says Judah. "There's not any bargaining table. You got me those three testaments and I gave one to Maggie. There's nothing to sit down around and nothing to draw up or change."

Light: the gradual accretion of it, sift in an hourglass weighting the time scale, first the seckel pear tree, then the tamarack then elms ignited, their twig-tips silver in the moon that is diffuse then fused from the east through that cloud bank, there, and then suffusing everything. He sees yellow leaves on the willow, and deadwood that he's notched but not had time to cut, sees the rooster distending to crow, saw cockfights in the silo they'd cut down to head height and covered over with chicken wire and used for a testing arena, but not with razors on the spurs. Then they moved the better cocks to Hamilton's old barn and bet on them and tied the razors on. Judah saw blood on the sawdust and cock's wings and sheets they soiled together, sees dishtowels he had used as tourniquets that time he hemorrhaged, and stumps that had been rooster spurs, both sinew and gristle gone black. The blackness swarms and rises and settles, buzzing, so what he took as guarantee was only the promise, at eight-to-five odds, and with men milling about him impeding the view, that this false dawn is light . . .

He sets out for the barn. The path is familiar. He has been robbed of his youth. He feels in his shirt pocket for the peanut brittle. He crumbles it with his right hand and pulls a fragment out and licks at his fingers. There is earth on his fingertips also. He coughs and hears the sound as if it were a stranger's—dim, tinny, high in the throat. He wonders is that what they mean by a death rattle? Ian, holding rattles, had been fierce. He pounded on the high chair's tray with a sounding cackle, Ian is left-handed, and no Sherbrooke was ever left-handed that Hattie can recall.

So Judah gauges his steps. Once he ran the mile circuit for kicks. For the joy of it he'd spot Maggie a third of the distance and try to catch her and half the time succeed. She'd be a wheat-colored blur by the sugarhouse, then resolve into component parts at the corncrib, then become all legs and jostling laughter as they shared the finish stretch. She could outrun him, nearly, for the sprint, but he was slow and steady and had the better wind. So he'd catch her as she lay back for him, laughing, head over her shoulder, feet dragging, elbows out.

The house is behind him. He steps from its shadow. There's a ring around the moon; it's two days off from full. He studies his shadow. It moves. He lifts his hand, and the shadow's elongated hand entices him, and he thinks, *Look, I'm a rabbit, look a giraffe, look at the antelope horns.*

"Make me a rhino, Daddy," Ian said.

He made a rhinoceros head, and horn.

"It's got a little one too, Daddy."

He let a knuckle protrude.

"Make me a unicorn."

He rearranged his middle finger.

"Now make me a rabbit again!"

His breath is plumes. His feet take root where he stands. At the tideline, standing in sand that the current subtracts then adds to his ankles, watching the water's pitch and yaw, sinking where he weights the shore while she, Maggie, is a quick glimmer in the surf beyond him, Judah knew just such stability in the middle of giddying motion. The world is a careening thing; the moon and sun are its outriders, and he hunts for solid footing since his balance has gone bad. Time was he'd walk the barn beams, quickest way to cross to the hayloft without even seeing the forty-foot drop; time was he'd top the pines by climbing them, right hand holding the saw.

"A morning's constitutional," Peacock wrote, "should not exceed one mile. That is a sufficient distance for the soul's repose and the body's repast to settle and assert itself. The gentleman avoids excessive exercise before and after meals. Provide a one-mile path. In His eyes there can be no distinction twixt the camel and the rich man mounted on the camel's back, in terms of distance travelled they are of course coequal. For the camel bears the passenger as burden, whereas the Passenger is burdened with the spirit's apprehension, and the task of guiding his insentient chattel through the endless sands. Lo how elusive proves that promised fount where each might slake his thirst, and where the Weary Traveller might bathe. How myriad are the Phantoms and False Lures. How often do we think ourselves within the Oasis of Grace! We stoop to drink of lambent and sparkling elixirs, wherewith the Soul might cleanse itself and raise the liquid Illusion to our parched and avid lips but find it dust. Dust the dream of surcease, Dust the hope of Merit that it might earn mete reward, Dust the ardor that enkindled this proud pilgrimage, all ashes and dry husks. So might we not need Compasses; might it not be Useful to have the path marked with Flagstones and not, as in the fairy tale, breadcrumbs for vultures to swallow. Should those who go before not leave such signposts for the Quick?"

"Hey, Ian, what about this baler?"

"What about it?"

"What are you doing now?"

"Nothing."

"Give me a hand," Judah said.

"What's wrong?"

"Just hold this."

"I need gloves."

"You don't need gloves."

"I do. I've got to practice after."

"Hold the twine then," Judah said. "Only hold it while I fix the goddamn feeder."

"You said you fixed it yesterday."

"It didn't work. It cuts off short."

"Why don't you get it fixed? Why don't you get Harry or someone from Allis-Chalmers to fix it?"

"Screwdriver."

"Yes, doctor. Scalpel at your service, doctor."

"Not that one." Judah shook his hair back. "The one with the Phillips head."

"Sorry."

"The big one. Look at this screw."

"Well how was I to see it?" Ian asked. "Under all that grease?"

"All right."

"All you had to say was Phillips head."

"All right."

"And anyhow it's raining." His voice slid an octave again.

"Hand me them pliers."

"Sutures, doctor."

"The socket wrench. You don't know your ass from your elbow."

And holding, forcing with his left hand, Judah overpressured with his right and came down hard on his own wrist. The Phillips cut a star shape just between his palm and wristwatch; Judah stood there, bleeding, letting the blood spout and clean itself out, watching his son go white-faced with his white hands full of string.

Now he shuffles forward and attains the sugarhouse. There he gathers up his things—the newspaper, the match tin, and the can of kerosene. For years he made leaf piles and burned them and inhaled the smoke, and there'd been nothing wrong with that until they called it dangerous, so you had to burn leaves on the quiet, coughing, tying handkerchiefs across your mouth and nose. The smoke was the color of mother-of-pearl, and it had dimension against the blue sky-shell. But you saw that less and less often lately and the smell was strange—boys raked leaves into bags and twisted them and stacked them on the paving now for trucks. It was a waste of compost, and Judah figures they burn the leaves in some landfill anyhow. Somewhere he hasn't been to there's a leaf-burning pit, and men stand by with asbestos boots and gloves, but there isn't any danger and they break open bourbon at three; at four they sniff and drink their fill and watch the sky go cloudy with its own opaque sweet-smelling sunset; at five the smoke would be lighter, not darker, than the night air it eddies through, and at six o'clock they'd huddle to the many-layered embers, taking comfort in the color and the perfumed heat.

"The Preacher calls it vainglory," Peacock wrote. "And vanity indeed, of all the Large or Venial sins, seems dangerous to him who builds. For Foundations are quicksand, not stone."

He wants to be by that landfill. He wants to be where everything is buried, with a group of workers like Hal Boudreau, not talking except with the no-talk that beats back silence, not needing to claim or reclaim. He'd sniff the acrid sour flame and drink the acrid sweet bourbon from a bottle that is everybody's bottle. Men would pass and raise the liquor and tilt and swallow and pour a final cupful on the flames.

"Judah, my wild one. The Lion of Judah."

Somewhere off in Africa, he's heard, they have embalmed Haile Selassie. The little emperor he's named like, half his weight and half his height— Maggie always said it helped your feet to walk in sand; like emery board sand took the dried skin off.

"What I mean is, what I meant . . ."

Outside it is colder. He hurries to the center of his woodpile and drops down the paper and matches and kerosene can. There is gray light now, and the kerosene sloshes lightly out of the air hole. He breathes. His inhalations are willful, since his throat is a streambed in August, with the springs dried out. He brings air in like water, sluicing it across his teeth like rock. They salvaged everything these days, so why not salvage teeth? There are landfill operations and operations for hearts and lungs and kidneys; a woman could go to a sperm bank and sleep with some pure stranger in a tube.

"And therefore," Peacock prophesied, "there will be stately progress in the Park. I seem to see my grandchildren's grandchildren curtsy, see them laugh at some Bright pleasantry or knit their brows with concentration at some sportive Feat. We shall build a brown Pagoda in the Chinese vein."

Her cheeks would flush; her throat, too, flushed; she could run barefoot, often as not, on ground he'd have to pick his way through, even wearing boots.

"Let the park be Glade and Bower for the gladding of the wakeful Mind; let there be Enticements such as Benches by the Grotto, and Japanese maples in profusion, since they teach us scale."

He continues. Peacock's grandchild's grandchildren are Ian and Seth. Ian has been gone for years, and Seth died in the house.

"Don't go," he'd said the final time.

"We're leaving," Ian said.

"You're making a mistake."

"I'll make my own from now on," Maggie said. "With your permission, Jude."

"And what if I don't give it?"

"That's exactly why we're leaving."

He looked them over. "I'll miss you."

"We'll miss you too."

"So stay. Save everyone the trouble."

"I'm eighteen," Ian said. "I can make up my own mind."

"Is that what they taught you in school?"

"I'll get the car," Ian said.

They had had what Maggie called a *pied-à-terre* in New York City for years. It was on Sutton Place South. She saw the river, she told him, and if he came to visit they could take walks and go to concerts like they used to and she'd arrange for parking so it would be only four hours, door to door. It was a point of principle, he told her, and not practicality; he never again traveled south.

When Ian started Exeter, Maggie also moved away, leaving Judah in the house. They both came back for Christmas and part of the summer and maybe a birthday or Thanksgiving to make a show of unity. But it had been sham unity and nothing to anticipate or, looking back on, remember as fun. And he had been in part relieved when Ian left for college in their final summer, and Maggie for New York.

"So this is it," she'd said.

"Yes."

"You're welcome in the apartment. Whenever."

"You don't mean that."

"I do."

"I'd give you warning," Judah said. "So you could clear whoever's in there out."

"I wouldn't require it."

"One thing I hate"—he tried to shift his feet but they were rooted, stuck with gum-sap to the Persian carpet.

"What's that one thing?"

"Is other men's coats in my closet," he said. "You know."

"Yes. I do know about that."

"So there's not a whole lot left to say," said Judah.

She made a motion toward him. "You've got the address and telephone number. You've got Ian's address and his number. Keep in touch."

"Be seeing you."

"It's not fair, Judah, just to let the boy go off like that. Without a word of luck or love or anything."

"I don't want to talk about it."

"Well, it's Labor Day," she said. "We'll have a ton of traffic on the road. We'd better be going."

"Good-bye."

And so she went off down the steps and into the car and that was all he heard or saw of her for seven years. He sent them checks through Finney for schooling and clothes and vacations, but never for the rent.

Now he walks into the hay barn and picks out a bale. Time was he'd walk with one in either hand or lend a hand at stacking and not notice when the lunch break came; now a single light-packed bale is overmuch to manage, so he cuts the twine and takes the hay in sections, clump by clump. He carries it assiduously to the stacked locust wood and uses it as chinking where the logs let too much wind in; he spreads himself a pallet in the center of the square. There are burrs and thistles in the hay; there is too much weed for use as anything but bedding, and he is glad for that. He wouldn't have wanted, he tells himself, to use feed hay for a pallet; it would have been a waste.

What pure grass they have is timothy, and he calculates which field this cutting comes from. The Shed field had been planted in timothy three years back, and Judah decides it will be time, this spring, to turn it over into corn. He coughs; there is chaff in his throat. He comes across a garter snake, crushed by the baler, and what was likely a chipmunk that is pressed now and extended like a carpet of itself. He hawks and spits.

("Judah," they told him. "We got enough now."

"It's coming on rain."

"Maybe just a little bit. No more than a wetting."

"Not enough to mention. To say so."

"Dinnertime."

"Suppertime."

"Smoke time. I need me a cigarette."

"Jimmy Slocum's cousin said he seen a camel. Like that old workhorse, Clyde, they called him, only humpbacked and not swaybacked and spavined and maybe three times as big."

"Judah. J. P. Sherbrooke. Mr. Jude."

"You got a name to match each name they give your wife."

"Except maybe vixen and harlot and Abishag the Shunnamite.")

His sleep this night was troubled, and his digestion troubles him, and everywhere he aches. "Flesh of my flesh," he intones. "Betrayal on betrayal." He likes repeating words for the sense of solidity, and balance; he feels himself a tightrope walker using words as a way now to ward off collapse. He extends both arms. There are spotlights trained on him, and he tries not to lose his focus on the necessary end; the inner ear, however, is the root of balance and he prays that his hearing will hold. "Flesh of my flesh" means sons, though what he planted in her was more a seed than flesh. He pictures his seed clinging to her womb wall like a cockleburr, or swimming, and then it was not "it" but Ian, and then not "it" but Seth, and Seth reverted.

"Of the various infirmities," Peacock wrote, "I hold with those sages who hold loss of Faith the Gravest, since belief in Wrongs is tantamount to the belief that Wrongs shall be redressed. Yet without the latter conviction, Man is but cast ashore as if he were a Castaway upon this Life's grim Strand, nor can sumptuous food or welcome or a bed of goosedown and Satin be the jot and tittle of True Comfort by Compare. Therefore for every Inward Arch I wish an outward Pillar, and for each circle a square or rectangular Shape. It is necessary in this monotonal Era to provide Relief. When tired with a long day's wrangling in the dusty offices or glittr'ing Courts of Law, I sometimes for an hour at work's End seek diversion with fencing; then do I see on the target before me not some dancing bobbin or Image of th' Adversary, but rather Delirium's Fancy: my house in Female Shape, its outline dark yet definite, and with one single window lit there on the Second Story's left-hand passage where reside the Heart. I lunge and pierce it through. There is an Awful Glory in the sight. Long past what we Inheritors have come to Know as the Expulsion, the light of incorruptibility still flickered—and as I lay my foil to rest I seem to see it beckon me, the Devil's very handiwork tricked up as foxfire. Gleaming."

When Judah finishes he pulls the barn door to. It squeaks and complains, and he tells himself the rollers should be oiled. The struts in the barn rainbow out. There are springs beneath it, and he'd cursed the siting often. They should have built above. There are springs that fill the gutter every time he cleans it, and one of them is strong and pure enough to bubble up above the rim; he's lost more lambs to water than disease. They'd cleared the barn of stock when he quit his serious farming, and now it holds only hay.

So be imagines himself in the gloom in the hay barn, with Maggie beneath. He would have baled and stacked three hundred bales that afternoon, and they would fill the top loft full, leaving only the drop-chute uncovered. There are tree trunks shoring up the barn with the bark still on them, and the braces and crossties are two foot across. The men would leave but his wife would be waiting, expectant, with wine and soft words and balm that beat horse liniment to stir the warmth in him.

That afternoon the sun would angle through the barn boards, roseate. She would fall on her back in the third rank of hay, in a level space he'd made when stacking, and where the sun illuminated air motes and her hair's wheat sheen. He, Judah, lowered himself. She spread and murmured "Husband," to the rhythm of his strokes, and there was pain and pleasure intermingled, fused, or more like cream and milk suspended in one rich solution, and he bent his head to kiss her and kissed the hay chaff and sneezed. There was a profusion of barn swallows; he counted six, then ceased.

Now Judah wads up newspaper and spreads it from his pallet to the wall. Hattie made what she called *Rutland Herald* logs. She twisted the paper tightly and tied it in three places and soaked it in the bath, then let the whole thing dry. She piled her paper logs in the corner of her closet, saying this will always burn and what else is it used for once you eat the headlines up. He should read in a mannerly fashion, and let the news digest.

The barn cats play about him, and the pigeons settle back. Chaff dances in the light; the air is wet but warm. He inhales it lazily. Maggie sleeps. She is his dream of consummation, light in the heart of the house. He throws his head back to study the vaulting and hears himself half singing, making noise in his throat. This is it, he tells himself. This is as close as man need ever get to where he's going, and still call it worth it, and still have a handhold on joy. This is more than most.

"Let there be chestnut and butternut wood; let the mantel be oaken, and every door be walnut of the House. Let there be Chinese Porcelains and statuary abounding, and fluted columns of the Doric Mode. I wish Lamps to be ceaselessly burning, in Continual Remembrance of the wakeful Husband that is Christ. Let there be four large rings and additional Cross Braces; let there be protective Skyworks to harbor the design from weather and Wind . . ."

He unscrews the kerosene cap and sluices his pallet of straw. Then Judah walks—the kerosene not racing out but not just trickling either, a stream he can control with his thumb on the air hole, a rivulet corkscrewing over the hay, a reservoir he dams and then, swinging, unplugs. He likes the smell. He likes the odor of resin, syrup, creosote, and the patterned wetness of the hay. He splashes his initials, then hers. He splashes a cross, then triangle, then circle, then paces the floor's dark perimeter until the can is empty. He wipes his hands.

("J.P. Hiya, how's my girl."

"Son of a son of a son of a bitch."

"They's dead in the ditches of France. Come here till I tell you, mister. Count to one one hundred. Two one hundred. Three.")

Such voices natter at him, dying, like casement flies in the window in winter: a black swarm falling as they rise. It wouldn't be so bad, he tells himself, if there were instruction in the prattle; Judah sits. They breed in the corners by the thousands. They live in his refracted heat and cannot be expunged. He works his toes in the boots. He loosens the laces, then removes them from the top eyelets and lets the ends hang free.

"Hiding in the pine lot. Hiding in the tack room. Hiding up under the roof."

"Ready or not," she repeated—and he was tenderfooted, naked, picking his way through underbrush. The leaves were wet. She hung her skirt and sweater on a low extended birch branch, so as not to soil them. She wore a yellow skirt. But he has lain with Abishag and shaken off the fleshly envelope and he knew her not. There is no luxury remaining; he has put back childish things.

So lying there he thinks the straw shape beside him is hers, the cold indistinguishable from that pervasive chill they'd known by the Walloomsack in their second marriage-winter, sleeping out. Wild nights, he tells himself and remembers how he wrestled with "Bear" Starkey, not losing. He tries his memory trick. It is April seventh, and he remembers that day a decade previous, then a score, then thirty years. He remembers forty years previous but only inexactly; he knows, of course, that he was living in the Big House even then, that there were hard times because Roosevelt knew nothing about orchards, and what he did know he forgot in order to build roads.

Judah remembers running from his mother's sickbed's side. Nose clamped against the smell of it, mouth full with air gone rancid, unable to swallow, he left the elevator's close enclosure and bounded down the steps; there on the portico breathing, there across the trellis with his lungs commencing to clear, there quicker than it takes to tell it in the tack room, taking his saddle and bridle and breathing in the smell of horse, out of this barn and already at a canter as he passed the gate. It had been he, of course, who found Lavinia Sherbrooke—hands crossed as though to save them the trouble, eyes shut, with only her tongue hanging out to instruct him, and nothing moving in the room except the long-fluked fan.

He tries the fifty states. He tries their capitals. Once he knew all the states and capitals and state flowers and could fit them lickety-split together for Ian's jigsaw puzzle. He knew the boundaries of Arkansas the way he knows the Shed field's perimeter, and remembers North and South Dakota, and North and South Carolina, but has the nagging sense that there are other pairings; New Mexico, New Jersey and New Hampshire aren't the only states, for instance, with the label "New."

There are other games to play. There is tick-tack-toe. He'd played leap-frog and Scramble and football in his time. Later he played hide-and-seek and Fuck the Upstairs Maid and then The Neighborhood Virgins and then Your Neighbor's Wife. My Lord, Judah thinks, there was gaming. Cards and horses and baseball and dogs and fighting cocks and you name it, he'd place a bet; given odds enough, he'd have bet against the dawn. Or at least that it was visible, or at least that it was visible past ten o'clock, and to a blind or sleeping man. He'd have bet his bottom dollar things would bottom out, that Roosevelt would get us into war and guns and profit and he, Judah, would do best by letting well enough alone.

"Let there be fifteen-hundred and forty component parts in the Stain Glass design. It was in the year Fifteen-hundred and forty that the descendants of Canute, the lineal cadet inheritors of that Excellent King Alfred, first considered travel from the Sherbrooke Seat. The actuall Pilgrim entrusts himself to ill-favored or favoring winds. The actuall Voyager will think of his body as a Boat and entrust it to the Isthmus as I myself have done, for what was lost is always found in Christ's pocket, and the accounting kept Completely in his ledger-book, if one might write of a pocket and ledger-book in this Connection. Then let us think of Him as a clerk of all souls, as an Adding Instrument that never makes mistakes."

Judah strikes a match. He does so negligently, not cupping his hands. The matchbook is damp, and the flame sputters out. He tries again. This time the match fails to take; he watches the sulfur-head disintegrate. His third match takes, however, and he protects it and tries to kneel. His body has gone clumsy, and as he shifts position the match is extinguished. He wonders, does that signify reprieve? He wonders, does it mean she seeks and yearns for him in their shared bed? His fourth match fails; his hands are shaking; he is an idiot, he tells himself, to have brought no lighter. The fifth match breaks in his fingers and the sixth shreds; the last has no sulfur-head.

Therefore he tells himself that he must ferret Ian out; he'll follow his son west. He turns. He stands and sets out from the barn, following the track from the sugarhouse to the garage and stealthily past the Big House porch and past the Toy House to the entrance gate. The moon is gone. He knows the path so well, however, he could walk it blind. He steps out unburdened, his bootlaces flapping. The iron gate is open; he closes it behind him. This takes some doing; he puts his shoulder in it, and the thing clatters clangingly shut. There are stone entrance pillars; they recede. The road is tarmac now; he sees the night lights of the village beneath him and starts down the hill. His neighbor, Willis Reed, sold farm-fresh eggs but never kept a chicken. He had a fifteen-foot-high elm sprouting in front of the house; nobody planted elms these days, but Reed's kept right on growing. He kept his hat on, always, and Judah knew the man was bald as billiards—Hattie said he wasn't human, with no eyebrow hair.

The slope is considerable. Judah picks up speed but steps in a pothole and buckles, nearly falls. There is no pain but he continues slowly now, favoring his ankle. The brick bulk of the Library is to his left and Morrisey's ahead of him, and as he hits the crossroads he sees cars. There is mud on the road. The curb is a perilous height. He wears his walking boots. He will shave this afternoon. The cars that idle at the light send smoke at him and at the mountain ash trees in the traffic island. There are, in that one engine, three hundred fifty horses shitting smoke.

Judah stops. He considers how best to head west. Hattie thought that west was always a left turn and north was straight ahead, since that's the way the map looked. He had tried to show her how west changed. "Nonsense," Hattie said. "The needle's broken. Every time you walk ahead you're walking straight ahead."

"What about south?" he asked her. "Does that mean you have to go backward?"

"How should I know?" she countered. "You've never taken me south."

"It wouldn't be backward."

"Turn right," she said, "and straight ahead you'll find New Hampshire and then Massachusetts and the sea. I know that much; it's east."

So he elects Route 7 where there's traffic. Ian might be in the bar, or driving past, or paying a courtesy call on Lucy Gregory and Elvirah Hayes. He remembers that you make a fist and put your thumb up for thumbing a ride. He wonders, should he hitch? West is New York State, then maybe he'd dip south and go through Pennsylvania, Ohio, Indiana, Illinois. A white car corners on two wheels and speeds off, blatting its horn.

And now he asks himself why ever he let Ian leave. The boy went off to college, and Judah could have driven there, could have shown up for the football games or plays or weekends Ian mentioned in his first few post-cards home. You could fetch him for vacations, Hattie urged. You teach a dog to fetch, said Judah; a son comes home if he wants to and shouldn't be begged. It isn't a question of begging, Hattie said, and Judah agreed that that wasn't the question and let's not discuss it anymore. All right? he asked. All right, she said, but started in at dinner till he laid it down as final that he'd neither fetch or visit unless Ian asked.

The boy was headstrong; he'd not deny that. Judah'd figured to outlast him and that Ian would come running back for his first college summer—or the second when the first went by with only a postcard from Boston and then one from a place called Elk in what the postmark showed was California. Then he instructed Finney not to forward college bills, but simply to pay them and leave it at that.

Some months later—four years back, he figures now—Judah got a bottle in the mail. He knew it on the instant for a liquor bottle, since it had the heft and shape. He unwrapped it carelessly, tearing at the thick brown paper that had been torn in the sending already, then tossing the cardboard and paper both into the fire behind him. It flamed. Only when he'd read the bottle's label, *Sherbrook Whiskey*, and broken the seal and tasted it right then and there, not liking it much, telling Finney who'd been there for supper that the family improved with "e," that the bottom of the silo tasted a sight better and twice as strong—only then, as the carton adhered to itself in its own ash shape behind him did he recognize what he had burned, or believe the clumsy fold and printing (in block letters, underlined, with blue-black ink and no return address he'd noticed) had been Ian's hand. He put his own in the fire to find it, but the form collapsed.

Now Judah imagines his son. He tracks him to some nightly revel, where redheaded women are dancing. They are drinking, wearing only sequins and anointed with perfume. He imagines Ian in prison or board meetings or the Blueridge Mountains that he'd sent a card from, once. He imagines him in concert halls, with his mother applauding from the second row. He gives Ian a moustache. Then Ian shaves it and he gives him shoulder-length hair and a beard and shaves it all off finally and has him in a raincoat, army coat, denim work coat, sports coat, and then what Sherman Adams got, vicuña, and sporting a cigar. He takes his hand; he takes his money and a kidney out of him for transplants; he has him dead in Vietnam and Memphis and then, miraculously, as he had done a quarter of a century before, gives Ian life. They hold conversations. They laugh. Bygones are bygones, and spilt milk is under the bridge. He will not, can he help it, die a wheezing, slack-mouthed fool. He will break his life off when the time comes like a piece of brittle, and the edges will be trim. "Let's neaten up the edge," Hattie says. "Just before we put it back"—and would take her knife and pare through pie or brittle or cake—"Just one more little bite." He tracks Ian to his mother's apartment on the edge of the East River where the sun rises and ignites them and they are drinking coffee on the balcony together, steam rising out of their cups.

A second car avoids him, honking. A mail truck speeds past. Judah has no money and no matches and not enough warm clothes. His ankle aches; his boots are loose. His estate is settled; he turns to see the cupola and wonders is that backward, is it south? He lifts his hands and opens and closes his fists. The palms are white. He peers at them. With a queer final fluttering, he drops his hands and puts them in his pockets and climbs back up the hill. The elms are black. The gate is too heavy; he skirts it and follows the wall. He clambers across where the rocks seem to dip and, negotiating purchase, jumps and tumbles back inside. He lies there for some time.

SHERBROOKES

I

When Ian returns to the Big House, it is for the first time in years. He does so as if by chance. Half his life ago, at thirteen, he followed Maggie to New York. She had offered him his choice, of course, but in a way that left him none: she was his mother and needy and fleeing Vermont for his sake.

Their visits to Judah thereafter were brief. They'd take the bus on holidays, or trains, or the limousine he'd send (refusing to drive or collect them—"It's fetch and carry," Judah would say, "I teach it to the dogs"). Then even that sham union shattered, and they stayed away. Since the Sherbrookes believed in plain speaking, said Judah, why not acknowledge their mistake and call a spade a spade: weekend families don't work.

Nor has he seen his mother since she elected this version of home. Maggie ensconced herself in the Big House as if they'd never left—as if such wounds might heal. Judah died soon after that. Ian knows; he's kept in touch, if only by message or letter and always at a remove. His absence, he intends to claim, was as accidental as his presence now—the logic of geography, not love.

He had not attended his father's funeral. He heard about it, however; Samson Finney reached him in Chicago.

"Thank God I've found you," Finney said. "We've been looking all week long."

"It's only Tuesday," Ian told the lawyer. "I wasn't hiding. Why?"

"It's me who's calling because—well, because your mother isn't up to it. She tried you in New York, and then we called around. I've been making the arrangements."

"Mr. Finney, you needn't apologize. We don't talk all that often."

"It's been a long while, hasn't it? Years."

"I recognize the voice."

"You should call me Samson," Finney said. "I hope you'll think of me as at your service, Ian. Should you require it. Not in business matters, I didn't mean that, though in the legal context also, if you want."

So it had come as no surprise when the lawyer said at last, "Your father. Judah's dead."

In the ensuing silence, Ian thought several things. He thought, That's that: seventy-six. He wondered how Finney had tracked him and how his mother was feeling and why she hadn't called. He thought about telephone static, how the crackle made it sound as though there were birds on the wire, poised, scratching.

Then he thought that Finney was not only an informant, but his father's friend who wanted consolation. The impulse to offer comfort displaced the need to receive it, and Ian cradled the pink lightweight phone and swung his legs out of the bed. "*Passata la commedia*," he said.

"Pardon?"

"It's Italian. It means things are over."

"The funeral's tomorrow," Finney said. "I'm calling to inform you."

He drew in breath. It whistled.

"Ian? You all right?"

He wasn't sure which way to answer, therefore said nothing and, sitting, crossed his ankles. It was—he consulted his watch—five o'clock.

"He died quickly," Finney said. "Peacefully. You couldn't have known."

"His heart?"

"Mm-mn."

"I knew about that. I did know."

"Angina pectoris," said Finney. "Your mother was with him. His sister, too."

"Hattie. How's she taking it?"

"About as you'd expect," said Finney.

But he expected nothing; they were strangers now. He had seen Maggie, of course, but neither Finney nor Judah nor Hattie for years. He felt as if his own heart were beating in his head; blood pulsed there so loudly it echoed.

"Your mother's all right," Finney said.

"When's the funeral—what time?"

"Eleven. We put it off as long as we could. The whole town will be there. I've been hunting you to hell and gone. Chicago—there's a connection out of Albany . . ." Finney trailed off.

He rubbed his ankle where it itched. He inspected the skin of his feet. Flocks settled on the wires, so he picked his words with care. "If I didn't see my living father," Ian asked, "why do you suppose I'd come to see his body? What makes you think I'd visit now he's dead?"

"It's not . . ."

"It is. Judah'd take no pleasure in the kind of thing you're after. He was ceremonial all right, but not for this sort of ceremony. I'm working here, I've got a job."

"You sound just like your father. Did you know that?"

"People used to tell me," Ian said. "But nobody here knows his name."

Passata la festa, Finney pronounced. "That's what you said, isn't it? I was in Italy during the war, and I understand the expression. We have a saying in America, you know. We say, 'Water under the bridge.' 'Don't cry over spilled milk.' 'Let bygones be bygones,' we say."

"I'm sorry," Ian said. "I'd be there in the morning if I could. But this is how it stands for now. I'll call Maggie and explain."

At five o'clock that afternoon the lights had been on in the street below, the traffic loud; he sat in the increasing dark while Finney's protestations turned to curiosity—what was he doing in Chicago? how long had he been there, on what sort of job? how long was he planning to stay?—and wondering, was he in truth like Judah? would Judah have refused to come to his, Ian's, funeral, and should he prove a point by going? would his mother be glad? would she consider his return a victory or capitulation—and for whom, to whom? So Finney had questions and Ian had questions; he hung up and turned on the light. He could see his own reflection in the room's one window—adrift, legless, surrounded by smoke. Judah had used a toast Ian proposed—lifting his hand to the mirroring window, invoking the thick, deep-voiced ghost: "May you live all the days of your life."

"You've been cut out."

"Of what?"

"The will," Maggie told him. "You'd have gotten everything if only you'd arrived."

"When? For the funeral?"

"No—when he sent that letter. When he asked us both to come, six months ago."

This phone was white. He had called her collect from Detroit. His company, he told her, was the bus-and-truck road show for *Excalibur*; next month they would start a swing south. They had been in touch before, but now the will was filed.

"He so much wanted you to visit," Maggie said. "We both did. You'll get what Finney calls a handsome settlement."

"I'm sorry I couldn't make it to the service."

"We didn't expect you. Not really."

Ian stretched the telephone cord, then watched it spring back, coiling. "What letter?"

It was eight o'clock at night, the day after Judah's funeral. He was standing in the cloakroom of the theater bar. There was so long a silence that he thought they'd been cut off. Finally she said, "You didn't get it?"

"What?"

"The letter Finney sent."

"Not that I remember."

"Try to."

"No."

"I knew he was incompetent," said Maggie. "I never believed him dishonest."

The cloakroom attendant was dressed like a French maid—black mesh stockings and a short white skirt, high heels and a black bow. She was forty, however, and fat.

"Who?"

"Finney. Not your father."

"It doesn't matter," Ian said. "I might have opened it and thrown the thing away." The cloakroom attendant tapped at her watch. She raised her eyebrows, shook her head. "It makes no difference."

"Darling . . ."

"I've got to go now," Ian said. "Entertain the troops."

"Do keep in touch."

"I will," he promised and hung up. He did not call again.

Arriving at the Big House, therefore, he tells himself it's unplanned. He could have kept on driving, could make it up to Burlington or Montreal by nightfall, or any of the towns between: Rutland, Middlebury, Montpelier. He could find a friend or make a friend or buy a bed to lie in—but that would have been avoidance. Though he's managed to avoid this corner of

Vermont for years, he finds himself unwilling to tuck his tail under and run. Habits are for breaking, Judah said. And Ian knows the road; his two hundred forty horses know the way.

Yet the roads have altered. What had been dirt is tar now; where the pharmacy once stood is a McDonald's. They've put a highway through, and when he noses past what used to be the Parker place he sees a concrete overpass. There are cloverleafs for trucks; there's a pink haze in his rearview mirror that he assumes is sunset till he sees the sun off to the west. Shocked, he reconnoiters; the village is a township now, creating its own evening light; the Sherbrookes' thousand acres have been bordered by cement.

He drives the land's perimeter. He knows the access routes and is unreasoningly pleased to see them blocked. There are *No Trespass* and *Private Property* signs, and locked gates everywhere, there is a high stone wall for half a mile, then a four-strand barbed-wire fence. He stops the car on the edge of the road, gets out and locks it, and decides to enter the grounds of the Big House on foot. As his father might have done, he checks the tight-strung wire. Finding a rusty stretch with give to it, he holds the bottom strand down with his shoe, lifts the second strand up, and slides through. There is snow on the north-facing slope in front of him, but the earth is soft and wet. It is early April, and he smells things breathe and thaw. Someone has been spreading manure on what he calculates must be the Shed field to his right; the breeze comes from the east.

Ian leans against a silver birch and collects his breath. It's not that he's short-winded, but his belly's in his throat, there's more to this, he tells himself, than he bargained for. He'd been a city boy the last half of his life. Yet it's like swimming or riding, he thinks, once you've learned how to do it, you never forget. You grow stiff with disuse or lose the edge that practice gives, but you know the silver birch from beech, and recognize that oak tree there in front of you, at the edge of the stand of split-leaf maple. A freight train down by Eagle's Bridge gives four pulls on the whistle as it shunts across the roadbed; it's a sound that heralds bedtime, as it did when he was six.

So Ian sits. He finds a boulder to sit on and pulls his knees up and supports his elbows on his knees. He rests his chin on his hands. He faces the house a half mile away and summons up his education to do battle with the breath-stopping, summoning glow of it all. This is absurd, he tells himself: the Prodigal Returned. You can't go home again; home is where they have to take you in; what goes around comes around—it's every cliché in the book.

This does not work, however; he cannot make such fun or mockery of homecoming as to make it simple to go home. He sits wreathed to himself on a cold April night (the very picture of his mother in a man, Hattie used to say, but a chip off the old Sherbrooke block) and fights for breath as once when he had asthma, and inhales for the count of eight and holds. He sits there for some time.

"Don't go."

"We're going." Maggie had taken his hand.

"Don't."

"You come too, Judah. Or visit us at least."

"No."

"Please . . ."

"Leave and you take yourself with you," his father said. "Go, but don't ever come back." Judah, not quite pleading, would plead for his young wife's attention, and she gave him that but never what he truly asked for, never let herself be bound by what Hattie called tight marriage ties and she a hangman's noose. Though Ian had not understood the terms of the discussion, he heard the words and saw them argue and knew it was more than a matter of language. Their argument had been impersonal, nearly— as if they liked each other well enough, loved each other always, but stood up for ways of being that could not be wed.

Maggie was flirtatious, Judah stern; she was gay where his father was grim. Although they owned the largest house and holdings in their corner of Vermont, her vanity had been to do without possessions. He was tight-fisted and she open-handed; he was white-haired and Maggie a blonde. She took pleasure in cities her husband abhorred, the art and music he derided or refused to discuss. When telling Ian about Woodstock or "the summer of love" or the civil rights movement, for example, she had been sympathetic. Judah's politics, his wife declared, were to the right of Attila the Hun; he had never met a piece of legislation he believed was worth the fuss.

But she believed the government could prove a force for social good, and was worth respecting. Judah, a New Englander, voted for Republicans; she was a Democrat. Ian heard workmen in the fields or coming out of bars or barns tell jokes about old Sherbrooke's young bare-naked wife. He merely had to show himself to silence their backslapping hilarity, but this happened often. Maggie admired those who shared things, while her husband was retentive; she had hoped to travel; he to stay at home. She had been beauty incarnate, and they gossiped in the town.

Yet there is much he does not, cannot understand—how leaving and loving, for instance, are two sides of the one coin. For Maggie came back in the end. A year ago exactly she had returned to the Big House and settled in again. She who proposed a different kind of sharing had shared in her husband's last months. They had lived apart for seven years, but hadn't once mentioned divorce. Then Judah bought her back. If Ian has not been what others would call dutiful, it is in part because his mother occupies the place she hauled him from and made him think of as a golden prison-cage.

He wonders why she came. Was it for safety only, for some shibboleth of duty and the Golden Rule, or to collect what Judah put up for grabs? He wonders why he's come. He tells himself reunion is not always reconciliation, and it's as good a place as any to return to. He's not estranged, he tells himself; they're simply out of touch. They need to catch up on old times.

A hoot owl flies across the clearing, so close that he can feel the susurration of air beneath its wings. "Polly want a cracker?" she had said to him on Sutton Place. "No matter how you play it, that's the song we sang. You can tie a bunch of ribbons on; it's still a gilded cage."

So Ian is nobody's son. He's learned the lessons of withdrawal better than his teacher, been rootless while Maggie returned to take root. He's held no job that counted, been in no city or country he'd come to call home, lived with no one he'd nurse through their six final months. He is twenty-six years old, a sometime stage manager and bit-part actor with a private income. Sometimes he plays backup bass. Once he wore a moustache and three times sported a beard; once he shaved his skull entirely and walked the Cordilleras for a month.

He had attended Exeter, then Harvard. He wrote a freshman essay on *The Masses* and the men who founded it. He admired what he learned about Floyd Dell, Max Eastman, John Reed, and Lincoln Steffens; he wanted to be big and bluff, to travel and write poetry and articles that shake the world. It was 1969. So after two years at Harvard he spent two years being—as he called it then—political. He knew he was riding the ebb of a tide, on a bandwagon that had slowed down. Yet Ian joined a *dojo* and trained himself in unarmed combat and the use and maintenance of guns. He renounced his piano playing as a mark of caste. He spent those hours that he once would spend at music on the streets instead. In Texarkana, however, he saw bodies in the wreckage of a fire-bombed Mercury Monterey coupe and became a pacifist. He returned to Adams House, was graduated in 1973 cum laude in government, and hit the road in earnest for four years.

The hoot owl shifts and settles, opposite. It is deep dark now; Ian stands up. He will rehearse his history for the women in the house; he has been to several continents since he saw them last. He knows Fats Waller's repertoire and a good deal of Shakespeare by heart. He has had trouble with his teeth and finds it harder now to kick the habit of cigarettes than, two years previously, he found it to kick cocaine. "You have an addictive personality," one woman said to him once. Her name was— Ian lifts his arms and stretches, remembering—Alison Clark. She was a social worker who used jargon when he angered her or failed to stay the night or praise her crabmeat salad. "You've got a character disorder, did you know that? Your surround just doesn't make it, baby; you're not a person to trust."

He starts down the hill to the house.

"You're spoiling him."

"No."

"Yes, you are. You've got him tied so tight to you he'll strangle on those apron strings."

"You're wrong, Judah."

"Prove it."

"It isn't a thing you can prove. There's no such thing as too much love; it isn't how children get spoiled."

So then they'd squabble over their son; he'd furnish their argument's text. He'd be the leverage they used in the seesaw bickering that made their separation a relief. Yet if Maggie spoke harshly to her husband and bitterly about him, she tolerated no dispraise from others and no single nagging syllable when in that separation Ian had attempted to console her by attacking Judah. She had the right, she seemed to say, to quarrel with her life's one mate; he'd earned no equivalent right. If he had nothing kind to say, she'd rather hear nothing at all.

Therefore silence was their rule, and Ian held his tongue. On the question of spoilage, for instance, he learned that there are many ways to spoil a broth. You can add too little seasoning, too much, or have too many cooks. You can have too thick or thin a stock and she—who was a first-rate cook—had shown him the trouble with watering down.

The spruce tree Judah planted in honor of his birth would have been taller than he as an infant; then Ian remembers looking down on it from the height of his young vantage; now it's grown at least a foot for every year of his life. So the tree that had seemed small is tall, and not yet fully grown. The poplars he is walking past had seemed to scrape the sky. They were enormous, heaven-aspiring, the biggest four trees on the place. The house that huddles beneath him grows larger as he nears. His grandfather's grandfather built it—Daniel "Peacock" Sherbrooke—arranging its grandiose proportions all the way from California in letters sent by sea mail and the railroad he helped to complete.

It is part of Ian's legacy. He knows the terms of Peacock's injunctions by heart. The magnate, too, had aspirations to heaven, but he praised the Lord in a complicated manner, passing ammunition to the envious and letting them take potshots at the inordinate house. Four stories high, surmounted by a cupola, with a servant's wing that once held thirty and outbuildings that housed thirty more, "Peacock's Palace" used up one whole quarry's seasonal production of black roofing slate and—so the legend had it—all of Woodford Mountain's hardwood for its paneling and floors. There are fourteen fireplaces, marble walkways, and a mile-long circuit that surrounds the buildings of the compound—the carriage barn and hay and cow barns and sugaring house and stables and the Toy House where his father used to sit.

Peacock Sherbrooke, who ordained all this, died on the day he came home. Like some latter-day commercial Moses who speculated on the promised land and lived to see it reached, built, tenanted—but not by him—he expired at the entrance gate in 1869. He had had pneumonia on the journey east. But in some fashion Ian only partway comprehends, his own father completed Peacock's venture by never venturing forth. Judah's was a holding action, and it held. The thousand acres he'd inherited remained the farmland that it first had been, though ringed with superhighways and gas stations and motels. He threatened those who left the house—even his wife and son—with expulsion, extirpation, the biblical language of exile. He treated the mile circuit as a magic circle, and those who went beyond it had to do so without his protection.

So Ian put it all behind him when he left. His mother had been family enough. New York City had been world enough, and then there was the world to see and inward voyages to take with the help of his white powder. In college, he met classmates with names that were grander than

Sherbrooke and houses that made his seem small. He contrived a kind of willed forgetfulness, and soon that contrivance was fact.

"Ian Sherbrooke, please."
    "Who's calling?"
    "Hello? Is this Mr. Sherbrooke?"
    "He's not here."
    "Would you know where we might reach him?"
    "No."
    "Might we leave a message, then?"
    "Okay. Shoot."
    "Would you tell him Samson Finney's office—he's got the number—is trying to contact him? And we'd be grateful if he'd call."
    "How do you spell it?"
    "Finney?"
    "Yes."
    "*F* as in Frank, *i,* double *n* as in nobody, *e, y.* Finney."
    "I'll do that," Ian said.

There is a fire in the library; he sees it as he nears. The room flickers at him, beckoning; there are open drapes. The Big House has a porch that runs the length of its southern and western exposures; he climbs the side steps lightly; still, they creak. He edges past the wicker rockers—set out already in April, he notes, so there must have been a thaw and the snowfall would have been recent, or perhaps they're careless now and leave furniture out all year long. Ian steps past the green plush glider. He stands by the library window, in the shadow of the drapes.
    Hattie is knitting. He has not seen her in years. She has a skein of blue wool at her side and a shape on her lap that enlarges—something, he thinks, like a shawl. She sits ten feet away, beneath a reading lamp, her

glasses on a chain around her neck; she who once seemed large to him has shrunk. His aunt purses her lips in concentration, making motions with her mouth that correspond to her fingers' knitting motion, and the way she works suggests a frail rigidity.

He moves; she shifts accordingly, and he wonders is this what they mean by a picture window? He scans the room; he thinks how many times how many in his family had no doubt done such staring from the reaches of the porch. He sees a second pair of legs and hands in the leather chair that Judah used—a block chair with a headrest: umber, huge.

The chair is canted sideways from him, and the woman within does not stir. He wonders how he knows the hands and feet are female—since she wears no nail polish, is wearing pants and boots. He asks himself why it is so certainly his mother in the chair. Then she bends forward, firelit, as if in instinctual response, and he asks himself why ever he needed to ask. She is fifty-two years old. He is half that age, has been around the world and with more women than he can count or name; she is beyond compare. Hattie says something, her lips moving now in counterpoint to the motion of her yellow needles and blue wool. And Maggie, bending forward to answer, offers her hair and profile and arms as if for Ian's inspection. He starts for the Big House door.

II

"May I come in?" he asks.

"Who is it?"

He has opened the door; now he knocks.

"Just a minute," Maggie calls.

"Who is it?" Hattie asks again.

"It's me."

"Who's me?"

"Ian."

Hattie's voice is querulous. "Speak up! We can't see you in the dark."

"Ian Sherbrooke," Ian says.

His mother is beside him. "Darling! Welcome home!"

She is nearly his height. He kisses her on both cheeks, in the European fashion.

"Are you all right?" she asks.

"Fine, I'm fine. How are you doing?"

"It's so good to *see* you. Such a surprise."

"I just got east . . ." He trails off, irresolute. They are like conspirators, he thinks, whispering in the hallway.

Hattie approaches. "I never . . ."

"How are you?"

"I never in all my born days."

As she limps toward him, he removes himself from Maggie and steps forward to embrace his aunt. She still holds the knitting needles, and wool unravels behind her.

"Ian Sherbrooke! You rascal!"

He bends to kiss her also; she smells of caraway. The powder on her cheek adheres to his lips thickly.

"What a surprise!" Hattie says. "Margaret, turn that light on. Let's get a proper look at him."

The chandelier ignites. He remembers when it held candles, not bulbs. The hall clock strikes resoundingly: eight.

"You've eaten?" Maggie asks.

"Yes."

"It's not true," says Hattie. "He could down a piece of pie, I'll bet. Look how skinny you've gotten . . ."

"I'd have room for that."

"Pumpkin," Hattie crows. "You know it's just about a miracle you're here. We do have pumpkin pie. I never take a bite but I remember how you used to take three helpings and then look around and see who hadn't finished theirs. Just yesterday, I guess it was, I said to Helen Bingham they don't sell pumpkin worth buying anymore. You remember when we used to keep them on the porch? When you got so scared of jack-o'-lanterns we used to have to blow the candles out? Maggie, go get him a piece."

"Not just now. Let me look at him."

Yet Hattie is insistent, garrulous. "He's *starving*, you can see his ribs. He ought to have a piece of pie. I'll get it; you'd cut it too small. Coffee?"

"No, thank you. I've had some," he lies.

"Doesn't do to drink too much of that. Not after lunchtime, anyways. I never take a cup but Sanka now. They tell you it doesn't make a difference, but it does. You're right. A piece of pumpkin pie, a nice cold glass of milk.

So Hattie bustles out, and they have a minute alone.

"Hello."

"Don't mind her, darling, she's just so excited to see you. I haven't seen her skip like that in months. You'll have to eat the pie."

"I'll manage," Ian says.

Now there is silence between them. He studies his mother's face. The chandelier is less generous to her than was the firelight, or his previous distance; she does show the traces of age. There is a network of lines at her eyes. The centers of them—that he'd always thought of as blue lakes, so clear she'd see him in Kabul, or when he'd had hepatitis those months in Tunis—have leached away. The bones of her nose are pronounced; the cheekbones he's inherited are bound less tightly in their skin. It is as if the whole flesh-wrapping has gone slack, gotten weary; Maggie stands less straight. She bulks a little at the waist. She appears to be supporting something almost alien by the set of her bent knees.

"Silver threads among the gray."

"The gold," he offers, gallant.

"Gray." She takes his inspection with grace. "It doesn't bother me, you know. It's not important."

"Beauty?"

"That too," she says. "It loses its importance. A winter in this climate and you forget about beauty."

"So what do you remember?"

"The hospital telephone number. The oil burner emergency number. The way to turn your wheel when skidding; the school bus route along the roads, so you know which ones get plowed."

He is compelled; he spreads his hands. "How did Judah die?"

"Not now," she says. "I'll tell you later. Hattie will be back in just a minute."

"Of a long illness; of a brief illness; suddenly," he says.

254

"Excuse me?"

"That's what they do in the newspaper files. You fill in the appropriate blank; you only have to check the box."

She turns from him and enters the library.

"I'm sorry." Ian follows her. "I didn't mean to upset you. I know I'm sounding stupid, but it's—well, it's funny to be back."

"Funny strange or funny ha-ha?" This had been his childhood distinction.

"Both. A friend of mine works for a newspaper. Writing obituaries. They have boxes for at home, in such-and-such a hospital, or where the accident took place."

"Let's change the subject," Maggie says.

"All right."

"It isn't much more pleasant than the topic of my beauty."

"I'm sorry," he says again.

"Don't be. You have the right to ask. It's only that I thought you'd forfeited your membership."

"In what?"

"We have a club." She turns to him. Her eyes have lost nothing, are dry. "It's called the family. You have to pay up on your membership dues. Then they send you proxy votes, newsletters every two or three weeks, requests for your opinion every month. Subscription blanks, circulars, everything . . . Oh, I know it's not a membership that anyone can forfeit, not the sort of club we let you quit." She drains the glass of water on the table by her chair. "But you did a better job of it than I ever managed, darling, you've been what we call 'inactive.' An 'Associate Member,' maybe, and it's just a little much to hear you at the annual meeting—so full of questions all of a sudden, so anxious to know what you might have been asking me all winter long. It's not funny ha-ha. It's strange."

Hattie returns. She carries a thick slice of pie, a bowl of cream, and a glass of milk. She has a napkin rolled in what he knows will be his napkin ring. The silver platter has handles in the shape of fruit that curve to form an S.

"You eat this. You look half starved," she says. "Pecan, I guess it was. Your favorite."

"Maybe he'd prefer a drink."

"Not till he's taken nourishment. Not till you've eaten every little bit of this here pie. And then we'll see," Hattie offers. "We might just celebrate."

She loves him; he knows that. She took up his education when Maggie was away and Judah in the fields, or sullen; she read him bedtime stories while they argued down the hall. Her voice would go strident with emphasis, Ian remembers—but never quite cover the din in their room or the following fierce silence. She had tried to fill the breach his parents made in love. Judah said, "You watch it, boy, you're buying her notions whole hog now. But you're buying a pig in a poke."

First the houses down the hill were outsize castles that he couldn't run around. There were neighbor moats and enemy ambushes, and woods and deserts and fortified walls all through the town. But then Hattie taught him comparative size: they were none of them big as the Big House, and his was the top of the heap.

His mother never noticed, even, that those other houses existed; he'd tell her he was going to the Frasers or the Andersons or Sloans, and she'd say, that's nice, dear, where do they live; that's good, do you need a ride? Later he knew it her leveler's instinct, that no one made her smile or notice if she didn't find them worth it, and Maggie's sense of worth was not the world's. But back then Ian had believed it meant what Hattie meant instead, that we're too fine to notice; our family was sitting here when theirs came up in wagons, and they took their shoes off when they came into our parlors, and it was a shoe that still fit.

So then the hill's houses looked small. Then he only noticed they had fewer rooms than his, and his property consisted of a thousand acres, which was hundreds of times more acres than any other house. He was, his aunt assured him—not quite saying it aloud—a prince. He let himself out of the gate like a drawbridge, and the ditch was protected by sharks; no one would dare approach his castle without an invitation, and he drifted down the hill to school like a general making the rounds.

Hattie understood all this and seemed content—seemed to want him, Judah joked, for the youngest member of the D.A.R. But Maggie was a careless mother; occupied with other things, she scarcely would notice if Ian wore socks, and let him wear his Levi's till the seams and knees were ripped. So Hattie made certain his clothes had been pressed, his buttons on, and that he was awake in time for Sunday school. She made sure the cooks and housemaids wore proper uniforms and did not smoke or swear. When he started in to smoke and be raucous and fight and whistle and swear, she said, "Boys will be boys."

Judah held him by the hand. His father's hand was huge, enfolding, and it manacled his wrist. Ian did not dare pull back, nor haul so hard in opposition that his bones would give—but neither did he help. The roof was steep. Slate has to have a certain pitch, Judah explained. Otherwise the snow gets in and then it melts and freezes and you'll lose a roof in just one winter, since when water freezes it expands. Take a look at ice cubes; fill the tray to almost full and by the time it's frozen the ice will be over the top.

So Ian clambered heavily after his surefooted father; Judah leaned sideways against the roof's pitch; Ian crouched. His sneakers slipped. They were on the Toy House roof but not so high you couldn't jump, since the Toy House was a replica of the Big House, its cupola and windows cut to scale. That winter there had been leaks. There were fragments and sections of slate on the ground. This was something you attended to before it got away.

"Daddy."

"What?"

"Did you ever fall?"

"From where?"

"From here?"

"Not that I remember. But it's like horses; you got to fall so often you learn not to care, you can't remember even when you took the tumble."

"Would it hurt?"

"Depends. You bend your knees; you tuck and roll; let your body be a spring. No point in fighting it; you'd telescope your legs."

"From how high?"

"Any distance if you do it wrong. From falling down a step."

"Thirty-two feet per second," Ian offered. He shut his eyes. He looked up; he had learned the speed of free fall and the force of gravity that week.

"You should have seen," said Judah, "Billy Eakins drunk and falling. Believe you me, he did so from a sight higher than this, though he slowed up once or twice bumping his way down. Well, we left him lying there until he slept it off."

Ian pondered the story. Did it mean a drunk should climb on roofs, or you'd best be a drunkard to fall? Judah took replacement slates from the pile on the scaffold; he demonstrated how to nail them neither too tight nor too loose.

"Lean back. Get yourself some purchase."

"How?"

"If you're going to hold on with both hands, boy, what'll you do with the hammer? You'll fall for certain like that."

"No."

"You'll want some space to breathe," said Judah, and he took Ian's hand again and forced him out over the roof. Now Ian knows it wasn't force, it was a calculated angle and small risk, but then—in the dizzying rush of it all, in the instant that he dropped his hammer and watched it bounce on the paving below—he felt himself a lamb in eagle's claws. The eagle has a wingspan larger than the lamb; it can pick its victim up and, great talons curved in the already-broken neck, flap to some unattainable eyrie and settle there to feed. Eagles drowned, he'd read, rather than give up the salmon they'd caught; they struck terror in the hearts of herds with just their shadow overhead. So Ian bit and fought for air till Judah said, "Okay. All right. I just wanted to show you it's nothing to be scared of."

Then he stood upright again, feet planted square on the scaffolding board, one rung higher than his father and therefore the same height. And with absolute assurance, having ascertained the angle—thirty-two feet per second meaning it would take him maybe three quarters of a second if he chose to land feet first, then tuck and roll, providing he had legs to tuck and arms to roll and shoulders that would take the weight— he jumped.

"So tell us where you've been?" Hattie asks.

"How did you get here?" asks Maggie.

"I could use a maraschino cherry now," his aunt says, as if offhand.

"Let's celebrate." Maggie winks at Ian, doles out two.

The pink stain spreads across the china plate. Hattie picks up the cherry between her thumb and middle finger, letting it drip. "Artificial coloring."

Then, while Ian picks and pours from decanters on the sideboard, his aunt describes her ills. It is a catalog of ailments—fear of cataracts, blood pressure way, way up. She can't see in the dark these days, and the house is dark. She limps; she doesn't sleep; she's frightened of sleepwalking and the stairwell; if she ever has to get on too much medication, she appoints him, Ian, a committee of one to take it away. She wouldn't want to go the way some members of their family have gone.

"What do you mean by that?" Maggie asks.

"You know."

"No. What?"

"You know perfectly well what I mean. And who," says Hattie, purse-lipped, contentious, and he wonders has he caused this fight or do they jockey for position always anyhow.

"Not perfectly well, no. You flatter yourself. Tell Ian. Do you mean the way that Judah died?"

"He went as he was bound to go," the old woman says. "I'm not saying that."

"What *are* you saying then? Implying?"

"Ladies!" Ian says. "I thought this was a celebration."

"Yes."

"But . . ."

He has his back to the fireplace now. He plants his feet in what he also knows had been his father's stance. He raises his full glass to each of the women in turn, then drinks to the discordant interval between them. "Let's celebrate," he says.

He is twenty-six years old by now and not a child; if only by default, Ian tells himself, he is the man of the house. Yet he finds himself thinking of onions where you peel and peel and find no core; just layers of transparency, a shapeliness adhering to itself. He feels that way. He tries to explain this to his mother, telling her how actors take on borrowed personality, and it's a habit for bad actors also—an accent, posture, a gesture that falls short of true. Or take dubbers, Ian says: the better you are, the less someone hears you; the perfect dubbing job is something that nobody knows has been done. You work till you're not noticed; notice the lighting designer, and he's failed to do his job.

"All right," she says. "I grant you."

Mummery: it's what he used to call his work—the half-derisive, half-defensive way he'd termed what working men call make-believe and not a profession at all. But memorization and ranting and mimicry are outworn notions, he explains. When the world stopped being a stage, it became a three-ring circus, and he'd turned to Living Theater, Open Theater, theater in the streets. Only that too faded, he still had to organize not improvise road tours and do the advance work and paper the house. If the Grand Lama of Tibet were suddenly to visit us, he tells his mother, you'd be putting on the dog. His Worshipful Holiness would still be hunting contributions for the cause, and there'd be someone on ahead to slap up handbills and do the radio spots.

"We don't keep dogs," says Hattie. "Not any longer. There's nobody to exercise them."

He has not planned to stay, Ian says, but has nowhere urgent to go to; he's, as they say, "between jobs."

"Just try and leave," says Maggie. "Now that we've got you."

"Where we want you," his aunt joins in, and he feels them fashioning alliance as once they might have done with Judah in the room. The bickering is over, anyhow; he smiles. He sees himself in the mirror with gilt Cupids, and pulls at his right ear. "If that's how you feel about it . . ."

"Yes," Maggie says. "We do."

"We most certainly do. Didn't I tell you, Margaret? Wasn't I right for once?"

"Um-mn."

Hattie flushes with the pleasure of her verified prediction. "I told you so. I always was certain you'd come on back home."

He picks up the fireplace brush. "You know how it feels when the plane drops too fast? Or the elevator stops climbing, or you thought there was an extra stair and you make adjustments, brace for it? Except there isn't anything." The bristles are black. He turns to Maggie. "No extra step, I mean. That's what I feel all the time." He yawns. His palms are wet.

Then Maggie advances toward him. Her face is the pattern of comfort. "Poor darling. You're tired."

He yields his glib assurance and his inward mockery: *whatever is coming must come.* He falls upon her neck and whispers, "Out on my feet."

"Glad we got you," Hattie says.

"I'm glad to be back," Ian says.

III

In the days that follow, however, he does notice change. Where first he found things constant and his recollection consistent with the aspect of the place, he soon observes how much has been abandoned. Remembrance is a trick time plays; what Ian sees as shabby he had thought of as ornate. His bed creaks. It sinks on its springs in the center, folding the mattress around him so there is no extra space. The plaster pineapples on the ceiling look bulbous; the marble fireplace-facing has cracked. Last year's oak leaves litter the path; the flower beds are choked. His mother is weary, neglectful. She takes no pleasure in the maintenance that had been his father's passion, hires no one to keep the house up. He asks her why they have no help and she says they have a cleaning woman, Mrs. Russell, every Thursday, and between times she and Hattie rinse their dishes, make their beds, and don't kick up all that much dust.

The gutters have sprung leaks. He watches the downspout in the first hard rain; it is clogged. The parquet has splintered; the carpets seem threadbare; the chandelier that cast its glow upon their first encounter has six broken bulbs. He hunts the reason all this worries him. It isn't that he's used to luxury the house no longer represents; even run-down and in desuetude, it's much more elegant than where he's been living these years. Neither is it that he's come back home to see the myth debunked; the house is exactly the cavern and canyon, a grandeur clogged with bric-a-brac that Ian left behind. Nor, since the days he could not remember of his infant brother's death, had there ever been much entertaining in the halls.

He is not disconcerted by the silence of the place. Its pretension does not shock him, or its shabbiness. He fears no daylight ghost. Rather, some picture intervenes—some notion of the legacy this structure had been built to serve. One night, attempting sleep, he remembers what they called the Rana palaces of Kathmandu. Enormous private houses—on a scale that dwarfed the Big House as the Big House dwarfed the Toy House—they had bedrooms for seventy wives. The Rana palaces had been converted to the Nepalese government buildings and hospitals and hotels. He had been invited to dinner in one of them once; the walls had fat-armed archers aiming their arrows at breasts. The ceilings were murals of sunset and clouds; the peak of Saga-Marta was a pottery motif. The ambition of the Rana nobles was to build the largest private houses in the world. In this they had succeeded, yet their legatees were clerks.

Maggie has changed. He pretends, for the first days, that all is as it was. She asks him to play music for her and he does so, clumsily, on the upright piano in the solarium. There had been a Steinway Grand; then that piano was destroyed and Judah bought a player piano to replace it. He tells her that his instrument, the few times that he's played these years, has been the bass. She lies in a chaise longue, eyes shut, face drawn. He cannot play the pieces she requests. He plays Jelly Roll Morton, and ten minutes of Art Tatum. Her silence is restless, resistant.

"What's the matter?" Ian asks.

"Nothing."

"I can stop, if this isn't what you want to hear. Or how you want to hear it."

"No."

He pulls the squared lid out, then down. "Tell me," he urges.

"I would if I could," Maggie says. "If there were anything simple to tell."
She shuts her eyes and turns from him; sun stripes the flesh of her arms.

"Is it too hot for you?" he asks.

"The model son."

"We do what we can," he acknowledges, making it a joke.

"You're so goddamn solicitous," she says. "Did you know that? Your father dies; for six months we don't hear one single syllable and suddenly it's
'Mother, are you warm enough; could I adjust the Venetian blinds; may I
fluff up your pillow?' It's surprising, Ian, it takes some getting used to . . ."

"I'm sorry," he offers.

"You're not. You're so proud of yourself you're bursting. Whatever else
you're thinking, I'm not an invalid."

"No." He places both feet on the pedals and pretends they belong to a car,
not a piano. He accelerates straight through the gearbox, reaching fourth.

"I'm sorry," Maggie says. "I didn't mean to snap at you. It's just I'm not
used to attention. I've forgotten what it means to answer a question like
'What are you thinking?' Or 'What do you want to do today; which kind
of music would you prefer to hear?'"

"It can't be all that bad," he says.

"It isn't now. It can be, though. It was."

Ian wishes manhood were a line to draw. He has a birth certificate and
passport to prove he's no longer a child. The definitions vary—he stiffens
his pectorals, flexes his thighs—but by most definitions he's a man. He has
lost one parent and lived alone for years; they call him "Sir" in restaurants.
Friends get divorced or die.

Yet there's been no rite of passage, no moment when things changed.
Little by little he grew up, thickened out; he repeated jokes, and then the
jokes were stories of his own receding past. He had seemed to suck in
worldliness at Maggie's side, they called him "little man," since he was

Judah Sherbrooke's boy. He wishes there had been some sort of test: something to prove that manhood was a line to toe, then cross.

He knows a man who made six million dollars by the age of thirty. He'd invested carefully, then gambled on coffee futures, and both the reticence and recklessness paid off. The man had a beautiful wife and two fine children, and purchased an apartment on Central Park South. One day he was riding in the park; his horse shied, and he fell and hit his head on a rock. From that moment on, he had been an infant. They thought the concussion might pass; they thought perhaps it was amnesia or a state of nervous shock. But he wept when left alone, wept from fear at the doctor's arrival into the room where they kept him, in a private hospital north of White Plains. His wife was loyal and hopeful and brave; she took a small apartment in the suburbs, so as to be near him for her daily visit.

Ian drove there with her once. This had been going on, Muriel told him, for twenty-three months; she was at the end of her rope. They visited her husband's ward together; his room had bright bay windows and a picture of Roy Rogers taped to the side of the color TV.

The occasion made no sense. The man's face was impossibly handsome still, the jaw smooth-shaven, eyes keen. Yet they showed no hint or flicker of interest in Ian, and, largely, distrust of his wife. All the patient could manage, in the stiff intervals of conversation (how have you been and how are things going, Ian asked, do you remember me; I'm the one who bobbled that grounder at shortstop when you were playing second, remember; I'm the one who dropped spaghetti sauce all over that flower arrangement), was "Peeps. Peeps. I need to make a peeps."

"You know what they say," said Muriel, departing. " 'What the Lord giveth He taketh.' Can you imagine that? Some people find comfort in thinking that way. I wish *I* could." She squeezed his hand. "Dear Christ, how I wish I just could!"

So Ian has been busy stripping skins. He picks at the flesh of his feet. He feels that he can slough off skin like garments, and that accent makes the man. He had worn an actor's motley till he recognized true talent in an actor playing Iago while he stood by hefting spears. He had professed

265

romantic passion till he found out passion's spasm was an act of discipline, like learning how to land a jab or sink a left-hand hook shot fading away from the net. What do you do, he asks himself, when the dragon gives up and turns tail? There's a padded lair it lives in and the armchair seems to fit; there's whiskey waiting in decanters, a fire set and banked back just the way you like it, and the maiden you've been asked to rescue seems to be enjoying her predicament. The tournament director has taken his knights and split south.

One morning, after breakfast, he explores the carriage barn. The storage room has sliding doors, and he puts his shoulder to them, since they stick and creak. Inside, it is dark. Ian shivers in the sudden gloom and rolls down the sleeves of his shirt. The air is stale and wet. There is a jumble of carriages and sleighs. He peers into the dusty dark, wondering how it could have happened that he'd been at home these weeks and forgotten or neglected what had been his treasure cave when young. This was his secret place. It is where he ran to hide or dream, pretending to be a nobleman or highway-man or just his great-great-grandfather, driving the team four-in-hand.

The brass has dulled. The leather has gone moldy, and cobwebs festoon the windows of the winter coach. The wood of the sleighs feels wet to the touch, and Ian finds a bird's nest on the high seat where he perched. Swal-lows flit away from him, frantic, enraged, and he hears the quick startled flurry of mice. Still, he takes comfort in these stacked, packed remnants as a stay against confusion: in the dark bottom of the carriage barn things are as they had been.

The north wall of the space is stacked with steamer trunks. He had pried them open when young, or worked the padlocks free. They seldom had been locked, but the moment he opened the trunks was full of expectation and delight. He had come to know their contents over time. And later on he came to think of that expectant lifting, that thrill of confirmation when he pulled open the trunk lid, as some sort of cognate to sex. He loves the act's preliminaries—the unbuttoning, opening out. There is an oxcart and plow. There are the blades of a windmill Judah had planned to repair. He climbs inside a curricle and sits on the stiff red leather where when he was twelve years old he used to picture Ellen Portis naked beside him, whispering endearments.

She left the village first, to go to boarding school. The school was in Concord, Massachusetts, and once he drove to Boston with his mother and they passed a sign for Concord and he thought of Ellen, free, a foreigner. They visited the State House and the ships in Boston harbor, and his mother introduced him to her cousin Jack. "He's a distant cousin," Maggie said. "So you won't remember him, probably. We'll just drop by for a minute."

Jack lived on Beacon Hill, where the sledding was terrific as soon as the cobbles got iced. In the wintertime, Jack said, there isn't any hill in Massachusetts that can beat out Beacon Hill. They call it that, he said to Ian, because it's where we hoisted beacons when the redcoats came a'calling; when Johnny Redcoat came to town this was the place we saw it from, and signaled Paul Revere.

So Paul Revere had saddled up and ridden off to Lexington and Concord, where Ellen Portis went to instead of the sixth grade. She would learn Latin there. She returned, tormenting him with Latin and Pig Latin and stories of the way they all smoked cigarettes in Concord, just behind the cannon, after dark. Later she returned with friends and flounced her way toward him, giggling; later still her face got splotchy and sallow and Ian also left. So she never sat beside him on the red leather chair.

As Hattie had predicted, he does become the town's prize. They welcome Ian at parties as if he's come back from war. When he mentions Portugal or Bali or France they make him feel like Marco Polo—an intrepid trader returned to share the spoils. He tells the truth or makes up tales and it makes no difference; as Sherbrooke's son he is eligible everywhere, a catch.

"Watch out that they don't eat you up," Maggie warns. "They'll serve you up in little chunks. In cream sauce."

"How's that?" Hattie inquires, approaching.

"I'm telling him to take it easy. He doesn't want to wear out his welcome."

"Nonsense. People are glad."

"About what?" Ian asks.

"That you're back. That someone's here who's been away but decided to return. You're showing your family feeling; you're putting down roots, Ida says."

"Well, Sally Conover is pleased to have a dinner partner anyhow. We can't really blame her," says Maggie.

Hattie sniffs. "She must just thank her lucky stars that Ian's come to town."

"Whoa," Ian says. "Hold your horses. May I remind you, ladies, we haven't even met?"

Maggie refuses invitations that ask her to accompany her son. After his return, however, he finds her in the kitchen, waiting up. She prepares warm milk and honey for him, and they talk. He tells her who was there and what they had been wearing and does imitations of the hostess till his mother laughs. She has the best of both possible worlds, Maggie declares; she has the pleasure of the parties, but doesn't have to sit there being bored.

He goes to dinner at the Conovers that Saturday. Ida Conover calls Hattie and suggests that Ian come; her grand-niece Sally has offered to cook supper and it'll be potluck for all of them, so why not Ian too? At the last minute, however, Hattie pleads a stomach cramp and sends him off alone. He finds the house and rings the bell and waits in the entryway, stamping. The girl who answers is tall. She wears a blue jumpsuit with a red line where the zipper runs, and has dark brown hair. She greets him with a sense of prearranged alliance, as if they are not strangers but long-established friends. Her hand is cold. "A crazy climate, isn't it?" she asks. Her eyes are brown, lips full. She wears three strands of pearls; the pearls are varicolored and irregular.

Miles Fisk arrives next. "Our babysitter's late. The wife will be along shortly." He nods at Ian. "You must be Sherbrooke. Welcome."

"Thank you."

"Fisk's my name," he says. "Miles. It means soldier, not how far you travel."

"What are you drinking?" Sally asks.

"Whatever's on offer. But lots of it." Miles winks. He wears rimless glasses and a tan corduroy vest.

"Ian." She touches his sleeve. "Would you do the honors, please? The bar is in the pantry."

"What's whatever?" Ian asks.

"Bourbon. Wild Turkey by preference. Water and no ice, okay? Just a splash."

"Of water, or bourbon?"

"The man's got a sense of humor," Miles announces. "Sally, my congratulations. Just a splash of water, please."

In the pantry, she detains him. "Don't mind Miles. He's such a tease. Being the local editor . . ." Sally touches his tie. "And promise me two things."

Ian measures, pours.

"First"—she drops her voice—"that you won't hold all this against me."

He looks at her. "All right."

"Promise?"

"Yes."

"And there's a second thing." She runs her tongue around her lips, then smiles at him. "That you won't look at his wife."

Samson Finney arrives. His neck has thickened, and his eyes have glazed. His hair has gone; there is hair in his nostrils and ears. He takes Ian's hand and pumps it, saying "My boy" several times.

"Mr. Finney," Ian asks, "are you still drinking whiskey?"

"What a memory! The answer is affirmative!" He rumbles over to Elizabeth Conover's chair. A big, bluff man wearing suspenders, he seems Judah's image, though dim. They talk about the weather, the mobile home zoning ordinance, the incidence of swine flu since Legionnaire's Disease.

Jeanne Fisk enters the living room, and Ian takes her coat. She calls to her husband, "Betty Boop was doing homework. I couldn't blame her, really; that's why she came late. Or the excuse she gave . . ."

"What may I get you?" Ian asks.

"It doesn't matter. Red wine, if you have it. Thanks."

"How *are* the children?" Finney asks.

"Fine. Kathryn lost her bicuspid. I was the tooth fairy and I gave her a whole dollar—inflation, you see. I remember being pleased if the tooth fairy forked over a quarter."

Sally appears with cheese. It has been cut into bite sizes, and toothpicks protrude from the segments like quills. "Do help yourselves."

"She's so proud," Jeanne Fisk continues, "she calls it her 'gap.' She keeps pointing to the space and saying, 'See my gap!'"

"And—what's the other one's name?" Finney asks. "Amy?"

"Yes, jealous enough to knock her own teeth out. Or tie them to a doorknob."

At dinner, Sally keeps him by her right-hand side and tells him her own story. She'd lived in Paris for two years, taking whatever jobs were on offer, hoping to break into films. But that meant teaching English to the children of the upwardly mobile; it meant being a gardener's assistant in the gardens of the rich. Her boss, she says to Ian, was a male model who pulled only the fanciest weeds in Passy; they'd be invited in to cocktails, often as not, and she'd take off her gardener's smock and pretend to be at home. It was one way to practice French and also earn your keep.

Then after that she'd gotten bit parts riding in the movies; she'd been a stand-in for a starlet ill at ease with horses, and she rode a roan mare six straight days in the mist in the Bois de Boulogne. The movie was never released. They laugh about this, comparing notes, and Ian says that by and large she'd done better in the world of entertainment than had he. Still, Sally says, you understand what made me want to do it, what made me need a life like that. I understand, he says.

They compliment the lamb. Then Finney toasts the wanderer come back. "The Good Lord threw away the mold when He made your father. Sometimes I tell myself that that's a reason to be grateful because two of Judah Sherbrooke would be more than one small state like ours could handle.

He'd fill a room so full you had to leave the windows open just to get some air." Finney raises his glass. "Absent friends."

Ian walks the Big House rooms; slowly he charts the four floors. He remembers childhood games along the halls, and which closet was the better hiding place because you could hear all the way to the kitchen, through the dumbwaiter behind it. One afternoon, in Maggie's room—he is not prying, just passing through, curious about what kind of bird is building in the copper beech outside—he sees a book. It is bound in red vellum, and a marking pencil lies on the open page.

Picking it up, he finds a collection of letters on yellowing paper, in a trained yet free-flowing script. Ian reads a signature and date, then recognizes the letters that Anne-Maria Sherbrooke Sheldon sent home. Peacock's elder daughter married—shortly after her father's death—a man named Willard Sheldon, in 1870. The Sherbrookes are Episcopalians, but Anne-Maria, in the single act of impulse and rebellion in her otherwise devout, chaste youth, took up with Willard Sheldon when the family lived in San Francisco, and she was eighteen. Ian knows the story; it's a tale his aunt told often. Willard Sheldon was an upright man, an associate of Peacock's in a silver mining venture that succeeded. He was a bachelor from Salt Lake City, but not, he liked to say, confirmed in the condition of lifelong bachelordom. He was red-bearded, thirty-three years old and, by all accounts, scrupulous and even-tempered. He was made welcome in San Francisco when he arrived for consultation as to silver shipments that Peacock prophesied would dwarf the Comstock Lode.

There was one problem, however. Sheldon escorted Anne-Maria in the park, or riding. His manners were beyond reproach, his language unobjectionable, his demeanor properly solemn yet, at the proper moments, openhanded. The problem was belief. Peacock, usually meticulous in matters such as this, had altogether failed to see the fellow for the devil's very agent that he was. Willard Sheldon was a Mormon; his family had followed

Smith and Young. The taint of such belief, Peacock later wrote, should have clung to his apparel and made itself known in each heinous pronouncement. But by the time he, Peacock, came to rectify the damage, much damage had been done. His daughter had been smitten in her heart of hearts. She would gladly have been Sheldon's thirtieth wife, her father fumed; she would have followed the heretical lubricious ape to Zanzibar or Guiana or wherever his mission might take him, and would wear no clothes.

So he forestalled this and sent Sheldon packing. The house in San Francisco was declared off-limits; the corporation books were shut, the chapter closed. Peacock gladly took this worldly and financial loss, he wrote, in order to recoup on otherworldly gain. She might mourn with her innocent's misapprehension of truth, but the seeming rigor with which her father locked her up was in reality a fond man's fancy that she might prove free. There was even some suggestion that Peacock chose to travel east and home in order to keep a continent's breadth between his daughter's salt-thirst and the man she had chosen to slake it. He took a private, guarded coach. If he died contentedly (and Anne-Maria by his side recorded that his final words had been, "I am content . . ."), it was in part because he felt his darling younger daughter would stay in Vermont and be saved.

His elaborate precautions did not work, of course. Perhaps he knew this also and gave up his own ghost contentedly because, for some few years at least, he had stayed fate. Or perhaps he thought his daughter made of common time-bound stuff. Yet Anne-Maria had inherited, together with her portion of the Sherbrooke fortune, her father's headstrong fixity of purpose. The Church of the Latter-Day Saints was making converts everywhere; she would and did convert. She married Willard Sheldon on the day of her majority—three years after they first met, and over her elder brother's resistance.

Ian studies these letters. He sits on the edge of his mother's unmade bed and leafs through them, deciphering. It appears, for instance, that the family objection had less to do with polygamy—though that is what Hattie had stressed in her version—than with the almost-outlaw nature of the group. Smith himself had been shot in a jail; the Mormons trekked through wilderness; brigandage and persecution everywhere attended them. David Sherbrooke—Peacock's younger son, and a member of the Vermont State legislature—did what he could to have the marriage disallowed. He made stirring speeches where the similarity of "Moron, Mormon, Mammon, and Moroni" did not pass unnoticed, and he claimed that the tablets appearing to Smith had been fabricated in an ironworks in Seneca. He had privy information that the massacre in Illinois was at the "saint's" behest.

Anne-Maria, daunted but not apologetic, wrote to her sibling at home. She had inherited Peacock's ornate prose style also—as if language were a bulwark against the inroads of modernity. Maggie has been reading this; he reads the passage she has checked, in red:

". . . though much of this seem strange to me, or but newly plausible, I must endeavor so to make it seem to you as if we were yet intimate. For this high Purpose I hold several Reasons. First, it was always our wont to Share, and had I not the perfect Faith this revelation brings with it, why still I would require that the Doubt be divided amongst us. Since I am not at present nor ever may be other than a Missionary's Wife, and since we are instructed to embark with the first fair weather on what are to me Uncharted seas, nor do I know what reception the Waters or Natives accord, I must take the chance whilst yet I trust to proximate delivery of this my message to send it: I embrace you, brother and friends, with faltering but steadfast Heart. It is my husband's Duty to acquaint you with the Word. It is mine alone to render you acquainted with the detail of our life. For if familiarity be a bog where the Mosquito breeds yclept contempt—as our dear father used to say—why then I think it also true that too great Distance breed Disdain; it is an arid, stony Soil, one I water daily with my eyes."

IV

Ian turns the page. Anne-Maria wrote on onionskin, with ink that has faded to brown. Except for the excess of capital letters, her hand had been well trained. He wonders what his mother hunts; she had not seemed family-proud. Judah hated Roosevelt for reasons of his own. He said the man wrecked orchards in order to build roads; he said that peddling apples was a whole lot better commerce to take place on street corners than what they peddled now. But Hattie hated FDR because he was disloyal to his class. "What business does a man like that have," she'd ask, "consorting with such riffraff and appointing them to Cabinet positions?" So Maggie had reminded her, in Ian's hearing, of the way the President started his speech to the D.A.R.—"Fellow immigrants," he'd said.

"There are many Servants of the Lord. Many have been Prosecuted in the service of their Faith. But it is mine that Charity be greater yet than Faith or Hope, and that you would not leave your sister lonely in Most need. Our father made his millions by unceasing vigilance. Many were the dawns I'd rise to see him in his evening clothes still, pen in hand, lit only by the candle glow or some sputtering oil lamp, but illumined from within. With Works. With Aspiration. If these things be as I think them, then it is more than passing Strange we should grow so Lazy in the service of the Word. My Willard says we have a gift it is Damnation not to share, Salvation to distribute. We embark for the Indies this week.

"There are instruments. There are the Urim and Thumin, stones in silver bows. God preserved them near the village of Manchester, Ontario County, New York, so that our messenger could avail himself of Aid in the effort of translation. He bade our prophet carry the Tablets always with him and to guard them zealously against those who steal or profane. For their number is Legion (indeed I think we numbered amongst them once) who set themselves 'gainst Change, for fear it is not Comforting as what they knew before. Therefore the prophet was hounded; his bodily Person was shot. And we who follow in his wake do so most willingly (though you know me too well, brother, not to know the trepidation I experience in front of Watry Peril and the fear of Shipwrack) since Hazard is our true Condition on this Earth . . ."

Now Maggie enters the room. "Hi," she says. "Reading my old love letters?"

"Not exactly."

"Written testimonials." She advances, stands by the bed. "Dear Dr. Carter, your little liver pill has been working wonders; dear Dr. Pepper, yours is the best drink I've ever tasted; dear Dr. Smith, let me have another box of cough drops, please. Or is this the first Mr. Smith?"

"What *are* these?" Ian asks.

"You know. Your great-grandaunt—last of the seafaring Sherbrookes. I found her letters in the attic. May I sit?"

"I'm sorry," Ian says. "I wasn't snooping. I didn't mean to, anyway; it's just that I got interested. Weird woman, don't you think? Anne-Maria . . ."

"It's all right," Maggie says. She sits. "How long are you planning to stay?"

"I don't know. I hadn't thought."

"Think about it."

275

"Why?"

"It makes a difference," she urges.

"As long as you want me to . . ."

"Weeks? The whole summer?"

"Forever and ever amen." There is something in her manner that he has not seen before. He tries to name it to himself—nervousness? embarrassment?—and peers at this strange figure settling by him, the intruder, on her single bed.

"It's a beautiful morning," she says.

"Yes."

"Have you been outside?"

"Not yet."

Maggie picks at the coverlet. Her face is worn; she is wearing a red woolen shirt. He wonders, was it Judah's that it should hang so loosely from her shoulders and bunch around her waist?

"Do you still ride horses?" she asks.

"Not lately. They're not all that common in your average metropolis. We have horseless carriages these days."

"I mean would you like to?"

"Sure."

"And get some air?" she asks.

"Yes. But where do you keep horses?"

"We could borrow some," she says. "I have the use of two of them. Why don't we ride together this morning? I could use the exercise; we both could, probably."

"I'd love to," Ian tells her. "Give me ten minutes."

"That's fine," Maggie says, and is gone.

"There is one further reason. Even at this distance, while I prepare our trunks and grips for Embarkation unto I know not truly where, I feel myself at home with you in those Myriad rooms and Houses we have all called

276

home. There is naught that may dissever what blood and birth conjoin. My husband is a Man both resolute and kind. He is an excellent Dancer who has renounced the Dance. All imputation otherwise basely imputes his name—our shared surname now, let me remind you—and is a mote plucked out of not the Neighbor's eye but him who sees Imperfectly. Comparison is base. I compare myself most Basely to those of our Belief who have received Revelation. I must transcribe for you verbatim our Prophet's Words, when Moroni came to visit him in his impoverished bedroom, in the Night. It is even so I first saw Willard Sheldon, and so I see him yet:

" 'He had on a loose robe of most exquisite whiteness. It was a whiteness beyond anything earthly I had ever seen; nor do I believe that any earthly thing could be made to appear so exceedingly white and brilliant. His hands were naked, and his arms also, a little above the wrists; so, also, were his feet naked, as were his legs, a little above the ankles. His head and neck were also bare. I could discover that he had no other clothing on but this robe, as it was open, so that I could see into his bosom.

" 'Not only was his robe exceedingly white, but his whole person was glorious beyond description, and his countenance truly like lightning. The room was exceedingly light, but not so very bright as immediately around his person. When I first looked upon him, I was afraid, but the fear soon left me . . .'

"Comparisons are base; I acknowledge this once more. You will think me foolish; you have always thought me foolish, brother, a giggling, unsteady girl. But I swear by everything we held together Holy, by the Sacred memory of our parents and all I will never Profane; I swear to you on pain of ridicule and chastisement, even so do I look on my Willard when he in his Nightshirt appears."

Ian goes to the hall closet and selects his father's riding boots; his own, from half a life before, are pinched and small. Judah's boots stand upside down, on stretchers. They have been recently greased. From years of usage, the soles are worn thin; Ian wears two pairs of socks. "Will you, won't you join the dance?" his mother used to say. She would recite him the Lobster Quadrille, then take his hand gravely, inquiring, "Will you, won't you; will you, won't you?" and drop him a curtsy. He does deep knee bends in the boots, then bends the ankles in and out, then jumps and clicks his heels together, twice.

He has forgotten the pure beauty of it all—the way the clouds accumulate on Woodford Ridge, or how a firebreak slashed down a mountainside completes the green design. The cows and barns in the far distance seem perfectly positioned, and the meadows are a tilting patchwork stitched by stone. The lilacs and the fruit trees are in bloom.

Maggie drives him to a trailer he had not remembered. It has the look of permanence, however: on cinderblocks, with a young box hedge to the front and a paddock at the rear. Split wood has been stacked between two stakes, and washing hangs from the line; long underwear flaps like a flag. The trailer's trim is red; there are curtains. The door is shut. There are bicycles and a yellow slide-set in the yard.

"Who lives here?"

"You know them. The Boudreaus."

"I don't remember," Ian says.

Again he senses that constraint in her, as if she has grown vigilant in order to set him at ease. Maggie hands him the car keys, then opens the door to get out. "Hal Boudreau. He used to work the place. Still does odd jobs for us—when he's not drinking, that is." Tossing her hair back, she takes his arm. "Doesn't matter, anyway. It's the horses we've come to visit. There!"

Two Morgans stand underneath the maples at the paddock's farther reach. She whistles to them, shrilly, putting her small and index fingers to her teeth. Ian is startled: his mother seems a hoyden now, the girl his father might have known when first they rode together. Her skin is flushed, her movements quick; the horses hurry to her and she pats and scratches at them, then points to where the tack hangs on the rail. Before he has his bearings, nearly, they are inside the gate, and Maggie has managed the saddles and bridles, and though he has the larger animal he can see it's not her favorite, is sluggish by comparison. He fiddles with the stirrups. She slips off her own horse, adjusting the leathers, then back before he can contrive some smart-aleck cowpuncher compliment about how well she looks today, how well he remembers she rides.

"Yours is Daisy, mine is Maybe," Maggie says.

"Who named them?"

"Hal—they're his. They need the exercise."

And she is off and out the gate, her horse ahead, its tail raised while it drops great steaming gouts at Daisy's feet; Ian, busy with the reins and the adjustments his muscles must make, fastens the latch to the paddock behind. Then he regains his seat and turns to see his mother break into a canter up the first small slope. He thinks he sees a man's face at the trailer door. It stares at him; he waves at it with his free hand, taking both reins in his left. It is a red beard, possibly; a trick of the light; not there.

They reach a footpath on the property that widens into bridle path, and they draw abreast. The paths are familiar, not strange. Peacock has ordained, she reminds him, that the land be circled with such roadways— in concentric circles, the circumference of the inside circle being precisely one mile. They come to the property's limit. The woods are thin and, in this second week of May, just starting to sprout and fill in. He sees Woodford Mountain to the north, then the Green Mountains ringing them, then the river that bisects the valley where they live. Through the birches and the oak and locust trees Judah left for hedgerows, Ian sees the town. Yet motels and shopping centers are low-lying things; he sees only spires and mills. His grandfather's grandfather also would have used horses for travel, would have worn such riding boots and breathed the morning air.

"What are you thinking?" she asks.

He looks at her.

"Deep thoughts?"

"Only that these woods are second cutting," Ian says. "Third cutting, maybe. So they look about as young as whenever Peacock bought this place."

"In eighteen sixty-nine," she says. "There were family farms on it before, but that's the year he finished up. I'm the historian now."

"I know. That's what I was reading. But I wondered why . . ."

"Got tired of *Little Women*," Maggie says.

He looks at her. She sits more heavily. "If you're tired," Ian offers.

"No. The walls have ears. I don't mean Hattie eavesdrops, but I never get to feel alone with you inside. I wanted a chance, just once these weeks, to tell you what's been going on; to ask you what you think of it without the Sherbrooke portraits frowning down at me, the Sherbrooke family chairs complaining when you sit on them, the Sherbrooke carpets kicking up dust . . ."

"We're both of us Sherbrookes."

"Yes. So I put you in as close as we can get to wilderness, and you talk about the time that Peacock lumbered it. Or how these horses constitute the past. Oh, Ian, you don't know how sick I get, how weary of pretending . . ."

She halts, she drops her reins and lets Maybe pull at leaves. There is sweat on the Morgan's brown neck. He halts beside her, feeling his heart go out to her who always seemed beyond the reach of pity. Ian reaches for his mother's arm; the horses shy. He turns Daisy in a circle and brings them nose to nose.

"Why don't you leave?" he asks.

"That's not the question . . ."

"Why not? For vacations, anyway. Why don't you bring friends up?"

"It isn't all that easy."

"Not that hard."

"You're wearing Judah's boots. Don't you know why Hattie keeps them greased? Because she's sure he walks the halls at night. How do you think she'd take to an actual visitor? To any gentleman caller who actually called on my room?"

"She'd get used to it."

The horses snout and nuzzle at each other, not gently.

"I wouldn't," Maggie says.

He watches a squirrel behind her freeze, then bolt, then freeze again.

"Some days," she continues, "I wake up sick. I always used to think the mornings were just wonderful—I'd wake up every single morning full of just the most extravagant intentions about how to spend the time. But it's as if some switch gets crossed, or some connection missed—whatever. I can't face it, Ian, every little duty, every detail, every invitation or meal or telephone call or arrangement. If this is all it is"—she spreads her hands out, dismissive—"then it just isn't enough."

"There's music," he suggests.

"It's worse when there's music around, as if some hole has opened out and this whole place will break apart; it all goes hollow if I hear Schubert, for instance. The day you came, I'd been sitting the whole afternoon just listening to the Impromptus, just a wreck. Why do you think we're here?"

He follows the line of her hand. She points to a near thicket, and he sees now what she means by "wreck." There is the fire-ruined, vine-twined hulk of a Steinway grand piano ten feet from him; there are raspberry bushes beginning to get green.

"I didn't notice."

"No. But you remember."

"Yes."

He wipes his face. He shuts his eyes; Daisy stamps and chafes at the bit. His father had had the piano hauled out here and burned. Ian followed him, protesting; they rolled the thing up on a hay wagon and he ran behind the farmhands, in their tracks. By the time he'd reached them he was winded; Judah had dislodged the piano, dumped it, and sent the others back. It was a clearing then. Using sheets and rags and paper, his father stuffed the body of the Steinway. It had been raining. The woods were wet, and Ian, watching, was drenched. His mother had left three days before, after one of those arguments he'd half heard down the hall, though his head was underneath the pillow and he'd held his ears.

Then Judah lit a match. It took some time to catch; it guttered out. He lit a second, and a third; he rolled a sheet of paper tightly and made a torch. His father worked with such deliberate purpose, unhurried, precise, that Ian knew there'd be no hope of holding him back.

So terror became fascination, and he kept out of sight. Judah lit the piano legs. Then he ignited the keyboard. They watched together, though Judah did not know himself accompanied—or, more likely, chose not to acknowledge that anyone surveyed him from the trees' wet tent. The varnish on the piano stank; the flame was sheets, then rags, then fingers interlocking. He watched until his father too had finished watching and stood and stretched and pissed and headed home. Then Ian crept forward, came down. He touched the hot crepitant keyboard. The pedals were poured metal, and the white ivory was cracked and black. He pocketed two keys.

"Sometimes I think," says Maggie, "it's what we call the 'change of life.' You know, it happens to women my age."

"Yes."

"And sometimes I think something else."

He watches her again; her face is pale, heavy; she frames the words with caution.

"What's that?" Ian asks.

"You won't believe me."

"What?"

"I don't believe it, really. I'm not expecting you to—but I have to tell someone," she says. "You *are* my son, it might as well be you."

"All right."

"It's crazy," Maggie finishes. "Don't think I don't know that much. It makes no sense. But I do know the feeling, after all; I've known it twice before."

"What feeling?"

"This. What I've been talking about."

He lets impatience surface; he is haunted by the spectacle of flame. "What *have* you been talking about?"

"I'm pregnant," Maggie says.

V

Time passes, Hattie thinks, like something in an hourglass. First it takes forever for the sand to look like anything, falling; then it seems abundant, then there's nearly nothing left. Next someone comes along and flips the thing—or maybe it's on a balance, one of those wooden rigs that turn themselves around—and everything flows back again; each grain of sand you feared you'd lost is present and accounted for. She'd been sure that her time had run out. She'd been certain, anyhow, the Sherbrooke line was cut. It's not a dying name; there are plenty of the Sherbrooke clan in Canada, where they'd made a city; there are collateral cousins in England and Wales, and no doubt some leftover Sherbrookes in San Francisco or Freeport or New Orleans.

But her nearest and dearest are gone. Judah is dead; she'd never thought to have outlived him, had been unprepared for that. She was five years his senior, and he had been strong as an oak. The largest and the loveliest are the first to fall. The oak gets leveled, Hattie knows, before the unimportant reed that flattens itself in high wind. So too with Seth, who had died in his crib; there'd been insufficient time for him to put down roots. He got lifted up and carried into the airless center of the storm. She's never seen or been in a twister, but she's heard that it fells everything, and in the cyclone's center there just isn't any air. Therefore the infant suffocates, and later the head of the family topples—while she, the reed, bends and survives.

Survival of the fittest: sometimes she preens on that. It would be dishonest to pretend she didn't triumph in the pure plain gift of survival, and how her teeth stay sound. Her hearing has failed; her eyes are failing; her digestion is not what it was. But she's eighty-two-and-a-half years old and has kept every one of her teeth. She walks without assistance, though her left knee is arthritic; she could go out dancing if Ian would ask her to dance. Dr. Davies said there's nothing wrong with you, Miss Sherbrooke, a glass or two of sherry won't fix, you come on in for whirlpool treatments if that knee hurts too much. She'd asked him if they'd need to cut it, and he said he didn't think so; nothing appears to be rattling around, just a stiffness of the joints.

She has sciatica, too. That can be a cross to carry when the nerve acts up. When she sits in one position for too long, it feels like she's been folded and her very bones have creased. Sometimes Maggie offers her a second Manhattan for the pain. Sometimes the maraschino cherries that have been her principal indulgence go sour in her mouth. Or they cloy or clot her throat, and she fears when she swallows she'll gag.

So survival has its drawbacks. Hattie has not married; it isn't a question of that. Had she done so and provided heirs, their names would not be Sherbrooke and their home wouldn't likely be the Big House, and maybe they'd not even live in Vermont. The storm she means is a discriminating wind; it picks and chooses carefully, leveling menfolk and leaving the women alone.

Maggie did return, of course, and the two of them rattled around together. They were each other's company. They have been companionable, even, though there's thirty years between them, and many gulfs between them that are wider than just thirty years. Sharing their meals, the roof, the heat from the fire at night, they are close the way two animals in stalls are close: each locked in place, for better or worse, in sickness and health—but staring straight ahead. For Margaret Cutler is a wed Sherbrooke, not born, and careless enough anyhow about her marriage vows.

Hattie believes in forgiveness. She thinks Maggie maybe never knew and can be forgiven how much trouble and indignity she caused. There's forgiving and forgetting, however, and Hattie can manage the one but not the other: Maggie had abandoned them. Her return failed to cancel that out. She could come back twenty times over and never make up for her going; she could be relied upon to be unreliable, and that's why she'd provided only Ian to the Sherbrooke name: a scapegrace and a runaway with fifty percent Cutler blood.

Still, Ian had returned. The hourglass tilts back, pours on; he walked into the house the spitting image of his mother when she first bore him, twenty-six. There are differences according to sex, of course, and Margaret wore her hair longer and had a higher-pitched voice. But Hattie sees the similarity beyond the difference, notices his way of standing (hand on hip, feet slightly splayed, head cocked) is how his mother used to stand when contravening Judah, or in sham agreement. His features are his mother's, though hers have coarsened over time; when Hattie sits across the table facing them, or in the study at night, it is as if she sees two photographs like those in the newspaper advertising weight loss: after and before. Or like the time she had the portrait of Peacock Sherbrooke restored by cleaning; it had darkened, the restorer said, in the parlor air and because a hundred years of fireplace smoke builds up a layer of soot.

So she had Peacock cleaned. She'd washed him, Judah joked, behind the ears and scrubbed him till he shone. But it had been a shock to them—how what they took for brown was yellow, what they'd thought was dark blue turned the color of an August sky at noon. His cravat had been shockingly red. The white hairs of his beard turned yellow also, and the whole thing glistened under varnish in a way that made Hattie ashamed. Daniel Sherbrooke stared at her—stared down at them from his place above the mantel—like a well-dressed stranger with a gleam in his bright eye. It was brassy, bold in a fashion that made her feel timid, as if time would avenge itself because she'd hoped to cheat. The man who cleaned and restored him said, "You see, Miss Sherbrooke, this is what the artist saw. This is just how your ancestor looked." But she could not get used to it; her great-grandfather was younger than she, a man in his glinting and peacock-bright prime. She wanted to rub ash on him and make him once more grave.

Therefore Ian makes her nervous not because he's her grown nephew but because of what has happened lately to his aging mother. It's as if they fashion an alliance just as Maggie did with Jude. She, Hattie, knows herself excluded; she's the third and three's a crowd. They share secrets, she knows that; she hears them whispering in corners or in private rooms. When she says, "Don't whisper, please," they talk so loudly they're shouting and it's impolite. It's disrespectful: everything time tamed in Maggie has come again uncaged.

"I'm having the bridge party Thursday," Hattie says.

Maggie makes no answer.

"Well?"

"That's nice."

"Would you care to join us?"

"This Thursday?"

"It's my turn, it's been a month. Ida Conover hasn't been feeling up to it. It's her turn actually, I suppose you do know that, I imagine you counted," she says. "But I thought as long as we were able we could jump a week; we'd just skip Ida's turn."

"Of course."

"Well. You don't have anything scheduled, I suppose?"

"No."

"Will you join us? It's about time, I should say."

"I thank you," says Maggie. "But no."

She does not insist; if Maggie feels excluded that will teach her what exclusive means, and maybe she'd stop muttering in corners, jostling, giggling with her son. The bridge game comes and goes. Maggie helps with preparations, as she used to do—making food and setting up the coffee tureen and helping arrange tables—but when the guests arrive she simply isn't there. Neither is Ian; they are nowhere to be found. They might be found had she, Hattie, sent up the visiting party to traipse through the halls of the house. They are in some upstairs bedroom, locked away and laughing together; she can hear them through the ceilings that are also floors.

Hattie wins that night. She and her partner, Mrs. Doctor Davies, hand Ida and Helen Bingham the worst drubbing they've had in months. But she drinks too much Sanka, or something goes wrong with the angel-food cake; triumphant, standing on the porch to wish her guests good evening, chaffing them about the time she'd made her bid of three no trump, telling them that soon enough she'll win the county tournament, the taste in her mouth anyhow is tin.

Then, as spring progresses, things change. Ian too becomes a customary presence in the house. He spends long days out alone on the land, just as his father had done. His sweetness surfaces once more; he shelves his city ways. He is the last male Sherbrooke, after all, and if this branch of the family is to spread and blossom, it's up to Ian to make sure. She reminds him of that.

"Marriageable ladies," Hattie says. "There must be plenty in this town. They flock to you, I'll bet."

"Not so I've noticed," he says.

"You don't go out enough."

"I've got two women in this house."

"That's different."

288

"Why?" He teases her with his pretended innocence; he purses his lips and cocks his head.

"Ian Sherbrooke," Hattie says. "Don't play the fool with me."

"I'm not, I'm just reminded how you used to tell me to stay home. Not to go out dancing all night long."

"Is that what you call it?"

He smiles. The smile is like, she thinks, the one you use for toothpaste ads or graduation photographs.

"Old enough to know better." She sniffs. "That's what you are. There's only just so long a man should wait. If you get my meaning . . ."

"I do."

"Well, anyway, you won't object if Ida Conover comes to visit, and brings her daughter's niece."

"You ask whatever company you want. It's your house," Ian says.

There are other changes, too. She invites the Conovers, and Ian proves polite. Ida arrives with her daughter, Elizabeth, and her grandniece Sarah. "Call me Sally," Sarah says. She has just the most marvelous figure; breeding will out in the end. She'd been to Wellesley College, which is, Hattie understands, an upright place to go. Then there had been some years abroad and something about an unfortunate marriage—some reason anyway that brought the girl back to New England. They sit together on the porch, eating apple pie with cheese and cream.

"I hope it's not too forward if I say this, Ian," Elizabeth says. "But we're all delighted you're back."

"I knew you," Ida offers, "when you didn't come up to my knee. This place does need a man."

Hattie breaks out sherry too. "His mother made this pie," she says. "Perfectly good. I couldn't do better myself." Maggie is not with them, but she gives credit where credit is due. She'd taught Maggie everything about baking, of course, but nowadays could scarcely fault the results—although she faulted Maggie in the eating. She must just pack them away. There'd be rows of pies one afternoon, setting on the rack to cool, and next day Hattie would come for a slice and there'd be nearly nothing left—just empty tins in the drain.

Ian tenders his mother's regrets. She was called off unexpectedly to see an old school friend. She expected to be back home in time to say good-bye to them, and meantime said hello. Hattie knows this for a lie, but also common courtesy; they couldn't declare how the woman's upstairs, too proud or busy or bored or whatever to come on down and have the common courtesy to even say hello. The crust is flaky and, if you ask her, too dry.

Elizabeth is talking of the way they'd tarred her lawn, simply dropped a stream of tar right down where they should have followed the curve. No matter how she fusses about it, her white rocks are black, and every single blade of grass they'd planted there so carefully is no doubt dead, so they have to seed again come fall. Just imagine, she tells Hattie, I called Bottomley so fast he said he'd be right over, and he only came next afternoon and by then I was fit to be tied. By then I gave him a piece of my mind, you can wager. I told him what I thought of his crew; they'll tar your lawn and fill in holes that never needed fixing, but do you think when winter's here they'll bother to plow out a person? No such luck; the snow can melt before they'll even notice or quit their coffee break. Sometimes I think between time off for coffee and time off for lunch we're lucky to get three hours of work for our taxes by now, in what's a working day. Hattie looks up over her knitting glasses to agree, to offer them a second serving and sees—she could swear it, plain as day and twice as bright, although her eyes are worrisome, because they'd moved to the glider and are creaking back and forth, but only she could spy it from her angle in the chair, Ida, and Elizabeth are spared, or mercifully ignorant, or used to it, or blind—the Conover girl drumming her fingers (vermilion nails they are; she should have known) right smack in Ian's lap.

Then things get worse. He takes to spending time in bars. She knows it, since she smells his breath, and sometimes he returns with mud down the back of his shirt. "Gone for a pig wallow?" Hattie wants to ask. "Been rolling with that harlot in the hay?" She separates the clothes for washing—light from dark—in two wicker baskets. That way Mrs. Gore, who comes to collect them and still can't tell the difference between Irish linen and Orlon, and never knows which one to iron and is color-blind to boot, won't make the fabrics run. So when she goes through Ian's clothes she finds cigarette papers and blood. She isn't prying, she wants to tell him, she doesn't mean to pry—but pray tell me, Ian Sherbrooke, if you plan to be disgraceful all your days.

She pretends nothing happened, of course. She cannot trust her eyes. She asks him offhandedly, later, how he likes the Conover girl and he says he likes her well enough. She tells him if he's short of funds and wants to buy prepackaged cigarettes, why she'd be happy to help; he needn't roll his own. She asks, "Have you been dancing?" but he does not answer and she will not pry. At the Library Committee Meeting the first Wednesday afterward, she asks Elizabeth how long her charming Sarah plans to remain in the town. The woman spreads her hands (her nails are pink and clean, but Hattie thinks, it's in the family, degenerate; she shouldn't splay her fingers so, what right has she to preen on them?), the cuffs on her blouse have been frayed. "Sally," Elizabeth says.

Hattie leans forward, says, "What?"

"It's what she calls herself now."

"I remember it as Sarah."

"Yes. She changed it back in college. You just can't imagine—I'd get these letters; every month a different name; once she even called herself Aquarius; can you beat it?"

"Yes," Hattie says. "Indeed I can. Mrs. Judah Sherbrooke had so many other names I'd never know which one to call her—Maggie, Megan, Meg. Margaret. They're peas in a pod," she continues. "I noticed it right off."

"Well," Elizabeth says. She pulls out her handkerchief. The meeting comes to order. Orvis Thatcher beats his gavel on the rolltop desk—hard, proudly, so often you'd think it would crack. "Is that a compliment?"

"Beg pardon?" Hattie asks.

"I'm glad you think my niece is like the present Mrs. Sherbrooke. Whatever she calls herself now."

That finishes it; she puts her fingers to her lips and hisses, "Hush."

Her doctor says he wants her eyes checked; he has urged her to make an appointment. He mentions specialists and words like macular degeneration and depth of field and cataracts and remedial elective surgery, but Hattie barely listens. She is a specialist in darkness anyhow these days. She puts her whole hand on the table, first, in order to find the right fork.

"That glass," says Ian. "Watch it."

"Watch what?"

"It's chipped, I think. Here, let me see."

She has been preparing to drink. He reaches over the table, taking her water glass away.

"I'm sorry," Hattie says. "I didn't notice."

"No."

"It must be a trick of the light."

She holds her hand out for the glass, runs her thumb around the edge until she feels the crack. She goes to the pantry to fetch a replacement and, coming back, watches him watch her. "Crystal," Hattie says. "It always needs replacing."

"Yes."

"One of these days"—she smiles at him—"we'll buy a whole new set."

"Are you all right?" asks Maggie.

"Never better. Yes, of course."

Evenings, Hattie reads to them from the ancestral papers, pointing out which of Peacock's ventures succeeded and which few failed, using the present tense. "He's a stubborn sort of man," she'd say. "Just like certain other Sherbrookes that we all could name. He's got a willful way about him, old Daniel Sherbrooke the dreamer."

She believes her brother met his end the way John Garfield did—in the arms of a hired fancy woman, and in bed. This was true of Garfield and English barons by the wagonload and many men in power, she is certain. They die with their boots on, perhaps, but wearing nothing else and in a sinful embrace. So Judah purchased Maggie's charms and paid the price of pleasure, expiring of love. She is his legal wife, of course, but Hattie thinks there ought to be another kind of law. Maggie killed him with her beauty's edge as surely as if she had whetted an ax-blade or sickle or scythe. Facing her, he'd come to have the stunned look of a cow who doesn't even know it's dead, whose skull has been crushed by a twelve-pound maul but doesn't yet feel it—standing there blinking, feet splayed, head lowered, eyes up.

Judah said that sort of blow is merciful; the animal won't know. But she knows what hit him, all right, as surely as she knows that her Redeemer liveth since He willingly gave up the ghost, not like some dumbstruck Angus dreaming of clover, then smashed. Hattie has observed it. She witnessed such slaughtering often. And she therefore has no trouble seeing how his eyes would glaze, would tilt and ride back in their sockets when his lawful wife advanced on him, her skirts raised like a hammer and his heart just not up to the shock.

They haven't discussed it, of course. There are certain things you can't ask a person, no matter if you know the answer off by heart. But the woman reeks of guilt as once she used to reek of perfume, and Hattie thinks she maybe ought to sue. There ought to be a law that says you cannot take advantage of those feebleminded, great-limbed men who have been disadvantaged by lust. She would win the lawsuit if there were justice on earth.

But justice is a matter for lawyers and judges and newspapermen, and no doubt they'd act precisely as Judah had acted before. One day in court and Maggie would have each of them agreeing with her, licking the salt from her palm. No matter how you try, you cannot legislate equality before the law courts in this life. Every dog will have her day, and Maggie's the queen of the pack.

So Hattie keeps her dignity before the law. But it's been pure plain torture not to say what she's screaming to say and what the woman ought to hear: *You killed him. He was healthy when you came to town and dead not six months after, and who's the cause of that? You made him your plaything. You made him humble himself to you, making him kneel—you, who weren't ever good enough to lick his boots!*

She is accustomed to dismissal, to being someone's maiden sister, then sister-in-law, and aunt. She knows what Ian does with Sarah Conover is not her business, really, nor her duty to control. She had hoped the girl would prove enticing, and her wish has come only too true. Make certain you know what you're asking before you ask for it, the fairy godmother warns; don't buy a pig in a poke. She'd hoped that Ian would return and settle in and maybe settle down, but he is so much Judah's son and Maggie's look-alike there seems no end of trouble to her granted wish. He comes home at all hours or sleeps in what he says are fields; he reminds her, sometimes, of her reckless first beau, Jamie Pearson. With his liquorish gallantry and high-stepping ways, Ian sure as sure is riding for a fall—and she, Hattie, tries to warn him off. She tells him how Jamie Pearson died: in an alley, in the winter, behind the Village Inn. His liver just plain quit. There had been no one left to watch him when he froze.

"Hospitality," says Ian. "It's what people here don't understand. They don't know what it means to take a person in."

"That's not true," Hattie says.

"It is. Believe me. Try and find a bed in this town if you weren't born here."

"We always give a helping hand . . ."

"To those who don't need help." Maggie speaks up on Ian's behalf. "To anyone who's a neighbor, why we might prove neighborly. But it's not what he means."

"What is then?" Hattie asks.

"Soup for the starving," he says. "A bed for Jamie Pearson if he's sleeping in the gutter. Your daughter for a black man, and maybe a junkie to boot."

"You're just being foolish."

"No. Extreme. If you won't give up your daughter to a hophead then you don't know hospitality."

"I myself have got no daughter"—Hattie has their measure now—"and if I did I'm sure she'd know a good deal better by herself. Than ever you imagine, Ian Sherbrooke."

"You get my point," he says.

"No, and I'm not sure I want to, besides."

He turns to his mother. "Do you?"

"He's saying," Maggie says, "that if we didn't own this town he'd have trouble getting gas. Or making it past the stop sign where Thatcher's looking out for license plates."

"We do not own this town!"

"Well, half of it, wouldn't you say?"

"I'd say"—Hattie sniffs—"the Sherbrookes own what they paid for and have a right to keep. In the face of taxes and developers and young do-nothings like yourself. I don't exclude you, Ian, it's a fact."

Next he tells them that the house should be transformed. "Turn it into a museum," Ian says. "Charge ten cents a visit, or a dollar fifty; do it for free. Whatever. You can show the strangers every instrument of torture, every hassock Peacock bought on mail order, those lamps that never worked. Every rug his children scuffed their shoes on, the paintings bought in job lots. And even the ormolu clock," he finishes.

"I'm sorry you feel that way."

"You're not, and Mother's not. If you were sorry you'd change it from feeling like a crypt," he says. "A place for embalmed attitudes. It's no sort of house."

"You show me how to change it," Maggie offers, "and I promise you we'll change."

"A box of matches," Ian says. "That's what we need."

Hattie is shocked. He seems to know, however, that he's gone too far and doesn't mean it; he takes her hand and strokes it gently, telling them, "But then we'd start again."

Now Hattie sees a thing she had not noticed. You live with someone every day and take them so for granted you forget to look. She sees (and triumphs noticing, since the woman was always pole-slim and perfect before, even at fifty-two, even eating too much pie—yet there is regret mixed in, since one of the things she has lived with is beauty in the Big House) her sister-in-law in the chair. Things change; somebody tilts the hourglass while she isn't watching, and sand runs the other way. Maggie has grown fat.

VI

She cannot quite believe it. It took her weeks to admit to herself, then weeks to think it possible, then weeks more to articulate to Ian—as if *saying* were *being*, was proof. It was like see-no-hear-no-speak-no-evil, or like the ostrich principle; stick your head far enough in the sand, and nothing seems a threat.

There are other reasons, of course. The odds on conception for women past forty are small; the odds against pregnancy for a widowed fifty-two-year-old are high indeed. Far more likely, Maggie knows, that what was wrong is menopause—and the changes she's been going through are the "change of life." Or even hysterical pregnancy—she's not discounted that. Nor were her periods regular. Nor, in her two previous pregnancies, had she been quick to conceive.

So logic argued inattention; it meant she didn't have to take her bodily promptings for fact. Of all the jokes time played, this would have been the crudest—and she chose to ignore it, not laugh. Of all the ridiculous problems, this would have been the worst—the widowed Mrs. Sherbrooke standing at a small-town small-time carnival, her face framed in the cardboard picture of some sort of clown, her belly pressing up against the backdrop while neighbors fling pie at her face.

Still, she woke up queasy. Still, she felt that quickening separate life inside her she'd not known for a quarter of a century. She'd felt it with Ian, then Seth. She told herself it is this pitiless mansion that makes a parody of how she'd been in her blithe wifehood, young. By the third year of their marriage, Ian had been born; two years later, Seth was born and then was dead in his crib. In one way or another, everything is repetition and empty echo since. She'd known it all along, of course; we all are born to die.

So Maggie would wake with her hands on her stomach, sweating already, going faint as she stood by the stove or in the middle of some meal with Hattie, or chatting on the phone. The world would take up its giddying motion while she stood rooted and still. Or it was she who was twirling, feet crisscrossed, toes down, arms raised, but the world neglected its rotation. So she had headaches and backaches and could not hold her food down, but was gaining weight.

She knew it wasn't ulcers; people with ulcers don't gain. She knew it wasn't cancer or colitis or peritonitis or any of the wasting diseases that might cause a woman trouble with digestion. One of the problems in this town was whom to use for a doctor—someone in whom to confide. She had Fred Wiggins over for supper, since he'd been her husband's friend and doctor and she had known him ever since Seth. But the man was ponderous—Hattie's speed, not hers. He had the face of a Basset hound; his hands were damp with too much washing, and his last medical textbook was probably *Gray's Anatomy*—or Galen, or Hippocrates, whoever wrote the first.

She asked around. She met Dr. Fifield at the Harrises' for cocktails, and asked what were the symptoms, for instance, of cancer of the womb. He said that wasn't a "for instance," that if she had any suspicions she should turn herself in straightway for testing. But then he said that hysterectomy was overpracticed in this country, if you wanted his opinion. If he were a vet, the doctor said, most any farmer would forbid him to perform a mastectomy on cows, but the selfsame farmer was ready to cut off his wife's teats, for instance, at the slightest trouble; begging your pardon, he said to Maggie, but I'm a plain-speaking man. She told him the analogy was only too plain, and sexist, and he might try in the future not to draw too pat an equal sign between women and cows. He blushed, fiddled with his pocket watch, and tried a joke. "You know the one," he asked her, "about architects and doctors? Architects cover their mistakes with ivy. Doctors just do it with sod."

"And women," Maggie said. "You forgot that."

"How do you mean?"

"The third part of the joke. You're supposed to say, about women, they cover their mistakes with mayonnaise."

There are, in this little town, no doctors she can trust.

For weeks, therefore, she lived with her suspicion of disease. Then that too faded from her, and she suspected the presence of life; she needed an obstetrician and gynecologist, not a stomach doctor. She thought of going to New York, but lately had feared traveling as much as Judah ever did, and Hattie needed her, and besides her New York gynecologist had moved to Santa Fe.

Then she heard, at a dessert party it was their turn to give, of an East Indian doctor who had just settled in. "He's devilishly handsome," Helen Bingham said. "Catch me letting my daughter take off her clothes in front of him!"

"Not likely," Ruth Whiting said.

"They want him for the hospital."

"He's Pakistani, is he?"

"No, Indian," said Helen Bingham. "You learn how to tell them apart."

"Is he married?" Hattie asked.

"Mm-mn. I do believe his wife is always with him in the examining room. Less risky that way," giggled Ruth.

"It's the law," said Helen. She had been a registered nurse.

"Well, anyway . . ."

"This is excellent cake," Maggie said. Hattie had provided it, and she changed the topic to the quality of eggs.

"I declare," Ruth Whiting said, "it's criminal the way they make those laying hens stay up. You can taste it, too, in a factory farm; they just never get any exercise or a chance to rest."

Maggie heard enough to seek the doctor out. He was sufficiently a stranger and good enough to have been courted by their hospital, despite what the board of directors would think of as his handicap of race. She made an appointment next day.

His office was in his house. He received her at the front door, beaming, full of exaggerated courtesy about the pleasure of her visit and apologies that things were not quite up to adequate yet with reference to furnishings; he had a singsong, high-flown rhetoric she thought of as a comedy routine. He said "okay" continually, as a concession to slang. He wore white shoes, white pants; his face was round and brown and soft, with a rabbit's quick twitching alertness; she found him neither devilish nor handsome and felt at her ease.

He introduced her to his wife; they came from Orissa, they said. Theirs had been an arranged marriage, and Dr. Rahsawala praised the tradition of arrangement, since he said—his wife beaming, short and boneless by his side—that no decision he had ever taken on his own had been so marvelously correct as the decision their families took. "Now what, is the problem, okay?" he inquired. "What are you wanting to examine, okay, this afternoon?"

She had long since grown indifferent to physical examination and some stranger's dispassionate probing. But now she felt as secretive as when, nineteen, she had been fitted for a diaphragm: as full of shrinking sin. Maggie settled to the stirrups as if onto a rocking horse; she closed her eyes and pictured Ian riding. Then she limned his features—focusing on the nose and its resemblance to her dead husband's—then thought she'd take him riding on the property. She pictured him in Technicolor next, as Dr. Rahsawala's gloved fingertips pressed and prodded and stretched her. She told the doctor she suspected pregnancy; he nodded, not amazed. He asked her for the first urine of tomorrow's morning, and told her he would have the answer by next night. Habitually evasive, she had had to face it then; she drove home, slept well, but woke up feeling giddy and sick. She took him the sample and left it with his wife; she was, she realized, as old as the two of them put together, since Rowhena was nineteen. Maggie did not return to the Big House directly. She drove along the Old East Road, hunting memories of Judah and how this came to pass.

There is a family legend of the golden-hearted whore. Peacock's elder son, they said, ate up his substance with loose women, and there were opportunities abounding in the city by the sea. Peacock was an upright man, one of the fledgling community's pillars: "The strong right arm of Probity," Anne-Maria wrote, "had no firmer sinew than Daniel Sherbrooke our father. We honored him daily alive as we honor now his dear departed Memory, secure in the availing grace of his person and Thought."

Yet Daniel Sherbrooke, Jr., was an errant son. The letters mention him often, then rarely, then not at all. He mocked his father's piety and gambled and rutted and drank. His I.O.U. was good at expensive gaming tables, since Peacock would honor the note. His name sent thrills of expectancy through the bars or whorehouses, since the drink would be abundant and the custom lavish and lavishly rewarded. He was, they said, prodigious in the consumption of women and pink gin and hundred-dollar chips.

Maggie imagines him. He would have had Jude's height. He would have wax mustachios and pearls on his vest and a pearl-handled revolver and a diamond stickpin in his tie. His teeth would glint in firelight and his belly-laugh would shatter glass; he would be expert at dancing. He could kick his heels three times in succession in the hornpipe jig. There was an octoroon, they said, who became his sporting favorite. "High yaller and high-spirited and low-life to beat all," he boasted. "That's my girl."

She styled herself "Belle Amour." He asked her what that meant and she said, "Guess."

"I know what Bella means," he said, "I know about the moors."

"You don't know French," she chided him.

"Not worth mentioning."

"Well, Belle Amour is French."

"Oh, pardon me. *Pardonnez-moi.*"

She pardoned him and they went waltzing and later he performed his hornpipe jig. "My lady of the Indies," Maggie imagines him calling her. "My precious golden calf."

"You'll spoil me, Dan," she warned.

"Can't do that."

"Why?"

"You're spoiled already."

"Spoil me worse," she said.

"What's worse than worst?"

"You'll spoil me for the others." She laughed her throaty laugh.

"That's my intention, chicken. It's my idea, Bella Moor."

So Maggie imagines them courting, with her hardened heart softening to him, and his visits frequent and always on soft sheets. She supported herself on his arm while they brazened their way past Peacock's office building on Montgomery Street. He displayed her like his cuff links, and there were many who took umbrage, but none who dared take umbrage to his face. He had been a crack shot. He was famously quarrelsome and could shoot fish heads from a seal on the Pacific rocks without injuring the mouth of the seal, using only his handgun and not bothering to aim.

Daniel Jr. stayed in San Francisco when his father traveled east. He was written out of the will. He set up Belle Amour in private apartments and spent his leisure hours there—and since all his time, they said, was leisure time, the two were seldom separate or gone from love's lush bower; their laughter would mingle with the sound of ice in glasses, and the glittery tinkle of jewels. "This ain't half bad," he'd say, approving, and she'd always answer, "Dan, it ain't half good." He would cackle and slap at his sides.

If she bore him children, they went unrecorded. There were deaths at birth and deaths in childhood often enough in that city and those years. San Francisco, Peacock wrote, though it be a city on the waters, was a city of the plains; "Sodom and Gomorrah were seats of Equity and Faith when held against th' Invidious Standard of the Present time, and the lewd deportment of the women on the docks."

She has shown no lewd deportment. She had been surprised by grief when Judah died; she ought to have prepared for it and had thought herself prepared. The reason she came back, indeed, was that he lied he was dying, and had had Finney call to offer his Boy Scout's motto: "Be prepared." Yet she stands accused in the eyes of the neighbors and remaining family, since she never has worked off that first accusation: *You're Judah's whore: you're money- and man-hungry, go back to your bed by the docks.*

In those last six months, however, Maggie tended her husband unstintingly. It had taken half a year before his lie proved truth, before the heart attack he'd faked to bring her up from New York City was actual and fatal and permitted her return. Except she did not leave. By that time New York seemed an alien place (it would have been leaving, not going home, she explained to those who asked her; it would have been beside the point). She did go twice in order to pack up her things and have them shipped north. She gave up the apartment. The second time (standing on the balcony, barefoot, watching the East River and deciding not to take the window boxes) she felt something like regret.

The moving men arrived. They gathered her accoutrements in only three hours—picking the place clean. They asked, "Is that all, lady?" and she told them yes. It would take a company a month or more to pack up the Big

House, and all of its vans. Her own few objects, however, added nothing to the bulk of where they were delivered—and Maggie, in her empty rooms, felt elegiac in advance for how she'd traveled light. There was an upright piano, a record collection, some photographs and books and plates and watercolors, and six suitcases of clothes. The seven years she'd lived apart from Judah were canceled by the smallest truck Neptune could provide.

The way her husband took her back had been on his own terms, of course. It meant those years could not exist—that he never mentioned New York City or their time apart. It meant if she referred to streets or concerts or friends he had not shared with her, his face would tighten and his fingers curl; his silence would be absolute or right hand rise to his chest. She had known something about that already, arriving to play hostage to the collapse of his health; she knew she was his prize possession ransomed back.

But in the six months since his death she'd come to understand such separation—how the sections of her life remained disjunct. It was maybe a function of age—that she could remember her ten- or twenty- or thirty-year previous self as some alien someone in some other place. Or the Big House did to her what it had done to Judah—its boundaries became the limits of her easy ranging, its rooms became the only rooms where she could take her ease.

There is comfort in that, Maggie thinks. Things do not alter if you have the money and time to preserve them; things stay as they once were. But every once in a while she'd felt so suffocated by the present way of living in Vermont that she embraced the headstrong past—went dancing or to concerts to console herself for her husband's death. When she packed up Sutton Place she spent the night at Andrew Kincannon's, and they played their lust-parts clumsily again. They heard a Schumann symphony, then ate a light postconcert supper at the Russian Tea Room; they walked to his apartment hand in hand as if it were a decade previous or when they'd started their affair, with his first wife in Barbados in—she calculated—1959.

"You've ruined me," said Andrew. "Do you know that?"

"How so?"

"For all other women." He raised his eyebrows and sighed. "For any earthly happiness, my angel."

"Oh, Andrew . . ." She released her hand.

"Oh, Andrew, what?"

"You're being theatrical."

"Just properly dramatic, Meg."

"*Im*-properly. Most people would be happy with such ruination. You're richer now than then."

"Don't mock me," Andrew mourned. But his tone was so sepulchral that she knew he meant it as a joke, and that their practiced coupling soon to come would be something to grin at, not mourn.

Still, the following morning, he had wanted her to remain. They ate Sara Lee croissants. She told him no; he asked why not, she said because she had to follow Neptune north; he asked her, please, to stay. This time he sounded serious and so she teased him, saying, "You can't mean it, Andrew. Not after all these years."

"I mean it. What else do we have?"

"What else I have is solitude," she said.

"You're being romantic. First you call me melodramatic and then you offer your own secondhand sentiment. From a third-rate novel." He drummed his fingers on the tabletop. "Have some orange marmalade."

"To sweeten my disposition." She smiled at him. He understood, he seemed to be saying, that this was the last time they'd meet. It was— Maggie hunted the word—indecorous; two aging spangled acrobats on all fours in the net. When she returned to the Big House, she would be its mistress alone.

Yet the habit of companionship dies hard. One of the things that died with Judah was someone's near body at night. She missed it, missing him. Then too, men had thought of her as a man's woman for so long that she came to think of herself that way also—half of some sexual whole that required a male for completion. She had been an ornament, so practiced in the fashions of flirtation that she draped her solitude around her like a peignoir. She wore it like a housedress with nothing underneath.

It wasn't a question of liberation; she had been a "liberated woman" since long before the term. But what that meant to men was promiscuity; what that signaled was the willingness to wager her freedom in some sort of contest, to make it the stakes of the game. And many men did battle with her or were suitors for her dangling hand or brought their spears and drinking gourds to the Big House parlor like lazy preening aspirants. They loitered in the door. They expected to be fed and made much of and flattered, or to warm themselves by the marble-fronted fireplace as soon as they hauled in the wood. They thought she would beg for the chance. She joked about herself that way—calling herself Penelope beset by preening suitors while she darned her absent husband's socks and dithered on whom to select.

Only it did seem a second-rate joke; Odysseus was dead and in the family plot. Telemachus was traveling and hadn't been back to the Big House in years, nor had she seen him lately. The theme was old, fidelity irrelevant, and all Maggie wanted was peace. There were blue-tick hounds around to play at being Argus, and Hattie could serve as the faithful retainer—she gave it up; she wasn't some contemporary queen who undid every night each day's artistic industry; she was a fifty-two-year-old with all her bridges burned. Moats and drawbridges and golden hair let out of towers were not now the point.

She tended the greenhouse instead. She grew hothouse grapes. She read old Sherbrooke journals, or the laundry lists of maiden aunts, or Anne-Maria's fanciful phrasing from her missionary trip. She drank coffee to begin the day and wine to go to sleep.

"Dear brother," she would read, "I need not tell Over the perils we passed, the Sea's vast surge about us for these Weeks or school you once again in how the Flying Fish were sure Harbingers of Mercy, seeming to relish company in such trackless Waste. I speak personally; it appeared track-less to me who never could discern the Wind nor which direction Tides Elected, having all I could manage to distinguish Dawn from Dusk, there-fore the East from the Westering Sun. And yet those sturdy Mariners who manned the ship were cheery and steadfast in Persuasion, recognizing Rock-face or Tide-Pool or Variety of Water when it all seemed confusion to me, a blank Map.

"But the comparison is just. Even so do some of us wander like inno-cents abroad upon the Map of Faith, not knowing that the paths we tread are well-worn Stages indeed. Even so perhaps do you peer out of the House portals, making nothing of what seems to me significant. God's Sign. I trust that this will change."

VII

Then, when she no longer coveted surprise, Maggie had been taken by surprise. It has always been that way and will be, she thinks; she herself married too early and become pregnant too late. You fill the freezer full with garden produce—having worked all summer storing, canning, amassing—and the machine breaks down. You let your guard down lazily, luxuriously, and that's when they throw the cream pie.

In his last years, Judah had relinquished his own attempt at farming and rented out the land. The crops and cows belonged to someone else. There had been a succession of tenants, she learned, since Judah was irascible and watchful and knew the place inside out. Once Sammy Underwood's prize bull was penned in the wrong enclosure and broke into the vegetable garden. Judah made the farmer—right in the middle of haying, when he had no time to spare or waste—repair the pen and paint the chicken-house siding that faced it and tie back four rows of beans. Sammy Underwood gave notice then that, come season's end and as far as he was concerned, the arrangement was over; the chicken house had needed painting anyhow, and he never signed on for painting. "You can save yourself the trouble," Judah said, "in case you didn't know. I wasn't about to let you have it next time around."

Will Banner's Jerseys ate his watercress; they forded the stream behind the duck pond—not in front of it, where Judah's herd had always gone—and that finished that. Willis Reed planted corn in the shed field and then his wife got sick and he spent the fall having to cook and clothe the kids and never got to plow it under or seed the acreage down. Judah made him harvest the thistles the following spring—when he'd intended to be seeding bottom land. Finally they let the place lie fallow and he hired Hal Boudreau just to do the haying and keep the barns in shape. Hay was a dollar a bale; they did better that way anyhow, he said.

Boudreau worked for Judah for years. He was sure-footed and careful enough to satisfy the old man's particularity, but without ambition of his own. You don't want a man drinking up his wages, and this one has a liquor problem, Judah said. Give him any money and he's done for; give him cigarettes and food and a roof for his head and all's well.

Hal Boudreau was married and had had four children. One son was killed in Vietnam, one daughter worked in the state mental home, and one lived in Arizona. Maggie inquired what she did there, and Hal was reticent. She made jewelry, he said; she peddled some sort of turquoise trash the Indians produced. His fourth child, Harry, was eleven and lived in the trailer and helped out with the chores. What Maggie noticed first about them was how alike were the father and son: their coloring looked similar and their sauntering walk was the same.

This caused her to think about Ian and Judah—how she wished they might have shared some sort of occupation. Harry had the feet and hands of someone who would shoot up soon—the gap-toothed grin that shortly would be stained with nicotine, just like his father's, the ears that protruded and mouth that turned down. She saw them at the pump. Hal worked the handle, his breath steaming in December air, until a trickle, then a rush of water came out, while Harry held the pails. What was it, she asked herself later; what aspect of their labor could have compelled her attention?

"Morning."

"Morning." Hal tilted his cap's visor back.

"You could use the tap, you know."

"Lines froze," he said.

"Where? Here?"

"No. Up to our place."

"Oh." Maggie paused. They watched her. They wore hunting caps. Hal had a deer license still pinned to the back of his red wool shirt. "Well, can't you run a line?"

"Ground's froze."

"A hose?"

"Ain't got one," Harry said.

She wondered, were they teasing her; she remembered that Hal was a drunk. His nose and cheeks were red so that they blended with his beard and all his face was ruddy, glowing, but she knew herself too flame-faced from the winter wind, and told them they could take and keep whatever hose they found. They had snowshoes; they padded away. For weeks thereafter Maggie kept the image of the two black shapes, their backs to her, holding pails and hose and shuffling up the hill to their tinny retreat; she wondered, was Hal still married?

He was; she found that out. His wife showed the effects of age—heavy with the diet that, like Jack Sprat's, left Boudreau lean. Maggie met her at the grocery and, as the woman commenced to haul her shopping bags on foot back up the hill, offered a lift. Mrs. Boudreau was voluble—"Amy," she said, "that's my name, that's what they've called me ever since I can remember anyhow, though my real name's Amelia, it's French." She was French Canadian and had met Hal in Maine. They were both potato farming near the

Alagash, that's the nearest river Mrs. Sherbrooke would have heard of anyhow, and she, Amy, was a Catholic and a Democrat and that's why no one talked to her in this whole town. There were other reasons. There were Democrats enough in the woodwork; you found that out come election time, except no one admitted it, not till then, and not too many Catholics were serious, if Mrs. Sherbrooke understood what serious Catholicism meant.

Maggie rolled down the window, wanting air. "How's Hal?" she asked. "How's Harry?"

"The boy's fine. Leastways as good as you can hope for with those kidneys. But that husband of mine—I know you've befriended him, I know you're not the sort to take this wrong—well, he's a cross to carry. He's my own burden to bear. Oh, I wouldn't want it known, you know, that I'd be caught complaining, but it's why we got no car. Give him enough money for a tankful and it goes to fill him up instead. At that wicked, wicked place." She nodded at the Village Arms they were passing, on their left. "We lost two cars besides. One on payments and one because he hit a tree; if he hadn't been inebriate—it's the word for it, Mrs. Sherbrooke, pardon my French but I call a spade a spade, inebriate is what he was, three sheets to the wind, if you follow my meaning—why the good Lord knows what injuries he would have had from the crash. We found him there, sleeping it off."

"I've never seen him that way," Maggie said.

"No. You mustn't mind me telling you these things."

"I'm sorry," Maggie said. She drove through the Big House gates.

"It's the other reason no one talks to us in this whole town. But your husband understood, he never lifted his voice once against my Hal. He might not have been a Catholic, but Judah Sherbrooke was a proper Christian, and don't ever let anybody tell you different. It's why we stayed. It's why we got this trailer here backed up on your land; he paid in heat and clothes and cigarettes but never once in money, or only to me; he'd let me charge the groceries and suchlike against wages; it's a cross to carry, let me tell you, if your husband drinks every red cent."

Maggie eased to a stop. "Do you want help with those?"

"No. We're managing, I thank you. It's been a pleasure meeting you. I'm so relieved you're back. Mrs. Sherbrooke, we always wondered if you'd decide to stay—you know, it's what everybody wondered, though none of my own business, and you can tell me that."

In the weeks that followed she saw Hal often; he was always at a distance, tinkering, polite. She came to make a point of walking past the barns, of bringing him a morning thermos of black coffee and watching while he wiped his hands and pulled his cloth cap back off the red tangle, then wiped his mouth with his sleeve. He'd be meticulous, deferential, and she saw no trace of drunken wildness in him; he wore blue coveralls. Hal had filled the barns with hay that fall and was waiting for a bidder, he explained; meantime he'd tend to the tractors and balers and spreaders, doing it for her dead husband's sake, since Judah always kept the things in apple-pie order, and why not continue.

She complimented him. "You know what you're doing."

"All my life," he answered. "Two weeks behind the crops. Seems like I spent every minute of my childhood under some machine. Seems like there's nothing you can't fix with chicken wire and twine."

"And patience," Maggie said.

His deliberateness pleased her; after washing he used bay rum. He was fifty-two years old, he told her, and she said, "Why, that's just exactly my age!"

"You don't look it, ma'am."

"Not a day over fifty," she joked. "My name's not ma'am. It's Maggie."

Setting the pails down, he blushed. "It don't sit right."

"I met your wife," she told him.

"Oh?"

"At Morrisey's, the other day. We drove back up together." She offered this as explanation somehow, but wondered what she was explaining; Hal's beard was trim, and he had shaved.

"I heard."

"You need a car to help her with the groceries," said Maggie. "Please take mine."

She thinks *Bermuda* to herself, or *Mexico, New Zealand*, somewhere where indulgence thrives and where it wouldn't matter if she was a widow with a child born late. She could tell new incurious neighbors that her husband had died suddenly, too soon to know their baby; she could live there as long as she liked. And if the notion took her to return, why then she'd claim the child was hers by her new foreign husband, or only by adoption, or a foster child. She'd resume her maiden name.

She could, of course, notify Andrew. He would do the proper thing. She smiles at the formula, using it, and thinks how far from proper their shared behavior has been. Yet he is marriageable, wealthy, witty, a man of the world. He had proposed to her, half-serious, for years. He would urge an abortion or marry her or come to the hospital and be her comfortable consort in their shared old age. Maggie weighed such gain against loss and found it insufficient. She would tell him afterward, perhaps.

For all this effortful preparation feels useless to her otherwise. She's weary in advance as she'd surely feel in fact; why pack to leave, she asks herself, in order to pack to come back? The Big House is her home again, and she'll not be hounded out of it for mere propriety's sake. It doesn't matter, Maggie thinks, it's just not worth the trouble, I'll tell him or leave when I'm up to it, if . . .

She leaves the *if* alone. It means too many things. *If* means if she does not miscarry, if the baby's born alive and well, if there's opposition in the town that doesn't fade away. There are myriad alternatives to *if.* It means if Ian also leaves, or the school system fails to improve, or if she meets someone from Bermuda or Mexico or New Zealand who makes her want to move.

That someone is some male stranger, however, and Maggie feels ashamed. She's lived too long in such subservience to embrace it willingly again; she needs a woman friend. There are none in this town. And those she's claimed for New York friends have their own kind of trouble by now, or their families have been dispersed, or their projected beginnings are not how she wants to begin.

When she forces herself to walk through town, nobody notices. She's self-conscious as a girl at her first dance. She remembers how each nerve end seemed exposed at the skin's surface, and the tingling temerity of self-exposure. In India, she's heard, midwives follow pregnant women from the moment of conception; they can tell from the way a woman walks if she'll be a likely customer.

But Maggie makes it through. "I'm thinking of adopting," she tells Elizabeth Conover. They wait for the same teller at the bank.

"Adopting?"

"Yes. A Vietnamese child, maybe."

"You can't."

There is a discussion going on ahead of them; the girl behind the window is uncertain.

"Why not?"

Elizabeth coughs. "Persons of color. There's trouble . . ."

Maggie advances. "A nigger baby. Injun. The only good one's dead."

"Don't raise your voice," says Elizabeth. "That isn't what I meant."

"What *did* you mean, then?"

"Obstacles. A single parent . . ." She flutters her hands, flustered, "At our age, you know."

"I don't know." Maggie chooses peace. "I've only been thinking about adoption. I haven't made inquiries yet."

"Well, when you do," says Elizabeth—handing in her bank book, saying "Afternoon" to the new teller at eleven—"that's when the trouble begins."

So she carries her secret through town. The third month, she has a fainting spell, and Mac Andrews from the filling station drives her home. "Something I ate," Maggie says. The air revives her, and she thanks him so effusively he stammers out, "No t-trouble, ma'am; a p-p-pleasure."

"You know, the strangest thing," she says. "I don't know if your name's Mac Andrews or MacAndrews. Mr. MacAndrews. After all these years."

"Got it right the f-f-f-first time," Mac brings out.

"Yes. Thanks."

He sprays gravel at her, leaving, showing off the car's acceleration, and she puts her head between her knees.

Then she takes a call for Ian, from Jeanne Fisk. The local chamber-music group wants to invite him to their practice session Thursday night. "I know he's busy," Jeanne says. "But he might be interested, and we need another player. Would you give him the message, please?"

"I'm sure he'd be happy to come. He isn't all that busy."

"If Sally lets him. I've never seen a girl keep tighter rein." There is petulance or malice in her voice. "She should share him, don't you think? With the rest of us poor unfortunates. But they're not married yet."

"I'll give him your message," says Maggie. "Thursday night."

She hangs up, heavily. Maggie is shaking; she brushes her teeth. She scrapes the bristles on her gums until they bleed. She discovers in herself such jealousy of her son's young lover that she has to hold the sink. She studies her blear scrubbed reflection, then sticks out her tongue.

The next day Sally Conover appears at the Big House. Maggie remains in her room while Ian answers the bell. She hears laughter in the porch, then in the kitchen, then silence; then Ian returns. "What did she want?" Maggie asks.

"To borrow sugar," Ian says, and deals the hand of rummy it is his turn to deal.

"You like her, don't you?" Maggie asks.

He moves his head so that it seems both nod and shrug.

"You find her—attractive?"

"Enough," he says, discarding. "Your turn. Knock with four or under."

"Enough for what?"

"Your card."

"Why won't you talk about it?"

"Enough to sleep with." He takes her discard. "If that's what you're asking."

She feels her stomach tighten, then release. "Not exactly."

"To go out to dinner with. Your turn. To give a cup of sugar to."

She picks up a seven of hearts. Of all the cards she might have drawn, this is the least useful; she discards.

"What's the problem?" Ian asks.

The child within is hers alone; she will not share it with her son. She picks the king of clubs. "No problem."

"She's just who's here is in this town at this time. You understand." Ian gives his sheepish, theatrical grin. He offers her the eight of diamonds: a stranger, some other woman's man.

"Jeanne Fisk called yesterday," she says. "I forgot to tell you. About this Thursday evening. She hopes you'll call back."

"All right. Your turn. We don't have to finish."

"We do. What was the knock card?"

"Four."

"I'm sorry," Maggie says. "I suppose I'd thought of you as . . ."

"Without alternative? Lonely? Gin."

Now Maggie asks herself what was the point of her abashed insisting that the Boudreaus accept what she gave. It was as if she ratified her own existence in the gratitude of others—saw herself only in mirroring eyes. And, since Boudreau regarded her as generous and honest, she could see herself that way. He gave his gap-toothed grin at her, and she smiled warmly back. He told her stories of the Alagash, how he loved pumpkin pie with catsup on it, how he'd never say no to a good piece of pie. She baked them for him, Thursdays, according to the available fruit and left them by his lunch box if he were out in the fields. Harry wanted to be a mechanical engineer. He studied mechanical drawing in school, and she gave him Judah's felt-cased compass set. Hattie looked askance at that, and Maggie reminded her that charity begins at home, that there was a blessing on alms. "It's expensive," Hattie said. "The boy won't know what to make of it. Why don't you buy him one at Woolworth's; why give him one so old and good?" Maggie settled the discussion by insisting, although she was not certain, that Judah would have approved.

Thereafter she kept her small charities secret—telling Hal to rent the tractors out and keep the rental fee. She put fifty dollars monthly in the safe for Harry's schooling, moved by his earnest self-betterment. She was shamefaced, always, in front of Mrs. Boudreau's voluble thanks and complaint, saying Judah would have wished it, saying she was only doing what he'd asked her to. She paid them more for pasturing and tending to the horses than the horses had been worth—and watched the man and boy on the bridle path together, evenings, after chores.

Then, starting in the end of March, Hal went on a two-week drunk. She did not encounter him, but heard the clucking disapproval of Hattie and her friends. He had been found in ditches or asleep in unlocked cars; his wife locked him out of the trailer, and he walked the streets. He was harmless and incompetent, they said; he wouldn't hurt a fly. But it was shameful anyhow, the way his clothes got muddy all over, the way he'd look at you and not say anything but start to cry, his brain so addled with the stuff he'd not known Jeanne Fisk's name when for some crazy reason she offered him a ride. You'd have had to fumigate the car, they said; they stopped his credit at the Village Arms. But he'd gotten hold of cash and walked down to Hoosick and paid for his binges there where they didn't know him and would not refuse a customer. There was trouble enough in this country without the men in it drinking themselves glassy-eyed or falling-down foolish and maudlin. They should refuse to serve him, Hattie said; the police should lock him up and let him sleep it off.

On the second Thursday Maggie found a lunch box by the sugarhouse and opened the door to find Boudreau inside, sprawled full length on the floor. He sat up, blinking in the shaft of light, focusing, and said, "Well."

"Well."

"I was hoping to fix these buckets," he said. "There's holes in them."

"Yes."

There were a thousand sugaring buckets, with holes worked through the base.

"Mr. Sherbrooke wouldn't stand for that," he said. He shook his head; she bent above him, helpless, trying to seem helpful. "He'd want them fixed by sugaring time. Them maples ought to be tapped."

"You'd need a soldering iron."

"Ayup."

"He did it by himself, you know, my husband told me so. Destroyed them. He wanted to let the sap run."

"I never . . ."

"It's all right," said Maggie. "You just sleep. You come on in the house and take a shower, if you'd like."

"No," Hal said. He shrank from her. "These clothes . . ."

"I'll clean them. We've got a machine."

"No." He built himself up to his feet. There was a bench behind them; he sat on that. "I'm drunk," he said. "I was. I'm so ashamed. I never . . ."

"You don't have to tell me," she said.

"I want to. Leastways, sit."

She shrank from him, but he patted the wood. He did so till she sat.

"Now shut that door."

She did his bidding once again; the sugarhouse was dark, sweet-smelling.

"There's stories I could tell you," he said. "Things you ought to know about."

"All right."

"My father died when I was ten." He coughed. "And there were eight of us, you see, so Mother had to farm us out, this was 1936. The bottom'd fallen out, grown men were grateful for work. And I stayed with people called Baker—Germans they were, north of here. Up by Burlington. He was a good enough man—big, jolly, but *distant,* if you follow; he'd put his arm around me and there'd be no warmth to it."

Boudreau shivered. He sucked an unlit pipe. He looked at her, but seemed to see instead the farms by Burlington; his eyes were wide.

"What was Mrs. Baker like?"

"A hard woman, mean . . . She worked me so long it's a wonder I've still got the stomach for farming. Outside I was farmhand and inside the house I played maid. Scrubbed those steps for her; polished the porch. But mostly I remember how she was too cheap to even buy me boots. All winter long we'd spread manure from off a sled, you see, hitch it up to ponies and just walk along in the fields. All winter I'd be wearing ankle shoes and I remember that I used to pray for dawn; dear God, I'd say, just let the sun come up."

He blew out ashes from his pipe bowl. Startled by this loquacity—he had never spoken to her at such length before—she put her hand on his hand. Boudreau coughed; there was a white dried crust around the edges of his eyes.

"Milking was like that way too. Except at least the cows were warm; I had to milk five cows every morning in the dark. But by the time I'd got my things and moved about a bit it was warm in the barn, sweet-smelling to me, Jesus; I'll need a cow to milk when I'm eighty, else I won't know I'm alive. I'd just lean my head against them, tell them my troubles, and pull . . ."

He breathed so slowly, deeply, that she doubted he was still awake, and when he clasped her, shuddering, she was not certain he knew. His body was slack and hair lank. She felt her stomach heave, and held her breath and breathed through her nose, shallowly, because he reeked. Still, Maggie whispered to him, although he did not listen, that she was there, was hoping to help, and fitted her limbs to his limbs. One year before, returning, she had clung to Judah in just such a fashion and, when her husband tried to lie with her, mastered the impulse to flee.

At ten o'clock, however, cramped and cold and queasy, she disengaged herself and left the barn and walked back home. And when she saw him the next day, Boudreau's manner was sober, reverted. He apologized for his behavior, sleeping in the barn and such, and said he was a burden for his wife and family to bear. "A cross to carry," Maggie said, and Hal announced, "Yes. That's what she calls it—misfortunate. It's just exactly her words."

VIII

"Say something. I'm pregnant," Maggie repeats.

"You're not serious," says Ian.

"Yes."

"You've got to be joking."

"No."

"You're sure?"

"Not absolutely. But it's a very good guess," she says.

His horse drops its head, sidestepping.

"Might I ask . . ." Here Ian too drops his head. He raises it again, with a queer half-grin, and stares at her, assessing.

"Go right ahead . . ."

"Who's the father?"

"You might ask that."

"Well?"

Her horse shifts for forage, stamping. Maggie releases the reins; Maybe turns three-quarters around.

"Anyone I know?" says Ian.

"The odds are for miscarriage. You ought to know that. And I'm not certain I'll carry the thing—be able to. It seems unlikely, doesn't it?"

"I wouldn't know. I've never been pregnant, you see."

A rabbit bolts past them; she lets her horse walk. There are felled trees by the trailside—cut up into log lengths, but left there to dry. After some time, Maggie says, "I'm glad you find it funny."

"Not funny, no . . ."

"Amusing, then. There's so little humor in the world these days."

"I didn't mean that."

"What *did* you mean?"

The trail is wide enough; he rides alongside. "I'm sorry."

"Don't be. Just tell me what you meant."

"I was thinking," Ian says, "how many ladies might have hauled me to the woods to tell me some such secret. But in my generation, you see, they take precautions. Pills. An I.U.D. . . ." He ducks, avoiding a branch. "And there's no Judah left to make a shotgun marriage out of it; there's no way I can help you, really, except to grin a little. I meant to laugh *with* you"—he finishes—"not at."

Now Maggie hesitates. Should she fall in with his attempt at levity or tell him that she needs his help—that she's a frightened woman with no support system in place? Birds shriek at them, departing. "My man of the world," Maggie says.

"I'm sorry."

"Don't be. You're all I've got. You're my only comfort, Ian, no matter what you think."

"No."

"Yes. Believe it. You won't remember Seth . . ."

He puts his hand up to his shirt and buttons it.

"You can't, of course, how could you?"

"I was two years old," he says.

"Well, I've been pregnant three times in my life," Maggie says. "Whatever the younger generation thinks; whatever precautions you take. It was as if, when Seth was taken from us—strange, I still think of it that way, 'passed on,' 'passed over,' whatever; I can hardly read the words 'crib death,'" Maggie says, "much less say or think them—*crib death, crib death, crib death*—maybe I should practice. When Seth died, at any rate, it was like my body put itself on birth control. It was inconceivable, Ian. There seemed nothing left to conceive."

He is silent. The branches that brush them are wet; the fallen wood cracks wetly under Maybe's hooves. They follow a carpet of leaves.

"You want this child?"

"I want to talk to you about it. If I were certain, I wouldn't be out riding; if I knew for sure, I'd spend the next five months in bed. With my feet on a pillow, understand."

"Are you planning to marry?"

"No."

"Does the father know?" He cannot keep levity out of his voice. "Are his intentions honorable?"

"Or maybe I'm trying to kill it, that's what. That's why we're riding, after all." She faces him and shakes her head. "You've been giving a pretty good imitation of Judah, my friend; you're conducting just the sort of inquisition he'd have approved of . . ."

"Do you know the father?"

She kicks her horse, holds back and releases; it canters away from him, flinging up mud. Ian holds his own horse to a walk. Something startles in the brush; it beats off, heavily. At the hill's crest Maggie halts. "No."

"Well, what do you want of me?"

"Nothing."

"Permission?"

"Not really."

"Some sort of green light?" He is angry now; his voice goes high. "Some kind of cheery approval? Yes, Ma, go right ahead, go have a bastard and let me call it brother, sister, *Seth*. You must have been busy these months, not even to know which . . ." He stops, spits, wipes his face. There is a sudden flurry up above them, in the trees. "What did you expect—that I'd be jumping up and down, saying surely, by all means, get off that horse, let me carry you home, let me put you to bed and bring you breakfast till the baby's term time comes? Just exactly what's the point of this, that's all I'm asking; do you want me to get you a doctor?"

"I've done that," Maggie says.

"Then tell me," he insists, "just what the hell you require."

"Help. Someone to say I'm not crazy."

"You're crazy," Ian says.

Now they ride in silence. They skirt a hay barn she has nearly forgotten—half collapsed and empty, its slate roof cracked into seams where the building has buckled beneath it, its foundation bellied out so that the whole east wall bows. Next they pass (this is the homeward turning, she tells him, the outer extent of the farm) the shell of a house she has truly forgotten—white clapboard, slate-roofed also, its windows target practice for the neighborhood children. The brick chimney teeters. There is a front porch with four support columns, vine-choked. Maggie jumps down lightly and tethers Maybe to a column of the porch. He follows her, stiff.

"Who lived here?" Ian asks.

"No one I ever knew. Your grandfather bought it empty, I believe."

"I don't remember. When?"

"Way back. When this was a separate farm."

They sit on the porch steps. He puts his hand out gingerly; she takes and squeezes it, says: "Do you forgive me?"

"For what?" Ian asks her. "For nothing."

"Not nothing."

"I like this place," he says. "Greek Revival?"

"That woman, Anne-Maria. The one whose letters you were reading in my room . . ."

"Yes."

"This was her dower house, I think. It was built for her and Willard Sheldon. But they never lived in it."

"Why not?"

"They stayed in Guatemala. They lived in Salt Lake City. She was never welcome back, or maybe they kept on drifting. The family sold it to spite her—then Judah's father bought it back. Who knows . . ."

"I'd like to look inside."

She thinks she hears a flute, a far-off intimation. She distinguishes scales, then practice runs, then only the pigeons Ian startles as he swings the entrance door open; the house is wet.

"If it's all the same to you," she says, "I'll wait. It's warm here on the stoop."

"Okay. I won't be long."

The floorboards creak, complaining. She watches as he enters, letting whatever nests there scuttle off for cover. Then she too steps inside. There is a fireplace to the left, a warren of rooms to the right, and a central hall with only the studs remaining, a freestanding stairwell, no plumbing or electric lights. The banister is intricately carved. Ian paces the length of the house, his footsteps echoing. She asks herself what memory he hunts in this abandoned place, beneath the roof (she can see up to it, through it, where the lath has given way and there are only crossties and a few cracked slates) that seems never to have offered shelter to the intended occupants. Perhaps some tenant farmer or those who came to help with haying had been billeted in the small upstairs rooms; perhaps some family idiot or mistress had been consigned to this space.

Ian makes his way back down the stairwell and, three rungs from the landing, puts his foot right through the wood. She watches him draw back, then jump. He picks a long pine splinter from his leg. "Does it hurt?" she asks; he tells her, "No." Upstairs the rooms are ten by eight, six of them—he's counted—each giving on the hall. This is not the time to make a full inspection, they agree; the horses whinny and nicker. But the abandoned house compels him; he will make it, he tells her, his own.

Her father, too, has died. In the last year, Maggie thinks, and with the exception of Ian, the men in her life were outlasted. His death had not been peaceful; he had had a tumor of the brain. She found him raving, in the hospital at Hyannis, sure he was the captain of a whaling ship, and with a mutinous crew.

Maggie had been notified by the hospital staff that her father's health was critical and she should come if possible. She drove to the Cape on a clear August morning and did not stop for gas until the Sagamore Bridge. Then, more slowly, reined in by traffic, she made her way to his side. When he did not greet or recognize her, she felt as if there's no escape, there's nothing that you ever get for free. Your husband who had shammed disease to bring you home lives on with dignity; your father finishes that. He had been a cheerful man, full of mariner's stories; as a widower he'd moved to Wellfleet and grown a full gray beard. They put him in a single room because he shouted so.

Maggie blamed herself. She thought, maybe what she'd taken as his harmless eccentricity had been the death-dealing tumor. Had she tried to question him (not listening nodding, subservient, unable to say Dad, you've never been to Hatteras, you never did use flensing tools), had she taken his headaches as actual, perhaps they might have caught the swelling in his brain. He howled "Avast, me hearties" and knotted the bedsheets like rope. He called his pillowcase a gag and swore he'd make his way by compass and main force through the Barrier Reef.

She shared his last three days. It was more time than she'd spent with him for years. But he had been unreachable—a shrunken, dapper person with water in his eyes. When he died she half believed that he was only resting, and she told the nurse who came to check just not to bother or wake him, please. When the doctor certified his death and signed for it, Maggie thought she saw a stormy petrel fly past the hospital window. She scattered his ashes secretively, later, behind the Harbormaster's Office of the Wellfleet Dock.

There were Pekin ducks on the back pond behind the garden wall. She'd left them out that winter, not bothering to coop them, but only setting up a windbreak and leaving them cracked corn or crumbs. They could fly, she'd said to Hattie; they could deal with the foxes this winter by themselves. "Sleep, shit, and screw, that's all they ever do," was Judah's barnyard rhyme. So she helped them with cracked corn, but not protection; they could keep the pond from icing over and deploy to the safety of water if there were a fox.

Therefore she'd made her way, every second morning, to the pond. It is behind what used to be the icehouse, maybe forty feet across. The house had been built out of brick, with a slate roof. There is a small stream feeding the pond, granite ledging on three sides, and a mud patch where the pond had silted in. She'd feed the ducks. They yawped and scurried from her and swam to the water's far edge. She'd check for fox tracks every morning and find none.

Then there was a cold snap, and the pond iced over. Maggie took a walking stick—Judah's heavy locust cane—and went and found, as she rounded the icehouse, fox tracks. Six duck carcasses lay by the windbreak. There was webbing left, and everything above the neck, and feathers and feet. The frozen blood looked brown.

She could not help admiring the precision of such slaughter—how the one night when the ducks could find no refuge was the night the fox had struck. She supposed the animal had reconnoitered while the ducks eluded it in the center of the pond. They'd huddle fifteen feet away, in water, and wait out his visit. On ice, however, there'd be no escape, and the fox prepared for that.

There was a riddle about pilgrims with a fox, a rooster, and grain. There was one small conveyance only, and the pilgrim had to cross a river with only one of the three as his cargo; otherwise he'd sink. The problem was to choose his route and companions—since if he left the rooster with the grain, the rooster would consume the grain, and if he left the fox and rooster, the rooster would be eaten in its turn. This was true on either side, though salvation waited on the farther bank.

There was a solution, she knew. She tried to remember the riddle. You take the rooster first, leaving behind the fox and the grain. Then you come

327

back and bring the fox with you, but take the rooster back. Then you ferry the grain across and come back empty-handed and return with the rooster and take up the journey again.

Just so, and just as carefully, she has tried to organize cargo. She has done double journeys and kept things separate and attempted to keep slaughter down. But the solution argued wakefulness; it meant she had to stay with one while loading up the other, meant the rooster would not dare to eat in the pilgrim's supervisory presence. And Maggie feels herself, these days, unable to furnish protection. Let them eat each other or die of starvation, she thinks; what happens happens anyhow; it's only a question of time.

Judah's death, for instance, had come in the fullness of time. This was Hattie's phrase, and then the minister's, though Maggie knows that Hattie thinks his death was premature. The doctors talked of surgery; they had talked of implanting a pacemaker; they warned him off too much to eat, and exertion and smoking, but he said a shot of whiskey drove the angina away. They said, "With luck, you'll live a good long time, and with any luck at all at least a dozen years."

But then he had his heart attack and everything was blockage, stoppage, old age fisting fingers through his arteries like ice. Then he was on borrowed time, with credit running out. Then he was at every instant's mercy, and his sister doled out blood-thinning pills. Maggie watched. He winked at her. He gave Hattie maraschino cherries in exchange, and she said the Lord's mercy abounded, and he himself had no real fear of credit running out. He said the Lord was not an accountant with favored clientele; you don't tally debits and credits for angina pectoris if you've reached the ripe old age of seventy-six.

"You take that pill now," Hattie urged. "It's just one extra swallow in the day."

Judah choked the white pills back. He gagged on them, Maggie knew; though they were smaller than anything else he ate, they would enlarge in his mouth. They filled the space behind his tongue and thickened as his throat thinned down, and he tried to feel his thick red blood go watery because of the helpful effect of the pills. In their shared room, at night, he spoke to Maggie about it. He wondered should he go on living if living were a hardship, and wondered when he'd know it had become a hardship that wasn't worth enduring, or was too hard to bear. "You'll know," she told him, and he puckered the skin of his cheeks and furrowed the skin of his forehead, concentrating, attempting to know.

They trot the first mile back. Then, at the trail's highest point, she halts, and her son draws up beside her while they survey what they own. "I like things best in spring," she says. "You see the contours of the land, the edges—that river there, those foothills. It's such a green profusion in the summertime; everything crowds together. In a month."

"I sneeze," Ian says.

"What?"

"In a month I start to sneeze," he reminds her. "For all of June."

"Still? I thought you'd outgrown it."

"In cities it isn't so bad. There ain't no pollination in cement."

Maggie smiles—her overgrown infant, faking bumpkin chatter in the breeze. "You could have shots."

"No."

She looks at Ian sidelong, studying. He wears a red shirt, has gray-blue eyes; his horse is brown. The fields are umber and ocher and a translucent green. "I lied to you," Maggie says.

He rolls his sleeve down, carefully, then buttons it. He shifts the reins, then does the same, less carefully, to his left sleeve.

"About what?"

"My pregnancy."

"I thought maybe," he says. "Menopause. You're not pregnant, are you?" There is relief in his voice, and she hears this with regret. "I am."

"Then how did you lie?"

"It isn't maybe," she says. "It's definite. And I do know the father."

"Who . . ."

"I got the tests back yesterday. The rabbit says 'yes.' Yes."

"Well." Ian masters himself. "Just you and me and baby makes three."

She takes his tone. "That's what I'd hoped you'd say," she says.

(Maggie had called the doctor. She introduced herself, and they discussed the weather—the astonishing quantity of rain, okay; and how are you feeling this morning, is it still like this next month in your country, this part of the country, okay, it's devastation elsewhere, Walter Cronkite says, because of the drought; his wife had never seen such activity, moreover, as with the cows at auction, they went Wednesday night, where we come from such animals are sacred—while she waited for her breathing to quiet, for the hint of yes or no or maybe that would organize his prattle into prophecy, her fate. He told her in his singsong fashion that they hoped to have some cousins come, their relatives would visit just as quickly as the passage could be arranged, okay, and has she been to Albany to see the mall like Delhi's, and would she recommend Las Vegas as a vacation destination since his wife had a passion for gambling, okay, unfortunate, but true. Finally she asked him outright, and he said, "Congratulations, Mrs. Sherbrooke, you're a very lucky woman, you must give your husband my compliments. Yes.")

"This is the last ride," Ian says, "the three of us will take."

"Yes, *sir*," she says.

"Hang on."

There is a passage in the letters that she knows by heart. It gives life to that archaic language, those beliefs she does not share, and to her present hopes. Anne-Maria wrote:

"Guatemala is a Pleasant Land, with what I venture to approve will be a Healthfull Climate and a people anxious to receive the Call. One tale I wish to tell you, brother, in the Belief it signifies; down here there is a Native Child who has had his tongue spliced from some Harsh Foreman's cruelty. Who knows the cause? I could not ascertain it, nor do the parents willingly speak of the case (if indeed they be his Parents under whose thatched roof he lies and whose fire he tends, whose food shares). Perhaps it was the common treatment for some childish Deviltry; perhaps indeed he was born thus, as some in the Village make claim. He is a silent boy— ten years old or thereabouts, lissome in contour and gait. We could not make him Speak to us, though Willard is adept at speech, the dialect no obstacle, and I have always had—as I trust you will grant is plain Truth and not Boastful—a way of talking with the Young.

"Still, Jo resisted. I call him Jo because his actuall name is far far longer, a disharmonious series of x's it is difficult to write. I would bring him little gifts and sit by the Fire he stirred (Evil comes to these huts if the hearth-flame Expire) and Eat of his corn-cakes and drink the milky water here from the one tin cup. I will not bother you with details of my talk. I spoke of the Green Mountains where in America we live, and how someday I hoped to show him railroad trains such as our Father possessed. I spoke of the tablets of Mormon, and how it is our fast Belief that revelation per-sists—that even in these latter ages God may speak to man. He listened, his lips closed. I must confess that, as the weeks continued with no utterance from Jo, my resolution failed. I thought perhaps the forked tongue was the Sign of some Satanic presence, not an attentive Child. Imagine if you will how when he wiped his lips, having shared our frugal repast or proffered me his own, a segment of his tongue caressed the upper lip whilst simul-taneous with that a segment licked the nether. Yet in the third week he said, 'Hold'—in the fourth 'Urim and Thummin'—in the fifth said, 'Mrs. Sheldon, you are a good woman to me.'

"I wept; I weep to write it; there is grace abounding in the farthest reaches of our Earth."

IX

She keeps it a secret as long as she can, and for many reasons. First, she's superstitious. Keep your head in the sand, she tells herself; don't count a chicken till hatched. If she does not identify the future's danger or delight, it might not come to pass. She dismisses Mrs. Russell so the cleaning woman cannot see her; if she is not seen, she tells herself, her stomach is not visible. Because of Ian's presence and the mess that a third person makes, Mrs. Russell is willing to go.

There might be complications. Maggie does not know this pregnancy will come to term; the odds seem strongly against it. But in the fifth month of gestation she takes the test for Down's Syndrome; whatever is in her is whole. She passes; *they* pass; she feels as if the doctor is a hard taskmaster, testing her. He slaps the needle on her stomach like a ruler, and she waits for his verdict like grades. Then he becomes a guru and benign; she feels herself falling in love. He and Ian are the two men in her life, the only two who know. Ian keeps her secret, she is sure. And in the fifth month she requests Dr. Rahsawala not to tell; she tells him how she hopes to give her husband a gift. For the same reason, Maggie says, she does not want to know the baby's sex. He offers her the option, but she says she's superstitious and would rather be surprised.

The road to his office is magic. It takes forever to arrive and no time at all to return. Then, when she falls in love with him, she drives there in an instant and takes forever to crawl home. In July he says, "Mrs. Sherbrooke, I know you're a widow, okay, I do not mind." He sits behind the desk, his brown face smooth, his hair slicked back, drinking Coca-Cola from a coffee mug. She bleeds a little the next day, and calls him, and he tells her not to leave her bed. She does remain there, attempting to read until the spotting stops. For the time it lasts, however, she contemplates miscarriage, and learns past contradiction—from the heart-stopping sorrow that wells up in her, and the tears she cannot stop—how much she wants this child. She is afraid of bearing it but terrified of losing it; the tea Ian brings her is too strong to drink. She studies herself in the bedside mirror—a wild, aging woman who's come to this pass, who'll stay in bed if necessary till her baby's born.

It has no sex. It is neither he nor she, but *it,* unnameable. Her life's blood is its drink. She eats for nourishment, not pleasure, and remembers how, when half this age and carrying her second son, she had been ravenous. Judah bought her raspberries, and she ate two pints at a sitting, with cream. He'd bring her garden produce, and she'd go through a whole plate of greens. Now Maggie's appetite is gone; now there seems no room inside her for food, and she keeps it down just long enough for *it* to eat. She is, continually, ill. Hattie notices at last but thinks it is some past-due change, some retribution for the way she used to guzzle but put on no weight. "You're eating too much pie," the old woman says, and Maggie dares not reveal that she bakes pie for the Boudreaus but cannot take a bite. If she makes it till her seventh month, she knows, the baby will likely survive.

But seven months means September and an eternity away. The summer has grown hot. The house is well shaded by maples, but there's never air. July has been so wet, she hears, that the corn's drowning. Her room in daylight is an incubation cell. At night, with the electric fan and lying on top of the sheets, Maggie can find fitful rest—six hours of surcease. She never sleeps longer than that. She leaves the Big House only to drive to the doctor's house, and only once every two weeks. He is solicitous—talkative and watchful both at once. By August she knows love for him is only for his office—that it has become her safe haven. He has not seen her in her slender previous integrity; he is not shocked. The room is white. There's a photograph of Everest and one of llamas and a woodcut that he tells her represents the dancing Krishna. He tells her that she must relax her mind, okay, and for the rest of August she fears not her body but mind.

She finds herself walking the house. It is not truly sleepwalking, since she does not sleep. But in a kind of trance she finds herself in laundry rooms, or in the greenhouse they emptied last winter, or in the back halls and attic. The cellar is a comfort, even with troublesome pumps. Water beaded on the walls where it had always beaded, and dry rot on the support beams of the cellar (she recognizes the traces now, since Judah had pointed them out) still leaves enough support to hold three times the weight. She knows the flooring—cement or dirt or, in the laundry rooms, linoleum tile—is backed on solid ground.

But the attic is a trial. There everything has been jumbled together, and crates strewn every whichway, with spiders and bats in the eaves. Attics are the place, says Hattie, closest to God and most heaven-aspiring. It behooves a person to maintain a cleanly attic, because otherwise a person is in secret disrepair. Yet the Big House attic is not beyond reproach; Hattie reproaches herself for that; she was always promising to make sense of the storage bins and organize the shelves.

For Maggie feels herself discarded, up in the heights of the house. She fingers instruments that no one plays or tennis rackets with strings snapped and even their wood presses warped and everything askew. She uncovers baseball gloves. Their webbings have been torn. She finds newspapers and magazines retailing early, simple times when nothing was a relic yet that now she moves past gingerly, her head against the beams. There are music stands and curtain rods and Venetian blinds. The closet is a receptacle, a space to fill with litter that is only not-quite waste. There are swallows' nests. She hunts their skeletons and can find none; they must have followed a favoring wind right out the eyebrow vents.

Once, the previous winter, when she and Hattie went to tea at Helen Bingham's, there had been a break-in at the house.

"Why don't you join us this afternoon?" Hattie had asked. "Helen would be pleased to have you, and we could drive over together."

Maggie, though she despised such gatherings—the wax floral centerpiece, the women cackling over someone else's troubles and clucking over their own—had just this once agreed. The snow was powder-pure. They stayed till dark and followed a snowplow back home.

There had been tracks on the porch. The kitchen door was broken, and one chair pulled near to the potbelly stove. Nothing had been stolen and nothing else touched; she liked to think of some cold traveler, meticulous but needing rest, grateful for the kitchen's dark quiet—apologetic, really, about that single smashed lock.

Hattie wanted to call the police. "We'll catch him, sure. It's easy to track fugitives in snow."

But Maggie refused. "Breaking and entering. That isn't such a sin."

"It is," Hattie told her. "He ought to spend the night in jail. He had no business here."

"How do you know it was 'he'?"

"A person knows."

"Well, what if it was Ian? Or somebody like him?"

"I'm shocked," Hattie said, "that you could even think a son of yours would do such things. That you'd harbor such a criminal."

"Don't let's call. They'd never catch him anyway. You'd just be sending the police all over creation in this weather."

335

"If it's what you want."

"Yes."

"Mollycoddling criminals . . ."

Maggie—so giddy with elation she almost wished the intruder were up-stairs, in some closet and not, as the tracks on the porch plainly showed, gone—raised her hands. "You got me dead to rights," she said. She tells herself she welcomes each invasion and escape.

Boudreau trims lawns; he circles their house like a drone. And when he mows the meadow grass he attaches a wagon to the tractor and sucks and spits up weeds with what Maggie thinks of as a giant vacuum cleaner. Judah had invented it years back. He'd built a wire housing on a wagon to hold the catch, and she delighted seeing the green swaths he cut through thistle. In the early mornings now, or at dusk when she knows she might wander unnoticed, Maggie walks by the tamarack and willows and through the river-birch stand. The air is palpable—so thick with gnats and pollen that it feels like netting parting where she walks. There are odors in the air she feels she might swallow or drink. Sprinklers chirrup at the flower beds, and everything enchants her with its hot somnolence. The stone walls of the property appear to her as if they are both parapets and moat.

Then Finney calls. "I haven't seen you." He coughs, as if announcing himself at an untended counter. "Not all these weeks."

"No."

"Months, it feels like."

"And you're just checking in," Maggie prompts.

"Yes. Something like that."

"Well, we're fine. Don't worry on our account, Samson; you've got more likely candidates for sympathy."

"I don't doubt. How's Ian?"

"Fine, we're fine. Is there something you wanted to ask?"

There is silence on the phone. She pictures him, considering, tamping down his pipe or rearranging stacks of sheets within the rolltop desk. "I only thought I ought to warn you," Finney says at last. "I'm a small-town lawyer. Licensed in Vermont. I don't know what they do down there in that fancy Manhattan of yours—though if you ask me they don't either, if you push us to it we'd get ourselves a verdict half the time. That's my opinion, anyhow—put small-town savvy at the bench with big-city smarts, and small-town savvy can win. That's how I've lived my life. Or tried to."

Maggie waits.

"But I have to admit it, I'm stumped." His voice has a queer weariness, as if admitting to confusion has confused him further. "Judah was—well, I don't need to tell *you*—he was adamant about divorce. Which meant remarriage, far as he saw it. So that carried over, Maggie, and he didn't want you marrying after he was dead. Now this could be challenged, I daresay"—his voice cracks, and she hears him sigh, exhaling—"by one of those lawyers, who'd no doubt be glad for a cut. But it boils down to loyalty—stay Mrs. Judah Sherbrooke and you keep the whole estate. Get married and it's gone."

"How could I have signed that?" Maggie asks.

"You didn't have to. It was Judah's signature we needed."

"Well, how could *he?*"

In Los Angeles, Maggie finds herself remembering, there were Santas slung from palm trees and a sleigh with reindeer rigged above the boulevard. She sat in a car in Bel Air, warm, watching joggers, waiting at an intersection for the light to change. She mentioned that it did seem strange: a plastic Santa leapfrogging traffic. Her companion said, "Yeah, that's California," and put his car in gear.

"You take my meaning," Finney says.

"Not really. No."

"Do I have to spell it out?"

"Maybe," she tells him. "It's not what you think, Samson, I'm not planning to marry just now."

"What *I* think doesn't matter. My opinion doesn't count." He breathes so that she hears it, as if inhaling probity. Maggie senses he behaves this way in the courthouse, and the claim of weakness is a move he makes by habit, falling back. He makes his counter-claim. "But there's rumors going round. Things people see and say."

She remembers, also, a woman in a sable coat. The woman wore leg braces and blue hair. She was sitting on a park bench with two tethered Pekingese.

"What kind of rumors?" Maggie asks.

"That Judah has a baby coming. Just a little late. I don't deny or confirm it, you understand, I know nothing about it at all. But I do believe *you* should know," Finney says.

She uncoils the black cord, then twists it again.

"And remember you can't remarry or the Big House goes on the block. Dismantled. Correct me if I'm wrong," he says, "but there's two options that I see. Providing there's a grain of truth in what we're discussing. In which case, of course, it's something to celebrate, right? You mustn't mind me saying this, but—well; it's either a Sherbrooke or bastard. Correct?"

"You accept the rumors?"

"You haven't let me visit." His voice is steady now, official. "I'm talking hearsay, not eyewitness evidence. If it's the prior instance—Judah Sherbrooke's child—then it may be tongues will wag; there may be a few difficulties—but no legal problems, follow?" He pauses. "At least not in this state. At least not in this town. No objection I can foresee. If it's the second instance, however," Finney says, "the testament obtains."

She tries to pay attention as he talks about the options consequent on birth. He wants the child to be Judah's; he is willing to believe it, because that's how Sherbrookes behave. She is not shocked. She wants to feel—or simulate—shock, but knows he'd take her protestations for guilt. What's guilty in the land's law is, for Sherbrookes, innocence. Though she could sue to keep the place, and the presumptions and precedents are in her favor, says Finney, there are certain battles it seems smarter not to fight.

"'Let sleeping dogs lie' is my motto," he says. "Or pass it on to Ian while you can."

So once again, thinks Maggie, she's being controlled by her husband and is bending to his will. If she raises the child in the Big House, it has to be called Judah's child. She supposes that this happened with some frequency in 1500, on feudal estates; women lied about their children's parentage. But this is not 1500, or feudal estates, and she's trying against odds to have what's hers to hold.

It could have been wind chaff, or sperm in a bathtub; she reads of a mother who claimed to be a virgin, and that she'd been impregnated by some total stranger's emission in the swimming pool. There are those who swear to virgin births; an egg is activated by a needle, Maggie knows. It had been inadvertent. She could have slept with Andrew or not slept with Andrew, could have told him or not told him how they had conceived. She tells herself that Andrew was the swimming pool, or needle; the child is hers alone. With every week and month she waits, the temptations of her privacy increase.

Then Judah rises from his testament like a gray ghost, canny, canceling her independence from his deathbed as in life. He claims prior possession. He still possesses the Big House since her own ownership is revocable and based on good behavior. He speaks in the tongues of townspeople, and in the name of the law.

Returning from her father's funeral, Maggie stopped for gas in Taunton. A street fair had started up, and a fat black man in a chef's hat was barbecuing chicken. He offered her a section. "On the house," he chortled. "Compliments of the chef." He was splendidly astream with sweat; he mopped his neck and chins with the apron's underside, then fed the fire with a stack of paper plates. "Nobody's here," he announced. "You're the first customer I've had; seems like we can't get *rid* of chicken in this town."

"I'm not much of a customer," she said.

"Pretty woman like you are hadn't ought to pay."

She thanked him and tried the charred meat. He licked his lips in pantomime, then said, "Excuse me a second, will you. I got things to attend to inside. If anybody happens past, just give them a chunk. On the house." He laughed again, hugely happy. "You follow? On the *house.*"

So Maggie waited in the street, finishing her chicken, wiping both her hands. A girl with lank black hair and wearing what looked like a nightgown appeared. She had rope sandals and carried a net bag; she wore fingerless gloves. "Everybody's at the races," the girl said. "Believe it, the dog track. I should have set up there."

"Would you like a piece of chicken?"

The girl eyed her doubtfully.

"Free." Maggie said. "On the house."

"In that case . . ."

"Help yourself."

So then they ate together, watching the street. There was a ring-toss stall opposite, and a table with four chairs. "I tell people's fortunes," the girl said. "I'm a palmist, mostly, but I also do the cards."

"Do mine," said Maggie. "Please."

The girl narrowed her eyes, shook her head. "They tell you what's important. It's no game, believe it."

"I believe that," Maggie lied.

"Like them races." She waggled one finger. "I could handicap them wicked if I wanted. Greyhounds and a mechanical rabbit. I ask you . . ."

The girl sat down and shuffled the deck. Suddenly formal, she pulled back a second chair. "If you'd care to take a seat."

A truck went past, backfiring. Maggie smelled the gas.

The girl spread out her cards in silence. Then, exhaling, she declared, "Death. There's lots of death here. Jesus. This is wicked difficult to read."

"What's difficult?"

"You got to get rid of it, lady, that's the point."

Maggie was shaken. "How do I do that?"

340

"The cards don't give advice." The girl crossed her arms, rubbed her elbows and looked, Maggie thought, like a raccoon. "It isn't like they tell you 'Fire the chauffeur' or 'take a long sea journey' or any of that shit. It isn't fortune-cookie shit, it's where your life is at." She bent her head, assessing the frayed diagram: there were towers and princes and cups. "Big changes, lady. Let loose."

Still, Judah proved hard to dismiss. His weight was on her when she slept; his will endured. She thinks perhaps the reason that he seemed so gentle those last months was that he'd known he'd trapped her and had claimed full possession: take me and mine, he seemed to be saying, but nothing when you go. It is not avarice. She has no need of what wealth he provided, nor the trappings of the house. If she wanted to be greedy, there'd been occasions for greed. Rather, Maggie tells herself, it's how she's grown to love the place, to feel at peace within its walled perimeter. The single thing her husband asks is that she call the bastard his; then the protection extends. He wouldn't have put it that way, of course. He'd envisioned her remarriage, not a child. No one envisioned that. But this is what it comes to, Maggie thinks: tell the little white lie that it's Judah's; let the lawyers do arithmetic and fudge a figure here or there, relinquish your own independence and call this madness sanity and all is as before.

Are these, she asks herself, the arguments of death? What kind of child would be born of a corpse; what womb-wrenching injury derives from such a covenant? Would she rather yield paternity to Andrew than her husband, get a second husband in the bargain and therefore leave Vermont? For days and weeks she waits.

Now the madness proves its guile. It turns the walls around. The memory of pain is fleeting as the aftertaste of pleasure; it is impersonal. She comes to think of herself as something separate, an entity within the house that sometimes bears her name. Once, in the New York apartment, she had painted Ian's room. It had been winter, and she left the window shut and all morning long inhaled paint fumes. Only when she left the space did Maggie lose her balance—feel the world whirling, the East River vertical—and the iron grillwork of the balcony seemed suddenly strawlike, light, bent.

She kept away from the railing and stayed carefully inside. Nausea too seemed wavelike and impersonal; she vomited without implication in the action of her throat. Systole and diastole—she found the words and chanted them, feeling her stomach constrict. Systolic, diastolic—everything was foreordained, mere muscularity, a structure she'd be part of till it spat her free. It did; she rose. She had been ready for Ian when he returned from school. He had noticed nothing but the newly painted wall.

But mostly she distrusts herself; her silence comes from fear, not shame. She consults her horoscope in magazines, and *Ripley's Believe It or Not!* She finds she's not even close to the age of the oldest woman to give birth, yet that is scarcely a comfort. Few of her friends have children still home, and none of them had babies past the age of forty-five. She'd been old before her time, she thinks, and now is young too late.

"I send you *The Pearl of Great Price.* It is our testament, brother, with revelations given to Moses and vouchsafed to Joseph Smith. There are writings of Abraham also. Happiness is, we believe, the Proper Lot of Men. The Book of Mormon says, and I urge the point upon you, 'Men are, that they might have joy.' Willard speaks to heathens here of *the dispensation of the fulness of times.* I would do likewise with you. There will in that fulness be Order provided, and all that seems but Accidental now or foolish must make sense; do not therefore glut yourself or Block your senses with whiskey and smoke, for fear the Sanctified Processional will pass your way and you will be incompetent to join it, since as with so many here the drunk and debauched men sleep, their slatterns beside them in the fields where wastes the Food that properly requires Harvest if virtue pass not out of the kernel in the Corn. To everything there is a season, as you know. Why not then store Sobriety against the Winter's ravages, and the Importuning Fingers of the frost that even in this southern clime must chill us all?

"We knew our father as a man of Strong Belief. That he did not know the Prophet greatly grieves me, since I think it likely he would have found both *light* and *truth*. 'It is impossible for a man to be saved in ignorance,' and I have lately come to terms with what his everlasting apostasy portends. Still, what though he spat on it, I pray he comes to be enlightened in the tenets of our Church. This is not impossible. Willard concurs. There is the possibility of conversion, brother, *after* death. Time and Eternity continue, so why should not our father have the chance, though mortal clay, to constitute himself again in what our leader cites as the Authoritative Way?

"It vexes me, a muddleheaded woman. I cannot sort the matter out. There is Doctrine for it also, but I am less well instructed in the issue than my husband would wish. What of those who—according to their own lights—found salvation, but did so in apostasy? Should we deny them reprieve? Ought we dash ambrosia from their lips and bleed them till the final drop of ichor spill? I trust you will answer on this."

Maggie thinks it gibberish. She holds neither Peacock's nor Anne-Maria's belief. But there is something in the conviction of the woman, some urgency that signals her to turn the yellowed pages with their perfect fading penmanship until she finds some meaning in the century-old preachment, "Men are, that they might have joy." She will never be a convert; she has embraced no faith. But as her world goes inward—as even her son, returned and intimate and everything she'd hoped for, becomes a callous stranger—she thinks what she has feared as madness is the need to know her own worth.

She has been prized all her life. She has been praised and courted and counted on until courtliness and praise are both beside the point. She runs through the kitchen and, seeing Ian, stops. She is in disarray. "You're still here," Maggie says.

"I promised, didn't I?"

"Yes. So you did."

"And promises are made to keep," he pronounces, with that sententious air of his, that whiff of Sunday school . . .

"I'm glad."

"You were running. Be careful," Ian says.

They come to tea with Hattie, or to dinner and bridge. Hiding, she will not descend. Her pregnancy would be the town's chief morsel, and they would gobble it whole. Sometimes Maggie wonders if she's being unfair; she's tempted to make herself public and find out. There might be Samaritans amongst them—those who'd wish her well. But when she studies their faces from the landing, or hears the shrill clatter beneath her, she knows it isn't likely, and it's sensible to hide.

Within the thousand acres, within the Big House and her upstairs chamber, it is no problem for Maggie; there is space enough around her, and company enough. She thanks her luck for Ian, since she might not have made it alone. Instead she fixes on him with a grasping fixity she knows he is embarrassed by but cannot contravene. She fears she is becoming a reclusive older sister; she will provide him with a child he might as well be father to, in age. And therefore Maggie waits like some self-tormented spinster in this tower of her building, patting her round stomach and dreaming that straw strands are gold.

X

Fat is not the word for it; she's bulging, Hattie sees. She's got a lump beneath her breasts the size of what in other women Hattie would have to call
twins. And Maggie's face is pinched, drawn in; there's nothing plump in
any other part of her. She can't and won't believe her sister-in-law is pregnant; she's unmarried and too old. So there must be something wrong with
what she eats, and Hattie tries to warn her off of pies. Or her digestive process has gone wrong, and everything gets stuck in the upper intestine. Or
it's hysterical pregnancy—Hattie has heard about those. She's seen it, once
or twice, in dogs. After the Willis's spaniel was spayed, she blew up just like
Maggie—a pathetic balloon where her babies should be and would never
ever arrive. The spaniel lay around all day, bloated, breathing heavily. Ellen
Willis said it would have been better to just let her breed; this breaks my
heart to see.

She's heard about a woman up in Shaftsbury—Greta Harrington's cousin,
what was her name? Hattie hunts it: the one who married Nickerson over

by the Old East Road—who swelled up just like this. They thought it was overmuch candy and water; they gave her pills and put her on a diet, but she kept right on growing. They thought it was glandular, then something in her blood, and then Agnes—that was it, Agnes Nickerson, the one with the strawberry birthmark—went pure plain crazy and they had to send her to the Brattleboro Retreat. There the doctors told her that what she had was cancer, not the child she swore she had been carrying; what she was birthing was death.

But Maggie will not discuss it, so Hattie keeps her peace. She yearns to be of use, awaiting her dead brother's child, if that's what Maggie's hatching like a broody hen. It would be a miracle, the Good Lord giving what he took; she'd go down on her knees and give thanks. Yet you don't speak till spoken to; she's long ago learned that. So it's a strange strained family they make these days—Ian out at all hours and Maggie never leaving the house, who'd been a gadabout before. They eat in silence if they eat together, and Hattie excuses herself by eight o'clock or at the latest eight thirty and shuts herself into her room.

The days are shortening; there's heavy dew most mornings and it grows darker sooner at night. She puts up peas and beans and corn and pickles; she cans tomatoes and makes jam. It's more than they need; she knows that. The pleasure has gone from preserving, and she works with a bone-weariness she hasn't known before. Morning after morning, week by month, she's been at the kitchen counter, chopping and boiling and putting things by. Sometimes, when she sees the asparagus patch or the berries they'd planted, or horseradish—things that are perennial, that last, so you couldn't say, "This season let's just not bother; let's forget about the garden this once"—sometimes she yearns to tell Boudreau to plow the whole thing under.

But you couldn't do that—or she, Hattie, couldn't; there's been too much love and labor expended on the asparagus patch. There'd been too many years it mattered to have homegrown food. Not because they couldn't always buy whatever they wanted; not because it was ever a question of need.

But for all those years Hattie'd known what she ate—known when it was planted and cultivated and who had been in on the tending. It is a satisfaction. She's tasted the fruits of her labor, which is a taste no supermarket or Morrisey's can sell. You sow and thin and prune and stay up nights all summer for the satisfaction of such tasting when the world gets wintry later on. You do it for the future's sake, and not for present gain.

"Good night," she says.

"Good night."

"Night, Aunt." Ian scarcely looks up.

"Sleep well."

"You too, Hattie." Maggie consults the clock. "It's early yet."

"We could play cards," she offers. "We could invite somebody in for a fourth."

"No," Maggie says.

"Why not?"

"I'm not in the mood. Not tonight."

"You never are, lately."

"I suppose that's true."

"If you don't mind my asking, is there a good reason for that?"

Then Ian intrudes. He puts his foot right in his mouth where it has no business being. "She does mind your asking."

"Well, I'll be off to bed then, thank you very much."

"Okay. Good night," Maggie says.

"You two." She bets they cackle together now, playing two-handed rummy, misunderstanding, thinking she'd told them, "You too."

She yawns in her room, purposive. She's heard that yawning is contagious. If you yawn a'purpose you can set a whole supper party to sleep. If you raise your voice, the others at the table raise their voices also, and soon there'll be a din and clamor and people shouting to be heard. If you drop your voice, however, the person talking to you will drop her voice in turn, and you have a mannerly gathering with no need to shout.

It doesn't work. She isn't sleepy. Hattie itches to be down in the kitchen, or already at the silver chest that had been tomorrow's project. There are coffee spoons and serving knives and ladles she hasn't polished in months; she keeps a list in the chest's inside lid of how many pieces the service contains, and when they last were cleaned. She is shamefully behind. Maggie wouldn't notice, and if she noticed would anyhow not care or mention it—but Hattie is responsible and doesn't want the silver service tarnishing. It would have helped to pass the time; she should have thought to bring the chest with her, and silver polish and rags.

Evenings, and in order to protect against intruders, she locks herself in. By the time she is inside her room Hattie means to stay inside and unmolested, thank you very much. A man's home is his castle, and a woman's home is twelve by twelve, but there should be a drawbridge to that too. She leaves the key in the lock. They could rattle at the door and pound on it and ask, "Is everything all right?" They'd be concerned and speculative and insisting that she answer, but she'd press her hand to her mouth while the perturbation in the hall increased.

It increases everywhere; the town has gotten shabby and they ought to hose it down. There are no typhoons or tornadoes in this section of Vermont, but Hattie nearly wishes for just such fearsome ruination. It's just as well, she sometimes thinks, that Judah didn't live to watch the world decay. There are exceptions, of course. She could set her watch, still, by the way Ted Fraser walks from the bank to the post office at nine and, come nine fifteen, walks back. There might be carpenters with pigtails who you'd swear had sworn a holy oath against deodorant; gas station attendants who spit on your window or use their filthy sleeves for rags; there might be girls wearing nothing under T-shirts that advertise beer—not to mention what they've done to where Bill Saunders used to live, piling their junk up like some sort of flag, keeping twenty cars out back behind the Bar-B-Kew, or how the elms are dying so that Main Street is a scandal—still, rain or shine, Ted Fraser will come walking by to get the morning mail.

"Let's have the Conovers to supper." She tries that gambit too.

"Ian?" Maggie asks. "How do you feel about that?"

He shrugs his shoulders, indifferent-seeming. Hattie says, "He'd love it. He's only playing hard to get."

"I can speak for myself, Aunt."

"Then do so. We're waiting."

"How do *you* feel, Mom?" he asks.

She also shrugs. It is amazing how they are look-alikes, peas in a pod.

Hattie says, "I thought it might be nice, is all. Have some people over, since you don't ever want to go out. Not that I want to butt in—you know, intrude."

"You're not intruding," Maggie says.

"Ida Conover and I've been friends since before you were born, Ian. Since before either one of you were born, practically. We've worked together on the Library Committee and heaven knows what else for thirty years, and I only thought for once in my life I might return an invitation. Just because that girl's in town—Sally, Sarah, whatever you call her—just because she's visiting *her* relatives doesn't mean I can't invite my old friend to the house. *Ida's* not to blame."

"For what?" Ian asks.

Hattie arranges her shawl. It has gotten cool these nights; soon enough there'll be first frost. "For anything. For what her daughter's niece does or doesn't do."

"Nobody's blaming her," says Maggie.

"Well."

"Invite them if you feel like it."

"And what does Mr. Sherbrooke say?"

"Whatever you want," Ian says.

It is amazing how they band together against her, how they fashioned an alliance and make her feel three is a crowd. She had been sarcastic, calling Ian *Mr. Sherbrooke,* but he took it as his due. It reminds her of those autumn nights thirty years back, when Judah and Maggie had scarcely been able to wait to be alone together till the dinner table was cleared. There'd been no decent interval till they'd go up to their room. They pawed at each other in corners, in every empty bed and corner of the house. No doubt the straw on Maggie's clothes had come from their meeting in barns.

Hattie knows it's possible. If Judah died the way she imagines he died, this child could be his child. There's no use pretending the sun rises in the west. There's no purpose in denying what her eyes see plain as plain: Maggie is pregnant again. And since everything gets slowed down with a woman in her fifties, since it took them more than twenty years to make another baby, why shouldn't this baby be slow? She remembers Judah talking about baby banks, where you keep a child in test tubes, on crushed ice. He'd been joking with Finney about it; Hattie remembers the joke. "Hey, Samson," Judah asked. "You hear about the tests they've done? On test-tube babies?" Judah was expansive, clicking his teeth. "Turns out that they don't work as well—don't make as much sense, anyhow—as babies made in bed."

Finney said, no, he hadn't heard. "Which only goes to prove," said Judah, "spare the rod and spoil the child!" They laughed together, cozily, thinking Hattie hadn't heard. She'd heard, all right, and it wasn't funny and hadn't been funny the first time she heard it. She scorned their pridefulness, while they chortled in the corner over Scotch. They talked about bull hormones, and she wouldn't be surprised at all if Judah'd left a test tube for his wife and widow to use.

Or possibly the woman is further along than she shows. Or possibly the child is small, or will be stillborn. Perhaps it lies embalmed in the amniotic fluid that should have given life. She doesn't like to think that way, but has to think it through. She wants to say to Maggie, "Do you feel the baby kick-

350

ing?" or "Are you gaining enough weight?" or "How does little Sherbrooke seem to be feeling this morning?"

But Maggie smiles that dazzled, inward smile of hers, which means she'd make no answer to the question if she heard it, and likely wouldn't hear. She is carrying the family heir, and either it is drowned in there or studying the proper time to come out wailing in this world; she, Hattie, has to prepare.

Therefore she drops a hint or two at bridge games that the Sherbrooke line seemed over, but is maybe beginning again. The branch would sprout new shoots. They think she means Ian, of course. The women ask who Ian has his eye on and if she approves, but she says the whole thing's a secret, he'll have to announce it himself. She drops the hint that Judah died with a trick or two remaining, and nothing is quite what it seems. "It won't be Sally Conover," she says, "you mark my words." She makes ready for the baby's birth as though they could be proud.

"That Ian," Helen Bingham says. "He's a deep one. Quiet."

Hattie agrees.

"You'd have thought he had his eye on no one but his mother," Helen says.

Hattie quarrels with that. She says, "Still waters run deep. He's just the flirt he always was." But in the very instant that she bites on Helen's sticky bun, the way keys turn in locks, she knows what half her mind has anyhow been thinking all along: *she's right.* That's why they're always in those corners, whispering, eyes for no other living soul, with laughter that's exclusive, not inclusive. The roof of her mouth is gummy with Helen's concoction; she swallows. The way to explain it is incest: Maggie's carrying a Sherbrooke from the Sherbrooke who's her son. It's Judah's child and grandchild both at once.

This stops her. Helen asks, "What's the matter, is something wrong?" and Hattie says no, she'd just bit her tongue. The filling in her right front molar acted up. "You ought to see the dentist," Helen says.

She excuses herself. She goes to the washroom and locks the door and stands, staring in the mirror, not even seeing herself, but only the gilt fixture behind: a deer whose antlers hold washcloths and towels, the monogram stitched just so in the center of each fold. Helen keeps a proper house. Then Hattie thinks, *What if Ian fathers his own brother on his mother, what sort of Sodom does it mean we live in?* She tries to work up rage. She watches the white wingtips of her nose flare and redden, clenching her teeth. She stamps her foot, but softly, so as not to alarm Helen in the living room, then turns the cold tap on full. She squinches up her eyes and stares at herself in the mirror: the son would be father and child.

This fails. She can't be angry at the notion; she wants to smile instead. She remembers a riddle that Ian once asked: "If Moses is the son of Pharaoh's daughter, then Moses is the daughter of Pharaoh's son." He'd needed to know, "How come?" He'd repeated the question and cocked his head, waiting for her explanation as if she were his grammar teacher, not aunt. She'd known the answer, anyhow. There's nothing complicated if you write it down, but say the sentence aloud and it seems like gibberish, making Moses both daughter and son. It's a question, she told Ian, of the possessive apostrophe; he had been learning punctuation marks in school. The "daughter of Pharaoh's son" means the son of the daughter of Pharaoh, not what it sounded like; you have to watch for the possessive, Hattie said. So Moses could be *both* the son of Pharaoh's daughter and the daughter of Pharaoh's son; he was all those things when still only a baby, floating in the bulrushes in a wicker basket with fine linen. He was what he was, all at once.

There was another riddle. "Brothers and sisters have I none, yet this man's father is my father's son." Hattie mouths it; she turns off the tap. The answer to that one—she puzzles it out for a moment—is "my father's son" means "me."

Now she studies her half-smile in the mirror. She adds a coat of lipstick, pats it dry. What business could she possibly have reciting schoolgirl riddles and amusing herself with no care in the world when the world turns upside down? She makes a mouth. And as she brushes back her hair, half-singing, giggling, she understands the reason is that Judah would applaud. He would have found it funny, would be glad to solve a riddle like their "father's son."

"Are you all right in there?" Helen inquires.

"Mm-mn. Just freshening up."

"Well, that's fine then. You had me worried. That tooth."

Iniquity abounds, of course, and she'd not countenance or be related to iniquity. Yet the result will be a Sherbrooke child—born out of Judah's test tube or late or slow or because of bull serum or his son; it's six of one, half a dozen of the other, she thinks—and how to keep Judah alive. She comes larking out of the washroom so full of fun she doesn't remember, when Helen asks if her tooth still hurts, to blame the sticky bun. It's the one way that Maggie will stay. The Big House will take root and blossom once again, and the halls will be full of children she prays—devoutly, snickering, telling Helen that she has to go and can't remain for supper—will look the way her brother looked. When the century was young and they were young together, he was just the most beautiful baby; she can *see* him in the bath.

"My land, I'd no idea how late it was," she says. "You'd better call me a taxi—I'm way overdue at the house." Consulting her watch, pretending she's expected, she's the oldest of the Sherbrookes at the oldest of their games: outlasting time.

Hattie knows, of course, that Ian arrived too late to make this baby; the months don't work out right. But who's to say they didn't meet in New York City earlier, or when Maggie went to her own father's funeral? She wouldn't put it past them. The evening Ian first came home, neither of them acted like it was a surprise. Maggie met him at the door almost as though she had known he'd be coming, and they'd made the agreement before. So just because he wasn't in Vermont didn't mean he wasn't there when she got pregnant; he'd go where the wind blew, that Ian. He'd follow the favoring breeze.

And since they lied by habit, who's to say she hadn't lied about the month of birth? Who's to say she's not protective of a son who could be jailed? Hattie guesses that he could be subject to arrest. She sees their bigheaded baby, sitting naked in the dust, licking flies from his idiot's face. If the conjoined Sherbrooke blood went bad with age and incest, Hattie thinks, she'll have them all in jail. If what they did meant weakness in the baby's head or body, then she'll let them know no quarter from the law.

But she cannot imagine a Sherbrooke born weak. She sees splay-legged shaking children at the candy rack in Morrisey's: boys as fat as pudding, girls who slaver and suck thumbs. Ida Conover says the reason for it all is lead. She declares lead poisoning is bringing Vermont to its knees. It destroyed the Roman Empire, she says; that's why all those emperors went mad. They drank from lead-lined cups and were proud of their plumbing's lead pipes. They drank from aqueducts that had lead lining also, and therefore the nation was crazy.

Ida says the same thing's happening here in Vermont: Those old pipes have poisoned the wells. And where you have town water then some Communist shovels in lead. It's why you see those girls in pigtails rocking, humming everywhere, and why New Hampshire's safer if you want to die half sane.

"Their parents love them anyhow."

"Who?"

"The handicapped," says Ida.

"I suppose."

"That's what I've heard. They just stay in diapers forever."

"Imagine."

Judah had a similar theory, she remembers, about Ireland and potato blight. He said what really caused the war there was the way potatoes were rotten, and poisonous, and what can you expect of Catholics and Protestants who've got mashed potatoes for brains? But with a proper diet and Mountain Spring Water to drink, Hattie's certain the child will be fine. It's a gift for her old age. It's a present Maggie makes, and she will attempt to be grateful. She knows they'll name it Judah, if a boy.

That night, at dinner, watching the way Ian tends to his mother—how he fusses over her, making no obvious fuss, but attentive the way a watchdog might be, or leashed like a Seeing Eye dog (Maggie in her blindness sits half asleep at table, toying with the broccoli, rearranging the food piles but making no dent in them, humming)—Hattie is convinced of it: *Judah dies, Ian returns.* The interval had been an empty one; the house was plain, blank space. Nothing could be born or come out of such emptiness; Maggie needed Sherbrookes to conceive.

So whether it is Judah's child or Ian's makes no difference, she tells herself, and attempts to say so: "There's worse fates." She butters her bread.

"Than which one, Aunt?"

"This."

"Sherbrook whiskey," Ian is telling his mother. "You know, I sent a bottle up here once."

"When?"

"A long while back," he says. "For Christmas. I found it in some cut-rate store and thought maybe Judah'd be grateful."

"He never mentioned it," says Hattie.

Ian takes a second slice. "I wouldn't expect so."

"Why not?" asks Maggie, rousing.

"Because it's not that tasty. And because I never put on a sender's label or a Christmas card."

Hattie drinks. What sort of message has no name attached, she wonders; what kind of gift don't you claim?

"Sherbrook," he says. "Without an *e.* The cadet branch, understand."

Maggie ignores the salad. She will not touch a leaf. Hattie returns to the subject; she wants them to know, she announces, that for her part she'll welcome the patter of small feet. She hopes they can trust her; she's kept her own counsel and will continue to keep it, but if they'd like her opinion, all they have to do is ask. Maggie seems asleep again, ruminant, and Ian starts in on some story about the way Miles Fisk could fix his perfectly good newspaper, and the problem with New England is a boom-or-bust mentality, where the southwest sets the standard but the northeast has water and wood. Ian thinks wood and water are on a pendulum; eighty percent of New England is wooded now, and half could be cut without ecological harm, to the area's benefit even. He hates to think what will happen to Phoenix when the water table sinks; like those boom towns turned to ghost towns since the Gold Rush, this one is a failure describing itself as success. He looks at her, expectant. He cocks his head with Judah's gesture, saying "Well?" Hattie gives it up. If he wants to change the subject, why that's all right with her; if he wants to act like this is high-school debating class, let him pretend what he wants. Maggie's child has made him childish, though he's its father also; he's a baby in the bulrushes, kicking at the basket to see if it will float.

She considers the layette. She knows that Maggie gathers up old baby clothes and blankets, and the whole house smells of mothballs for a week. Hattie will not interfere, and she won't help until asked. She could fix frayed bunting in the dark, with both hands behind her back. But she's not inclined to lift a finger until Maggie shows she's helpless and at least admits to that. The curtains in the child's room should be washed. The paper in the room has faded, and if things were done correctly they'd repaper the walls. Her right eye flutters, aching, in what had been Seth's room.

But she's superstitious. The whole house holds its breath. She won't say that it can't be fixed, has never liked to think that way, won't let herself be frightened by the unproved-say-so possibility of things. And she's got no use for moodiness—can't understand, for instance, how some people say they're positively evil till they have a cup of coffee. She wakes up every morning feeling just the way she felt before and will feel tomorrow morning, thank you very much.

And it's the same with opinions; consistency counts. She's always said and will repeat that Ian has the sweetest disposition you could ever hope to have. She won't account for moodiness. It's like those girls with oversize glasses—you think you see their eyes, but instead they're wearing two round moons made out of mirrors. The Conover girl wore a pair. If she looked at blue sky, then her eyes were blue; if she turned toward you, you saw yourself watching; if she studied the porch floor her eyes—the windows of the soul, no less—went blank and brown. Hattie understands how some women might prefer such glasses for protection. So she can't blame Sally Conover; it's a cosmetic blankness, though Hattie suspects that there's nothing behind it, no signifying glance to let you know what's what.

But that is the girl's business, not hers. If hiding from the world is what she calls attractive, then let her hide from the world. What worries Hattie is Ian. That reflecting blankness—that gaze which has nothing behind it but mirrors: his eyes have the same flat stare. He looks at you like a wall, looks *through* you like a wall; if eyes are the soul's window then his soul has blinders, shutters on, and the shade has been pulled down.

There are bats in the dining room chimney. They've been nesting there since summer, and she cannot smoke them out. First she thought it had been thunder, but the sky was clear. Then she thought it was chipmunks or squirrels, but they wouldn't nest this early. Then she thought it was maybe a trapped starling; there'd been owls in the chimney before. But slowly—from the rave and squeak and way their wings would worry at her eardrums, flapping—she concluded it had to be bats.

Her own room is above the dining room, and the chimney passes through the wall. All night she scarcely sleeps; the creatures hunker just behind that double course of brick like what she used to think was Seth's unearthly presence; like some small but terrible avengers they survey her through the plaster, she is sure. There are spaces in the brick just broad enough for bats to pass through, folded, and then unfold their wings. She knows they keep mosquitoes down. But no matter how she reasons with herself, no matter how many Manhattans with a maraschino cherry she might swallow before sleep, the sweetness furled inside her throat, she cannot find repose. Her ghosts are unrelenting and she cannot smoke them out.

So she decides to ask her nephew to help her with the bats. Hattie unlocks the door again and steps down the hall to the elevator shaft, deciding to save herself the trouble of the staircase. Inside she flutters her fingers against the oak walls, imagining herself a nocturnal creature with its wings outstretched. Their mother had used the elevator, in her final sickness, for inspection tours. She would patrol the house in her wheelchair, hunting evidence of slackness in the maids. Hattie remembers watching that shrunken old lady she cannot believe is her junior by now—that image of shriveled age who died seventeen years previous to the age she, Hattie, at present possesses, bedridden, allowing the nurses to lift her to the chair or chamber pot, but allowing only Judah to carry her out of the room—and thinking, "Persistence. Do unto others. Good taste. Those are the rules I have lived by, and where does it get me?"

She presses the elevator button, descending, holding on. If they catch her, she decides, she'll tell them that she's only come to fetch her knitting or for a drink of water or to gather up the tarnished silver from the silver chest. If Ida and Elizabeth and Sally Conover—three generations of women who, after all, are used to decent silver—accept for teatime on Thursday, then it's best to be prepared.

Therefore she remains immobile inside the hollow oak cube; she presses it open a fraction. Excluded, scarcely breathing, she listens to the two inside the room. There is just enough air; she can hear them conversing, alone.

"How long now?" Ian asks.

"I'm not sure."

"What does the doctor say?"

"One more month, maybe. Forty days. But it doesn't feel that far away."

"It's not a guessing game," he says. "You ought to have a pretty good idea."

Then there is silence between them. Hattie holds her breath.

"Maggie, I've been thinking . . ."

His voice trails off; she waits.

"I could be married. For all you know, I *have* been married," Ian says, "and for all that anyone here knows, I *could* have had a wife."

"All right."

"If that's so"—Hattie edges the door a fraction wider—"then she could have had a child."

Maggie waits. Hattie waits behind them, breathless.

"I mean a lawful child. My wife and I had this one child, but she died in labor."

"You don't mean that."

"Why not?" Ian raises his voice. "She died in labor and the baby was premature and I sent it off to the in-laws so that I'd have time to be alone with my grief. That's why I came back home—we could say something like that. I dealt with it by coming home and now we're ready, now we want to raise the child up here. In the Big House where it belongs."

"She didn't die in labor," Maggie says.

"I'm sorry, I don't mean to make you nervous. Only it occurred to me . . ."

"I know what you're thinking. It makes no sense."

"But no one in this whole town knows you're pregnant," he persists.

"Finney tells me there are rumors. Hattie knows. So everybody will."

"She won't object," says Ian. "All she wants is to preserve the family name."

"The family."

"No. The family name. There's a difference."

She closes her eyes in the box. They bury the poor in mass graves. Undertakers are arrested, Hattie knows, for taking money from the state, then burying poor children by the dozen in a box. This box is a mass grave for Sherbrookes; they are buried with her, soundlessly, in tiers on the oak walls.

"You may be right," the woman says. "She thinks *you're* the father, you see."

There is silence. Then Ian says, "You're joking."

"No. I wish I was. Or *she* was, anyhow."

They laugh, and Hattie hears the madness in their laughter—chittering, high-pitched. She presses her eyes shut, but opens them again; nothing changes; nothing's changed; this is her nightmare's truth.

"Even better," Ian says, "if we do it my way. Then the child is mine and you're its grandmother, not mother. A proper Sherbrooke baby."

"They'd believe that," Maggie says. "It does make more sense." But then her voice shifts register, goes flat. "And what about the baby? Would you tell the baby you're its father?"

"I don't know. I hadn't thought it out."

"Of course you did. The child grows up not knowing who's its mother, not knowing who its father was; you have an extra added burden, darling, on those broad, broad shoulders; it's a *splendid* plan. I'm the one who's being unreasonable, I know that." She pauses; Hattie needs to sneeze. She presses her hand on the bridge of her nose, fiercely. "Just a muddleheaded woman who thought this baby's hers. And had a right to stay that way."

"I'm sorry," Ian says.

"Who didn't want to lie. Tip-top," Maggie says. "A-okay."

It is possible, Hattie thinks, that the elevator shaft is—what's the word for it? She concentrates, reaching for it at her tongue's tip like a cherry—*conical*. That would mean the square she sits in sits within a circle. That would explain why she whirls. That would mean there's world enough, a sufficiency unto the day; it's why she's twirling on the bottom of this shaft like rings on a raveling string. You tie a string to your finger and tie it to the wedding ring and hold your hand perfectly still. This pregnancy test never fails; it's a guessing game she's made young women play forever, and in fifty out of fifty she's guessed right. If the ring twirls left, why it's a boy, but if the ring twirls right, then it's a girl. She's hanging on like that, although the cables are steel. A hangman's noose has thirteen knots; she presses the button, ascends.

360

XI

They take a second cutting from the fields in August. Ian helps Hal Boudreau. There's not much talk between them, since they are behindhand and would have to shout—but they catch each other's rhythm, stacking hay. One man unloads; the other piles and places it, and when a wagon's empty they sit in the barn's shade and smoke. Hal has theories about the weather's worsening, that it's either drought or too much rain and all because of polar ice caps and nuclear bombs.

"The government's been studying," he says. "I heard about it just the other day. They figure we're in for fifty years of trouble. You know; floods . . ."

"Still, fifty years," says Ian. "That's hard to predict."

"The ozone belt . . ." Hal falls silent, considering. "I recollect we used to walk through head-high snow when I was a kid. You can't say it hasn't warmed up."

"The Van Allen radiation belt . . ."

"Well," Hal says. He flicks his cigarette. "Your dad'd have us working a whole lot harder. We ain't exactly busting ass, now are we?"

"Listen—that farmhouse. The one at the edge of the place—over by Bailey's. You know about that?"

"The honeymoon house."

"That's what they call it?"

"I don't imagine your father did. But it's the way it was intended."

"For whom?"

"Can't say as I've been there in years."

"You used to, though?"

"Everybody did." He has left his bite-plate out and grins without teeth. "Half the county anyways, one time or another . . ."

His voice fades. He swings to the tractor and starts it up. "You coming?"

"Not this load," says Ian. The other waves and winks at him, then clatters off.

Each story starts, "A stranger came to town." Or maybe it's that someone leaves for points unknown, then learns to know and conquer strangers or is instead enslaved. What we have here, folks, thinks Ian, is the oldest two-bit tale: it's come on back and find your father dead, your lands lying fallow, and mother again in the family way. He is astonished at how easily his previous world fades; he steps into his childhood bedroom, scarcely breaking stride. He makes a phone call, writes a letter, returns the rented car. He has few friends to notify, and no permanent address to change. He was between jobs anyhow, he tells his aunt, when she inquires if they're missing him at work. "Regression," Maggie calls it, and he tells her, "No. Progression. I'm starting all over again."

One day he adds a saw and a scythe and a twelve-pound sledge and a wrecking bar and hammers to the toolbox in the truck. He does this offhandedly, on impulse, but has been deciding to do so for weeks. It is August seventeenth. He makes his way to what he thinks of now not as the "haunted" or "honeymoon," but Anne-Maria's house. He drags the few sticks of furniture free. He has trouble with the mattress; it collapses on him, sighing, as he lifts it through the door.

362

There are two cane chairs, a packing crate that served as table, and, in-explicably, a lamp. Ian scythes a clearing in the high weeds by the house. There he spreads out the mattress, then adds the lamp and crate and chairs. He takes his wrecking tools into the entrance hall and commences to clear the place out.

This is slow work. There are nails to watch for, and glass shards, and great chunks of plaster that come away in sections. He satisfies himself that the "best parlor" wall is not a bearing wall, and attacks that, accord-ingly, first. The plaster shreds in his fingers; the lath is dry enough so that it also crumbles; he finds horsehair and corncobs throughout. The posts bristle with nails. He pries free the nails that tie the posts to flooring, then takes his sledge to the post-base and knocks the columns onto the diago-nal. They hang from the ceiling, then drop. He carries these posts to the pile. The day is bright and hot; the downstairs windows and the door blow plaster dust at him like smoke. He waits for it to settle, but it does not settle—remaining suspended, seemingly, and thickening the air.

Ian labors through the afternoon. His arms and clothes are white. When he catches himself in a window, hair stiff with the white dust, it is as if he sees his father's face. He takes pleasure in this business of leveling, bring-ing down two walls and the ceiling that first day. At six o'clock he knows he will be late for dinner at the Conovers, but continues anyhow. When it grows too dark for him to work in safety—hands and legs trembling, eyes uncertain in the wreckage—he piles his tools by the fireplace wall.

"You're late."

"I know. I'm sorry."

"You could have called."

"I'm sorry. I just wasn't near a phone."

"What were you doing? Or should I ask"—Sally asks, her voice flat—"with whom were you doing it?"

"I was alone," Ian says.

"You haven't answered my question."

"No."

"You selfish son of a bitch."

"Hey, baby, be easy," he says.

"What for, when we expected you? Why?—give me one good reason."

He is placatory. "Because I didn't mean it. I just got distracted."

"Two hours late . . ."

"I'm sorry. I did want to see you."

"Well, I called to tell the Harrises that Ida wasn't feeling well and that we'd have to cancel. The Fisks are coming Saturday; come then. Or you could come alone right now . . ."

"I'll do that," Ian says.

"What were you doing?"

"Nothing."

"Come on," she wheedles. "Where were you?"

"It's a surprise," he says.

The trouble with plays is the third act, Ian thinks; what do you do when the hero goes home or is dead? There's room on room of vacancy he's planning to fill full. He would tell Judah if he could that all of this has been badly arranged; he hadn't planned to be fatherless so early, and now's the time they'd get along; now everything is ready for the recognition scene. Except the road crew struck the set; they're packed and waiting in production trucks, and even Stage-Door Annie has gone home. So Ian has to play his reconciliation scene alone. Judah should be hale or turned from stone to flesh to greet him or emerge barely changed from the woods. He should fling back his greatcoat, revealing true identity, and they would fall into each other's arms, and all would be forgiven and each mystery revealed.

As the weeks pass and his mother withdraws, Ian finds himself often alone. The elms are dying, and tent caterpillars breed in the pin cherry tree. The rot is generative, however; things spawn behind each stone. He discovers, in a book of lists, that five thousand five hundred mothers out of every million in Albania are over fifty—or so the government claims. He shows her pictures of a sixty-year-old woman holding her baby. Maggie fails to find instruction in such facts.

She has been halving beans. He watches her cut off the stems, then slice them French style, expertly. What bothers him, he tries to say, is how she plays no music now, how the pianola and the upright piano fail to add up to the burned concert grand. She makes a small, dismissive gesture. "It's the strangest case of rivalry," he says. "Twenty-six years between siblings, and we fight over who gets the crib."

"Go on," Maggie says. The knife is Japanese. You sharpen it, he knows, by wiping the blade with paper.

His vision blurs; he blinks. "I'm not exactly joking."

"No." She studies him.

"Let me help you."

"I'm finished now, it's done." She fetches a colander and pot; her hands seem green. "This isn't easy for you, is it?"

What wells up in his throat is something he must swallow. "Boats in bottles," Ian says. He makes a mound of the discarded stems, then scrapes them off the table into his left palm. "That's what I've been building all my life."

"The taxes," Finney tells him, when they meet at Morrisey's. "You can't keep on forever. They'll assess you into bankruptcy."

The aisles are narrow and the light above them flickers. Outside, it rains.

"Your father knew about it," Finney says. "He was so pigheaded stubborn he chose not to listen, is all. He made the kind of will that's just an invitation to disaster."

"You drew it up." Ian has been buying beer.

"Don't remind me. I did exactly what he asked me to. But this is the twentieth century, boy; like it or no, it's a fact."

"All right."

"We ought to talk about it. You should have some legal recourse. A procedure we agree on, that we plan . . ." Finney coughs. He keeps his voice low, standing at Ian's elbow in the checkout line. "I mean about taxes. For the eventuality. In case it should eventuate . . . You studied political science?"

"I'll stop by your office. We'll talk."

Ian works at the house, thereafter, with a fixity of purpose that takes him by surprise. He is compelled. Whatever it was that had made him lethargic now makes him unable to sleep. He wakes at dawn and sets out for the site, hauling the tools he thinks he'll need from Judah's old toolshed by the sugarhouse. He is excitable, jumpy; his nerve ends feel filed. Yet the procedure he follows is methodical; he guts the whole house in two weeks. Each morning, on arrival, he sets fire to the accumulated refuse of the day before—saving out and setting apart the wood that might serve to rebuild. He has a childhood fear of rusty nails, since lockjaw means you'll never talk again. And he remembers how Ray Bolger as the Tin Man needed oil to move, how tetanus can stiffen all your joints.

So he is careful, laboring. He pulls the nails from every piece of wood he saves, and keeps that stack free of the ground. He cuts the cracked panes from the windows and gathers up the glass. He removes the rotted sills. When he leaves he chokes the fire embers with plaster; where he works he sweeps. He had had, Judah told him, no skill with his hands; he had been all thumbs. Therefore the simplicity of gutting the rooms is a comfort; he exults in his precision and has all the time in the world.

Upstairs, he leaves things intact. Where the plaster has already fallen he removes a section; where the ceilings belly down he pulls them down entirely. He loves that last suspended instant prior to collapse—it is as if the wood holds back and the plaster bands together, as if their opposition to his leveling act is animate. He works in silence, but humming, happy in the house.

Now his image of Judah grows huge—not shrunk-shanked like Finney, or manageable. He knows, of course, how memory enlarges: Judah might in fact have been less sizable than in the stories about him. Long after Adam left Eden, he knows, the light in their shared house burns on. The way that Maggie looked at him was not how a mother should look. When she said, "They think *you're* the father," her laugh had not been guiltless. Was she embarrassed at a white lie that she helped to foster, or at its plausible truth? Had she countenanced the rumor, or simply turned blushing away? He needs to know, he tells himself, he has to find out what they're saying, and who said it first.

So he attempts to locate the true father of her child. Ian assumes the man is married, unavailable. He imagines candidates. He thinks of the men who came and went on Sutton Place when he last shared her life. There was a flutist from the Philharmonic, a real-estate broker, a professor of law. He remembers their names. They brought flowers and wine to the apartment, and sometimes stayed the night. More often they did not remain. At eighteen, he remembers, he took a cruise with his mother and Sam Elliot to the Caribbean for two weeks. The boat was Dutch; they stopped in Puerto Rico, Saint Thomas, Jamaica, and Aruba, he remembers how the trade winds bent the trees in Aruba at ninety degrees. He remembers the name of the tree—divi-divi—and how the taxi driver in Aruba spoke five languages. The three of them drank rum swizzles and played games of shuffleboard; Sam Elliot wore flowered shirts and bought him a watch at the duty-free port; he called Ian "son."

"I'm not your son," he protested, and Sam said it was just an expression, a word. They had been lying in deck chairs by the ship's saltwater pool. Sam did leg-raisers and sit-ups before accepting broth. He said, "Your mother's marvelous," and Ian said, "I know."

"Sometimes I wonder," Sam said, "if you see what she's been going through."

Ian flexed his stomach muscles, but did not raise his legs.

"You're my chief rival, understand. I wonder if you're cognizant of that."

"I do have a father."

"Yes. Well. You see what I'm getting at, don't you?"

"It's hot. I need a swim."

Maggie joined them, glistening. She wore a pink scarf on her hair, and her profile, Ian thought, looked like a raised medallion. "Whew," she said. "If it wasn't for this sea breeze . . ."

"There's no breeze," Sam said. "It's just the forward motion. Ian and I were getting acquainted. We've reached agreement, you might say."

She found her dark glasses. "On what?"

"On nothing. On the fact that you're marvelous, Mom."

"That isn't nothing," she said. "I thank you, gentlemen."

He dove into the pool's green depth and swam the length of it without surfacing, shutting his eyes against salt. Sam Elliot ate turtle steak near the dock in Kingston. All through the homeward journey he complained of stomach cramps; he took rumba lessons, and tried to teach Ian the steps.

Charley Strasser was a psychologist with the White Institute. He spoke about the virtues of Sullivanian group therapy, and proffered books by Harry Stack Sullivan. "But you've got to want it," Charley said, "or it's just a waste of time. You've got to work at confronting the self. It's hard work, let me tell you. By comparison, I'm telling you, digging ditches is a breeze."

He, too, wore flowered shirts—open-necked, with a moonstone pendant and a bracelet of jade beads. He told Ian that encounter groups were where it's at this season, but to accept no substitute for the painful private thing. "I'm involved with your ma, kid, you're hep to that. Or I'd take you on myself. But that would be unprofessional. The best I can do is refer . . ."

Everett Armstrong was a banker with a private plane. He took Ian flying in the Catskills and over the Hudson, telling him, "It's just the thing for morning-after headaches, or to clear your head. Up in the blue empyrean. That's how I like to describe it, you see. That's what it feels like, not sky: the *blue empyrean*."

Maggie asked him if he minded what she called her "gentlemen callers." "Because if you'd rather I don't see them," she said—"it isn't any problem when you're home from school. I'd rather see *you* anyhow, of course."

"The penalty for incest in the State of California is fifty years' imprisonment."

"That's useful to know. What else can you tell me?"

"I worry about Judah," Ian said.

She turned to him. "You mean it?"

"Yes."

"A little late to say so . . ." Smiling, she touched his arm. She studied him as if his were the one face she ever saw, the single voice she hears. Maggie retains—has always had—the gift of concentration. Judah must have reacted to it; Ian does so now, and feels, if not identity, the same vein beating in his temples, the same pulse-quickening anger that Maggie has been shared. It's what men do with beauty, he thinks; it's why they hoard and lock it up and nail No Trespassing signs on the gate; it's how they end up mastered by what they'd planned to own.

He confronts her anyway. "Who's the father?"

"You asked me before."

"You didn't answer."

"And won't. It's not important, Ian, surely you know that."

"Is it that you don't know or aren't telling?"

"We're not playing twenty questions either, and I haven't been planning to offer up clues. The point is this baby is mine."

"You don't know," Ian says.

"I do. But as soon as I gave you his telephone number, you'd be on the phone. It would be easy enough. All you are is curious; all you want is answers to a crossword: Fill in the blanks. What Hattie wants is the assurance that the man's a Sherbrooke, or at least of the same class. And all *I* want, my darling, is to be left alone."

"By him or me?"

"By you both. By everybody's neediness; by everyone who's staking claims. *I* claim this child. Okay?"

Still, the paradox of ownership is that he must relinquish things in order to have earned them. He'd been born with silver spoons that left the taste of tin. So now he practices rebuilding a deserted home with his two hands, no power tools, and being someone's son who had been fatherless before. It is not that he hopes to be Judah's replacement or to replicate the past. It is as if the past had been unfinished business, a creditor whose note is due—some debt he has to settle with in order to begin.

And Maggie seems disorderly; she has a craving for frog's legs, she says; could he possibly find frogs? She wants them with garlic butter and parsley, pure, the way she used to eat them at La Grenouille. She asks repeatedly. He visits the town's supermarkets, and Morrisey's, to see if they sell frozen frog's legs. "I'm sorry, sir," the clerk in the Grand Union says. "It's just not a popular item."

His mother is disappointed. She wonders if the local restaurants have frog ponds, and he says no local restaurant he's been to offers frogs. She's had such trouble eating and her appetite for frog's legs is so keen, she confesses, that she wonders if he'd mind fetching their very own batch. Now that the Pekins are gone, the frogs are multiplying, and anyhow they keep her up at night. So Ian takes his waders and a net. He catches half a dozen with little difficulty—fat outraged swimmers, scissoring jerkily through the green slime. The first two jump out of the pail. He catches them again and weights his shirt across the top and, in fifteen minutes, accumulates her meal.

But preparing them is Maggie's job; he leaves them by the sink. When he comes back from the mud room—having hung up his waders and replaced the net—the frogs are on the floor. One of them is cut in half; it wriggles. His mother has a cleaver in her hand. Her face is white and strained. "I just can't manage," Maggie says. "You have to skin them and slice them up, and cut off the feet. That's what you're supposed to do, then soak them in water—it just isn't worth it. I'm sorry . . ."

He has always been what Hattie calls a ladies' man; he has returned, he tells himself, to walk down a street where he's known. Yet there is nothing he now wants to share with the prying villagers. They see in him just Judah Sherbrooke's prodigal, just the soon-head of the house. And the Big House sets a standard that is not his to follow, its beds and halls and silver make demands. Each antimacassar *signifies*—or does so to Hattie, who would have him take his place as the reverential guardian of the family estate. Maggie has no reverence, but requires him there also, as a kind of guard. It's not his place, he wants to say, it's for the ancestors or heirs and assignees to come.

Therefore this shell on the shore of their holdings; therefore he will try to live within the Sherbrooke acreage, but in an abandoned house. Sometimes, in the village bars, he watches men come in to fight for the exercise—having had a drink or two and nothing else to do. They shout and swear and maybe break a chair and, in the morning, pay for it, and nothing's gained or lost.

One day he finds a cornered cat in the carriage barn, spitting at him, snarling, its eyes like agates and its every rib protuberant; he leaves the sliding door ajar and hopes it might depart. Next day the cat is dead.

"I don't have to stay here," says Sally.

"No."

"It's a bullshit town," she says. "If I opened that boutique I'd sell one dress a month."

"With luck."

She taps her chin backhanded, then spreads the fingers. "Up to here. I've had it, Ian."

"We're talking oil and water. Time ain't nothing to a hog."

"What's that supposed to mean?"

"This city slicker stops to ask directions from a farmer, see? And he's standing by an apple tree, holding a hog in his arms. The hog is eating apples from the lower branches. So the stranger says, 'Why'd you do it that way?' and the farmer says, 'Why not?' 'Why don't you shake the apples down and let him eat off the ground?' 'The apples would get bruised like that. He likes them off the tree.' 'But it would save you energy,' the stranger says, 'and time.' 'Well,' the farmer answers—I got this from a farmer, the one who works my mother's place. He scratches his chin, considering. He squints up at the sky. 'Time ain't nothing to a hog.'"

"You're telling me to go," she says. "You know that, don't you?"

"Yes."

XII

"I rise at 4 A.M. and help the Natives weed their Patch. Juan Alonso is grim this season, since he says we're overdue for rain. I tell him trust in the Lord and be Certain of bounty but I confess to you, brother, that with every day and week of Drought I wonder whether Bounty is a term applicable to heathen land and think more longingly than ever of our own Green Hills. I recollect so well the contours of home. In the blinding noonday sun here sometimes I seem to see corn in abundance, the cows in ample pasturage, the limpid streams that feed the Bottom land and there where the river incessantly flows, where we kept our rowboats, the picnick place beyond the willows. It is a vision afforded to few. Here the cattle—what few we control—graze on hillsides so steep as to rival a Cliff, and the rivulets are dry. Vermont is earthly Paradise; believe you me who am at Great remove.

"Then I chastise myself for weakness, and would not confide such faith-lessness to Willard for the world. We lack for nothing in these parts because the Lord is with us and His bounty is all-plentiful even without grain. I write you therefore secretly, and because I must needs share with someone these my secret Doubts. The boy I wrote of—Jo—has reverted. He speaks no more when preparing our fire; his mumble and chatter is mute."

In the second winter of their marriage, she and Judah snowshoed down to the Walloomsac. The afternoon had had that brilliant clarity she knew the presage of a cold snap, bringing minus ten at best and maybe minus thirty. They had watched the sun go down and moon come up in tandem, and Maggie turned to him and said, "What would you say if we spent the night here; could we manage it?"

He answered yes, with luck, with matches and a bunch of scrap wood to burn and saplings for a lean-to, but it wouldn't be much fun. She said, "Let's do it," and he said, "You're crazy."

"Maybe," Maggie said. "Let's try."

So he humored her and gathered wood and said you break it up in sections and strip those pine branches there. Judah had his pocketknife and fire-starter and matches, but they had no hatchet. They settled on a space protected by a stand of pine, under the lee of the hill. There were six inches of crusty snow, but the spot was level. He cast wide circles, using the last light and saying he could use the light of the fire to find nearby deadwood later. Starting in the pine lot, she gathered a head-high pile of deadwood, warming to the work. Judah took off his snowshoes and stamped the branches with his boots, splintering them into usable lengths. He showed Maggie how to lash them, and she built a windbreak. "You sure you mean to do this?" Judah asked. "It's not turned cold yet. Not even halfway there."

"Will we survive it?" she asked.

"What time is it?" She had had the watch.

"Four forty."

"We'll know in twelve hours," he said. "They won't be a whole lot of fun."

"Not if you take that attitude. If you don't want us to try."

So Judah had been challenged and was grim. "What if trying doesn't work?"

"We'll walk on home."

"Not easy."

"Oh, someone will come out and find us."

The dusk was blue. She wondered, when would her teeth start to chatter.

"I feel called upon to ask this," Judah said. "I've been in cold weather before."

"How bad?"

"This bad and worse."

"Well, you survived it," she said. "My frosty hero. Right?"

"But I had sleeping bags. And a tent."

"Will we die?" She dropped her head to look at him. He stood a full head higher, and it was a trick of flirtation; it made her look up through her lashes.

"Not likely. But there's frostbite. You might lose a finger or two."

"There'd be eight left." She waggled her hands.

"Toes," he said. "How good are those boots?"

"You gave them to me for Christmas," Maggie said. "They'd better be good."

"They are," he adjudged them, remembering.

Then time slowed. Then he ceased to ask the time of her, and the night sky had no meaning, and she watched the constellations not knowing which quarter she watched. Wind rose and died, and she registered its arousal and subsiding. They had a flame in front of them, and a lean-to that sufficed. There were raccoon and rabbit and deer tracks and one two-footed track he couldn't name. It appeared to snow, but the constellations were manifest, and therefore she knew it the wind, not sky, that had produced the snow. She pondered the distinction between the wind and sky. She remembered pictures of the wind with bellows as puffed cheeks, with its white hair streaming and a gunnysack. Wind was a god toting trouble, and forced to let it loose.

"Eight o'clock," Judah said.

"Yes. Eight o'clock and all's well."

You take, she knew, a stitch in time. Flexing her fingers, Maggie wondered how you best stitch time, and what kind of needle it took. Judah, kneeling, seeming legless in the snow, was a furry creature she would have her children by. There were bears. He would take his leave of her when there was insufficient meat, and wander off outside and lie down uncomplainingly on the pack ice. The old and the infirm were luxuries, he said. Respect for age and infirmity was a mark of abundance, not strength. Those tribes that could afford to honor their elders were the best tribes to attack. They would be easy prey in the lean winters, he said, clustered to the fireside like flies in wet spilled sugar. There were rock abutments. In the hollow of the rock he hollowed still more deeply, and made a place to drink. There had been owls. She listened to them. She observed, for the first time, how alike are the cries of owls to those of railroad engines. She said this to her kneeling husband, but he was oblivious; there had been ice on his eyes. She wanted, obscurely, to wipe her own eyes. Kneeling beside him, Maggie attempted to wipe off the ice, but her gloves were thick and stiff and snow-encrusted also. Therefore she smudged his face further, attempting to cleanse it, and he blinked at her and whispered it was eleven o'clock.

"Time flies," he said.

"No."

"Maybe we should move around."

"Yes. What's absolute zero?"

"The temperature when nothing moves."

"And how cold is it?" Maggie asked.

"I don't know. It's difficult to know yet. Maybe five below."

"No. Absolute zero."

His cheeks seemed splotched with measles, his forehead had been charred. "Not sure of that one either," Judah said. "They can't ever reach it."

"Why not?"

"Because the thermometer moves. Because it's absolute."

"There are no absolutes"—she tried the joke—"absolutely not."

"Two hundred seventy-three degrees below zero, I think. Centigrade."

"This is cold enough also." She clapped her hands. There was snowfall from her wrists. She watched his lips. They moved in opposition to his chin. They were not malleable anymore, and if he touched his knife to his lip's flesh the knife blade would adhere. He spoke of men who gutted bear, then slept within the fur and fat and ligaments. They used the paws for gloves. They coated themselves with flesh grease. The two of them had bear-paw snowshoes not five feet away. These tilted against the hill's angle and were rimmed by snow already. Maggie looked for falling snow. She raised and lowered her head. The wind abated, and therefore she distinguished falling snow from snow that had fallen already and was dropping from the laden branch. There was no falling snow. She looked for the snowshoes again.

Heat hurt. The side of her that faced the flame was warm. Judah bought her a rotisserie, since she wanted one for Christmas. There where her world was in shadow, there on the dark eastern edge she could not feel, there was no tingling quickness in her arm. She turned. She thawed herself. One fourteen, he told her, and said we should keep on walking or decide. The fire spat pitch, and the green branches seemed like filaments of sap. They embraced. They fitted together. She was grateful for the duck down in her coat. He clasped her with his bulbous, shrouded arms. The firelight was yellow. She was without sensation. He rearranged their legs.

In this fashion they weathered the night; it was not as long or cold as Maggie had feared. She could layer the sky, but not wind. Wind was a wrestling match in progress, all over itself, arms and legs. You couldn't tell the cold wind from the warm, but the night was windless and the two of them did sleep. She woke to guttered coals. She could not see the moon. There was light enough to see. Judah lay snow-marbled, but she knew her husband breathed because his breath was air. His nose was alabaster and his hair had been blasted, then chiseled, then rubbed. She wondered, should she light the fire, and decided no. It was warmer where she lay than when she stood. She flapped her arms and stretched and attempted jumping jacks. Her left leg hurt where she had lain on it; she waited for pain; she stamped her feet and saw and listened to them move.

"The heat is extreme here these months, though dry. Indeed one would wish there were moisture, that the parched land might drink. At eleven A.M. we cannot support it and lie in the hammocks in Shade; it is that hour now. Willard lies in the hut while I pen these lines to you, dear brother, in the fervent hope you read. Amongst the people here He shines like a beacon, but dimmed. When down the terraced hillside I see some weary husbandman, his short-legged stride always—or so it seems to me—an attempt to remain Upright on the mountain, or pigs snouting in the wallow that is behind each hut, wherever earth retains a sufficiency of moisture so that it become muddy with trampling, then do I measure His arrangements with Wonder, Who watcheth over all. The clean and the unclean are both within His purview, those who build enclosures and the Beasts enclosed.

"This day I am barely able to write. I wanted to tell you one thing. When Willard's stay is over and he wakes from this long Sleep, we will return to the Green Mountains gratefully indeed. I dream of our father's House. The shutters fasten and the door bolts fast and there is privacy abounding in the upstairs corridor, no shameful doings open to the world. If you saw what I had seen. We live in a barnyard here, among the Tribes."

The people in this town, she thinks, set too much stock by face. A facing cord was half the wood you used to call a proper cord; farmers' barns are painted on the street side only, if they need to save on paint. There are houses with dirt floors and no plumbing that nonetheless have imposing façades; why paint the portico, she wonders, if you require a floor? Her sister-in-law puts stock in "face," and always asks, with that sideways slant to her mouth that means gossip, "What can you tell me that's new and different?" Although they don't discuss the child, she knows—by the way that Hattie sniffs and arches her eyebrows and harps on the Ferguson girl's pregnancy—that Hattie knows. And therefore it's a toss-up if the town does too.

Judah, when she met him first, was thirty-eight years old. Then ten years intervened, and she met and married him when he was forty-eight and she was twenty-three. So she is older now than he had been, who seemed old to her when she was truly young. She finds a cardboard carton full of letters that she sent. Telegrams and postcards proclaim eternal love. There is her carefully copied version of the Shakespeare sonnet that begins, "Let me not to the marriage of true minds . . ."

She cannot bring herself to read the letters through. They are stacked at random in the box; Judah had been retentive but careless, jumbling the years. The passionate phrases she does read (in her open penmanship, the Papermate unfaded) make her want to weep. They are so certain (she was so certain; she's uncertain now how all this altered) things would work out well. They promise to carry his child. They say how wonderful his arms and nose and teeth and hair feel to the touch. They reek of musty innocence, and she finds it hard to recognize the print. "I'll love you forever and ever," she wrote. "Oh, J. P. Sherbrooke, wait and see."

Yet *see* means hearing Hattie tell how Nathaniel Shotter preached this morning on the subject of lice in civilized lands, and how licentiousness was Christ's true text when he urged the Magdalen to put off the ways of the flesh. As far as Hattie is concerned, the only true license is marriage, and those who are licentious without it are the cattle of this earth. Why else does darkest Africa remain in such a shadow; what else keeps all those Indians from improving their God-given lot? It's not an accident, the preacher says, that Our Lord refused the ministry to women—though his attitude toward women, taken within the context of the time, was progressive and positive and kind. There is an ancient Latin proverb that is appropriate here: *"Quod licet Iovi non licet bovi."* Hattie says the minister says that, in free translation, the proverb means, "What's feasible for Jove is not permitted to the cow." She repeats this to Maggie in various ways. "What's good for the goose is sauce for the gander," she says. "What is licensed by God is licentiousness in beef."

See means watching from her window while a picnic progresses beneath her, on the lawn behind the Toy House where the elms afford protection. The blue-haired ladies, Hattie's peers, wear cloth coats and keep them buttoned. Their laughter and chatter and gossip assault her as she spies; they are plumper, each of them than she in her sixth month. *Wait* means accept how they guzzle that cucumber salad and cider and pie.

Her retreat is a long, slow season; she tries to give up cigarettes and fails. Cleaning, Maggie forces her body through paces that were painless once; she has too many aches now to name. Therefore she mourns her youth. She exercises every day, but her whole system complains. And the sense of beauty fled, of all her agility winnowed away, is with her like a bulbous shadow every step she takes. The letters that she used to read—attempting to establish kinship, poring over Anne-Maria's pleas in the faith that they presaged her own—ring hollow now, or false. She remembers a woodcut she studied once, of a spotted cat biting its tail. There is no starting point or end point to the cat; it swallows itself, and its tongue is serpentine, a second girdling chain. She believes herself that beast these weeks, and is her own extinction as she grows.

So *see* and *if* and *wait* become her litany; she chants them to the waning moon, then to the crescent and full. She tries to teach herself the shapes of stars again, and when the constellations would appear. Now all she knows are the Dippers, and they tilt and careen past her room.

She calls her doctor. "How is it going?" he asks.

"All right."

"Okay. What are you feeling?"

"It kicks," she says. "I'm not nauseated anymore."

"Do you sleep?"

"Yes. Not all that well."

"Any pain? Any particular problem you notice?"

"No. But . . ."

There is static on the line. She remembers when even the Big House phone had been a party line, how she always had the feeling that the operators and the neighbors listened in. Now the right to privacy is guaranteed, they say; now operators cannot listen in, even if she asks for verification; we're not allowed to verify, they tell her—it takes a court order for that.

"But what?" he asks.

"Is it possible it's twins?"

"Except we did the sonogram."

"Yes."

"I might be wrong. There's always a margin of error, okay. But I should call it unlikely, Mrs. Sherbrooke, you're producing twins."

She lights a cigarette. She knows that, she wants to tell him; it's not what she started to ask. What she wanted to know and to hear him assert is whether it's certain she's having a child, or whether they've somehow been fooled. Because this makes no sense, pleads Maggie; it's out of synch, it's a jumbled-up time. She feels herself a creature and receptacle of other people's expectations, not her own. Love is a word she's used so often in those letters to Judah that it has been used up.

She shifts the phone. "Thank you."

"You're quite welcome." His voice is high. "Is there anything else?"

"No."

"Quite certain?" he inquires.

"Yes."

"You are coming to see me"—she hears him rustle papers—"next Wednesday, remember."

"I remember," Maggie says. "Good-bye."

But she cannot remember next Wednesday; she barely remembers last Wednesday. You cannot remember the jumble of time yet to come. In the future someone else will empty out the contents of that cardboard box, will know how a girl who signed herself Megan, then Meg, then Maggie wrote impassioned letters to a man as dead as she. Love lives, she had written;

our love cannot die; love always and always, my love. To that future some-one Megan too will seem a wasteful stranger: I love you love you love you, she had written, till the twelfth of never; love you deeper than the deepest ocean, taller than the tallest mountain, I'll love until language runs dry.

Now Maggie adjudges herself. She presses her eyes shut and sees what she saw in photograph albums and magazines and men's eyes. She sees herself on horses and in concert halls, or with her father on the dock in Wellfleet at high tide. She sees herself dancing, or in the Balmain gown she'd bought last year in defiance of the winter in Vermont. She sees herself mending fences with Judah to keep her Morgan in, leaning so hard on the wire it feels she too must stretch. She sees herself holding Seth. When he died of crib death something inside of her withered that never thereafter could flourish; those innocent love letters became (on the rare occasions that she wrote—having left her husband for some necessary foray and then on some pretext and then for her New York apartment) the pattern of es-cape. The world was sterile for her, though its population doubled and would redouble by the laws of population growth more quickly this time through. There is a kind of quiet, Maggie thinks, that's peace, and there's the calm before storms. Ian wanders the rooms like a caged, clawless leop-ard, padding the same circles as if home could seem a cell. She tells him he could leave.

"No."

"If you're restless here . . ."

He shakes his head.

What is it then? she wants to ask, but Ian veers off to the kitchen, peeling a banana. He seems much younger than his years, more of a child every month; fecundity has mocked her and is doing so again.

"It is not a barren labour we here do. It is bound to yield up dividends to an Accounting for our Lord. But brother, dare I confess it, there are days I think Arithmetic is senseless, that each soul on the positive side of the ledger must be counterbalanced by some subtracted soul. My recovery, for instance, might mean your disease. This is heresy and, what is worse, unfair to my husband, who Labours unceasingly, albeit now he sleeps. It is what they call dark night; I write to you though perhaps I will think better of sending these secrets. At this hour I am barren; *I do not any longer believe.*"

XIII

Ian drinks at Merton's Hideaway. The waitress went to grade school with him, and he recognizes faces from the grocery and bank. Solitary by habit, he keeps to himself; he's too young to be a regular and, at twenty-six, too old to be just passing through. Hattie says they say he's uppity, but she tells them he's just being shy. Miles Fisk appears and hails him, then brings his bourbon over and sits down.

"Mind if I join you?" asks Miles.

"No. Glad for the company."

"We never see you at the house."

"No."

"Drop by some evening," Miles says. "Don't be a stranger." He loosens his tie. He discourses on the problems here with zoning, the Rotary Club's attitude to senior citizens, and the possibilities for solar energy investment in Vermont. Miles is a firm believer in coal; were he the speculating sort he'd speculate in stocks that deal with solar energy or delivery systems for coal.

Because it's not so much a question of mining equipment as equipment for delivery, and that includes the railroad system and the barge canals; it isn't a question of whether, but *when*. By comparison, Miles says, the Alaska pipeline is an expensive mistake. We're just getting over the summer, he says, and no one understands we're in the middle of a full-fledged energy crisis; or what would happen if the Arabs organized a full-fledged boycott next time through. Never underestimate the power of a boycott, Miles maintains—why even his advertising revenue goes down each time he runs an editorial that advocates surveillance of the price of oil. It's common sense. He's not a trust-buster, mind you, he's not even advocating price control—just a sort of watchdog attitude and wariness and full-fledged utilization of this country's coal and oil shale and solar energy resources. There's only so much oil to drill before the well goes dry; there's just so often you can dip a bucket in.

"That's true," says Ian.

"Yes. I thought you'd say so. I knew we'd see eye to eye."

His stare is baleful now, unblinking.

"About this?" Ian asks.

"Oh, everything. I knew you for a man of education and good taste. You went to Harvard, didn't you; I knew we'd agree."

"Maybe . . ."

"Not maybe. For sure," Miles says. He stands and slaps five dollars down. "My pleasure talking to you, Ian. I'll tell the wife I saw you. She'll be pleased."

"Give her my best."

"I'll do that. Do drop by."

He leaves with the decisive stride of a courier whose message is delivered. Ian dawdles, staring at the worn brown booth in front of him; he orders a third drink. The cashier asks him, "Been here long?"

"Not long," he says.

"How long?"

"Three months or so. Maybe more."

The man makes change, incurious. "What brings you to these parts?"

"I was born here."

"That so? Whereabouts?"

Ian jerks his head. "Back up that hill."

"Which house?"

"The one at the top. The Big House."

This conversation ends as do the others—in silence, a nodding withdrawal, a separating out. They think him a liar or a Sherbrooke, and in either case exclude him; their world is not his world.

He tries to leave. It is the beginning of leaf season; the roads are full. He drives the Packard into town, needing to buy Sheetrock tape and nails and a tub of patching plaster. On Route 7, however, and because the hardware parking lot is clogged, Ian swings north. He settles back to drive, settles in, and has made a hundred miles before he asks himself in which direction he's heading, or why. He empties his mind, travels east. In New Hampshire he fills up again and checks the oil and transmission fluid; the attendant admires the car. "Don't see too many like this one," he says, cleaning the windshield with care.

Ian continues. By four that afternoon he reaches Maine, coming in sight of the sea. There are roadside stands for shells and saltwater taffy and Lobster-in-the-Ruff. There are Katch-Your-Own and Reddy-Packed and Lobster-Roll huts. North of Mount Desert Island he pulls still farther east, through pine lots to a village harbor that is a dead end, boardwalked, doubling back on itself. He works his way out to the bight. It is high tide, and he picks his way over the rocks. A cold fog envelops him; he watches the few houses go hazy, indistinct. His boots are wet. Ian asks himself now why it is the Sherbrooke home became a charmed confinement, and what it is that holds him when he could so readily escape. There are shells at his feet. Gulls circle, screaming, where two draggers ride at anchor out at the edge of the visible. He squinnies up his eyes and hears their engines cease. He wants a drink. He wants a smoke. He wants some sort of clarity where everything instead has shifted and is smudged.

The harbor slips are vacant; green spume batters the pilings. His hair is wet; he breathes fish-reek. This is as far as you get to, he says to himself; this is all there is until it's Labrador or Ireland or maybe Portugal. He does his Porky Pig stutter for the absent audience: "Da-d-dats all, folks, dere ain't no more." He cuts a caper, clicks his heels, and turns back to the car.

Returning, Ian is weary. He drives south through Boston, then follows Route 2. It is after midnight by the time he comes to Athol, and he stops for coffee at a diner, then climbs into the back seat of the Packard, stretches out, and sleeps. His sleep is fitful, brief, and at first light he heads home again. Twenty-four hours after his departure, he pulls up to the hardware store—the Packard clicking like clockwork—and buys the Sheetrock tape.

He has been, he tells himself, in pursuit of something all these years; now he recognizes he has also been pursued. Judah was the hunter and Ian the quarry who's trapped. Things change. He'd come to make his obsequies and peace, like his mother one year previously, although she with the living and he with the dead. He can lie in the haymow smoking, dangling naked from the rafters like the kid he never was, to fall on all fours in the prickly softness of the threshing floor. Therefore, to establish manhood means to slay his childhood's guardians, go to dinner parties where they serve iced tea, build again the crumbling house on the outskirts of their land.

He understands three things. First, Judah's sense of self was rooted like the maples back beyond the carriage house—it would go as far as wind would take it, or seeds on the seat of the carriage, but insentient, insensate, not in conscious quest. Second, he himself had been a wanderer whose travel term has come full circle to the place where he began. Third, his choice is to acknowledge how he'd had no choice.

"Let me put it this way," Finney says. "I was in Buffalo last week. The motel was—I don't know how to put it exactly—like a sound box, a sort of echo chamber. So I had trouble sleeping and pulled out the Gideons' Bible; there

387

was nothing else to read. And what do you think I see on the flyleaf; what do you think some other customer had written there in pencil?"

"I can't imagine," Ian says.

"'The chambermaid fucks.' That's what they tell you on the first page of the King James version nowadays. 'The chambermaid fucks.'" He winks. He wags his head. "I'm not an idiot, understand, I know it's a message worth getting—but in the *Bible*, Ian, right there on the first page? Hell in a handcart, that's where."

They are in his office, at the rolltop desk. "You've heard about the foolishness," Finney continues. "All over town. At Page's place, for instance. It's a wonder they're not selling tickets for where the old fool got stuck in a tree. Or where she rigged her bushel basket, fixing to brain him with apples. Or the time old Jim MacKeever died, and his wife—who hasn't so much as *talked* to him for twenty years, who wouldn't answer any of his letters anyhow—no sooner is he dead than she's up at the house changing locks. Can you imagine?"

Finney shakes his head. The lines in his brow furrow; not quizzical, Ian thinks, not even outraged, just tired. "He hasn't been buried yet, and this woman and her New York City lawyer take a drive on up to change the locks. The whole thing—lock, stock, and barrel." He sighs. "MacKeever never did divorce her, so she's got the right."

Ian furrows his brow also, lowering his right eye, then the left.

"So anyhow," says Finney, "they lock the cleaning woman out. Augusta— you remember her—a redheaded woman, portly, the sister-in-law of Dick Rudd, the one who lives over by Bailey's? Anyhow, it doesn't matter; they locked her out, you see. And she's left her portable radio inside. The one she brings to work on Wednesday, only this particular Wednesday MacKeever has a heart attack, so, understandably enough under the circumstances, Augusta leaves her radio behind. You follow? All she wants is the radio back; she isn't even asking for her pay." Finney sighs again, soundingly. He studies his hands, then wiggles them. "So I've got to go to court, asking Alice MacKeever for permission to recover a portable radio."

His voice trails off. He broods on this, letting Ian savor the indignity, letting him have time to comprehend the impropriety of it. He, Samson Finney, doesn't hunt for clients now. He's on the verge of retiring, but still in a position in the Small Claims Court to take on New York City lawyers and beat them hands down or talk to a standstill; don't count old Finney out. Except he has to spend his time on radios that won't cost twenty dollars to replace. He's asking for punitive damages, court costs, and the like, when he'd rather be out bowling or at the nineteenth hole.

"It does seem silly," Ian says.

"This town. I'm glad you agree." He nods at the window shade: ocher, half rolled, the pull on it raveling. "What I wanted to tell you is this. You think it's foolishness, that story about the MacKeevers? You think the James Page people won't likely appeal? Wait until they get around to you, my boy. Just wait." He sighs again, squints, taps his pencil on the Formica between them. "The trouble with family lawsuits is you almost never get to settle out of court. Else they wouldn't have gotten to court in the *first* place, if you follow."

"I follow," Ian says.

"I'm not naming names, understand. But maybe that's the trouble with the whole damn thing. Your father's will. When the state highway people start asking permission, don't say I didn't tell you. When they're working on putting Route 7 through the barn. They'll put a goddamn Indian on the road crew, understand; they'll say he's the grandson of the nephew of the grandson of the squaw who sold the thing to Peacock way back when. They'll say it's his by quitclaim right, and all you Sherbrookes have been doing is squatting on the state's own land this century. You mark my words"—he snaps his yellow pencil—"hell in a handcart, that's where."

He reads about his college classmates in the pages of *Newsweek* or *Time*. They are makers and doers and movers and shakers, becoming prominent. Or some girl that he'd slept with once, who'd shaved her pubic hair in order to do the chorus kick more decorously, now has her own TV series and stares at him from the cover of *Coronet,* by the cash register. Or Morrisey's nephew—the one with the cleft palate that they never fully fixed—is M.I.A. in Vietnam and they mount a statewide petition to find out his fate. It's curious, he thinks; it's the years' tricks played upon his grade-school pals, who now are older than their teachers who seemed old.

Ian lacks ambition, Hattie says; why, Helen Mattock's husband is an advertising executive who flies all over the world. He was invited just last month by the South African government to play golf with Gary Player and other executives. Imagine, she says, taking all those pretty women to Madrid or Venezuela or wherever they advertise Coke; imagine being paid for that and calling it a job. She cannot imagine, she says.

His father, too, had lacked ambition; he'd exalted staying power where other men praised change. He'd held what he was born to hold, and that seemed enough. So Ian watches forward motion from his sideways vantage, and the fuss and bustle of it make him sad. For himself, perhaps, who has so little envy in him, yet such a share of jealousy; for others, certainly, who run along a treadmill they construe as track.

Therefore, when Maggie tells him that she's willed the house and grounds to him and him alone, Ian takes it as his due. She might die in childbirth, she says; she might not be free from entailment—it's best to be prepared. She mentions the estate and property and inheritance taxes. She tells him Finney is fearful they will be bankrupt soon. Her testament explicitly leaves the whole house to him, and not to be divided by claimants or alternate heirs. "It's what Judah wanted," she says.

Love—Ian distrusts the word; it has become emptied of meaning except perhaps as echo or as mockery. The spirit of adventure is, for Sally, the spirit of intrigue. When he enters the honeymoon house, she is there.

"Hello." She stands in the living room's center.

"Hello."

"It wasn't locked."

He carries plywood sheeting and rests it on the banister.

"Are you surprised to see me? I was just . . ."

"Yes." He straightens, faces her. "A little bit."

"You thought I was going?"

He nods.

"I am. I'll leave you alone. After this. Don't be nervous."

Her perfume is so strong he smells it from his ten-foot distance.

"It's coming along, your construction." Sally lifts her arm. "Our house."

There is sawdust at his feet. He spreads it with his foot.

"I always thought of it that way. It's funny now. Imagine. *Our* house."

"You look beautiful," he offers.

"Do I? You didn't know that, did you? How I thought this place was ours."

He rearranges the plywood. He lays a two-by-four as anchor at the pile of sheeting's base.

"Don't be nervous," she repeats. Her dress pattern is of climbing roses; they are red and yellow and the leaves and stalks are green. The fabric gathers at her breasts and then falls free.

"No. It's hot in here."

"Yes. Hot."

"We don't have air conditioning. Sorry . . ."

"Don't be." She releases her hair.

"I've been framing windows. They're nailed shut."

"Let's go outside." She walks in front of him—four feet ahead, her shoulder blades pronounced—and settles in the clearing. He sits beside her; she kicks off her sandals and draws up her knees. To quiet his own breathing, Ian inhales for the count of eight, then holds for the same count of eight, then exhales. He makes the ground a sounding board and beats out three against four.

"I'd like to have heard you play music . . ."

He stirs circles in the uncut grass. "Shabby."

"You don't mean that."

Ian pulls at the raspberry bushes behind them. "Alexander's ragtime band. I was lead boy for the tympanist. You know: playing piano on a flat-bed truck for funerals."

"You didn't!" Sally claps her hands.

"That's right, I didn't. But ask about Duluth. Tallahassee. St. Louis; Reno; ask me if I've been there with seventeen overworked dancers, one stand-up comic, and forty-two suitcases."

"You don't have to tell me."

"Well, there we were," says Ian. There are goosebumps on her arm, and all down the length of her legs. "Seventeen overworked dancers, one stand-up comic, and forty-two suitcases. Not counting the timpani, of course. Not including cellos and the makeup bags and Angel's pet ocelot; you should have been there. You would have loved it. Tallahassee. In a snowstorm. The second one this century."

She edges away from him, chastened. "Why are you so secretive?"

"Because I have nothing to hide."

Now even in the instant of his glib rejoinder, Ian recognizes truth in it and feels ashamed. Keeping silent, he has kept her interest—making mysteries where little of value was hidden, with his penny-ante expertise at pretending there's a rabbit in the hat. They are both enacting fantasy; he knows that too. He knows she half-expected sex and that she carries underclothing in her Halston carryall; she had planned to go back afterward to what they call "the big bad world." There, with his semen leaking out of her, she would continue to function, as he would continue to function, and they would think themselves the secretive elect.

The maples in the clearing have exploded: every color he has ever seen in trees.

"Except this can't go on." He had not known he'd say it, but knows it to be true.

"You mean that?"

"Yes."

She makes a pile of pine needles. "Why?"

"There's just no place to go. Or hadn't you noticed?" he asks.

In one swift, heart-stopping gesture she lifts the dress above her head and stands before him naked. "That's better," Sally says.

A shaft of sunlight lights her. She waits with both hands at her sides, the left hand holding the dress, motionless, as if the impulse—if it had been impulse, Ian thinks, and not preplanned—has exhausted her inventiveness, and the next move must be his. Dust dances between them. He is irresolute. He advances on her, takes the dress, yet does not want to put it on the grass. He folds it into her bag.

"It doesn't matter," Sally says. "That dress."

"I've been using you, you know. Faking it. It's this dream of escape we share."

"All right."

"All right to what?"

"All right we're using each other. You didn't seem to mind."

He looks at her—this lean totem, offering so nakedly what is not his to take. And he remembers with a kind of love—a passionate nostalgia— what it had been like to be uncertain, trembling-fingered, full of the foretaste of adventure that first evening when they met.

"I'll say it," Ian says, "as clearly as I can. There's nothing you need that I'm able to give. There's no way—not now, not these weeks, at any rate— I'm going to provide it. This town"—he waves his arms, encompassing . . .

"You're not really leaving," she says. "I don't believe it."

"Why not?"

She hesitates. "You know those creatures—water skates—who stay on the surface of things? The ones with feet that float? Well, that's what we've been doing." She lifts her eyes. "On ponds."

"My cup runneth over," he says.

"I'm twenty-five years old. I've been married and divorced, I'm here in limbo waiting for some sign of feeling from you. Something real . . ."

He places his hand on her thigh. She removes it. "No," Sally says. "That isn't what I meant."

But he reads dismissal as its opposite: please stay. Please fascinate me further. Compare the still life that we make to *Dejeuner sur l'herbe*. Or try for Omar Khayyám; make me laugh.

"'A jug of wine,'" Ian pronounces. "This picnic tableau. 'And thou beside me.'"

"Stop it!"

"... 'In the wilderness.' The wardrobe mistress ain't been busy overtime." He winks. "Fine costume, though ..."

"Stop it!"

He obeys. Yet the litany continues in him, with his escapist impulse, *loaf of bread*. Let us mourn together, Ian thinks, the disappearance in this nation of literacy, plain dealing, and the garter belt. There's gain and loss in every act, and the point of this encounter is just to stick with gain. He takes a stick and snaps and quarters it.

Leaves fall. The bones in Sally's feet are working as if she ran in place.

"I'm sorry," Ian says. He reaches for her hand.

"I need a cigarette."

He offers one, then lights it. Her hand shakes.

"It seemed so easy—so automatic, almost, that we'd get together." Her voice is low. "But it didn't turn out that way, did it?"

"No."

She studies her cigarette ash. "Why?"

He makes no answer.

"What kept it from working, Ian? Are we so different, such ..."

"Similar," he says. "So similar."

"You mean that?"

"Yes."

"What's wrong, then?"

"We've been trained." The breeze shifts and he smells perfume. Sally's nipples have puckered, are brown. "Ever since I got here I've been following directions. That's what it feels like, anyhow. You know. Some other Sherbrooke's part. Playacting."

"You've been very good at it."

"You too."

This makes her smile. "It's funny, isn't it? I've never felt so close to you. Not once. And it's all over, isn't it? You want what you can't get."

He cannot speak. After a moment she strokes his hair with the flat of her hand, as one might soothe a dog. In Kyoto or Izmir he had felt this way as well: the signs were in a language he could not comprehend, the characters indecipherable, and the natives knew a language he would never know. Ian thinks of those improvisations (done so ardently in acting class, with partners or as solo) that have to do with sensory impairment: be a blind man painting or a deaf one at a concert or a paralytic playing basketball . . .

"What are you thinking?" she asks.

He shakes his head; he smells cigarette smoke.

"Tell me."

He looks at her. She tosses her hair. It is a gesture that seems practiced, as if she knows her hair shows to advantage when swirling. The engine of the pickup is still ticking, cooling on the path where he left it. He listens to that, then the birds. A woodpecker batters a tree.

"I'll miss you," Sally whispers.

"I'll miss you."

"Yes."

"More than you imagine."

"Maybe. I wanted what you wanted," Sally says.

"No."

"Yes. I want what you want right now."

"Leave. Please go."

"Good-bye."

In the clearing now, alone, he confronts his empty house. Sally has moved off, naked, accumulating grace with distance, not looking back over her shoulder. It is early afternoon. He wants to call to her, to court and cover her, but keeps his precarious peace. He wonders where she will present herself at three. Obscurely, he feels jealous and whistles to catch her attention—three low notes, deliberate, spaced. She does not turn. Soon he loses sight of her and enters the house once again.

You get in a boat, Ian thinks, or on horseback or jump a freight or plane. Or maybe what you choose to do, he tells himself, is live alone in empty space. After insulation comes the Sheetrock; after Sheetrock comes the tape, then paint, then hanging pictures, then the choice of furniture to match. You borrow twelve dining-room chairs. He sees it in anticipation, as if already done: he'd take the straight-backed oak chairs six by six in the back of the pickup; he'd buy an oval table, set up portraits of his ancestors, inherit the hall chandelier. So he'd replicate the Big House and the Toy House and be a pilgrim washed back up like flotsam to the starting point; it isn't worth it, Ian thinks, not without a woman there, not this afternoon.

He has imagined himself on the edge of the woods, repairing as a craftsman might what had been long untenanted. But now it seems beyond him—past his energy or competence or enduring interest to build. He gathers up his tools and places them, their handles touching and the tools' extensions radii—so that the wrecking bar and crosscut saw oppose the hammer and ripsaw and drill—in a circle on the bedroom floor. He has no power tools, and, therefore, nothing he fears will be taken. Ian leaves these ancient implements where he had wanted his bed. He does not lock the door.

XIV

Images afflict her; she cannot keep them from coming. They inflict themselves upon her eyes like headlights in a mountain pass at night. For survival's sake, Maggie has to peer ahead. She sees clouds that seem like smoke, are smoke, billowing about the house. Judah stands in the firelit center, fists black with coal, his forearm muscles knotted as he grinds the lumps to dust. He blames her, Hattie says, and they huddle in the kitchen. But since he will not voice his rage—has lost his voice, she fears, is strangling in there, his vocal cords cut—she herself accepts no blame.

So when the house explodes it is in a dream of vengeance, not justice, he's dreamed. He appears surrounded by fire—has always been. Once she told him, joking, that he'd missed his calling and should have been an arsonist, but Judah only stared at her, his maul and wedges in one hand, three split ash logs in the other, wondering, was that a joke? He'd deliberated so; he pondered all her offhand levity and wrecked it, laughing late.

She sees her infant, Seth, caught in the same explosion while he choked for air. In the final passage, Maggie knows, the infant has to be ejected quickly so that it suffers no brain damage from scant oxygen within her—but has to shoot forth gasping, filling its lungs. So she dreams a tunnel dream—like crossing the Lincoln Tunnel or through the Simplon Pass when there's a traffic jam and smoke fills her eyes with cinders, with New Jersey or Switzerland up ahead like bright salvation: sun. Seth died in his sleep—which is saying, she tells the doctor, that you die of life, that something starts in killing you the instant of that starting breath. You die of death; it doesn't tell you anything; you die of crib death, crib death, crib death like an auctioneer's recital: going once, going twice, going, gone.

She sees herself in flight. Air and water are her elements, as Judah owned fire and earth. Therefore she took planes and boats with abandon, confident that where she went would prove a welcoming shore. Her father, the fierce mariner, never had ventured to sea. He took slow tacks about the Wellfleet harbor, under sail or with the outboard, while Maggie goaded him to enlarge ambition. "Jeremy Point," she'd say. "The whole of Cape Cod Bay. It's not enough. Dad—let's get where the waves are; let's try for Nova Scotia."

He would adjust the sheets and check the wind and pretend not to hear her, preparing. "Ready aboot," he would say; or, suddenly, "Jibe, ho!"

Maggie kept him company. But left alone at the tiller of his Rhodes 19 ("The perfect day-sailor," he'd say, "for an old codger like this one, a length one man can handle, and not too much upkeep besides"), she would head directly for the outer channel and bay. There, where things were treacherous, she felt alive; she was her daredevil thirty-year-previous self. Fish slapped at the water around her, and the winds were various, and rocks she'd had no notion of loomed fifty feet to port. Judah was an inland person, and her father lived along the shore, but Maggie dreams unbroken sea or depthless, cloudless air.

Yet always there is this house like an anchor. There is an albatross called Hattie to wear around her neck. There is a baby on an umbilical windlass within her, and her belly is a cargo hold, since she's become fat as a blimp. "Oh, Ian," Maggie wants to say. "It used to be so easy; it used to be just going, going, gone."

Therefore she lives with images that dance upon the countertops like something in a windstorm or whirlpool or bird that's blundered somehow into the Lincoln Tunnel or the Simplon Pass. She sees Judah ringed by flame, Seth in his receiving blanket, then herself at Hattie's age, anticipating visits from her wastrel unborn child. It is Ian's look-alike but mute.

The six months she shared with Judah until he died were equable; it was as if they'd used up all their squabbling frenzy years before. They'd grown so used to silence in the seven years apart they could keep a companionable silence together once she returned. People are like puzzles, Maggie thinks; it's a question of fitting edges together, of sanding the sharp corners smooth. It worked; they'd worked at it. He who had been threatening made no threats against her, nor reproaches or demands. She nursed him without stint. So now, looking back, she sees their marriage in its final light—a calm thing, placid nearly, and without menace. Judah would take both her hands in his one hand and squeeze. The flesh was liver-spotted, flaccid, and his grip felt weak. She could remember when his hands would pinion her and how she feared he'd crack her bones as easily as turkey legs or, with one swift motion, wring her neck. But that was nightmare history, and never came to pass. When he died, on the late afternoon of November seventeenth, 1976, it was a gentle death. She had been by his side. He breathed more slowly, gently, relinquishing, and she never knew the instant when his breathing ceased.

There is a pileated woodpecker she hears like a drum roll each day. It has settled on the property—somewhere in the pine lot to the east; it beats its beak like fists against a tree. She feels her ears' membranes stretched taut. She feels she has to find the bird and answer its summoning call.

So Maggie sets out on a walk. It is a clear October noontime, and she takes pleasure in the exercise—pleasure also in the possibility of tracking such a noise. She knows that pileated woodpeckers are common to the South. She knows—or believes—that it is among the oldest living species, in direct descent from the pterodactyl. She allows for a degree of echo and magnification in sound. But the woodpecker that manages this huge tattoo must be of no common variety; Judah said he saw one once, and she will try to today.

The woods are wet. There are mosquitoes about, and she startles fat squirrels and toads. She remains on the path that last she rode with Ian; the bird calls every two minutes or so, and she pictures it in the interim, digesting its speared grubs. From the regularity with which the call resounds, Maggie assumes that the bird does not move—has picked a single tree and will stay till the trunk-meal is done.

Yet distance confuses her; the sound seems now to come from every direction, not east. She asks herself why should she wander so far from the house, so perilously close to term, in search of one bird with a beak. She crosses a long pasture—hayed now, its gates open—where the Holstein herd had grazed. She remembers when the herd was Ayrshire, and how they used to chase her for the sheer sport and curiosity of watching this yellow thing run. The fencing has rusted; weeds choke the third strand of wire. She mourns so much life lost.

Beyond this field, and rising again till it dips to the river, Maggie sees a hill with a dead standing tree. Then she hears that summoning tattoo, that single havoc-wreaker wrecking what she thinks was maybe once a beech. She stops, keeps still. The pounding resolves itself off into echo while she peers up and across. It is, she thinks—and knows herself foolish even in the superstition, even in this formulating instant—a sign.

So Maggie waits immobile in the middle of the haying field for the bird to batter out its signal once again. She attempts, in the near distance, to distinguish tree from bill, the shape of that survivor from the branch it thunders on.

Her baby shifts position. She folds her hands upon her lap, though standing, and warms it; something moves across the edge of the field to her right. A crowlike shape resolves itself from the highest branch and she hears a laughing, leisurely caw. Maggie steps forward to see. In sudden silence and with a quick lift, the bird—a pileated woodpecker?—flies off. It makes for the thick pine lot behind, and all she manages to see is the span of its retreating wings. There are berry bushes all around her, and she notices how they have scratched her legs. Again she hears the bird's slow call, but now is not tempted to follow; she turns.

Head down, oblivious, not fifty yards away, a naked woman walks across the field. Because there are thistles and she wears no shoes, she picks her way with care; Maggie stares at the retreating form. It is a brown-haired image of herself when young—the same straight back, thin hips, and long-legged gait. Now Maggie discerns a leather bag slung dangling from her forward shoulder—within which, she assumes, the woman must carry her clothes. Sun dapples the field with cloud shapes, but floods it like bright water where she walks. The breeze is at their backs; therefore her footfalls make no sound. The woman appears deep in thought. Her body is a single shade—sienna, Maggie thinks. Next, from the field's far edge, a whistling comes. The woman lifts her head to listen, but refuses an answering note. Her pace increases, though she does not hurry. Maggie is elated, watching, though she cannot name or place the stranger's grace; they are acquaintances possibly, but the woman wears her nakedness like a disguise. She diminishes, walks on. The angle does not change. Without breaking stride then, suddenly, she breaks into a run. Maggie starts to follow, then stops short. It is an apparition; she exhales. It makes a purposive diagonal from what she now remembers is the maple stand that shelters the abandoned house she'd stumbled on with Ian months before. It flees from her son.

"What did you do today?" she questions him that night.

"The usual." Ian smiles at her. "Nothing worth mentioning."

"No?"

"Not really. Why?"

"I just wondered. How you pass your days these days."

"A little of this, little of that."

"It's the *that* I was asking about. How's the house?"

He studies her, suspicious. "Coming along," Ian says.

"Don't you want some help with it?"

"No."

"Not my help, for heaven's sake." She laughs. "But we could hire . . ."

"No. In fact, I think it's finished. For the time being, anyhow . . ."

"I didn't mean to grill you."

"You weren't."

She studies the decanter between them. It is a glass pyramid; the stopper is an octagon of cloudy glass. "It's just," Maggie says, "I get around so rarely. I would like to visit that house. To see what you've accomplished."

"You're welcome," he says. "I'll take you there. Tomorrow?"

"If it's a nice day. Not raining."

"It won't rain," Ian says.

The first time she slept with Judah, he was more than twice her age. She told herself she'd wearied of the younger generation and consequently ought to give the middle-aged a fling. Yet the truth was, Maggie knew, that he touched some nerve in her that only he rubbed raw. Behind the muddle of emotions she tried to explain by means of Freud, reading *Beyond the Pleasure Principle* as if it were a code to solve, some unslaked impulse to marry her father, so that her life with Judah was the "future of an illusion" and her sweat-soaked agony beneath him a compound of pleasure and pain—beyond all such reductiveness was passion she could not reduce.

She fought it in several ways. She fought his grim unyieldingness with laughter, saying, "Where's that feather mattress?" when he covered her in barns. On the mattress, in their nightly rampage, she felt as if her body were a field he'd determined to clear. If she brought him lunch or coffee where he was plowing, or cutting back brush, he'd lean her up against a tree and say this was what he wanted, the only break worth taking in a day. She wore no underclothing, and loose skirts. She ached, continually. He was big-muscled, blockish, and the mass of him insistent in a way that made all other flesh seem light.

She tested this. She fought her frightened certainty, in the months before they married, by returning to New York on some shopping pretext and sleeping with the lover she had left. Dan was wistful, a photographer, twenty-six years old. He said, "Megan, since I've seen you, *Life* bought a picture. Skyscrapers at sunset, the first big break; it's a beginning, isn't it?" But when she took the bus back north, it was if nothing had happened; she remembered having the hiccups in bed.

And later, when they married and the marriage was a battle, she'd been unfaithful to him in the effort to break free. He exaggerated this, of course, suspicious as a watchdog sniffing prowlers. He had had his hackles raised. But it wasn't any contest, never was. The Judah-current was too strong; she pretended to escape from him but knew it for pretense. She'd lie on beach towels sunning on some other suitor's beach, but behind the membrane of her eyelids Judah flamed. She tried to say, and could not: "I love you, Bill, I love you, Sam, I love you, Dan." It had no chance of working, never could. She had had to laugh.

So when she returned to the Big House—to Hattie's disapproval, Ian's puzzled pleasure if she'd gone alone—it was always with fear and relief. Judah would wait by the fireplace, maybe, or whistle from the Toy House roof (she remembers him looming above her that way, hand extending into hammer, black against the snow-colored sky) or come in from sugaring. He took no notice of her. He pretended that her absence meant no more to him than presence, that she'd visited some cousin or been at a conference for one of her committees.

And when she left for Sutton Place, taking Ian with her, it was as if they both had disappeared for Judah—been swallowed up. He did allow them to come north but refused to travel south; she wrote him that Manhattan's East Side was not a world away, that she'd be glad and Ian grateful if he came to visit sometime. He dealt with her like fencing: something to cut and patch up.

Therefore, until her son was grown, she fought a losing battle with a dawning certainty: her passion equaled his. She came to admit that, in time. "Your oversized and undereducated farmer," Andrew said. "Your Lawrentian gamekeeper. What was his name, Mellors? Who happens to own the lodge."

"Me too," she told him. "Me too."

He thought she meant "joint ownership," Maggie supposed. But what she was saying to Andrew—who turned away, half satisfied, having heard an explanation that made his kind of sense—was that Judah owned her, lock and stock. She belonged to him as helplessly as land. And because her every instinct battled with such ownership, there was carnage in their bedroom: lamp oil and long yellow hair on the carpet, the ribs he broke while squeezing and the thumb she dislocated once when pushing him away. His sleigh bed was a captor's tent; his hands would weight her wrists until she feared they'd crack. Judah was her lover, first and last.

The next day dawns wetly, and she prowls the corridors of the Big House, more restless than she can remember having been in months. The rooms cannot hold her, nor her work on the layette. When they meet at lunchtime, Maggie cannot eat. "Why don't we go driving instead?" she asks. "I'll suffocate in here."

"Sure," Ian says. "Any particular place?"

She wants to tell him. *Anywhere. Just out of this huge prison, into air.* Instead she offers, shyly, "Why, no place in particular. Unless you've got an errand. And just for an hour," she says.

So he gets the Packard and they set off together, Maggie in her raccoon coat to mock the fifties feel of it, and her own elegiac sense of what she'd wear with Judah in a windy fall. Also because it's a shapeless enclosing disguise—she makes herself recognize that. "I haven't been outside these gates for *weeks*. Three relics," Maggie says. "This car, this coat, this dame."

"Where would you like to go, really?"

She casts about for a plausible answer—some end that would give purpose to her sudden need for flight. She is, she wants to tell him, without destination. She wants to go no public place or any of their ancient haunts; she had tramped around enough the day before. "Just drive," Maggie says. "How about that?"

"It's apple-picking time," says Ian. "Let's go to Bullitt's orchard. Maybe up that hill if it's clear. We'll get some cider anyhow."

"Perfect!"

In the refracted light of her passenger window she sees herself reflected: a wild-haired, puffy-faced person in motley, fluffed up in ridiculous fur. She used to drive like royalty, the top down, waving at the world. Judah had offered true fur coats, but she hated both the slaughter and the affectation of it, keeping only this memento of what was anyhow a pest. The apple orchards span the hills that lead to Woodford Mountain; the road is deeply rutted, but they raise no dust. Ian drives attentively, so she keeps a grateful silence by his side. Up here, these few hundred feet higher and ten miles north of the Big House, the trees are nearly bare.

"The old people's home," Ian says. He points, and she follows his finger—seeing what nestled at the orchard's base—a long, low clapboard structure where they keep the county poor. It is wet weather still, so the porch rockers are full. She sees them sidelong as they hurtle past: the companionable relics, waving caps.

"Have you ever been inside?" he asks.

"Not yet." She manages a smile. "But we used to drive this way often. Have you?"

"No. How many does it hold?"

"This home? Twenty, maybe. Twenty-five."

"It's half the size of ours," he says. "Not even. They must keep close quarters."

"Yes." Maggie closes her coat. The apple trees in ranked rows now appear around them; Maggie scans the hill's far reaches where the pines make a green mist. She is again in terror's grip; she struggles to name and dispel it, says, "Stop!"

405

He looks at her, surprised.

"Please!" Maggie begs. "Just for a minute. It's just I need some air."

"Of course." He brakes and cuts the motor, then is out the door and opening hers. She puts her forehead to his hand and feels its heat. She shuts her eyes, inhales the orchard air, and feels the tensile quickening of Ian holding her. She sees black tractor tires stuffed with marigolds. They circle the old people's house. There is a pile of empty tires and a stack of firewood for sale. There is an American flag. The clapboard has been painted white, but the window trim and door are red; there are brooms and, prematurely, a snow shovel by the door. The screens are off the windows and storm windows wait, ready for mounting, beneath the northerly eaves; there are ladders in readiness also. How could she have seen so much, she asks herself, in that brief instant driving by; why does she picture it still?

And knows the answer and her terror's source at once, and says to Ian, "Go back, I have to see that house."

"Which one?"

"The one we passed. The retreat. Oh, hurry, and I'll tell you why. Please!"

He responds to her shrill urgency and turns. A half mile down the hill she tells him "Stop!" again and clambers out the door to stare down at the home. There is sunlight upon it; the roof is of slate. There are ventilation pipes and chimneys and she focuses so closely she can see the birds' nest in the gutter. Now Maggie shifts her gaze to the men on the porch. She stands with clenched fists, fervent, waiting while the jumble there comes clear.

"Is it someone we know?" Ian asks.

She ignores him, staring.

"Mother . . ."

"Ssh-sh." And lets him think whatever he chooses about her whims or pregnant madness; she walks down the dirt road and waits. Maggie displays herself on the hill's first turning.

An old man disengages from the white wicker rocker, laboriously. He clambers down the four steps of the porch. He is fat and short, and wears a bright red hunting jacket. He has on a white cap, black waders, and appears to be wearing a scarf. As he nears her she determines that the scarf is his white beard, its ends tucked into the collar of his thick woolen shirt, He wears rimless glasses; his forehead and hands are pink. No other flesh is exposed to the air, but in the sudden sun the afternoon is hot. She grins, awaiting him.

The man strides purposively up the hill, and with a practiced gait. He does not seem to notice her. Watching from the slope above, Maggie asks herself if the figure who approaches might be blind. His eyes are red-rimmed, bulbous, huge. From her fifty-foot distance, she lifts her right hand in greeting, but he does not respond. It is as if this ancient takes his constitutional in wind or weather, regardless. Maggie waves. Then everything changes and is rearranged—the man stops, smiles, rocks back on his heels, hoists his cap.

He does this as a puppet might—jerkily, all limbs engaged. His beard pops free of his chin. His grin is toothless and it splits his face. He waves his cap in circles three times at his arm's extent. Then he reconstitutes himself—jams his cap back on his head, tucks beard into shirt, and turns. Maggie is radiant, watching. When the old man has regained the porch, he turns and waves once more. Again that sudden lift and stretch, as though triumphal crowds were passing; again no word exchanged—Maggie walks up to the car.

"So you did know him," Ian says.

"No."

"Well, he certainly recognized *you.*"

"In a way. In the way that I know him. We used to wave at each other, that's all."

He starts the car. "But why were you so frightened?"

"That he wouldn't be there," Maggie says.

"How may we best establish Meaning in this Life? It is a conventional question, a query one hears more and more in households that think the sun a collection of vapours & gas & flame, not God's Manifest. Willard says Redemption lies in Works. We are engaged in irrigation Labor here, and shall reclaim this land for those whose livelihood depends on it. I had a child; I lost it. This explains my silence. They did such butchery upon me in the local hospital as to make me unfit to conceive. You asked for news. You have it. Implements we would reject rather than use for scraping the bristles off hogs were those they used upon your sister, and Willard says it is a happy Chance I did not die of the infection. I did not think so, then."

So they return to the Big House without apples or cider, contented. She kisses him and says, "Now run to whoever you run to, darling. I'm grateful we did take that trip."

Ian garages the car. She watches him from her own porch—efficient, orderly. He drives off in the pickup through the woods. She remembers Judah's funeral. "The whole town attended," Hattie had said. "Everyone who's anyone is here. It doesn't pay to set stock in these things, but when you come to think of it it's the best kind of tribute, really, the sort of compliment he'd value. Every single person that he'd call a friend . . ."

Yet to Maggie the crowd of survivors seemed thin—the bald and palsied and bent who clustered to her, condoling. They pressed her hand as if receiving alms; they shook in the weak wind like the last oak leaves above her in the churchyard where he lay. And later, in the Big House, while they filed past the table for coffee and pie, while they came up turn by turn to tell her how they grieved, could understand her sorrow, but wasn't it lucky he went how he went, the list of names and platitudes came somehow to seem like a petition: tell us you'll come to our funeral too; promise when the time comes round you'll remember and attend.

The baby shifts position. She settles on the daybed in the late-afternoon light. She pats the sack beneath her breasts as though to offer comfort, then pats herself with her left hand and makes circular rubbing motions with her right. It is a question of coordination, Maggie knows. It is a problem of the right hand not following the left. She has received three signals in as many days, and her task is to make sense of them, to resolve these images once more. The child subsides; she dreams.

There is a pileated woodpecker, a naked walking woman, and a mad old man. She does not know why she thinks him insane, but it is an assumption she's lived with for years: a glad, waving, wordless madness she welcomes in this world. Ian's lean brown lover and the bird that summoned her belong to private systems that she cannot share. She is her own sufficiency this afternoon on the porch.

XV

So when Hattie accuses her sister-in-law, calling her a Jezebel, the woman will still not repent. Hattie says, "You're pregnant," and Maggie says, "That's right."

"And not with Judah's baby."

"No."

"Have you no shame?" Hattie asks.

"What does that mean?"

"Shame," she repeats. She musters all her spitting venom and pronounces, "You don't even know the meaning of the word."

"Not in this case," says Maggie.

"No?"

"No."

"How *can* you? . . ."

"Children get born every minute."

"Not in this village," says Hattie. "And not to a widow."

Maggie lights a cigarette. The smoke hovers at her head; it will not rise. "But you didn't mind before."

"When?"

"When you thought it was Judah's. Or Ian's, maybe."

"Mind? Of course I minded. But there wasn't anything to do about it."

Hattie knows her answer makes no sense. She didn't much mind and she still wouldn't mind if the child were a Sherbrooke, not bastard. Yet she feels allowed to lie in the face of brazen falsity; she'll fight fire with fire; they'll see.

"But what can I do now?" Maggie's voice is—she could swear it—amused.

"Farm the thing out." Her own voice has gone querulous, whining, like a girl about to cry. "Have it adopted."

"It's not a *thing*."

"Put it up for adoption. Or else . . ." The threat is empty, Hattie knows. There's no "or else" to threaten her with, nothing to insist on but the force and weight of decency, and decency doesn't apply.

"I'd like your help," says Maggie. "I'd be grateful if you felt the way you felt before."

"What about the father?"

"No. He doesn't know."

"How can that be?" Hattie asks. "He's a stranger?"

"He just doesn't know," she repeats.

"I wasn't born yesterday. How's that possible?"

"It is."

Hattie summons control. There's indignity enough without her having to debase herself by asking what Maggie won't tell. Let him who is without sin cast the first stone, said Our Savior, and she'd cast no stone. But that didn't mean she couldn't disapprove; it didn't mean she had to countenance or take part in such shamefulness, it meant that sin abounded in her once spotless house. Nowhere in the Bible did it say you had to welcome Jezebel, or take Mary Magdalen in. And that Judah'd willed this house to Maggie, who kept her here on sufferance, was just her fool brother's mistake. Lot's daughters were a whorish pair, no matter what reasons they gave.

There is nothing left to do but lock herself into her room. She gathers up her knitting and her cocktail glass. The others can weep till the carpets are salt; she herself will not descend.

"The difference you're making makes no difference to me," Maggie says. "It's *my* child, understand. It could come from a stork, if you'd rather. Or"—she gestures—"Hal Boudreau."

"I never . . ."

"And I'm not *saying* he's the father. That isn't the point. The point is you've been wanting all these weeks to credit Judah. You've not done the addition. Credit me."

"But Ian . . ."

"He's no more the father than Boudreau." There is anger now in Maggie, and whip-snapping severity. "I got it from the whorehouse where I worked."

"Which one was that?"

"In Guatemala. Last week. Now if you don't mind, I'm tired. I've got to entertain the football team."

"I shouldn't wonder."

"You should."

Yet Hattie feels a queer desire to prolong this talk, since when it's done all's done. She stamps her foot, then taps it. "You've killed me," she says.

"No."

"It's the same as murder. This is the death of me."

"It's not the same."

"It is. You listen to me, just this once. A person's name is their way of living; a person's good name is his life. You've taken ours and dragged it through the mire—that pig wallow where you're at home. It was the last thing left us. Now there isn't anything left."

"Oh, Hattie, it's not true!"

"What is then? What's your sluttish truth?"

Maggie swallows. She is white as if they've just passed Christmas, not Columbus Day. Her cigarette is out. "There's my child," she says.

"Who? Ian?"

"The one I'm carrying. It's in the service of life."

"So you say. I don't believe it, I . . ."

But Maggie ends this argument by shrugging, veering off. "Suit yourself," she says. It is as if the woman mocks her—saying words can't kill, ideas can't kill, a name or child or shame can't kill; you'll live to be a hundred, Hattie, wait and see. She will not wait. She'll never ever speak to Jezebel again; she's told her so in no uncertain terms.

Once the world was lovely; once she only had to hear a stream in order to tell Judah, "Isn't it beautiful; isn't it lovely, that sound?" Then everything was cause for celebration and the world chock-full of celebrants; she remembers how he used to light up Roman candles and sparklers and pinwheels come Fourth of July. Ian would watch big-eyed, *bug*-eyed, corking his ears with his thumbs. And Maggie would be out there with her husband, a quick shadow on the grass, a shape that darted in to light the fuse he offered her, and they would huddle together while the fireworks went off. She, Hattie, would stay on the porch. She'd sit in the rocker or join Ian on the double seat or just stand at the railings and look down on their intricate dance.

Once, on Ian's seventh birthday, Judah forked a haystack in front of the Toy House. It bulked there in the middle of the driveway, and she wondered what he meant by that, who always salvaged hay. She'd have to beg a bale from him for garden mulch, even though the barn held thousands—yet here he piled it head-high. The night of Ian's birthday, when his few invited friends had left, Judah gave a match to him and said, "Here. Light it. The whole heap's yours."

Ian was frightened of fire, as he had good reason to be. But Judah led him to the hay and held his hand and made him light it at the kerosene-soaked rim. Black smoke snaked up and billowed around them, and she wondered would it catch, because the hay was green. Then suddenly the smoke went white and then was red, was fire, and Judah stepped back. Ian encircled his waist. That had been his way of asking for protection; he did it with Maggie too, hiking her skirt.

She remembers wondering why Judah planned this pyre—what had been his purpose that night. There wasn't much risk, really. The driveway was broad, and she noticed he had hoses ready, and the flames went straight on up. But ash was floating all around them, and charred wisps of hay would litter the flower beds, and it did seem a pure plain waste.

Then the first sparkler went off. Then a Roman candle exploded, and fireworks she could not name—great whorls of green and red and purple rockets and yellow ones unfurling all the way above the cupola of the Big House. The four of them watched, rapt. Judah had filled the haystack with so many fireworks it made the Independence Day display seem small. Ian crossed his arms and held them at his shoulder blades and rocked. His eyes, she said to Maggie, were like sparklers also; he'd been so blazing proud. The haystack burned until ten o'clock; she remembers consulting her watch.

It is that hour now; her cuckoo clock chimes. The Big House crests the highest hill for miles. It has four floors, counting the attic, and a walk-in cupola. There is a widow's walk around it, and the rooftrees shape a cross. Peacock was a pious man and planned his house to be a signal beacon to the weary traveler; he wanted his heaven-aspiring edifice to stand truly rooted, four-square.

So Hattie thinks she might ascend—slip out the door and sneak through the attic and up to the cupola, taking a megaphone, hanging herself from the highest crosstie and proclaiming shame to all the town beneath. She would shout till breath was done how the Sherbrookes were dishonored by that widow-whore. She would dangle like a belt-end from the wooden hips of the roof. Her feet would dance in circles and her face would suffuse and be black.

Then Hattie thinks that Maggie would be glad of this—relieved the household guardian was gone. She'll not give such satisfaction; she'll endure. Yet she might take the midnight air, might slip out of the house the way Judah used to and go for a stroll. She ponders this. It would be undignified. She could not creep past those watchdogs outside, or set out unopposed. A locked door locks both ways. Yet in the very instant that she sees herself as prisoner, Hattie chooses to escape; she will oppose the ancient ways to all of this tinsel modernity and see who wins out in the end.

So she contrives a plan. Just because they've shut her in doesn't mean she'll stay that way; there are windows and drainpipes and fire escapes. She's high-hearted as she hasn't been in years; blood races in her veins. She imagines herself a princess preparing to elope—thinks she'll take the bedsheets and knot them together and tie them to the bedpost and let herself down. She imagines herself on this ladder of sheets, and the tower cannot hold her, and she drops in her billowing gown to the arms of some prince on a princely white steed.

Or she could call the fire company. She could raise a false alarm, and men from the village would come on her say-so and stand beneath her window with a circle of stretched canvas while she leaped. She would bounce like an acrobat up from the hoop, then say, "Thank you, gentlemen," and just walk away.

Then she remembers—there's a fire ladder in a box on the top shelf of the closet. Judah had purchased ten for the house and placed them in each likely room and instructed her in their use. She'd mocked him, saying, "Can you imagine? Me on that rickety thing? Don't be silly, Jude."

But he'd been insistent, showing her how the metal rungs would hold three times her weight, and how the hooks on the ladder's top end would fit to the window frame snugly. She'd never tested it, of course, but now's the time for testing and she fetches the web-encrusted dusty box down from the topmost shelf.

There are instructions for use. There are little chain links between each aluminum rung. She lifts the thing out carefully, making certain not to twist it, making no noise. Then, cradling the bundle as once she would her nephews, with her hands squeezing so the handles can't slip, Hattie lets the ladder fall. Its lightness pleases her. It is thirty feet long, and reaches. She adjusts the curved hooks to the sill; they hold. She jiggles and tests it; it holds.

Next Hattie composes herself. Such flight would be madness, she knows; it's a girlish fancy and she's eighty-two years old. She's not the type and never was to shinny up drainpipes or climb down a ladder or a tree. But she hunts sense in nonsense now, and every argument she musters is its own reproof; why should she hide in her one room when there's a wide world glimmering beyond? The men who threw gravel up at her window have long since been buried, and there were few enough of them to begin with; why worry about catching cold? The Big House shelters wastrel sons and unwed mothers; why shouldn't she escape?

The ladder hangs away from her like something in a pool. It bends with the line of the house. She is not afraid of heights, but not partial to them either, and the descent would be perilous in her high-heeled pumps. She therefore takes sensible shoes. A hoot owl—or something very like a hoot owl—cries in the middle distance, and she hears it as an invitation and gathers her shawl.

Ian comes to the door. He tries the handle, finds it locked, and stands in the hallway, saying, "Aunt. Are you all right?"

"Do you remember," Hattie asks, "the time we came back from—where was it, Wardsboro? And it was Memorial Day. My land, yes. And the woods were full of campers and it snowed?"

He tries the door handle again. She takes it for encouragement. She will not look at him, but will not be silent either, since he's come to listen.

"Then those hills at Wilmington. And how you jumped on out and pushed? And we skidded past fifty stopped cars?"

"Yes," Ian says.

"We'd never have made it, but for you shoving," Hattie finishes, uncertain.

"Open up, I can't hardly hear you."

She smiles. She is on to his tricks.

"Please!"

"California is the fastest-growing state," she tells the door. "Its capital is Sacramento and its largest city is Los Angeles. The highest point in California is Mount Whitney, and the State Flower is the Golden Poppy."

"I'm sorry," Ian says. "I just can't hear you through this door."

"It's in the Hammond Atlas. Everything's there."

She sits back, concentration released. The door is oak; he could batter at it till he breaks his wrist.

"You're certain you're all right, aunt?"

"Yes."

"Can I bring you anything?" She hears, perceptibly, relief.

"Not now. Tomorrow, maybe."

"We'll see you in the morning . . ."

She tells him "No," so softly that he does not choose to hear.

"For breakfast."

"No."

"I'm sorry, aunt," he says.

She shifts her position, crossing her ankles and crossing her wrists. "For what?" She has a hundred answers to that question; Ian offers none. He raps at the door with his knuckles, so hard the mirror on the inside shakes; she sees herself framed in it, shaking. "Why are you sorry?" she asks him again, but Ian beats a jaunty closing tattoo on the door-frame, says, "Sleep well, anyhow," and leaves.

Hattie arranges herself on the bed. She folds her brown wrap precisely and wonders how she otherwise might pass the time—how to beguile the hours, days, and weeks till her heart cracks. There are books to read and serving silver to polish, and Betsy Ferguson's niece will not stop having babies, so there's receiving blankets to make up. She sits alone with her mirrored second self for company, and talking to keep up her courage. "*I'm* not the one who's pregnant," Hattie says. "*I* haven't brought dishonor on the house."

Her digestion has been troublesome. There's only so much wormwood you can swallow before your stomach hurts. It's like a hardened artery or a sclerotic vein—although she has neither, thank goodness. But the bitterness and gall accumulate; they pinch in your lower intestine; they lie there like a self-accreting ball of bile. She wishes she could hawk it up and spit it at Maggie just once. But she is a mannerly person and therefore must swallow her knowledge and answers; she has to bite her tongue. She has done so before every meal. She speaks with honeyed sweetness, saying please and thank you and might I have another maraschino cherry, if you please.

Maggie has been companionable with her in the months since Judah's death; Harriet acknowledges that. They'd shored each other up in isolation like a doorway frame you find somewhere standing in the woods, with everything around it burned or rotten and torn down. They'd formed a kind of arch, she thinks, standing upright and separate and at a certain point starting to lean. They leaned together, falling, and were each other's support. Then you looked inside and saw the forest, looked outside and saw the forest, looked below you and saw only the lintel, then weeds.

Still, some magic is at work; it's a wonder she's having a child. Stranger things have happened, but none so strange since Hattie could remember hearing, or ever in the Big House. There's bravery in it, she has to admit. There's bravery and recklessness mixed in so close together it's not like the sides of a doorframe, but more like cream and milk. And now she knows the ghost she fears is just the vanquished past and Maggie's way of saying what's important is anticipation, not remembrance, is every tomorrow to come. Hattie can admire this, but cannot accept it as true. She has to give credit where credit is due, and her sister-in-law can take credit for this: nothing in eighty-two previous years had made Hattie take to her bed. Her parents and brother and nephew have died; she never had married, and has outlasted all her suitors anyhow; the most part of her friends are dead, or in hospitals and on the way. But nothing—not two wars and one Great Depression and Lord knows how many setbacks, recessions, the flu—you could knock her down with a feather, Hattie thinks, you could blow her over and just leave her, she's never in all her born days . . .

She wears cleanly night things, since they should not be embarrassed when they come to lay her out. It is a tester bed, handed down from her grandmother's aunt. Her eyes are bothersome. If her eyes had been better, she thinks, she would have spotted this coming, could have seen it a mile down the road. She still could sue. She is not litigious—not like Judah anyhow, who'd jump into a lawsuit like a boy into a swimming hole, feet first and whistling, shutting his eyes, delighting in the thump and splash and wetting everyone who watched. Then he'd come up grinning, dripping, saying what the hey, that worked or didn't work and let's just try again.

Yet Samson Finney himself, she knows, would counsel against such a suit. It would cost the family whichever way, and the only ones to benefit would be the newspaper people. You wouldn't want a fuss like that, not in this town at this time. She supposes the lawyer is Judah's watchdog still; Miles Fisk would take an item like that and run a two-column lead.

So Hattie determines to go. She folds her hands, interlacing her fingers on the lace bodice that's laundered and pressed. Jacob's ladder ascended to clouds. In the picture book she'd used, and then the one she gave to Ian, heavenly ladders got lost at the top of the page in a sunburst that could dazzle you—so bright the rungs seemed silver. She will forgive them their trespasses, though Lord knows they've trespassed enough. She wishes them joy in the house.

"Hattie."

This is the next visitation—foreseen.

"Hattie. Are you asleep?"

She presses her lips shut.

"Can you hear me?"

She twiddles her thumbs.

"She's sleeping," Maggie says. So Hattie knows there's two of them outside, not only her sister-in-law. She reverses the direction of her thumbs, twiddling toward her own neck.

"Hattie?"

She holds her breath.

"I meant no harm," says Maggie to the door. "I didn't mean to hurt you, and I do apologize."

She stops her thumbs' rotation.

"I should have told you earlier. You had a right to know."

The walls require paint; their rose tint has faded to pink.

"I just wasn't certain, is all. It might have been Judah's, I thought."

There are cracks in the plaster besides; she's watched the house disintegrate. The shape on the ceiling above her is like a spring-tooth harrow, and she imagines it dragged the whole length of the room. It's as if the plaster were an ice-smooth field to plow.

"I could use your help," Maggie says.

She has trouble restraining herself; she presses her palms to her ears. If she wanted, she could tell them both a thing or two.

"We all could."

She hears Ian withdraw; his steps have Judah's pace to them, although not the weight. Hattie cups her palms harder; she wishes that she had her conch shell handy, where you listen to the sea. If she started to talk she would burn off their ears.

"Well," Maggie says.

She lies back and listens. Her pillow is horsehair, flat.

"Good night then."

The mattress too is horsehair, and long-lasting, though it ought to be repacked. She imagines the horses that shed her mattress to be a matched, picked team. The stable hands would curry them for profit, selling off their coat.

"Sweet dreams," Maggie offers. "I'm grateful for your attention."

They would bear her away in the coach. She tries not to laugh out loud. "It's been such a pleasant chat."

They would carry her out of this dark place, through the gates. Maggie and Ian could taunt her forever, but she would be upright in the carriage, trotting smartly, not able to hear.

"I know you're in there listening," she finishes, "so hear me out and then I'll go. I'm in pain tonight and wish you'd be willing to help me."

It is as if the oak has no protective density, no deadening resistance to her voice; it is as if the keyhole where she whispers is a trumpet. "Good night," Maggie says. "Wish me luck."

Now she arises like smoke. Hattie has no fear of cold or heights or what the neighbors would say if they chanced to see her on the ladder, no fear of falling when she swings out over the ledge. She has decided to escape and is not indecisive and has no regrets. They conspire in the corners, thinking that they've locked her in, but she has a trick or two left. She finds herself giggling, delighted, as she lets herself down rung by rung. She sneezes twice, and sways. The ladder takes her weight as if she were a schoolgirl or lover eloping; it lets her down springily, resilient, and she noses past the dark bay window of the dining room.

The house is warm. The clapboard's slats retain, it seems, the sun's heat from that afternoon, and the ivy rustles so as to cover her clinking descent. Her hands are cold, however, and she does fear cramp; she counts five rungs, then rests. For an instant, dangling there, halfway from the window, she yearns to climb back up and clamber into bed. But she does not have the strength to rise; she tries one rung, and it's all she can manage to lift her first foot. There are lights above her, but the downstairs floor is dark.

"Hot night," says Judah.

"Yes."

"We're not supposed to feel it, but we do. Sometimes I sweat like a horse. The weather's changing hereabouts."

"State your purpose." Hattie confronts him. "Tell me what you're after and I'll let you know what's what."

"Still the same old girl," he chuckles. "No monkey business."

"That's right."

"In some things anyhow."

"What do you mean?"

"What's going on in this house?" Judah asks. "What's happening beneath my roof?"

Those had been his final words—the last time that she spoke to him before he fell asleep, or seemed to, and Maggie took over the watch. He had been suspicious, but she, Hattie, was without suspicion and tiptoed out, never dreaming he would die that day or have nothing else to say, with unanswered questions.

She continues her descent. She cannot see. She drops her shawl. Her left foot misses, and she flails out for a further rung but misses, toes the ground. She stands in the shadow of the head-high yew trees, safe.

Next Hattie gathers up her nightgown like an evening dress. She holds the pleats so that they will not rustle, and she steps forward alone. Seth is a bat; Judah a fading, fire-rimmed presence; and her tester bed is not a carriage but a sleigh. She summons all her hardiness and plunges through the stream with Jamie Pearson once again (his red hair flaming in front of her; his drunken cackle making mock of her bared breasts) and shivers while Widower Powers warms his ring-bespangled hands in front of the coal grate.

Hattie advances. She follows the flagstone path. The moon has sunk behind the house, and it takes her several steps to come out from its shadow. She skirts the Toy House, then the sugarhouse and carriage barn and, keeping those buildings at her back, sets out for the pump house and pond. She raises her left hand as if there were partners and does a box-step fox-trot. She hums to keep up her courage, and does not retreat.

And all her great-hearted elders—Tommy Sherbrooke lost at sea; Peacock fording the isthmus, though in the death grip of pneumonia, to return to his imagined mansion made actual for his children, and his children's children till time out of mind; her mother in a wheelchair and father asking permission to light a cigar—ride on every side of her, escorting. They are without fear. There is an inland sea she's heard of, coming around the mountain: it is where they're going to, her father says. They have donned bathing gear and brought umbrellas and picnic hampers; they've all prepared for such immersion. There is balm and sense-soothing liniment about; there are birds in abundance.

"Last one in's a rotten egg," cries Judah, and she wants to warn him that his wife has been unfaithful, that she's spawning Sherbrookes who have no true Sherbrooke blood. But he is happy, oblivious; he does his flutter kick. He splashes and whoops and, in the water, stands on his head. The horses graze contentedly; there's been no damage, Judah says, emerging again to dry off. He shakes the water off him like a dog. The horses shift and stamp. He blows and sputters and wheezes hugely, saying, "Do you hear me? There's no damage, sister. Nothing. None."

Therefore, at the pond's near edge, she does not slow her pace. She rucks up her gown a tuck higher and tiptoes through the cattails. The marsh grass is springy; it gives. She is dancing splendidly; she whirls and twirls and floats. Wild ducks flee from her and fly off south; she hears their wings. And now the water welcomes her; it is a bevy of partners, and she embraces each in turn. They yield and sing and sink.

XVI

"When in the cool of the evening we walk by the arroyo here—for such they call the stream bed that is dust and gravel now which once must needs have been mighty indeed to hollow these hills—Willard discourses to me on the workings of the Covenants, and how the Doctrine pertains. Let me impress upon you, brother, that the only begotten Son of God in the flesh is nonetheless part of a purposed and principled unity, one in three. Scarce half a century ago, the church of Jesus Christ of Latter-Day Saints was organized at Fayette, and see what progress we make: heathen by the hundreds flocking to our fold! As if the Melchizedek priesthood— which as you know was directly bestowed by these resurrected apostles, Peter, James, and John, upon the prophet Joseph Smith and also Oliver Cowdery—as if this priesthood, I say, and also the lower Aaronic orders, were herdsmen watching over the lambs and the large-bellied goats. We run around the pen. We follow the leader in circles, close to. But just about and outside of the gate, remaining there for our protection against the importunate scavenging Wolves, is the whole of which the Shepherd seems but part: godhead and good appetite, an ignorance dispersed."

The dawn is late, with that irresolute lingering dark that means the end of October. Ian walks out by the barn, where Hal is stacking wood. He labors in the shadows—bent-backed, stooping, and chomping on his unlit pipe; Ian remembers, embarrassed, how yesterday he'd promised help but had forgotten.

"Changed your mind, did you?"

"I'm sorry."

"Had better things to do this morning?"

"Mm-mn."

"Well." Boudreau blows his nose. He checks the wind's direction. "It's not getting any warmer."

They work together in silence, stacking and facing off cords. Hal has backed up a wagon, with split maple wood and ash. "You can tell me anytime, shut up. Just mind my own business," he says. "But what's it like, I wonder."

"What?"

"How old are you?"

"Twenty-six. Why?"

"No reason." Boudreau studies the alignment of the wood, then says, "We'll keep this section clear. Back the wagon on in later."

"All right."

"I just thought I'd ask you, is all."

Ian knows there's no use rushing: that impatience in him will slow Boudreau down. This is the spring's dead wood, ready to burn. So he signifies his willingness to answer, saying nothing, sneezing in the barn's thick outer air.

"Because maybe," Boudreau says—he ties twine together, slides the barn door shut again, and drapes his loop on a nail—"maybe you been to the Alagash?"

"No."

"God's country, that is."

Ian has chaff in his throat. He hawks and spits.

"You know what my boy told me? He learned this in biology, he says; you know how your body cells die. Well, every seven years exactly every one of them is changed; you're not the same person you was. There's not a single cell alive in you that was living here seven years back." Boudreau marvels at this; he thumps his chest. "This heart of mine even; it's been eight different hearts. You figure fifty-six is eight times seven, right? You figure every time you change it takes you seven years; you've got to figure I been eight different people, seems like. Seven, anyways."

There are pigeons in the barn. They settle on the flashing, unalarmed.

"You're an educated person," says Boudreau. "I want your opinion on that." He holds his right hand up and ticks the fingers off, working backward to the thumb. He folds each finger down in the service of arithmetic, intent. "So what I want to know is, are you figuring to stay?"

"How long? For seven years?"

Boudreau nods. He studies Ian closely now, eyes large in the dim light. "And what sort of partner do you think you're like to be?"

"Partner?"

Hal nods again. He plays with the brim of his cap. "I figure I got the know-how and you got the money and land."

"For what?" Ian asks. He can hear the pigeons flutter and ruffle, settling.

"For anything you've got a mind to," Boudreau says. He looks like a cardplayer now—cagey, holding his cap to his chest.

"Development?"

"Maybe."

"A shopping center?"

"Why not?"

"A bowling alley," Ian says. "I've always been partial to them. We could use the bottom land."

"If you've got a mind to . . ."

"Parking lots," he continues. "We're in need of parking lots around here."
Boudreau seems less certain now.

"Shit," Ian says. "Stock racing. That's what we could do with it. Build us a track!"

"If you want to . . ."

"The answer is no."

Maggie runs to meet him. Her strides are panic-lengthened, and she wheels her arms. She appears to find no rhythm, swerving, jostled, jerked along and not quite falling; she has not run in months.

"Where's Hattie?" she cries out to Ian. "Where've you been?"

He sees her terror, takes her arm.

"Where *is* she?"

"Wait," he says. "First catch your breath."

She stands beside him, panting, flushed, sweat starting on her face; she leans on him and shuts her eyes. "I'm certain she's gone. I was so sure you had left me."

"No."

"But *she* has. There's no answer there, no matter what I say to her. It's not the same sort of silence, Ian, not like last night when we knew she was listening."

"Let's look at her window," he says.

Maggie is calmer now; her breathing subsides. But as they walk around the house, Ian supporting her, she says, "There's no one alive in that room. I tell you I can feel it; she's gone. She's killed herself."

"Take it easy. We don't . . ." They round the corner and see the fire ladder and the open window and her shawl on the yew bush beneath. Maggie stops. She starts to laugh. Her laugh is high-pitched and irregular, on hysteria's edge. "I told you so," she says.

The ladder hugs the clapboard as if pasted on. There is no wind.

"Well, anyhow, it's one way in."

"It's one way *out*, you mean."

"No," Ian says. "I mean I'll climb on up and take a look. It's easier than knocking the door down. You meet me back inside."

"I'm staying here."

"Please. You were racing up that path to meet me; you're shivering now. I'll climb up and unlock the door. That way . . ."

But Maggie takes the brown shawl from the branch it dangles on, and swaddles herself and says, "No." He cannot argue with her; he has come to share her dread. So for something to do he tests the ladder, puts his weight on it and pulls. It holds; it seems securely hooked across the sill. He starts to climb.

"It's useless," Maggie says. "She isn't there, I know it. She's gone—can't you understand anything? Why can't you understand that?"

Ian continues to climb. As he clears the yew bush it comes to him that his mother's right, that he's some playacting suitor making his way up to vacancy. The window gapes above him, open, and she would not leave the window open were she still inside. He thinks perhaps he'll find her corpse, and that she's let the cold air in so as not to stink. This is absurd, he tells himself; this is as silly as believing she eloped. But he cannot keep from shaking as he clears the final rung; the ladder clanks beneath him and he hears Maggie talking, but not what she says. He puts his head above the ledge and, eyes shut, tumbles in. The room is unlit, rectangular, cold; there is nothing in the room.

Maggie looks about her. Whenever she attempts to rest, the baby within her is restless; it's used to motion, she assumes, and prefers being rocked when she walks. She holds her side and tries to keep the panic in, staring up at the ladder and wall. Her son has disappeared. There is some sort of order, apparently, in what she sees as order's absence; it is like those number series she'd been tested on in grade school, to test her gift for patterning. It's the sort of game that Judah liked, according with his sense of how things fit. The simplest questions showed a simple sequence; if the list ran two-four-six-eight, you could answer ten. If it ran four, fourteen, twenty-four, thirty-four, you could answer forty-four comes next. She says these numbers aloud.

Her child will deal with all of this. Her child will bring vivacity into the dead surrounding space—bringing frogs and teddy bears and friends, wearing so rapid a sequence of clothes that Maggie cannot quite determine if it is male or female, young or old. It wears pajamas, nightgowns, jump suits, snowsuits, pants, skirts, blouses, sweaters, and has an assortment of hats. It is an infant, little girl, stripling, youth and debutante at once. It cries, wails, drinks from her breast, then from a bottle of gin without interval and is married, then both a mother and father. Her child eats Easter bunnies' ears, then jelly beans and pizza, then selects a lemon tart from the dessert cart at Périgord Park. She tries to watch such fantasy unreeling like a series of home movies with the focus not quite right. Whatever it is, it is soon.

For Jude the future's guises had been threatful, indistinct. He saw plots behind each tax hike, and inroads every time they tarred a road. She has begun to understand how all his self-taught caginess about the law was meant to throw a smoke screen up—not against her own behavior but government authority—not to save the money but to thwart the I.R.S. Had he died intestate, Maggie as his lawful wife would anyhow have gotten what his maneuvering offered: the house and the land for life. And the trust funds were an ill-named joke: they signaled lack of trust.

Yet Finney, with his chitchat about provisos six and nine, was heralding the future's toll and telling her to watch out. She has a vision, suddenly, of their impoverished children's children squabbling over resale rights, and who would get to keep what piece of tract land after the developers were done. They would have to sell the place in order to pay inheritance taxes; they would divide and subdivide and end up with the Toy House only, staring through a picket fence at the mansion-turned-museum that had been their family home.

"How might we best live after those who go before? What remedy or comfort can we discover—with our great fathers dead, against this Present

Age? It is my dream of waking that we follow their Example and survive. When Father died it was as if the light of the world went out for me, and all delight was snuffed. Things used to seem so *organized . . .*"

Ian reappears. His head is framed by the window's white frame. The wood requires painting. "I'm coming down," he calls. "She's not here."

"I know that."

"Yes." In the silence she can hear doors opening and closing; Maggie knows it is too late to follow Hattie's tracks. Her sister-in-law is light-footed, and she'd have gone off alone. Like those aged Eskimos that Judah said got up and left the fire's circle, heading out to freeze, she must have headed for the hills, not town. It's just exactly like her, Maggie thinks, her way of having the last bitter laugh.

Ian comes out from the house. "Should we call the police?" he asks. "When did you notice this? When do you think it happened; how long has she been gone?"

"Last night sometime. I thought maybe you'd run off together."

"We do have to notify *someone*; we'll need help."

"I can't have them ogling me, Ian. Not this morning, I can't face them now."

He studies her. She is floating, inward, arms on her stomach as if it were buoyant. It may be a fool's errand but he'll make it anyhow, and spend the day hunting his aunt. There are flashlights in the car. Maggie nods at him and, trailing the brown shawl, walks past. She enters the house like a hospital hall; irresolute, he follows.

"Well, go if you're going," she says. "I'll wait." So once again he gathers up equipment for the car—keys and blankets, a bottle of rye. He drives the land's perimeter as he had done six months before, arriving. The stone walls of the property are bare. He has half expected, somehow, she'd be sitting by some gate. Or that he'd meet a car whose passenger seat she occupied, turning in the entry drive—sure she'd told them of her plan to spend a night after bridge with Doris, or that she'd gone to Arlington to visit Laura

McKechnie who'd been begging her to come since Lord knows when. She'd feign innocence in any case, pretending not to know she'd been in any way missed or remiss; she'd scold him for his fretful search and say she knew the reason. "Just because *you* want to leave doesn't mean I'm leaving, mister. Don't call a kettle black until you've cleaned the pot."

But the few cars he encounters do not slow down; the village beneath him is quiet. He drives through Main Street twice, in case, where the houses yield no secrets to him, and the bar would not contain her, and the post office and grocery are empty. Nor does he think it likely that Hattie— who called departure "trespassing"—would leave. Still, there is the ladder and the evidence of escape. So she'd let herself down and gone for a walk and not returned for twelve hours at least, he calculates how far she could get in that time.

She might have gone in circles. She would have stopped to rest. She might set out on what she took to be the path of least resistance, and find it was a marsh. There are paper streamers dangling from the trees, festooning them for Mischief Night; tomorrow will be Hallowe'en. There are exploded pumpkins on the southerly approach road, dropped from trucks. Ian parks and finds himself where first he'd parked, returning. He vaults the fence and is again at the shed field's far edge. He stands beneath the oak, hears what he swears is the same hoot owl calling, and studies the Big House a half mile below. He paces the field's width, then length, and, hunting his aunt's traces, crosses the field and continues.

That afternoon she takes to her bed. She has known for weeks that she will deliver the baby at home; the local hospital is stuffed with aging gossips, and the maternity ward has four-bed rooms, not singles or even a room with two beds. Ian protested it might be risky, and she said more babies have been born at home than ever came from hospitals; she'll run the risk on that.

She used to sing him "shortnin' bread." She used to chant the verses over and over until Ian slept; then Judah would yank on the rope to the

431

cradle and set it steadily rocking. He'd sing the chorus with her in what he thought was harmony, but was a separate tune. She could remember "shortnin' bread" and also the song that went, "You push the damper in, and you push the damper out, and the smoke goes up the chimbley all the same." All it is is repetition; all it means is turning twenty-five-year circles until you start again.

But try as she might to imagine her child, the life within her—even in continual motion, even with the hiccups—stays abstract. It is an alien memory, how twenty-five years ago she fondled two male babies and breast-fed and fed them formula and changed their clothes continually and handled their bodies with intimate ease. Since Seth died in his crib, she has made a point of forgetting what those early years were like; now she finds herself hunting the memory. She has readied the old, stored layette. She polished the metal fittings on the cradle and put lemon oil on the slats. She kept herself busy for all of October—folding and unfolding the child's receiving blankets, then washing and ironing and folding them again.

Yet it is the exercise of duty, not desire. Maggie wonders what she'll do and how she'll manage with this child. All she knows is that she'll have it, willy-nilly, and even if it has two heads to match its two splayed feet. She believes in abortion, of course; she's a member of Planned Parenthood, and the future of the planet depends on birth control. But she has to have *this* baby, has never had any choice.

XVII

"On June 27, 1844—a heinous day, and I blush to have shared breath with those who breathed that afternoon—men blackened their faces with Cork. How far much blacker, however, were their souls to have counselled such Action! Even now, with Willard's intercession that I learn Charity, that Meekness and Forgiveness and Obedience to things ordained are Christian virtues truly—and the Prophet shows us that much Evil springs from Ignorance, that it is not wicked but witless behavior we largely should disdain—nonetheless I find no charity within me when I consider how that mob, that rabble, that canaille broke into Carthage Jail. 'To Carthage then I came,' writes Augustine, says Willard, 'where an unholy fire burnt all about mine ears.' How much less holy, even, were the brands and flaming torches that these brigands flung about them, as if their insignia forever and ever must be the light of damnation, the heat that devours. When the scuffle was over, John Taylor was hurt. But Willard Richards escaped. Yet those lawbreakers had as quarry the leaders of us all, the Latter-day prophets themselves, and were it not profanity thus to blaspheme his title, I should call Joseph Smith indeed a pearl of Great Price among peas.

"The First President was brutally cut down. So too was Hyrum Smith. But whether with axes or long knives or rifles I do not know; it is all one. They cannot harm his free fleeing, whatever baying pack they constitute themselves: we are ascendant, brother, and shall survive even this! To be accused of Treason who was eminently Faithful; who was lieutenant general of the Nauvoo legion, pacific in men's eyes! To have been vilified and fettered whilst these blackamoors moved freely against him, sneering, using I know not what vile imputations and piercing the Dear Flesh! Who uses the term Treason in any other context but to call such mob in Treason's thrall traduces even language, much less its purposed intent. No. Governor Ford pledged protection. This pledge was empty, duplicitous. He is a latter-day Pilate whilst the Smiths are Saints. I cannot rid myself of rage—of sorrow rather, that His Presence is denied us who had every right to worship it continually. We are bereft of such huge-hearted men as walked this land before . . ."

She had gone with Andrew, last year, to his country place in Westport. It was an eighteenth-century farmhouse, with white siding and dark green trim, and there was a heated outdoor pool. They ate at a waterfront restaurant, hearing foghorns, sampling the paella and the salad bar. Afterward they drove back home, and she watched comedians and chorus girls, the eleven o'clock news and the Johnny Carson show. The house was sparsely furnished; Andrew was deciding, he said, what sort of motif to employ. He thought the thing to do was to have an ancient house with only the most contemporary furnishings—or vice-versa, to have a modern house furnished with only antiques. Lately, he confided, he'd determined that perhaps one could also manage to marry the two, since Mies and Shaker styling share a principle; in both cases, less is more.

Maggie had had trouble sleeping. She watched a late-night movie, fitful, half alert. She turned the sound off but retained the image—of six boys in a boat in the South China Sea, becalmed, without water or oars.

They depended on one compass and a coolie for directions; when Maggie switched the sound off he was telling them his rickshaw was more suitable conveyance. She shut her eyes; she slept. At three o'clock, however, she was awakened from a dream of burial by the sound of something thrashing. She shook Andrew awake; the television nickered at them, indistinct. Then Andrew pulled the window up and she heard grunts and sloshing sounds outside. He said, "Christ, something's in the pool." She said, "You've got a cover on," and he said, "Yes. But it's plastic; it floats."

They ran outside, wearing raincoats; the night was opaque. The fog was thick, and somehow it refracted sound so that the grunting and the slosh-ing seemed to come from all directions; he turned the pool lights on, but they too were refracted and she could barely see. Then she saw, at the pool's deep end, what seemed to be a remnant of her dream. A buck with horns high as the diving board was caught in the water and plastic, writhing, snorting, panicky. She also panicked and began to reach for him, but An-drew shouted: "No!" Its horns were huge; it slashed at her, she drew back from its fearsome reach.

The water steamed; the buck was black and tangled in the torn blue cover; Andrew had the pool net out—the one he used for cleaning leaves—and was wielding it like a flimsy aluminum spear. The buck backed off; they drove it into the shallow end. There, on its knees and scrambling, slipping, the animal broke free at last and, charging up the three pink steps, impaled a plastic deck chair on its horns.

Maggie laughed; she heard herself—a thin, high wail on the edge of hysteria. Stamping, streaming, the buck reared high with its white plastic garland and, with an upward thrusting, flung the chair into the pool. Then it was gone. It leaped into the darkness back behind the lights. She was not sure, for an instant, if such fierce animality had indeed been trapped or willful, but she held to the diving board, listening, rapt. Andrew said, "Shit. It's been shitting all over the pool."

So then he started up the vacuum cleaner, and they pulled the deck chair out and took away the plastic cover and, for an hour, while she sat at the pool's edge and watched, he vacuumed deer shit from the depths. If he didn't catch

435

it now, he said, it would be slime by morning. The night was cold; she shivered, watching; he worked with a shocked thoroughness that imitated calm.

It was simple, Andrew said. The buck had walked out on the pool blanket, trying to drink. In summer they came for the roses; there was less food in the Westport woods than the herd required; the town dogs were leashed and garden fences were low, so they'd get used to foraging in people's backyards—he'd seen deer before. "But in swimming pools?" she asked.

"No. And nor a buck either."

"I tried to pull him out," she said. "I was reaching for those horns."

"You must have been sleepwalking."

"This isn't working," Maggie said. "I—I need to go back to the city. Please."

"We just got here!"

"It isn't that simple."

"Of course it is. Take sleeping pills; have a Grand Marnier. Anything. For Christ's sake, it's *my* furniture he wrecked!"

"Judah wants me to come to Vermont. Finney called to say so this morning."

"Who's Finney?"

"Our lawyer. Yesterday morning, I mean."

Andrew had remonstrated with her. He had said she was upset, said six good hours' sleep would fix it and just because her husband's lawyer said she ought to come back north didn't mean she had to jump. As far as he could see, said Andrew, she was making a mistake; she was cutting herself off from diversion just when she needed diverting. But Maggie—on the diving board, legs tucked beneath her and her raincoat buttoned to the neck, watching the water spread and ripple with his extracting motion—had known she would return. Her husband was dying, she said—trapped and dying in the Big House—and she'd write him in the morning to tell him she'd be on the bus.

She conjures up Andrew Kincannon. She has not done so in some time, but now that the baby is descending and her contractions start, she concentrates on its father. He shifts his shape, however, and is not palpable; it is as if he were wind chaff or pollen spores caught on a screen. Nor does she know, these moments, if what she feels is gratitude or scorn. Judah haunts the house in ways far more corporeal than Hattie's daytime prowler or her lover in Manhattan: his foot has worn each floorboard, his back grazed every wall. She ranges the rooms—bearing something within her she'll choose to call Sherbrooke, waiting for some indication of her dead husband's feeling toward it, feeling it kick. It still would be simple to leave. She could go to New York afterward, she tells herself, or New Orleans, or some other country, and raise the child in peace. There would be attentive doctors, solicitous new friends. She would be nobody's whore, but a widow, well provided for, and in a suitable climate. She could fly to Guatemala, where Anne-Maria once went. But she knows she will remain instead; she will suckle her baby this winter, when the grass is sere and branches stripped, and never leave the house.

Maggie remembers a display in the Natural History Museum. When they first settled in New York, Ian had been young enough to want to examine the dinosaurs and reconstructed tribal totems and animals of the veldt. Later he loved weaponry and rocks. But she recollects, this evening, a cross section of New England farm soil such as hers. The exhibit showed seasonal change.

The farm in spring was as she knew it, but the farm in winter showed a burrowing collection of things that seek protection from snow. The mole tunnels, for instance, were shown behind glass, and in the last such tunnel lay a mole. There were field mice and worms in abundance, and everything sought shelter from the frozen surface of the earth. She tells herself the blind snug mole is sensible; she remembers Judah shooting groundhogs, then stuffing them back in their holes. It is all a question of what sort of questions to put. If Andrew calls, she decides, she'll tell him—but not until he asks.

For he is as alien to the life around her as she herself would feel now on Fifty-Seventh and Fifth; they share nothing she wants to acknowledge they share. The child inside her is the child she had been robbed of, earlier; it compensates Judah for Seth.

Maggie supposes her dead husband is phrasing what she'd not quite phrased. Her teacher still, he squints at her: Adam's curse was also a blessing, and labor a God-given thing. They would make snow families. Maggie lay on her back at the garden's far edge, arms akimbo, waving. Then, jumping to her feet, she would leave angels incised in the drift. Ian would use coal and carrots and potatoes for the snowman's features. He had been a purist, eight years old.

She remembers their squabbles at play. Ian wanted only snow and made elaborate ice carvings on the snowman's chest—undoing Judah's tie. Judah used a tie with orange and black stripes and a Windsor knot; Ian couldn't reach the knot and couldn't untie it anyhow and therefore he yanked at the tie's ends and severed Joe the Snowman's head.

"Now look what you've done," Judah said.

"Look what you made me do, Daddy."

"*I* didn't make you."

"You did." Ian stood there in pure opposition, lower lip trembling, left mitten holding the tie.

"Like father, like son," she had said. They turned to watch her approach; she had been muffled, walking.

"Thank God we've got no daughter," Judah said.

She bent to Ian. "Don't you pay any attention. The chip on your daddy's shoulder is a chip off an old, old block."

Judah patted Joe the Snowman's head back into shape. "No-neck Joe, that's what we'll call him. No-neck, no-necktie Joe."

"Mom? Let's make snow angels in all different sizes. In every direction. Okay?"

"Okay."

Ian peered from his snowsuit, consoled. "In every direction there is."

Birds fly left to right outside her window, and she tries to remember if that brings good luck. She lets the curtains fall. They hide her from sight; she is grateful for that; she moves within the room like a portly, aging vestal; Judah'd called her "Sacred Vessel" when she bore his sons. He did so

438

half joking, of course, but beneath the banter there had been awe. So she tells him now, saying it aloud, "Hey, husband, the vessel done cracked." She sees the wild ducks settle, early, on their southward flight. Before they were uneasy—squabbling with the Pekins for possession of the pond, settling on the edge of it for respite only, not rest. Now they appear to remain.

Boudreau has reported to Ian that this was a good year for hay; we made it while the sun shone, the man says. The barns are piled to the rafters, the five silos full, and he will sell it in the winter when the others come up short, he's sold a thousand bales already to make room. Ian returns to the car. He has walked all day, or nearly, crisscrossing the fields and following bridle paths and the sounds of startled creatures in the brush.

He hears nothing human, however, and if his aunt is on the place she— like so much else, like everything he'd planned to keep—eludes him. Ian asks himself, has he elected recurrence? Is he being put through paces that his father ran? "What begins as mystery completes itself as politics," his fifth-form teacher said. "Péguy. Charles Péguy, gentlemen. I trust your French is adequate. *Tout commence en mystique et finit en politique.* That's what the poet-warrior observes."

Ian remembers nothing else about Péguy, nor what the phrase applied to. But he sees Mr. Kay again, bifocals at his nose-end, purple sweat-moons under his armpits, tapping his ruler for emphasis: "History repeats itself. That's one of the reasons our esteemed Henry Ford called it bunk. He thought that interchangeable units increased efficiency, no doubt, but could be controlled. Witness the assembly line. Witness the shameful yet self-congratulatory miracle of Detroit. What are our Fords and Chryslers, gentlemen, I ask you to consider—(and be prepared to do so on Monday at length, for our little written exercise)—what *are* our Fords and Chryslers, I submit, but instances of Péguy's formulation, not Ford's: an idea outlasting its time.

"Let me put it to you this way." Mr. Kay pushed back his spectacles. His blue serge suit had chalk stains and his buttons had popped and cuffs frayed. He spoke with such weary precision, however, that Ian thought him noble—a daunted guardian of standards waging battle five mornings each week. "Putting aside the question of the motor car, of the internal combustion engine and what havoc it creates in the atmosphere, what pride of place it gives to oil and the possibility of corruption; putting aside the astonishing truth that soon we will have paved over, in this nation, an area the size of France and go hurtling over concrete at a breakneck pace to—where? oblivion? the Sunday picnic?—I offer you a second formula, my friends: those who do not understand history are doomed to repeat it. Your essay should be five pages minimum, typed, and with a cover sheet." Their teacher finished with a flourish, straightening his cuffs. "Class dismissed."

So Ian asks himself, should he remain on the land? A question for him one last time, though it had not been for Judah, it seems his father's question nonetheless. Is his mother's photograph at thirty (yellowing, the birch trees brown, with Ian peeking at the camera from her knee's protection, her hair unbound and her hands on her hips, elbows out) the emblem he hunted in Sally but had failed to find? Hattie and the villagers have locked him so entirely in place that he fears his own identity is gone.

Everything that's mystical ends up manipulation; all early authority fades. If man is a political animal, as Ian once believed, then he has been caged. He imagines his mother behind him, and he takes her hand. Her knuckles go white when she squeezes, and he asks her, offering, *What kind of help can I be?* What do you want of me; what can I do, how can I be of best use?

When labor begins, Maggie does not recognize it as labor—only her accustomed tightening previous to sleep. Then the contractions come in earnest: a band of muscle wringing her as if she were the washing squeezed to dry. There are gigantic hands around her, fingers interlaced. She holds her breath, then breathes shallowly. She is unprepared. She has intended somehow, someway, to prepare herself for this. She has bought books about Lamaze, the methodology of painless childbirth, yoga, and breath control. There is a book by a Frenchman who insists that babies come out smiling if they come in darkened rooms, and she agrees with this: being born is enough of a trauma. Therefore she leaves the room lights off. We don't need hospitals and people shouting and instant vitamin shots; she's said this to Ian, persuasive, but Ian is not in the house. Hattie is dead in the attic, she fears. Her child will be a stillborn girl, and she will die in the process of birth, and Ian would return to find three generations of Sherbrookes to bury: the women of his line.

Maggie musters self-control. She calls the doctor and he tells her to time the contractions, to tell him how long between contractions and call him back, okay. She hears the noise of his household on the other end; then he hangs up. She understands that her own household produces no similar noise; she stares at the hands of her watch, forgetful of her purpose in such staring. The contractions cease, Ian will be home, she tells herself, before things can get serious; her labor with him took two days. She waits eight minutes, twelve, fifteen, and calls the doctor to confess there's nothing yet. He tells her therefore not to worry and to try to get some rest. She has a wakeful dream.

Maggie is with Judah on just such an evening, though thirty years before. They are courting, have not yet been married. He shows her how to twist the wires of a barbed-wire fence together so they tighten, using a stick of wood as lever; he is repairing a gate. On the far side cows file past; they have beaten the path brick-hard. The cows have eaten everything but thistle; the pasture is infertile now, he tells her, more a place to exercise than feed. She will be Mrs. Judah Sherbrooke in two weeks. She wonders how the animals decide to cluster to a path, and where they decide to fan out. In certain meadows they walk single file, in sequence; in others they graze without order; this is also true of sheep. She listens for Ian, for Hattie, for the noise of the furnace or toilet or pump. She is alone in the house. She brushes her hair at the dressing-room table, tallying three hundred strokes. Her arms go weary; she rests them on her stomach and pats the jumping, kicking thing inside. Again she has a contraction—thinking herself those wires now, with the twisting child a stick and everything rotated tightly, taut—but cannot remember how long since the last. Time is not sequential, she decides, but circular. The light that dusk, with Judah beside her, had a kind of thickness to it that she supposes was dust.

In this fashion she prepares to pass the night. She is provided for, fenced in; she will let the doctor sleep. With such security about her, Maggie cannot bring herself to dial his number yet again.

On school mornings, Ian remembers, the table offered everything a man and boy and two women could eat. Judah was back from the barns. He'd drawn feed for the cows, if it were winter, and milked them and set them out to pasture in the spring and fall and would come in for breakfast steaming, slapping his hands. But his father would wait to eat breakfast until he, Ian, arrived. There had been orange juice and milk and mugs of coffee that he learned to like. "Time was," his mother told him, "when you wouldn't take your bottle unless it had some coffee in it. To color the milk."

There had been cornbread and blueberry muffins and cheese and every sort of jam; there was bacon or sausage to go with the eggs. The eggs were scrambled one day, fried the next; therefore on three school mornings every week—Monday, Wednesday, Friday—he'd get scrambled eggs. He preferred once-over-lightly to sunny-side up, and always added catsup to the egg mush he made. "Don't do that," Hattie said, "it's not good manners, Ian."

"I'm not," he used to answer her. "It's my fork that's doing it"—pressing the tines through the yolk.

On Sundays there'd be pan-fried potatoes also, with sometimes a thin slice of steak, and sometimes both bacon and sausage if there were company; the morning sun would shine on the juice so that he'd see the orange pulp and pits and squeezings in his glass. He'd shift the butter so it stood in the path of the sun. That way it would be warm enough to spread without forcing and making his muffin collapse. There had been conversation, but they told him not to talk with his mouth full, and what he remembers is not what they said but only the mumble and hum. There were cooks who came and went. There was always a scraping and clatter and weather forecasts and Hattie asking if he'd done his schoolwork to the teacher's satisfaction.

"How can he tell?" Judah asked. "It ain't been graded yet."

When Ian brings the Packard back, it is full night. He is shivering; the sunset has been wintry. He garages the car, then sets out for the house. He hears Boudreau calling, turns and sees the man emerge stoop-shouldered, bearing something white and limp, coming from the stock pond. Ian does not trust his eyes; he waits. But presently the aspects of this conjoined figure settle and resolve themselves; soon enough he sees the limbs and lank hair of his aunt, and slime across her gown.

Boudreau carries her with little difficulty. He has got her in a fireman's carry, slung around his neck like a young lamb. The men are constrained; it is not clear who should hold her, for instance, or how to effect the exchange. There is some echo of their morning's argument, perhaps; they seem to be in opposition as they meet. Boudreau is soaked; he has waded in the pond to fetch her, and his clothes are streaming with the water that her clothes disgorge. "Don't weigh nothing," he says. "It's amazing how little she weighs."

"I'll call the doctor."

"Too late for that . . ."

"No—what I mean is," Ian says, "for a postmortem. An examination."

"You do that. But let me tell you, this is death by drowning. Any fool can see as much. And it wasn't accidental, neither. I got her from the pond."

"Of course. I didn't mean . . ."

Hal holds his left hand up, hieratic; the corpse shifts. "She was a long way in."

They lay her in the carriage by the Packard, on the hard red leather of the open seat. Ian closes her eyes. He had expected the lids to be brittle, resistant, but they slide easily shut. "We'll need you for a witness," he says to Boudreau. "I'll go tell my mother, then go into town."

"Don't wake her."

"Who?"

"Your mother. Let her get some sleep. She hadn't ought to see this."

"No."

"Well." Boudreau clears his throat. "I'll get help. You stay here."

He watches the man amble off. Something in that upright carriage is a puzzle to him still; there's swagger and humility combined. It's as if Hal learned a shambling imitation of Judah himself—but forgot to keep his head up when he walked. His shoes make wet, sucking sounds. Hell is full of thirsty devils, Hattie used to say; it's what they mean by firewater when you're doomed by drink.

He cannot look at her. He hawks, spits, shuts his eyes. He kneels and puts his ear, Indian fashion, to the gravel drive. He knows there is no sense to this, but holds the position anyhow, needing the sense of solidity it gives him, pressing the earth as though perhaps Sally lay there also. He sees himself as Boudreau might, from the dark windy distance: a grown man on all fours. He pivots on his knees since the entrance drive is circular, and listens in the four directions for some sound. He thinks he hears his mother screaming in the house. There is a beaver bog by Glastonbury, where the flat flap of tails on the pond resounds as does his heart now, thumping. Ian rises and enters the house—its uncontested master who must arrange for burial—taking stairway treads three at a time.

Boudreau is wet, soaked through. He's shivering so he can't make it home, or call for the police just yet; he shelters in the hay barn and takes off his coat. Then he pulls his boots off and peels back his socks; his feet are blue. He wheels his arms, then slaps his hands together and slaps his legs and belly until he feels his hands. When he saw Hattie floating like a drowned sheep in the pond, he'd thought to leave his pipe and matchbook on the bank; the matches are still dry enough to take. He lights the kerosene lamp by the door. He pulls a bale free from the stack behind him, sits on it, and smokes. He tamps the pipe and says, "Strange doings, Mr. Sherbrooke," to test the sound of it.

There's wind inside the barn. He pulls the door shut. The runners need oiling; they squeak. He sees a stack of feed sacks, takes one, and rubs himself down. He's taking off his shirt to let it dry out also when he sees what he's known all along awaits him, his consolation and reward. He trims the wick; the flame is steady now. It's how you remember a man's name, he thinks, not knowing you remembered it, but knowing that you *knew* it anyhow, like when the light strikes slantways on a house so suddenly you recollect that thirty years ago this Christmas you were inside at the drop-leaf table, eating pie. He busies himself, remembering. There was old Jamie Kerr and Lewis back from Arizona—"Airizona," Lewis called it—where they sent him for his lungs. Judah'd just got married to that amazing girl, so busy courting her he'd not had time to make a proper wedding, or not bothered to, because any time they were upright and in public must have seemed a waste. He himself was down from Maine. Engaged to Amy, hunting work, he'd not known that this town would be their town forever; he can *see* the rhubarb spilling out over its crust.

Boudreau stops shivering. He relishes the time it takes to sidle past the bottle. He bends and lifts it clear, unscrews the top and sniffs it and swigs, holding his pipe in his left hand now, his right hand in his beard, temptation dangling from his fourth and pinkie fingers like an extra length of flesh. Drinking, he sees the Alagash. There's wide, fast water where he'd pitch his camp, where he came upon his daughter once asleep without her shirt on, with the fishing rod lashed to a tree. He'd known he'd never see her again when she went off to live with Indians, doing what her postcard said was government work. How come, he'd asked his wife (who'd made no answer, had pretended she was busy with the stove top and scouring pad), how come she could afford to send those turquoise bracelets, tiepins, cuff links, necklaces? On *government pay,* he said, I'd like you to answer me that.

He tips the gin. He whistles, wishes for the thousandth time that Billy had had asthma when they drafted him, not gone, not gotten over what he'd suffered with through all of seventh grade; knows as he always has it's futile, finished, milk spilled so long ago you can't even see where it spilled, drinks, thinks the old woman had willed it, heading fifty yards through cattails like a hunter for his blind. Sweet suffering Jesus, he thinks, you were a rare one at your age wanting to learn how to swim.

But sorrow does not die with its occasion. Grief lasts. He is not drunk. There's not enough to get drunk on, only warm. If he wanted to get drunk he would. He'd walk to Merton's Hideaway or the Village Arms and tell them a story they'd pay for, tell what's been happening to Sherbrooke women lately, how one of them drowns and the other fills out like a mainsail; it's only three fingers of gin. He drinks. His wife will be waiting, incurious, and he'll let her wait. Harry's home. He'll be sitting by the TV, not watching, drawing circles, making triangles inside the circles, then circles inside the triangles again. Loss endures. Hal waves his pipe. There's room enough, if he's careful, for both the pipe and bottle in the circle of his mouth, and he spends some minutes shaping things so that they fit. The bottle's neck is a circle, and he puts the pipestem in; he lies down in the haymow, balancing. He hears the Coleman lamp hum. There's things to juggle in this world, he tells his old employer, there's problems like the ones that he and the boy were discussing: *bowling alley, shopping mall.* He'll fix it in the morning when he's dry. He has one inch of gin, one inch of tobacco remaining, and must not confuse them; this white wet certainty of comfort is what they want you to swallow. He strikes his final match and settles back.

Labor: she savors the word. It is both curse and blessing, her portion again. It is a rack she's pinioned on, but willingly. Maggie enters a hall with a great fire burning at the room's far end. She shuts her eyes and rides with it and will not scream; she screams.

Ian comes to the door. He has something to tell her; she tells him, "Not now. Call the doctor. Please." He does as she bids him, and dials; the doctor answers on the second ring and says he will arrive. Ian's hands feel wet with pond slime still; he wipes them on his pants. He touches the bed, and it also is wet. He takes her in his arms.

STILLNESS

PART I

I

His dream is incomplete, and he knows this even as he loses it. They are riding gondolas in a cold wind. His skis feel cumbersome. These pines are snow-white pillows he will have to rearrange. The alarm means travel, always, like a wake-up call; Andrew switches it off. The room is dark. He lies in his king-size bed, on the diagonal. The drapes are floor-to-ceiling, though last night Eloise had asked, "Why call them that? They start six inches from the floor and they certainly don't reach the ceiling. And anyhow they drop, they drape—that means they *should* be called ceiling-to-floor."

"Don't be so literal," he'd said.

"Why not? What's wrong with that?"

"It's pretentious. The cognoscenti's game of innocence."

"Talk about pretentious . . ."

"What time did you say you were leaving?" Andrew had opened the hall closet. "I've got to get up early. Thanks for coming by."

He dials the weather number: WE 6-1212. A male voice wishes him good morning: it is minus six degrees. There is light to moderate snow falling as of six o'clock; the snow will taper off to flurries by midafternoon. The wind is north-northeast in Central Park.

His sheets have a diamond pattern; the blanket is Hudson Bay Blue. The mattress pad is electric and keeps him sufficiently warm. He wears a silk kimono stitched with crescent moons. The bathroom door has full-length mirrors on each side. He will have to call his office, canceling the lunch date; he tries to remember with whom he's supposed to be eating, and where.

Andrew Kincannon is fifty-six years old. Lately he finds himself forgetting details like who's where for lunch. It's not that he misses appointments or that anybody notices—or, if they should happen to notice, would they call him to account. He is not forgetful. It's just that he can't bring himself to feel it matters much: Kincannon Associates would get along without him, and probably as well without him these next months. There are fifteen people in the office he could send instead.

Andrew turns on the shower and smiles. Waiting for the water to adjust, shedding his kimono, he imagines sending all fifteen to La Grenouille. They'd jockey for position near the guest. Who *is* it anyhow, he tries to remember, then does: that reggae singer's manager. He shrugs, yawns, tastes his tongue. Maybe Kennedy's shut down; maybe the man from Jamaica's scared to go out in a storm.

He touches his toes. He likes his spray hot, strong. Some of his best thinking has been done in showers. He used to tell his clients this, announcing that he's changed their strategy the way a Speakman Anystream can change from mist to faucet strength, although it's always water, always Speakman Anystream, so what we're going to do, love, is try a different mix. But he does not want to concentrate—and concentrates, therefore, on soap.

Soap too is various. Some prefer rich lather; others prefer soap scented or with the promise of medicinal benefits: as "natural" as plausible or as artificial. Benita, his first wife, liked Camay soap not because of its ingredients or shape, but because she liked the raised medallion and attempted to keep it intact. For weeks Andrew would notice the way the soap shrank—as if she used only its edges, or the portrait's underside. He prefers Roger & Gallet. He shampoos his hair, then rinses.

This also fails. He's fully awake now and cannot keep from thinking of the day and trip to come. He tries to remember Benita's phone number, and her cousin's middle name; he tries to remember their hotel in Barbados in 1959, then the name of the reggae man's manager's son. He succeeds: 222-3732, Alison, Sam Lord's Castle before the renovation, Bill. Still, he must drive to Vermont.

Stepping out of the shower, toweling down briskly, he decides that he is grateful for the storm; it will be something to concentrate on. He selects a tape of Sylvia Marlowe playing Couperin; the harpsichord's clear regularity enables him to pack.

The call surprised him yesterday. He'd answered the phone the way he often did, half hearing, checking the notepad for calls. Suzy bunched his message slips according to three categories: Urgent, Urgent Urgent, and Call Back. He was checking through that last list when the home phone rang.

"Hello? Is this Andrew Kincannon?"

"It is."

"Hello. I tried your office."

"But you got me here instead."

"This is Ian Sherbrooke," Ian said.

Andrew stopped crossing names out. He capped his Montblanc pen again. "Hello."

"Maggie gave me the number," her son said. "Or, at any rate, I took it."

Andrew lit a cigarette.

"Don't blame your secretary," Ian said. "I told her it was serious, an emergency even—but she wouldn't give out the number. Your unlisted number, I mean. I got it from my mother."

"All right."

"I'm calling . . ." Then he paused. "She doesn't know I'm calling. Understand?"

Andrew nodded. "It's been a long time."

"That's why I'm calling. I thought we could change it." His voice was low-pitched, his elocution excellent—an actor, Andrew remembered. "Or you could, anyhow."

"Where are you calling from?"

"Home. Vermont. From the carriage barn, actually, so Maggie can't listen."

Andrew struck a second match. He held it to the cigarette. "What's wrong?"

"You ought to come on up."

Ian would be thirty, Andrew thought; it had been a dozen years since they last met. He had seen Ian's mother since then, but always in private—and the last time he had spied on her she did not know he watched. "Why?"

"It took till yesterday until she told me it was you."

He put his thumb on the crossed rackets. They were embossed on the cigarette box lid.

"That's how I knew she'd let me call. Three, *four* years," said Ian. "Have you known about it all this time?"

Andrew made a movement of impatience. It was as if he'd come into a play mid-act, with the exposition over. "Why call me now?" he asked.

"Tomorrow is tour day. That way you could wander through the house. You could just simply show up, and we'd have to let you in."

"You're losing me."

"I'm sorry. Of course." There was the crackle of static, and Ian's voice increased. "You don't know I've been living here. You didn't know that, did you?"

"No."

"Well, the Big House is partway a museum now. I have to open it every second Thursday of the month. I'll explain it to you when you come. But we could get you in."

The cigarette box was silver. He'd taken second place in the mixed doubles tournament. At match point he'd missed an overhead; Andrew put pressure on his thumb, then lifted it. "Thanks."

456

"It isn't the reason I'm calling."

"Listen." He let irritation surface. "I'm a personal manager, right? And an old friend of the family, if that's what you want me to say. But I don't handle mystery writers. Just tell me what you're after."

In the ensuing silence he had a picture suddenly of Ian as Maggie's look-alike—hand poised beside the wall phone, knuckles white where they clenched the receiver. "Right." The voice went flat. "A funny thing happened to you on your way to work tomorrow."

"What?"

"You didn't get there."

"No? Give me one good reason."

"Two."

Andrew controlled himself. He counted five, then told himself to hang up. He told himself this call was a mistake from the beginning; he needed a drink. Then he chose to have some sympathy, to be more welcoming to someone who did after all have a claim on his attention. He started to say, "I'm sorry . . ." when the stranger in a carriage barn changed the conversation utterly.

"Two reasons," Ian said. "If you're still listening. Because the mother of your child is going crazy. Come."

Dressed now, he opens the drapes. There is no snow falling, but his balcony is lined with snow—three inches like white foam atop the railing. It will not clear. The sky is gray and cloudless, with a density that augurs permanence. He had dialed Maggie's number the minute Ian hung up. The line had been busy, however, and Andrew heard the buzzing with relief. He poured himself a full glass of Wild Turkey; he would not have known what to say. It had been early evening, and he watched the first flakes, calculating: four years since they last met. Her husband, Judah, had recently died. Andrew could not understand why Maggie planned to remain in Vermont, she'd come to Manhattan that week to pack up her apartment. He protested when she left the final time.

457

"I don't understand," he had said. "Why should you go back up there?"

"It's home."

"Not now. It doesn't have to be."

"It does."

"But I'm not married," Andrew said.

"Not this week, maybe. I give you a month."

"Marry me."

They had been lovers for years, faithful to their shared ongoing infidelity. She took his hand, half smiling. "I'm *supposed* to be the other woman. Right?"

"Wrong."

"Andrew, this is silly. We wouldn't know what to do. You forget how often I've been hiding in that closet."

"You could trust me."

"Yes. As somebody else's husband. When I was someone else's wife."

He studied her. There was a kind of logic in her instinct, always, and he'd known it inappropriate to bother her that week. She was paying off old debts—Judah's dutiful fond widow, embracing sacrifice. They ate Sara Lee croissants, and Andrew prepared cappuccino in his new machine. Maggie had been radiant that morning: fifty-two years old but looking half her age. Her parting kiss, Andrew remembers, had had the taste of marmalade; she touched him where he'd failed to shave, promising to stay in touch. She would follow Neptune north and see what she could see.

He himself has long been expert at avoidance. If she embraced such behavior, he thought he also could; he'd leave her—them—alone. They had started their affair in 1959. She was taking piano lessons in the city, and he met her in the Russian Tea Room every month for lunch. Maggie had had few illusions. She kept at the piano for the music's sake, and not because she dreamed of a career. He would order kvass and blini while she ate an omelet and drank tea. She'd talk to him of Judah's hovering possessiveness, and how from time to time she had to leave the farm.

"Funny, isn't it," she'd say. "The air's so clear up there I need to come south just to breathe."

Later, when the British coined the word "bird," he'd called her Judah's bird who migrated twice a month. "But always heads back to its nest," Maggie said. "Is that what you're implying? Like a homing pigeon, correct?"

"Correct."

"Let's change the subject," she said. "How was Barbados? How's Benita?"

"Fine." he said. "Still there."

It is February fifth. He takes the elevator to the basement and walks through to the garage. The attendant has his Volvo ready, and he's grateful in advance for how it handles snow. Andrew has a country place in Westport, and he'd bought this station wagon the previous fall in order to carry antiques. Dark green in its reflection, he stows his bag and offers Hank a dollar.

"Bad out there," Hank says. "You heading to Connecticut?"

"Vermont. I'm taking the Taconic."

"Drive careful, hear?" Hank squints down at him. They discuss the weather, always, and which direction to take. "Road's slushy is what the radio says. Slick."

"I will," says Andrew, and buckles his belt. *The mother of your child.*

He has been married twice but has produced no children. There was a time when this seemed like a problem, and Benita and he had discussed it for years: whether to try, to try harder, to have tests or to adopt. In those years, however, Andrew loved his work. And she had been an only child who found the world too crowded. Those friends who urged them to have children did so with the urgency of self-justification, as if "family" were a gospel that required spreading. If he and Benita had no children, they appeared to say, their own sons and daughters would be threatened; their deliberations over schools and clothes and camp and orthodontia lost all meaning unless shared.

His second wife was a dancer and worried about her career. When she shattered her kneecap skiing, and was forced to quit, she said, "Well, maybe we should have kids now. What else am I good for? What else is there?" Andrew answered, "What else there is, is divorce." Marian agreed. She had gone skiing against his advice and with the ballet master's boyfriend. They had married each other on impulse, and when the impulsiveness waned they were strangers who disliked each other. They were divorced in Mexico, on their second anniversary; she told him that the doctor said her knee would heal.

Then his friends' children grew up. They went to college or dropped out of college or attended law school and medical school and married and had children of their own. At fifty-six, he could well have been a grandfather. He slept with a series of women who could have been his daughter's age—in a kind of abstract incest, pressing flesh that stayed resilient while his own went slack. Andrew had nephews to visit on Christmas, and that had sufficed.

The FDR Drive has been cleared. He takes the Major Deegan till the turn for the Saw Mill River and the Taconic Parkway; there the snow begins again. He turns on his wipers and the rear-windshield defrost. He listens to the weather forecast and learns that the brunt of the storm is ahead: eighteen inches fell in parts of northern Dutchess County, and a travelers' warning remains in effect. "Time to dig, kid." The announcer makes a jingle. "Those who've got someplace to go will get there if they take it slow: turn your wheels in the direction of the skid."

Andrew keeps to the cleared right lane. Scrupulous in nothing so much as self-analysis, he hunts the explanation for this trip. He could have gone antiquing or returned instead to Westport. Yet he feels the half-forgotten gift of anonymity, of no one knowing where he is; he needs to get out of the city; he wants to see Maggie again.

That's the explanation, of course, and has been since his heart's quick lift when Ian spoke her name. The truth that Andrew halfway sees, the knowledge he's attempted to dismiss, is that Maggie still astonishes him, and has done so from the start. He dislikes inconclusiveness and is driving north for closure. The young Mozart, he remembers, is supposed to have lain sleepless when his father left off playing—waiting for the chord progression to resolve. But his father had a visitor, and they got into conversation, and Mozart had to creep downstairs to sound the final note. Then he went back to bed, according to the story, and fell happily asleep.

So Andrew tries to tell himself that Maggie will be pleased. He feels the station wagon skidding, slows again, and follows the sand track on snow. She will accept him in her house for old times' sake if nothing more, and they will drink and chat together, catching up. "There's so much to tell you," she'll say. "I just don't know how to begin . . ." They share a past by now as long as his statistical future; he's known her for as many years as he can expect still to live.

Meanwhile, he has proved a success. He fiddles with the radio again. He can tell her, if she asks, how he's doubled his firm's profit in four years, with inflation factored in. He has been in *US* magazine, dancing with a disco queen; they've mentioned him twice in "Around and About." Nor are his achievements all that flashy always; Kincannon Associates remains firmly grounded in artists' management. He's taken over one or two actors for friendship's sake, and because his legal staff has expertise in maximizing artists' incomes for the years that they make money. Life may be brief and art long, Andrew says, but the longest shot of all is art when it comes to investment. He himself never buys with investment in mind, but only the pleasure of the purchase—can he use it, can he sit on it or lie in it or stack faience on its shelves?

Still, something in the calm congruence of furniture does move him. It makes him buy past his need for the object, with the result the Westport farmhouse now seems stuffed. He buys Shaker pieces, mostly, and mixes them in with Breuer chairs. Of such disjunction he makes a motif: the past and the present conjoined. So a formica Parsons table stands catercorner to a seventeenth-century trestle; a water bed is on the porch and sleigh bed in the guest room. In this welter and profusion, Andrew feels at home.

On the anniversary of their last night together, he dialed Maggie from his office. When she answered, he said, "Hello, it's Andrew. How've you been?"

461

"*Andrew* . . ."

He held a coffee cup. The cup was Styrofoam, and he broke off a piece with his nail. "Just thought I'd get in touch. It's been too long. A year."

"Exactly," Maggie said. "About something in particular?"

"What?"

"Did you think you'd get in touch"—she pronounced each word with the exaggerated precision of his grade-school spelling teacher—"about something in particular?"

He incised the rim. "No."

"Where are you calling from?"

"New York."

"It's a good connection. I thought maybe you were here."

"No."

"Well," Maggie paused. "You must be busy."

"No." Andrew tore the cup in two.

"The weather has been fine," she said.

"That's fine."

"Yes." Again she paused. It was as if he'd squandered his initiative by dialing—as if the gesture might be self-explanatory, and the single word "hello" would shock them into fluency. "We have a daughter," she said.

"*What?*"

"I thought you should know."

"You're joking."

"No."

"A *daughter?*" He divided his half into quarters, then eighths.

"Yes. When I stayed with you that time. When I packed up my apartment after Judah died. She's three months old. She's wonderful."

"Why didn't you tell me?"

"I would have."

"*Would* have?"

Maggie did not hesitate. "Except you didn't ask," she said. "Not once this year. This is the first time you've called."

He pressed his eyes. Muzak intervened; the receiver squawked like startled geese, and then the line went dead. "Hello? Hello?" he said.

"I hear you."

"Maggie?"

"Yes."

"I can't believe this. I . . ."

"Believe it," she said. "That's when I got pregnant. I didn't believe it myself."

"A daughter."

"Yes. Jane Sherbrooke."

"All alone? You had her all alone?" Dimly, at the back of his brain; the enormity of what she'd done and failed to do came clear.

"Ian's here. There was a doctor."

He lit a cigarette. He deliberated, smoking. "What you mean is, don't you, that I wasn't good enough."

It was as if she'd rehearsed her response. "This child is mine, not yours. It's been a year now, Andrew, and you've remained in your life. Don't be hurt. I wasn't trying to hurt you."

"You've succeeded," Andrew said.

Again the Muzak intervened. When Maggie came back on the line, her voice had shifted pitch. "I'm sorry you feel that way. It wasn't my intention."

"Jane," he said. "A daughter. Jane *Sherbrooke,* you call her."

"Keep in touch." Then she hung up, so he had to realize how she meant the opposite: you cannot touch me. Good-bye.

The next day—a February morning chill as this one, three years previous—Andrew flew to Albany. He rented a car and drove east. Moved by some notion of cunning, he parked at the Big House entrance gate and approached through the first line of pines. He saw Maggie in the window of the Toy House and advanced. The Toy House was a replica of Peacock Sherbrooke's mansion, built five hundred yards away from its original and to the children's scale. He stepped quietly around a shaped yew by the window and waited there knee-deep in snow. She did not hear him or turn. She was studying a stove, it seemed, and its relation to a cradle; her breath steamed faintly in the inner air. He strained to hear the song she sang, but it was nearly tuneless: "*Mama's little baby loves shortnin', shortnin'; Mama's little baby loves shortnin' bread.*"

Andrew stared. He waited in shocked disbelief while flesh of his flesh existed on the far side of a window like the window of a hospital. It would be three months old. It had its eyes open or possibly shut, but was facing the other direction. He pursed his lips and kissed the glass and lifted his hand, then retreated.

Maggie sat. She lowered herself into the chair and pushed to set it rocking; she changed the cradle's angle several times. It was empty, with no blankets, but the question of position appeared to be important—she adjusted the cradle repeatedly and was not satisfied. She extended her foot, nudging the cradle this way and that, then let it come to rest on what seemed the diagonal between her bentwood rocker and the cast-iron cook stove. The griddle had been covered with toy canisters marked Flour, Sugar, Salt. Her humming was continual; he heard it through the pane. He told himself, when she changed songs or ceased her earnest rocking, he would enter and make himself known. "*Mama's little baby loves shortnin', shortnin'*"—Maggie sang. Whatever she held was so thoroughly swaddled he could not see its face. He wondered, had she lied to him and was this child a doll? He wondered, would she be nursing out here, then wondered if Maggie had milk.

Snow fell. He looked up at the Toy House slate roof. A sharp sense of exclusion assailed him, as if Maggie had been right to say he had no place in the Big House, no presence in their family that would not feel intrusive. He told himself it was his right to meet and greet his daughter, if only this once while she slept. He pictured her eyes and small hands. He could take her wordlessly, examine Jane's features, and leave. He would do so once Maggie held still. The rocking, however, continued. If he knew some code word, Andrew thought, some answering tune, some way to arrive without

464

disruption, why then he'd enter the Toy House as if it were not locked to him, in a simple act of entry, since he held the key.

He had no key. The door was not locked and the window not nailed, but the Toy House resisted him palpably nevertheless. He waited for perhaps ten minutes in this attitude, crouched and shivering, unable to decide if he should claim his daughter or disclaim all interest. Maggie did not want him there and would not know he came. He would put all this out of his mind. He had ejaculated children elsewhere also possibly; there might have been Kincannons he never knew existed. Andrew turned. If he left, he can remember thinking, he could leave unchallenged; he withdrew in his own recent tracks.

At Newburgh the snow starts in earnest. The sides of the Taconic are heaped high. There is diffuse sun, however, and a glaucous sky glows brightly; the snow shines. It is nine o'clock. Andrew reaches for sunglasses from the glove compartment and adjusts his driving gloves. He tilts the rearview mirror down and is not displeased. The face in it seems purposive: a trace of tan still from his January stint in the islands, gray at the temples and sandy, short-clipped hair. The nose is wide and flat, and sometimes he pretends he broke it in a barroom, the teeth are capped. He wears a dark green turtleneck and uses a cigarette holder; its band is silver, stem black. "You're past the mid-life crisis," Eloise had taunted him. "You're at the male menopause."

What bothers him of late, however, has been the absence of crisis. The weeks become months, the years decades, and everything seems foreordained. While his friends and secretaries shift from est to Zen to Transactional Analysis, Andrew prides himself on constancy, whatever else he is, he is not a convert. "*Nouvelle vague*," he'd say. "You're just riding the wave crest, pal. New vague." Pleased with his bilingual pun, he'd make a point of translation. "You understand that *vague* means wave; that's what I mean by hanging ten on every wave crest. And it's, what's the word, a wipeout. Like Studio Fifty-Four."

So although he cannot prophesy which fads will take stage center, he knows they will succeed each other as night follows day. And even though he makes his income in part off of such faddishness, he feels the scorn for fashion that a servant feels for service—knowing well enough how wind-scraps follow a prevailing wind, and what appears like luck is organized by men like him, in offices, ten months before "the first big break." He's tired of his work. He has grown weary of his clients' inflated fees, and fame. He slows for a gas station that looms whitely to the left of him and unlocks the gas tank for a boy in a black parka. "Fill it up," says Andrew. "Please."

"Right," the boy says. "Check the oil?"

"Okay. You got a telephone?"

"In there." He jerks his head. "I notice yon got no snow tires."

"Radials," says Andrew. "Four of them."

"Right. I notice your wiper blades're iced."

"Right," says Andrew. "It's snowing. You notice?"

Hunting a dime in the change he pulls out, he feels ashamed of such impulsive condescension; he'd had no reason to mimic the boy. Using the credit card, having to repeat the number to the operator, he calls his office.

"Kincannon Associates," says Sally. "Good morning."

"Good morning."

"Mr. Kincannon?"

"Himself." And, pleased with the timbre of her voice, pleased also that she'd known his own voice from the two words of his greeting, Andrew talks to the switchboard, canceling lunch. He's out of town, he says, and won't return till Monday; they're turning the Taconic into a toboggan run. She is worried. He tells her not to worry, they have the snowplows out and everything's fine. For the next twenty-four hours, however, he cannot be reached, he will call again tomorrow at this time.

He steps out of the phone booth and pays for the gas. He shivers. Until the instant he made light of it, the weather seemed a joke; now, for the first time in his journey, Andrew feels uncertain. He kicks at his four tire treads and brushes off the roof. Slush has frozen thickly on the fenders and the doors. Why is he going and where does he go to; what will he find once arrived? North, where the road has been blasted through rock, the ice slides are multicolored; he follows the Taconic until Route 295.

Surprise: she had astonished him when she first came to his apartment, not flirtatiously, in 1959. "Judah would kill you. You know that, I suppose." She had taken off her clothes with the unembarrassed competence of a nurse preparing for some surgical procedure—as if someone else's body were at stake. He had adjusted the lights. He could not tell if she was joking or attempting to enliven their adultery with fear. "We might as well get on with it," she'd said.

Years later, returning to Judah, she wanted to wrestle a stag. It had blundered into the swimming pool in Westport, and Maggie reached for it barehanded. He screamed at her to stop, and she had done so, shocked. They watched together while the animal escaped. She sat on the diving board, arms around her knees, in his raincoat; he had had to vacuum the pool. The blue plastic cover was shredded, a deck chair's fabric ripped. Next morning he insisted they drive to New York, diverting her announced intention to go north to Judah. So when she did leave she blackened his walls, writing "NIXoN LIvES!!!" with rags and shoe polish on the plaster; she had known he planned to have the room repainted anyhow that week.

The roadside is heaped with brown snow. He listens to the eleven o'clock news and turns left on Route 22. The houses here have woodsmoke spreading from their chimneys; the restaurants have closed. There are school buses in the school's front parking lot, however; a police car idles in the main street of New Lebanon. He stops and folds back the map. He is hungry; he will stop at the first open diner and get himself something to eat. The temperature is minus twelve; the towns bear names like Pittsfield and Chatham and Lebanon Springs. He is farther north already than the Catskills and the Berkshires; he approaches the Green Mountains and the villlage in its foothills that Maggie circled for him twenty years before.

This is a new map, of course; the roads have changed. Route 7 is being enlarged. But he traces the map's routing and sees, as clearly as if printed there, a red circle drawn in crayon around her house. Andrew shuts his eyes. The world he watches daily is the world of fashion—a swatch of iridescent mediocrity beneath his gloved right hand. He stares at this dark central spot.

II

On the wall behind the silver chest or there above her bed, using whatever wide whiteness the house has retained, in the laundry room when she
folds sheets, on the bare peeling plaster of the stairwell to the cupola that
Ian has been promising to whitewash now for months, by the greenhouse
door where straw hats hang, filling the space between pantry shelves even,
on oilcloth, she sees as if in continual rerun (the hand rifling back through
the photograph album, lending by its motion motion to the fixed still
sequence, knee raised till it offers the semblance of stepping) that night
again: fire and slime. The inside of her eyelids unfurls like a furled screen.
Maggie plays it over whenever she closes her eyes.

That night: the flame she saw beyond the window that Ian assured her
was coming from town, was nothing, was somebody's bonfire maybe
set at dusk in some place like the shed field to keep warm—it had been
Hallowe'en and someone was scaring the kids. So she heard shouts and
whistles, saw flashlights bobbing, but was herself so racked and screaming

she could not distinguish fear from celebration, the volunteer firemen from those who came to trick or treat—and sees it that way now again, though in flashback and from an angle she had never known, lying in her own bed three thousand feet from the barn, the wind in her direction while Boudreau escaped.

For that had been the cause of it, Maggie came to learn. Their hired man fell asleep in the hay, knocking over in his stupor the kerosene lantern he carried, drunk, half-naked in the straw because his clothes were soaked. Or maybe just his pipe ignited chaff; his beard caught fire, they speculated, and everything caught fire though he'd had the sense to run—the corolla of his face hissing and popping and sparking like some ignited scarecrow's—and dive into the frog pond and be saved. All utterance was screaming then; the doctor in the hallway had been called to help Boudreau instead, whose jaw had been so badly burned they had to knock him out. The men with hoses by the barn and lead lines to the pond would yell their orders so she swore she heard them from the house—though Ian said it's nothing, nothing, hold your breath, breathe deeply, don't worry, you're doing just fine.

Therefore when she shuts her eyes to see Hal fling himself like a ship's anchor overboard, she sees it both outlined in flame and doused, snuffed on the instant—sees Hattie also where he wallows, lying in the cattails that she'd breasted hours earlier to die before Boudreau could fish her out, then threw himself back in to live. He did live, she visited him in the hospital, later, Hal lay bandaged and unseeing, swaddled as her child had been and not a whole lot more competent; they fed him intravenously for weeks. His mouth had burned so badly it hurt him just to moan. Or maybe that was what he said in order to earn silence, peace while they waited to question him, time to consider what answer he'd make. But meantime, for those weeks while he lay in his hospital bed and she in her bedroom, she thought about it also and told Ian not to ask. Let's not bother him, she said, with the details of the bottle the insurance adjuster discovered. What valuation could they set on one hay barn to set beside and overbalance the years of

Boudreau's service; why trouble him in his time of trouble further than need be?—let's let the man heal. The Sherbrookes lost a single barn, but the outbuildings were saved. The carriage barn and sugarhouse and smokehouse and Toy House and silos still stand; he did the haying, didn't he, she asked; it's his hay and profit we lost.

Nor did she see Hattie in her box. They kept her from that also where she lay. So now in her mind's eye she pictures the weed-covered woman, age scrubbed from her by water like the dirt lines from a palm, hair rinsed, pulled back, extended like some lady underneath a parasol on beaches in daguerreotypes where white is yellow and black, brown. Ian could have offered arguments when the Boudreau family promised to leave: *this* is home, the burns will heal, are half-healed already judging by the bandages; you pulled Hattie from the pond and we're grateful, we'll make it up to you: stay. But when Boudreau emerged again, they did not talk about it, keeping an embarrassed silence while his wife said they were quitting, heading for the Alagash to try potato farming.

The barn burns like a gas jet, steadily, straight up. Maggie sees it that way when snow makes the meadow a screen. The sugarhouse and carriage barn and Toy House where Judah would sit—the ring of buildings around the Big House that face the four directions—form her picture's frame. Yet the firewood fails to ignite. Hattie lies in the middle of the circle, and her sheets are sodden. Maggie grips the doctor's arm so fiercely he winces; Dr. Rahsawala, his round face gleaming like a new brown penny in a pool, says, "Not to worry, A-okay. What will you call it, have you decided, Mrs. S., what will be the baby's name?"

He bends to her, enlarging, but she makes no answer. She sees it in the bathroom tiles: one woman kills herself because another woman will give birth, and the number of the Sherbrooke clan therefore stays the same. She does not like to think this; there are certain topics it is safer to avoid. But it's like a childhood game of avoidance—missing the third piece of paving, avoiding the lines of the pavement, or trying not to think about the word "rhinoceros." No sooner does she try to ignore it than "rhinoceros" is all she thinks: a great horned warty thing that lumbers up from the swamp.

Hattie killed herself because the baby was not Judah's, and would bear the Sherbrooke name with no born-Sherbrooke blood. It was as simple as that. She was eighty-two years old and, except for cataracts, in perfect health. She never had married or moved from the Big House because no other name or holdings would suffice. Her pridefulness was absolute, but it had been impersonal—as if she set herself to be the household guardian, a witness to the probity of Sherbrookes since they first settled in Vermont. She organized family archives, filing letters from her great-great-uncle and photos of Ulysses S. Grant. When Calvin Coolidge rode one morning in the Sherbrooke barouche, she knew his coachman's name. Judah used to claim that she knew laundry lists from 1900 by heart; she took her relatives to bed at night like hot-water bottles.

"You're making fun of it," she'd say. "But you're as proud as I am, Jude. Less willing to say so, is all."

That too is true, Maggie thinks. She might believe in progress or the chance of new beginnings, but Judah'd seen the Great Depression and a series of recessions and the way the world went around. He was twenty-five years older, after all. What she had called discovery he called repetition; it's why the world's a circle, Judah said. You can whistle till the cows come home about the way things are changing and have changed; all it means is maybe there'll be no more cows. Don't blame the cobbler for his last if the last's made out of plastic and the leather's synthetic or the stitching needle's tin; don't blame a shoe for its fit.

"That's a nice baby, Margaret. A *beautiful* baby."

Maggie had smiled. "Well, thank you, Louise."

Elizabeth Conover patted her hair. She wore glasses on a ribbon around her neck. "Takes after you," Elizabeth said. "How much did she weigh?"

"Five pounds, eight ounces. If she'd weighed any more I'd have burst."

"I bet you're glad though. Proud."

"Yes."

Louise bent closer, leaning over the shapeless thing in blankets. "Eyes just like her mother's. Your mouth too."

"All babies look like Winston Churchill," Maggie said. "Or maybe W. C. Fields. I think she favors Churchill."

"Such clear skin. A beauty."

Elizabeth Conover straightened. "Her father would have been proud."

"He always wanted a daughter, Judah did."

Maggie cleared her throat. "Not so you'd notice."

"Excuse me?"

"Not so I noticed."

"Oh, that was just his way," Elizabeth maintained. "I knew him longer than *you* did, my dear. Not better, of course, I'm not saying that. But I can say for certain Judah Sherbrooke wanted daughters. I'm certain of that as can be." Elizabeth patted the crib. "He used to tell me way back when—before you were married, before you'd even *met*, I daresay—daughters would be fine. A ladies' man . . ."

Louise agreed. Maggie had smiled at them, feeling her mouth stretch. These were her first visitors, ten days after Jane had been born. Her pregnancy had been an ill-kept secret, but a secret nevertheless. At first she could not believe it; then she believed the baby would fail to come to term. It seemed too strange a joke, too much of a biological accident; she'd seen no one but the family and Dr. Rahsawala for months.

Jane had been born three weeks early, the night of Hattie's death. By pretending, later, she was late, Maggie made it possible for lawyers and neighbors to label the child Judah's. The weight of five pounds, eight ounces, for instance, could herald weight loss in the womb and not Jane's prematurity. She never called her Judah's girl nor countenanced such chitchat about her father's fighting spirit and the same cleft chin. But Maggie did not gainsay it either and therefore endorsed the white lie. When Elizabeth Conover and Louise Hutchens came to call, she had received them politely. They bustled about the nursery like customers for a layette—fingering, assessing. They brought blankets and a rattle and a windup mouse that played Brahms's lullaby and twitched its tail.

"She'd break his heart, this little thing," said Louise.

"Yes."

"And Hattie's. What a shame she didn't live to see her niece."

"Yes," Maggie repeated.

"It breaks my heart to think about it. So much sorrow in this family when there should be rejoicing."

"So many deaths," Elizabeth said. "It's like the Kennedys. It makes a person think."

"I try not to think like that . . ."

"There's trouble attached to each blessing." Elizabeth went on, undeterred. "Triumph and tragedy. That's what I've been thinking about, ever since you mentioned Mr. Winston Churchill's name. That's his phrase, if I recollect. 'Triumph and tragedy.'"

"What the Lord giveth He taketh away," said Louise.

"I need to feed the baby now."

"Of course. We shouldn't stay too long."

"We didn't mean to," said Louise. "We've overstayed our welcome."

"No. It's just I'm very tired still."

"You ought to have some help here."

"Ian helps."

"I mean a nurse. A trained person to take things over every once in a while," Elizabeth said. "Helen Bingham knows a nurse."

"We'll think about it," Maggie said. The baby snuffled, sucked in air. "Thank you for your visit. And the gifts—they're exactly what we need."

"Should I have Helen call you?"

"No. Not now. Not yet."

She did indeed hire a nurse, three weeks later and for the first months. She used an agency, however, that provided trained personnel from New York.

They had the perfect candidate, they said. And since she didn't have to deal with Helen Bingham's curiosity or face someone who'd known Sherbrookes since before she came to town, Maggie welcomed such assistance. It would help.

Then Eleanor Mason arrived with her Mexican Hairless, Lassie. She proved officious. Her hair was blue as Hattie's had been, and as tightly curled. She was a licensed child nurse, she explained, what the English call a governess or nanny. And as far as she, Eleanor Mason, was concerned, the word governess was fitting: it meant you had to fix things and arrange them just so. Who ever heard of governors, she asked, that governed only one part of the state—it mattered what her charges ate, mattered how the kitchen had been cleaned and whether it was clean. She didn't mind telling Mrs. Sherbrooke that some of the great names she'd worked for (names that made people stand up and notice, names like Vanderbilt and Whitney and others she'd as soon not mention) kept their kitchens no cleaner than stables and therefore encouraged disease.

Miss Mason sniffed, loudly. She reeked of disapproval, trailing it after her presence like toilet water; she made Lassie roll over, lie down. Her charges were entitled to a cleanly, germ-free house—and if her charges didn't care or were too rich or ill or used to it to notice, she, Eleanor Mason, noticed anyhow: taking care of children meant you also took care of the mop. Drafts mattered. They mattered all the more in winter, what with the snow coming on. In a rickety old house like this one, you kept the windows open though you thought you'd nailed them shut.

Maggie only half-listened at first. Those first four months she hardly even heard what Ian said to her, much less some chatty stranger. She walked as a somnambulist might walk, waking only to Jane crying in the crib beside her bed. Eleanor said this was wrong. No mother in her condition should have to wake up three times nightly for the sake of an infant she, Eleanor, had been hired expressly to feed. "You take it easy, dear," she'd say. "You leave all this to me."

She bathed Jane after lunch. The child was placable, attentive, and Eleanor took credit for each smile. She clipped Jane's toes and fingernails, bending over her charge in the light so that Maggie felt shouldered aside. "Her mother doesn't know what to feed her," she overheard the woman say on the phone. "If it wasn't for me, that poor little darling would starve. Imagine. Trying to feed her creamed carrots at *this* stage, and being surprised she spits up. And leaving her all wet in that diaper. If it wasn't for me—and her brother, Mr. Ian, I have to give him that . . ."

One night Jane scratched herself. She woke up bleeding, unperturbed, but the scratch was near an eye. The welt was one inch long. Eleanor said she'd trimmed the nails on Friday and this was only Monday, and no other baby ever had grown fingernails so quickly—but Maggie raged, implacable, till Eleanor said, "Well, Mrs. Sherbrooke, if that's how you feel . . ."

"That's how I feel," Maggie said.

"Is this a dismissal, dear?"

"It is."

Miss Mason gathered her things; it had been the end of the month. Her sister needed help in Westerly, and she herself was sixty-five—too old for this kind of trouble. She'd had enough of cranky folk who thought because they raised a child or two they were more expert than the experts. Because you built a bookcase would you try to build a house, she asked; because you made a dress one time would you set up in business? She had letters from the Vanderbilts and Whitneys and others she'd as soon not name that praised her competence; babies scratch themselves and have been scratching themselves since time began and will go on doing so no matter how often you cut back their nails. She had been planning to give notice anyhow. And now she'd used the word, said Eleanor, now they were finally having this conversation, she couldn't help *noticing* things in the house: how poorly they'd been managed. If Mrs. Sherbrooke wanted Jane to grow up sad and wrong, why she should just continue doing what she'd done.

The Mexican Hairless was sick. It gagged and heaved. The nurse was trying to salvage some sort of dignity from the dismissal, but her dog was trembling and her suitcase would not shut. She struggled to preserve her precarious hard-won disdain; she tied up the suitcase with cord. The way some people treat you, Eleanor said, it's enough to make you sick; it's not the way a person ought to treat their dog. She's sorry if she spoke her mind, but she's a plain-speaking person, always has been and will stay that way: a knife that won't cut melted butter is the sharpest one you've got. And she'd rather go to Westerly where value given was value received than stay with those who don't appreciate her one single additional night.

It had made Maggie sad to see the woman go. Such garrulity was harmless, after all, a way of filling up the space that silence made. So when Miss Mason left (setting out in her Volare like an unloved upright Mary Poppins, telling Ian that the drive was hard on Lassie, harder than he'd ever guess because the motion made her frantic, all that high-speed humming and exhaust: dogs' ears are sensitive, that's why she seems so nervous now, their sense of smell is acute, they know a lot about the world without having to see it) she kept Jane in her bed.

That night, at midnight, she awakened to a full moon outside her window and a caricature cheese-face imprinted on the pane. A squirrel chittered in the eaves; she heard the freight train shunting down by Eagle's Bridge. Her daughter slept, untroubled, surrounded by pillows. There were flowers on her sheets. Moon shadows invaded the room. They formed rabbits and skeletal shapes—the magnified figures of twigs. Maggie can remember thinking, as clouds scudded past and the furnace clicked on, as the clock continued in a different register, *Help me, I'm falling apart.*

Helen Bingham said, "She's wonderful. Wonderful, really."

"Thank you."

"I'm not exaggerating. I'm not the kind of person who exaggerates. So lively, such a handful . . ."

"That's true enough," Maggie said.

"I marvel at it. So alert." Helen Bingham turned to Jane. "Come over here, will you." Jane came. "How old are you?"

"Two years old."

"And when's your birthday?"

"October thirty-one."

"A smart one." Helen nodded. "That's Hallowe'en, you know."

"I know." Jane looked at them unblinkingly.

"What will you be this Hallowe'en. A princess?"

"No."

"A witch?"

Jane shook her head.

"The whole world dresses up for her birthday," Maggie said. She studied her fingers.

"Not me."

"Not you?" asked Helen. "Why not?"

Jane raised her shoulders, shook her head.

"She should have playmates."

"Yes," Maggie said.

"There ought to be some other children in this house. Have you looked into play groups?"

"No. Not yet."

"Cinderella?" Each time Helen spoke to Jane, her voice would rise an octave. "Is that who you're going to be?"

"Susie," Jane said.

"Who's Susie?"

"My imaginary friend."

Helen clapped her hands. "Did you hear that? *Imaginary friend.* My imaginary friend. Oh my . . ."

"It's time for your nap," Maggie said.

Jane approached the couch they sat on, wordless, purposive and took her yellow blanket. She took her bottle also and lay down. Her eyes were blue, long-lashed; she did not close her eyes.

Barns get pegged, Judah had explained to her, not nailed. That way the whole thing has some give, you watch a barn creaking you know what I mean—the whole thing's likely to collapse sooner than any part of it. So wall by wall in

Maggie's vision becomes rectangular translucency, a shapeliness adhering to itself: she watches planks go brown then black, with Boudreau stretched full length on the hay like some stone warrior, only drunk, only forgetful, the third side of a triangle whose other leg was Hattie, their junction that point in the pond where he dove to find a corpse and would dive again.

Did he run blindly? Maggie wonders. Can you keep your eyes open if your beard and hair are burning? Hattie, the night before, left her eyeglasses behind. She had known the way. She breasted a path through the collapsing foliage that Boudreau, tracking her, would tread again, its density in any case diminished by the season; so perhaps he raced through cattails that had been parted before. Drop a plumb line from the apex of the figure that they make; make that apex the conjunction of Boudreau's hands and Hattie's when he hauls her to the mudbank, dead; bisect such painful symmetry and out comes Baby Jane.

It had been Hallowe'en. Seabirds that ride on the ninth wave from shore are the souls of the dead, sailors say. She remembers when she used to dress up like a witch and climb the tree on Hallowe'en, with cooked but cold spaghetti in the pot. There would be light from the Toy House—enough to show the stars on her crepe cone. Children would gather beneath her; she would lower the spaghetti to them like a rope of worms. Ian—who had been in on the joke—would stand by her side twisting his fingers, cackling when she cackled: "Take, take, take." She wore a nightgown, Hattie complained; they could look up her legs in that tree.

"Well, what will we call her?" Ian asked. He was back in the room, by her bed.

"Her?" Maggie was crying. "Her?"

"Your daughter," Ian said. "This little lady here."

"Is she all right?"

The doctor bent above her. His teeth had the luster of pearls. "I told you so already, Mrs. Sherbrooke. A fine healthy baby girl."

"Yes." The tears were independent, alien, some other someone's water squeezed from her. She forced them out like afterbirth.

"Congratulations," Ian said. "We'll call her Baby Sherbrooke for a while."

"Jane," she said. "Plain Jane."

"You mean that?"

She heard sirens. She attempted to sit up, but Ian pressed her shoulder. "I'm not joking," Maggie said. "Just Jane."

"Jane Sherbrooke." He turned to Dr. Rahsawala. The baby was wailing, convulsive, gasping for air that would prime the lungs' pump—that fear allayed on the instant, though in weeks to come they took her to the hospital for every sort of test. There was silver nitrate in her eyes. The choked, high-pitched lament Maggie heard across the room meant severance, a chorus: best of all not to be born.

The Big House has four floors. The attic, Maggie warns herself, can lift at any moment in a southeast wind. It is moored to the house by the frame's insubstantial anchor only, and wind whistles through it like a signal to hoist sail. She hopes the snows increase. If it's bad enough and they fail to get the entrance plowed, then nobody will come. They can open the doors to the building, and two o'clock will come and go and three-thirty come and go, and she can say to Ian, "See. I told you so." He'd scowl and lock the door again and say, "Just wait till springtime. That's when you get your first tourists." The mud room will hang no strange shapes.

The first time they hung coats in there, Maggie had been shocked. She carried Jane out of the house. They drove away just as the second set of visitors arrived, and returned as the last car departed. She had refused to countenance his plan—his crazy way of circumventing roads. What you do is build roadblocks, she said, not invite the world under your roof. What the government gives you with one hand they take away with the other; she distrusts the National Register of Historic Places and their letters of approval and their plaques. What you do is keep strangers away, not ask them in to eat your porridge and sit in your chair.

Then shame possessed her for her adamancy, her sounding so like Judah that she could *hear* him approve. Those had been his arguments, not hers;

x

480

that had been his way of toting up accounts. He had been more litigious than their lawyer, Samson Finney; he wrote simultaneous testaments, then decided which one should apply. Maggie urged her husband to share and share alike, but with his homegrown sense of equity he tacked up No Trespassing signs.

So she yielded to Ian's insistence. He convinced her that his strategy was sane; in order to keep out traffic they had to open the gates. She called the paying visitors their "guests." The second Thursday, when guests arrived, she stayed upstairs with Jane. There had been noises beneath her, and the sound of scuffling feet, and when Ian rang the gong to tell her that the coast was clear, the coast was covered with mud. She vacuumed all that night. She had time before the next invasion, and she wanted no strange fingerprints on the counters or the walls. She mopped the kitchen floor. Ian said he'd had six visitors, and nobody entered the kitchen; she said the floor required mopping once a month. "At eleven o'clock?" he inquired. "Mrs. Russell does it, doesn't she? And she's coming tomorrow."

"But I'm not tired," said Maggie, rinsing, "and I feel like doing something."

Ian bought mannequins. He knotted scarves. "Jane will love this stuff," he said. He spaced dummies in the sewing room as if at a tea party, and dressed them carefully. The room was a success. He called it "Touch and Try," and left a heap of jackets and bonnets and shawls on the ironing board. There was one blouse with thirty-eight mother-of-pearl buttons down the back; there were riding habits and a collection of collars. When she set the room straight, afterward, the mannequins would have been moved. Their wigs had come uncurled.

A woman with a plastic face pauses at the church in order to remove her hat. She holds a parasol. Another bends to stoke a stove, and her face is black. Happy huntsmen come through woods with a stuffed deer slung from a pole; children sit around a table, raising pewter spoons to bowls half full of papier-mâché eggs; there's a slab of cardboard bacon on each plate. These are reconstructions she has seen in the local museum. She stands behind the cord or glass and watches her own vividness go dim: mother and children, a *tableau vivant*—note especially the shark's-tooth's necklace on the three-year-old. This may be an amulet intended to ward off evil. Note also the harpoon on the wall, and the trout net by the snowshoes; a trapper's implements have been set out for cleaning on the workbench to your right.

Maggie tells herself Jude's stories. There is the one about the beekeeper followed everywhere by bees. When they swarmed they swarmed to him, and he was honey all over. There is the one about the crow who thought it was a duck, and the dog that found its master five hundred miles from home, in Boston, on a subway car. Her heart is beating rapidly; it hurts. She opens the door to her room. This is Thursday; she has to prepare. There is the story of the bank clerk who increased the balance sheet of anyone he trusted and considered deserving. He'd embezzle fifty dollars at a time and spread it through the accounts. They were little windfalls, always, not enough to query or get curious about—but enough to make a difference for a birthday celebration or a fine wedding present or maybe a new coat of paint. He was forty when he started, and went on till retirement without being caught. Afterward he told Judah that he'd done it to plow back excess profits—to do what he said the bank *should* do for the community it serves.

Maggie listens for some sound from Jane. She is not distracted. There's the one about Sebastian who was a night watchman at the plastics plant. One night the boiler exploded. They put out the fire with help from every volunteer department in a twenty-mile circle; Judah had been there, and it took the best part of a night. Once it was possible to get inside, they hunted for Sebastian and could find no part of him. They called his daughter to see if he'd maybe stayed home, and his daughter said no, but could she give him a message? No message, the firemen said.

Then Judah found a watch. It was waterproof and fireproof and shatterproof, and registered twelve fourteen. They identified it as Sebastian's watch, and then they found a piece of what was once a shoulder, and a metal shoe tip that had melted into toes. They held a full-scale funeral, but the only thing they buried was his watch.

"Those aren't the right stories for Ian," Maggie had maintained. "Tell him something sensible."

"Why not? What's wrong with the stories I know?"

"They're pointless," Maggie said.

"You sit around and listen." Judah bit his right thumb's cuticle. "That's how you pick things up."

"Tell him about animals. And unicorns and maidens and maybe knights in shining armor who beat up the dragon. Whatever you want. Gypsy stories about kings who were beggars before."

"Once upon a time," said Judah, "there was a unicorn. There was a maiden and a knight in shining armor who beat up the dragon. He became king of the gypsies. I don't know stories like that."

"Invent them," Maggie said.

An old woman lived in a shoe. Cats went to London to visit the queen, people rode a cockhorse to Banbury Cross, then opened the cupboard to find it was bare and so the poor doggie had none. Except lately all such rhymes feel cruel to her—with Jack tumbling Jill and broken eggs and blackbirds baked alive. Someone is licking platters clean at some other someone's expense, or riding pell-mell through the streets in order to light lamps or sweep chimneys clean with the bodies of storks or force the children to sleep. People are plunged into pots; spiders wriggle inside, or thumbs come popping out of pies, or ladybird's house is on fire and she has to hurry home.

Slowly therefore, scuffing the floor to find splinters and keep the parquet shining and because she might as well get use out of the hallway runner before it goes threadbare beneath strangers' boots, leaning on the banister for much the same reason, not weakness, Maggie approaches the stairs. Judah used to walk that way. She had started on this stairway more than half her life ago, at twenty-three, though blithe, though skipping, her ungainliness what he called grace as, lumbering up after her, she heard him wheeze and snort. The first time, when thirteen, lost, and finding the Big House, she'd not gotten past the kitchen—but more than forty years later Maggie remembers how he'd risen from his work desk like a wave, towering over her, then crashing down. The stairwell has paintings. *Jude*, she wants to tell him. *Look what's happened in the house.* There is a cowboy chasing buffalo, and the pink sun sets behind a canyon wall. There is a stand of birch trees, then a painting of a stream. There is a group portrait—worked up, perhaps, from photographs—of the Transcontinental Railway where the two halves meet. Men pose in top hats or shirt-sleeves, and one man in a cutaway holds a spike and sledge. High noon casts gray light anyhow upon the celebrants; they are shadowless. Maggie holds her housecoat closed and raises it a little; otherwise, she'd slip. The man in the cutaway grins. She drifts past him and studies a cow; its eyes are lakes in which this particular artist has seen fit to paint brown trout.

The second floor is cold. She wears knee socks. Her housecoat has pink quilting that has faded to near-white. Her flannel nightgown is blue. From outside, through the twelve-pane window, past the laden maples and the tamaracks, she sees herself positioned in the tableau's center: a great glass dome above her, and a farmhouse and flag and glued-down grazing animals above the thick flat base. You buy this toy for Christmas and you give it to your daughter and she shakes it like a rattle till there's snow.

Hattie's door is open, as it rarely was during her lifetime; Maggie enters. The furnishings have been placed on display. William Jennings Bryan wrote a thank-you note that's in a silver frame on the bed table; the hooked rug reads "Home, Sweet Home." The pillow on the rocking chair is a sampler saying "Rest" that Maggie has not seen before; the oil lamp has been burnished and the candlesticks hold candles. The curtains have been drawn and fastened with a pink silk cord.

This is the window she escaped from, Maggie thinks. *This, that he's hiding.* She undoes the cord's loop, separates the curtains, and peers out. "Come in the evening or come in the morning; come when expected or come without warning," was how Hattie put it. She said "hospitality" and "openhandedness" and "Sherbrooke" used to mean one and the same.

Maggie had been openhanded, been a partygiver and a partygoer and the life of every party till her husband could not stand it and shut the Big House door. But she agrees with him now. She wishes she could tell him how reclusiveness prevailed. She balls her fists and stares out at the yew trees as conical as igloos with new snow. It had been easy to leave. She'd left him overnight, then for weekends, then for weeks. Then finally she left for seven years. Now she is just as much a prisoner in this enormous cage as she had ever laughingly called Judah, or the portraits of the ancestors that loom by Hattie's bed.

Now she descends. She sees Ian in the kitchen and constructs a smile. They will pay to see her mummified, bending at the waist but swaddled in silk and chinchilla; the legend says that that's what Judah's wife should wear. She wonders what there is for breakfast, since the Froot Loops box is empty—only pastel crumbs inside, only the sweetened broken arcs of circles that Jane insists be whole, returning each morning's measure of breakage because she will not swallow it. Ian has been making coffee. The pot steams. Maggie hopes so hard for snow she feels herself shiver: every second Thursday let there be blizzards till June.

III

Ian hears her shuffling progress. When his mother comes into the room he smells her from a distance; he will have to urge her to wash. Her hair looks like a squirrel's nest—lank, tangled now, and graying, with Hattie's tarnished silver comb protruding from the bun. The skin beneath her eyes is puffy, darkened, as if she has been pressing on a bruise. He does not regret calling Andrew. For weeks he'd gone to sleep each night resolved to take some morning action—to shock Maggie back to competence, if she could be shocked. She had been his image, always, of efficient sanity; now she holds her housecoat closed because the buttons have been lost.

She raises her shoulders, exhaling. "Is there coffee?"

Ian pours a cup. He adds both cream and sugar, then justifies himself again, as he feels the need to do each time they open the house. "It's the legal minimum. If they look at it too closely, we might not get away with it. It's just a way of saying this is public property for six hours a month."

"I hate it," Maggie says.

"You used to have more people visit every weekend than we ever get these days on tour."

"Except they were invited."

Ian looks at his hands. "The government protects us, that's how we keep Route Seven away. As part of the Historic Preservation Act. You know all this, we've got no choice."

"We do."

"Not much."

"We don't need the money."

"Agreed."

Maggie sighs. She dips her head like some slow schoolgirl learning long division.

"It *has* to be of public value. That's what Finney says." He pours himself more coffee. The mug has been chipped; Ian runs his index finger twice around the rim. "Section one-oh-six: the effect of the roadway must be determined by the head of the relevant federal agency. Otherwise they can't release the funds or issue the license and permits, remember; otherwise we'd be sitting ducks. 'In practice,' says the handbook, 'a mediated solution has usually been achieved.'"

He repeats this as though he's persuaded; it's a lesson he learned six months back. Yet the truth that Ian hides (with all his talk of National Historic Preservation Acts and the National Register of Historic Places and house museums and Advisory Councils and easements and Tax Reform Acts) is he's just as lost as she, and flailing at the future with words about the past: *preservation, trust.* "Well, anyhow," he says, "that's what Finney figures."

"Not upstairs. Not in Jane's room."

"No. But we can rope it off."

"Not my room," Maggie reminds him. "Not anyplace we live in."

"Have it your way," Ian says. "Have it the way Miles Fisk wants. Let them put an exit ramp right through the south-facing gate. Past the shed field;

that's where they'll put Sunoco and a Hojo's if we're lucky. We could harvest plastic bottles and tin cans."

He watches her. His father would have strung barbed wire or stood in the roadway with shotguns. But Ian too is fighting for the Sherbrooke property, with more modern stratagems: petitions and incorporation papers and a listing in the National Register of Historic Places. Maggie goes to the window. "It's snowing."

"Someone may arrive today," he says. "You mustn't worry."

"I'm not worrying."

"Don't be afraid," Ian says.

His condescension shocks her, he sees, though it comes in the guise of compassion; that he should tell her not to worry seems far more a cause for worry than the statement by itself. She advances on the window and smudges it by breathing. She draws a triangle in the opaque pane. "I've had strangers here before," says Maggie.

"Yes."

"But a *museum* where we live? I've seen them," she whispers. "Tracking salt all over the carpets. Using up the well."

Outside the wind increases, and what had seemed like light drifting snow drives at the window and sticks. The knuckles of her hands are white; she sucks at them, two at a time.

"You'd better get dressed," Ian says.

First, she could ride horses better than anyone—better than his father, even. She made him chocolate cake with chocolate icing and filling, and wrote with whipped cream on the sides and top: this is IaN'S EverYBodY ELse HaNDS OFf! He would watch her, pleased and proud, while she extruded the thin round line and cut it off at each word's end; when she offered him a turn, all he himself could manage was globs and splotches and leaks. She was a better pianist than anyone—and Judah gave her, when Ian was five, a concert in the house. He brought a violinist and a cellist over from Boston; they were both professionals, but Maggie played the piano part. They played Beethoven and Dvořák, and then sight-read Haydn trios; he had been enthralled. Maggie sat three-quarters facing him, her face flushed; someone turned the pages at his mother's nod. She played with her lower lip sucked in, swaying, and was the most important person in the trio, with the loudest part.

He had adored her. He leaned forward, rapt. He was just learning to play. They had hired fold-up chairs and put a hundred in the hall, outside the music room. Some man he didn't know, behind him, said, "How did she get the musicians, I wonder?" "Judah paid," said someone else, "or they damn well wouldn't be here," and the lady with him said, "Ss-sh, that's her boy." Ian flushed and fled.

They found him in the kitchen. He would not cry, he said to Hattie, and she said, "Of course not. You're too big for that. You're five, and five-year-olds don't cry."

"And three-quarters."

"Five and three-quarters. Let's go back."

"I want . . ." he said and stopped.

"Want what?"

"Promise I can have it?" Ian asked.

She had been distracted, hearing the music beyond. He heard his mother's solo passages, and she missed every note.

"You know," said Hattie, "I can't promise anything when I don't know what you want."

"Promise anyhow," he pressed her.

"Maybe." In their negotiations this meant yes.

"I want that man out of the house!"

She looked at him, shocked. He stamped his feet. He folded his arms on his chest.

"I can't, Ian. You know I couldn't do that."

"You promised!"

"Which one?"

"The one with the flat nose. The one right behind me."

"Who, Andrew? That's Andrew Kincannon. But he's your mother's friend," she said. "Why ever would you want him out?"

"Because."

"Because why?" Hattie was growing impatient.

"Because of what he said."

"About?"

Ian considered. "About the music. He said, 'Judah paid . . .'"

"Oh, don't pay any mind to him. Not Andrew. He's just jealous."

"Of what?"

Hattie studied the ceiling. She pursed her lips. Even then he'd known she knew more than she was letting on about his mother's friend, but knows now how much more there was she didn't dare to guess. "He's in the business," she said. "A professional person. He wishes Judah had asked *him* to arrange the concert, probably. You mustn't mind his talk."

So he had been mollified and went to his room hating them, hating the piano. Later, when his father burned it—though by that time Ian was using the Steinway to practice—he'd understood a little of the reason why. When the fire quieted, he salvaged a black key and a white key that had been cracked and blackened, and hid them in his bureau, in the socks.

In December he had discovered his grandfather's daybooks in the attic, in a cupboard with sealed shelves. There were a dozen volumes, and Ian leafed idly through. The handwriting was clear, the pages lined. The books were leather-bound. In his open-faced, right-slanting script, Peacock's grandson kept accounts, each ledger comprising a year. His principal occupation had been that of banker, and he supervised the workings of the farm with fitful inattention. He planted apple orchards, organized the Elgin Creamery, and undertook to ship milk to New York in refrigerated trains. There were three such trains a day. He reduced the flock of sheep and increased the herd of cows.

But Joseph Sherbrooke was a meditative man; his entries attested to this. After each row of figures at week's end, he would unburden himself. And as his affairs grew more complex he kept a separate ledger for the workings of the farm, recording in his daybooks only the daily weather. Full of schemes for social change he never quite effected, he focused on his family with a kind of abstract earnestness. "If I had my preference," he wrote in 1900, "this century so well arrived would last a thousand years. My darling wife and daughter thrive, the barley yield was excellent, the season's syrup sweeter than any I can remember tasting. Business prospers. The proper irrigation of the bottomland is now in Leahy's charge. We are in good health. I have one wish remaining, with which to greet the Year: may the child we await be a son. If so, we are agreed. We will call him Judah; that is praise. For Judah is a place and tribe as well as single man; it is an hilly fastness and an ancient name. For Leah 'conceived again and bare a son, and she said. Now will I praise the Lord: therefore she called his name Judah, and left bearing.'"

The radiator leaks. He studies the discolored floorboards at its base. He wonders if they should put their best or worst foot forward when Andrew arrives; should he urge his mother to use makeup, for example? Would Andrew respond to Maggie's collapse or the brave guise of endurance?—Ian does not know him well enough to know.

"Kincannon," she pronounced, three days before. "Andrew Kincannon."

"Who?"

"Do you remember him?"

"Not very well."

Maggie lifted her head from her hands. "Try to."

He did, and Andrew acquired definition: the full lips, the expensive clothes, the ears that Ian had seen to be lobeless. "What about him?"

"I can't handle it. Not by myself."

He could not remember Andrew's eyes. He spent some time attempting to remember and, failing, concluded that Andrew wore glasses. He imagined horn-rimmed glasses, tinted glasses, bifocals, hunter's glasses, goggles, and even a single black patch.

"You've got to tell him," Maggie said. "I can't handle it alone."

She spoke to her fingers. He looked at them also. "You're not alone."

"No."

He made those assertions of comfort he'd been making now for months. "We're with you. We're in this together."

"Yes."

"You'll get better. Wait and see."

She shook her head. "I can't describe it. There's so much pain, it's every-where . . ."

He lit her cigarette. He flicked the lighter additionally, twice.

"Like an operation," Maggie said, "without anesthesia. So you know what's happening and feel it, *feel* it, Ian, but have to stay strapped to the bed."

"Jane's fine, she's thriving. You mustn't feel guilty. You're in a safe place here."

She put away her cigarette. He continued with the blessings that she ought to count, and why anxiety was inappropriate; she took a strand of hair and combed it with her thumbnail, then curled and uncurled the hair. "It doesn't help," she said. "You used to want to find out."

"What?"

"The name of Jane's father." Maggie spoke carefully. For the full term of her pregnancy, he'd asked her that, and she refused to tell him, saying it didn't matter, wasn't relevant: she'd had this child to have this child, not to have another husband. "You used to want to know."

"So Andrew . . . ?"

"I need help. I can't pass an open window, Ian, or go near the medicine chest. Oh, I don't mean to frighten you, but I might not make it. Some days . . ." She stopped. It was as if, even thick-tongued and in pain, she felt ashamed to admit it. "I don't mean you, you'd be all right. But Jane. She ought to have what help there is. Christ knows it isn't likely but he might provide some help. It wasn't *his* fault. Andrew Kincannon."

Ian reached his hand out, but she placed both her hands in her hair.

"Why this uneasiness?" Joseph Sherbrooke wrote. "Wherefore this sense of impending disaster, as with the silence that precedes a storm? Three elms fell in last week's wind, and this morning's stillness is the portent of motion not peace. Thirty-one degrees. The very sky beyond my window is glazed with an additional glaze so that one might think it lacquered: layer on layer of preservative that suggest fragility not strength. Just so did we when children pierce an eggshell with a needle and blow out the liquid contents—thereby retaining the retainer that otherwise would crack. I was always clumsy-fingered, but could perform this feat. Therefore, with the pleasure of skill elsewhere denied me, I would eviscerate dozens of eggs. The women of the household painted them, vying with each other in intricacy of stencil and design—so that by Easter they displayed whole shelvesful of such objects, a rainbow of color refusing to fade.

"My prey was the hen house no fox ever entered. They dared not because of the dogs. But the dogs were acquiescent while I their young master wreaked havoc—there was in any case a superfluity of food. There are stone eggs also that my aunt collected, and the semiprecious ones called Fabergé. But mine appeared more precious still, at least in my youthful accounting. They were the reward of chores, the final product of a morning hour. Things change. I have changed. I am thirty-eight years old today, with one child born and another arriving. We will celebrate. I smoked two cigars after lunch. The maids set out the birch log on the table, with its twelve drilled holes for candles and the twelve white tapers. It is the hollow center I fear, however, the perfect preservation—year by year unchangingly the birch log!—that suggests decay."

The snow is unrelenting, and the ground has been buried for months. Ian has reasons to go to New York, and he proposes that they travel there together, then take some southbound plane; they have the means and leisure to go south. But Maggie seems as rooted as ever Judah was. "If I can't get to Morrisey's"—she tries to make a joke of it—"what's the point of New Orleans?"

He says there's a difference between a grocery store where everyone knows you, and a city where nobody does. "The trouble with travel," she says, but does not complete the sentence; she turns from him, lifting her hands.

He skis across the meadow or on the woodlot trails. Jane enjoys it when he takes her piggyback—not on the skis but snowshoes, scarcely breaking the new crust. She flails her mittens at his ears and chortles, "Giddyap." Once he took a tumble and she fell head first into the snow, feet sticking up like flags. He'd righted her, but the snow had been too deep for damage, and all Jane said, when he'd finished drying her and swung her back onto his shoulders, was: "Careful, horsey. *Careful.*"

Her snowsuit chilled his neck. He had wanted to hurry back home. But the sun had been unimpeded that morning, and soon enough the liquid on his chest was sweat, not melting snow. They built a snowman instead. They built a different creature every other day. It was their way of populating the hills. She got to choose when they set out whether they'd carry oranges or carrots or potatoes from the kitchen. She selected buttons or bracelets and told him if he should or should not bring a corncob pipe. They built snowmen and snowladies and snowbabies, turn by turn. Her favorite was babies, and they built them near the Toy House, in a patch defined by tamaracks they called the nursery. Jane had been learning to count. She counted all the carrot slabs that made the babies' eyes, and could go as high as twenty-nine but then said twenty-ten. If a baby had been ill-assembled and toppled in the night, or if the sun caused its ears to melt and fall, Jane put her hands on her hips the way that Maggie used to, and would say, "*Bad* girl!"

When they build snowparents, however, they elect separate spots. He lets Jane do the choosing. She never chooses a site near the house and never puts a snowman next to a snowlady. One morning he asked her why not. She said, "Because," and he asked, "Because why?" and she said, "Because they're different, Ian. *You* don't understand the rules."

The rule, he tried to tell her, is that snowmen and snowladies and snowchildren make a family, and they might as well be in one place. It saves on the telephone bills. It means if you have bad dreams in the middle of the night and you wake up calling "Mommy" or "Ian," they'll be around to hear. It means that though the Daddy snowman's in some distant field, there's family enough.

She had been unconvinced. "It's *my* rules," Jane had answered. "I get to do the choosing in this game. You get to build. I choose."

"You help me building, don't you?"

"Mm-mn."

"So why can't I help you choosing?"

Jane had been adamant. She bent to miss a laden pine branch, but the snowfall brushed them both. "Because it isn't fun."

Ian has been hoping for months to keep both Maggie and the house intact. The problem is they seem opposing problems. She wants no interfering strangers in the rooms, and his application to the National Register promised community use. He says that there are doctors who are trained and paid to help; the help she wants, she tells him, is to be left alone. When he consulted a psychologist up in Manchester, the doctor said, "Except for a formal institutionalization, Mr. Sherbrooke, there's no way we can work with a patient who resists. And even in the former instance—which is a drastic one, at least at this juncture, and one I gather you wish to avoid—admission must be voluntary. Unless she breaks the law."

The doctor spoke as if by rote, as if telling an illiterate person to fill out and file applications; Ian thanked him and hung up. He remembered that his mother had a lover, once, by the name of Charley Strasser who had been associated with the William Alanson White Institute. Ian could not reach him. He reached the Vice President for Staff, and the Vice President for Staff said yes, he recollected Charley, but Charley went out on the farthest twig of the renegade branch of Sullivanian analysis—and Mr. Sherbrooke no doubt understood what happened to such people; he's not with us now.

So he buys books. He reads of postpartum depression that may last for years. He reads about the common and uncommon psychic side effects of menopause. Anxiety and dysfunction are "commonplace concomitants" of depression, but he cannot think about his mother in terms of commonplace concomitants. Therefore he waits in ignorance, telling himself he can handle the house. It has stood upright and solid since 1869. When the east wind brings the sound of plows, or nighttime comes with Maggie still in her nightgown, drinking coffee in the window seat; when the furnace gives out and the pipes in the laundry room freeze, and the greenhouse roof crumples in that January ice storm like tin in tin shears, Ian pits himself against the weather. He tries to be a kind of father to his young half-sister, trying to make up to them for all his time away.

The nightgown Maggie wears has elastic at the wrist. She pushes back the fabric and stares at the new mark. Then gravely, as if vitality were ratified because the flesh receives impressions even on a window seat, and the pink line left by elastic might serve as a bracelet of pain (this mark is there and wasn't there this morning and will not be there tomorrow, so I exist in time, and time was things were easy and Jane will grow up happy), she readjusts the sleeve.

"February 4. Temperature at six o'clock, six degrees. To suppose no connection exists between the present and future character is to take away the uses of the present state. High wind, north northwest. The sense of prior history is requisite for any sense of destiny. To freeze time is to embrace stagnation. It denies progress as well as decay and weakens the hold on men of moral investment in the future. To the animal the past is blank, and so must be the future. But to the inquiring mind the present is comparatively nothing. I see within this block of ice the stilled springtime freshet, the watering hole. To suppose that the bones of a Mammoth unearthed means somewhere now a Mammoth walks, and Mastodons inhabit icy regions to the north, is too great credulity.

"My father hated Charles Darwin. It was no personal distaste, no animus against the man but rather I think against the enforced expectation of change—not so much the fear of having been descended from a Monkey as the fear of what the Human Race will presently become. I fear it also. My child will be dead by the millennium. This girl born a century after her great-grandmother might perhaps have a grandchild surviving by then, or if longevity be afforded to her child: what strange and marvelous visions will they find familiar? Five years ago there were no more than four horseless carriages in the United States. Today they number thousands and tomorrow in the millions—shall we therefore forfeit feet?"

A dog has been found floating in the local reservoir. The water pipes are high in lead content, and the previous fall it appeared as if lead poisoning might reach epidemic proportions. The town manager drank water from every shop on Main Street as if to prove public fears groundless. This drink-in was reported by Miles Fisk. The local paper ran a photograph of William Ellison holding an eight-ounce water glass and toasting the populace, smiling. "Hydrophiles, Unite!" the caption read.

William Ellison's day-long drink-in took place on a Friday, however, and on the following Monday he did not report for work. He claimed it was a family matter, then admitted he was indisposed, then checked into the hospital for tests. "I've got sick leave coming," he told Miles. "And I'm overworked. Can't you give a guy a break?"

Disease-control and prevention experts arrived from Burlington. They too sampled the water, but under laboratory conditions and not by drinking it. Miles gave front-page play to the story, quoting Ellison's excuses, running the photos of a test tube and of the suspect eight-ounce glass on adjacent columns.

Then Peacock's aqueduct was unearthed. They found the moss-grown, perfectly arched viaduct on Cold Spring Road; it testified to masons' skills a hundred years before. Peacock had wanted water closets on the fourth floor. Since his house crested the highest hill for miles, he had had to bring the water down from Woodford Mountain. It worked. When Joseph added wells, however, the aqueduct was disconnected in 1921.

Now, experts claimed it would prove serviceable still. Jim Brockway, who'd retired from the Army Corps of Engineers, said the line could be cleaned up. Hank Woburn, the dowser, said the apple trees on Cold Spring Road were stunted for one reason only: they headed down to where the water was. Walt Newcomb, who built the dam up at the reservoir and had had to take his chain saw to it during dredging, said if Jim and Hank agreed on water, only a fool disagreed. When Ian got a haircut, Vito the barber, speaking for the selectmen, said the selectmen concurred: it would be worth a feasibility study. They needed his permission, said Vito—busy with the razor he was stropping—but they figured they had his support. You could say, said Vito, we'll trade you off the water for that exit ramp.

Then the town's water cleared up. They diagnosed a case of colitis in William Ellison; they said the decomposing dog contaminated nothing, and likewise the dead floating deer. So the selectmen turned elsewhere, and the feasibility study was dropped. It would have cost three thousand anyway, said Vito, it would have been throwing worse money after bad.

"Most people using that expression say 'Good money after bad,'" he said, "but you notice I say 'worse money after bad.' Because it's a question of worse after bad, not better after bad, it's a question of cutting your losses—what all of us are doing in these parts. Vermont's a place," said Vito, "where everything becomes a problem lately of worse after bad." He shook his head, confiding; he doesn't understand how any of them stand it; he himself will be in Naples by this time next year.

That was a threat he'd made since Ian could remember, and had made to Judah since the end of the Second World War. But Vito loved winter, and the alpine slide at Bromley. He hung a sign on the door every Wednesday that read: "Gone Sliding Down Bald Mountain. Had to Shut up Shop!" His daughter who did greeting cards—the one who stayed at home because the leg brace made her shy—painted it. The first letter of each word had red-and-white stripes, and the exclamation point after "Shop!" looked like a barber pole.

Yet whether Vito goes or remains, whether they hook up to the aqueduct or not—whether the selectmen endorse the bypass and the shopping mall or oppose them—makes small difference finally. Now, holding out means mostly holding on. Ian is the last male Sherbrooke, and the first male Sherbrooke settled before Houston or Los Angeles had names. And he has to face New England's decline: had Peacock kept that acre of Montgomery Street in San Francisco where he worked, the single acre would be worth far more than these thousand acres he retained.

"Stucco on a postage stamp," says Morrisey. "I tell you I seen it. The price of property out there." He has returned from Disneyland, and postcards of Pluto are taped to the cash register. "A 'For Sale' sign in California"— he shakes his head. "Either you're a millionaire or don't even bother to knock."

This is a cold region, and they're pouring warm water on ice.

"February 6. Rain for the first time this winter. Temperature at six, thirty-six degrees. Mercury falling, however, and already I see sleet. Aunt Anne-Maria died this morning—or rather I learned of her death by this morning's post. She was by all accounts a virtuous woman, one whom it would have been worthwhile and a pleasure to know. Her wanderings took her far afield, to Surinam and Guatemala and even, if I remember rightly, Siam. This is recollection at second remove, since I have nothing but the haziest personal image of her (nor do I know if I remember the woman or remember having been urged to remember). When she married Willard Sheldon, she found the Mormon Faith and was lost to us entirely. The memory I do have is of Father reading her letters aloud—sent from Surinam or Guatemala or perhaps Siam—shaking his head. It deeply grieved him, I believe, to feel at so wide a remove. Proximity and distance are riddles we must learn to solve: the very objects on this writing desk attest within a four-foot reach to oceans and deserts traversed. In its leather parts the blotter is Italian, the pen French. The meerschaum comes from Holland, the tobacco from Virginia—and so on and on around the girdling globe. There is no collector's volition at work, nor the conscious purpose of catholicity—but I am perforce more near to the savage digging roots and fashioning this ink than was my father to his sister once she traveled to her tropics in an alien belief. If my daughter has a brother when our second child arrives, may it not prove so with them!"

Ian turns on the entrance hall lights. He sets the pianola roll to "You Are My Sunshine." He unlocks the storm doors that give onto the front porch. He picks three china oranges from the display bowl on the sideboard and spends some minutes juggling. Then he replaces the fruit. If Andrew arrives, he tells himself, they will have a consultation; pleased by the near-rhyme of "confrontation-consultation," he repeats this several times. He listens for Maggie and Jane. In the "Hudson River Valley Dawn" attributed to Bierstadt that he looks at, inattentive, a horseman emerges from pines. Ian has not noticed this before. He looks at it more closely and sees the man's black hatbrim, the ocher gleam of saddlebags, and the brown withers of the horse. The horse's neck is wet with sweat; the man may carry oil paints in his pack. He sits the horse as if they have been traveling some distance, his body in a practiced slouch, the rifle protruding at thirty degrees. There is nothing to do now but wait.

PART II

I

"February 17. Ten o'clock P.M. Train prompt. Felt unwell at supper, discarded cigar. Must see Bill Robinson—not half so decent as Joe Miller, but more than twice the doctor. Came across a letter from Anne-Maria this morning. She lost a child in infancy amongst the Andean tribes. She wrote my father that they butchered her with knives, and she never again could conceive. Her husband Willard Sheldon seemed insensible to grief. He did not leave off work. But nowhere was it written that a missionary's wife need prove equally insensible or, dare I breathe it, unbending. I am ignorant of burial procedure amongst the Mormons overseas—if indeed they have a burial procedure—but will cause a stone to be erected in the infant Sherbrooke's honor. This should be done in private. In the orchard, not the churchyard, where such stones are ours to ordain. The death is unrecorded and more than twenty years old: my phantasmal cousin. A gravestone fails to mark the place of the body's abiding. That place is in the heart."

Downstairs, a door slams. The noise there increases. Maggie remembers Judah's song, the one she'd overhear him whistling and would urge him to put words to, but he'd claim he couldn't sing or didn't know the words, till finally—half-shy, his voice sticking, uncertain, deep in his throat, and higher than she'd ever think that bass of his could travel, Judah sang: "*Way down in yon valley, in a low lonesome place, where the wild beasts do whisper, and the winds they increase . . .*"

She'd tease him, her head on his shoulder or in his lap, saying, "That's not how it goes, that isn't the verse." He'd try again: "*Way down in yon valley, in a lonesome low place, where the wild beasts do whimper, and man seeks his peace . . .*" It was a song, she knew, about a wandering laborer who loved a woman, Saro Jane. She loved him too but wanted land, and therefore she was going to marry some rich landowner with servants, houses, security. The singer understood, and got on his horse and went west.

Her memory of Judah will not fade. He stands there, increasing, solid as the flesh he was and intervening always in her hope of breathing space, her ranging through the Big House rooms and up to the stone gates. He will not let her leave. He is her guardian in death as much as ever in his life, except that she accepts this now and does not seek release. She'd failed to take his measure at the time. She'd taken him on her own terms, or tried to anyhow, opposing his possessiveness with years of dispossession, assuming when she went away she could leave Judah behind.

Yet all those years he'd kept her on a leash. She'd broken free, of course, but only in terms of geography; in all the ways that counted she'd held back. Maggie learned to love confinement, though she called the house a cage. She'd come when he whistled, tail wagging, nails clipped, for all the world like some prize apricot poodle groomed for a dog-show display. He'd petted her, made much of her, and she'd been puppy-eager for the feel of his hand on her neck. She took a photograph of Judah holding the keys to the truck. His face had been in shadow, but sunlight glinted from the key ring in his fist. It was fat as a jailer's, she'd teased him, bristling with duplicates, with keys that opened doors and trunks he'd long since left unlocked, or junked cars, or tractors traded away, though he kept a second set in case. "In case of what?" she'd ask, and he'd tell her if the Nickersons were fools enough to lose their keys or leave the tractor in some ditch he'd have to help them haul it from, or maybe he'd be standing by the icehouse, not planning to have opened it but needing to get out the ax.

Judah was wearing his corduroy jacket. The earflaps on his cap were down since it was early April. She can remember standing on the porch steps shivering, come back for good—not ten feet away from him and not five years ago. He bent to the key ring, attentive. She sees him this way, finally: an old man in love with exactness. There's nothing that he needs to lock, no one for miles who'd trespass and no robbery she's heard of in these parts. Yet Judah knew what opened what and rested secure in the knowledge; he'd make his rounds like Keeper Dan at feeding time in the book Jane liked.

"*My love, she won't have me,*" he'd sing, "*and I understand*"—not understanding how she kept him with her always, and the landowner she wanted was him, and the winds that increased where the wild birds do whistle were in their own green valley, *here,* not lonesome since she still was lying by her only husband's side, not lonesome even now because of Jane.

"We knew Mr. Sherbrooke," says Lucy Gregory. She drops her voice, confiding. "Your father was a perfect gentleman. He used to bring us pears."

"That's why we're here," says Elvirah Hayes. "We thought it's time to say hello. It's been so long."

"Too long. We never once *entered* this house."

They introduce themselves to Ian. Before the switch to automation, before the phones were worked by computer, they worked the village phones. Now they have been retired with no more than a by-your-leave, a handshake for their years of service—fifty-three if you put them together, adding

Lucy's twenty-nine to Elvirah's twenty-four. Never sleeping through the night if somebody's youngster was poorly, answering questions, delivering messages so that generally speaking, says Lucy, and taking turns working the night shift, they spoke for the whole town. Before he, Ian, knew how to talk they'd heard folks talk about him; they must have made connections with every corner of America the morning he was born. So what they hope he understands is how much they miss Judah, how his father used to bring them bushels of the fruit they couldn't grow at home. Home was Church Street, the third house down, the one on the south side with brown trim and the knocker in the shape of a Dalmatian. He shouldn't be a stranger—now that they've been to the Big House, why they'll expect him in theirs.

There is a third visitor. Examining titles, he stands by the bookshelf. He has gone directly to the books.

"So anyway," says Lucy. "Here we are."

They used to raise Dalmatian dogs; his father took an interest in the breed. He knew the finer points of breeding, Judah Sherbrooke did; when he walked through a kennel, it was as if you invited a judge. You couldn't hope to have a keener eye. He'd spot a problem with the hip before there was a problem; once he said he *smelled* distemper clear across the yard. They ask Ian if he keeps dogs now, and shake their heads when he says no; Lucy says those were just the most marvelous pears.

"We knew your aunt too," says Elvirah. "Of course."

Harriet Sherbrooke was her age exactly, Lucy says, though Elvirah's five years younger, and for fifty years they lived a mile apart—since she, Lucy, moved to Church Street from where she was raised in Londonderry, and Harriet never budged. They'd met fifty times if they'd met once; though not exactly what you'd call friends they were not exactly strangers, my land no, says Lucy, let no one imagine that. For half a century she'd not set foot inside this house but it wasn't for lack of intending to—just the right time somehow never came up; we belonged to different choirs, understand, a different church, and played bridge with a different crowd. The term for it if Ian knew dogs is "run with a different pack."

They'd looked at each other, they'd looked at the snow. They had nothing else to occupy this Thursday afternoon. If he doesn't mind their asking, asks Elvirah, would his mother be about? He blows his nose. He wonders, should he offer to return their entrance fee? The third visitor—bent, white-haired, of indeterminate age—from across the room is saying, "This complete John Greenleaf Whittier you got. The spines ain't even been cracked."

"And what about your little sister?" Lucy asks. "We were hoping we might get a glimpse. A chance to pay our compliments."

"We brought her a present," says Lucy, "It's three years late in coming, but better late than never. A person can always use scarves."

"She knitted it," Elvirah says. "She's too modest to admit it, but it's her handiwork."

Lucy dips into her bright-green bag and pulls out wool. It is thick and pink, with fringes. He cannot tell, by its length, if it has been intended for Maggie or Jane. She rolls it up again. "On a day like this one," Lucy says. "I myself always wear scarves."

"Thank you. I'll give it to her later. I'll tell her you made it."

"We were hoping . . ."

"When was this place wired?" The stranger in the corner points to the light switches. He pulls at his ear. "When did they put plumbing in this house?"

Ian offers information. He talks about the chandelier, the parquetry, the steam-heat system Peacock bought that seemed so dangerous insurance underwriters refused to underwrite it. The system prospered, Ian says, as did everything that Peacock touched—the man was a Midas for silver. When he touched rock, the rock split open and, hey presto! what we have here, ladies and gentlemen, is the Comstock Lode. He sees himself in the dining-room mirror, expatiating, gracious, and thinks maybe Maggie is right: this isn't worth it, he needn't make Jane curtsy for a scarf.

Yet these are chosen visitors, the ones who come in when it storms. He should maybe offer them coffee. Ian points out plaster ornaments, and the tooled-leather peacocks on the walls. He shows them where the speaking tube emerges in the butler's pantry, and how each bedroom in the house is numbered so the maids could know who wanted them where. He says, as if for the first time, trying to sound unrehearsed: "One way or another, we all make a museum out of our past. My family just happened to retain it more than most."

The dried hydrangea in the pot are evidence of shape inhering, how the lifeless residue of what had once been vital holds for wintry seasons what it had burgeoned into seasons previous, how what has faded here is neither shape nor size but color, the white integuments turned to ocher, not the texture but the tint of watered silk. Maggie stares at the nine blossoms massed beside her bed. She counts them repeatedly, making certain that the ninth though short-stalked is actual, not imagined. Hattie called them snowball bushes, that's what we call them in these parts, she said, not hydrangea; hydrangea bloom in June and July, but snowball bushes come along in August and September. So even the name of the flowers by her bedside is uncertain, even their number from her vantage changeable; she studies the deep-blue cone beneath that has a crack so it would hold no water, were water requisite.

Hattie said they ought to chuck it out. Her expression had been grim. She couldn't bring herself to part with anything her brother owned, so instead consigned this relic to her bookshelf, saying well why not, there's room enough, what difference does it make? Judah used to say that what you give a gift in is as important as the gift, part of it, so when he brought back flowers, they were in a vase to keep.

Then, months after Hattie's death, cleaning the bookshelf, Maggie saw her own face staring back at her in the ultramarine glaze. Her reflection was foreshortened as it might have been in water, she picked up the vase and dusted it and traced the hairline crack positioned to the rear. A network of spiderweb-thin filaments in the patina fanned out from that central one. She remembered how the water beaded on it, then was a ribbon, then a small puddle beneath. Hattie had been shocked, disbelieving that a thing so simple could make such a complicated mess, thinking probably she'd overfilled the vase or tilted it when setting it down, or the cleaning lady, Mrs. Russell, had been careless dusting.

Maggie stands. The blue-and-ocher shape beneath her now looks like a blossom-ball. She should roll it downstairs. She should make an entrance scattering crockery and petals all over the staircase. They would fall to their knees, collecting shards, apologetic, gathering the remnants of what was her regal nine-sided bouquet, but find no water, hunt for it, expecting that the oak treads would be slick with droplets, the carpeting soaked. She would tell them: "Rise"—descending, insouciant, stepping on flowers and clay.

Mexican bark paintings hang in the bathroom: bright riotous assemblies of women waving gourds, of cats entwined with birds and men on burros holding guitars. Red dogs gnaw yellow bones and blue parrots watch from vines that establish the border. Everything is drawn in profile, and the primary colors are bright. They come from bins in curio shops. She had purchased ten of these mementos, she remembers, for whatever five dollars had been worth in pesos in 1948.

It had been nighttime—so hot the long-bladed fans above her seemed to stir the air, not cooling it, like a spoon in tea. In the near distance a radio blared; bullfrogs and cicadas chorused out beyond the plaza; cars made a paseo, backfiring, by the water. She ate turtle steak and drank quantities of rum: her final day in Isla de Mujeres. Something of that seaside languor haunts her still this morning when she studies the bark paintings where they hang above the tub. Life was easy, sweet, and short: a cigarette, a dance, a hammock for the night. She had been the beautiful "gringa," and a pilot in Mexico City flew her down to Merida, then Isla, for what he called the payment of her company, no string attached. She had been his single passenger; the plane delivered mail.

Did she know, he asked her, that "gringo" comes from the Spanish-American War? When Teddy Roosevelt's army went through, he said, singing "Green Grow the Rashes O!" the natives could not understand and thought they sang, "*Greengo* the Rashes, ho." Maggie had not known that, and she told him so. "I remember everything," he said—she struggles for the pilot's name: Jorge?—"about your presidents. Jefferson, Madison, Harrison, Taft. Zachary Taylor, even. Martin Van Buren was the number eight. Millard Fillmore, what sort of name is Millard for a man? Is it instead a duck?"

Maggie raises the blinds. Her window is opaque. Jorge had sported a moustache and looked, she told him, just like Howard Hughes. "You know him?" Jorge asked. "Is my hero," the pilot said, preening. "Is better than your Lindbergh. Lucky Lindy. Wiley Post."

Life had been so easy once: she repeats this to herself. Why now is it an act of will to stand, to dress, to keep from crying; what keeps her from a winter's flight to Isla de Mujeres this year? Hotels, she's heard, are everywhere along the beach; she could phone for a brochure. Why should the susurrus of voices beneath her be more threatening than jungle sounds; why, if she took that stranger on, should she close her door to neighbors? There were leopards in the wilderness just beyond the plaza, Jorge said; there were reasons to carry a gun. He slapped his hip with nonchalance so that she might admire his holster; it was studded with turquoise and tin. Where had all her gay vivacity been buried, in which cranny of the house?

"February 18. Slept late and felt unwell. Temperature at eight o'clock reading twenty-one degrees. Wind southerly. Four weeks more to wait until delivery. If we have a son and heir the question will present itself: how best to educate him? What precepts to instill and which to let lie fallow? Nature versus nurture. In this land of opportunity—for still I so account it, notwithstanding recent turmoil and the fear of future such: alarums and excursions on the field of liberty, so that man becomes a slave who does not recognize his bonds, in Satan's thrall nowhere so much as in our refusal to recognize Satan (whose greatest stratagem is invisibility and who delights in our belief that he has been dismissed, this blithe modern dream that all evil is done)—Judah will have opportunity to choose. I'll carry him with me pickaback as soon as he's able to sit. He will be higher than my head by the height of his own head. Then turn by turn, as has been the case for fathers immemorial, I shall exact the tribute Aeneas gave Anchises. Could use a hoist today. Cigar too loosely packed. Tastes bitter, draws like weed. Who imitates the *Aeneid* fails to properly to imitate Virgil. A strange and troubling visitor this morning. I must conserve my strength."

The doorbell rings. The Fisks appear. Miles has a ten-dollar bill in his hand. "Two will get you ten," he says. "There's four of us. That's eight dollars we owe." Jeanne stands rigid next to him, wearing a beige parka; her daughters' parkas are pink. "They canceled school," Miles says. "A little bitty blizzard and they cancel the whole damn day. Well, as it happens, Ian, I was home for lunch, and I've been meaning to do a story on this place—so I said to Jeanne here, come on, what with Amy's broken ankle skiing's out."

Amy offers him her ankle for inspection. She pulls up the snow-covered cuff of her jeans, and advances a signed cast. "I busted it," she says. "The metacarpals, too."

Jeanne's face is red from what might have been the wind. She unzips her parka, stuffs her gloves in bulbous pockets, and, in a single gesture, shakes her black hair free. "We don't want to trouble you. This *is* the right time, isn't it?"

"No trouble," Ian says. He indicates the others. "It's what I'm here for."

The twins are lean. They have their mother's dark intensity, and their father's features. Their eyes are large, their cheeks bright pink; snow melts on their berets. They too unzip their parkas and are wearing the same sweaters—turtlenecks from Scandinavia, with white chalets. Their names have been embroidered: "Kathryn" and "Amy" in red.

"Just go ahead," Miles says. His voice echoes in the hall. "We'll tag along." He nods at the two spinsters, recognizing them. "You can catch us up to what we've missed some other time. Didn't mean to interrupt."

"Mr. Fisk," says Lucy. "Am I right?"

He nods. "And this is my wife, Jeanne. This here is Kathryn. Amy."

"Elvirah Hayes," Elvirah says. She titters, tentative. "All present and accounted for. We're quite a party, I must say."

"Your mother around?" asks Miles.

Jeanne has not moved. Unblinkingly, she watches her husband, then gives a small shrugging lift of her shoulders. "It's hot in here," she says. "Could we take off our coats?"

Ian indicates the cloakroom. Miles admires the brass hooks. He fingers the miniature deer heads, their antlers extended for coats. "That's what counts, I tell you. Detailing. Carpentry. It's attention to detail that tells you what's what."

He turns to Ian now and claps him on the back. The blow is hard, unnatural. "That's what I admire, friend. You look around you long enough, you get to see what's what. A person gets to notice things he just hasn't noticed before. Those silver-plated hinges. These hooks, for instance. Deer heads, horns. Terrific." He raises Ian's arm, as if proclaiming a new champion. "I bet our Mr. Sherbrooke here screwed them in himself."

Judah had mistrusted prophecy. He said fortune-tellers told him nothing that he hadn't known before, and palmists just tickled his palm. He told Maggie he trusted prediction—the way the rain would likely follow when the wind came north-northeast, or what the groundhog's shadow meant that day in February and when geese traveled south. These were signs and portents, and he accepted them. When he first heard of the Manhattan Project, for instance, he'd predicted the world would explode. There were sufficient learned fools to blow the earth apart. It was only a question of time, said Judah, and not a long time either, and the portent would come to fruition and be a prophecy fulfilled.

Yet prophecy was not the same as omens; he put no stock in omens and walked under ladders to prove it. Black cats could cross his path forever and he'd notice but not mind. You see yourself, he said, better in mirrors than crystal balls—providing you learn to look straight. It was like the law of averages and the law of probability. He, Judah, never had a car crash in his life. He'd fallen off horses often enough, and tractors, and broken his leg and collarbone falling in the barn. So every time he went out driving, the law of averages was for him and the law of probability against. He'd explained it to her once.

"Let's say you take a quarter," Judah said, "and flip it."

"All right."

"Well, odds are fifty-fifty it's going to come up heads."

"Or tails."

"Mm-mn. It's always fifty-fifty and nothing changes that."

"What if the coin's not balanced? What if you throw it up sideways or don't flip your wrist?"

"The law of probability," he explained, "is always fifty-fifty when the odds are one to one. Now let's take averages instead. Let's say for some strange reason you've spent the night flipping quarters. And you've thrown ten thousand times and it's always turned up heads."

"Five thousand should have been tails," Maggie said.

"Correct. And the odds are good you'll start a run on tails—bet on it. You've been batting a thousand but you ought to bat five hundred. So you're likely to start flipping tails."

"Sounds likely." Maggie smiled at him. He was proud of his analogy, intent.

"So you'd figure, see, the next thousand or two thousand tosses would mostly turn up tails."

"I see." She had tried to understand why he loved arithmetic and so enjoyed accounting and was meticulous keeping the books.

"But you couldn't *bet* it that way because the odds on every toss are still just fifty-fifty. That's the whole problem with doubling. That's why it's difficult just to play odds. And you see why driving gets more dangerous the same time it gets less."

She'd known he was half joking. She knew he'd left out some variables, but Maggie didn't know which. He'd flipped his car keys in the air, then caught them and opened the passenger door. "Get in," he'd said. "Let's go."

Ian shows them through the house. Miles subsides. After his first outburst he has little left to say; he follows nodding, smiling, scratching at his hairline with a hand festooned with rings. The twins are inattentive, whereas Jeanne inspects each item with slow care. The white-haired stranger coughs. He looks about him hawking, swallowing. "Name's Kerr," he says, "Jamie Kerr. You won't remember me." To this gathering of visitors, Ian delivers his speech. He praises the glazing in the French doors, the downstairs fenestration, points to the Vermont marble in the fireplace, the Persian carpets his father called rugs. He makes glancing reference to the girth of Peacock's wife, at least as evidenced in the portraits and the dressing gown ballooning on the dressmaker's dummy upstairs.

Amy favors her foot. "I've got snow in my cast," she announces. "It's melted. The plaster feels all squooshy."

"Mommy, she's complaining." Kathryn hops up and down.

"If you knew how much it hurts . . ."

"I know."

"You don't!"

"I do."

"She doesn't, does she, Mommy?"

Kathryn does a ballet turn to prove her own agility. "You tell me all the time. You never quit complaining."

"I *wish* you knew how much it hurts. I wish it was *your* ankle . . ."

"Stop it. Both of you," Jeanne says.

Ian indicates the cupola. It soars two floors above them, its stained glass snuffed by snow. The doorbell rings. He excuses himself; he half expects Andrew Kincannon. Instead a group of neighbors enter, stamping, blowing on their hands. They make a relieved commotion. Advancing singly or in pairs, they ignore the goldfish bowl with its few dollar bills. He greets them in the entrance hall. They tell him, "Power's out . . ."

The snow seems a white wall outside; it travels laterally. Wind causes it to rise. Past the columns of the porch it is as if snow gathers, advancing, and they watch from the trough of a wave. "You've got 'lectricity," says Samuel Coffin. "Heat."

"The whole hill's out," says Helen Coffin. "Since early morning. Seven o'clock."

"Mm-mn." Peg Morrisey smiles at him, toothless. "We were talking, Helen and I, and she swears she's seen the lights on here, and we take a look from the upstairs window and sure enough it's Thursday, you're open anyhow, so we thought we'd come and make that visit we've been promising. But mostly if you didn't mind, just sit and wait it out." She coughs. "I've got this winter flu. Can't seem to shake it, the weather's not helping . . ."

Miles returns. "Of course," he says. "You're welcome. Public invited . . ."

"They'll fix it," says Elvirah. "By nightfall, anyway."

"A pipe don't take too long to freeze," says Coffin. He turns to Miles. They are adversaries. "I was you I'd write a article about it. Folks thinking they can get away without 'lectricity full-time. But not if they've got running water in the house."

Miles pats his pockets. "Matches?"

"Here." Coffin owns the Furniture Shoppe on the corner of Willowbrook Drive. "Delusion," he pronounces. He is on the proposed Mall's planning board; his shop is in the center of the present cloverleaf. "One don't exclude the other, it's all part and parcel, you see. Like the way a farmer nowadays needs gas. For his tractor, his combine, every damn machine. Petroleum derivatives." Samuel sighs, disgusted. "You think Mobil Oil or Texaco or Exxon give one damn about America?"

"The multinationals," Miles offers. He tamps his pipe.

"Standard Oil of New Jersey, the Esso that turned itself into Exxon." Coffin squares his shoulders. "Rockefeller money, all of it. It's shameful. What in hell did we fight that war for, anyhow, so they can kick the dollar

around? The German mark. Go begging to the Russians so's they conde-
scend to buy our wheat?"

"The Japanese . . ."

Ian wonders if he can ask Maggie for help. There are more arrivals, bulk-
ing in the doorway. He waves them in.

"So you need a blowtorch just to keep the pipes from freezing. So you
lose your whole damn stock to chemicals. Then some outfit comes along
and offers to pay damages. *Damages*." He prods at Ian with his index finger, fiercely. "What kind of compensation is damages and court costs when
you're dead? When some farmer gets to bulldoze a whole herd of dairy
cows used to be making good milk?"

The hallway lights flare. The furnace rumbles, firing, and the lights
go dim.

"Water too," says Lucy Gregory. "It isn't drinkable. It's like we lived in
Mexico or some such place."

"Iceland more likely," says Sam. "You got to boil it twenty minutes just
to wash your hands . . ."

"February 19. Temperature at six o'clock, twenty-seven degrees. No wind.
Ache in throat and stiffness in joints, but less. Peculiar encounter yesterday, and this morning with my fever done it seems almost like something I
might have imagined, a dream. *O lente, lente currite noctis equi.*

"Let me reconstruct it. Peacock Sherbrooke had a son, Daniel Jr., who
disappeared in San Francisco thirty years ago. Unlike his sister, Anne-Maria, he left no trace behind—sending no letters or Christmas gifts to those
who stayed in Vermont. His parting was not amicable, apparently. Peacock
enjoined the whole clan to return on his last journey, and the profligate de-
murred. He had business in the brothels and at the gaming tables; he had
credit in the bars. How much of this was true I can only surmise; my father
must have felt abandoned in this house. But if so he never spoke of it—nor
of the other two sisters who died of pleurisy. So father alone survived of all

who journeyed east with Peacock, coming home to this new domicile. And he alone had issue, and this is the line of descent.

"Or thus I had assumed till yesterday. It is now an arguable question, according to my visitor—who claims to be the son of Daniel Sherbrooke Jr., via an octoroon mistress later become Daniel's wife. Who came here for the dual purpose of reverence for his paternal homestead, as he called it, and the not-so-pious but keener purpose of extortion. He called it remedy. His frame was thin, complexion dark, and his eyes had the glitt'ring intensity of madmen convinced they are sane. He showed a pair of pistols— unloaded, I am glad to say—with mother-of-pearl inlay on the handles, and the letters D and S. He said these were his legacy, together with one diamond stickpin long since exchanged for gin (this latter conclusion was mine, since it took no nose to notice what was reeking from his mouth). He said his mother passed away in rags on the rain-soaked California docks, and though she never breathed one word of bitterness at bitter usage, he himself was not so saintly or without a sense of justice and recourse. We were cousins, he said, and equal under the eye of God and the American Constitution, and it offended him that there should be inequity so grievous between blood-kin. He sat at his ease on the couch. He rearranged the cushions. His mother had had skin to match the color of her reputation, but an unspotted purity of countenance to those who knew her well."

This time Andrew parks by the carriage barn; his is the only car. His tire tracks are deep; snow reaches the base of the door. There are many footprints on the driveway, however; he tucks his pants into his boots. Split wood has been stacked to his left. Exhaling, he watches his breath.

A woman appears on the porch. He approaches. She is dark and slight, not Maggie; she raises her hand with a stranger's politeness and asks, "Cold enough for you?"

He nods. "But at least the snowfall's stopped."

"Yes."

"I'm Andrew Kincannon."

"Jeanne Fisk."

He climbs the stairs and stands at her level one full step down from the porch. Her black hair is thick and her eyes are large; the look is, he tells himself, Hepburn—Audrey and Katharine both. "The world's inside," she says.

"A party?"

"More or less." The woman shrugs. "It's Ali Baba time. Open Sesame."

He hears laughter in the hall. "Not your kind of party, I take it."

"I needed some air. Do we know each other?"

"No. Pleased to meet you; I'm not from these parts." ·

"My family's inside," she says, as if her presence does require explanation. "What brings *you* here?"

He releases his pants from his boots. "Antiques. I'm a collector."

"Well, you've come to the right place. Antiques." Conveying somehow that the audience is over, that her attention has been long enough bestowed, Jeanne turns toward the door. "Except they're not for sale."

"You go on in if you want to," he says. "I need to stretch a little, I've been too many hours in that car."

Absurdly, till she disappears, Andrew does torso twists. The Toy House bobs and weaves; he straightens and the landscape readjusts.

In Westport, he has a collection of quilts. He drapes them over the rafter and admires the myriad folds and pleats, the fringes shaking slightly in the updraft from the furnace or an open door. "What's the point?" Maggie had asked—the last time she visited, with her husband still alive. "They're useless or ought to be used."

"Spoken like a Sherbrooke?"

"No. Judah would approve. Our house makes this one seem frugal, you know that. But if I don't admire hoarding in him, why should I like it in you?"

"Beauty," he had pronounced. "There's nothing wrong with hoarding it. Acquiring it. Preserving it."

"These quilts"—she shook her head. "They're meant to keep things warm."

"All right." He reached for the diamond-pattern above him. He pulled, and quilts cascaded. "Let's take them upstairs and see."

Such plenitude in emptiness, however, has come to bother him. He feels, each time he arrives in Westport—alone or with companions— that Maggie had been right. He sees himself becoming that stock figure: the aging, wealthy man-about-town who collects. It could have been stamps or Dresden figurines or statuettes of owls; could have been quartz or Tibetan woodblocks or any kind of collectible that would attest to choice.

"Form follows function," Maggie joked. She ascended the steps behind him. The colored stuffs on her arm caught the sun; he turned and watched her at the window where she paused. She stood there clothed in light, bedecked with quilts, and Andrew can remember thinking: this would be what marriage to her means.

He tells himself he's not prepared; he should be bringing gifts. Retreating, he makes for the Toy House once more. The snow above the flagstone path is less high than the fallen snow on the surrounding ground.

Someone starts the pianola, and it beats out "You Are My Sunshine," tinnily. Peg Morrisey joins in the chorus. Ian counts a dozen faces that he's seen when walking, or in the supermarket aisles, or behind the drive-up window at the bank. The villagers have gathered here like people under siege, believing that within these walls they will find heat. He excuses himself, goes upstairs. He knocks on his mother's closed door. She calls, "Who is it?" and he answers, "Ian."

"All right."

"Can I come in?"

"It's not locked."

He opens the door. She sits alone, still in her quilted housecoat and on the edge of the bed. "I was just getting dressed," Maggie says.

The blinds are drawn.

"Are you all right?"

She makes a gesture of apology, then places her palms as if for balance on the mattress. "I have a headache. I took two Excedrin."

He watches her. "Where's Jane?"

"In her room. She's got company."

"Oh? Who?"

Now Maggie turns her hands again and moves so that the bed springs squeak. "What time is it?"

"Three thirty."

"Girls," she says. "Your visitors. She doesn't seem to mind. Jane, I mean . . ."

He turns on the bathroom light. One bulb in the vanity fixture has burned out. There is water on the floor. "I showered," Maggie says.

"Do you want me to check on her?"

"It's all right. I listened. Two dollars a head." She says this with a rising inflection. "It's worth it, don't you think?"

"For company?"

"For company. I *was* getting dressed," she repeats. "I only put this robe back on because I had to think."

He comes to stand beside her. "There's no power down the hill."

"So that's why there's a party." Her smile is fleeting, inward, as if she has been proved correct.

"It's not a party."

"No?"

"No."

"Then what do you want me to wear?"

There is laughter down the hall. Maggie lifts her head, suspicious. "Whatever you want," Ian says. The laughter is high-pitched, multiple.

"You haven't answered my question," she says.

"Which one was that?"

"What do you want me to wear?"

"The hell with it," he says, exhaling. "I'll go down alone."

Maggie stares at her hands.

"A dress. Shoes. Anything. Something to show you can get up and dress."

"I can," his mother says.

Judah was cagey in argument, always, with opinions he'd come to before she was born. He had habits she just couldn't break. He wore his boots to supper, over Hattie's objections and hers, no matter how muddy or how much they reeked of manure. He bought no books but Fix-It manuals and tolerated no TV and went to concerts with her as a kind of bodyguard, watchful but not listening. She sometimes thought any kind of performance was irritating to him, a cause for suspicion: the lewd embrace of audience and ego in the stage-lit dark. He took it as a personal affront. A thing's the thing it is, he seemed to say, not something else or more because some magazine or press agent says so: if you walk naked in the world, don't try to prove you're dressed. When Lady Godiva went riding, she didn't make the populace admire her new clothes.

The wall behind the dressing table shakes. She thinks of walls in California where she had dinner one evening and the soup bowl had its own volition, jiggling on her plate. Their host said, "San Andreas," as if that might be an answer, as if such agitation might in the act of naming be dismissed. "It's just the fault," he said. "Not to worry. If it comes, it comes. There's nothing we can do about it."

Maggie steadied the tureen. He had a white beard cut in emulation of an eastern sage. "Tomorrow you should look at it. The fault, I mean—up there in Point Reyes. Take a little walk until you find the place it cracked. Not much," he said. "Hardly worth mentioning. Just a shift in the landscape is all, a zigzag pattern in the fence." His table had ceased shaking. The light increased. "But think about that six-foot shift and what it does to cities. That's why San Francisco fell and why downtown burned. That's where the whole helter-skelter civilization will get swallowed up. In just that six-foot difference: the measure of one tall man."

Maggie had been skeptical. She told her own companion, later, that their host was posturing, that all his high-flown rhetoric about our six-foot final home had failed to explain why he patted her ass in the hall or pressed his knee to hers when pouring herbal tea. The earth is not a fabric where you sew a zigzag pattern, a geological fault is not some sort of metaphor for sex.

Her own walls continue to move. She remembers a cruise she took with Ian and Sam Elliot, when Sam invited them in 1969. That year was the first she'd left Judah, and the Christmas holidays included no trip north. Sam Elliot called, saying, "I've got two extra tickets for a Dutch tub leaving next Monday—why don't you come along?" His own wife and daughter at the last minute elected Zermatt. Sam was divorcing anyhow, and he preferred to send his women to the Alps than listen to their endless bickering; he was sick to death of it, he said, and cognizant that the bitch's lawyers would jump on this trip and make him pay in spades. "But what the hell," said Sam, "I'll end up paying anyway—so why waste the tickets?"

Maggie asked Ian, and Ian agreed. They made a strange threesome that winter. It was a two-week cruise; the S. S. *Maasdam* put in at Jamaica and Saint Thomas and Puerto Rico. On the way to Aruba, Maggie remembers, the stabilizer equalizers failed. Again they had been eating, and by then she was accustomed to the ship's slow tilt and rise. Yet there was nothing rhythmic in the sudden dive they took—the crash and hurtle of her cutlery, the way the chairs skidded and slipped.

Sam fell. He picked himself up, cursing, his Cuba Libre all over his shirt. Then the ship dipped in the other direction, as if sliding down gigantic waves, and tumbled in a trough of seas gone virulent. China broke. It smashed and scattered everywhere; waiters lost their trays. "Let's get out of here," said Ian, and they struggled to the deck.

The sky was blue, the air hot. Deck chairs had been upended, and the water in the pool lurched over the pool's lip. The sea appeared calm, however, and she could not understand it till a steward said, "The equalizers. The stabilizer equalizers, madam. They're stuck."

For half an hour then, while the crew worked to free the stabilizer equalizers, she clung to a guardrail and watched the world veer. Things careened about her that had possessed stability—and all this in a sea without whitecaps, with a gentle breeze. Sam Elliot explained that stabilizer equalizers worked like fins, or training wheels on a child's bike; they roll on ball bearings, counteracting the waves' pitch. "Imagine," he had marveled, "what it must have been like to sail a clipper ship. Before they invented these suckers. Every minute of the trip would have been as bad as this."

So she imagines the earth without balance—a catamaran with two hiked prows or gyroscope about to topple as its orbit slows. Walls shake; rooms are upended; the constancy to count on is no constancy but change. The dried hydrangea in the pot retain both shape and color, yet they crumble to the touch.

Now Maggie rallies. She has wasted too much time. She selects her clothes efficiently, as if to prove all suspicion unfounded; a cowl-necked yellow blouse, and her three-piece Kimberly knit. She sets the outfit on her bed and, returning to the table, addresses her white staring face.

"February 19. Four P.M. I told him I was ill. I said he was welcome to soup. He said he wanted half our property in order to withdraw. I said such excess must be born of desperation, and it gave me pain to have a man however sick and drunken take the name of Sherbrooke mistakenly. He said he was not sick or drunk but well within his rights. Half the property was modest as a settlement, since my own line was provable cadet.

"There was an eloquence about him—the usage of the term 'cadet,' for instance—that belied his rough demeanor. And I restrained my immediate impulse to throw the man out. Have him thrown out, I should admit, since the fever coursing through my veins would have rendered me incompetent to eject a fly. Furthermore, he made small fuss—startling no members of the household, lounging on that couch as if to the manor born. So I sat and listened while he fabricated claims—that his father, Daniel Jr., had made and lost more fortunes at a single sitting than our prudent Eastern husbandry amassed. My knowledge of poker is slight. The bizarre intruder used its terminology, however, to describe his life—in a sort of *Nicomachean Ethics* of the gaming table. It is for this reason principally that I doubt I dreamed his visit, since I would not even in nightmare call the dear dream of America a 'four flush' or 'inside straight.' He said he was down on his luck. He said the deck was stacked. He said he could not deal with such a bunch of cardsharps holding a dead man's hand—two aces and two eights. He drank my tea in insatiate gulps and wolfed my four slices of bread. I gave him what money I had.

"Perhaps indeed when young he met a man called Daniel Sherbrooke, perhaps he won those pistols on a bet. My head is light with the exertion of even these jottings. Sleep."

Ian continues. Jane's door is open, and he stands for a moment in the hall. "*That* isn't how to do it," Jane is saying. "Not inside."

The twins respond. She is on her tricycle, turning circles in the room; she veers around the toy shelf and sees him in the door. "Amy hurt her foot," she says. "That's why I'm riding."

"Hello, Amy. Kathryn."

"In a *accident*," says Jane.

The twins smile, sheepish to be found with someone so much younger. Jeanne Fisk sits on the bed, upright, surrounded by stuffed rabbits. "Hello."

"Hello. I wondered if you'd left."

"The master of the house," she says. "No. I was resting."

"I'm glad you're here."

She leans back and crosses her legs. She selects a teddy bear. "We thought we'd skip the guided tour. Skip out on it, anyhow."

"It won't last much longer," he says.

"The stuffing's coming out. Mr. Bear has popped his buttons, he's so proud."

"We played Candyland," says Jane. "And guess who came in second."

"Bill," he says.

"No."

"Sam."

"No." She giggles. "*I* did."

"I'd never have guessed it."

"Ian's teasing," Jane confides. "He always teases."

"What would you call this?" Jeanne asks. She indicates the bed, its litter of stuffed animals, and the three girls intent again on Candyland. She lifts a giraffe, then makes a space for him in the circle of rabbits and pats the quilt smooth. "A harem or menagerie?"

He sits. "A guided tour. The public one."

"Yes."

"Miles is taking notes downstairs."

"I know, he wants a story . . ." She smiles at the twins. Amy turns up double-red and passes the ice-cream sandwich. Kathryn turns her card and gets a single blue. She pouts, reluctant—in spite of her announced scorn for such childishness as Candyland—to be last.

"I've got to go," Ian says.

"Here. Take this." She hands him a seal. Its nose is red, its body black, and its eyes are orange marbles. "Something to remember me by. There's an antiques appraiser downstairs. Go ask him what it's worth."

"He seems angry."

"Who?"

"Your husband."

Jane leans forward, concentrating. She turns up the gumdrops and has to lose ground.

"You're very observant, Mr. Sherbrooke. I knew you'd notice, sooner or later. Men are so observant." Jeanne addresses the three girls, "That's what I always tell Miles." They pay her no attention. She smiles at Ian falsely, showing her teeth, and hands him Minnie Mouse. "Now run along and play."

The Toy House door is locked. There is deep snow at the entrance, and a broken windowpane; snow has been drifting inside. It lies on the hooked rug like dust. There are watercolors on the walls; Andrew leans forward and looks. A St. Bernard uncovers a man in a snowbank; the dog's tail appears to be wagging; a barrel labeled Brandy is fastened to its neck. The rescued traveler, already pink-cheeked, smiling, reaches for the flask. A second picture shows the St. Bernard at home, nursing roly-poly puppies; a third shows the dog itself eating a bone that is its ample reward. A chalk sketch titled "Mother's Little Helper" hangs above the cast-iron cookstove; it shows a golden-headed girl with brooms and clothespins and a pail. There is a picture, also, of the girl saying her prayers. She kneels with her back to the artist, a candle in her hand and a pet duck on the floor beside her; a kitten peers out from under the sheets.

Despite these ornaments, however, the Toy House seems abandoned. Sheaves of newspaper cover the chairs, and a drop-sheet hides the couch. The miniature cupboard is open, but the canisters are upside down and there are empty trays of D-Con on the shelves and floor. A depression in the snow beneath the roof's perimeter indicates where snow has, melting, dropped. Andrew walks around the house three times, obliterating this line. Brown icicles fall from the eaves.

II

Ian had spent time onstage since he first studied the piano; he expected to stand in the spotlight and receive applause. He was not an accomplished musician, however, and the few times he played in public were as back-up bass. Then for some years he was an actor, playing bit parts at the Cleveland Playhouse and at A.C.T. in San Francisco. He could recite much of Shakespeare and said the song from *Cymbeline* had taught him everything. "Fear no more the heat o' th' sun," he would pronounce. "Nor the furious winter's rages; Thou thy worldly task hast done, Home art gone, and ta'en thy wages. Golden lads and girls all must, As chimney-sweepers, come to dust."

Though his love of the theater persisted, he gave up attempting to act. He saw true talent in an actor playing Iago at the Guthrie, and understood himself to be, by contrast, third-rate. The most he'd had was presence—a kind of watchful wariness that made those around him respond. The actor who was Iago made a living, later, as a doctor in a TV serial on hospitals; then he played the DA in a serial about hard-hitting cops.

But Ian had what Hattie used to call the gift of gab. He loved the way words edged together, the clashing jangling sounds they made. His ear was good. He could manipulate accents, speaking as a German might, or a Spaniard or Cockney or Indian out of Oxford; his inflections were precise. He had some trouble with Italian accents as distinguished from the French, but he embellished Italian jokes with gestures that worked well. All this, he knew, was just the gift of mimicry; he could imitate a barnyard also, crowing as the rooster crows or sounding very like a dog or cat or horse. He amused Jane greatly by being a cow and teaching her the goat's distinctive bleat. His repertoire included jokes about a chicken crossing roads. The closest he had come to truth on stage was in the title role of *Charlie the Chicken*, wherein he was transformed; he did the same with less success in *Rhinoceros* and *The Dog Beneath the Skin*.

Yet such transformation had its limits, finally; he was Ian Sherbrooke and not an entertainer. He would be no one's parakeet or parrot when they came to lift the curtain from his cage.

Once settled back in the Big House, he occupied himself in several ways. He did the shopping and cooking and spruced up the place. He enjoyed the work of restoration—simple household tasks of carpentry and maintenance. Over time the house gutters and rainspouts had filled; the north-wall paint had peeled. Judah used to deal with one exposure every year, painting first the north wall, then east, then south, then west. Ian found his father's metal scaffolding stored in the carriage barn. Having assembled it, he scraped and primed and over two weeks painted the north wall.

The flat fact was he had no need to work. There was in any case no employment in town, or none that suited him. He rented out the land. After the hay barn burned down, and with Boudreau's departure, Ian saw no point in managing the farm himself. He yielded the task with relief. A family three miles away came to the acreage daily on tractors, and he saw them in the distance plowing, seeding, harvesting; they waved and were respectful. He checked the fence lines every so often and discussed with a show of interest which field to plant with what.

Then Alan Whitely approached. As president of the local drama club, he made a proposition. Since the carriage barn was not in use, and since they required a stage, would Ian consent to let them use it for rehearsals? They wanted to mount an open-air production of *Desire Under the Elms,* with the inside of the carriage barn as the inside of the house. They might build a proscenium, but it could be dismantled later; they would repair the flooring and rent all the necessary chairs.

Jeanne Fisk was the group's treasurer. She called one evening in order to discuss the financial arrangements: whether he required guarantees and what sort of contract to draw up. He said he needed no guarantee: it was a goodwill gesture in accordance with his plan to make the Big House available for community use. He consulted with Samson Finney, however, and called Jeanne back to say they would be grateful for a letter of intent. She said they could discuss the details over lunch; she wondered, also, if he might be interested in becoming a participating member of the group. He said he'd finished acting, and she said, "Nonsense, it's still in your blood—a drug. I know that much."

"Why?"

"Old actors never die," she said. "And young ones most certainly don't."

"They fade away, though. It's called 'Honorary Withdrawal.' They turn in their Equity cards."

"We're not a professional company. We do it just for fun."

Ian played a parlor game. Take any roomful of strangers and attempt to pair them off: does like attract like, or do opposites attract? Is that blonde in the corner, inclining to fat, the wife of that man with brown sideburns wearing a vest, or will she remain with the host? He had met Jeanne Fisk six months before, at dinner at the Conovers'. Jeanne seemed dissatisfied not so much with Miles or her position in the world as with the whole enterprise of satisfaction; she confided to him that a supper party like this one made her want to smoke. She mimed the process of inhaling and, looking at him, held her breath. Then she released the air and shut her eyes and wet her lips.

At first he'd been the town's prize catch—or so Hattie assured him and so it appeared. Jeanne called to offer picnics and chamber-music soirees. One day he met her in the checkout line at Morrisey's, in the five o'clock half-light. It had been raining hard.

"You never visit," she reproached him. "How many times do we have to invite you?"

"I'm sorry . . ."

Jeanne pointed to the shallots that Morrisey was weighing. "I *can* cook. You promised you'd come by for lunch."

In profile her face had a difficult beauty: dark, strained. Her hip grazed his. Later when he tried to pinpoint how their banter shifted, how that casual encounter came to seem shot through with meaning, it had to do with just such tactile contact. She had reached across him, needlessly, for bread. "Do come to visit," Jeanne said. Departing, she rested her hand on his arm, as if to seek help with the door or seal a bargain struck.

At lunch, however, he repeated his refusal to act; she served him a leek quiche. The twins were at school and Miles at the office; a pair of prisms hung in her dining room window. This time by way of excuse he told her he was writing plays, an author, not an actor. She called his bluff. "How wonderful! I'd love to hear what you're working on. Please. It would be wonderful to stage a play you wrote. We could do that, couldn't we?" Jeanne asked.

She wore a scarf that hid her hair; her forehead and features were smooth. Some provocation in her challenge—their courting dance in its first steps—encouraged him to answer yes; he'd show her and they'd see.

When Jane was born, he'd planted a blue spruce. It was a family tradition, and Ian did as much for Jane as Judah did for him. It was late in the season for setting out trees, but the weather had been mild. He bought the best blue spruce in Quinlan's Nursery. Quinlan said with luck and water and a protective casing the tree might make it, and not need to wait till spring, and in any case there'd be a guarantee. October was still fine for planting, but November might be touch and go. "You plant a hundred-dollar tree in a ten-dollar hole," said Quinlan, "and it's a ten-dollar tree. The way I see it. You plant a ten-dollar tree in a hundred-dollar hole, and it turns out fine. I guarantee this beauty: dig her deep."

He followed those instructions. He chose a sunny swatch of lawn thirty feet from the Toy House, and dug. He fertilized and soaked the spruce, then banked it with peat moss and hay; he covered it after the snow. The winter proved hard. The tree's blue spikes lost resilience and went brown. He tended it continually, banking it with hay and dreaming that when spring arrived at last it might have proved successful. It did not. The spruce was blighted, sere; he could not coax it to life. So he went back to Quinlan's and exercised the guarantee for a replacement. Jane was too young to notice and would anyhow not care; Maggie would have noticed but had not been in the garden. In the same spot, laboriously, Ian planted the substitute spruce, using a pickax to enlarge the hole, then dropping totems in: a silver dollar, a daguerreotype of Peacock's face, and a penciled unsigned note to Jane that read: "I love you. Flourish." This tree grew.

A Greek Revival house at the property's edge had been intended as a wedding gift for Peacock's younger daughter. But Anne-Maria married a missionary and did not return to Vermont. Ian spent months renovating the place, sleeping in it from time to time with Sally Conover, but there too his interest waned. He had been boarding up windows when Jeanne tapped his shoulder. He turned; he had nails in his teeth.

"I didn't mean to startle you."

He spat the nails into his palm. It was early April.

"I was out walking," Jeanne said. "And I heard this hammering . . ."

He wiped his face with his shirt. He hooked the hammer in his work belt and replaced the nails. "Welcome," Ian said. "You walk this way often?"

"Not often."

"My house is your house," he said. "Would you like to see it?"

"Please . . ."

He showed her through the empty rooms, their vacancy reproachful and the sun blocked out. He had sanded the floors but not sealed them, so they took off their shoes. She praised his carpentry, the turnings on the banister, and he said he had ten thumbs. In the upstairs east-facing bedroom, where light still shone because he had not boarded up the windows, she asked if this was where he'd planned his bed and if he needed one; she had an extra mattress. It was no use to her, she said, it only gathered dust.

"Would you be willing to share it?" he asked.

Her hesitation moved him. Smiling, she shut her eyes. There was a passionate demureness in the gesture. For an instant, watching her, he wondered what he'd gain and lose: if this game was worth the candle or he understood the rules.

"I thought you'd never ask," Jeanne said, and lifted his hand to her breast. They fell on each other, then to the floor, like starvelings after food.

Ian wrote a play for voices, a play for ventriloquist and dummy, and several play beginnings that faltered on the page. He had had, he claimed, an excellent first line. The curtain would go up and reveal three actors in a living room. They would clear their throats and fold their papers and cross and uncross their legs. No one, however, would speak. This has to continue, he said, past the point of anxiety on the audience's part; it must provoke boredom, then rage. It must continue till the customers rise and fill the aisles. Then an actor would put down his paper, shake his head, and say: "Well. We seem to have run out of things to say to one another."

He could not continue. He wrote a madman's monologue titled "The Twenty-Fifth Clock." This man sat in the center of a circle of clocks, each timed an hour previous to the sundial of its neighbor. By rotating on his chair coincident with the play's action, the actor could always face the same instant and claim to have annihilated time. An Orpheus clock known as Georgi came creakingly to life. "No one cares to sing about the sordidness of loss," it sang. "The self-deception of a backward look, and all the little bargainings of fear. I am Orpheus. I care." This lament, however, dissolved in a cacophony of cuckoo clocks, their works sprung and wheels clogged. The actor at scene's close was spinning counter-clockwise on his barstool in the dark.

He wrote a play about Pygmalion and Galatea in reverse. The sculptor so embraced his craft that every woman he approached became a Muse or artifact instead; his kiss turned flesh to stone. At a retrospective of his work, which transpired in the second act, the sculptor propositioned women at the Guggenheim. They clustered to the eight-foot-high anthracite phallus by the entrance desk. Stroking it, they murmured praise that pointed out the fruitful conjunction of aesthetics and pornography. Ian tried to write about injustice—those things that sent him to the streets when an undergraduate, and kept him on the road thereafter: poverty, repression, war, disease. But there his gift of mimicry felt forced; he could not write of revolution in the accents of belief.

He tried a play about a playwright trying to write plays; he wrote about himself as the prodigal son. He wrote a play for children, calling it *King Ed* and updating Oedipus; he tried an Orphic mystery with a grape-guzzling narrator that women tear apart. All these failed. He knew enough to know how poor his early efforts were, and to keep quiet about them. On his twenty-eighth birthday, however, while drinking scotch and soda with Maggie on the sleigh bed on the west-facing porch, he realized just how secretive he'd been. His mother did not know he wrote; he had not dared admit it. Whether this was shame or pride seemed unimportant somehow; he had accumulated nothing in the years away. They had been five-finger exercises; Ian clenched his fist. He studied the pattern his fingerprints made on the glass. He told her he would like to write, and she said, "Yes. Why not?"

Already she seemed inward-facing, barely able to muster attention for Jane's breakfast or a soiled crib sheet. Yet she had not been indifferent. Her "Why not?" acquiesced. Those family occasions where he had had to toast the guest, or write a birthday poem for his aunt, the years of magic shows or wild imagining occasioned by some steamer trunk, its lid sprung, costumes in profusion in the attic, where he was Wild Bill Hickock, Captain Marvel, then d'Artagnan in outfits worn to school—all these seemed sufficient preparation. Maggie assumed (with no lift in her eyebrow or hitch in her rocking motion) that he could do and be just what he'd care to: a Sherbrooke does not bite off more than Sherbrookes chew.

Her "Yes. Why not?" gave him his measure; it contained no shift of emphasis, no sudden assertion of change. She would have questioned, certainly, his decision to become an engineer or to take up golf. Yet this seemed foreordained. He bought a set of notebooks and began on the following day.

Jeanne was both his audience and critic; he met her at the Dry Goods Shoppe and helped her load the car. As a member of the Cooperative, she spent Tuesday afternoons behind the counter and stocking shelves. She had purchased beans and dried fruit and fabric and cheese; he handled the two bags.

"You want a family," she told him. "That's what you really want."

"No."

"Yes, you do. You can't marry your own mother, so you're after me."

He opened the car door, then placed the grocery bags on the floor.

"I'm serious," she said. "You want a family, lock, stock, and barrel; that way you'd be getting three of us for the price of one. A bargain."

"And in the neighborhood," said Ian. "You're right, it's an advantage."

She fumbled for her keys.

"I never did want to change diapers. It's simpler this way, isn't it?"

She put on dark glasses, bent, and entered the car.

"All that fuss and bother—formulas, midnight feedings. I'm doing it for

536

Maggie's child, so why get all involved with children of my own? Croup. Measles. Misery. Who *needs* it?"

"I'm sorry. You can stop now . . ."

"I was only getting started. School bills. Migraine. Nagging backache."

"I told you I'm sorry."

"I hear you," he said. "If you want to back off, just back off."

She looked up and over her glasses' black rim. "I have to go now."

"Right."

"Ian, I don't want to. It's that they're expecting me."

"Mm-mn."

"You're making it more difficult."

He did not answer, stepped away.

"When can I see you?" she asked.

"You'll find me. I'll be the one with baby powder in my buttonhole. Wearing a pink Dr. Denton's . . ."

Savagely she stepped on the accelerator. The car roared. She swung into traffic, not waiting. He walked along the river, past the covered bridge and sewage treatment plant. Then he broke into a run.

His subject was Judah, he knew. He had imagined his father for years, had tried to come to grips with just such proud constriction—the way that Judah drew a magic circle around the farm, saying thus far and no farther, then raise the roofbeam high. When Alan Whitely suggested that they use the carriage barn, he saw his father there. The image was corporeal, flesh dense with blood and bone. Judah turned in greeting, holding neat's-foot oil and rags; he had been working on the carriage rigging and the horses' tack. He lifted his free hand, hieratic, in a compound of menace and welcome that Ian saw as clearly as when last he'd seen it in fact. The gesture was silent, however. He had to muster the right language, to have those talks with Judah that their reticence denied. Judah bent back to his task. The leather was supple; the carriage rails gleamed. Light slanting through the barn seemed palpable and thick with dust; the smell of horses hovered in the empty stalls, and the zinc washing bin and brushes and the currycombs and pails awaited use. They had not been used in ten years. He watched his father stride through the clutter, then tried to make him speak.

This proved no easy task. His father was closemouthed, always had been, and Ian remembered no modulation; he remembered Judah muttering and then at shouting pitch. But his silence had been eloquent; it was action and example far more than speech. Some such character as Hattie could provide the background chatter as she did in Judah's life. She could be garrulous by contrast and deliver homilies that Ian had no trouble writing: incessant, homespun-glib. She would take the mailman or the plumber as her audience, if there were no family, and no friends arrived for a lunch date or bridge. Failing any audience, Hattie would talk to herself.

So Ian had two figures for his action. One figure spoke too little and the other spoke too much; he needed to disrupt their troubled lifelong truce. He turned their harmony to discord by introducing Maggie, though in the play he called her Jane. He filled two ledger books with notes. Early on, he found a title. He called it *The Green Mantle,* suggesting Edgar's speech in *Lear* and signaling the fecund rot that is the slime of algae on a stock pond with poor drainage. "Tom o' Bedlam" would eat frogs' legs and drink from this green standing pool—his inheritance suggested also by the title as a verdant passing-on of fields if not authority. The action had a grace note therefore of renewal in collapse; it augured generations as well as spring in fall. For weeks while he began to write, he carried with him heavily the weight of such pronouncements as "Nothing comes of nothing," or "Never, never, never, never, never," and "Still through the hawthorn blows the cold wind."

Jeanne asked him to show her the play. He told her he needed more time. It was, of course, his own absent presence he tried to imagine—his role in this drama as other than author, and what they argued over when he was not home to listen. He saw Judah as a warrior preparing his own bier. He ringed himself with hay and cattle, sticks and leaves and logs. His armor and favorite objects and women were arrayed in order of importance so the best would be the last to burn; he scrambled up on this improvised pyre at the first-act curtain and stretched out on top. He scratched at his armpit; he sniffed. Judah looked out at the audience with a queer cunning, lighting matches, waiting as the suicide so often waits for someone to shout "Stop!"

The next time they met he was contrite. Jeanne found him by the sugarhouse; he had been stacking wood. "I'm stuck here," Ian said. "I've been feeling sorry for myself, that's all. I shouldn't take it out on you."

"I started it."

He waved a birch log at her like a peeling plump baton.

"Escape," she said. "That's what you mean to me also, I suppose." Jeanne smiled. She gave him a letter. "Is this what you're after?" she asked. The Sage City Players were grateful for free access to the carriage barn and wanted to convey their thanks to Mrs. Margaret Sherbrooke and Mr. Ian Sherbrooke for the community spirit involved in such an offer. The production of *Desire Under the Elms* had had to be postponed due to the unforeseen absence of Alan Whitely. He had been offered a summer stock role in Falmouth, and therefore the company was temporarily without its president and leading man—but she, as the group's treasurer, was confident she spoke for everyone when signing this testimonial; they hoped to take advantage of his offer at some future date.

"Thank you," Ian said. "Has Miles seen this?"

"No. Why?"

"Because he wants the place shut down. The highway lobby . . ."

"Look!" Jeanne pointed to the west. A hawk was wheeling, gliding; it plummeted. The sky was white. She shuddered, touched his arm. They stepped inside the sugarhouse. He closed the door and drew her into the sweet-smelling darkness, then down.

The second act came easily. It was a magic interlude, or meant to seem as such. In the first act the action had been plausible—a little daily round of life in one old man's set circle. Yet language was at odds with gesture:

Hattie's chatter, Judah's silence, the descriptive couplets and archaic rhetoric all had been extreme. Now the action went balletic while the diction became that of everyday discourse. Judah climbed down from the hayloft cursing, scaring witnesses, the barn roof had leaked and a section of prime hay had spoiled. The hay that he'd figured for feed in midwinter would prove to be bedding at best; he found six-packs of beer in the eaves.

And now these creatures moved as they had sent him hopping when a boy. Judah, Hattie, Maggie (who would dominate the second act, whose agony was its subject as she tried to mediate between her dying husband and sister-in-law self-appointed as nurse) became real. He wrote a scene with the five senses figured forth in deprivation: the clear-sighted man going blind, the keen-nosed one who lost his sense of smell, the musician who went deaf. She who prided herself upon her sense of taste lost her taste buds utterly; she who had great tactile skill went heavy-fingered and slow. Together they comprised the senseless individual.

This dance took place in silence while Judah spoke downstage. He had been honing an ax. He accused his wife of making it with stablehands, of getting locked in the First Congregational Church with the minister, then taking on all four members of a string quartet during intermission at their concert. He repeated this list of betrayals. It did not devalue Maggie nor make her the butt of some joke. The second time through, it was clear that Judah gave no credit to such rumors; his was a boastful litany that praised her foxy worth. There was a shaving mirror by the sink. He pulled it from its nail and studied himself, stage center, patting at his jowls the way a barber might. He muttered to himself, inaudible. His wife gained added value from her value in men's eyes. He felt the ax-blade's edge. He sank to his knees and said, "Love."

Love was not a word to trust. It was too easy, too often abused, a substitute for lust or amity or even loving-kindness. Ian had experienced these things. He had known puppy love and had made love and, when forgetful of their names, called semi-strangers "love." Yet the word's proper usage came hard. Maggie and Judah had known love, perhaps, and he felt untrammeled love for Jane, Because of his face and his money and a certain athletic insistence in sex, he had heard several women use the term. Once a woman chanted "I love you" with such abandon, writhing, that Ian gathered up his clothes and left. They had met at a party three hours before and would not meet again.

Love is a passion, he wrote, a weak-kneed knowledge that the earth is tilting and the world well lost. It is a bordering, protective solitude, a hunger and invasion, a series of clichés. It manifests itself in several ways: Jeanne became the pursuer pursued. Walking past her house—on the corner of North and School Streets—he listened to her play the flute like an enchantress warming up. She was always waiting for him, always the first to arrive. She had to juggle errands and appointments and cover her tracks, while he had the whole day. He watched her with her children; the girls were six years old, she had been married for eight. They made a unity from which he knew himself excluded. They could display open affection, and such a display (Amy holding to Jeanne's knee, her brown head buried in the bend of it, one brown eye staring out) was denied him. He imagined her house in the mornings—with the twins at their mother's side and Miles already occupied, preoccupied, suited up for the day's work. He listened to Jean-Pierre Rampal endlessly in the Big House music room, wearing Maggie's patience thin and needing to replace the needle on the phonograph. Jeanne insisted he keep her secret, and the measure of insistence was how he measured distance; she would not leave her husband for the interloper, him.

This was so clear that they rarely discussed it. She apportioned him his time like some efficient allocations clerk. The truth of all those walks, he claimed, was she had to fix it with the babysitter first. She was busy tending to her family or guests. Jeanne appeared hedged in by need; her husband needed her and the children needed her and he, Ian, was an indulgence— her private neediness administering to itself. She who made their beds wanted every other afternoon to lie out in a clearing, on the blanket of his clothes. Returning from the PTA when the weather changed again, she required the seat of the Packard, or the hayloft when it snowed.

For seven months they did not see each other. He completed the play. Then, as if without interruption, they met and coupled again. He tracked her footsteps after rain and wanted to carve their initials on trees. Miles wrote and printed anonymous Letters to the Editor about the Big House boondoggle, and how the National Landmarks Commission wouldn't know a landmark if it ran aground on Plymouth Rock. He wrote signed editorials that weighed the pros and cons, and—during the months that Jeanne stayed away—came down on the side of the safeguards in Section 106. Ian guessed she was an ardent partner to her husband also, that their afternoon encounters enkindled her for night. Or that she separated out devotion, as he himself had learned to separate the roles of brother, lover, son. "Like cream from milk," he complained.

"It's the reason that you stand for this. You never hear me slam the dishes. Or scream."

"Or snore."

"I don't do that." She seemed half hurt, and he realized again how precarious was the esteem between them, how taut-stretched the tightrope they walked. "I was only thinking of an actual bed," he said. "One whole night together. It's a fantasy."

"Oh, Ian, dream it true." Her eyes were wide, voice soft. Yet for all Jeanne's seeming pliancy, he knew, she'd leave within five minutes of the time she'd planned to leave. She was using him, he said, like a liberated woman run amok.

"I'm not," she said.

"Of course you are."

"Not using you," Jeanne said. "Not liberated enough."

"Amen to that."

She pecked him on the cheek. She said, "If I don't go, the children will be home before me," and was gone. He did leg-raisers, watching the sky.

The third act brought him home. Ian wrote the scenes with fluency, hearing how his father and his mother made their peace. They discovered this was fragile because the world went mad. Their son was killed in Laos—or so the telegram said. Judah's first child, from his first marriage, had been killed at Anzio, and such recurrence broke him; he painted the barn door a havoc of colors and then produced a rope. He worked with an old man's shuffling persistence, fashioning a noose and using the hayloft's block and tackle and a ladder as scaffold; he stood on the ladder's third rung, staring over fields that he in delirium took to be beachheads, while with jerky puppet-like gestures he urged his babies on.

Then Maggie in her youthful guise appeared. She told him to come on in by the fire, he'd catch his death of cold. She said she needed charity, but he had none to spare. She said she needed comforting; he railed at her for the delusion that there was comfort to give. He'd lived to see his first son die, and then she came along and picked up the pieces and patched them together and made him a second son in her guileful image. He would not be beguiled. He had had enough of it; the world was bereft of all reason; it killed his second boy as it had killed his first. And what was left to live for, Judah said, was not worth having; it was by-your-leave and thank-you-ma'am and a jar of cold cream for Job's boils.

She pleaded with him, piteous, but he was deaf to entreaty; a hangman's noose has thirteen knots, he said, and he was busy tying them, she needn't hang around. Her pity turned to anger and, soon enough, a kind of scorn. She said that he was selfish, every suicide was selfish, it was grandstanding, the easy way out, it left the survivors to muddle along with their shame in the town's eyes, and guilt. If he used that rope, she warned, he shouldn't plan to have her cut him loose. She washed her hands of all such death-in-life.

Judah stood irresolute. He said that she was shaming him, twisting what she called his weakness the way she twisted everything and him around her little finger. He told her to go back inside. She would not leave. They bickered at each other as if over coffee, and how hot or strong to serve it in which cups. It was not serious. It was vaguely comical, as if Judah threatened suicide each time his will was crossed. This bickering continued while Ian walked on stage. He carried a duffel bag, limping, then sat on the duffel and unlaced his boots. They took no notice of him till he lit his corncob pipe.

Maggie did not seem surprised. She threw up her hands; "Oh, you're impossible," she said, then turned to Ian and said they should drive to New York.

He had not been killed, of course. The news of his death was some bureaucrat's error, he had been wounded slightly and sent home on leave. They questioned him; he temporized. He had shot himself in the left knee. What did it matter? he asked; what mattered was he'd come back home alive. He asked about the dairy herd, naming the cows with tenderness, asking which cow had freshened and what was the milk yield and what was for supper that night. He was so hungry, Ian declared, he could eat a horse.

Judah studied him. Maggie did not seem to mind, was kneeling beside him and stroking his hair, saying, "Baby, baby," while he smoked. "A dishonorable discharge?" Judah asked. "You might call it that," Ian said. "What would *you* call it?" Judah asked. Ian said he'd just as soon not name its name but let sleeping dogs lie and bygones be bygones; what mattered was the prodigal come home to stay and the three of them could learn to laugh, making everything up to each other for all those years apart. "They did their best to slaughter me," he said. "But I made it anyhow. Let's celebrate the world."

Jeanne met him in the carriage barn. She wore wooden clogs that resounded, and her skirt was long, with a pink fringe. He told her how Jane that morning had given up her bottle, saying bottles were for babies, but could she keep just one for her play kitchen when she needed it? Jeanne put her fingers on his cheek and splayed them there. "Don't worry."

"No."

"I tell myself two things."

"What are they?"

"First, that I'll get over you. Not right away, of course, but in twenty years or so. And, second, you don't mean to hurt me."

"No."

The hand that rested on his cheek had weight; she let it drop. "I'm indecisive, Ian, is that such a crime?"

"No. And you're not indecisive. You want two things at once, that's all."

"You too," she said. "You too."

"I'm simplicity itself," he said. "I want you to leave Miles."

He had not said this before. He had not planned to say it, but knew it for the truth. "That's what I want," he repeated.

Her eyes were wide in the scant light. They had the largest proportion of pupil to iris, he thought, of any eyes he'd seen. "Do you mean that?"

"I do."

"I'm older than you are, remember? I have two children and one husband who won't want a divorce."

"Do you?"

"That isn't the point. It's called desertion. If I left him, we'd all have to leave."

"All right."

"We couldn't live here." She raised her arm, embracing air, and indicated the barn. "Not now."

"I've left before, I can do it again."

"Yes."

"Just think about it," Ian said.

"I think about it all the time."

He placed his hands on her breasts. She did not move toward him but did not move away. The barn seemed peopled suddenly with Maggie and Jane and the twins and their bags; a porter approached. The floor was a platform, the carriage a train, but Ian could not say for certain if the scene he witnessed were composed for greeting or farewell. "I think about it every day," she said again. "Ask me what I think about, and there isn't anything else." The space felt vast, echoic, and he could hear mice scurry in the walls.

Hattie entered in the final scene. She carried a whisk broom and mop. But she dropped her cleaning implements—seeing the rope at Ian's neck, his mother in an attitude of mourning, and the block-and-tackle feeding line while Judah hauled. She advanced on her brother, fists on her hips. She scolded him for being a tease, for playing with rope as he used to with fire. If he knew what was good for him, he'd put that noose away.

The quartet that followed took some time to write. Ian knew his play depended on the final scene, and the disjunctive modes of it had here to be combined. He sounded his various themes. It was not to be a play about a single family within a single corner of New England. It was to be—or fail in trying—a tone poem celebrating constancy, the age-old song of ageless-ness in youth. Therefore these legacies: this paved and fenced dominion where the wilderness was sumac, where trash trees and raspberry bushes ran wild. Therefore these legators, who thought that they could keep possession by not giving and yet gave. When Judah bent to place the noose around his, Ian's, neck, he did so almost tenderly, as if his son were sculpture of inestimable worth. Maggie's eyes were marbles; they rolled along the sockets of her skull.

He wearied of this soon enough and tore up the first draft. The sonority and rhetoric was, after all, mere sound. He scored this last scene several times, conceiving of the voices as stringed instruments. He knew no one would notice and did not want them to—but wrote it that way anyhow in order to distinguish Hattie's querulous treble from Judah's bass. The four spoke contrapuntally; they took up a figure and phrased it, and though intonation differed the phrasing was the same. Vermont was earthly paradise, and progress the snake in the grass; Vermont was a fool's paradise, and progress that four-lane highway; there was nothing wild enough to tame.

Ian confronted his father. He wrote the recognition scene he had returned too late to play. They quarreled over roots. Judah said without a taproot any tree will topple in the first important wind. Ian said that's fearful, it's an argument for constancy that takes no note of change. Judah said the only trees worth mentioning are those that last, the almond tree, black walnut, oak; and Ian said it's a question of what kind of growth we're discussing. This century began before the motorcar or airplane or the Zenith

Chromacolor II television set. It started when intrepid men might span in a season's hard traveling the distance a satellite shows on the six o'clock national news. The man who hears that news while driving from the World Trade Center to his home in Katonah will girdle the globe just commuting this business year—in what way, Ian asked, should radical deracination come as such a shock?

Big talk, big talk, said Judah, the more things change the more they stay the same. They say a baby whale's six foot by fourteen; you want a preachment, Ian, that's what I'll teach you to preach. You start out big you stay that way, since those that have shall get. And them that's not shall lose.

Jeanne's face in animation was a face he could not scan; it was too mobile, a quicksilver series, five women, in one that he watched. Miles went salmon fishing for a week, and Jeanne deposited the twins with her sister-in-law in Dorset, saying that an old school friend was dying in New Haven. She met Ian in Manchester Center, and they drove across New Hampshire into Maine. There was constraint between them, a taut expectancy. He drove with his hand on her knee; she covered his hand with her own. She told him that she'd first met Miles when they were both eighteen. He'd been a wonderful dancer, she said, he'd swept her off her feet at Comus; he'd been visiting New Orleans since Jeanne's brother was his roommate, and they both flew down from Dartmouth for the ball. She remembered to this day the way he looked in evening clothes, a bouquet of white roses in his fist. It was that image she'd married, she said: his slicked-down sandy hair, his praise for Lyndon Johnson as the great conciliator, and how he wore his raincoat like a cape.

They married five years later, when Miles was graduated from journalism school. Both of them dreamed in those first years of foreign postings for UPI or *Time* or *The New York Times*; they would live in Lagos or Rio de Janeiro or Hong Kong—anywhere out of this world. Jeanne pictured herself serving tea, or riding through a game preserve,

or making servants happy in the scrubbed and newly painted compound back behind the house. They settled for this small-town post
as if it would be temporary—bought the house and had the twins as if
merely marking time.

She didn't mean, she said, the twins were unimportant. She'd wanted a
child more than anything, she loved them more than anything. With every
year and change in them she loved them all the more, her fledglings about
to take wing. But Kathryn had been born with a dislocated hip. She spent
the first four months in a cast, and Jeanne remembered feeding them—the
one so light, the other so heavy with plaster—and feeling how she'd caged
herself, was body-bound, how the tropics or the Orient were dreams she
must defer.

Miles had been helpful, of course. He was a devoted husband and father;
he wanted what was best for them, insisting what he wanted most was just
her satisfaction. She fell out of love with him when they were twenty-eight.
It had not been fair. She stayed at home all day all week, imprisoned by a
pair of Barbie-doll enthusiasts; she cooked and cleaned and dressed and
washed and dealt with them continually. Yet when Miles arrived for dinner, striding through the foyer like a guest in his own house, they fled toward their father like hostages set free. He grew sideburns, then a paunch.
He took long scalding showers, using all the tank's hot water, and did not
unclog the drain. She knew these things were trivial; she felt disloyal telling him that was how love died. Love faded like the last light of the sunset
on Kowloon she would never see except in travel posters; it disappeared
like panthers from the edges of a water hole where some other someone's
husband advanced in order to take photographs. It scattered and grew
separate like a pair of growing twins.

They reached Mount Desert Island in the dark. They registered as man
and wife, then walked along the harbor streets until they found a restaurant. They entered and ordered and ate. The lobsters were ready for molt-
ing; he told her how he'd watched them molt and how, with their shells
shucked, they were lighter than the water and would rise. "That's when

they make the best eating," Ian said. "For fish, at any rate. And it's the same with soft-shelled crabs; you catch them while they shed."

The waitress had tied napkins to their necks; the napkins bore the legend "Lobster-in-the-Ruff." Two lobsters shook claws across Jeanne's breasts; she accepted her bib the way a child might, poutingly. They ate baked potatoes and salad and drank bitter white wine. "Do you realize," Ian asked, "that this is our first date? I mean we've been having our—whatever we've been having—for nearly two years now. And we shared meals in public way back when. But it's the first time we've eaten alone since you asked me to your house for lunch." He dipped a claw in butter, cracked and sucked it while she watched.

She told him how at thirty she'd asked Miles for a divorce. He had been shocked, not suspicious. He'd asked her what was wrong and could she pinpoint and discuss it, so that he could have it fixed. He'd used that expression, Jeanne said, as if marriage were a faucet that required a new washer, or a car that needed lubrication every three thousand miles. She told him "have it fixed" was not a way to solve the problem, but proof of the problem itself: he rolled up his sleeves and consulted a maintenance book.

Miles had been baffled. His self-esteem was shaken, and it hurt her to see how he hurt. He'd asked if she were having an affair, and she answered him truthfully—this antedated Ian—"No." He'd asked if she would like to take a vacation, go somewhere without him, or go to a doctor, or maybe go to the movies more often. She told him that the trouble was pervasive, not particular, not something you get to have fixed. They had settled down together, but it was unsettling; it was Kansas she traversed. There was beauty in it, certainly, and much that was fruitful and rich. But looking out her kitchen window—past the geraniums in the window box and past the swing set, the sandbox, the hedge, past the white Congregational Church steeple all the way up to Mount Wayne—seeing the swatches of pine and rock and maple like a crazy quilt, then the sky like a bedspread and clouds like white tassels, she still saw the landscape of Kansas, only Kansas, an interminable flatness she was doomed to forever and ever.

Jeanne smiled. She emptied her glass. She'd been unfair to Miles, of course, not to mention Kansas. She had never visited the state and there was no reason to condemn it out of hand. But equity was not the question; landscape and weather and travel and doctors were not answers for her then. She could not explain it. She yielded when he pressed her and they stayed together for convenience's sake, and for the twins. It would have been absurd to go. She had nowhere to go, and nothing to go to, no reason for leaving she knew how to formulate: only Kansas, always Kansas, and the loss of joy.

That was, Jeanne said, when they met. That was when she came to dinner at the Conovers'. She had been unprepared. She had prepared herself for Samson Finney, for the old ladies and gossip and jostling and, since it was Friday and fresh seafood day at Morrisey's, for the shrimp remoulade. She had reconciled herself to Miles, and staying on. She concentrated on the twins' ballet, and the flute. There had been enough to do just cooking and cleaning and transplanting the geraniums; there was no room for restlessness if she re-papered the room.

She should not tell him this, Jeanne said, it was unladylike. It was not the way that thirty-year-old wives and mothers from New Orleans are trained and supposed to behave. But she had wanted him so badly when they said good night (he'd taken her coat from the closet, remember, his hands were on her shoulders while she fumbled for the sleeves) that she had nearly propositioned him right then and there in the Conovers' hall. He, Ian, was just back from wherever he'd been wandering, carrying his strangeness like a shield and the reserves of distance like a spear. Did he remember how Miles went ahead, was warming up the car? She could have fucked on the floor.

He ordered a second carafe. The lobster shells lay ransacked in the bowl between them; there was butter on her chin. He wet his napkin in the finger bowl, then wiped her chin and cheeks and lips. She submitted in silence; he tore her bib free. He put his fingers in the warm lemony water and touched her eyelids. "I love you," Ian said.

"I know."

"I love you very much."

"Yes."

"This isn't the end of that story."

"No."

"It's a beginning. We're beginning."

"Maybe." She kept her eyes closed but reached up for his wrist. Her fingers closed on his watchband; she squeezed. "I'm trying not to tell you more than you deserve to hear."

"Deserve?"

"Mm-mn. Some of what happened just happened. Some of it might well have happened anyhow. And some of this belongs to Miles, not you or us or me or anyone."

"He'll deal with it."

"I wasn't prepared. I'd planned on something else that night. I'd planned on being Mrs. Fisk and chatting with Samson Finney and the other guests and drinking two glasses of wine . . ."

The lights went out. There was a sudden gust of wind, a darkness all around them, and loud rain in the street. The waitress came with candles. She apologized. "Seems like there's always trouble with that power company. Seems like whenever it storms we get to watch it in the dark."

"It isn't a problem," Jeanne said. Her voice was high; it broke. She was crying, he saw, had been crying perhaps since the waitress arrived, was sitting in the candlelight with her eyes awash. He reached out his hand, but she pulled hers away. "Poor Miles," she said. "He doesn't deserve this. I'm going home."

"Now?"

"Tomorrow. First thing in the morning."

The waitress returned. Her name badge read Nancy; her nose had been broken and badly reset. She wore an Ace bandage on her right forearm; he asked for the bill. "You folks passing through?" she inquired. "Don't mind me asking but are you from Canada?"

"No."

"I could have swore it," she said. She returned to the counter. Jeanne stood. "We're going to argue," she said. "Let's not ever argue. I'll leave in the morning without you, if you'd rather. I could rent a car."

"We'll go together."

"Ian, I'm sorry," she said. "I didn't mean to act this way. I wanted to be free for you. I meant to be. I'm sorry."

He paid. Outside the moon was bright and the rain had ceased. They walked the length of the dock. He skirted the small puddles and listened to the harbor's noise—the clamor and whistling and racket of seabirds and clatter of buoys and boats. Their motel had a Coleman lantern as its only light. He fumbled with the lock. The door when it swung to was heavy; Jeanne entered behind him and, wordless, lay down on the bed. She kicked off her sandals and kept her legs crossed. He kissed her ten toes, then her knees.

Love: what Judah felt for Maggie in his bristling proud possessiveness and she in turn gave back to him unyieldingly, then yielding; what Peacock would call ownership as husbandry, then sumptuous thrift; what Anne-Maria and Joseph and the others of his family had called a kind of stewardship not sacred nor profane but proper to those who have holdings; what Hattie had deemed merely fitting and appropriate to Sherbrookes, a lifelong burden of behavior and expectation fulfilled; what he at his return had been unable to give Sally Conover and at first withheld from Jeanne—the glad renunciation of this separate thing, *Ian,* and the arithmetic of passion which, combining two, makes one—love became his subject then and had been all along.

He wrote a courtly scene. He made Judah and Maggie conjoin in a circle of fire, swearing fealty while villagers watched. He had them meet by accident—the woman knocking on a door in order to gain entry and an escort through dark woods. He composed this scene several times, transposing it to Europe and varying their ages and casting the encounter in the several lights of amity, suspicion, or lust. The complicating factor in romance was marriage, and he wrote of that repeatedly also. In one draft: Maggie married someone else, and her need for Judah was illicit, entailing divorce. In one draft she was pledged elsewhere but married to Judah instead. In the third draft she was muddleheaded, trying to make up her mind. The task was how to reconcile fidelity with freedom, to enter in the tournament unpledged. The problem was how best to keep a keen-edged sense of chivalry when lists were laundry lists. Maggie had ten white handkerchiefs; she waved them with abandon while the warriors preened. One handkerchief was knotted to each finger, and she waved them as extensions of her hands.

So Jeanne seemed unattainable, though the physical fact of attainment happened early on. He battered at her ceaselessly. There was distance that he sought to bridge, an inward reticence that had nothing to do with restraint. The sex was unrestrained. What he wanted to demolish was her self-regarding separate self, and it was long until he learned such demolition works both ways—that boundaries once crossed are boundaries erased.

They drove that autumn to the roadbed for Route 7. Following the Old East Road past Matteson's, he came to road signs reading: CONSTRUCTION AHEAD, ½ MILE. Ian parked his pickup on the road's dirt shoulder. There were power lines. Jeanne descended lightly, unafraid; if someone recognized them, she would say they were scouting locations for next season's children's play. She had explained this to Miles and packed a picnic lunch. They walked past a trailer with a placard that read: PUBLIC WORKS. It was a Saturday, and therefore the site was abandoned; there were yellow trucks parked in rows. They followed the construction path up over a small rise.

It had been raining all week. The access road was mud. As the slope increased, however, the roadbed grew firm; the tractor tracks seemed baked brick-hard, and the drainage worked. They crested the first hill. The view was immense: Green Mountains in the hazy distance, a rainbow of maple and oak in the valley beneath them, barns positioned to the west like pins where meadows intersected like green sheets of paper. There were cumulus clouds. Crows flew. A mile or so down this east slope they were constructing a bridge; cranes flanked the space like sentinels. A conduit stood ready for assembly to their left.

A dog barked. Ian looked for it; it barked three times, then ceased. Beneath them, on a transverse path, a girl on a bicycle weaved into sight. She pedaled effortfully through the mud. They waved, but she did not look up. Bears hibernate, he said to Jeanne—or so his father used to say—in the ruined Glastonbury Inn; they sit in every single chair and sleep in all the beds. They got charcoal pits for smelting there, Judah said; this town required that mountain. We'll go up and get us a bear.

After some time, they settled in a clearing. Jeanne spread out a blanket, and they sat and ate. She had cold chicken in the hamper, and bread and hard-boiled eggs and fruit and cheese and wine. He talked to her about the play, about his dream of character that would not prove restrictive.

She lay back, adjusting her skirt. The gesture was domestic, practiced, a single swift twist of her hips. Her black hair had leaves in it; he plucked them loose. He spread his arms. The clouds between the sun and Woodford Mountain made patterns on the slope's green surface; their shadows moved like whales. "The peaceable kingdom," he said.

"You make me want to live with you. It does feel right."

"More than that. It feels complete."

"I'm happy. You do make me happy." Jeanne emptied the bottle. She added ice. The wide-necked thermos had a picture of a boat at anchor. "I wish it could go on like this."

"I love you," Ian said.

She made no answer, swallowing.

"This isn't working, is it?" Ian asked.

"No."

"Why not?"

She shook her head. Averted, it was once again a dark medallion—minted in a foreign land, a currency he could not translate into use. "I stopped that road," he said. "From going through our property, at any rate. But it's still being built. It makes no difference, does it, that I want you to leave Miles?"

"It does," she said. "But not enough. Not yet."

The road became an ocher strip, then crested a hill and was lost.

He saw her two days later at the County Fair. Sheriff Joe was demonstrating how to split a bullet on a knife-edge and pop two balloons at once. Then, wearing a black blindfold, he held his rifle upside down and still punctured a balloon. After each trick his wife held up a piece of paper with one bullet hole to prove he wasn't using scatter shot; she broke the bottle whose cap he shot off to prove that the bottle was glass. There was a stall purporting to show the world's largest steer—"Ten Thousand Hamburgers *Alive!* On the Hoof!" A wire cage held rattlesnakes, with cows' skulls and tumbleweed blown all the way from the Old West; for seventy-five cents you could fish five minutes in a trout tank and keep whatever you caught.

He wandered past the Swimming Pool Display. There were tractors for sale, and whirlpool baths, and chances on a brand-new Mustang; three Hondas would be sold to any single customer for the price of two. There were portrait painters and photographers and fortune-tellers on the midway; at four o'clock a demonstration of dressage was scheduled for the stock-car track. Men waved at him, a man alone, to try his luck at ringtoss and at basketball; he shot six electrified geese. He hit them on their beaks so that they squawked and fell. Men hawked kazoos and key chains and T-shirts reading "Dung's Deli" and "Disco Sucks." They sold balloons and food and hats, he bought a cowboy hat for Jane, and a leash that clamped on air and was called "The Invisible Dog."

While he was receiving change, Jeanne touched his arm. "Hello."

He pivoted.

She offered him a Sno-Kone. "That's Amy over there," she said. "Behind the cotton candy."

"Amy. Kathryn. How are you?"

"We get to spend two dollars," Kathryn said. "We get treats."

"Two rides on the carousel," said Jeanne. "One upset stomach from a pizza, and a Kewpie doll."

"Have you been here long?"

"Not long," she said. "A year or so. You came alone?"

He showed her the hat. "Jane's too young."

"There's animals," said Amy. "Off in that direction. And a girl I know won first prize in the 4-H eggplant contest."

"And Debbie Korey's goat got second place," said Kathryn.

"It did not."

"Did too!"

"What's so good about just *second* place?" Amy put her head back and twirled the cotton candy like a majorette. The pink concoction remained on its stick. She stuck out her tongue.

"Is your father with you?"

"It's Monday," Jeanne said. "No."

"Could I treat you to the Ferris wheel?"

The twins jumped up and down. In their first display of unison, they clamored to be taken; "Mommy, *please*," they said. Jeanne was wearing a white scarf. She wore white sailor pants and an azure tank top. "It won't kill you, lady," said the man who had sold him the leash. As if they were a family, they walked to the Ferris-wheel gate.

In the ensuing minutes, Ian thought several things. While he paid and escorted and fastened them in, he thought how he was buying time, how time itself was purchased by the woman at his side—Jeanne looking so much younger than her peers at the concession stands, so much the bright beginner still—how as they settled back and joked about the cage and bar and bench, the girls half fearful and then wholly so with the permission to clap hands and scream, how as the world turned upside down she reached for him, the rush of wind and roar of equipment providing, somehow, privacy—saw in that reaching instant cotton candy on the seat, the glint of copper in the fold of Amy's left penny loafer, a Pentel heart and telephone number complete with area code on the bench beside him, the legend claiming "Samantha Sucks," greenhouses in the distance and the meadows full of cars, a Coca-Cola van unloading crates, the shins and stalls beneath them gone kaleidoscopic, with himself the turning lens—thought, *This is the woman whose life is my life, joy my joy.* At the top of the circle, she called out his name. They hung there poised, suspended, and then dropped.

"Mommy, you were crying," Amy said.

"Not really."

"Yes, you were."

"I got something in my eye."

"Did you two like the ride?" asked Ian.

"Yes."

"Say thank you," Jeanne instructed them.

"Thank you."

Kathryn shook his hand. "Thank you, Mr. Sherbrooke."

"Ian. You're welcome," he said.

"We have to go now."

"Do you? There's a lumberjack who was the world champion. He's putting on a show in twenty minutes."

"We have to," Jeanne repeated. "It was excellent to see you. Good-bye."

She adjusted her handbag and turned. She walked between the twins and guided them toward the exit gate. He watched them till they disappeared, then made his own way to the lumberjack. A tree had been stripped of its bark. A fat man in a red shirt sliced a piece of paper with his ax. "People often ask me," the man announced, "if I can shave with this ax. Well, you can't see me shaving, so I just want to show you all how fine this ax can cut."

When *The Green Mantle* was finished, he sent it to New York. Apollonius Banos, the theatrical impresario, had been his roommate at Harvard, and they had kept in touch. Apollonius would claim to be in Ian's debt. "I owe you, buddy," he had said the last time they met. He lowered his head and raised his eyes and gave his upward-staring glare, his chest hair curled out of his shirt.

Banos used to say he had the dirtiest act in Adams House; it got the little ladies where they lived. He had majored in Social Relations, and he had a theory that Harvard was a whorehouse purporting to be something else. "Put ten thousand young adults in the same place, and what do you have?" he would ask, going falsetto on "young adults." "Faggotry, careerism, and the biggest gang bang in Boston."

He quoted Miller and Donleavy and *The Story of O*; he doused himself with musk oil and wore a jockstrap over his pants. It was his ambition, Lon said, to make it with more Radcliffe girls than any previous Soc. Rel. student in the major's history; he kept statistics on the wall above his bed. It was more than just an ambition, he said, it was a mission and jihad; it was Cabrini Boulevard's revenge on Central Park West.

Molly Benson came from Ipswich and was shocked at Lon's insistence. "It's not that I mind the idea," she would confide to Ian. "Don't get me wrong. But all that leather and garlic . . ." She tossed her yellow mane at Lon and told him to get lost; she said he never gave himself wholly, but was a dog marking trees. They had raucous arguments, and Ian as the witness would be implored to judge.

Apollonius came from a family of furriers. "That means," he confessed, "it's cut and stitch, it's warehouse time in Washington Heights," He worked holidays and summers in a pizza parlor, and attended Harvard on full scholarship; he was determined, he told Ian one evening—when Molly was in Widener, preparing for her orals—to marry rich. "It's the sexual revolution, right, so why not get paid for the pleasure?" He did his Tambo imitation. "I'se *tired* of licking hind tit."

Lon was magnetic, Molly said; he was an evil flower in the cultivated garden. But his problem was he didn't know, for instance, she'd just cited Baudelaire and Voltaire. He knew Kluckhohn and Erikson, perhaps, but did not know French. "Evil Flower" derived from *Fleurs du Mal,* and "cultivate your garden" was a phrase out of *Candide*; she knew more about Homer and Apollonius of Rhodes than his Greek family had ever known; she hated feta cheese. She despised retsina wine and that ridiculous deposed king so proud of his karate and Scandinavian wife; the language was boring to study, boring to listen to, boring to read. "Worry beads and olive oil and fascism," she'd say. "That's what you offer, and it just isn't enough."

They married, however, over her family's objections and two days after Commencement. Ian served as the best man. Her father took Ian aside and said, "I don't mind telling you. I wish it wasn't happening. But we'll make the best of a bad business, and what I want from you is a phone call if anything goes wrong. Her own inheritance," he said. "That's what's the trouble, right? My Molly." Mr. Benson shook his head and drove north to Ipswich, refusing champagne. Ian stood on the steps of Memorial Church, surveying Harvard Yard and all he would relinquish, not envying Lon's cupidity but envying the sweet sad look that Molly gave as she raised her veil and let him kiss her; when Ian left Cambridge, thereafter, he left no forwarding address.

In Rome he got a postcard, at American Express. "Wish you wuz here, fella. You and me and baby making three. I'm working for her old man now and on my way. C. U. Soon." In Kabul he got a letter from Molly, saying how much they both missed him, how very little laughter there seemed to be these days; in Delhi he received a telegram from Mr. Benson, saying they sought an annulment—and would he make a deposition at the Embassy?

The grounds were nonconsummation, Mr. Benson said. Apollonius was impotent—or would be once the lawyers had got through with him. Molly was hysterical, sitting by her father's side, and when she spoke to Ian all she could manage to say was, "I don't want to see you. Don't come." Ian waited by the phone in Delhi, trying to distinguish the sound of her breathing from static, trying to determine if she needed him or needed him gone.

He drove to visit her in Ipswich as soon as he returned. The Benson house was set back from a feeder road for Crane's Beach; he and Molly walked there, in a November rain. Her mother had not wanted them to go. "You'll catch a cold," she said. "On top of everything else."

"Please, Mom," said Molly. "It's all right."

"All right. But come back quickly, hear? And do please bundle up."

They left the house in silence. Her hair was cropped; her speech—they discussed the weather, his whereabouts since last they'd met, and college friends—was slow. Her body had thickened; she leaned on his arm. "It was awful," Molly said.

"We don't have to talk about it."

"Oh, but we do."

He kicked a stone; his shoes were wet.

"We have to," Molly said. "It was awful. What he did. What he was doing . . ."

"Who? Lon?"

"My father says"—she said, as if reciting—"that he was lucky to stay out of jail. Nobody else will hire him, if they know what's good for them. He's gone to Hollywood. It's oil and water, father says, our kind and his don't mix."

He turned to her, shocked. "Molly . . ."

"We're divorced," she said. "I should have married you. Oh, Ian—my parents don't know that, of course."

She leaned on him more heavily but focused on the ground. She moved inside her slicker like an animal at feeding time; her eyes avoided his. The rain increased. He had indeed imagined this blockish, glazed girl as his own lover once but shrank from Molly now. Whimpering, she stepped away. What shocked him most was not such shrinking but that he was also aroused—Ian felt drawn to this woman as he had not, earlier, to the golden senior on his roommate's bed.

"It was awful, awful, awful," Molly said.

"I wish you could tell me what happened."

"My father knows," she said. "I've gone bananas." She wriggled. "This is my banana boat."

"But Lon . . ."

"Ss-ssh!" She put her hand on his mouth. Then something curious happened. She rolled her eyes, stuck out her tongue, made a "cuckoo" sign at him, and winked. Her face settled into sane calm. It was as if she'd mimicked madness; he shared her secret, she seemed to be saying, they both could take a joke. A woman like herself would not lose equilibrium because of a husband like Lon.

Returning, they drank sherry. Mrs. Benson offered cheese. She hovered near them, then withdrew. "Your father will be home at six," she said to Molly. "He can stay for dinner, if he wants."

Ian thanked her and said no. There was a fire in the living room. Molly put on "Pages from the Notebook of Anna Magdalena Bach." "Do you still play?" she asked. He shook his head. "No pianos in the Hindu Kush, is that it?" Molly asked. She adjusted the volume, and paused. "You could have written," she said. The room felt like a cage; she stared at him, unseeing. An automatic light clicked on—he stepped toward her, stopped.

Then her uncertainty passed. She reminded Ian of the sherry served at Apthorp House, and how the first time that the three of them went to a football game together, Apollonius got falling-down drunk on port wine. She laughed with unaffected ease and kissed his cheek, departing, with what seemed like cool affection. He wanted to sleep with her then. She said, "If you see Banos-baby, tell him things are fine. Tell him I hope he makes millions, and everything's under control." She shut the door behind him, and watched him through the mullioned windows while he walked away. He left with this sense of shut doors: a chance missed, road not taken. Whatever message she was sending was one he would fail to convey.

For weeks that final winter, Jeanne avoided him. When he met her in the street, her smile seemed forced, voice loud. Her children had the German measles, and though better now than later it was still a worry—they never took turns being sick. It was simpler, she supposed, to nurse them both at once, but they took a lot of nursing and she, Jeanne, was out on her feet. The January blizzard hadn't helped. Miles needed the jeep just to get to the office, and her own car wouldn't start. She hoped he'd understand; she had lists of places to go and people to see and phone calls to return and groceries to buy, and it had just been the busiest month, she couldn't seem to find the time to do what needed doing with her friends.

Ian heard her out. He focused on her lips. When she faltered into silence, he kissed her. She withdrew—a startled sudden motion—and backed against the plate-glass window of the Automotive Accessory Shop. There was a sign that read: SNO-TIRE SALE 4 FOR 3! There were radial tires and snow tires forming a black igloo on the bench behind the window; there were tire irons and sets of wrenches and wreaths and leftover Christmas lights. He said, "Just being friendly. The holiday spirit. Good-bye."

Jeanne called him the next day. "I can't see you," she said. "But the girls are getting better, and I did want to talk."

"How are you?"

"Fine. Just fine. Terrific."

"I'm glad to hear it."

"No. You're not glad to hear it, and I'm not terrific. I'm frightened, Ian, it's falling apart."

"I didn't mean to frighten you." Jane came into the room, carrying her Sesame Street puzzle set.

"You did. You do. I don't know the rules of your game."

"I'll help you," Ian mouthed at Jane. She sat on the floor and upended the box, then turned the yellow cardboard shapes face up. "I don't know them either," he said to the phone. "It isn't a game."

"Not for me."

"I know that. I wanted to kiss you. I'm sorry."

"Don't apologize," Jeanne said. Her voice was flat, constricted, as if she had determined to erase all modulation. Jane sighed and, with a gesture copied from Maggie, scratched her hair above the ear. "Strangers kiss me all the time on Main Street, in full view."

"Ian?" Jane asked. She held up a corner piece, pointing. "Is this a square?"

He shook his head.

"Rectangle? A edge?"

"Look, can I call you back?"

"No."

"Happy New Year," he said. "There was mistletoe still hanging from the power line. You were standing under it."

"I wanted you to do it. I want to be able to, Ian. I can't."

"I know that," he answered and, saying it, knew it. "It isn't your fault. We did try." *So this is how it ends*, he thought, *this trouble with timing: good-bye.*

"All right," said Jeanne. "I'll stop."

"Yes. I'm glad the twins are better. Give them both my love."

"Thank you, I will. Give our best to your mother."

"I will."

An odd formality possessed him then, as if their reluctance to speak face-to-face was mannerly and apt. Had she stood in front of him, he would have kissed her hand. He kissed the receiver instead. "I have to go now," Ian said. "Big Bird requires fixing. Jane is working at it, but she's got his tail on backward."

"Good-bye."

"I lied about that mistletoe. Just one goddamn peck on the cheek. Just one kiss in public," he said. But Jeanne was hanging up, was telling him she loved him; he listened to the silence, then the hum. Jane had managed Bert, but Ernie was eluding her. She held up a piece of the puzzle, its shape a soft-edged star. He bent and touched her hair. "Is this a edge piece?" she asked.

When Apollonius wrote, it was to say he'd call. He was working on a series now about a shipwrecked boat with twenty chorus girls who'd been heading for a tryout at the Folies-Bergère. If Ian felt like coming down for consultation, sending in a script about the complications caused when, after their fourth month on the island, Suzy announces she's pregnant and needs a balanced diet and gets so dizzy in the morning she can hardly keep her halter on, why Ian was welcome to try. Lon himself was in the islands checking out locations and the local scene; his girl could do the limbo on a mattress all night long. *The Green Mantle* was at present with a pal of his who was very well connected with the Shubert Organization and the Public Theater; they'd be in touch with him soon. The problem was talent, Lon wrote; there's little enough in this town. You got a shred of talent and they call you Emperor; you shake it hard and fast enough and they call you Queen for a Day. The salutation—dictated but not signed—was their old college slogan: "Arse Gratia Artis. Go for it."

They had last met four years before, in New York. They had had lunch at Lutèce. Lon was buying, was being expansive, waving his snifter like a tankard. He had a winter tan. His hair was thinning and he'd grown a moustache; he wore a velvet shirt and leather pants and patent leather boots. Festooned with chains around his neck, he looked entirely Greek. The divorce had been easy, he said. All that talk about annulment was just talk. They could have carried it off in Italy maybe, or Chile, or someplace you can buy the Church, but any decent Catholic was fitted for an I.U.D. these days; it would take a team of fingerless blind men to call his wife a virgin. He, Lon, felt no bitterness about it and no bitterness toward them— but the marriage just didn't work out. Why not admit it instead of ignore it, he asked: that's the ostrich principle, that's what drove her crazy with her see-no-evil head in the sand and ass in the air up there wiggling, you can call it quits without calling God and the Pope as your witness, no wonder she lives in McLean's.

"McLean's?" Ian asked. "The hospital?"

Apollonius sighed. He took a cigar, then replaced it in his pigskin case, unlit. "That's where they've been keeping her. Last time it was Austen Riggs."

"I didn't know."

"Yes, you did."

"I guessed it."

"She told me you came by. To Ipswich."

"What else did she tell you?"

Apollonius extracted the cigar again. This time he bit the end and lit it. "Nothing."

"Nothing?"

"*Nada*. She asked to be remembered. She's getting better, they say." He smiled, showing teeth. "Afraid *I* don't see it." His signet ring was emerald, and the setting was intertwined snakes. "I'm thinking over nightclubs now. Atlantic City. Heading there this afternoon; you want to come along?"

You cross a line, thought Ian, and do not know you're crossing it but know you can't turn back; you sit three feet away from someone and the distance is unbridgeable, the past no sort of prelude and the intimacy fake. They dusted off their anecdotes and drank to them, revolving their shared memories like glasses in the light. They smacked their lips and smiled and toasted friendship, and Lon said several times, "I owe you. Don't forget it." Yet they were drinking dregs.

She came to him in dreams and was his constant witness, as though a man might fashion his own muse. Thirty-two years old, her shoulders settling forward with the added weight he placed on her, the albatross he joked he was, Jeanne played both mother and wife. He puzzled out fidelity. He knew that in his fashion he was replicating Judah's plight, repeating Maggie's wrangle with deceit. He did not want to lie. He wanted to take Miles aside and tell him, "Look, I love your wife. I want to marry her. It's not her fault, it's not your fault, it isn't mine. It's just the way things are."

But things were not that way, were ragged-edged instead. She occupied stage center in his play invisibly; there was no denouement. This did not change. They climaxed together each time they made love, but the climax solved nothing and slaked no desire. They stayed unsatisfied. He remembered his own first assessment of Jeanne: how she reveled in dissatisfaction, happy to think herself sad. She wanted what she could not keep as if by prearrangement, as if the only thing worth grasping would be out of reach. Ian knew what he was saying; it was his own behavior he described. At first he labeled it immeasurable longing and a romantic refusal to sell each other short; later he would call it childishness and petulance and just plain being spoiled.

He had no one to talk to but Jeanne. Secretive by habit, he had made no friends in town. He might have talked to Maggie but she listened only, always, to some inner echo and for Jane's insistent cry. She had no advice to give him or any attention to spare, and he kept his secret from her in something like reprisal for those months she would not name Jane's father's. So Ian and Jeanne rehearsed their affair like a scene. They discussed it all a dozen times, having nothing else to do as soon as their bodies broke apart in physical satiety and having nowhere else to go, no public place to visit or business to share. She blamed him for his restlessness; he blamed her for her ties. They agreed that they both were to blame.

Then Apollonius called. His voice was reedy, faraway; he was talking from St. Croix. After some minutes he said, "That title. Change it."

"What?"

"*The Green Mantle.* Shit. It maybe would sell tickets to a fireplace convention, or some faggot seminar for decorators, baby."

Ian paused. "Is there anything else?"

"Lie back and enjoy it." Lon laughed. "We said you were the only son of Arthur Miller, and your mother's Marilyn Monroe, and Tennessee has got the hots for everything you do to him. We're working on your uncle, David Rockefeller, for a contribution to production costs. You got an agent to handle this stuff?"

"No."

"Get one. You need one. You will."

They talked some minutes more. Apollonius was optimistic; the play would be produced. He promised, guaranteed it; what counted was talent, he said. He himself did not believe that undiscovered masterpieces lie around in some desk drawer in some hick town in the hills. No genius starves in a garret—talent will up and will out. It helps to have friends, understand; they pump a little hot air in and *up* goes the balloon. Ian was a lucky man; he was going for a joyride soon and ought to hold tight and hang on.

So strong a sense of the implausible was with him through the call that Ian barely listened. He thanked Lon and hoped they would meet soon again, and said he would buy the next lunch. He hung up and lit a cigar. He paced the kitchen, smoking, and asked himself how often he would need to learn the lesson that his world was not their world. Four years before—or six, or ten—he might have trusted what he heard and held his breath, expectant, waiting for the management of A.P.A. or someone from the Shubert office to come north. They would not find him anymore. He had traveled, standing still.

"I can't leave him," Jeanne announced. "I'm trying, but I can't."

"All right."

"The children . . ."

"You said 'him.' Miles."

"Don't be impatient," she said.

"Long calls," he said. "Long-distance calls. That's all I get these days."

"I'm just around the corner."

"Far enough."

In the ensuing silence he heard children in the room. Amy and Kathryn were shouting; he shifted the receiver so it nestled in his neck. Jeanne said, "I want to see you."

"Yes."

He would spend his life in this kitchen, he said, preparing meals and chatting with people whose lives were led elsewhere. He felt so full of pity for the figure in the pantry mirror—darkened and sent back to him by the glass pane above the sink—that he lifted his hands to deflect it. He laughed.

"I don't find this funny," she said.

"No."

"And I do want to see you again."

"Of course."

"We've said all this before," she said, "I just can't wipe away ten years. Or all those years before we were married—I've known him so much of my life."

"I understand," said Ian.

"Do you? Kathryn, *stop* that! Right now or you go to your room." Jeanne shifted pitch and returned to the phone. "I'm sorry," she said. "What were you saying?"

It occurred to Ian that the modulation for courtship was just as pat and standard as the one employed for children: with him her voice was soft and low, when scolding it went shrill. "We were discussing avoidance," he said. "And telephones. I can't romance Ma Bell."

"That's the reason I stay home."

"Agreed. We've been saying good-bye since we first said hello."

"Yes."

"Good-bye."

He imagined her with Miles. Miles picked his feet and picked his nose and did not clean the bathtub drain; Miles was getting corpulent and going no-where fast. Yet it had been no contest, never was. Ian played the handsome stranger in this script of his devising, but the home that he was welcome to would not be Jeanne's. He imagined her house; he peered at them through the calico curtains and eavesdropped when they woke. Miles made break-fast on the weekends, Ian knew, and they shared an English muffin. He preferred jam on his muffin, whereas Jeanne liked cheddar cheese. He but-tered their muffins, then spread his own section with jam. He used the same knife for her cheese, and the trace of raspberry on cheddar drove her wild; it had driven her wild now for years. She suggested remedies, since problems like these could be fixed. There were several ways. She could make the muffins as she made them every weekday; they could use separate knives. He could slice her cheese before he spread the jam. He could use a different sponge to clean the counter from the one he used for cutlery, he could separate the garbage so the paper bag for cans and paper would not get soaked and split. There was a plastic garbage bag and a separate garbage pail for everything that leaked.

Miles promised to reform. He would pay attention for days. But his habits were deeply ingrained and her remedies were not. Soon enough she'd clean the second pail or wash utensils twice or throw out her muffin section in a mild wildness that failed to persuade. He said they could afford two plastic garbage bags. They had two pails, and he saw no point in division; they did not have a compost heap, and everything was thrown together anyhow outside the house. He was forgetful, he admitted that. But the gesture was what counted, and the thought behind the gesture, and he offered her her breakfast out of kindness not unkindness; she should give him credit for the thought behind the deed. She gave him that. He liked his eggs over easy, and she liked them sunny-side up. She could not stand a broken yolk, and he preferred it sometimes or never seemed to mind. She liked her coffee weak and fresh; he liked his own so strong it tasted bitter.

Ian took his parka from the mud room and went out. The wind was high. It battered at him, freezing, and he made for the ruined burned barn. The charred stumps of beams had been stacked and lashed down; the tarpaulin that covered them was piled high with snow. Such opposition, Ian knew, was a domestic argument that argued domesticity; the Fisks would stay together while he remained apart. One doorframe was standing, though the section behind it was gone. The door itself was useless, tilting crazily from one sprung hinge; snow adhered. The structure gave on nothing. Ian wrote it down. He would reconstruct it. He walked through this door to the haymow that was and would be.

III

When Judah had been fifty-five, Maggie had been Ian's age, and Ian had been Jane's. But she was Judah's trophy wife, and if neighbors raised their eyebrows they did so in silence, or snickering. Tongues wagged, of course; she knows that. Yet there was half-respectful envy in the jokes about old Sherbrooke and his pretty city girl; September–May marriages are countenanced, and a widower will often take an ambitious youthful bride. Particularly if he's rich; particularly if he's powerful in town; particularly if he's been the local catch, that aging bachelor will be expected to be caught by some slip of a thing in a half-slip and heels. It's what they expect in these hills.

But Ian as her consort is the subject of suspicion. He settled in as might a young husband and father: doing the shopping, making supper, spending hours with Jane every day. Strangers would have thought them to be three generations, not two; that's why Maggie stays at home. She used to feel that way when Judah took Ian out to the fields—as if her presence between them was a function of biology, no other kind of need. She herself had been irrelevant, an instrument required so that Judah could have sons. He had denied this, of course. He pointed to his sister, how he'd lived alone for years, how he'd had no children before and not felt the need. He'd wanted her for reasons that had nothing to do with the making of sons, the way you pick a horse to ride and not as a broodmare.

"That's some compliment," she said. "You might find another example."

But Judah said he meant it as a compliment, and that's what she should hear. When their second son died of crib death and she was inconsolable, and life that was so joyful once seemed empty, hollow, tasting of tin, he said we have each other, we're a family of three. Ian had been Jane's age. The boy paid no attention and didn't much mind; soon enough the memory of Seth became, for him, like a memory of pet cats run over or dogs dying old—inextricably bound up with other memories of loss in a time of youthful gain.

Yet Maggie felt shunted aside. What went on between father and son wasn't pretty; they were at loggerheads often as not, and Ian disappeared for Judah's final years. Sometimes she thinks her boy will leave her also in the end, when she's old and homebound by necessity, not choice; it's in his blood. He'll prove the prodigal again, she tells him, wait and see.

Meantime however he is with her, an intervening male between the women of the house. He says he isn't leaving, and she says he mustn't think of it, he has to promise not to, ever; calm yourself, he says. She musters a semblance of calm. She says all right, I didn't mean to worry you, let's open the house to the public—some kindly handsome stranger will no doubt come along.

Maggie steps into her skirt. She examines herself in the mirror. One thing about anxiety, she thinks; it's caused her to lose weight. No diet could have done better; she's back to what she weighed before she married Judah and bore a pair of boys. She had been doing part-time modeling. She sat beneath a hair dryer, smiling at the photographer in an advertisement for—she cannot remember the product she had been supposed to sell. Perhaps it was for beauty parlors; perhaps for a cosmetics line; perhaps she had been selling the metallic-blue dryer itself. She remembers an advertisement for vacuum-cleaner parts, and how she fitted the stem into the steel-ribbed hose smiling, always smiling, bending over at the waist; it was mail-order catalog work. But now she would be hired as the matron, whereas then she was the young homemaker; then she was skinny, now gaunt.

When Seth died in his crib the world went bad. It has taken her years to see and say so, but it is as simple as that. Sons die in war; they die in ships or of liquor or drugs; more of them die on the highways each year than were citizens of Athens when Athens had been in its prime. Sons die as suicides or by mistake; they die when changing tires on their honeymoons. Helen Ferguson's son-in-law got out of the car on a mountain road in order to change the left front flat, and a truck coming past him crumpled the door where he stood. They die in their teens and their twenties and thirties, with mothers watching helplessly; some women have to bear five sons in order to have one survive.

So Maggie knows it's selfish, self-regarding, and improper to mourn a single death. Her husband and her father both have died. Yet she does not mourn them equivalently; they lived to ripeness and desiccation, and then their lifelines snapped. It would have been wrong to continue: the fig still hanging from its tree, the apple turned to rot in snow, the fruit ignored by harvesters sent north from Jamaica or Mexico as a team in autumn.

But Seth died in his crib. When the time came for Jane to be established in a separate room, Maggie chose the room right next to hers—not down and diagonally across the hall, in what had been the nursery space before. She attempted to ignore that room for years. But you cannot ignore what you know; she is not ignorant and knows beyond question the world has gone bad. She struggles with that knowledge—denying or disproving it, or trying to, seeming rich and well-favored and well. Strangers tell her she looks lovely; they admire her good humor in the face of recent trouble and the loss of her husband and sister-in-law. They see merely surface-truth. The reality is death.

On the first floor, there are new arrivals. Ian hosts a gathering that has its own momentum. The visitors are neither attentive nor calm; they mock his vision of an orderly processional through the downstairs rooms. He discourses on the carriage entrance and the porte cochere, how a mansion of this size would have had at least two entrances, and how the habit of a social call has been supplanted by the telephone; one dials one's visits today.

They ignore his explanations; they sit on spindle-backed dining-room chairs as if awaiting soup. The goldfish bowl in the front hall has tissue paper wadded in between the dollar bills. When the lights flicker and fade, Elvirah says, "I told you so."

The light returns. Samuel Coffin is triumphant. "If there's anyplace to be on a Thursday in a snowstorm, folks," he says, "it's here."

The porch door slams. The cold air, entering, seems spatial; it feels distinct from the surrounding acrid air. A tall man enters, stamping. Finger by finger, he peels off his gloves. Ian recognizes him but is half-hidden in the music room, and Andrew Kincannon approaches Miles Fisk. "Never thought I'd make it," he remarks, and offers a hand. "This last part was the worst."

Miles shakes it, cordially. "Name's Fisk," he says. "Miles Fisk. I don't believe we've met."

Andrew covers what must be confusion. He coughs, unbelts his Burberry. "I believe I met your wife outside."

As Ian advances, Miles turns. "All right to use the phone?" he asks. "It's in there, right? I should call the office."

"Long time no see," Andrew says.

"Yes. I'm glad you made it."

Andrew scans the living room. "I'm not the only one, it seems. You've got quite a party."

"The power's out all down the hill."

"Does Maggie know I'm here?"

"No. She's upstairs."

Andrew examines his hands. "The trip was slow, this last part especially. Should I go up?"

"I'm taking the whole crew up there. It's part of the package—open house."

"I could use something hot to drink. Or isn't that part of the package?"

"It isn't," Ian says. "But we make exceptions."

Andrew asks for black coffee, with sugar. Ian gets a coffee mug and, in the kitchen, pouring, says, "I do think we should talk before you see my mother." He hesitates, then pours a second cupful for himself. "Or Jane."

"Jane?"

"My sister. I recognize you." Ian drinks. He has carried the family's weight for so long he feels light-headed, giddy at the prospect of dividing it; his resentment of Kincannon bulks less large than his relief.

"And Jane," Andrew asks. "Does she know I exist?"

Ian wets his finger and circles the mug's rim. "I'm not sure," he says. "I've given it all up, nearly. You have to understand it takes some getting used to."

"What does?"

"Help. The idea of somebody else in the house."

Andrew raises his eyebrows; the eyebrows are white. "I don't exactly live here, Ian. I took a day off from work."

"Yes."

"Seven hours in a snowstorm—eight." Andrew balances his coffee mug, concentrating on it, frowning. "Let me meet your sister Jane."

"February 21. A night of fitful dreams, light sleep. Temperature at six o'clock, thirty-three degrees. Thawing, wind due east. Lavinia is restless these mornings also, and has peculiar hungers. Strawberries and cream for dinner, veal for breakfast. Argument with cook. Cook thinks she should be given adequate notice of what to prepare, thinks—though she dare not say it quite so openly—a child indulged thus in the womb will likely prove captious and spoiled.

"Train prompt. If he were actually my cousin, bastard or no, would it have been a kindness so to acknowledge him—would our consanguinity have bridged so wide a gulf? His ways are not our ways. The sores upon his cheeks and hands were loathsome, scabrous things. He appeared not wholly sane. All these are arguments advanced against such harboring, such wanton embrace of a man claiming kinship—and therefore I emptied the safe and paid for the pistol with what was contained there: a small sum that to him seemed large. I saw his drinker's greed tabulating revels with the exchange I proffered, and said the pistols would be loaded if he dared return. He left as quietly as entered. My conscience reproaches me since. I do not know his name."

"All the lighting fixtures were originally gas. Peacock was a daring man to put his faith in gas—before that were candles and kerosene lamps. He purchased the Levi-Stevens Patented Gas Machine: it produced a carbon gas that was piped to the fixtures directly." Ian points to a wall socket, and switches on a light. He has continued the tour; he and Andrew and the others form a group. "At the turn of the century, however, the Big House was electrified. That's when they stained this chestnut here to make it look like mahogany. And when they converted that coal-burning fireplace to make a proper parlor. Burning wood. Because the rooms have been continually occupied, it's a question now of preservation, not restoration."

"What's the difference?" asks Elvirah, an obedient schoolgirl at eighty.

"The house has been altered," he says. "The inhabitants made alterations all along. Like getting rid of the old steam furnace and installing oil. Like those velvet drapes; they would have come with 'modernization' in 1900 also. But the tassels came later, you see. It has something to do with the presentness of things, of living history, not living *in* it . . ." He gives his practiced half-smile of apology. "That sounds arrogant, I know. But it's why this place is worth preserving, or why I think it is."

"We knew your grandfather's maid," says Lucy Gregory. "The kitchen maid, that Swedish one."

"It never was," says Samuel Coffin—to Andrew, but loudly so that Ian overhears—"what you'd call a proper farm."

"Not the one your father fancied,"—Lucy squints, remembering—"the girl your grandmother kicked out. But Inger, *Ingeborg*, that was her name. Who couldn't speak a word of English when she got off the train. Not a single blessed word. And ended up marrying Huntington's boy, the pharmacist—you know, the one at the four corners." She puts her hand on Ian's arm, retaining him, and turns to Elvirah to ask: "Am I right or am I right? That Swedish girl who married Huntington . . ."

"Swedes." Elvirah is noncommittal. "Can't say I remember which was which."

"Mind I'm not saying," Samuel says, "they never farmed it. That's another thing. But only as a sideline until Judah come along."

"I remember," says Elvirah. "Used to be a family of Swedes in town every time you turned around. But *she* wasn't Swedish, not that one, not the one Mrs. Sherbrooke dismissed. Your grandmother Lavinia." She nods at Ian, sagely. "French was more like it. Remember how her fiancé was dead in the ditches of France?"

"Your grandmother," says Lucy. "She knew what was what in this house."

Her door is an oak Christian door. Slowly she approaches it, concentrating on the cross and where the wood needs painting, seeing how the painter last time filled the cracks—overfilled them, really, since the paint itself has ridged and welted, layer on layer imposing its own pattern on the pattern of the wood. For a minute Maggie stands there, focusing on this white space where once again the barn burns, Hattie drowns, and Jane is born: the figures balletic, in motion. Hal Boudreau extinguishes himself, guttering out like a candle in its own puddle of wax. Then Ian says, "I've got something to tell you," and the doctor beams at her, a brown moon saying, "Just imagine. By this time tomorrow you'll have another child"—as if that were encouragement, as if she could endure twenty-four more minutes, not hours, of such explosiveness, the sheets slimed beneath her, this pain—and by the time she understands he's not predicting the length of her labor but making conversation, by that time she's lost control of her breath and control of the contraction, and she screams.

"Hush," Ian says. "It's going to be fine." They shout beyond the window as if at the Rutland State Fair, and the volunteer firemen get free tickets for this sideshow, her. The rescue squad applauds and whistles and claps their smoke-blackened hands while she writhes behind the window on display. It's not true, Maggie knows, it isn't possible to see her where she spreads herself upon the bed, soaking the sheets and bleeding through the mattress-cover to the mattress, where much later she will find a heart-shaped stain the size of her daughter, ineradicable, the brown afterbirth imprinted on the Sealy Posturepedic; not true they stamp their feet for her or fondle themselves in the dark.

"It's been a long time, Mrs. Sherbrooke."

A woman appears in the hall. Maggie stops.

"May I call you Maggie?"

"You're Jeanne Fisk."

Jeanne laughs. She puts her hand to her hair. "Surely it hasn't been *that* long," she says.

"No. How's your chamber music group? How are the Sage City Players?"

"Two years," she says. "It's been two years. I saw you once with Jane. She was toddling then—you know, the way that they do, as if every step is both the first they've ever taken and will turn out to be the last. It was by the Post Office."

"Yes. Well."

"I remember the stroller," Jeanne says. "Orange."

The mirror at the stairwell's crest lets Maggie see the villagers. They have clustered to Peacock's gold-plated spittoon; they examine the framed piece of iron and a splinter from the *Merrimack*.

"Jane's growing up so poised," says Jeanne. "So much the little lady. My girls adore her."

"How are they? The twins."

"Fine." Jeanne nods her head, as if to offer reassurance. "They're fine."

"If you'll excuse me," Maggie says. "I ought to say hello downstairs . . ."

"Of course. But bring Jane for a visit someday soon. We live on North Street, Ian knows which house. The girls would love to see her. Please."

The cross upon a Christian door is meant to keep deviltry back. Where the white junction of the elevator door approaches (Maggie nears it, focusing, forcing herself to determine that the vertical slat is uninterrupted, five feet from base to top, the horizontal members cut to fit, not nailed athwart it, forcing herself to hear how the ruckus in the stairwell is a group of convivial friends), she briefly rests her head. Then she walks down the long corridor, hearing Jane and the twins in the room with the mannequins, and steadies her breath and descends.

"March 3. Snow. Temperature at six o'clock, seventeen degrees. Wind northerly, and it howled like a banshee last night. I walked to the bank through our fields and back again in my own tracks. Right foot turns out. Recognizable. Harriet broke her porcelain bowl at lunchtime; I reprimanded her, urging her to be more mindful since she is five years old by now, and she burst into tears. Unseemly. Why this heaviness about my heart, this stench about my body like a dying beast? Teeth hurt.

Shipment from Havana damaged in transit. Leakage. 'The man also that writeth Mr. Badman's life had need be fenced with a coat of mail, and with the staff of a spear, for that his surviving friends will know what he doth . . .'"

"I've got to be going," says Miles. "Did you see my family?"

"They're upstairs. Do you want me to get them?"

"No. I'm due at the office. Just tell them when they come."

"You walking?" Ian asks. "I could lend you the truck . . ."

"No, I'll walk."

There is something almost furtive in his attitude: a hurry to be gone, an eagerness that Ian has not seen before. Miles buckles his parka and pulls on his gloves. He tips his hat back rakishly, says, "Nice to meet you, Andrew," and departs. There is a cold wind at the door, but the snow has stopped.

Maggie appears. They stand together, watching her. She steps down as if buoyant, rising. "Well, well," says Andrew.

"Ian," Maggie starts to say, then sees Kincannon and stops.

"You know each other," Ian says.

"But how did you get here?"

"Just now," Andrew says. "I drove up."

He bends to kiss her hand. She stands two steps above him and offers the hand as if coached. "Did you come from New York?" Maggie asks. "Was the driving difficult?"

"The last few miles . . . I thought Vermont was famous for the way it kept roads clear."

"Not on Thursday afternoons." Maggie indicates the dining room. "That's when the road crew visits and everybody's welcome here. On Thursday afternoons they don't clear roads, they come inside instead."

"You haven't changed," says Andrew.

"No?"

"No. You look wonderful."

"And you. You always did lie through your teeth." At the word "teeth" Maggie falters, and Ian steps forward to help; it is as if this first false note rings true for him, the sound of his mother's distress.

Andrew says, "I thought I might pass by, since I was in the neighborhood. I hope you don't mind . . ."

"Mind?"

He indicates the library. Someone has broken out sherry and glasses; Samuel Coffin holds the bottle and is pouring drinks. He bends above the serving table, scrupulous, apportioning the levels so that each glass holds the same. "You've got a party going on," says Andrew. "I wasn't exactly invited . . ."

"That isn't true," says Ian. "Yes, you were."

"It doesn't matter," Maggie says. "What counts is you've arrived." She takes the final step and stands between them on the landing, gathering the lamplight for her entrance—poised between escorts and perfectly dressed. She smiles a smile so brittle Ian asks, "Are you all right?"

Samuel Coffin sees them and puts the sherry down. "Mrs. Sherbrooke," he says. "Margaret. No fooling. You look younger every day."

"Why thank you, Samuel."

"No fooling. Every time I see you I'm reminded."

"This is my day for compliments. I'll have to save them up."

"Fact." The old man turns to Andrew. "If I was your age again . . ." He offers his hand. "Name's Coffin. Samuel Coffin."

"Will you excuse us?" Maggie says. "We've got *such* a lot of catching up to do." She smiles at Samuel, then Ian. "Run along and give your tour. We *do* want all our visitors to get their money's worth." She swivels and presents her back, shuts her eyes an instant, then puts her hand on Andrew's arm. "You naughty man, you could have sent a postcard. Where *have* you been keeping yourself?"

In the final months of Judah's life, they attended the church oyster supper. He had been doing so, he said, since 1946. It wasn't the Sherbrooke church, wasn't even local, was twenty miles of dirt road into the next county and down by Hoosick Falls. But Judah said they served the best oysters from here to kingdom come, and it didn't matter where you lived and didn't much matter what faith you professed in order to have faith in this: Ralph Andersen knows oysters and where to order them cheap. He, Judah, cherished raw oysters. He'd be a double-dyed Baptist on Saturday, he announced, if they allowed only Baptists inside; if born-again Christians get second helpings, he'd be born again.

But though the congregation had first licks at the first feeding, there was always enough to go around. They sold tickets to the supper six weeks in advance. By two weeks thereafter they were sold out, and Judah was part of the list. He'd buy up a table's worth anyhow, and take Hattie and Samson Finney and Maggie, if she were willing. If the table was part empty, so much the better, Judah said, that means there's extra for us.

The feast was in September, and the afternoon was bright. They waited in a pew. Ralph Anderson announced the numbers, calling them off in tens, meanwhile trying to sell cranberry bread and fudge and relish in the vestibule where the ladies displayed baked goods. Maggie looked around her and was shocked. How could they all have grown so fat, she asked herself, so old in the years since she'd last attended, so blue-haired and bedecked with rhinestone finery? The ladies smiled and nodded. The men waved. The carpenter from Shady Hill had a new set of teeth. His mouth made appreciative separate motions as he praised the oyster stew. There would be raw oysters, then stew, then scalloped oysters, then pie. There were mashed potatoes and squash and rolls and coffee provided gratis, Hattie said, so all the Baptists had to pay for were the oysters brought north in bulk.

Their numbers were called. She helped Judah downstairs. He made space for himself, as always, and seemed the largest person there, though his gait was shambling and his bulk had been reduced. He busied himself, as he did always, assessing the evening's probable profit—the total take at five dollars a head, minus expenses. He worked out the figures aloud. "One hundred thirty-seven folks at a sitting," he said. "Four sittings, right? That's five forty-eight times five—twenty-seven forty. Not counting those who eat free. They clear fifteen hundred easy, maybe eighteen hundred, depending on the freight."

Their waitress knew the Sherbrookes; she filled their water cups. She told Judah how well he was looking, told Maggie it was wonderful to have her back again. She bet Finney he wished it was vodka or gin, told Hattie how the day before they'd had a hepatitis scare and thought they'd have to cancel—how someone down in Chesapeake had called up Adam Chamberlain and said these oysters came from beds the state had put in quarantine. "Not fit for local consumption," she said. "But okay to ship out of state—can you imagine?" So Ralph had been up half the night checking out the accusation, making certain there was nothing to it, making certain what they had were prime-grade oysters with no question mark attached. "Truth is," she said, "if I'd have to get sick, this isn't the way I would like to. Catch me eating them raw . . ." She shook her head and topped up Judah's plastic bowl. "Cholesterol," she told him. "Heavy on cholesterol, that's what oysters are."

Maggie picked and chewed. There had been bowls of cocktail sauce and crackers, jugs of vinegar. The oysters seemed stringy and thick. She had difficulty swallowing; the mixture adhered to her throat. Those in the group around her asked for second helpings; Maggie blew her nose. In the next instant, with her handkerchief still at her mouth, she blinked to clear her eyes. She could not see. Then Maggie saw the room as if through water, with the steel columns turned to kelp and the many-fingered children waving at her languidly. There were solemn-eyed strangers like fish, snouting up against their plates. There was coral all around her, and its edges were knife-sharp. The light above was like the light through water impossibly deep. She pressed her nose and fought for air.

Samson had a pocket flask. He uncorked it and poured whiskey in her coffee cup. "Good for what ails you." He winked. "It makes Irish coffee, is all." Upstairs the next set of celebrants waited. The minister waved broadly at Pete Ellison, whose boy won last week's football game with an interception, but said he had to practice late and therefore skipped out on this meal. "You know what practice makes," said Pete, "that Soskins girl, she's *perfect*—so I've got this extra ticket here if anyone's still buying. Practice makes perfect, get it?"

Maggie drank. The coffee failed to warm her but it cleared her sight. That instant she knew she didn't belong here and would have to leave. She hadn't known it then, of course, had only just returned. She'd thought life with Judah might last. Then when he died she thought to mourn him in the proper context; then she was pregnant with Jane. In the sixth month of her pregnancy, she dreamed nightly of escape, but there had been nowhere to go. Then for a while it seemed that staying would be pleasant and convenient; then her inertia mounted and she could not move.

Yet these faces and bodies repelled her, this white flesh wandering from feeding perch to feeding perch, these up-country citizens who hated her and would hate Jane. They inserted their new sets of teeth after the curried oysters and before the bread. They were her enemies. Their names were Harrington and Cooper and Hall: names on the stones outside that would be incised soon again. "If this is the salt of the earth," she said to Samson Finney, "I'm going on a salt-free diet."

He studied her, concerned. "They're good folk," Samson said. "They may be dull and pious and whatnot, but they're law-abiding folk."

Maggie checked her face in her pink compact mirror. "Bad for business," she said. She had tried to humor him, but he was unamused. These people would brand her if they dared, had branded her in their mind's eyes already, would run her out of town except she owned the town.

This last phrase is theatrical. She does not own the town. That was being proved. Nor do they bother her or call except on Thursday afternoons while she hides in her room. But they roil about beneath her like carp after bread, they lurch and snap and swallow indiscriminately. Jane cannot live here, she knows. Jane will have to leave, as she and Ian left. When the gong sounded and the five o'clock set-to arose, shuffling, scraping back their chairs, swallowing as if in unison that last chunk of lemon meringue, Maggie thought she would not make it, not climb up the stairs behind Judah—he needing no help now but striding, hands in his pockets puffing out the flannel, fetching his cigar case and telling Finney, "We might as well have us a smoke."

"Did you hear the one?" asked Finney, "about this king in Africa who got himself a modern house with all our foreign aid? So he had this fancy chair, see, with jewels on the headrest and leopard-skin pillows, and they looked through the picture window and saw it and deposed him. Killed the king." He paused. "Which only goes to prove," he said, "that people who live in glass houses shouldn't stow thrones."

Judah laughed. He threw back his head and repeated the punch line: "Stow thrones." His white hair was fluffy with washing; it bunched at the back of his neck. He winked down at Maggie and asked, "You ever hear that one? Stow thrones."

"She's heard it," Finney said.

The men bit cigar ends and spat. Hattie had excused herself, drifting off to visit with the Conovers. Judah and Samson traded jokes the way they traded cigars. They'd been doing so for decades, and Maggie scarcely listened, and she wondered if they listened to each other anymore—they must have known the repertoire by heart. It wasn't as if they collected jokes or told them well, it was more a ritual observance, a way of stating fellowship.

They were standing in the vestibule, and Maggie stepped outside. She'd brought no wrap because the afternoon was warm, but now she shivered, waiting. Judah collected his coat. The lights were on in the church and the parking lot was full and cars lined the dirt road. A policeman waved at traffic, and a woman in a wheelchair waited for a lift. Maggie saw white curling smoke from a chimney to the east, the sickle moon above her, and a far plane, blinking. She felt herself so alien in this country company—so balanced between shame and scorn—that she began to cry. She licked her lips and tasted salt; she would weep this way for years.

"Jane?"

Jane does not turn.

"Here's someone I'd like you to meet."

"Hello."

"Hello." Andrew offers his hand. She takes it and shakes hands, polite.

"Pleased to meet you," says Maggie. "Remember?"

"Pleased to meet you."

"I'm Andrew Kincannon, I've known your mother a very long time."

"Can we play 'Touch and Try'?" Jane asks. "Are we allowed to, Mommy?"

The hallway where they stand is dark. The wall light is shaped like a candle. It does not function. "Who's we?"

"Kathryn and Amy. They're in there already."

"If you put things away," Maggie says.

"We *have* been, Mommy. We're being careful."

"All right." She turns to Andrew. "There's a costume room. She loves to play dress-up."

"What are you going to be?" Andrew asks. "I mean, when you're in costume?"

Jane smiles but makes no answer. She is barefoot.

"A princess?" he asks. "Or a ballerina, maybe?"

"Can I wear high heels? Please? They're wearing high heels."

"Yes," Maggie tells her. Jane leaves.

"March 7. Temperature at six o'clock, eighteen degrees. Yesterday my visitor returned, I knew him on the instant, though his aspect was grievously altered; it is as if he had remained with me since three weeks ago when sick myself I showed him to the door. He has not left the region, it appears. He spent the sum obtained from what I consider charity and he called compensation (I speak of the purchase of pistols, those eighty dollars with which he established credit at some nearby tavern) in Drink & Debauching.

"Mine is not a fearful nature. I am not queasy. I enjoy my stirrup cup as well as the next man. But those who favor Temperance could choose no better instance than that poor supplicant who found me by the sugarhouse and asked for permission to sleep there this night. Demanded it, rather. Such permission—judging by the disarray of his face and hair and clothing—had been granted in advance. He raved. He tested my determination to be peaceable. He swore that *I* should take the sugarhouse or corncrib for dominion, when I told him how Lavinia lay close to term upstairs. He shook his fists. He swore the house was his by right of prior birth, with all of its appurtenances—including, if she met his fancy, though he reserved the right to change his mind upon inspection, since he had not as yet set eyes on her, my wife. He laughed. His right eye had been swollen shut, and viscous fluid bathed his cheek.

"I am thirty-eight years old. He is perhaps five years my chronological senior, but the ague upon him made him seem more nearly seventy. Disease can thus mock time. The sickly child may comprehend mortality as well as the hale ancient. Although he soon ceased flailing them, his fists shook of their own accord nevertheless.

"Mindful of my earlier remorse, I heard him out. I spoke soothingly. I touched his flesh that made my own flesh crawl. I said he should come in and eat and bathe and have a doctor tend his wounds both inward and external. He groaned. He said no human physic now could heal his sickness, nor balm relieve his scars. I covered him with sacking and went to summon aid."

Lucy Gregory is worried that the power won't come back. "Last spring," she says, "I remember, because it was the first day of spring, we had that freak storm. Though why we call it *freak* I don't know, it happens every year, I declare I should be *used* to it—the one that lasted three days. Well, we lost the freezer. Every single thing we'd packed in there so carefully. The meat. Elvirah went to get some chops, and it's dark down cellar, you can't hear the click on the machine if the machine's not running. So we used the flashlight, and we *thought* we closed it up again and never thought another thing about it. Till the smell started in three days after—I tell you the lid was wide open." She sniffs. "They say it's just one power line, and it takes them three whole days."

"We should be going," says Elvirah. "No point in putting it off."

Ian leads the group along the upstairs hall. Jane is in the costume room along with the Fisk twins; they wear pinafores and bonnets. Jane's whalebone corset brushes the floor; she drapes it from her shoulders like an overcoat. She is wearing lipstick also, and lipstick highlights on her cheeks. She smiles at him half-fearfully and takes three steps and puts her arms around his knees.

"We're playing," Jane says. "Pretend."

"Yes. I see that."

Kathryn and Amy seem abashed. They look at him through lowered lids, then look at the grouping behind him—Samuel Coffin, the two old ladies, Vito, and the rest. He puts his hand on Jane's head. "Having fun?"

Her reply is muffled. He feels like an intruder, in some stall where women dress.

"How old are you?" asks Lucy.

"Three and a half."

"A smart one." Vito waggles his hand.

"May she have her mother's looks," Samuel Coffin pronounces. "And her mother's brains."

"That's good," says Vito. "Very good. Her *mother's* looks, her *mother's* brains." He chuckles, memorizing this. "Except of course that, if he heard it, Judah'd have your head."

"It's a compliment," says Samuel Coffin. "I'd have told him to his face."

587

"How many sisters does Cinderella have?" asks Jane.

"Two," Ian says.

"These are my sisters," she says. "We're getting dressed for a party."

Lucy Gregory advances. "You'll turn into a pumpkin."

Jane seems undecided as to whether she should greet these strangers. She tightens her hold on his arm.

"Hey, Cinderella, your coach awaits you." He ruffles her hair. "Come on out."

The look she gives him then is Maggie's glance entirely: a baffled willfulness compounding fear and trust. Perhaps because of Andrew, or the villagers' gleeful scrutiny, or those twin hostages to Miles who stand beneath the goose-necked lamp in silk and hoopskirts staring up at him—Ian removes her arms. He bends to her and picks her up and shuts his eyes and buries his head in her neck.

The green grass cloth has faded where the picture hung, or rather not faded so much as retained coloration while the wall around it darkened in some process of response to sun that causes cloth to darken; Maggie sees the picture as if there (not taken off when the glass cracked and left unrepaired in the broom closet, stacked for salvage with those other objects Ian has not yet found the time or interest to redeem), its eighteen- by twenty-four-inch frame a lessening of contrast but sufficient contrast still, the cow and clouds and haystacks Hattie loved to point to, saying, "This is what it looked like when I first learned the way to look," and the protected rectangle therefore appearing changed, not constant, as if bleached by the absence of sun. The cow had been Ayrshire, clumsily painted, the sienna of its haunch and horn too stridently an aspect of the composition, not the true color of the cow, and its udder too absolute a complement to the haystack at the upper left. It had been done by Hattie's friend who'd read an article once on Corot, who incised the thick paint with the edge of her palette knife, bluntly, making barbed-wire strands and grass stalks. Maggie remembers those fields with regret, remembers how when young she seemed to be out in them always, always helping Judah or bringing him his lunch or walking to meet him or walking back as if from a secret assignation, though lawful. They'd made a joke of it: he was never in the house and Hattie never out of it, so if they wanted privacy they made love in the woods. And even in old age, when he couldn't wander far afield, he wore his work boots and bib overalls and that red-and-black plaid shirt she'd given him in 1958. He took himself laboriously off to the outbuildings, puttering, giving orders, making order, or to the Toy House, where he'd sit wrapped in sheepskin, ruminant, so that if she needed him she'd know to look outside.

"I'm sorry," Andrew says. "I should have told you."

"What?"

"That I was coming. Planning to come. It isn't fair to just barge in."

"You're welcome," she says. "You knew that."

"I didn't. Not really. The last time we talked . . ."

Maggie releases his arm. They stand in what once served as a solarium. There are bay windows on the southern wall, and ceiling hooks for plants. The plants have gone leggy, however, or brown; some pots hold nothing but dirt. "It's just too expensive," she says. "The cost of fuel oil. It isn't worth it, everything freezes, there's no point trying."

Andrew sits. He stands again. She indicates a brittle, leafless bush.

"Azalea?"

"Ian says it's cheaper just to buy new plants every spring. You've no idea"—she shakes her head. "Living in that southern place with someone else paying the bills."

"New York," he says. "It's not exactly tropical."

"No."

He watches her. A greenhouse is visible out to the right. An upright piano stands by the door; the piano bench has lost a leg. "May I ask this: how've you been?"

"Surviving," Maggie says.

"And Jane?"

"I wondered when you'd ask."

"How is she?"

"She's got your mouth. Your coloring."

"I'd like to spend some time with her."

Maggie moves to the window and fastens the drapes. The drapes are many-pleated, beige, and patterned with an S for Sherbrooke.

"I'm sorry," he repeats. "I should have warned you."

Ian skis cross-country. She used to do that also, and snowshoe, but it's been weeks and feels like years since she's braved the winter weather. The fields have gone so fat with snow they've thickened past the second strand of wire, wearing its barbs like a belt. While Judah lived and she was young, such fencing was not threatful, was simply an efficient way to keep the herd contained. It had not seemed an obstacle or augury of tetanus or reminder of the wars. "'Good fences make good neighbors,' as that rotten farmer said," she'd say, laughing at the notion of an Ayrshire in the tulip patch, or trampling the sweet peas and eggplant, blundering down gravel paths because the fence was bad: the dream of placid passage where the cow path had been beaten turned to her nightly nightmare of an unleashed animality, all burrs and flies and shit.

How explain this to Andrew, she wonders? How tell him how her world has been contained? He stands by her side like Boudreau. He has that same hangdog expectancy, that air of previous entitlement—as if his very manhood were a virtue, something to be honored though unearned.

There are differences, of course. Boudreau is a burned drunk living near the Alagash, and Andrew is what Hattie would have called "distinguished." He wears expensive clothing and his fingernails are trim. His body has the sort of leanness that signifies wealth—not the half-starved voraciousness of Hal in his long Johns swigging gin. In America, she thinks, the better off you are the skinnier you stay. She swallows, shuts her eyes. Judah or Boudreau or Andrew in this nightmare seem the same. There's a cat-o'-nine-tails and a set of ankle straps, a mirror and always the bed: there's beauty as booty, her force-fed submission as prize.

"It's been a long time," Ian says. "How are you?"

"Fine. Just fine," says Jeanne.

"We haven't talked since New Year's."

"The word was 'terrific,' remember? I used to say 'terrific' when you asked."

"I remember," Ian says. "Why was Miles in such a hurry?"

"To leave, you mean?" They stand beneath the cupola. "He's probably got an appointment. He wants to slip his secretary in between town meetings."

"Miles?"

"I told him when he asked. He asked about you finally. I told him there was nothing left, but there had been something." She examines her hand. "So he's making up for all those years of blissful ignorance—catching up. With secretaries, babysitters, even Bill Ellison's daughter."

"I don't believe it," Ian says.

"Why not? He wants an open marriage now—he read about how well it works. That's why he slapped you on the back and what he meant by leaving me here." She spreads her fingers carefully, then folds them to her palm in sequence. The thumb remains upright. "Or maybe you'd prefer Bill Ellison's daughter yourself."

"Not likely."

"No?"

"No." He waves at Samuel Coffin in the far end of the hall, then points for Samuel's benefit to a stuffed bison head. The bison's eyes are mottled and the size of billiard balls. "When did you tell him?" he asks.

"My New Year's resolution. I told myself I wouldn't lie. I'd tell him if he asked."

"And you said it was over?"

"I did."

Samuel makes his way into the music room. The hall is empty; Ian touches her cheek. "Then tell me why you're here."

"I thought the twins might help."

"Help?"

"Protect me." Jeanne smiles. "You know, remind me whose mother I am. And whose wife."

"I don't need reminding."

"All right. I came because I couldn't stay away."

Again he reaches out for her; again she makes a gesture of resistance. "It isn't over," he says.

"No."

"I'll call in the morning."

For an instant, standing there, he hopes she will refuse him. It would provide finality. Her body is bulky with clothing, and at a four-foot distance from his own. But any stranger watching them would know they had been naked together; Jeanne breathes as though beneath him. "Call at ten o'clock," she says.

"Am I forgiven?" Andrew asks.

Maggie imitates politeness. "What have you been up to? It's been *years*."

"I've missed you," he says. "Very much."

"You're sweet to say so. Where've you been?"

"Nowhere in particular. New York. I didn't mean I knew I missed you, but I know it now."

"A pretty phrase," she says. She cannot control herself. "You might have called."

"I did. I tried."

"Not hard enough. Once in four years."

His contriteness, too, is brief. "Well, where were *you*? Don't they have telephones here?"

"It wasn't up to me to call. My God, we're squabbling like a married couple."

"Marry me," he says.

This too is echo, repetition, a reminder of when last they'd met and he meant it, or seemed to, asking him to marry her because Judah had died and she need not divorce him and they had twenty good years left, with impediments removed. He'd used the phrase "impediments removed," and she asked did he mean Judah by that, and he'd hesitated, saying no, not really, just they were past fifty now and had no reason to wait.

"She *is* your child," says Maggie. "Jane."

Andrew puts his hand to the wall but seems to lean no weight on it. "Why didn't you tell me?"

"I did."

"Before, I mean." His hand rests where the picture had hung. "When it was happening, when you were pregnant."

Maggie has an answer, but it would take too long to say and is an ancient tale. Nor would it flatter Andrew. It has to do, she wants to say, with debts she'd tried to pay alone and the secretive pleasures of pride, with her aged shocked sister-in-law and a pileated woodpecker and much he had no notion of. It has to do with Ian's return, how he'd played Judah's surrogate, with the weather, the corncrib, the fresh coat of paint, with lawyers and doctors and busily inquisitive neighbors, the way she'd lain awake for months to hear Jane's every whimper till that solitary wakeful watch seemed sane.

Andrew coughs. "I should have known."

How tell him that she'd tried for weeks to put his face in focus, to make him more a presence than the dead man who still quickened her? Yet Andrew's face stayed featureless as that rectangle of grass cloth, a blankness that she'd tried to read till curiosity faded, till she told herself the baby could come from a sperm bank for all that it mattered. What mattered was Jane; what counted was the number they made, making two, making even Ian superfluous. How tell him she had waited for some second call or visit, some sign that she could answer with no fear of having hauled him north or playing the outraged maiden in a paternity suit? She'd managed; they'd managed; she had been doing just fine, thank you, till her managing ability collapsed.

"You've no idea . . ." says Andrew.

Maggie rouses. "What?"

"How peculiar this is. How strange it makes me feel. I drive on up because your son says you're in trouble."

She shakes her head. "You mustn't blame Ian," she says.

"And you look as lovely as ever. Untouched."

Her feet are cold. Her ankles ache.

"Does Jane know I'm her father?"

"No."

"Does anyone but Ian?"

"Not for certain. No."

"So everyone thinks she's a Sherbrooke." Andrew nods. "And for all practical purposes, *I'm* the one who's dead!"

"I wouldn't put it that way."

"Why not? What other way is there to put it? If I'd hung up on Ian, if I'd been out of town or happened to be busy, if I turn around now and go home"—he snaps his fingers—"why, this never happened. Kincannon just doesn't exist."

"You could do that," Maggie says. "I wouldn't blame you at all."

"This never happened," Andrew repeats. "If I drive back to Westport without you."

"It's your decision," she says.

"March 9. Temperature at six o'clock, thirty-one degrees. Wind moderate, southerly. My grandfather sent letters to strangers, the architects commissioned for this house. My aunt sent letters not to strangers but to her brother

594

my father. And I am grown so inward lately that my letters are this daybook self-addressed. There is correspondence at the bank. There are certain tasks it is my duty to perform. But I am struck by such a declension; how Peacock took for granted that his instructions would be followed the width of a continent distant. And how his daughter in her turn urged instruction on her near and dear though far. I am reduced. I write to myself in secret. There will be enquiries. The shame is inward only and confounded by relief. I whisper here what I would hesitate to confide to Lavinia—who knows nothing of the episode as yet, who must be kept from shock—and cannot tell the coroner: I believed our guest my brother when he died.

"His thin chest heaved. He lay on the sacking like Job on his dunghill; it was five o'clock. I brought him a boiled chicken, but he could not eat. In his Delirium he waxed profane—cursing me and mine and God and Theodore Roosevelt, pausing only to cough: a hacking, rasping sound I shall not soon forget. It echoes in my study still. He claimed that he was well not ill, was perfectly able to rise except he might be poisoned by a brother if he stood.

"The doctors were tardy. I had sent word with Benjamin to fetch Bill Robinson or, failing him, Joseph Miller. Yet they arrived too late. It transpired suddenly. No human agency, I am persuaded, could have saved him then. One instant he was talking of his mother's excellence, the way her hands were strong and gentle both at once, fit equally for soothing him or wringing roosters' necks. Then next he seemed to see her, raising up one elbow and speaking French endearments that I could not understand. Transfigured. It is the word. There is no other adequate. He reached for her as if for salvation, then fell back."

Big-bellied, protuberant, set back on his heels like a woman in her last trimester, Junior Allison walks in. He wears his duffel coat and boots; his nose is red. "Miles sent me," Junior announces. "Said I should drive these folks back home."

595

Jeanne enters behind him. She smiles at her daughters, "Time for supper. Get out of those costumes. Come on."

"It's easy driving now," says Junior. "No problem."

He drives the village taxi in all weathers, equably. He has been doing so since anyone can recall, and is "Junior" still at seventy; he used to help out Judah. His limousine is ancient, with a blue sheriff's light affixed to the top. The left rear fender is red, the windows have been shorted out and fail to shut. But Junior washes and waxes and dries his car with avid exactitude still, and his calling cards read: "Driver Service," not "Taxi." He does not stop for strangers if he does not like their looks; often as not he leaves the bus terminal as passengers arrive.

"Going so soon?" Vito asks.

"It's not soon," Jeanne says. "It's five o'clock nearly. This open house will shut."

"Four forty-five," says Ian. "I'll walk you out."

The girls have divested themselves. She hangs up their costumes, ignoring him.

"What about the power line?" Samuel Coffin asks. "Any lights back on down there?"

"Not yet," says Junior. "But they've got it located. They'll fix it by suppertime, maybe."

Elvirah Hayes adjusts her scarf. She fiddles with the buttons of her long black coat. "It's been such a pleasure," she says. "So interesting, Ian, such a nice way to visit. I particularly liked the scrimshaw. 'John Smythe. His horn.' Can you imagine . . ."

"Say good-bye upstairs for us," Lucy adds.

"I will. And this summer I'll bring you those pears."

"Seckel pears," Elvirah says. "The ones from the stand by the icehouse. That's not till late October."

"November sometimes," Peg Morrisey says. "They're mostly good for pies."

Samuel Coffin stands. He walks as if the parquet were a tightrope, wobbling, weaving. "Long as you're driving," he says to Junior. "How 'bout a ride?"

Allison grins, "*You'd* best not walk," he says. "You'd take a swan dive off that porch."

Ian turns to Lucy and Elvirah and Peg Morrisey. "Ladies," he says. "This is what you would have been wearing sixty years ago." He picks a single silver fox off the hook it dangles from and wraps it around Jeanne's throat. The fox has marble eyes and an open mouth and ebony teeth; he places the tail in the teeth.

"The not-so-quick brown fox," says Jeanne. She disentangles herself. Junior sets his blue light flashing; Jeanne bundles the twins in the front. Ian waits beside the car and helps the elder ladies in, then Samuel Coffin and Vito and, finally, Jeanne. She squeezes his hand, but he offers no answering pressure. She occupies the jump seat and leans forward to address her daughters. They leave.

Ian thinks of Joseph's dutiful recording—how the crops and temperature, the weather of those years was faithfully transcribed. His own middle name is Daniel, as befits an elder Sherbrooke son; Judah's middle name was Porteous, from his mother's side. If Joseph's visitor were truly Daniel Jr.'s son, and Joseph's ancestry had been—in the journal's words—"provable cadet," then they had indeed inherited the Big House by right of mere possession. Daniel Jr. had been written out of Peacock's will. He had been his father's first-born who did not return. He disappeared from San Francisco, heading west. West was on some fishing fleet or expedition after seals or oils or silk; west was the trading impulse, still, the face that faced a setting sun until it reached the Orient and east. West was nothing manifest and not in the family archives; it was earthquakes and fire and opium dens. There were bodies on the cliffs; there were bodies in the wake of ships and unmarked graves and potters' fields, a multitude of bodies like the crossties on the tracks. Daniel Sherbrooke Jr.'s name was legion: sand in wind.

Yet certain things continue. Ian imagines Peacock's will—a document he no doubt could find in Finney's files—as evidence of the old man's litigious zeal. Judah inherited that. He was forever revising bequests, as if each actual or imagined courtesy and slight should be attested to. Their father, Hattie used to say, had been considerate; he would ask permission of every lady present before he'd even dream of lighting a cigar. And Ian sees himself these days as both a scribe and witness, more kin to Joseph's mild-mannered abiding than he would have guessed. If Judah had been there to tell him, Ian thinks, he might have saved some time. He might have known he'd be his grandfather's own meditative ineffectual well-intentioned grandson, a stitch in generation-time but cut from the same cloth. He ascends the porch steps heavily, stamping the snow free.

Maggie asks herself what right he has, what forfeit of integrity his very presence posits; Andrew opens the door and it too makes a frame. It is both entrance to and exit from a space she's filled for years, this composition made of oak and paint and brass. The hinges are silver and six inches high. The door opens into the hall. There is a mirror opposite, and she sees herself reflected as she takes a final survey, turning as she'd turned from Judah once to dive from high dock pilings. Where she stands is split precisely, half in and half out of the hallway as in water— so that if he'd hooked her and she was his yellow fish, she might have been rising, not diving, or as if a hand-cranked home movie were being reeled backward, and she could do a swan dive up anytime he turned the wheel, emerging poised and dry and toes together from the sea. All she needs to know is direction: study that door. Does the woman enter it or leave? Is she familiar with her surroundings? Is she threatened by them, or do her shoreline certainties extend? Will she be pleased? What waits behind the door, at her sight's fuzzy limit, and will it harm or give her pleasure and how may she decide? The frame is eighteen inches above her head, since Peacock Sherbrooke built high, and twelve to either side, since he envisioned spreading skirts and swallowtail frock coats and persons of stature or girth like his wife's. The light has gone so dim, however, that what she extinguished was darkness not light. She shuts her eyes. The barn, pond, hydrangea, grass-cloth frame, and matron in a doorway disappear.

PART III

I

"March 12. Five days since our visitor's death. Temperature at six o'clock, twenty-one degrees. Wind due west. There is a beast within my body that seems to take pleasure in pain. It fattens on grief like a vulture on carrion, and the greater the carnage the gladder the feast. If Man were fully aspirant to sanctity and sanity, Angelic orders would have triumphed in their battle with the Dark. But no such work as Darwin's undertakes the soul. It does not seem to me Humanity progresses as the species Homo Sapiens becomes more broadly sapient. The 'Origin of Speciousness,' perhaps. We might have lost the usage of our toes to grip tree limbs, and excessive Body Hair with which to thrive in winter, but we never lose the bloodlust that sets humanity against itself to try to establish dominion. The stronger takes to wife the wife of the weaker he kills.

"He lay on the pallet, exhausted. I asked him at the end if he would call me brother. He did not seem to hear. He turned his head towards the wall and licked his lips continually, with the insatiate thirst of fever. I provided him water and cloths, I asked if Daniel his father had been as furiously quarrelsome as fame reported it; he was said to have been a crack shot. He nodded then and held out his hand—but whether in responsiveness I am unable to say. His fingers curled as if they held the pistol stock, and he took aim. I am reminded of those trading posts in Hudson Bay where Indians were called upon to pile their beavers high as guns, since this was the system of barter. The avaricious trader produced long-barreled rifles so as to receive more beaver pelts. And this in turn made the weapon's sighting more accurate—the longer the barrel the better the rifleman's aim. Greed in this manner may ordain its own extinction. That mine enemy grows older is small comfort if I also age—the mirror held so close to nature that breathing on it mists and must erase the mirrored face.

"I am accounted here, and not without reason in public accounting, an honorable man. Yet murder and rapine and pillage are my Intimates; nightly I riot with maidens called Envy and Lying and Sloth. What should such a creature do upon this earth?"

Jane comes from the kitchen and, seeing Ian, stops. "Can I have a pretzel?"

"What time is it?"

"Just for a snack. I'm hungry, Ian, can I?"

"It's after five o'clock," he says.

"I haven't eaten . . ."

She is in her sleeveless leotard and pink tights and blue denim skirt. She is wearing earrings salvaged from the costume room. "Since when?" he asks.

"Since breakfast just about. Not since my Froot Loops."

"You can have an apple."

"A pretzel."

"An apple."

"Oh, Ian, *please*," she says. Jane stares up at him, pleading, with her precocious insistence and that little-girl-lost look he knows she puts on for effect. But the automatic act of bickering over apples or pretzels, milk or

Coke, his fear of losing her now Andrew Kincannon has arrived, the fact of her hunting permission to eat and his having neglected to feed her—all this makes Ian mourn. He bends and embraces his sister; she tries to wriggle free.

"I want a hug," he says. She tightens her arms at his neck. "You can have pretzels," he says.

"March 14. Temperature at six o'clock, fifty-two degrees. Warm dark, surprising mildness, stood outside admiring breeze. Easterly. When my own child attains my age and I am twice my present one, what might we not have witnessed in the interim: the end of war perhaps, the end of famine certainly, the universal brotherhood of race and creed! All this seems possible—nay, plausible, on a day so full of promise, as if winter were extinct. No pestilence or hatred or remorse, no sleeplessness to trouble the dear dream!"

They return together to the kitchen. He reaches for the pretzels on the topmost shelf. She helps herself to two, then judges him correctly and extracts a third. All through the day he has juggled demands; he has been brother, tour guide, host. He holds such roles aloft and in suspension like Indian clubs or oranges. They have labels pasted on: friend, lover, rival, son. He has some skill at juggling and his reflexes are quick. His rhythm is steady, his concentration good, and he has been practicing for years. Yet there is always one orange too many, one trick where the fruit falls and splits . . .

When Ian hoped to be an actor, he had studied juggling and fencing and mime. "If you want to work at Shakespeare," his acting coach would say, "first thing you need to know about is how to handle blades. Edged weapons. It's got to be a third leg, kid, not just something you strap on for the big scene. Fencing, that's the ticket. The ticket is to know who's coming at you on what street."

"Can I have something to drink?"

"We'll eat soon," Ian says.

"I'm thirsty."

"Milk?"

"No. Pepsi."

"I used to ask for yogurt," Ian says, "when I was your age and we went out walking."

"The *twins* drink Pepsi. Every time they want it they get to drink Pepsi or Coke."

"That's because they've had their milk already."

"How do you know?"

"I know. They drink it first thing in the morning. When you're drinking orange juice . . ."

"I bet," Jane says. She licks her fingers for the salt. "What are we having for dinner?"

"What would you like?"

"Hot dogs. Hot dogs and ketchup and noodles with butter."

"Let me ask you something."

"What?"

"Would you like to stay here with me if Mommy went on a trip?"

"Where to?"

"Just a trip."

"Australia?"

"Not that far," Ian says.

"Where's she *going*?"

"She isn't going anywhere. I was only asking."

"Where *is* she?"

"Upstairs with Andrew."

"Andrew Kincannon," Jane says.

"That's right. Do you like him?"

She moves toward the refrigerator. "When's supper ready, anyhow?"

"Would you rather take a trip with them?"

Jane watches him, alerted. He starts the water boiling, then selects the open Mueller's thin-spaghetti box. "Not to Australia," he says.

"Where?"

"New York City, maybe. Someplace nice."

"Now?"

"I don't know. No. I'm just asking."

"What about you, would *you* go?"

He pours some oil and salt into the pot. He asks, "How hungry are you?" then shakes out the spaghetti. She waits. He sets the timer for eight minutes. "Can I stay?" Jane asks.

"Yes. If Mommy says so."

"With you, okay? They can go on their trip if they want."

"One hot dog?" Ian asks. "Or two?"

"One. And white meat from chicken. And ketchup."

"Please."

"I don't have to say it every time," she says.

"If you want good manners."

"Not *every* time."

"All right. You like the twins, don't you. Amy and Kathryn."

"Mm-mn."

"Milk in your Peter Rabbit Cup? Or in a wineglass?"

"A wineglass," she says. "It's its turn."

"March 15. Halcyon morning. Temperature at six o'clock, fifty-two degrees. Soft mist in the valley; fields breathe. When I was born this nation was engaged in Civil War; our father sent up thousands as a subscription for troops. Now there are few signs of strife and few such public levies, but I fear the torpor almost as acutely; where there is no Public Standard, the private banners wave. And so it is already in our corner of Vermont; men march to no music but gain. I see this in the Bank. We are rich and getting richer, but the wealth incites and does not assuage penury. I write this in full knowledge that I as Peacock's grandchild may turn up my nose at profit since his own nose was so keen. Nor is the Bank engaged in charity. But how much more gladly would I disprove than teach that conundrum having to do with riches and camels and needles and the Kingdom of God. My possible brother is dead. His stone will bear no name. I got it from a quarry in receivership in Proctor, and at a bargain price. Have purchased also from the same establishment a stone for Anne-Maria's child, dead long ago and far away. The meek may inherit the earth, but neither bottomland nor negotiable property; theirs will be the thornbush on the steep side of the hill."

The small mechanics of preparation have long since grown familiar; Ian busies himself with her meal. She pulls out her stool; he folds the napkin so it makes a triangle, not rectangle, knowing without asking she wants salt on her spaghetti, wants butter that's melting and ready to mix. Each of Jane's gestures seems freighted for him with the weight of loss, and he watches her as closely as he dares. Her hair needs cutting. It is tangled thickly at her neck, and the curls are brown: this is the color her hair turns in winter, or maybe she won't be the blonde that Maggie was. Her hair needs washing; he determines to give her a bath. Her snub nose is unformed, though the lines in it emerge, and she frowns in concentration as she mashes up the noodles with her poodle fork. The fork in this favorite set has a poodle for handle; the spoon has a dachshund, the knife with its blunt edge has what he imagines is meant to be some sort of bird dog, pointing.

Jane has lost her baby fat. Her ankles are thin and she sits with them crossed. Her knees show their structure; her shoulder blades show through the leotard top. Her skin has perfect paleness and is clear. She is a beauty already, as Maggie was a beauty, and he hunts some imperfection so she will not grow up vain. Her eyes are flecked with green. The lashes curl. She has dimples in her cheek; her neck is long. She is everything he hoped for in a daughter or a sister, and he tells himself he cannot bear to relinquish her just yet.

Ian scrubs the colander, then rinses it and sets it in the rack to dry, then towels it dry nevertheless. The house held eighteen servants once, but the dormitory wing has been removed by Judah's father who, in an access of democratic feeling or good architectural taste, or maybe in order to save on the heat, razed the servants' quarters and built a greenhouse on the foundation instead. It protrudes from the northwest wall. The panes are cracked. The louvers have rusted, and hothouse grapevines have languished untended for years.

From time to time, however, Maggie shows a fitful interest in this jumble—cutting back geraniums and starting tomato plants. She potted herbs. But then he'd find her with a broom in hand, her apron on, its pocket full of pebbles and a pair of hand-clippers and length of green string, her face gone blank in concentration, attempting to reconstitute the order once apparent. "I can't just give it up," she'd say, trying to repair the pots, to tape the glass or transplant shriveled roots. He'd help, he'd rearrange things till the wreckage bulked less large. But soon enough she'd stop and stare at the tables and dead hanging things, the Christmas cacti left to bloom two years before, the jade plant frozen, fallen, and the mounded dirt. "It's hopeless, Ian," Maggie would say. "I've got yellow thumbs."

There are plastic gloves in the drain. They point limp-wristed at the bowl he still should clean. He picks up the bottle of Joy, squeezes it, then lets the water run. Jane finishes her hot dog and tilts the plate toward him proudly, saying, "See? Now can I have my dessert?"

"What do you want?"

"A treat."

"What kind?"

"Nuts and raisins," Jane pronounces. "For a quick energy lift."

She has begun to learn from teachers that he cannot name. She too will leave the Big House, wearing clothes he has not bought in rooms he has not entered. "For energy," Jane says again and cups her hand. He drops some peanuts in, then raisins: the provider, his palm slick with soap.

"March 17. Temperature at six o'clock, thirty-eight degrees. Wind gusting northeasterly. A night full of difficult dreams: Daniel Jr. dressed in peacock-finery but starving, betting all he owned or could manage to mortgage on an inside straight. An apparition merely, the stomach's disquiet in sleep. Must inquire of cook regarding cream sauce served with veal. The public and the private man appear more separate than strangers, and that is why this daybook cannot fail to seem peculiar to the curious, if such there be. The daily round, the press of occupation is absent perforce from these sheets—when I work I do not write. I keep no secrets from my wife and all day long engage with her in conversation; therefore Lavinia is also largely absent from my text. It is only of an evening or in the early morning that I sit at ease, in silence, and pen these my secret thoughts: we are a nation fattening on calves that have been fattened for the kill. Who waits in what wings with which knife?"

"Shall we go find them?" Ian asks.

"Who?"

"Mommy and Andrew. It's time for grown-up dinner. We'll ask them what *they* want to eat. You help me cook it, okay?"

"Okay." She is out of the kitchen before him, half-skipping, slipping through the swinging door that leads to the back stairs. "Do *you* like him?" Jane asks.

"Who?"

"Andrew Kincannon."

"Why shouldn't I?"

"Because."

"Because why?"

"I love you, Ian," she says.

Her declaration announces a need. "You don't have to worry," he says.

"Can I tell you a question?"

"Yes."

"Why is Mommy going?"

"Who says she's going?"

"I know."

"She's lonely here. It makes her sad."

"But *we're* not lonely."

"No, But Mommy has no friends up here. That's why Andrew came to visit us."

"Can I make the salad dressing?"

"Yes."

"She looks like dress-up," Jane declares, "in the clothes she's wearing now. Except she's got no coat."

"Go ask them," Ian says, "what time they want to eat."

Jane had been incurious as to their mismatched paternity; it still sufficed to tell her that Judah Sherbrooke was dead. Since Ian had no father, and she has no father, their no-father was the same; she has been willing to leave it at that. She thinks of him as partway father anyhow, and he is more than old enough. Maggie said one parent and one brother is a multitude; family means family, it is a plural word.

Now he returns to the pantry. He takes out place servings for four. Ian pictures Judah at the table's head when they were four for supper—his father and Hattie and Maggie and he—pouring wine and cutting meat and passing salad, not making small talk because the business of eating was a full-time occupation for the time you sat to eat. Good manners meant you didn't talk with your mouth full; good manners meant you ate what was before you and asked for second helpings but did not simply reach for them and wiped your mouth before you drank and used the proper fork. His aunt had paid attention to proper place settings and plates. She hated stains and crumbs, waging a one-woman war on bad manners; the place for stains is napkins, Hattie used to say. Their tablecloths were linen, and she said no linen tablecloth ever looks entirely the same if it has soup stains or gravy, no matter how soon afterward you clean it and use bleach. It could hang on the line in the sun for two days and she would always know—when the time came to iron and fold the cloth back—who had been sitting where.

She hated wine stains worst of all. If someone at a dinner party spilled wine, Hattie would make clucking noises in her throat till she could not restrain herself, saying, "Excuse me," and getting up. She would walk with the saltcellar to the offending spot and cover it attentively, outlining the perimeter in crystals. She did this once too often, Judah said. He called for wine at a party when she'd covered Samson Finney's stain, and started to pour and kept pouring till the liquid splashed over the glass's rim and onto the table till the bottle was empty and the wine spread everywhere. His hand had been unwavering. Hattie started out of her seat, reaching for salt until she realized his intention and sat back and stared at the heavy red bottle tilting, the ruination of her cloth and pride of second place; Judah finished the bottle and, shaking it, said, "When."

There had been many such scenes. He remembers his father's fierce temper, and Maggie's continual watchfulness, and the way that Judah whetted knives preparatory to carving; he'd run his thumb along the blade and stare at Maggie's guests. Ian pictures (the last time he remembers Andrew Kincannon in the house) an argument with Maggie's piano teacher. They were discussing the techniques of Rubinstein and Horowitz and Artur Schnabel. Andrew insisted that Schnabel had more musicianship than either of his piano-playing rivals. He claimed that the greasy elision of Rubinstein's reading—in the key passage in the second movement—debased the line's raw elegance. Ian still can remember the phrases "greasy elision" and "raw elegance," and the piano teacher's disagreement while Judah sharpened his knife.

He wonders, now, just how much Judah knew of Maggie's infidelity. It had been a rumor in town. Tinkers and tailors and pot-bellied plumbers would joke about old Sherbrooke's wife; the lank-haired stuttering attendant at the Getty place would swear he'd seen her bare-naked in the middle of the cow barn, and not milking neither. There had been no truth in it, of course. She had been selective in her forays from the house. The men she chose were not of Judah's circle, and surely not his farmhands, and the gossip was ill-founded as such gossip always is—the envy of the clumsy-fingered for beauty out of reach.

He takes six twelve-inch tapers from the candle drawer. He inserts them in the candelabra, then sets out wine and water glasses. Ian thinks of this as, plausibly, their final meal together. For months his mother has eaten alone, or at the kitchen counter, nibbling at some salad like a rabbit, or squirreling sunflower seeds. She had seemed to swallow air. A cracker and a cigarette sufficed for her food for the day—with possibly the remnant of Jane's alphabet soup, or the leavings of a banana. She lost weight. Her face had that drawn-in expectancy of someone near starvation: flesh clarified like butter, ears transparent, eyes enlarged. The symmetry is absolute: he himself will sit in Judah's place, and Maggie and Andrew Kincannon will have a child between them wondering who leaves with whom.

"I'm thirteen," he had insisted to Judah. "I can make up my own mind."

"You can't," his father said.

"I can."

"Not legally. Not for five more years. You haven't got a mind."

"Stop it, Jude," said Maggie. "That's unfair."

"Who started it?"

"You're making this much harder than it has to be."

Judah turned. "One way to make it easy is don't go."

"Stop persecuting us." She reached for Ian's hand. "All we're doing is taking a place in the city. There's nothing criminal in that. Oh, Judah, why don't you *see*?"

"I see my wife who's leaving. Who's taking my one son." The edge of menace nickered in his voice like flame at paper: something that flared up, then fell. "Who's making him choose between us. And who won't be welcome back."

Then too Junior Allison was waiting at the door; he was to be their escort to New York. He barely knew the way. The upholstery was black. Ian remembers their departure as a kind of prearranged escape: he'd been sure that Judah would pursue them, in his pickup or the Packard or maybe even on horseback, fists raised.

Maggie sat on the stiff leather, motionless. She'd left the Big House often enough and taken him along with her on the shorter forays. But when they left for New York that time the severance seemed final, the sundering complete. It comes to Ian now (while he is distributing the napkin rings, the silver serving implements, and the trivet and ashtrays and candlesticks and salt and pepper shakers) that the departure he prepares is also a reprise: a second setting-out.

Returning to the kitchen, he takes three speckled trout from the freezer and unwraps the foil; he'd caught them last autumn in the Battenkill over by Shushan. For some minutes he busies himself with butter and lemon and almonds, making a final feast for Maggie in the house. Judah did not cook; Hattie used to claim he would have burned boiling water and couldn't manage an egg. Women had cooked for him all through his life; he had relatives or wives or hired cooks. But Ian learned to love cuisine and would prepare *truite almandine*; both of them are powerless to halt this one woman's escape.

Nor does he wish to, finally. There is this difference, at least: he has called Andrew, not Junior. If Maggie leaves she may return, but if she stays she'll die. He puts it to himself this way, taking comfort in the flat phrased urgency: if he loses her he'll find her, if she goes she can remain.

"March 24. Temperature at six o'clock, thirty-two degrees. It is possible the drunk who died here recently was engaged in a confidence game. He might well have taken me in. At the end of his tether, he would have nonetheless had strength sufficient for impersonation. I have heard of such cases before. He would have come to town and noted the name of the Bank, would make covert inquiries as to the age and nature of its president. Then, satisfied with what he would construe to be my gullibility in matters of this sort, he set about to make himself familiar with the Sherbrooke past. There are few enough of us. Of Peacock's children and grandchildren and great-grandchildren there is little to know; except for Daniel Jr., we are an open book. That page, however, is blank. Thus he would have fastened on the figure of my uncle, finding pistols with initials that might well have been incised there, say, by someone boasting to be a *Dead Shot*. There are explanations. It takes small wit to guess how small he deemed my wit. Yet I would have called him cousin and dear brother had he lived.

"Lavinia is come to term. I write this while she labors, in the quiet interval. Bill Robinson insists I busy myself elsewhere, as if there were sufficient distance in the house or in the village limits or the whole state of Vermont. I could travel the continent's breadth and not be at a hair's-breadth distance—they assure me all is well but I hear her down the hall. My hand is weak, my pen leaks black blood, my eyes cannot focus. Eleven-fourteen. I pace like a caricature husband, smoking like a chimney, wearing circles in the rug."

"They're coming down," Jane says.

"Good."

"Mommy isn't hungry."

"We'll make her eat anyhow, right?"

"Right. *I'm* still hungry."

"You can have trout."

Jane makes a face. "She says she might be hungry soon, but not just now, it's early."

"Is Andrew with her?"

She nods. He sets out the ingredients for salad dressing. She can handle salt and pepper, but the vinegar and olive oil require his assistance; he moves her stool till it touches the counter, then hoists her up. Jane begins work immediately, frowning, undoing tops, and pronouncing the word "ingredients." She chews her lower lip. He peels three garlic cloves, then helps her use the garlic press—squeezing not her hand but the handles. Lamplight casts a circle where they work.

Now Jamie Kerr enters. He is wobbly-drunk, he appears to have swallowed his teeth. His cheeks have white stubble, his hair is uncombed. He stares at them as if through smoke, his eyes are watery. "A fine house," he says.

Ian moves in front of Jane.

"Quite a place. Nice." Kerr points in the direction of the kitchen table. "Mind if I sit down?" Without waiting for an answer he scrapes out the nearest chair, folds himself upon it, puts his elbows on the table and his chin in his two hands. He squints at them. "You don't remember me, do you? I mean, not before this afternoon."

"No," Ian says.

"Time flies. That's what I always say."

Ian indicates the clock. "It's late."

"Mm-mn. I knew your father, understand. I knew him when the person here her size was you." His fingers tremble, pointing, and he cups his chin again. Then he extracts a paper napkin from the holder on the table and, loudly, blows his nose.

"You live in town?" Ian asks.

"Used to be," says Jamie, "this house was harder'n all hell to visit. Dogs." He fends off the air. "Used to be this place was like a bank on Sunday. No Trespassing."

"Could I get you a ride? The others have gone."

"I'm going, never mind. I'm not about to incommode you." He says "incommode" with emphasis, as though the word has lain in storage and is being aired. Jane watches him wide-eyed; he whistles and wiggles his ears. "No cause to worry," he says.

Caught between politeness and the impulse to throw the man out, Ian returns to his task. He selects two onions, peels and slices them. Slicing, he tries to have patience; when he opened the doors that afternoon, he tells himself, he had invited just such wheezing fretfulness to enter. "Mind if I smoke?" Kerr asks. He fumbles in his pants for matches, takes a single cigarette from his shirt pocket, unbends and licks and lights it, then leans back. He sighs; he has tobacco on his chin. Jane does not seem frightened now and shakes the salad jar. Ian runs warm water over the cold trout.

Jamie Kerr remembers how the Big House had had concert guests one year for Maggie's birthday. Judah'd penned the dogs that day so he lay out beneath the elms and listened to the sound of it, the music and the laughter and the clink of ice in glasses; just the sweetest sound, he says, you'd ever hope to hear. He used to come this way often. He remembers Hal Boudreau, and many nights they'd walk together downriver or across to Eagle's Bridge, discussing what it would be like to try potato farming—Hal discussing it, that is. As far as he, Kerr, is concerned, there's no percentage in that kind of work, no point in playing hostage to the seasons in a state like Maine—a place so godforsaken lonely by the Alagash even Indians don't want it. So they're hunkering along the shore with fifty million tourists and a Wigwam Lobster Roll Motel every ten feet, along what's mostly rock by now and tar and traffic jams. You ask him, Jamie, he thinks God's country still is this one where when it's snowing there's always a fire in somebody's chunk stove, and you know you're welcome if you wipe your feet. He's been a traveling man. He's been to Arizona, which is where you go for lung trouble; "Airizona" is what his friend Merriwether Lewis Shillington had called it. He's been more places than Ian could guess, has been to eighteen countries in the Second World War courtesy of Uncle Sam. He rode camels, for example, in Africa. You don't believe me, probably, he says, but there was a time he flew to Nairobi, Kenya, with the mail. There were girls of good family there waiting to greet him, he has photographs: East Indian girls, they were; he's seen the Pyramids.

Jamie Kerr sighs. He studies his hands. They are cracked and red, and his fingers are nicotine-stained. He has many memories about the Sherbrooke family—though always at a distance, nothing personal, no reason to make that girl there nervous; she looks the spitting image of her mother for a fact. In twenty years, you mark my words, says Jamie Kerr, she'll be the only other thing ever to compare for looks with her mother hereabouts. They broke the mold, he'd thought, but somehow glued it back. Sometime he'll tell Ian how their old aunt Harriet was young once also and went dancing. He'll tell how Judah's charity was secret so you never knew who paid for what until you knew you didn't know and therefore understood it must have been Judah—Judah Sherbrooke who'd donated trucks to the rescue squad, food for the hospital fund-raising square dance, books to the Library. He provided clothing to those who otherwise would go without, supported the Old People's Home up in Woodford where Jamie resided these days. And once a year or every other year or every five years maybe, it didn't matter when you got to be his age, he, Kerr, would feel so cut off from the world he'd wander into it and greet the survivors, the Sherbrookes who continue.

He hopes he hasn't intruded. He thinks Ian ought to crack the spines on that John Greenleaf Whittier. He came this way some winters back and wanted to pay his respects. But everyone was out. He'd sat in this kitchen, in this chair, not wanting to disturb the house or walk through without permission. After half an hour maybe he'd stoked the stove and banked it, then departed. History repeats itself, they say, says Jamie Kerr. And maybe that's true and maybe it isn't, but one thing's true for certain in this land of milk and honey—where the milk gets confiscated and you have to shoot the cows, or strontium 90 wrecks the bones of everyone who drinks it, and the honey's made from saccharine and artificial sweeteners and costs more than a swarm of bees to package in cellophane anyhow—you blink your eyes and blow your nose and what was up in front of you is way-back-when behind. It happens in an instant, in the winking of an eye. It's like riding a train and sighting some tree and standing up to get a closer look at it and in that standing-instant you find you've missed the tree. He himself would rather walk. The tree's still there, of course, and if you're walking or on snowshoes or even in the desert on a camel, why you'll have a chance to study it, to name the kind of tree it is and whether its planting was luck or intention, the way that stand of walnut grew, or the hackberry out by the pond. He's done that; he's walked through the house. He's had his cup of kindness—six of them, to be exact, and tasty too, and just the thing to oil the joints and make an old man supple as the boy he was. He bids them good night and goes out.

"March 25. Temperature at six o'clock, forty-two degrees. No wind. I drink my coffee peaceably; train prompt. We are in the maelstrom's center but it feels like peace. A poor sort of pilgrim, content to mind shop and spread the butter thickly on his raisin toast. The quartermaster might not seem important to those on the front line, yet without him the troops starve. May my son know just such peace, and may my daughter grow up beloved. It is a worldly prayer but the single thing I pray. Harriet and Judah. May their manners be courtly yet frank. May they have physical health, and long life, and sufficient comeliness to please the eye but not bedazzle it. May their learning be solid not showy, and their skills precise. May his work engage him; may they multiply. Let them continue in this house, as I have continued, and after their departure may they welcome the thought of return."

II

"You've got it all worked out," says Maggie. "Haven't you?"

Jane runs to her. Maggie puts her hand, splay-fingered, on her daughter's head. The curls are thick.

"Are you proud of yourself?" she asks Ian.

"No."

Andrew lifts his coffee mug. "The sun is past the yardarm, I believe. It's cocktail time."

"I could use a drink," says Ian.

"We all could, couldn't we?" Andrew is proprietary. He turns to Maggie. "What are you drinking?"

"Vodka," Ian answers for her. "Just vodka and ice."

"Show him where the ice is," Maggie says. "He might not be able to find it alone."

"There was a man here, Mommy. He just left, he sat in that chair."

"I'll find the ice," says Andrew. "It's the vodka that's giving me trouble."

"Here." Ian produces a bottle. There are glasses in the drainboard, and he sets out three. "If you're still drinking bourbon, it's in that decanter."

"Kincannon Associates." Maggie turns to Andrew. "You know, I never really thought of you as *management* before. But that's what you've been doing, isn't it? You and your associate here—managing me. Bringing me around."

Andrew has extracted ice from the freezer. He holds the tray in his hands, uncertain where to crack it.

"Maybe I don't want a drink," she says. "Maybe I don't want to go to New York. Maybe the patient's not supposed to notice how she's being treated with patience. Handled. You and your associate should think this through again."

"There's no collusion," Andrew says. "We haven't handled you."

She hears herself protesting that the deck is stacked, the game unfair; her very act of protest proves their point. It's the old trick of asking what cannot be answered, and then taking silence as the evidence of guilt. If she is docile they'll call it depression; she can't win for losing, she says.

Andrew turns to Jane. He changes the subject, pointedly. "Do you go to school yet?"

She nods.

"What kind of school—nursery school?"

She shakes her head.

"Kindergarten?"

"Play group," Ian says.

"Has it occurred to you?" asks Maggie—of no one in particular, of the space between the two men, bisecting it, interrogating air—"That maybe I know what I'm doing? That grief is—what would you two call it—an appropriate posture?"

Ian ignites the front burner. "I'm making supper," he says. "Jane made the salad dressing."

"The madness of our parents," Maggie mocks him.

"Trout." Ian has his back to her. "That's what we're having."

"When?"

"In half an hour."

"Fine," Maggie tells them. "I'll pack."

In her room again, alone, she does begin to pack—pulling out a matched set stamped LV and opening the luggage on her bed. She turns on the overhead light, then empties her six bureau drawers. Maggie works for several minutes with efficient inattention—not sorting things or folding them but stuffing each valise until it barely shuts. She fills her cosmetics case also. Holding the hair dryer, however—having trouble with the cord, attempting to bend and wrap it so the slipcase is positioned properly—Maggie sees herself reflected in the bathroom-vanity console.

She pats her face as might a blind person, feeling its contours. The cheekbones are sharp. She wiggles her nose. Maggie has to concentrate; she snaps the cosmetics case shut. In the kingdom of the blind the one-eyed man is king. But whom would he choose for a consort, she wonders, the blindest of the blind or the one who can distinguish dark from light? This is assuming, of course, that all the women are equally young, equally rich and attractive and adept in bed. She presses the lobes of her ears. The parable does not make this explicit, but it is implicit: the terms of success are sight and sight only—therefore all else must be equal.

Or perhaps the one-eyed man in the region of the blind is damned, not saved by sight. Perhaps he alone can see devastation, how the landscape around them grows withered and sere. He in all that countryside must meditate on blight. If beauty is in the eye of the beholder, and the beholder has no eyes, then how might such beauty survive? She tries to remember and cannot remember if the phrase is "country of the blind" or "kingdom of the blind." She busies herself, remembering. If she does not remember, the men in the kitchen conferring beneath her will win; her problem these past years has been retentiveness.

Maggie smiles. She touches her teeth. She is retentive enough, Lord knows, but what she retains makes no sense. She remembers a man in a

diner who wore a thick cord sweater and ordered coffee next to her, closing his hands on the mug. He turned to her and confided how he liked
sugar first, then cream. That way the sugar could dissolve at leisure in the
hot brew above, and all he needed was a spoon for stirring. Most people
prefer to have their coffee poured first, and then they add cream and sugar.
But his practice was the reverse. He had had to explain this, always, to
waitresses or people who offered him coffee. She remembers his theory in
detail, and the sensuality with which he praised the sugar's diffusion—the
way it rose to the surface, permeating everything from the bottom up. For
the life of her, however, Maggie cannot recollect the man's name—or the
diner, or whether they arrived together or ever met again. Perhaps it was
no diner but a restaurant or airport lounge; perhaps the stranger was a
dream-transfigured lover or man in a TV commercial.

She does not know. She does not need or care to know; it is a composition without frame. But she wakes up with the taste of sugar, the coffee so
thick it is viscous, her mother telling her to have some manners and not to
pile her spoon so high or take a second spoon. The amount of sugar that
she seems to need is appalling; it's probably a sugar imbalance, or maybe
it's pure gluttony and will make her fat. Her father tells them never mind,
it's good for the folks in Jamaica, and he brings her sugar cane to chew.

The Cutlers have maids from Jamaica. Maggie's childhood is an unbroken memory of maids—all wearing white frilled aprons and green uniforms that button at the neck. Their names are Netty and Alice and Gladys
and Bess; they meet her in the hallway when she comes home from school.
Later, they tell her their troubles. They have glass in their thumbs or pins
in their hips or seventeen cousins in Runaway Bay, and problems with men
and rheumatism in the winters in this city made out of steel and cement;
she might not believe it yet, but soon enough she'll learn. Steel and cement
soak up water like nobody's business, and when the winter comes it gives
that dampness back, that's how a city breathes, that's why it's smart to wear
rubber-soled shoes. She sits at the kitchen table, on a stool the twin to
that which Jane possesses now, head cocked, winding spaghetti around her

fork and smearing the pasta with ketchup. Or she's ladling Netty's special sauce that's orange and milky and just how she likes it; her mother tries on Saturdays but never can equal the taste or consistency—so Netty makes up a batch on Fridays and they keep it in the freezer, just in case.

She attempts to find instruction in such scenes. She knows that in Manhattan she will seek help, and the help will ask her, at sixty-five dollars an hour, to conjure up that full-time help to whom her parents might have paid sixty-five dollars a week. These are the facts of inflation, not value. Maggie packs her boots. She takes four pairs. She evaluates her parents' absence. It had been easy enough, in the years when she wanted to exorcise Judah, to label him some father-surrogate, some ratified totem of incest with no sexual taboo. It had been easy but untrue; the two men were the same age but otherwise unlike.

She knows an analyst might argue that their very opposition is proof of similarity; she's picked her father's opposite number out of a kind of ambivalence. But the truth is the two men were fond of each other; they would have gotten along. Maggie remembers, still, the contrast at her wedding: Judah huge and rumpled, Mr. Cutler slight and neat. He sported a Thomas E. Dewey moustache that he later enlarged to a beard.

Judah did not travel, and her father was unwilling to intrude. He had tried to avoid taking sides. And since their marriage was continually a question of which side to take, he'd kept to the sidelines and covered his eyes; he had welcomed Maggie when she fled from Judah, first, but urged her to return.

Her mother had been dead by then—having had an aneurysm at fifty-six. There had been no warning. Maggie remembers picking up the phone, and her father's choked announcement, and her disbelief: her mother died at luncheon, drinking tea. "She never knew what hit her," was the phrase he used. Maggie can remember how she pictured some crazed waiter wielding the teapot as a truncheon, wreaking havoc in Le Pavillon and scattering the customers like chaff. She herself is fifty-five. She thinks perhaps the women of her family are doomed to early death. Her mother had been prudent and had paid attention to her diet and gone to exercise class. She had been (she liked to say, with a self-deprecating moue) "well preserved." And they had not been intimate—so that Maggie, thinking back on it, thinks possibly what troubles her now is retrospect and augury, a punishment for her at-the-time indifference to her mother's death. She had worn mourning, of course; she comforted her father and played the dutiful daughter for months. Still, the quick of her remained untouched; she could not help half smiling at a term like "well preserved"; it was redolent of candied yams and pickles and vegetable permanence, not health. She had broken from her mother with a break so absolute it had appeared to heal.

Yet nothing is that simple, she knows now. No such fracture mends. The image of her mother—stern-seeming, brittle, sitting with her long legs crossed and reading the *New Yorker* their one summer in Vermont (when first, at thirteen, she'd met Judah; when her family elected once to take an inland holiday but hated it, hated the heat and the flies and lack of salt water and seafood; "We tried," her mother said. "We gave it every opportunity. You have to give us that.")—is an image of life lost.

And although she now might see herself as her mother's look-alike and has tried to offer Jane what she herself never received, her father was not Judah—never was. She loved him without reservation, but he made her smile. Even in his final years, living in retirement in Wellfleet and careless of his clothing, fixated on his Rhodes 19, even in his deathbed rantings (paranoid in the Hyannis hospital, convinced the doctors were trying to torture him, trying to make him yield the secrets of the *Bounty*'s mutiny and whether he had been responsible, had horsewhipped Fletcher Christian, had given a sufficient ration of the shipmates' bonus rum), the man was more comic than fierce. The Cutler in her had been banished when she married Judah Sherbrooke, and she wanted it that way. She put all that behind her when she entered the Big House.

Maggie walked on marble then. Peacock's walkways had been marble, brought from the quarries at Danby or Proctor, and the path he laid out through the grounds would shine beneath the moon. The village, too, had had marble sidewalks. North Street and West Street and Main Street used the broad slick stone for paving—and since there were no streetlights, such a sheen was an advantage. She remembers the bright reach of it like wake behind a boat, the feel of her heels in the slight corrugations, and how the facing had pocked.

But the elders of the village thought such grandeur commonplace; you couldn't give marble away. It was slippery when wet. It made Elvirah Hayes so nervous she walked in the mud by preference. Agnes Nickerson fell down in front of Morrisey's and cracked her knee open and fractured her hip. Samson Finney said that marble had three uses only: it's useful for statues and tombstones and sinks.

So two years after Maggie came they cracked up all the paving or levered it off to the side. They joined the state sidewalk program, getting cross-walks and poured-cement slabs. That was an improvement, Finney said, though not so good for lawsuits or the tourist trade. Then trains stopped coming too. When Maggie first arrived there had been nine trains heading north per day, and nine trains heading south.

The village is a losing proposition; Samson tells her why. The price of fuel oil and the price of gasoline is prohibitive and getting worse; real es-tate's too high. Industry goes south or west, or simply goes bankrupt and quits; the Route 7 bypass won't work. It will take tourists past the town, not cause them to stop off and visit; our industry is tourists now, he says. Half the state is paying for the other half to live on welfare; it used to be seventy-thirty, but now it's fifty-fifty. He's seen breadlines before and he'll see them again if he lives. I'm telling you the truth, he says, as if she might not otherwise agree; you'll see fighting in the streets before you see our welfare system fixed.

Samson has aged. He comes to visit once a month and calls her every week; his visits are ceremonial always, and he brings a gift for Jane. He is her only visitor and one authentic guest. He sits and reminisces in the leather block chair Judah liked, the strongest link to Judah left, telling his widow

626

how they would carouse, drinking Irish whiskey neat, and patting his lips with his tie. "To hell in a handcart," he says. "It was Judah's expression. Or mine. I'm not sure I recall which one of us began it—but every time I'd use the phrase, he'd say you mean handcar, not handcart, and we'd argue over that. Or maybe it was me who'd say handcar and him who'd say handcart, I can't remember." Finney blinks. "It doesn't matter anyhow, it's just an expression. The world's gone to hell in a handcart is what we used to say."

His suits are threadbare now, his socks are at his ankles, and he walks with an umbrella as a cane. In the chair across from her, he scratches at the armrest. "Nothing's what it seems like anymore. You build a road, it hadn't ought to be a one-way proposition, not only be a bypass and take you somewhere else. You mark my words," he says, "I'm telling you God's truth." Main Street won't be any use to anyone but bicyclists, weeds will make it to the middle line and daisies push up through the cracks. What the state can do to pasture if it puts a highway through is only one side of the coin, says Finney; they'll be grazing off of Main Street soon enough. He can remember when the airport was a cabbage field—thirty acres planted in red and white alternate sections. Up there from Mount Wayne it looked like Frederick Matteson was playing checkers with a giant, he had it planted so perfect. So when the runways crumble, it can be a cabbage field again.

The town's been good to him; he isn't saying otherwise, and he's settled something on Jane. It won't make her rich, Finney says. She doesn't need it anyhow, but it makes him feel like when he's gone he'll keep on going with that girl; she, Maggie, mustn't mind. Old men are forgetful, he says, but one thing they remember is mortality. He, Finney, recollects that clear as clear. One thing he remembers is the way she looked in '38, her Calamity Jane outfit on and riding that merry-go-round like it was an actual horse.

Andrew comes to the door. "Can I help?" he asks.
  "What did Ian say to you?"
  Andrew hesitates. "Not much."

"But enough," Maggie says. "When he called . . ."

Andrew nods. She hears his hesitation as if it were speech.

"You needn't have worried, mister. I'm not about to jump just yet."

"You don't belong here."

"I did. I've not been"—Maggie pauses—"well." Her tongue is thick. It fills her mouth. "Not well. So frightened, Andrew, so anxious all the time. You say it's easy to leave, but nothing has been easy. Ian does the shopping. I don't even go out shopping."

"What keeps *him* here?"

She offers an archaic phrase. "Filial duty, perhaps."

"He said he was working on something."

"Yes. I'm glad he told you."

"That's all he said," Andrew says.

The stubble on his chin is gray. She sees this with relief. He draws his hand across his eyes and starts to speak, then stops.

"We'll leave with you," she says. "If you'll still have us, now you've seen the—what would you call it?—situation. We don't have much choice."

"Where I come from," he says, "we call it common sense."

"Where *do* you come from, Andrew?"

"We can spend the night in Westport. We could make it back."

"That isn't an answer."

"It is. Let's get you packed."

Maggie looks at him in the diminished light. The storm is over, anyhow; she hears cars pass on North Street out beyond the gate. She had not thought him generous and is unsettled by his presence in the doorway. "I'll be right down," she says. "You go and keep them company."

He will provide for Jane.

She sits. Her luggage tilts toward her, and she steadies it. She remembers finding Judah on the night of her return. They'd been apart for seven years; then he informed her he was dying, and she took the bus north and stayed.

That night he tried to sleep with her and failed. She fell asleep beneath him and woke to find him gone. His departure had been noiseless, and her first waking thought (who had lain alone for seven years, or mostly, staying with her lovers only on occasion, with Andrew for a week or two, living with no one but Judah though she lived on Sutton Place and he never visited) was that she'd been dreaming. The room had the dim light of dream. When she realized that the weight that breathed on top of her, the dead weight pressing on her breasts was Judah's proved reproof—when she realized that he'd left her bed but had been an actual presence, she dressed herself and followed him and went to set things straight.

He was not in the house. She tried every room, from basement up to cupola, not wanting to rouse Hattie or signal her alarm. But she had been alarmed. She switched on the lights of the house. She looked in every closet, in the elevator and the basement, leaving only Hattie's room unlit. The place seemed huge, illimitable, a cave in which she hunted him but knew there'd be no trace.

Maggie tried the pantry last. The storm door to the back porch had been insecurely fastened; the door had slipped its latch. Then she knew on the instant how Judah escaped; he'd done what he used to do often, leaving the Big House behind, walking off the heat or shame or argument or airlessness of life within such walls. He was out on the land where she never could track him, and his privacy endured. He had invited her into the mansion—invited her in 1938 when first they met, when she was lost; invited her again a decade later when they met at Morrisey's by seeming-accident that they soon enough, in the talkative sessions of their new nakedness together, agreed to call fate; invited her to marry him and enter countless times thereafter, to come back from Providence, Boston, New York, to come back again in April, 1976, and have the house declared—in Ian's absence, Finney's acquiescent presence, Hattie's powerless abiding—her own.

Yet the land remained utterly his. She owned it outright also, but she could not bring herself alone to roam its thousand acres as she did when at his side. So all through the dawn of her first day's return she waited by his exit door, wearing her traveling clothes, drinking coffee in the kitchen and huddled to the stove. The world might be no merry-go-round, nor memory a carousel—but Maggie was assailed by circularity. He had been as lost to her as she had been to him before, when fled south to Manhattan. At eight o'clock that morning, while Hattie was stirring above, while she was on her third cup of coffee and her stomach would not settle, Judah walked in from the porch. His step was slow. His lips were blue. His boots were unlaced, and bits of straw clung to his duck-hunting jacket.

"Still here, I see," Judah said.

"Still here."

"Sleep well?"

"No, I didn't. Did you?"

He made no answer but blew on his hands. She rose and poured him his coffee.

"I thank you." His hands had been raw. He folded his hands around the mug so she could not see the mug, and steam rose from his thumbs. They made a kind of peace together, drinking, silent, and it lasted. Later that morning she did go outside. She found hay bales drawn up on the ground, and some of them were loosened where he'd made the hay his pallet for the night. And Maggie had known (again on the instant, not needing to confirm this by the matchbook lying there, the few charred stalks and shocks) that Judah had endured the April watch by the barn, relinquishing the house to her for what would prove forever.

But forever was five years. Six months later he was dead, and six months later Ian came back, and six months thereafter, more or less, Hattie left the Big House and threw herself into the pond. The circle was complete. Then the hired man did burn the hay and burn the barn and burn himself, though drunk and not intending to, not conscious of the carousel and how his action finished what her own return began.

Maggie watches herself in the window. It is deep dark outside, and the light behind her renders the pane a dark mirror; she sticks out her tongue. The women of the house, it seems, are those who leave, whereas the men remain. She buckles the first two bags. *Forever is five years*, she thinks; there's nothing but death that endures. And short of such finality all action is irresolute: Judah failed to burn the hay, Boudreau survived his burns. Ian has gutted the honeymoon house—the Greek Revival shell on the edge of their land he'd planned to renovate. But soon enough he left it and returned, his father's son, to where they both began. And now that she, Maggie, is leaving, he will feel free to marry and start the Sherbrooke line again. She wishes her older child well. She tells Ian good-bye. She'd thought that four years previous she'd said good-bye to Andrew, but he's drinking in their daughter's presence and about to eat *truite almandine.*

Jane, plain Jane, Calamity Jane, Jane Jane come in from the rain—Maggie rests her forehead on the glass. It is cold. She has wanted to jump. Often in the months gone past she'd thought such pain could not be borne, need not be borne, and breathing was too much to ask. Hattie had quit; she could too. There's nothing in the pure plain fact of continuity to praise. Death lasts beyond all lastingness, so why put pancake makeup on the age lines in her neck?

Jane is the answer, of course. She is the single reason, and it suffices. Maggie cannot jump—cannot open the window even for fear of the sweet whiff of freedom in jumping. She tries. She sits on the bed's edge and writes, using her yellow notepad and the toilet case as surface, using a ball-point pen. "Darling," she writes. "I don't expect you to understand it now, but maybe later on you'll understand. Keep this letter, please. It will tell you sometime what you'll want to know—I loved you, love you, will continue loving you until there's no life left. My death does not concern you. It should be set apart. It mustn't worry you. It . . ."

Maggie stops. She is not serious. She tries this letter on for size like an ill-fitting dress; its lines are not her lines. She takes a second tack. "The only thing that frightens me is that you'll feel responsible—not now, I mean, not now when Ian and Andrew will take care of you. I've gone on a trip, they will say. Remember when we gave you goldfish for your birthday? And you woke up the next morning saying you were just so lucky that the goldfish could be pets? Well, they'd died that night—it happens to fish often on their way from Mammoth Mart. I tiptoed in that night to see how you were doing, and they'd floated to the top. We flushed them down the toilet, Ian and I. But you wouldn't take no for an answer. I had to lie to you—it's the first time, maybe the only time I can remember doing that—and pretended they'd gone for a swim. They were fish that belonged in the river, but they'd surely be right back. You went back to sleep, it didn't seem to bother you. It bothered me. It would bother me if Ian or your father says that I've gone on a trip."

She takes a second sheet. Her handwriting is clear. "You never asked about Judah, so I didn't have to lie. You never knew him so it wasn't a loss, really, and Ian has been wonderful and Andrew will be wonderful and everything will work out fine. If you don't feel responsible. Going back to New York means beginning again, and I'm not sure I can manage it. But *you* must manage it, my darling."

Maggie stands. She folds the sheets, then tears them twice and lets the letter drop. She turns off the light and goes out.

Andrew is discussing the work week in Manhattan, and how his junior partners all are workaholics. "Fifty hours a week by Thursday," Andrew tells Ian. "They log ninety hours by Sunday, and what they do for relaxation is, you know, jogging. Five miles around the park for lunch, then back to the desk. It's crazy, it's no good. What I do is shed load. That's what I advise them—you're no good after ten o'clock, so why take the office home with you? Wrecks your home life if you've got one, wrecks your health, wrecks your digestion sooner or later." Andrew wags his index finger, admonitory. "The more we work, the less we produce."

She watches him debone his trout. Perhaps he too is haunted by the ghosts that once ate supper here and held such opinions; he might cite Judah's attitudes in order to impress the son and wife.

"Don't fence me out," says Ian. "I agree. It used to be the other way around."

"Used to be," says Maggie. "The emptiest phrase in the language. It's worse than might have been." She shakes her head, then pats her lips and drinks. "Used to be that there was smallpox here. And people died at fifty if they lived that long. And what we're eating now would feed a family of twelve. And this was virgin land."

"All right," says Ian. "I was talking about limitation. Fences."

"Why? Because you used to be so dead set against them? You open this house to the public because you hate Route Seven?"

"Don't shout," Jane says.

"We're not shouting, darling, we're having a discussion." But Maggie too can hear the anger in her voice; she takes a cigarette. It is an echo of her argument with Judah, she wants to explain to her daughter. She is preparing to withdraw, and this is how she's done it always—breaking things, smearing the walls. "I didn't mean it that way," she offers. "What I mean is, Ian, it's yours."

But he has turned to Andrew, as if they are in league. They talk about load-shedding and the danger of cult sects and recession and inflation; they talk about the weather and the best road back to Manhattan, or the best road down to Westport, according to which destination Andrew picks. They discuss the advantages of four-wheel drive or front-wheel drive and what to do with cable television when it fails, and whether the Taconic or the Thruway makes more sense; she has difficulty breathing; she keeps her eyes closed. Ian calls it a national madness, there's no gas left to speak of, and those mammoth rigs that take a gallon every yard are digging roads to nowhere every chance they get. It's like the difference, says Andrew, between a circle and ellipsis, a rectangle and parallelogram both failing to be square; it's like parallel lines that fail to meet but intersect in infinity; they're, what's the word, *asymptotic?*

This is what she must return to, Maggie thinks, these are the ways of the world. Her father puts her feet on his, and she is tall enough to hold him around the waist already and bury her head in his vest, and he moves her through the room to an imagined orchestra. Her feet are on his burnished shoes, and they do the box step so she follows where he leads.

Now once again she is without volition. She'll go where Andrew takes her, and when. The men are staking claims. She has no claim to stake. The pair of them drink wine and water together, lifting their glasses like legs. She is the tree that they mark.

III

Andrew excuses himself. He finds a bathroom, enters it, and switches on the light. It is early still, not yet seven o'clock, and he feels little hunger; he is accustomed to eating at eight. The windowpane is frosted glass. He cranks it open; it resists. Outside, the blackness appears palpable, as if the line of light his window casts had texture and solidity as well as shape, as if solid geometry were indeed a factor in his life. He smiles. He has not used words like "parallelepiped" in decades; what was he trying to prove? Maggie barely listened, and Ian disagreed. So whom did he want to impress with his half-baked memories of asymptotes and tetrahedrons and collapsing circles where the foci fuse?

Maggie had a second son, she told him once, who died in infancy. He remembers how her face went loose when telling him, as if the lips and nose and eyes were held onto the skull's smooth plane by glue that came unstuck. She shook. Her words were clear, but her lips made additional motions. She wet them continually. Seth had died of crib death, and she had one remaining son who had, she said, no use for her.

"It's a phase," Andrew responded. "All boys go through it. Especially in college."

"Did you?"

"What? Run away from home?" He considered the best answer. "Metaphysically."

"Nonsense," Maggie said. "You either leave your parents or you don't."

"Well, what about your husband? You leave *him*, but you don't."

"He's not my parents."

"I don't have a son," Andrew said, "But I've *been* one. Right?"

"Right."

He remembers wondering why she should oppose him so—why her self-abasing confession turned so rapidly to scorn. "Listen," Andrew said. "You're inventing trouble for yourself. That's what's wrong with you. You imagine that you ought to be upset about him."

"Ian," Maggie said. "It's his name."

"About Ian. Then you discover, if you're honest, that you're not upset. Right?—and that makes you upset. It's a vicious circle."

Maggie extracted sunglasses from her handbag. She found a Kleenex, blew on each lens carefully, and wiped.

"The trouble with you . . ."—Andrew pursued his advantage—"it's interesting. It's what makes an artist. Very many of my clients seem to share this trait: you've got no superego. Or a weak one—you're all ego, Maggie, no wonder the kid took a trip."

She tested the glasses. "Smudged," she announced. She took them off, then folded them again. "You've been marvelously helpful, Andrew. Thanks."

"I mean it . . ."

"Apparently."

"All ego and no superego," he repeated.

"Marvelous. It explains just everything. Why Seth died in his sleep, for instance, and I never see my son."

"I never said . . ."

"Nonsense. I know, that was my word." Maggie stood. "And thank you so much for your help."

The bathroom window is ajar; he breathes the winter air. The snow has ceased. He has a sudden image of himself as Jane's sweater-clad white-headed father, bending over her exercise book in the lamplight that helps him to read. He assists her with her algebra; he solves the problem that her sixth-grade teacher sets. In the room they occupy, there's a whiff of woodsmoke; he tells her Michelangelo could draw a freehand circle as accurate as a compass-drawn circle. He did it, people say, with either hand.

"Who's Michelangelo?" she asks. Andrew tells her about Michelangelo—enough to pique her interest, but not enough to keep her from the problem of apples and oranges that ten minutes ago had her stumped. He urinates. The bathroom he had used this morning feels a world away. He could slip out the back door and drive back to Westport or Manhattan, and none of this need have occurred. Eloise would welcome his return. They had parted peevishly before, and her gratitude when greeting him had been well worth the argument. She would ask him to forgive her, and he'd ask her to forgive him, and she'd say—not understanding or with the barest glimmer of suspicion as to where he'd been and what acquired, what relinquished in the interval, the wife and child he'd never had, then had, then left—she understood. She shouldn't have mentioned the drapes.

Andrew washes his face. There is no soap in the soap dish, and the towels are wet. He thinks "paternal instinct," and wonders, is he supposed to have paternal instinct with no practice of paternity? He likes Jane well enough. She's pretty and perky and quick. She's quietly attentive, also, as if she hears why people talk as well as what they say. But he'd be lying if he said that he felt shivers up his spine when introduced to his daughter, or that her every word engaged him and her glance had been instructive. He would have failed, no doubt, to select her from a playground or room full of children; she would be a stranger for months.

Such an instinct must be earned, he thinks; the strangeness dissipates. It takes place over time. It has to do with bottles and wailing importunity become some sort of greeting, with pride and delight at the first word or tooth. He has shared none of this. He never wanted to. He had averted his eyes from the peephole at the Toy House and lived the intervening years without regret. He runs his tongue over his teeth. He has many faults, but one of them is not the lust for repetition. Having embraced avoidance, he need not do so again.

He opens the door. Jane is there. For an instant they assess each other. "I ate already," she says.

"Yes."

"When it was *my* suppertime. I don't like fish."

"Does Ian cook often?"

She nods.

"Does your mommy cook also?"

"Froot Loops. She used to," says Jane.

"Or do you go to restaurants? With your mommy and Ian?"

"Only Ian."

Andrew gets to his knees. He is conscious of the gesture, the stiffness in his joints, the patterned oak beneath him, and her height now consonant with his. "Would you like to take a trip? And visit many restaurants?"

She watches him. "With who?"

"Me. And your mommy."

"And my brother?"

"In New York City," Andrew says, "there are many restaurants. Friendly's, for example. McDonald's. And so many others you'd think you could burst."

"He doesn't want to."

The floor is cold. Andrew's knees hurt. He stands again. "Who doesn't?"

"Ian."

"How do we know? Did you ask?"

"It's emeralds," Jane lifts her right hand to show him. "This ring."

"He doesn't have to come, you know. It's not that far away. Or he could join us later."

"Mm-mn."

"He's been to New York City. So now it's your turn," Andrew says. "We'd better go back for dessert."

She takes his hand, returning, as if to tell him that he's won her momentary fealty. Maggie's face seems smooth in the candlelight; the lines in her neck are erased. Jane sits in the chair next to his. He counts the chairs; this table could seat twelve.

Sitting, he is weary; he moves his toes in his shoes. Last night Eloise declared (putting on her coat in the foyer, jabbing at the elevator button with her vermilion index fingernail) he should get in touch with his feelings. He mouths the phrase, attempting to get back in touch. But he cannot touch feelings; he can only feel, touching, and he finds that touching enough. He makes a little ditty of the idiotic syllogism. A fashionable distaste for fashion, he tells himself, the kind of person who watches TV in order to disparage it—that's who I am. He had attended a wedding that week where the rabbi instructed the couple to "Tickle. Touch. Unzip." Andrew had controlled himself. It was his client's daughter who stood there nodding solemnly, promising in silk and lace to tickle and unzip. The rabbi had been plump, with turquoise chains around his neck and a Vandyke beard. "A solemn marriage contract it isn't," her father had said later. They clinked glasses. "Four daughters I've got, Andy. But just one *kaddish zoger*. There." He pointed to a boy in a white jacket, with a red carnation and a pompadour. "That's the little *pisher*. My *herzkind*. About the daughters, Andy, I'm exactly in touch with my feelings." He clapped his hand upon his heart and pulled a wallet from the tuxedo's inside pocket. "Talk about a soft touch, Andy, it's five thousand dollars a feel."

"Do you remember?" Ian asks, "when they had actual trains here?" He turns to Maggie. "When they whistled at the house?"

"No. They'd stopped doing that."

"According to his daybook," Ian says, "Joseph set his watch by the train whistle. He shot his shotgun off at them if they were late."

"Well, not exactly *at* them," Maggie says. "Up in the air."

Andrew rubs the tabletop. He makes conversation with Ian, as once he had tried to with Judah. He asks about the crops and cash value of hay these years, and what the land is good for other than dairying. "Developers," says Ian. "Bowling alleys on the bottomland because it's flat."

"You don't mean that," says Maggie.

"Or parking lots, maybe. You see"—Ian reaches for the pitcher of water—"to those who live their life on a farm, it isn't so romantic. It's a losing proposition, and you get burned in the bargain. You wake up one morning and find yourself dead; you find out the cows have mastitis and the feed's run out and prices have been raised for everything but milk. You go downtown to wrangle with the Agway man, and while you're gone the vet shoots the herd and says it's for taxpayers' safety. Shit." He drinks. "It's nothing personal, you understand; my father knew enough to get out from under, at least. I'm talking about the whole region. Ski slopes. Picturesque fishing villages. The best New England ever does is almost as good as it used to."

"What keeps you here?" Andrew asks.

"The chamber of commerce somewhere asked a caterer to reproduce the first Thanksgiving feast." Ian has grown voluble; he crosses his fork and his knife. It is as if he wishes to accumulate conversation, to hoard it for the silence soon to come. "At today's prices," he says, "and with no profit margin, the estimate was one hundred fifty dollars a head. They screamed at him, they said he's crazy. But he told the city fathers that he'd cut it close. He said you've got to figure lobsters, goose, and turkey—all the trimmings; applejack brandy, wine. They ate themselves silly, those Pilgrims."

"Is that an answer?" Andrew asks. "What *are* you working on?"

"It is. Because I don't believe it. I believe they ate a little leftover cornmeal and turnips and maybe the first of the hams. Maybe Samoset brought in some feedcorn from the storehouse."

Maggie rouses. "We've been sold a bill of goods," continues Ian, and she says, "I've heard that before."

"Yes? From whom?"

"Your father."

"I don't remember."

"He had this theory about Roosevelt. He used to say how Roosevelt's historians made picture books of settlers bringing in the sheaves. Sitting down to celebrate. When nothing grew that time of year—it was never harvest time in Vermont in November."

"Well"—Ian smiles—"that's one thing we would have agreed on."

"Entirely," says Maggie. "And more often than you think."

Andrew, drinking water, has a sudden vision of the winter when New England was true wilderness, not with roadways plowed and salted and honeycombed with motels. Men with names he can barely remember—names in front of libraries or state capitols or churches, names like Hooker and Mather and Shepard and Cobb, Bradford, Bradstreet, Edwards—names that conjure broadcloth and a broadax in conjunction, the preachers felling brush the length of the Connecticut Valley, the men who founded colonies not so much in the image of that England they left as in the image of a New Jerusalem, a place where faith and works, where faith *in* works was manifest: he sees them dreaming.

The air would be clear. It had the depthlessness of dream. Sight followed it until the horizon was lost, was blue, remaining in the mind's eye like the kingdom of the just so properly proportioned that it required no king. No tree there stood so tall it seemed distinct, nor mountain peak that belittled the hills, nor cataract that made the stream a tributary merely. The world was frozen, cleansed, air like a knife-edge where such settlers drank. They broke the ice each morning that forbade reflection on the wells. What they saw when bending to the surface of the ice was not their nearing features but a rippled visage of perfection: purity.

641

It cracked. Evil attended. Evil was corporeal; it had both face and frame. It passed elderberry wine and pumpkin pie and hiccuped, holding its stomach. It continues. It waits leering, stinking, its collar undone, its grease-thick fingers on the rump of some pink parlor wench, using the King's English and the Bible to calumniate, using gin and water to incite the children sleeping on the bear pelt by the door, feeding slops to the redskin or dogs. It lights its clay pipe and stretches, edging the girl to the fireplace coals and the nearby mattress of straw ticking it can spread her on, and thinking: *soft, soft, soft, from here on in it's soft.*

She does not resist. She joins him there with glad abandon, having no reason not to. Men drink. They hoist pewter tankards like the ones on the mantel behind him. They build with wood, then brick, then quarry for marble and slate. Men ford rivers without bridges and make pasture out of forests, and they lay out roadbeds and trainbeds and canals. The firelight was similar; a chicken tracked under equivalent tables for crumbs. The minister attended. Someone sang. A child succeeding in sleep at the far edge of that trestle, her head cradled in her arms, has hair astonishingly like Jane's; it spills like liquid amber over her crossed wrists.

Maggie stands. She snuffs the candles. Evil and his serving wench were always of such company, but there is another presence. It remains. It makes no noise. Andrew would banish this sight if he could, and he blinks his head to clear it—turning once more to the group in the room, these generations of his newfound family. He smiles. He licks his teeth. Yet the spectacle persists. It intervenes. A figure high as houses is standing in the moonlit dark, right hand resting on an oak, left hand hefting an ax. The ax is double-bladed, eight feet long. The handle is polished up under the blade where the right hand would grip. Its splinters have the girth of logs, and the presence looming at the edges of his vision strokes the blade with fingertips that must themselves weigh pounds. Its shadow fills the door. It does not menace him, however. It studies the tableau within. It appears to ruminate—testing the edge of the blade with an automatic motion, following no rhythm Andrew can establish. It could bring the Big House down as if such toppling were routine.

He is disregarded. Judah ignores him. For Andrew has no doubt it is Judah he senses—out of a compound of weariness and travel and whiskey, a ghost he can't believe in since he can't believe in ghosts, a trick of the light or his tension or memory, a hovering persistence—but Judah nonetheless. His grandfather's grandfathers hang on the walls, so Judah clings there also. And yet he is outside. Judah has no use for him and pays him no more heed than he might a mosquito—noticing his, Andrew's, presence possibly, and poised to slap and squash, and tracking Andrew's progress from the corner of his eye, but not alarmed, not fretful, concentrating elsewhere, knowing if the insect drank its fill there'd still be blood to drink.

Andrew waits. He too can take his time. What he's hearing is the wind, or maybe the furnace or some unfastened shutter on the second floor. Such seeming fixity in Judah is a form of weakness, since he does not notice how his adversaries prosper. Andrew notices. The opposition multiplies. He sues for Maggie's hand as if her hand were Judah's to bestow. He admits to his previous guilt. He should not have coveted his neighbor's wife nor, having seen his child that time, have left without a word. And because of this admission perhaps (or weariness and travel and whiskey, the persistent hovering and ax-edge in his retina), they are not adversaries. Instead, and to Andrew's relief, they are in league. He wishes Judah well. He wishes him rest and release. His vision fades. It smokes like the snuffed candles and goes dark.

"Are you all right?" Ian asks.

"Yes. A little tired."

"Do you want coffee?"

"No. We should be going."

"It's early yet," says Ian.

"We?" asks Maggie.

"Yes."

She accepts the plural. Jane is asleep in her chair. "I can't explain it," Andrew says. "I think we should leave here tonight."

"This isn't house arrest," says Ian.

"No."

"You're welcome to stay." He smiles. "Lord knows, we've got the room. And if you're tired, or worried about driving . . ."

"Oh, Ian"—Maggie turns to him—"won't you be lonely without us?"

"Yes."

"You could come too!"

Ian takes her in his arms. "I can't."

"You can. You could."

"Not right away. Maybe later."

"Soon?"

"Soon."

"It can't come soon enough," she urges. "Do think about it. Please."

From his vantage in the passageway, Andrew increases the light. The chandelier works on a rheostat; it hums. Ian seems calm. He breathes in the same rhythm as his sleeping sister, and his eyes also are closed. "I will," says Ian. "Maybe."

"Just let them build the road," she says. "The hell with it, really."

Jane mutters and moves in her sleep.

"We'll hire a caretaker—someone to stay here. Someone to make sure the lightbulbs are working and the furnace stays on. You have better things to do . . ."

They disengage. They each retreat two paces. Maggie says, "So much that's more important. Please."

"Do I?"

"Of course. That play of yours . . ." Her voice is without assurance. It carries no conviction, as if she knows he'll stay behind no matter how she pleads. "Custodian," she says. "It's just a fancy name for janitor."

Jane wakes. She stretches, staring, blinking, and takes her mother's hand. "It isn't bedtime, is it?"

"Yes."

"We're going," Andrew says.

"All right," Ian says. "Keep in touch."

Maggie precedes them. She walks through the halls holding Jane. As though the Persian carpet were a tightrope to negotiate, her balance seems precarious; she teeters, unused to high heels. Andrew watches. He has trouble focusing; she shifts in his vision from youthful to old, with the ripe dessication of agelessness—what she was she will remain. Maggie is the woman he has gauged his manhood by for years; there are changes in the mirror, but not in his mind's eye.

He has seen enough, however, to note clinical collapse. He reads the signals of depression like a contract, clause by clause. Her anger revives her—as it did with Ian some minutes ago—but without such anger or the habit of flirtation she goes blank. Her mouth appears dry; she licks it repeatedly. Her eyes have a wet glaze.

A change of scene will help, he hopes: somewhere less wintry with playmates for Jane. He pictures how next spring he'll teach his daughter to swim. The pool at his house has a shallow end, and he'll rope it off and spend hours with her till she learns to float. He can see himself bending above her, the sun on his back and his own trunks dry, he'll keep her so close to the steps. Jane will have a life belt on, and water wings; Maggie will be drinking fruit juice or Schweppes in her chair. The chair is yellow plastic, and its headrest and footrest are white. In the early mornings he wipes it dry of dew. She will smile across at them, this father and daughter so essential to each other and to her.

He gives himself pleasure by giving them pleasure; indulging his daughter, he feels self-indulged. There will be birthday parties, paper hats and noisemakers and magicians and balloons. He'll take her to the circus and *The Nutcracker* ballet and the Natural History Museum to see the dinosaurs. He'll ply her with presents from FAO Schwarz, making up for these three years, making good for what he'd failed at earlier. It was not his fault, of course; he'll try to explain that and justify his absence—but not until she asks. He will make the second bedroom in the farmhouse hers entirely; he'll buy only washable quilts. And in Manhattan they'll make room. It's possible, he thinks, standing in the dark hallway with mother and daughter before him, adjusting shelves and beds and furniture in the den, buying a Castro Convertible to replace the window seat; it's possible, they might just make it, might not have to move. But if there's insufficient room they'll find a larger place and settle down.

Andrew lights a cigarette. He has invented a future so much at odds with his own recent past that the present feels disjunct. How, for instance, should he introduce this family to Eloise, or explain them to her when she comes to claim her things? Her negligee is in his drawer, she would have worn it to welcome him back. Should he propose to Maggie and institute adoption proceedings or claim paternity for Jane? Should he wait till Maggie knows her mind or suggest intensive therapy or hospitalization; should they take a get-to-know-each-other trip? It has long been Andrew's opinion that the acid test for marriage is a hotel room in winter in a strange town with the airport closed; if you can get through that, he'd say, you'll get through fifty years. Make it in Omaha on Saturday or Tokyo without a hotel reservation, and you'll make it together till death do you part.

Yet the surprising thing about all this is how little he's surprised. It is as if he's been preparing for just such a change—has known since his chill vigil by the Toy House three years previous that he would bring them south. They'd parted breezily enough the last time they'd met (a peck on his cheek, reaching up, tiptoe, a half-wave as she lowered her head, the staccato heels). But nothing was resolved; it was a parting with false closure that had assured his return. He'll need an extra subscription to the opera series, and one for chamber music at Alice Tully Hall—but entertainment is his business, and there should be no problem. The Castro will fit, and the teddy bear Jane carries, and the trunks Ian promises to send: there is space on the shelves for Peter Rabbit and Big Bird and a Lite-Brite screen of Bozo the Clown she has finished except for the ears. He gathers these and stacks them in the vestibule.

It would have been so simple to pretend he had known nothing. He could say that Ian called one night and the next day he, Andrew, drove north. Then he claimed his daughter and took her to her rightful home and balanced the imbalance of their years apart. But Maggie had known otherwise; she knew that he'd known and done nothing those years. She could not know, of course, how he attempted to enter the Toy House and failed, how his first impulsive foray was repulsed by her seeming self-sufficiency when he saw her cradle the wrapped flesh of their shared engendering, back turned to him till he turned back.

The mother of your child, he tells himself; maybe Maggie's trouble dates from his own past refusal to help. He doubts this, but doubt nags. Had he come to her rescue when she told him three years previous that she was in Vermont with a child of their devising, her sorry recent history need not have come to pass. Yet she'd asked for no such rescue; she seemed to want the opposite. Had he brought a ladder to her window in the turret, Maggie would wait with her hair hanging down till he reached to embrace her, then kick the thing free. He, Andrew, would have toppled, he can feel it in his back. He had not been needed then. He hopes Ian does not know how he delayed three years.

His car, outside, has a light sheet of snow. Andrew starts it without trouble, then switches off the motor and lets down the tailgate to pack. The sky seems a black road with ice slicks for stars. Ian turns on the light on the porch, and the brilliance fades. Shivering, wordless, they load the Volvo. Ian brings his mother's suitcases to the car, and Andrew arranges them. The cold is absolute, and now his head is clear. He can smell and touch and taste cold weather everywhere; it extends from Lake Erie to Gander, and is unremitting. Jane is asleep again on the hall couch. "You're sure?" asks Ian. "You're very welcome to stay."

Maggie answers for them. "If we're going we should go."

"You're sure?"

"Yes." Once more, however, she sounds uncertain. "Understand," she says. "I love it here." Maggie rests her fingertips against the waist-high wainscoting. She bends her head. "I'm frightened."

"Of what?" Andrew asks.

She will not look at them. She runs her hand along the wall as if there are Braille markers there, and her future is embossed. "You don't know how I love this place. Ian doesn't. No one does."

"We can come back," Andrew says.

"Yes. But it's having to leave it . . ."

"You don't have to," Ian says.

Maggie turns to answer him. She has lost all animation; her mouth works without sound.

Jane puts her arm across her face and grinds her teeth.

"You're not being forced," Andrew says.

"I'll be a burden, Andrew."

"Yes."

"Ian can tell you . . ."

"He has."

Maggie smiles. Her face is white; the smile cracks her profile like marble. It is without mirth. "Don't think I'm not grateful," she says. "I know how—how *decent* you're being. Doing the proper thing, the honorable thing. But this is different . . ."

"Judah's dead," says Ian. His voice has Judah's weight. "He didn't burn the barn or burn his armor and his cattle. You can stop mourning him now."

"And you?" She turns to him. "What about you?"

His face, too, is marmoreal. It has no color, seemingly. "I've done that," Ian says.

"So what do we do? Just say it's over; decide it's finished?"

"Yes."

"Well, I *can't*. It's not that easy. It used to be. That plaque on the Toy House. It's not a National Landmark, Ian, not something in some register. It's where Judah sat."

"I know that," Ian says. "You'll come back sometime soon."

"No."

"When you're ready. If you want to."

Jane stirs in her sleep. Maggie shifts her attention. She turns to Andrew. "You poor man. You thought you'd just drop in on us. Now look what you're getting."

"Two women," he says.

"My white knight. My prince on a princely green steed. You won't regret it?"

"No."

"You can change your mind," she says. "That's allowed."

"I know."

"Let's go if we're going," she says.

Ian gathers Jane in his arms and carries her out to the car. He wears no coat, and his shirt is open. Jane sleeps where he settles her, on the soft leather seat and under a blanket; she holds her yellow blanket also, and her beanbag Snoopy. She does not wake up or respond when he kisses her goodbye; Maggie enters next. She sits beside her daughter, wearing a black cape. It has a black silk cowl. Andrew and Ian shake hands. "I've got something for you," Ian says. "To tell me what to do with, when you get a chance."

"What is it?" Andrew asks. He discovers a desire for Ian's good opinion; the desire is acute.

"*The Green Mantle*," Ian says. "My case in Judah's court." He smiles, half sheepish. "I hope it makes sense. It's why I'm staying, anyhow. I'll send it to you soon."

They shake hands a second time. When Andrew starts the engine, the smoke from the muffler is thick; it billows underneath the porte cochere.

Ian brushes snow from the rear window. His hands are cold. The last thing that he sees, as Andrew eases into gear and the car tilts forward, is his mother's staring face. She watches him, retreating, who stands immobile as they leave, who lifts his hand as she lifts hers. Her fingers fall. She says something at the window that he fails to hear. The cold increases. He has caged her for her freedom's sake; he has trapped this animal in order to release it. She sees him. She kisses the air.

AFTERWORD

I was born in England, of parents born in Germany, with an Italian name. It's a not uncommon story in this nation full of immigrants; mobility seems less the exception than rule. People move. We came to America when I was six; I have remained here since.

In my youth and young manhood, however, I traveled a good deal. The places my fictive family's scion, Ian Sherbrooke, visits—Iran, Afghanistan, Nepal—were stamped in my passport as well. My early books convey a wanderer's delight in distance; the first novel took place in Greece, the second more or less everywhere/nowhere, and the novel that preceded the Sherbrooke trilogy was set in the south of France.

At the age of twenty-four, I moved to southwestern Vermont. There, teaching at Bennington College, I fell under the spell of the landscape and dreamed a deep-rooted dream. Instead of change, I came to value constancy; instead of geographical variety, I wanted to write about those who stay put. Staring up at the Green Mountains, I grew vegetables and a beard, learned to ski and rototill, and began to think myself, if not a native, at least sufficiently immersed in it to focus on New England. I still can remember, and clearly, the day I decided to try.

It was 1975. I had joined the faculty of Bennington in 1966 and would remain there for ten further years. My wife and I were living in a farm-house on the grounds of the Park-McCullough house, a large and impos-ing Victorian structure in the village of North Bennington. I walked the trails and meadows daily and knew the property well. At a certain point on one of those walks—a fork in the road in a wood, as it happens, with a gate overlooking a pasture—I understood *this* was the place I had come to call home, not Greece or France or London or New York or Timbuktu. I can remember telling myself there was no point pretending otherwise; I was an American writer and needed to set a book *here*. Before all else, therefore, I knew my novel's location; it came prior to the story line or characters or any conflict between them. And since I knew the owner of the Park-McCullough mansion, I asked his permission to use the locale.

He gave it. His family had been retentive; they kept laundry lists and letters and records of business transactions from the nineteenth century, and he provided me with access to an attic full of documents. There were thousands of pages in boxes; I read and read. At some point in that pro-cess, however, I came to understand that these figures from the distant and the recent past failed to fire my imagination; they seemed—not to put too fine a point upon it—dull. To the degree that this is an historical novel (as in the letters of Peacock Sherbrooke, his daughter, and his grandson), that early research may have left its residue, but the generations of my family are each and all invented. So I began with two imperatives: use the land-scape of southwestern Vermont, and people it with people who have been made up.

Here is how I put it in a prefatory note to the first of the volumes, *Possession:*

> The author wishes to thank John G. McCullough for
> his generosity in making available the files of the Park-
> McCullough House. The location of this novel more or

656

less accurately describes the locus of that house—but I wish to make it clear that the characters within it are wholly invented, not real. It would be a poor return for kindness indeed if any reader were to confuse my imaginary Sherbrooke tribe with the residents of the Governor McCullough Mansion, present or past.

I would like, in the pages that follow, to provide a kind of gloss on what I believed I was doing and what I believe I have done. The Sherbrookes trilogy (*Possession*, 1977; *Sherbrookes*, 1978; *Stillness*, 1980) was a major project for me and, though I'd published seven previous books, felt like the end of a learning curve. When the third of those three texts was done I'd cut my eyeteeth as a novelist and was no longer a beginner. It's simple truth, not boastful, to say those books were widely reviewed and well received; by 1980 I could fairly claim to have finished my apprenticeship and entered in the guild. Yet more or less coeval with completion of the trilogy, I lost my bearings in the longer form and would not publish a novel again for fifteen years. I kept my hand in, as it were, and wrote short stories and non-fiction, but the well of the novel went dry.

So the opportunity to reconsider these old efforts is a welcome one. For openers, I'm now much closer in age to the seventy-six-year-old Judah Sherbrooke, the protagonist of *Possession*, than to the age of the writer who invented him; from my present vantage it has been astonishing to see how much I knew then and how much I failed to know. The British boy who impersonated a Greco-American and resident of Southern France next borrowed the garb of Yankee settlers and the accents of New England. But what was I up to, and why?

When John O'Brien (the publisher of Dalkey Archive Press) kindly offered to bring the trilogy back to print-life, there was a choice to make. Most authors, including this one earlier, are glad for the chance to reissue old texts and leave well enough alone. At worst, the errors of juvenilia are simply that; one fixes a comma or adds a footnote and the book exists anew. It's a record of a time and place, not something one should tamper with. Painters and composers often revisit their previous work and offer, as it were, variations on a theme. Some authors—famously Henry James in the New York Edition of 1909 or, more recently, Peter Matthiessen in his rewritten trilogy—do undertake a full-fledged overhaul of what they wrote before. But the majority of writers seem content to say, *Here. What's done is done.*

In my case, however, the three books were one, and I had conceived them as such. The structure of *Possession,* for example, mirrors that of *Stillness*—with *Sherbrookes* as a kind of second movement and pastoral interlude. The first and third book's actions transpire in a single day; the second deals with gestation and plays out over months. The seventy-six-year-old Judah whom we meet on page one has his birth attested to by a doting father at the end of Book Three. All along I'd hoped to publish them as a single volume, or a kind of triptych, and when invited to do so it seemed the right way to proceed.

Yet certain issues if not problems came immediately clear. First, volumes two and three contained passages of recapitulation—in order tell a new reader what happened in previous texts. (Judah dies in the interstices of *Possession* and its sequel, *Sherbrookes*; his sister Harriet drowns herself at the end of the second installment; and the reader of the third book, *Stillness,* would have to be aware of this. Secondary characters such as Samson Finney and Lucy Gregory make what seems like a debut appearance in *Stillness,* but have in fact been introduced some hundreds of pages before.) These repetitions felt redundant and could be edited out. This I did. But once I began with red pencil and scissors I found it hard to cease cutting; the entire text—sentence by sentence and paragraph by page—could be, it seemed to me, pruned. In the aggregate I cut roughly seven percent of the whole: nearly ten percent of *Possession* and less of the subsequent two installments. The book now comprises some 200,000 words—a long novel by any reckoning but not, I hope, bloated.

The simplest way to put it is this: I changed nothing important in *Sherbrookes*—retaining the second book's title as the title of all three. I added nothing of note. The characters and conflict and action and tone stay the same. The thematic matter (of which more later) is constant, as is the order of scenes. But no single page of prose escaped my editorial intervention; I'd written the sentences long ago and could rewrite them now. Why not, I asked myself, improve what needed improving; why leave a phrase intact when it could be with profit rephrased? The good news is—or so I told myself—that I'm a better writer now than when I started *Possession*. The bad news is the same. The youthful exuberance of Delbanco's prose troubled the older Delbanco, who has learned to admire restraint. Someday perhaps some scrupulous someone may compare the trilogy with this single volume, but at the present moment I'm the "sole proprietor" of the territory of *Sherbrookes* and can alter its property lines.

A few examples may suffice of what and how I revised. I bowdlerized the text a little and simplified it a lot. Some of this was a necessary consequence of present-day technology. My books were composed on a typewriter, not computer, and no previous word-document exists. So the pages all had to be scanned. That process has become increasingly precise, but there were many errors of transmission—"lit" for "hit" and "nickering" for "flickering" and, routinely, "r" and "n" conjoined as "rn" where the original letter was "m." Some passages were missing; others were reproduced twice. In effect, I was required to copyedit *Sherbrookes* more than thirty years after it came into print, and I worked my way through the three volumes with a proofreader's eye. Having done so, now, six times, I feel more or less confident of exactness—but in the process of such tinkering I could not keep from changing words as well as correcting their spelling: from fixing, as it were, the language as well as the text.

For example I substituted "the day after Judah's funeral" for "ten days after Judah's death," when Ian calls his mother at the beginning of *Sherbrookes*.

It seemed wrong for him to wait the longer period; he was conflicted over his duty to his dead father, not to his living mother. This is a small editorial intervention only, but it does register change. And I cut the last line of *Sherbrookes,* since it seemed over-explicit; we do not need, as readers, to be told: "They huddle together, as once they would with Judah, and are well."

The process of revision could be as simple as the substitution of "She said she'll write you it's her own idea to come" for the original "She said she'll write you that it's her idea to come." Or the alteration of the phrase "not to waste this time" to "not to enjoy this time"; the word "waste" seemed less clear than "enjoy." Or the substitution of "with glass and gauze between them . . ." for "with glass and gauze intervening . . ." I did try to fine-tune a character's diction: "*Who knows your reasons, lady?*" becomes, in Hattie's voice, "*Who knows your reasons, missy?*"

To this older writer's eye the younger writer over-ascribed dialogue; I cut perhaps a hundred usages of "he said" and "she said." These had been more a function of rhythm than necessity; in the first published version I used "he said" and "she said" as taglines throughout the spoken discourse, and they could be—with no loss of clarity—removed. At that period I had (still have, no doubt) an excessive fondness for semicolons and that often needless word, "that." Too, I used to love to turn nouns into adjectives by means of a hyphen; this seemed a habit to break. So by using an added conjunction I could substitute the phrase "comfort and temptation," for the invented compound word "comfort-temptation." To my present ear, this seems an improvement and slightly less mannerist prose.

Repetition is another habit I did try to break. When, for example, I had Judah both "triumphant" and "triumphing" in a single page of text I cut the former usage. And sometimes I would cut a phrase I liked because it called too much attention to itself: ". . . the farthest twig of the outermost branch of Sullivanian analysis," became ". . . the farthest wing of the renegade branch . . ."—which is more accurate as a description if less engaging as trope.

The bulk of what I excised was sheer rhetorical excess. I was too fond of metaphor and the abstract generality—or so I now believe. William Faulkner and Malcolm Lowry were my masters then; these days I'm more committed to power in reserve. A phrase such as the following seemed a candidate for cutting, with nothing but verbiage lost: "the past is as the present's shadow, shortening and lengthening and mutable in the terms of perspective, changing with sightlines or on hillsides or pavement or light—yet truly immutable, fixed."

Or, "He is haunted by flesh, not fleshlessness, and he twined his limbs' decrepitude around his young wife's limbs. She does not fade or stale; she took lovers twenty years her junior, as he had taken her. She tempts him now continually, even in decrepitude, and is not dead but quick."

For the adept at variora, here are some examples of what has been cut:

> There are those who train with horseshoes and can throw and ring the horseshoes as part of their performance. There are those, Maggie knows, who can drop one orange or Indian club yet not break their juggling rhythm. Some jugglers can stack cups on saucers without shattering the cups. She herself is more agile than most; she has kept a close inventory of relatives and lovers and the patterned arc they make, from throwing hand to catching hand, suspended.

> He cannot remember her out of the wind, now Judah comes to think of it, or ever less than airy light for all the years' stiffening additions—and remembers now the nursery rhyme about the oak tree near the ocean, and reeds: how everything is leveled in the last big wind but bending reeds, how roots and all mean nothing when the hurricane and thunder come.

So she kept *doing* and *talking* aloft. Things hung there suspended an instant, in perfect opposition to the force of gravity—only rotating, not rising or falling, and for that perfected instant she could keep three men convinced they were her only man, or persuade two aunts in the same room that they were her favorite aunt. At such times, she told herself, she could persuade a Catholic with seven children to embrace the right to choose, or vote for George McGovern since he'd bring the boys back home.

Ian would be staring at the traces of a lesson plan, trying to learn what he needed to know—while there was only her blurred mouthing, only the spoor of the sentence she'd thought and no blackboard and no chalk and nobody there to nudge him with the answer. Still, he picked it up. He lip-read, thought-read, read without reading; if only he'd been half the student in school that he'd been of her manners' schooling, Hattie said, why then he'd be adept at fractions and geography and penmanship also. He learned degree and size.

She yearned for him. She was, she told herself, in love. It wasn't a term she much liked. It was attended by guitars. It had meant *crush*—some hero's sock stolen from the basketball court, and treasured, rolled into a totem in her top right drawer. Later it meant four-leaf clovers proffered as they walked through fields, and later the wine bottles shared. So love became a pawing intensity—and the terms were making out, then making it, then making love. Later still it meant submission. It meant Billie Holiday singing "Hush Now, Don't Explain"—the whiskey seams in her voice come unstuck, a fiddler using nerve and hair ends for her strings.

It's not as though these passages strike me as poorly written—just that they seem excessive and at least a little ponderous. I was flexing verbal muscles then that now seem over-exercised; my guiding principle throughout the revision was, in effect, Less is more. In several instances (particularly from *Possession*) I excised entire scenes. I cut, for example, memories of Judah's grandmother, of Ian's escapades abroad, and Maggie's trip to Los Angeles since they failed to advance the tale's action—or were a gravitational side-drag upon it. Dialogue, too, went on too long, and I cut exchanges that seemed merely to mark time:

> "That's nice," she said. "That's complimentary."
> "It's the way I meant it."
> "Men do yoga too. The world's best athlete is a ballet dancer."
> "Who says?"
> "*Time* magazine," she said. "And they must be right."
> "I didn't call it sissy work. Just woman's."
> So, to spite him, she had kept at it. She taught Ian to sit in the lotus position.

> "Judah"—she would summon him—"what kind of tree is that?"
> "A birch tree, grandma."
> "Yes. What kind of birch?"

"A silver birch."

"What other kind would it be?"

"A silver bitch," he'd mutter, and she strained to hear.

"What?"

"A white birch maybe, but it isn't. It's a silver birch."

She'd have her notebook out, and wet the pencil stub.

"Beech, did you say beech?"

"No."

"Hattie knows the answer. She could tell."

He put his hands in his pockets. He balled his fingers to fists.

"Fess up, Judah, you said beech—that's a penny less this morning. That cancels out the elm."

"*Birch*, I said. Silver birch."

"You got the popple," she would say. "You got the cottonwood."

"Do it again," he'd ask her.

"Why?"

"It's fine to watch."

So she'd pick the limp lengths up again and turn her back to him and work her arms and then turn back with magic entanglements, fanning out and in. He wanted her to try with tinsel, but it wasn't long or strong enough. So he fashioned her, one Christmas, a tinsel necklace and bracelet and earrings and said, "They'll hold. You wear them," and she was his glittering creature lit by the Christmas tree lights. They made daisy chains from Reynolds Wrap, and Maggie said, "Imagine. There's country where it's warm enough so you can find real daisies in December." He imagined that.

I began with the assertion that I'd always thought of three as one; that is not quite the case. When I first tried to people the landscape of North Bennington, I started with a phrase—or, more precisely, tableau. For some time I had been thinking of the story of King David, and the great biblical description of that warrior-poet's old age. Fading, cold, and failing, he is offered the company of Abishag the Shunammite in his tent at night. But her body's warmth cannot rouse him. The Old Testament's indelible description reads: "And the damsel was very fair, and cherished the king, and ministered to him: but the king knew her not" (1 Kings 4). That last phrase engendered *Possession* and remains embedded in it still.

More generally, I had the image of a funeral pyre erected at a tribal hero's death. This is the sort of procedure collectively attested to in Norse mythology, Anglo-Saxon legend, Indian suttee, ancient burial rites and so on: the king lies arranged on a high pile of wood, ringed by wives and serving girls and soldiers and armor and chattel, the regalia of his eminence. Then the whole is set on fire in an all-consuming blaze. If there is water he sets out to sea, and the boat bearing him off too must burn, from keel to topmast: flame. It was the image with which I began and the first scene I wrote.

The manuscripts of my Vermont trilogy (as well as other, early papers) reside now in the Abernethy Room of the Middlebury College Library in Middlebury, Vermont. I have not consulted them. But somewhere in those cartons is the scene of Judah Sherbrooke, lying on a hay bale in the middle of his hay barn in the middle of his property and, by extension, the world. He sets himself afire and, operatically, dies. I wrote and rewrote till it seemed letter-perfect; even today, more than half my life later, I remember the satisfaction of that "pyrotechnical" prose and those funerary rites. The scene was, I was sure, triumphal: a set piece to make Faulkner or Lowry or even James Joyce proud. But I can praise it so unreservedly because it's in an archive and never exposed to the harsh light of print; in the event I cut those pages out.

Judah's elements indeed consist of fire and earth (his young bride's are air and water), and there are leftover traces of the language in Hal Boudreau's drunken fiery accident at the end of *Sherbrookes*. Too, at the end of *Possession*, the old man lies down on his pallet of hay and strikes a match or three. But by the time I'd lived with him and was fully engaged in writing the book, I knew this particular character would not burn down the house. He's too much of a skinflint, too property-proud and retentive to set the world ablaze. Instead, Judah brushes himself off, shambles up and down the street, then back into the kitchen to share a cup of coffee with his wife. It's a much less dramatic—even an anticlimactic—conclusion, but a more truthful one. During the process of composition I had come to understand that, far from destroying himself, this flinty old Vermonter would keep on keeping on.

And that's when I conceived of a second volume and why he does not die. Or, rather, he dies *between* the first two books and not at the end of *Possession,* just as Hattie dies at the end of *Sherbrookes* and Maggie leaves at *Stillness*'s end. It's a technical challenge, of sorts; the protagonist of Book One must be a presence in but not central to the action of Book Two; a central character in Two is absent from the action of the third installment. In that sense, these three books are not sequels but sequential, and that's when I understood I'd not be finished at *Possession*'s close but needed to resume the story. As Conan Doyle discovered when he tried to kill off Sherlock Holmes and was forced, by an avid public, to bring his hero back to life, it's best—if you do plan to continue—to keep characters alive. In my end was my beginning, therefore; when I scrapped the scene of Judah's death the trilogy proper commenced.

In Book Two the focus shifts; in Book Three it does so again. A single long novel would not perhaps be built this way, but no single figure here is *Sherbrookes*'s sole protagonist; rather, it's a collective and family history with—counting down from Daniel "Peacock" Sherbrooke—five generations in play. It's difficult if not impossible to ask a reader to shift focus and allegiance text by text; the boy who's wholly absent from Book One, for example, is wholly present for Book Three—while his father, Judah, who was thoroughly corporeal in the first book is, by the third, a ghost. I tried to justify all this in part because the narrative concerns itself with parents and their children, the presence of the past. And in part by having Ian Sherbrooke—the surviving son of his mother and father's fierce union—write the whole thing down.

The long middle chapter of the middle section of the final book—(which details Ian's romantic history and his attempt to write a play about his parent's intimate wrangle—is my favorite chapter in *Stillness*. (In *Possession* I'm most partial to Part II, section IV, which begins with the phrase; "Judah met her first, in 1938," and in *Sherbrookes* I like best chapter XIV, describing Maggie's emblematic visions: "Images afflict her; she cannot keep them from coming.") This is, of course, only one man's opinion, but the recapitulatory nature of Ian's rehearsal of what went before does seem to me a successful attempt to lend shape to the whole. It's a tip of the cap, I suppose, to the metafictional and self-reflexive strategies that were so common in the 1970s—an attempt to meld the modern and the more traditional mode. At any rate, when Ian summarizes his family's history (as well as, it happens, this novelist's previous publications) I knew that the book neared its end. Andrew Kincannon—that outlier—is meant to provide a kind of perspective to the goings-on in the Big House; when he and Maggie and Jane drive off at the end of *Stillness,* the ongoing agon is over and Ian's work truly begins.

A thing that surprised me, rereading, is the inadvertent way in which these pages have become "historical." It's strange to see that what one wrote when young is today a period piece and equally strange to read what proved predictive—how these character's imagined future has since come to pass. There are no cellphones in *Sherbrookes*, and certainly no iPods or computers; when people write to each other they write letters, not emails or text messages; when they need to make a call they find a phone. I'm struck, in

Stillness, by how Andrew Kincannon has to dial the weather number (WE6-1212) in order to get information on the forecast storm, and how he—generously, for the time—hands the garage attendant a dollar. Things change. In these three books, and even when pregnant, everybody drinks and everybody smokes. When Maggie *does* get pregnant at the age of fifty-two she's a medical anomaly; now that would be a bit less startlingly the case. The Packard Ian drives (and Judah purchased for his wife) is a conscious anachronism; the Plymouth Volare has become one also, but wasn't intended as such. Maggie reminds herself that "these are the facts of inflation, not value," but the price of a stamp or housekeeper's wages or psychoanalytical session has increased exponentially. Her sister-in-law is outraged that soda water costs thirty-five cents a bottle, plus deposit; we'd all be glad of that now.

By contrast, however, most of the geopolitical concerns remain pertinent—or have today surfaced again. *Sherbrookes* spans the years 1976 to 1980, but its characters discuss the price of oil and the possibility of boycotts or an OPEC embargo; they worry about global warming and the infrastructure's collapse. Many of the speeches about the trouble with and in America have, alas, the ring of current truth.

The thematic oppositions of Maggie and Judah—their ways of living in the world—have dulled a little, however, and lost some of their contemporary sheen. The novels deal with the then-much-more-vocal contrarieties of "flower power" and cultural conservatism, the ideals of liberation—particularly, here, in terms of gender—and the straitlaced desire to preserve what went before. I never really saw my heroine as wanton or promiscuous, but it's true enough that, by the standards of the time and place, she was a kind of revolutionary. Perhaps I should have been explicit about the clash of values and the way this specific family was supposed to embody the general national case; it's not an accident that Judah is seventy-six years old in our bicentennial year. At any rate I took for granted, and possibly more than I should have, the backdrop of the Civil Rights movement, the emergence of a drug culture, and the generational wrangle which put Ian and Judah at odds.

Other aspects of the story, though I here attempt to retrieve them, have been lost. Those years at Bennington were made vivid for me by the presence of John Gardner; we were close colleagues and friends. I showed him the manuscript of *Possession*, for example, and we argued over the spelling of Sherbrooke—John insisting that the final "e" was an instance of my Anglicisms and should properly be cut. He came up with a bottle of Sherbrook Whiskey in order to buttress his point; that bottle appears in this book. (The town of Sherbrooke, near Montreal, does have a final "e" attached, and therefore I retained my own preferred orthography.) John, who wrote at warp speed then, preceded me into print with a novel called *October Light*, which won the National Book Critics Circle Award for 1976. In it, he has *his* Vermonters joke about mine; his villagers tell tales about the goings-on in the Big House and mock old Judah Sherbrooke and his "bare-nekkid wife."

My own wife and I make a cameo appearance in the pages of *October Light*, and—like many other authors—I had been written about, flatteringly or unflatteringly, as a character before. But to have a creature of my invention be referred to in another's book did seem a kind of testimonial to the power of the written word, and I returned the compliment by having my townspeople in *Sherbrookes* gossip about James Page, Gardner's protagonist, as an "old fool" stuck up in a tree. This cheerful back-and-forth was noticed by a critic in, if I remember correctly, *Newsweek*, who complained about it as a form of literary incest, but the lines still make me smile.

Less happily, I took the title *Stillness*—having asked him for the use of it—from a manuscript of Gardner's he assured me he'd abandoned and was not planning to publish. (Other working titles for the third of my three novels were "Shoreline Certainties" and "Boats in Bottles" both of which appear as phrases and of which John disapproved. He was, I've no doubt, right.) After his death in a motorcycle accident at the age of forty-nine, it devolved upon me as his literary executor to usher into print the unfinished text of *Shadows*, the manuscript on which he had been working when he died. We paired it with his novel, *Stillness*, and there's an echo in these titles—though my own book appeared before Gardner's—which now sounds more mournful than glad.

So what, in my seventh decade, would I change and how revise—beyond the ways I've detailed here—these books? The models for my minor figures were sometimes not-so-distantly based on people I knew (Apollonius Banos and Junior Allison were portraits of, respectively, a college friend and a North Bennington taxicab driver), and sometimes an amalgam of townspeople; Elvirah Hayes, Hal Boudreau, and Sally Conover all had their distant counterparts in local village folk. The Old People's Home is an actual structure; the bank and library and grocery store exist. The pavements of North Bennington were marble once; no more. John G. McCullough is long since dead; so is his older sister (who bore scant resemblance to Hattie); the Toy House and the Carriage House and Big House now operate in fact as a museum and may be rented out for concerts and wedding receptions. When our younger daughter got married, it was in that very house.

In the way most writers, magpie-like, choose to line their nests with scraps of past experience and fragments of encounter, I borrowed attributes of men and women I knew or observed for the central quartet of characters (Judah, Hattie, Maggie, Ian). Yet this is no roman à clef or private code to crack. It is an amplification of that begetting image of a funerary pyre and the phrase about King David and Abishag the Shunammite: *but the king knew her not.* The countryside does play, I think, as large a role as I at first envisioned; the trees and stone walls and snow-covered meadows retain a kind of "stillness" on the page.

What emerges for me now, rereading, is how absolute these figures are, how uncompromising in their argument. Judah burns the piano Maggie played on, sells the truck she had incised a heart on in the fender's dust, and never goes to visit when she asks. Jeanne Fisk is much more a relativist, a modern woman caught between allegiances who tries to eat her cake and have it too. At its best this book does capture two ways of behaving and—though all this seems more clear to me as reader than decades ago as writer—the clash between the clenched fist and the open hand. The thematic matter of *Sherbrookes* consists, I think, of a young man's puzzled effort to come to terms with commitment: which lines to draw in what sand. It is a book about landscape and the lasting nature of love.

The language of the letter-writers (Peacock, Anne-Maria his daughter, and Judah's father Joseph) looks a little too elaborate today: more representative, I think, of the eighteenth century than the nineteenth. But this I largely left alone, since I hoped for a declension in the generations, and I used their rhetorics to mark the march of time. The language of the Vermonters (paradoxically the more so when they speak at length than when they go "Ayup ayup") is pretty close to the mark. Or at least it feels as near as I could come then and now. I did, I believe, a creditable job of describing Judah and his octogenarian sister, but overstated his sexual appetite and understated, a little, the old man's need for sleep. Maggie's behavior when depressed in *Stillness* feels more persuasive to me than her exuberance in the first two books, but that's no doubt a function of this reader's present age. And the character of Ian—closest, I suppose, to a self-portrait in these pages—appears to me more successfully composed today than I thought then; his efforts at self-definition seem more a function of personality than a failure of precision on the author's part. He's a beginner, our Ian, who grows up at novel's end.

His creator did so too. Not much happens in these pages: men and women live and die. They grieve and cleave together; they eat and argue and are selfish or selfless and cantankerous or kind. Yet (three decades after finishing the Sherbrookes trilogy) it has pleased me to revisit these old haunts and walk, as it were, those old meadows and trails. And, sentence by paragraph by page, to revel in the view.

NICHOLAS DELBANCO is a British-born American who received his BA from Harvard and his MA from Columbia University. He currently directs the Hopwood Awards Program and is the Robert Frost Distinguished University Professor of English at the University of Michigan. An editor and author of more than twenty-five books, Delbanco has received numerous awards—among them a Guggenheim Fellowship and two Writing Fellowships from the National Endowment for the Arts.

PETROS ABATZOGLOU, *What Does Mrs. Freeman Want?*
MICHAL AJVAZ, *The Golden Age.*
The Other City.
PIERRE ALBERT-BIROT, *Grabinoulor.*
YUZ ALESHKOVSKY, *Kangaroo.*
FELIPE ALFAU, *Chromos.*
Locos.
IVAN ÂNGELO, *The Celebration.*
The Tower of Glass.
DAVID ANTIN, *Talking.*
ANTÓNIO LOBO ANTUNES, *Knowledge of Hell.*
ALAIN ARIAS-MISSON, *Theatre of Incest.*
IFTIKHAR ARIF AND WAQAS KHWAJA, EDS., *Modern Poetry of Pakistan.*
JOHN ASHBERY AND JAMES SCHUYLER, *A Nest of Ninnies.*
GABRIELA AVIGUR-ROTEM, *Heatwave and Crazy Birds.*
HEIMRAD BÄCKER, *transcript.*
DJUNA BARNES, *Ladies Almanack.*
Ryder.
JOHN BARTH, *LETTERS.*
Sabbatical.
DONALD BARTHELME, *The King.*
Paradise.
SVETISLAV BASARA, *Chinese Letter.*
RENÉ BELLETTO, *Dying.*
MARK BINELLI, *Sacco and Vanzetti Must Die!*
ANDREI BITOV, *Pushkin House.*
ANDREJ BLATNIK, *You Do Understand.*
LOUIS PAUL BOON, *Chapel Road.*
My Little War.
Summer in Termuren.
ROGER BOYLAN, *Killoyle.*
IGNÁCIO DE LOYOLA BRANDÃO, *Anonymous Celebrity.*
The Good-Bye Angel.
Teeth under the Sun.
Zero.
BONNIE BREMSER, *Troia: Mexican Memoirs.*
CHRISTINE BROOKE-ROSE, *Amalgamemnon.*
BRIGID BROPHY, *In Transit.*
MEREDITH BROSNAN, *Mr. Dynamite.*
GERALD L. BRUNS, *Modern Poetry and the Idea of Language.*
EVGENY BUNIMOVICH AND J. KATES, EDS., *Contemporary Russian Poetry: An Anthology.*
GABRIELLE BURTON, *Heartbreak Hotel.*
MICHEL BUTOR, *Degrees.*
Mobile.
Portrait of the Artist as a Young Ape.
G. CABRERA INFANTE, *Infante's Inferno.*
Three Trapped Tigers.
JULIETA CAMPOS, *The Fear of Losing Eurydice.*
ANNE CARSON, *Eros the Bittersweet.*
ORLY CASTEL-BLOOM, *Dolly City.*
CAMILO JOSÉ CELA, *Christ versus Arizona.*
The Family of Pascual Duarte.
The Hive.
LOUIS-FERDINAND CÉLINE, *Castle to Castle.*
Conversations with Professor Y.
London Bridge.
Normance.

North.
Rigadoon.
HUGO CHARTERIS, *The Tide Is Right.*
JEROME CHARYN, *The Tar Baby.*
ERIC CHEVILLARD, *Demolishing Nisard.*
MARC CHOLODENKO, *Mordechai Schamz.*
JOSHUA COHEN, *Witz.*
EMILY HOLMES COLEMAN, *The Shutter of Snow.*
ROBERT COOVER, *A Night at the Movies.*
STANLEY CRAWFORD, *Log of the S.S. The Mrs Unguentine.*
Some Instructions to My Wife.
ROBERT CREELEY, *Collected Prose.*
RENÉ CREVEL, *Putting My Foot in It.*
RALPH CUSACK, *Cadenza.*
SUSAN DAITCH, *L.C.*
Storytown.
NICHOLAS DELBANCO, *The Count of Concord.*
Sherbrookes.
NIGEL DENNIS, *Cards of Identity.*
PETER DIMOCK, *A Short Rhetoric for Leaving the Family.*
ARIEL DORFMAN, *Konfidenz.*
COLEMAN DOWELL, *The Houses of Children.*
Island People.
Too Much Flesh and Jabez.
ARKADII DRAGOMOSHCHENKO, *Dust.*
RIKKI DUCORNET, *The Complete Butcher's Tales.*
The Fountains of Neptune.
The Jade Cabinet.
The One Marvelous Thing.
Phosphor in Dreamland.
The Stain.
The Word "Desire."
WILLIAM EASTLAKE, *The Bamboo Bed.*
Castle Keep.
Lyric of the Circle Heart.
JEAN ECHENOZ, *Chopin's Move.*
STANLEY ELKIN, *A Bad Man.*
Boswell: A Modern Comedy.
Criers and Kibitzers, Kibitzers and Criers.
The Dick Gibson Show.
The Franchiser.
George Mills.
The Living End.
The MacGuffin.
The Magic Kingdom.
Mrs. Ted Bliss.
The Rabbi of Lud.
Van Gogh's Room at Arles.
ANNIE ERNAUX, *Cleaned Out.*
LAUREN FAIRBANKS, *Muzzle Thyself.*
Sister Carrie.
LESLIE A. FIEDLER, *Love and Death in the American Novel.*
JUAN FILLOY, *Op Oloop.*
GUSTAVE FLAUBERT, *Bouvard and Pécuchet.*
KASS FLEISHER, *Talking out of School.*
FORD MADOX FORD, *The March of Literature.*
JON FOSSE, *Aliss at the Fire.*
Melancholy.
MAX FRISCH, *I'm Not Stiller.*
Man in the Holocene.

CARLOS FUENTES, *Christopher Unborn.*
  Distant Relations.
  Terra Nostra.
  Where the Air Is Clear.
JANICE GALLOWAY, *Foreign Parts.*
  The Trick Is to Keep Breathing.
WILLIAM H. GASS, *Cartesian Sonata*
  and Other Novellas.
  Finding a Form.
  A Temple of Texts.
  The Tunnel.
  Willie Masters' Lonesome Wife.
GÉRARD GAVARRY, *Hoppla! 1 2 3.*
  Making a Novel.
ETIENNE GILSON,
  The Arts of the Beautiful.
  Forms and Substances in the Arts.
C. S. GISCOMBE, *Giscome Road.*
  Here.
  Prairie Style.
DOUGLAS GLOVER, *Bad News of the Heart.*
  The Enamoured Knight.
WITOLD GOMBROWICZ,
  A Kind of Testament.
KAREN ELIZABETH GORDON,
  The Red Shoes.
GEORGI GOSPODINOV, *Natural Novel.*
JUAN GOYTISOLO, *Count Julian.*
  Exiled from Almost Everywhere.
  Juan the Landless.
  Makbara.
  Marks of Identity.
PATRICK GRAINVILLE, *The Cave of Heaven.*
HENRY GREEN, *Back.*
  Blindness.
  Concluding.
  Doting.
  Nothing.
JIŘÍ GRUŠA, *The Questionnaire.*
GABRIEL GUDDING,
  Rhode Island Notebook.
MELA HARTWIG, *Am I a Redundant*
  Human Being?
JOHN HAWKES, *The Passion Artist.*
  Whistlejacket.
ALEKSANDAR HEMON, ED.,
  Best European Fiction.
AIDAN HIGGINS, *A Bestiary.*
  Balcony of Europe.
  Bornholm Night-Ferry.
  Darkling Plain: Texts for the Air.
  Flotsam and Jetsam.
  Langrishe, Go Down.
  Scenes from a Receding Past.
  Windy Arbours.
KEIZO HINO, *Isle of Dreams.*
KAZUSHI HOSAKA, *Plainsong.*
ALDOUS HUXLEY, *Antic Hay.*
  Crome Yellow.
  Point Counter Point.
  Those Barren Leaves.
  Time Must Have a Stop.
NAOYUKI II, *The Shadow of a Blue Cat.*
MIKHAIL IOSSEL AND JEFF PARKER, EDS.,
  Amerika: Russian Writers View the
  United States.
GERT JONKE, *The Distant Sound.*
  Geometric Regional Novel.
  Homage to Czerny.
  The System of Vienna.

JACQUES JOUET, *Mountain R.*
  Savage.
  Upstaged.
CHARLES JULIET, *Conversations with*
  Samuel Beckett and Bram van
  Velde.
MIEKO KANAI, *The Word Book.*
YORAM KANIUK, *Life on Sandpaper.*
HUGH KENNER, *The Counterfeiters.*
  Flaubert, Joyce and Beckett:
  The Stoic Comedians.
  Joyce's Voices.
DANILO KIŠ, *Garden, Ashes.*
  A Tomb for Boris Davidovich.
ANITA KONKKA, *A Fool's Paradise.*
GEORGE KONRÁD, *The City Builder.*
TADEUSZ KONWICKI, *A Minor Apocalypse.*
  The Polish Complex.
MENIS KOUMANDAREAS, *Koula.*
ELAINE KRAF, *The Princess of 72nd Street.*
JIM KRUSOE, *Iceland.*
EWA KURYLUK, *Century 21.*
EMILIO LASCANO TEGUI, *On Elegance*
  While Sleeping.
ERIC LAURRENT, *Do Not Touch.*
HERVÉ LE TELLIER, *The Sextine Chapel.*
  A Thousand Pearls (for a Thousand
  Pennies)
VIOLETTE LEDUC, *La Bâtarde.*
EDOUARD LEVÉ, *Suicide.*
SUZANNE JILL LEVINE, *The Subversive*
  Scribe: Translating Latin
  American Fiction.
DEBORAH LEVY, *Billy and Girl.*
  Pillow Talk in Europe and Other
  Places.
JOSÉ LEZAMA LIMA, *Paradiso.*
ROSA LIKSOM, *Dark Paradise.*
OSMAN LINS, *Avalovara.*
  The Queen of the Prisons of Greece.
ALF MAC LOCHLAINN,
  The Corpus in the Library.
  Out of Focus.
RON LOEWINSOHN, *Magnetic Field(s).*
MINA LOY, *Stories and Essays of Mina Loy.*
BRIAN LYNCH, *The Winner of Sorrow.*
D. KEITH MANO, *Take Five.*
MICHELINE AHARONIAN MARCOM,
  The Mirror in the Well.
BEN MARCUS,
  The Age of Wire and String.
WALLACE MARKFIELD,
  Teitlebaum's Window.
  To an Early Grave.
DAVID MARKSON, *Reader's Block.*
  Springer's Progress.
  Wittgenstein's Mistress.
CAROLE MASO, *AVA.*
LADISLAV MATEJKA AND KRYSTYNA
  POMORSKA, EDS.,
  Readings in Russian Poetics:
  Formalist and Structuralist Views.
HARRY MATHEWS,
  The Case of the Persevering Maltese:
  Collected Essays.
  Cigarettes.
  The Conversions.
  The Human Country: New and
  Collected Stories.
  The Journalist.

FOR A FULL LIST OF PUBLICATIONS, VISIT:
www.dalkeyarchive.com

SELECTED DALKEY ARCHIVE PAPERBACKS

My Life in CIA.
Singular Pleasures.
The Sinking of the Odradek
    Stadium.
Tlooth.
20 Lines a Day.
JOSEPH McELROY,
    Night Soul and Other Stories.
THOMAS McGONIGLE,
    Going to Patchogue.
ROBERT L. McLAUGHLIN, ED., *Innovations:*
    An Anthology of
        Modern & Contemporary Fiction.
ABDELWAHAB MEDDEB, *Talismano.*
HERMAN MELVILLE, *The Confidence-Man.*
AMANDA MICHALOPOULOU, *I'd Like.*
STEVEN MILLHAUSER,
    The Barnum Museum.
    In the Penny Arcade.
RALPH J. MILLS, JR.,
    Essays on Poetry.
MOMUS, *The Book of Jokes.*
CHRISTINE MONTALBETTI, *Western.*
OLIVE MOORE, *Spleen.*
NICHOLAS MOSLEY, *Accident.*
    Assassins.
    Catastrophe Practice.
    Children of Darkness and Light.
    Experience and Religion.
    God's Hazard.
    The Hesperides Tree.
    Hopeful Monsters.
    Imago Bird.
    Impossible Object.
    Inventing God.
    Judith.
    Look at the Dark.
    Natalie Natalia.
    Paradoxes of Peace.
    Serpent.
    Time at War.
    The Uses of Slime Mould:
        Essays of Four Decades.
WARREN MOTTE,
    Fables of the Novel: French Fiction
        since 1990.
    Fiction Now: The French Novel in
        the 21st Century.
    Oulipo: A Primer of Potential
        Literature.
YVES NAVARRE, *Our Share of Time.*
    Sweet Tooth.
DOROTHY NELSON, *In Night's City.*
    Tar and Feathers.
ESHKOL NEVO, *Homesick.*
WILFRIDO D. NOLLEDO, *But for the Lovers.*
FLANN O'BRIEN,
    At Swim-Two-Birds.
    At War.
    The Best of Myles.
    The Dalkey Archive.
    Further Cuttings.
    The Hard Life.
    The Poor Mouth.
    The Third Policeman.
CLAUDE OLLIER, *The Mise-en-Scène.*
    Wert and the Life Without End.
PATRIK OUŘEDNÍK, *Europeana.*
    The Opportune Moment, 1855.
BORIS PAHOR, *Necropolis.*

FERNANDO DEL PASO,
    News from the Empire.
    Palinuro of Mexico.
ROBERT PINGET, *The Inquisitory.*
    Mahu or The Material.
    Trio.
MANUEL PUIG,
    Betrayed by Rita Hayworth.
    The Buenos Aires Affair.
    Heartbreak Tango.
RAYMOND QUENEAU, *The Last Days.*
    Odile.
    Pierrot Mon Ami.
    Saint Glinglin.
ANN QUIN, *Berg.*
    Passages.
    Three.
    Tripticks.
ISHMAEL REED,
    The Free-Lance Pallbearers.
    The Last Days of Louisiana Red.
    Ishmael Reed: The Plays.
    Juice!
    Reckless Eyeballing.
    The Terrible Threes.
    The Terrible Twos.
    Yellow Back Radio Broke-Down.
JOÃO UBALDO RIBEIRO, *House of the*
    Fortunate Buddhas.
JEAN RICARDOU, *Place Names.*
RAINER MARIA RILKE, *The Notebooks of*
    Malte Laurids Brigge.
JULIÁN RÍOS, *The House of Ulysses.*
    Larva: A Midsummer Night's Babel.
    Poundemonium.
    Procession of Shadows.
AUGUSTO ROA BASTOS, *I the Supreme.*
DANIËL ROBBERECHTS,
    Arriving in Avignon.
JEAN ROLIN, *The Explosion of the*
    Radiator Hose.
OLIVIER ROLIN, *Hotel Crystal.*
ALIX CLEO ROUBAUD, *Alix's Journal.*
JACQUES ROUBAUD, *The Form of a*
    City Changes Faster, Alas, Than
    the Human Heart.
    The Great Fire of London.
    Hortense in Exile.
    Hortense Is Abducted.
    The Loop.
    The Plurality of Worlds of Lewis.
    The Princess Hoppy.
    Some Thing Black.
LEON S. ROUDIEZ, *French Fiction Revisited.*
RAYMOND ROUSSEL, *Impressions of Africa.*
VEDRANA RUDAN, *Night.*
STIG SÆTERBAKKEN, *Siamese.*
LYDIE SALVAYRE, *The Company of Ghosts.*
    Everyday Life.
    The Lecture.
    Portrait of the Writer as a
        Domesticated Animal.
    The Power of Flies.
LUIS RAFAEL SÁNCHEZ,
    Macho Camacho's Beat.
SEVERO SARDUY, *Cobra & Maitreya.*
NATHALIE SARRAUTE,
    Do You Hear Them?
    Martereau.
    The Planetarium.

SELECTED DALKEY ARCHIVE PAPERBACKS

ARNO SCHMIDT, *Collected Novellas.*
  Collected Stories.
  Nobodaddy's Children.
  Two Novels.
ASAF SCHURR, *Motti.*
CHRISTINE SCHUTT, *Nightwork.*
GAIL SCOTT, *My Paris.*
DAMION SEARLS, *What We Were Doing
  and Where We Were Going.*
JUNE AKERS SEESE,
  Is This What Other Women Feel Too?
  What Waiting Really Means.
BERNARD SHARE, *Inish.*
  Transit.
AURELIE SHEEHAN,
  Jack Kerouac Is Pregnant.
VIKTOR SHKLOVSKY, *Bowstring.*
  Knight's Move.
  *A Sentimental Journey:
  Memoirs 1917–1922.*
  Energy of Delusion: A Book on Plot.
  Literature and Cinematography.
  Theory of Prose.
  Third Factory.
  Zoo, or Letters Not about Love.
CLAUDE SIMON, *The Invitation.*
PIERRE SINIAC, *The Collaborators.*
JOSEF ŠKVORECKÝ, *The Engineer of
  Human Souls.*
GILBERT SORRENTINO,
  Aberration of Starlight.
  Blue Pastoral.
  Crystal Vision.
  *Imaginative Qualities of Actual
  Things.*
  Mulligan Stew.
  Pack of Lies.
  Red the Fiend.
  The Sky Changes.
  Something Said.
  Splendide-Hôtel.
  Steelwork.
  Under the Shadow.
W. M. SPACKMAN,
  The Complete Fiction.
ANDRZEJ STASIUK, *Fado.*
GERTRUDE STEIN,
  Lucy Church Amiably.
  The Making of Americans.
  A Novel of Thank You.
LARS SVENDSEN, *A Philosophy of Evil.*
PIOTR SZEWC, *Annihilation.*
GONÇALO M. TAVARES, *Jerusalem.*
  *Learning to Pray in the Age of
  Technology.*
LUCIAN DAN TEODOROVICI,
  Our Circus Presents . . .
STEFAN THEMERSON, *Hobson's Island.*
  The Mystery of the Sardine.
  Tom Harris.
JOHN TOOMEY, *Sleepwalker.*
JEAN-PHILIPPE TOUSSAINT,
  The Bathroom.
  Camera.
  Monsieur.
  Running Away.
  Self-Portrait Abroad.
  Television.
DUMITRU TSEPENEAG,
  Hotel Europa.

  The Necessary Marriage.
  Pigeon Post.
  Vain Art of the Fugue.
ESTHER TUSQUETS, *Stranded.*
DUBRAVKA UGRESIC,
  Lend Me Your Character.
  Thank You for Not Reading.
MATI UNT, *Brecht at Night.*
  Diary of a Blood Donor.
  Things in the Night.
ÁLVARO URIBE AND OLIVIA SEARS, EDS.,
  *Best of Contemporary Mexican
  Fiction.*
ELOY URROZ, *Friction.*
  The Obstacles.
LUISA VALENZUELA, *Dark Desires and
  the Others.*
  He Who Searches.
MARJA-LIISA VARTIO,
  The Parson's Widow.
PAUL VERHAEGHEN, *Omega Minor.*
BORIS VIAN, *Heartsnatcher.*
LLORENÇ VILLALONGA, *The Dolls' Room.*
ORNELA VORPSI, *The Country Where No
  One Ever Dies.*
AUSTRYN WAINHOUSE, *Hedyphagetica.*
PAUL WEST,
  Words for a Deaf Daughter & Gala.
CURTIS WHITE,
  America's Magic Mountain.
  The Idea of Home.
  Memories of My Father Watching TV.
  *Monstrous Possibility: An Invitation
  to Literary Politics.*
  Requiem.
DIANE WILLIAMS, *Excitability:
  Selected Stories.*
  Romancer Erector.
DOUGLAS WOOLF, *Wall to Wall.*
  Ya! & John-Juan.
JAY WRIGHT, *Polynomials and Pollen.*
  *The Presentable Art of Reading
  Absence.*
PHILIP WYLIE, *Generation of Vipers.*
MARGUERITE YOUNG, *Angel in the Forest.*
  Miss MacIntosh, My Darling.
REYOUNG, *Unbabbling.*
VLADO ŽABOT, *The Succubus.*
ZORAN ŽIVKOVIĆ, *Hidden Camera.*
LOUIS ZUKOFSKY, *Collected Fiction.*
SCOTT ZWIREN, *God Head.*

FOR A FULL LIST OF PUBLICATIONS, VISIT:
www.dalkeyarchive.com